EDITH HERON;

OR,

THE EARL AND THE COUNTESS.

A SEQUEL TO "EDITH THE CAPTIVE."

BY THE AUTHOR OF "JANE BRIGHTWELL."

WITH FIFTY-TWO ILLUSTRATIONS.

DRAWN BY F. GILBERT.

VOL. II.

LONDON:
JOHN DICKS, 313, STRAND; AND ALL BOOKSELLERS.

INDEX TO VOL. II.

———————

INDEX TO THE ENGRAVINGS.

EDITH HERON;

OR,

THE EARL AND THE COUNTESS.

CHAPTER CLXXVIII.

HERON AND EDITH SEEM TO RESTORE THE DEAD TO LIFE, AND JONATHAN WILD IS CAPTURED.

"TELL me," said Edith to the boy, as she placed her hand affectionately on his shoulder—"tell me how you came here?"

"My father and I were forced at this inn to rest; and I went into the flower-garden, which

you may see from the windows of this room, to gather some flowers, when the man who looks like an ostler came after me, and caught me by the collar, and without speaking a word to me of the reason of such treatment, he thrust me into a stable and locked and barred the door on me."

"You called to your father?"

"Yes, dear lady, I did; but it would seem that he could not hear me, and I was a prisoner, and alone."

"You escaped?"

"I did. I climbed from one of the troughs of

the stable to the hayloft, and being so slight and slim as I am, I perhaps found my way where the people of this place never suspected it was possible for any one to go. I got on to some roofs, and from one to another I reached a window which led me into the room next to this; and then at the back of a cupboard I happened to discover a small sliding bolt, by moving which I opened the panel that has led me into this room to you."

This short and simple narrative was told with so much grace, and yet so much sadness, that it went to the heart of Edith.

"My poor boy," she said, "would that we could restore to you your father!"

"Have you seen him?"

"Alas, no!"

"Oh, what shall I do?—what shall I do? I am so friendless—so destitute!"

"Nay, do not say that," interposed Heron. "You shall never be friendless and destitute while you choose to call us friends. Edith, let me speak to you apart for a moment."

When the boy heard Heron say this he shrank back with intuitive delicacy out of earshot.

He spoke earnestly to Edith.

"Dear Edith, there can be no doubt but that this poor boy's father has met with the sort of fate here that was intended for us."

"Alas, no doubt at all!"

"Permit me then, at least, to make the effort to ascertain that fact, and to try if it be possible to save him."

"What would you do?"

"I want to go down that trap-door in the floor of the wardrobe, and see where it leads to."

"Oh, Felix, it can only lead to the dead, and perhaps to death."

"I do not know, Edith, but something seems to urge me on, and to promise me some success. Do you see these old silken bell-ropes, and the coil upon coil of ropes that holds one of the old chairs together. By their aid I can descend as far as prudence may dictate, and return with ease."

If ever in this world there was a man of action that was certainly Felix Heron. As he spoke, he had got down the bell-rope, and uncoiled the cord from about the chair, which, by the bye, fell to pieces when he had done so.

"Now, Edith," he said, "do not say anything to the boy; and I will descend and see where the opening beneath the trap leads to."

The boy looked on with a vague and amazed curiosity at what Felix Heron was doing.

By the assistance of a chair, Heron succeeded in propping open the trap-door, so that the counter-poise which made it come up into its place, and which was merely a weight and pulley and a cord, would not act.

Securely, then, fastening one end of the cord to the leg of the table in the room, he let himself slowly down.

In the depth of about twelve feet Heron found that he touched the floor of some apartment below him.

He had about him the means of procuring a light; and, in truth, it was much needed in that place, for it was most intensely dark.

At the first flame of the match which he had lit, Heron saw that he was in a sort of ground kitchen, which, from the appearance of the walls, covered with moss as they were, and the floor with green damp, had not been for many a long year used for any legitimate purpose.

He lit a small wax taper then, and looked more carefully about him.

Then Heron could not, even with all his well-strung nerves, forbear a start as he saw at some short distance from him a human form.

Sitting up, and looking as ghastly as death, if it were not an image of death itself, was a man.

As the taper light fell upon the pale, wan face, Felix Heron was struck even at that moment by the likeness to the young lad, with all the bloom of youth and beauty upon him, in the chamber above.

Heron stepped forward, and stooping low, he looked into the pale face.

Blood was upon the brow, but death was not absolutely there.

The lips moved.

Heron spoke.

"Let hope be the blessed word," he said, "that shall fan the flame of life and make it burn with renewed vigour!"

"Laura!" said the wounded man, faintly, and by a great effort. "Oh, heaven, my Laura!"

A look of agonized supplication came over the face of the wounded and almost dying traveller, and he again in low, moaning tones, pronounced the same name—"Laura, Laura!"

"I know not who or what you mean," said Heron, with sympathy in his tones. "But I have reason to believe that you had a son here, a fine, gentle-looking boy, of about fourteen years of age, with dark hazel eyes; and if so, I can tell you that he at least is safe and well."

A cry of joy—there is no mistaking the natural language of the heart—came from the lips of the injured man; and Heron saw tears coursing each other down his face.

"My Laura—my Laura!" he murmured. "Oh, how good is heaven!"

Heron could not comprehend all this, but he was specially anxious to get the wounded man out of that dismal place to the room above.

That, though, would be no easy matter.

But where there is a will there is a way to accomplish anything and everything; so Heron got the wounded traveller on to his shoulder, urging him to hold by him in any way he could, so as not to fall; and by an exertion of that great strength which he, Heron, possessed, but which in this instance was sorely tested, he fairly climbed up the rope.

"Help, Edith!"

She flew to the trap in the floor of the wardrobe, and most materially aided Heron to emerge from it with his burden.

Then, with a scream of joy, the boy ran forward and clasped his father in his arms, and sobbed, and uttered exclamations of joy, and gratitude, and thanks.

The father could not speak.

But as if then some sudden thought had come over the boy which he felt called upon him to put into immediate action, he left his father, and flung his arms round the neck of Heron and kissed him on each cheek.

Then he did the same to Edith, and then returned to his father, from whom, by the affection that beamed in his eyes, he seemed to say he would never more part but with his life.

Heron was surprised that the wounded traveller should be so satisfied to give up the Laura he had spoken of with so much affection; and he was in momentary expectation of hearing the name again, when the traveller turned towards him and Edith, saying, "Thank heaven, I am not much hurt! I fancy, while my dear Laura went to the flower garden, I was given some poison!"

" Your dear who ?" said Heron.

" My Laura !"

" Why—that—oh !"

The young boy, or the seeming boy, hung down his head, and a bright flush came over his face. Then he looked up with a smile at Heron, as he said, " My father and I travel so much that this boy's costume became convenient. I am the Laura that he speaks of. He and I are alone in the world !"

Heron bowed as he returned the smile, saying as he did so, " My dear girl, I ought to have felt quite sure that those eyes were feminine. But tell me, sir, how you came to be in that dismal place from which we have both just come ?"

" I hardly know. I drank some milk, and then found my senses leaving me, and I thought I was driven by a fall down some place; and then a deadly sickness came over me, which, in all probability, saved my life, by preventing the poison from taking effect."

Before Felix Heron could say a word in reply to these explanations of the traveller, a blow came at the door of the room, which was nearly sufficient to break through one of its panels.

At the same moment the brutal, grating voice of Jonathan Wild cried out from without, " And where does this door lead to, and be hanged to you all ? Open it, or I will know the reason why !"

" Hush !" said Heron, for the traveller was about to say something.

The voice of the woman now sounded from without, in reply to Jonathan.

" I will not open the door for any one, gentle or simple. A pretty pass, indeed, things are come to when I may not keep my own bedchamber door locked !"

" Bah !" said Wild.

" I tell you you cannot and shall not go in there !"

" Indeed !"

" Yes, in deed and in fact !"

" Woman !"

" Man !"

The virago temper of the woman was aroused, and she pitched her voice a good octave higher than Jonathan Wild's, screaming out her words with a vehemence that was quite terrific.

" Hold your row," roared Wild, " and open the door at once, or I will find a means to do so."

" Help ! help !"

" Oh, that's your game, is it ?"

" Help, Samuel !"

" Ha, ha ! Your Samuel would need be a fine fellow to interfere with me. My name is Wild, and I was christened Jonathan."

At this information, which, for the first time, let the woman know she was in the presence and the power of the famous thief-taker, she uttered a shriek of dismay, and would have fled but that he caught her by the wrist and detained her.

" No, ma'am, if you please; I would much rather you remained where you are !"

" Mercy !"

" Oh, of course, lots of it ! Will you open the door now ?"

" I cannot !"

" Or won't, which is all the same to me, so here goes !"

Wild had with him the heavy, short bludgeon which he never went without, and a collection of which he kept at his house in Newgate Street, and with the heavy loaded head of it he commenced upon the door.

Blow after blow about the region of the lock began soon to loosen and start every screw that belonged to it.

But Wild, in spite of the woman's remonstrance, went on, till the lock started from the door, in a complete state of dismemberment, and the door was open.

Wild dashed into the room.

It was empty.

Where was Edith ?

Where was Captain Heron ?

Where the wounded traveller and his daughter Laura ?

All gone !

The mystery of their disappearance was great to the woman, for she fully expected to see Heron and Edith there—not, of course, knowing them by their names, but believing that there they would be found, poisoned with the drugged milk.

She looked about her with amazement.

And so did Wild.

He could not imagine why he had been so pertinaciously excluded from a room in which there was nobody and nothing extraordinary.

But neither the woman of the " Woodman " inn, nor Jonathan Wild knew of the panel in the wall through which the whole party, consisting of Edith, Felix Heron, the wounded traveller, and Laura had passed.

There had been just time to effect a retreat in that direction before Wild was in the apartment, glaring about him like some ferocious animal baulked of its prey.

" What do you mean ?" he shouted to the terrified woman. " What do you mean by all this, and why was the door kept fast ?"

" I do not know."

" I will know, though, or there shall be a good reason why not."

Jonathan could not believe but that he was the victim of some trickery in which the woman had a share; although, if he had more carefully studied her alarmed and frightened appearance, he no doubt would have come to the conclusion that she was as much in the dark as he.

" Hark ye," he said; " if I do not get full satisfaction about all the secrets of this house, I shall take my own way of finding them out."

" Your own way ?"

" Yes. Do you happen to know what that way is ?"

" No."

" Ha, ha ! Then I will tell you. I bring down from London a small barrel of gunpowder—say about ten or twelve pounds—and I place it on the ground floor and set it alight with a slow match. It blows up the whole house, and then I and my men have a hunt among the ruins."

Too well for her safety she knew what was to be found among the ruins of that house.

" Oh, you don't like that ?" said Wild.

" We are poor, but honest people," was the reply; " and we don't see why our house should be blown up over our heads."

Wild made no reply to this speech, but going to one of the windows, he tried to open it.

" Why, what's the meaning of this ? Are all your windows made air-tight ?"

As he spoke, he dashed his bludgeon through two of the panes of glass, and broke down likewise the framework of the casement between them.

Thrusting then his hideous and revolting physiognomy out of the fractured window, he shouted to his men below.

"Hoy! Halloa!"

"Yes, Mr. Wild."

"Come up here, you Swiney."

"Yes. Mr. Wild."

One of the janissaries at once dismounted, and giving his horse to one of his comrades to hold, he made his way up the stairs to the room.

"Stay here!" was Wild's brief order to the man.

"Yes, Mr. Wild."

"And, Swiney!"

"Yes, sir."

"In case you should be dull, I will leave you this lady to keep you company."

"All right, Mr. Wild."

The woman of the inn from this felt that she was a prisoner. It did not require the sudden movement of the man Swiney to a station between her and the door to convince her of that state of things.

The fact was that Jonathan Wild had made up his mind to search the house, and he thought he should be ab'e to do that much more conveniently without the woman than with her.

Leaving, then, Mr. Swiney on guard, Wild made a rambling progress through the "Woodman" inn; but he found nothing to recompense him for his trouble but an old silver tankard, which he at once, upon ascertaining what it was, put into his pocket.

Wild did not propose to make any lengthened stay at that inn. It was only stress of weather that had induced him to stop at it at all; and he thought he would in reality lose no time if he waited until the heavy down-pour of rain had run off the roads and made them a little more passable.

Jonathan Wild was in reality bound for Epping Forest.

He did not think it likely that Felix Heron and Edith would venture to seek the forest until nightfall, and he had conceived the idea of holding possession of that same road to it, which he knew on two occasions before was the one that Felix Heron used on approaching his sylvan home.

That he might, by such an act of audacity and daring, succeed in making prisoners both of Edith and Heron was just probable enough to recommend the attempt to him.

Whether he was le ally justified, or not, in so doing, never troubled him for a moment. He suspected something wrong about the supposed reprieve for Edith, and when that something wrong came to be understocd, it would be a great triumph to him to be able to say that he would produce the prisoner again.

Nothing would be easier for him to do, provided he had Edith in his house, called Little Newgate.

His intention in regard to Felix Heron was of a much more sanguinary character.

Wild fully intended to take the life of Heron now whenever and wherever he could.

The pain in his neck from the half completed hanging at Castleneau House was still amply sufficient to keep that little episode in his existence fully present to his imagination.

The murder of Heron, therefore, was a something that Wild, over and over again, told himself he should not be happy till he had effected

Having, then, completed his search of the "Woodman" inn, and found nothing to reward him but the old silver tankard, Jonathan Wild went down to the little tavern in front, where his men were.

The rain was nearly over, and a brisk wind was scattering the few drops that remained of it, in the minutest particles through the air.

"Off, and away, my men," he cried. "For all I know, we have got no time to lose."

The janissaries tightened their grasp on the reins of their horses, and prepared for a start.

"Come down, Swiney," cried Wild—"come down!"

But Swiney did not answer.

"Come down, I say!"

Still no reply.

"Idiot!" roared Wild; "do you not hear me?"

As he spoke, Jonathan dashed into the house again, and not without a certain misgiving in his mind, rushed up the staircase.

He reached the room in a few seconds.

"Come down, will you, and mount? Who is to wait for you, I wonder?"

But no Swiney was there.

The room was perfectly empty. Both Swiney and the woman of the "Woodman" inn had disappeared.

Wild looked about him with surprise, and a sensation of fear began to creep over him.

The mysteries of that house were, just t en, too many for him; and that superstitious element which we have had occasion to remark was in his nature, began to make itself felt.

"What's the meaning of all this?" he said

He moved slowly towards the door as he spoke, for he did not like to trust himself further into the room than necessary.

"Speak," he added, "if you are anywhere that you can hear me—I charge you, speak!"

A deep, awful, hollow groan was the response.

Where it came from, Wild could not possibly divine. It seemed to be in the air of the room, exactly about the middle of it. It required no great stretch of fancy on the part of one prepared to believe in supernatural agencies, to think that it came from some being there present, but invisible to mortal eyes.

Wild got nearer still to the door.

"What? Who? What are you?"

There was no reply.

Wild rolled down the stairs, his hanger, that he wore by his side, rattling and bumping on the steps as he went.

"Confound the place!" he muttered. "I will come and burn it down, or blow it up, or pull it down, brick by brick, but I will find out what is the meaning of all this."

The disappearance of the man Swiney, and the possible peril that he might be in, did not give Jonathan Wild any concern.

The principle he went upon with his men was, that if they could not, or did not, take care of themselves, it was no fault of his.

Swiney was therefore left to his fate, whatever that might be.

But something more important than the disappearance of that man was yet to happen before Jonathan could bid a temporary good-bye to the "Woodman" inn.

His foot was actually in the stirrup of his horse, and his men were almost on the move, when, slowly approaching the inn yard, by a narrow path that led through a neglected garden, and terminated at a small gate, there appeared two persons.

Those persons carried stout sticks, which had evidently been recently cut from a hedge, and they had the appearance of being rather travelworn, if not weary.

CAPTAIN HERON RECEIVES INTELLIGENCE OF THE TREACHERY OF HIS BAND.

Presented Gratis with No. 53, of the New Edition of EDITH HERON, the Sequel to Edith the Captive; or, the Robbers of Epping Forest.

The approaching wayfarers did not seem to see the horsemen in the inn yard a moment sooner than they themselves were seen.

The fact was that the little path by which they approached had a curve in it which shut off the view of the open space in front of the inn where Wild and his men were assembled, until the two travellers almost actually reached the gate.

Then Wild uttered just such a shout as some ancient hunter might, perhaps, in the primeval forests of England have uttered when he saw his game in sight.

That cry was more than enough to awaken the two travellers to a sense of danger.

The surprise, however, of this encounter with Jonathan Wild and a strong party of officers, all that distance from London, was too much to be overcome on the instant by the two travellers.

They stood by the little gate as if they had been petrified.

Then Wild raised another shout of gratification, and tearing from the saddle of his horse the two holster pistols, he presented them full at the two travellers, as he cried, " Stir hand or foot on peril of your lives!"

He knew them well.

And who did they know in all the world better than they knew him?

They were old acquaintances—old acquaintances of Jonathan Wild, and old acquaintances of our readers.

They were none others than Ogle and Tom Ripon.

Taking advantage of a stage coach, which took them about a third of the way to Epping Forest, and completely clear of London and its environs, Ogle and Tom had resolved then to walk the remainder of the way.

Overtaken by the terrific storm, they had protected themselves as well as they could among the trees and hedges, but they had suffered sufficiently from the down-pour of that tropical-like rain to make it very desirable to find some temporary shelter.

Evil fortune surely had conducted them to the " Woodman " inn.

" Move hand or foot, and you are corpses!" yelled Wild again. Your pistols, men, your pistols! Don't fire but cover them well!"

Some half-dozen of the men who were with Jonathan Wild presented their pistols at Ogle and Tom Ripon.

The coolness and promptitude of action that characterized both of these personages had come back to them, and they had turned to fly.

But they saw at the same time what would be the consequences.

A volley from Wild and his men.

Now, an escape from one pistol, or even from two, hastily aimed in the open air, might have presented fair chances enough.

A volley from six or eight, though all random enough possibly, but yet filling up a good space, was decidedly dangerous at such close quarters.

" Stop, Tom," said Ogle.

Tom stopped.

He had great faith in Ogle and what he advised.

They both stood as calm and cool as possible by the little gate leading to the inn.

Wild stepped forward clear of his horse, and still keeping his pistols levelled, he said, " Yes, Ogle, and you, Tom Ripon, are my prisoners!"

" I don't know that yet, Mr. Wild," said Ogle.

" No more do I, Johnny," said Tom Ripon.

" But I know it," said Wild; " and I give you the chance of death here upon the spot, or of capture."

" I don't think," said Ogle, " that Mr. Valentine, the officer, who I see here, would countenance the deliberate and cold-blooded murder of any one."

" No," said the officer alluded to; " but if Mr. Wild has good cause to apprehend you, I cannot answer for accidents provided you resist."

" We don't resist," said Ogle; " but we give in to Mr. Valentine, and hold him responsible for our lives."

" No!" cried Wild; " that won't do at all!"

" I think, Mr. Wild, it will be better," said Valentine. " If you have any charge against these two persons, you had better give them into my custody, and then nobody can say anything."

" They are two of the most notorious of the band of Captain Felix Heron."

" Indeed !"

" Yes; and that man Ogle, you know, or ought to know. well, for he was once in my service."

" Well, I do know him by sight; but you don't mean to say, Mr. Wild, that the boy is a robber on the highway ? "

" I do!"

Tom Ripon looked as if he could then and there have eaten Mr. Valentine, the Bow Street officer. with half a grain of salt.

" If," he said, " a man falls into misfortune, he oughtn't to be insulted and called a boy." .

Valentine spoke then to Ogle.

" You had better not make a fight of it," he said. " What's the regular and precise charge against them, Mr. Wild ? "

" Highway robbery !"

" Very good! Then I advise you, Ogle, and you, my little man, to give yourselves up to me without more ado."

" Alls right !" said Ogle.

" Is it all right?" muttered Tom. " I should say its all wrong."

Ogle took Tom by the arm, and led him into the inn-yard, whispering as he went, " Don't be uneasy, Tom. Don't you know a live dog is better than a dead lion ?"

" What do you mean, Ogle ?"

" Why, I mean that as long as we are alive and unhurt we are all right, and have every chance of getting free."

" Oh, ah! yes!"

" And besides, it's worth while finding out what Jonathan Wild is about here, and so near to Epping with such a strong party."

" To be sure it is, Ogle; I'm rather glad he has nabbed us, now you put it in that light. How do you do, Johnny ? All right, old chap?"

Wild looked furiously at Tom Ripon, but he did not condescend to reply to him.

A whispered consultation took place then between Jonathan and Valentine, the officer; and then the latter said aloud, " Very well. Two can be spared easily enough, and well armed as they are, if you pick your men properly, they will stand no nonsense."

CHAPTER CLXX'X.

OGLE AND TOM RIPON FIND THEMSELVES IN CLOSE COMPANIONSHIP WITH DAISY.

WHAT really might have been the immediate fate of Ogle and Tom Ripon upon that occasion, it

Jonathan Wild had happened to be only surrounded by some of his own unscrupulous myrmidons, it is not difficult to guess.

No doubt their murder would have been accomplished.

The accidental presence, however, of an officer of the police, who was not in the immediate pay of Wild, put such an act out of the question.

Mr. Valentine was a Bow Street runner, and though not one whit more scrupulous than the rest of his class, he had none of the special motives of action in regard to Felix Heron and his band that held possession of Jonathan Wild.

The proposition, then, of the Bow Street officer was that two of the party should be left behind as a guard upon Ogle and Tom Ripon, while the rest accompanied Jonathan and him. Valentine, on the original expedition to Epping Forest.

To this Wild was fain to agree with the best grace he could put on.

He selected two of his own men, who he knew perfectly well would stop at no deed of violence for which they could see any excuse.

Casting his eyes about him then in the inn yard, he saw the stable into which Daisy and the horse that Captain Heron had ridden had been placed by the morose-looking groom, who had now disappeared, and was in hiding somewhere.

"Let the prisoners," said Jonathan Wild, "be placed in that stable. It's good enough for them, and empty, as no guests are at the inn."

Wild then added some injunctions to his men, which were quickly obeyed; and much to the chagrin of Tom Ripon, although Ogle took the proceeding with a calm serenity that specially provoked Wild, they were tied together by the wrists with a stout cord, and their other hands rather cleverly, by a turn of the same cord, made fast behind their backs.

Thus secured, they were thrust into the stable and the door closed upon them, and made fast.

The man of Jonathan Wild's party who pushed them into the stable, and who was one of those who were to remain on guard over them, never troubled himself to look into the stable to see if it were empty or not.

That was a fact which was assumed.

Tom Ripon tumbled down among some loose straw, and Ogle very nearly fell over him.

"Get up, Tom! You ain't hurt, I suppose?"

"Not a bit; but there's a hole here that I put my foot into!"

"Oh, it's an old place!"

"Hush!"

"What is it, Tom?"

"Murder!"

"Good gracious, what is it?"

"Somebody—something——"

"What?"

"Has got hold of my hat and all the hair on the top of my head. It's so precious dark here I can't see!"

Ogle stretched out his hand, the one that was fastened at the wrist to one of Tom's, and felt the neck of a horse.

"A horse, Tom—a horse!"

"The deuce!"

"No, a horse!"

"Let go! Let go, do! Don't! I mean let go! He's got it!"

"What, Tom?"

"My hat and half a peck of the hair off my head. Oh! oh! Ogle! Ogle!"

"What now?"

"If that isn't Daisy, I'm a Dutchman, or a Frenchman, or some other wretched being."

"You don't mean that, Tom?"

"Stop! I'll soon know, dark as it is in the place Daisy, boy! Daisy, lass! oh, which will you be? or neither? Daisy, my Daisy!"

Tom probably had more to say, but he was nearly pushed off his feet by the horse's head being placed on his shoulder suddenly.

"It is Daisy," he said: "I could swear to her nose."

"And now you can see to swear," said Ogle, as he, by stooping down, succeeded in finding a little sliding piece of wood in the stable door that was about large enough to let fowls creep in and out.

When once, however, that sliding panel on a small scale was removed, sufficient light came into the stable to enable them to see two horses.

One was Daisy.

The other Ogle at once recognised as Daisy's companion in the coach that had been left in Field Lane.

"Why, Tom," said Ogle, as he felt a fear of he knew not what as he spoke,—"why, Tom, what has become of the Captain and the Lady Edith, since these are the two horses they rode?"

Tom looked blank.

Ogle was fairly puzzled to account for the state of affairs, and it added no little to Tom Ripon's incapacity to hazard any conjecture on the subject to see how full of vague, and yet terrible, apprehension Ogle was.

"You don't think, Ogle—you can't think that anything has happened," said Tom.

"I don't know what to think."

"No more do I."

"But one thing is quite clear; and that is, that we must get this cord off us, so that we may know what to do, and be able to do it."

Ogle made a desperate effort to get his hand out of the loop of the cord, but it had been put on by persons of skill in such matters, and he only hurt his wrist in the fruitless effort.

"Stop a bit!" said Tom Ripon. "I know how to do it!"

"It is more than I do, Tom."

"Daisy will do anything I tell her," added Tom. "She hasn't yet asked me how I am, or made any remark about the weather; but I live in hopes she will some day; but she will do what I want her now."

Tom whistled to Daisy in a low, monotonous way, and the creature came close to him, and placed her head upon his breast. Tom then held up his hand along with Ogle's, on which was the cord, and said, "Bite, Daisy—bite, girl—bite!"

Daisy did not seem to know what was meant for some time, and seemed under the impression that Tom Ripon had meant some new game; but when Tom himself suddenly put down his head to the cord, and began gnawing at it, she comprehended that that was what she was wanted to do.

Ogle laughed.

"Oh, Tom! Tom!"

"What now!"

"We never thought of that!"

"Of what, Ogle?"

"Why, while we had our teeth left us. I don't think a hempen cord ought for long to have held our hands!"

"To be sure not!" said Tom; "and here have I been getting Daisy to understand how to do a something that we might do ourselves! Never mind! Only look, now—she knows all about it!"

Daisy's teeth were sharp, and she made her way

through the cord a great deal quicker than either Tom or Ogle could have done.

However, they set to work then upon that portion of the rope that so clumsily fastened each of their other hands behind their backs.

In about six minutes both Tom and Ogle were quite free from the cord.

"Bravo!" said Tom.

They both listened.

"Hush!" said Ogle.

"What do you want here?" they heard a rough, snarling voice say.

"If you only come a little closer," replied one of Jonathan Wild's men, "we will let you know."

Neither Ogle nor Tom Ripon, strangers as they were to that place, were aware that the rough, snarling voice belonged to the ostler of the "Woodman" inn.

"Be off with you both," he added, "or perhaps somebody will come to make you."

"Don't lose time, old fellow," replied one of the men. "Send for the somebody at once, will you?"

"Get out of the way!"

"Oh, indeed! And pray what for?"

"I want to come into the stable."

"You don't say so! May we presume to ask what for?"

"You might guess, since I am the ostler, and that a couple of horses are there."

"Horses, old chap! Ha, ha! You mean horses on two legs, I suppose."

The cross-grained ostler was thoroughly angry.

"I don't mean to say," he retorted, "that there may not be horses on two legs, since I see that there are donkeys."

The two myrmidons of Jonathan Wild laughed aloud. They were by no means the kind of men to be easily offended by freedom of speech, and they were rather pleased than otherwise at the rough humour of the ostler.

"Why," said one, "you are just a man after our own heart, you are, old one!"

"Oh, be off, do!"

"Not exactly. We would do a good deal to oblige you, but as to being off, that is just what we can't do."

"Then get out of the way."

"Well, if there are horses in the stable, we may manage so much as that; but just to make sure, I will go in and see, because we have a couple of animals there that Jonathan Wild rather sets store by."

This janissary of Wild's gave his companion a sign to be vigilant, and then opening the stable door a few feet, he put his head in, calling out as he did so. "Hilloa! hilloa! you two thieves in there! Have you the stable all to yourselves, or is there a horse there?"

"Come in and see," said Ogle.

As he spoke, Ogle caught the fellow by the throat with a clutch that effectually prevented any breath from passing its thoroughfare until he chose to release it, and by the same action, he pulled him headlong into the stable.

The door swung shut.

"I have one of them, Tom," whispered Ogle.

"All's right!"

The janissary who was still outside, had, in obedience to the private signal of his comrades, kept a sharp eye on the ostler; and although he certainly did hear an odd sound at the moment that Ogle pulled his comrade into the stable, it was not sufficient to make him think there was any pressing danger.

The ostler remained growling and grumbling, according to his nature, at the stable door, and the janissary still on the outside getting impatient, cried out loudly as he dealt the door a kick, "Hoy! what are you about, mate? Come out!"

No reply was made to this appeal, and the janissary, for the first time in the transaction, began to feel a slight shock of alarm.

He no longer cared for the ostler, but turning his eyes full to the stable door, he was about to say something, when speech was stopped short on his lips, and he stood like a man suddenly transformed to stone.

The cause of this phenomenon was amply sufficient for its production.

The stable door was open about a couple of inches, and through that small space there projected the muzzles of two pistols, that seemed to move about in a most mysterious manner, always keeping exactly in a space that would comprehend the head, face, or breast of the janissary.

A voice then added to the awkwardness of the situation by saying, "Move hand or foot, and you are a dead man!"

The janissary felt the full truth of those words, and the hand that had mechanically sought the pocket of his wide skirted coat, in which he had a pair of pistols, was allowed quietly to drop.

"What's amiss?" he said.

"Nothing," said Ogle, as, with Tom Ripon, he opened the stable door and stepped out.

They each had one of the pistols that had been in the possession of the janissary who was so unceremoniously pulled into the stable by Ogle.

Now the man belonging to Jonathan Wild, who stood alone outside the stable door, was a man of the world. He knew when he was beaten.

Without any special interest in the matter, he saw no good to himself in throwing his life away to please Jonathan Wild.

So he gave in at once.

"All's right, Mr. Ogle," he said; "you gain the day. I give in."

The ostler, however, had not the temper of this man, and he turned to fly.

"Stop," cried Ogle; "I want you."

But the ostler had his own suspicions that some of the murderous practices of the "Woodman" inn might possibly come to light in rather a disagreeable manner.

Ogle, however, in doubt and uncertainty as he still was about the fate of Edith and Captain Heron, was by no means disposed to let the ostler escape.

"Stop!" he cried, "or I fire!"

The ostler took his chance. He knew the premises well; and he thought that if he once got into the thick plantation that was around the house, he might easy baffle pursuit; but Ogle was one of the worst men in the world to trifle with.

When he called to any one to stop, he meant that they should do so.

At the moment, then, that the ostler was on the point of disappearing through a hedge, Ogle fired after him.

A yell!

The ostler rolled over and over, and then lay still as death on the green-sward.

"Not a bad shot, that," said Jonathan Wild's man, quite calmly, and looking at the ostler with critical eyes.

At that moment an awful cry came from the stable.

The door was dashed wide open, and out issued Daisy, with the janissary of Wild in custody.

Daisy had him by the hair of the head, and bolted out with him as easily as a cat could have done with a mouse.

"Bravo, Daisy!" cried a voice.

Both Ogle and Tom Ripon looked up to a window of the "Woodman" inn with astonishment for that voice was the best known to them in all the world.

It was the voice of Captain Heron.

"Bravo, Daisy!"

"Hoorah!" shouted Tom Ripon.

"Why, Captain," said Ogle, "can I believe my eyes?"

"Yes, Ogle; I am all right up here."

"And Edith—I beg pardon, I should say the Lady Edith?"

"I thank you, Ogle, for the first thought of one so dear to me. She is with me, and well."

"Then I, too, cry out bravo!"

In a few moments, Felix Heron, with Edith and the wounded traveller and his dear daughter, Laura, looking so charming in her boy's dress, came down to the lawn.

The mystery of the disappearance of Edith and Heron, and the woman of the inn, and Swiney, from the room above, will be evident to the reader, since the sliding secret panel in the old mansion, by which Laura had made her first appearance, accounted for all.

"To horse!—to horse!" cried Heron. "I am convinced that Jonathan Wild is on the road, with the intention to attack us. Quick, Ogle; get the horses out!"

Daisy was prevailed upon to let the janissary go, and Edith and Heron were soon again mounted. A couple of horses that belonged to Wild's two men accommodated the wounded traveller and Laura; and in another stable Tom Ripon and Ogle found two tolerable steeds, which they did not hesitate to take possession of.

"Off and away!" cried Heron. "Across country to Epping, friends all. We will visit this 'Woodman inn,' Ogle, some other time when we have more leisure!"

Both Wild's men were left to do the best they could to join their master, but as they were on foot, that would be but a slow process.

In another hour, Captain Heron and his little party reached the outskirts of Epping Forest.

CHAPTER CLXXX.

CAPTAIN HERON, ONCE MORE IN SAFETY AT EPPING FOREST, CONCOCTS A NEW PLAN OF OPERATIONS ON THE ROAD.

How fair and beautiful old Epping Forest looked beneath the summer's sun! How different from the jarring roar and tumult of the city!

Well might Felix Heron and his Edith stroll hand in hand, with rapture, beneath the shadows of the tall old trees, and dream that life passed in that sylvan solitude would know no pangs.

And Edith, as she now looked lovingly into the eyes of Heron, cherished a hope that the days of his perilous adventures had surely passed away.

She thought that henceforth they might be permitted, in the deep recesses of that wood, to live a life of peace and serenity, undisturbed by the cares of life or its ambitions.

Alas! how greatly mistaken was poor Edith.

The adventures and many hair-breadth escapes that Felix Heron had already gone through were destined to be far transcended by those that in the history of his career were yet to come; and at the very time when Edith was dreaming of such peace and serenity, circumstances were preparing which were to exercise the greatest influence upon her life.

The sun was in the west, however, as she and Felix Heron walked thus lovingly side by side among the old trees.

The slant beams of the sultry ball of fire in the west, growing each moment more golden and more crimson, shone sweetly through the trees, dappling the green sward on which they trod, with many fanciful colours, so that it rather resembled the *parterre* of some garden rich in floral beauty, than the mere ordinary grass of the forest glade.

Edith spoke.

"My Felix, we shall now know peace. The tumult of your life should surely now be ended, and we should be able to feel that rest and safety belong to us."

Heron sighed.

"Oh, Felix, why that sigh?"

"Because, my Edith, you have conjured up a vision which I fear will vanish like one!"

"Alas! alas!"

"Nay, fear nothing, my Edith; for I have still to seek on the heath and on the road those adventures which have already made the name of Captain Heron famous. I will do so, with a providential care for the life which owes all its value to me that it is dear to you."

Edith started.

A hurried footstep sounded close at hand.

The low hoot of an owl, as a signal that he who was so quickly approaching was a friend, sounded mournfully on the evening air.

Edith clung close to the arm of Heron, and he called out aloud, "Who comes? This way, bird of night, and fear no hawks!"

The approaching figure at once emerged from among the trees, and Heron recognised the face and form of Ogle.

There was a look of care upon Ogle's face, and yet of that full and trusting confidence in himself and in Captain Heron, which never departed from him.

That Ogle was the bearer of some intelligence of a startling character, Heron had a suspicion, and by a slight sign he warned him not to be too hasty in declaring it before Edith.

Ogle quite comprehended him.

"A fine night, Captain," he said. "I thought perhaps, you wanted to speak to me on some very important business!"

This was Ogle's way of letting Captain Heron know that he had important business to speak of.

But Edith was by far too acute and observant not to comprehend at once the artifice of these words from Ogle; and she spoke, before Heron could form a reply.

"Do not, Felix, keep from me anything that it is well for you to know. The important business mentioned by Ogle, means danger, and, as such I ought to know it."

"You are right, Edith, and shall. Speak out, Ogle, and say what it is!"

Ogle hesitated.

From that hesitation there grew, not unnaturally, in the mind of Edith, the opinion that what he had to say was, in truth, more than commonly important.

THE LADY ADELA TRELAWNEY.

No. 54.—EDITH.

And so in truth it was.

Ogle came close to Heron and Edith, and uttered one word which brought more of a pang to the heart of Heron than could any ordinary signification of danger.

The word seemed to find an echo among the old trees; and as it was uttered, the last ray of the golden sunset died away, robbing the foliage of all its beauty, and leaving the forest cold and desolate.

"Treachery!"

That was the word.

"Oh," said Captain Heron, "you have, indeed, Ogle, found the only word that in all the English tongue can give me uneasiness."

"And us too, Captain; but I have too good reason for what I say."

"One of the band, then, is faithless. Is it not so?"

Ogle shook his head.

"Speak out, then, and say what you really mean. I hope to heaven I am not doomed to hear that some one who is bound to me by no common ties of gratitude, is faithless to me?"

"No, Captain, it is not quite so bad as that. Tom Ripon, and old Mortification, and my wife and myself, are all with you the same as ever."

"Thank heaven! Cheer up, my Edith: all well yet be well."

Edith had turned pale, and was trembling, as she kept close to the side of Heron. It appeared to her that the closer she was to him, the more safe he was. And now, Ogle, advancing still another step, spoke rapidly.

"Captain, I have had my suspicions of several of the band for some time, and have kept a good watch on them, but it was not until an hour ago that these suspicions became certainties!"

Captain Heron did not speak, but he made a sign for Ogle to go on.

"I was hiding in one of the thickets, where the nut-bushes grow the thickest, and I overheard a whispered conversation between two of the rascals. It was to the effect that they were to hold a meeting to-night in the old cave or grotto, close to the spring. You know the place well, Captain?"

"Yes, yes."

"It is where that poor old crazed woman used to hide herself, who so long made a home in the forest."

"I know it well."

"To-night, then, Captain, the whole of the band. I take it, will meet there, to consider what they shall do."

"In what way?"

"The intention, so far as I could gather it, Captain, was to give you up for a free pardon, and share the reward among them."

A flush of colour came over the face of Captain Heron, which, however, in the fading evening was not perceptible.

But he himself felt it, and it was with a deep sigh that he said, "And so this is to be the end —this the severance of the tie that has held me for so long to these men!"

"It looks like it, Captain."

"Well, Ogle, what shall we do?"

"I don't see that we can do anything, Captain, but the right thing."

"And what, Ogle, do you take that right thing to be?"

"Blow them up!"

"What?"

"Blow them up, Captain!"

"No, no."

"Well, of course you can do as you please; but I should place that little keg of gunpowder I had such a difficulty in getting at the old powder mills at Bow, in the cave, and in the middle of the affair blow them all up, and so settle it handsomely."

"No, Ogle, that will not do; I will myself ascertain what they intend, and then we will act accordingly. Cheer up, my Edith, and fear nothing!"

But poor Edith was full of fear.

The evening however soon deepened into night, and a dark and blusterous night it became; for after the sun had fairly departed, and not the faintest scintillation of twilight was in the western sky, the wind rose, and moaned, and howled among the old tree tops of Epping Forest.

The secrets of the ruins of the priory were not all known to the band of Captain Heron. It was not that he had any particular distrust of them, for it was rather his nature to be trustful, and he was oftener inclined to err on the side of too much confidence than too little; but it had never occurred that there was any necessity for initiating them into a knowledge of all the secret ways about the huge foundations of the ancient priory.

This was now fortunate, inasmuch as the narrow and gloomy passages that led underground to the cavern or grotto by the spring in the Forest, from the ruins, being only known to Heron himself, afforded a sure and certain mode by which he could come unawares upon those who were about to plot his destruction.

And yet it was with a heavy heart that Heron, at about half-past eleven o'clock on that night, stood in one of the old underground rooms of the ruins, prepared to explore the hidden and secret way that led to the grotto.

Fain would Edith have gone with him, but it was the wish of Heron to go alone, and she saw that wish was so strong that she forbore to urge him to forego it.

Ogle said not a word, but only waited for orders.

Those Captain Heron soon gave him.

"Ogle, it would not be possible for me to lie down to sleep in Epping Forest with the consciousness that the air was tainted by treachery. If I find such to be really the case, we who are here assembled will leave this place together."

"Yes, Captain."

Ogle looked about him as he spoke, as though to take counsel of who it was that would make up the party.

There were himself and his wife, Tom Ripon and the young girl of whom he had become so deeply enamoured; the Rev. Mortification; and there might have been two more persons, but poor Amelia Staunton, the mother of Captain Heron, had passed away to another and a better world, and was at peace; and Mrs. Ripon had gone to London, to look after, as she said, her property, which she had placed in various secure hiding places, such property consisting of parcels of valuable plate, which she had come by in the way of business.

But still the party was a pretty large one, and

as Ogle counted them, he said to Heron, "Captain, we shall want all the spare horses."

"Yes, Ogle, let them be collected, along with Daisy, in the glade that we call the Spanish Walk, on account of the Spanish chesnut trees on each side of it."

"It shall be done, Captain."

"And now, dear Edith," said Felix Heron, "I leave you in command of the party, and Ogle will see that all your orders are obeyed. I have but one to give."

Captain Heron spoke in a tone that sufficiently showed the grief that sat at his heart.

Edith clung to his arm as he spoke, and he added sadly, "You all know the sound of the silver bugle horn that I have usually about me, and which I have always said I would never breathe into except at times of emergency?"

"Yes, yes."

"Then if you hear two notes upon that, mount and ride at once down the glade, and be assured I shall soon meet you all."

Edith turned, and took from the arms of the young girl (Tom's flame) the little child, and held its soft baby face up to the lips of Heron.

He left a kiss upon the fair young brow, and then another upon the cheek of Edith.

"Be brave, my Edith. This is but a passing cloud, from which we shall emerge into a bright sunshine yet; for the light in which we live, it appears, is the false one of treachery."

CHAPTER CLXXXI.

CAPTAIN HERON SURPRISES THE PLOTTERS, AND TAKES HIS DEPARTURE FROM EPPING FOREST TO LONDON.

THE hour of midnight has come.

From the thickets and bushes, and from the deep shadows of the tall old trees in the immediate neighbourhood of the grotto by the spring in the forest, there emerge dim and dusky figures, which, as by one accord, make their way towards the grotto.

With the exception of those persons whom we left in the foundations of the old priory ruins, every living soul in the forest assembled in the grotto.

The scouts upon the outskirts of the wood left their posts.

The prowlers, as those of the band were called whose duty it was to keep watch and ward about the old forest glades, no longer peered out from amid the nut-bushes or the tangled brambles.

All obeyed the summons to the meeting in the grotto.

They had no light.

No one could see the other, but one name—it was that, probably, of the one who had set this treacherous combination in motion—spoke in a low tone.

"Let each one here present," he said, "proclaim his number."

This was done to the extent of thirteen.

That was, excepting Ogle and Tom Ripon, the exact number of Captain Heron's band.

Then, looking like dim and silent ghosts, they listened to the man who was leading them from the faith they had all pledged to Captain Heron.

"You all know," he said, "that we are not making money. What are we here for, but to make money? What do we care for Captain Heron, or Captain anybody else, if he don't put us in the way of feathering our own nests?"

"Good!" said one.

"Well, I'm glad you all agree to that, for it makes what I am going to add to it come all the easier, you see. I propose that we make a good round sum at once, and begin life all afresh—after we have spent it!"

The orator paused at this point, in the hope that some of his audience would say something to break a little the harshness and cold-blooded treachery of the proposal which was on his lips.

But no one spoke.

"Well," he added, "since you will make me say it, I have no objection. What I propose is, that we all share and share alike, which will give us hard on to a hundred pounds each, if we give up the Captain."

There was an uneasy movement among the band, and yet each man had perfectly well known what was coming.

"If that's agreed," added the spokesman, "nothing will be easier than to make terms with the beaks in London."

"But the pardon?" said one.

"Well, that's what I mean. It must be a free pardon, and a hundred pounds a man. Not a penny less, I should say, and no sort of going back from the terms of the pardon. Then, you see, we shall start afresh in the world, with something to enjoy ourselves with."

"Agreed!—agreed!" they all cried, one after the other.

The leader counted this word, repeated ten times in different voices, and then, dark as it was, he felt satisfied that he had the assent of all present.

But little did he suspect, or they suspect, the auditor they had.

Felix Heron was at the back of the cavern, having entered it by the subterranean way, and he had heard all that passed.

It was with a faint sigh of regret that he felt now quite satisfied that the old forest, where he had passed so many happy hours, was no longer tenable for him and his.

But his mind was made up previously.

He controlled the desire he had to walk forth into the midst of those men, and ask them what he had done that they should betray him.

With a wiser decision and a calmer judgment he let them take their own course, and he made his way back through the gloomy passages.

Heron had secreted in the recesses of the old ruins of the priory considerable treasure, and he felt quite certain that there it might be safely left until he chose to bring it forth; and it pleased him to think that it was there as a resource for Edith and the little one in case destiny should snatch him from them.

Ogle and Edith herself, along with Captain Heron, only knew of the secret repository of wealth in the wood.

But with all this, it was with a feeling very nearly akin to desolation of the heart, that Captain Heron felt the necessity of making up his mind to part with those familiar scenes in the old forest that had so long been a resting-place and a haven of security and peace for him and his.

That parting, however, had to take place, and the reader will please to imagine Felix Heron, with Edith, making such brief and hasty preparations as were necessary for the purpose.

But where were they to go?

Where were they to find such another refuge as Epping Forest?

Alas! nowhere to the same extent of security or pleasure in occupation.

Edith looked sadly in the face of Heron, and although she did not in so many words ask the question, yet her looks plainly enough said, "Whither shall we go?"

And Felix replied to those looks.

"Edith," he said, "let us look for the safety we want, even in what shall seem the midst of danger."

"More danger, Felix?"

"No, dear one, I hope more safety. There is an old fable of a lamb who, fancying that it was about to become the prey of a wolf who was prowling a forest in search of it, strayed into a gloomy cavern, where it found security until the hunters came into the wood, and slew the wolf —that cavern being the wolf's lair."

"Yes, Felix, I see, you would say, we will seek for safety somewhere that shall seem so dangerous that no one will dream of there looking for us."

"Just so, Edith."

"And where shall that be?"

"I propose that it be in our town house in St. James's Street."

"Whitcombe House?"

"Even so, Edith. There can be no doubt that it is completely deserted; and I should hardly think that even our arch enemy, Jonathan Wild, would look for us there."

"Be it as you wish, Felix."

Edith shuddered.

Her recollection flew back to the terrible agony she had endured from the visit of her brother at that house, and she had a dread of again taking up her abode even in secrecy in its chambers.

"This shall not be done, my Edith," added Heron, "if it be repugnant to you; but it has advantages — one of them, and not the least, being that you will be sufficiently near to your dear aunt, Lady Castleneau, that, if much pressed by any danger, her mansion in Bloomsbury Fields would be a refuge speedily attainable."

"Yes, Felix—yes, you are right. We will go to Whitcombe House."

Felix Heron, in concert with Ogle, soon had all in readiness for starting.

Daisy and several other horses were ready saddled and bridled for the road.

Tom Ripon was quite in his glory, for he looked upon a residence in London as affording a scope for his abilities that no wood, or forest, or country place could possibly present.

The night was creeping on, and as Heron could not tell exactly what steps the treacherous band might take to his detriment, he resolved that as the midnight hour had come, he and his little party would start for the metropolis.

Heron calculated that in two hours they would easily reach London; and as it would then be two o'clock in the morning, the streets would be in their most deserted condition.

But all was not to pass over so peaceably as Heron imagined.

It wanted about twenty minutes to twelve, when Tom Ripon, who had been out among the old trees bordering one of the glades, came back to the ruins of the priory with rather startling intelligence.

"Captain," he said, "I don't know what to make of it exactly, but I have seen, at one opening out of the wood, some men on horseback, and they don't belong to the band!"

"Indeed, Tom!"

"Yes, Captain! I crept close to two of them, and I heard one say to the other, that he should give it up if the governor did not come soon."

"Ogle," cried Heron.

"Here, Captain."

"The wood is getting beleaguered, I feel convinced. Let us start at once."

"All right, Captain."

"Edith, are you prepared even now, this moment, for the night ride to London?"

"Yes—oh, yes—this moment."

Edith caught the child from its little bed, and wrapped it in one of her mantles.

The party were all collected at the extremity of one of the narrow entrances to the old ruins, and Ogle was in the act of making a way for the horses by pulling up some shrubs that he had only that day loosened in the soil, so that they would yield to a vigorous effort, when they were all startled by the loud clear note of a bugle.

Ogle paused abruptly.

Heron held up his hand for silence, and by the dim light of one lantern, which was in the care of the Rev. Mortification Ripon, they all maintained their various attitudes, and waited for what might follow the bugle note.

A confused sound arose from the depths of the wood.

A shout—a kind of triumphant hurrah from many voices.

Ogle spoke hastily. "Captain, I have it. Those rascals have been more prompt than we thought; and no doubt is in my mind but that bugle call has let them know of the arrival of a force to help them in their villany."

"Then," said Heron, "we are in danger."

"But that, Captain, is not exactly the kind of word to scare us."

"No—but——"

"Never despair, Captain!" added Ogle. "All's well that ends well; and I think we can contrive to hold our own in spite of these rascals."

"Hush!"

Again the bugle note sounded clearly and distinctly through the wood.

This time it was echoed, or, at all events, immediately succeeded, by a strange shout from Mortification Ripon.

"Yea, murder! I fear the Philistines are upon us! Yea! Oh, dear, what is this?"

From his neck, where it had slightly grazed his skin, but chiefly spent its force amid the folds of a huge cravat he had lately taken to wear, the Rev. Mortification extracted an arrow.

"Yea, what can this mean——"

"Silence!" cried Heron. "Ogle, see to this— it means more than it looks."

"I think so, too, Captain, for here is a letter of some sort wound round the shaft of the arrow."

FELIX HERON LEADS HIS TRUSTY FOLLOWERS IN SAFETY THROUGH THE BURNG FOREST.

Presented Gratis with No. 54, of the New Edition of EDITH HE the Sequel to Edith the Captive ; or, the Robbers of Epping Forest.

"Hold the lantern here, Mortification."

"Yea, I will."

Heron carefully unfolded the strip of paper that was wound round the arrow, and read as follows :—

'I, Jonathan Wild, beg to inform all whom it may concern, that I don't mean to harm or interfere with any one in the forest but Felix Heron, the highwayman ; and him I mean to have, so I advise that he be given up quietly, or worse will come of it."

"Is that all, Captain ?" asked Ogle.

"Yes, that is all."

Edith crept closer still to Felix.

He smiled as he looked upon her, and spoke : "Well, my Edith, this is but what we expected, and brings, at all events, no more danger."

"Yea," said Mortification, "it hath brought me a scratch in the neck that is unpleasant, for, as the Psalmist says——"

"Never mind the Psalmist just now, Mortification," said Heron. "Ogle, I want you to see to a little matter at once."

"Yes, Captain."

"Go and catch one of the band if you can, and we will make him tell us what is exactly expected to happen.

Ogle laughed.

"Yes, Captain, that will be the plan. It will go hard but I come back with one of the rascals at the end of a noose."

What Ogle meant to do was sufficiently apparent by the little hasty preparation he made.

That consisted in making a noose at the end of a rope about six or eight yards long, and, with that coiled up in his hands, like the lasso of the South American hunters, he went out from the covert of the ruins into the wood to make a prisoner.

It was impossible to divest the present state of things of a feeling of considerable anxiety, although, if Felix Heron had been alone in the forest, it would have cost him not one moment's thought or preparation to decide on what to do.

He would just have mounted Daisy, and then sallied forth and made an end of the whole affair by a gallop out of the forest.

But he had the safety of others to look to, who were far dearer to him than life itself.

Edith and the little child.

It was no time for rash adventures when their safety was the question at issue.

The silence that ensued while Ogle was gone on the somewhat hazardous and strange expedition was unbroken save by a few low whispered words between Edith and Felix Heron.

"My Edith," he had said, "I wish you to mount Daisy, and take charge of the little one, so that whatever happens you will have no great difficulty in riding to your aunt's house in London."

"No !" was the whispered response of Edith, —"no, Felix ; we will go together, or not at all."

"Nay, Edith, do not say so."

"I must, indeed."

"You unnerve me."

Edith grasped his hand in tears.

"Do not you, Felix, unnerve me by using such words. Together we can be bold and strong. If we separate, we shall each of us be a prey to so much pain and anxiety about the other that we shall be unable to cope with events that may call upon us for action. No, no, a thousand times, no ! We will not—must not separate !"

Felix Heron was fain to comply. He was full of admiration for the feeling that prompted Edith, while at the same time he was full of pain for her safety.

A scuffling noise was heard now at some distance off in the wood.

"Help, oh, help !"

A voice raised the shout, which, by its tones, seemed to belong to some one in the last extremity of evil fortune.

Then all was still.

"Yes," said the Rev. Mortification, "our friend Ogle hath captured a Philistine, or a Philistine hath captured him."

"Hush !" said Heron.

"Don't be an elderly goose, father-in-law," said Tom Ripon. "Ogle is not the sort of chap, I can tell you, for any what-do-you-call him to get hold of."

"Yea, I——"

"Silence !" cried Heron, sharply ; "some one comes."

An odd, scuffling noise was apparent among the shrubs and bushes.

Then it assumed the character of some wild animal in want of water and breathing hard.

The Rev. Mortification at once got behind Tom.

"Ogle," cried Captain Heron.

"Here you are, Captain !"

"As quick as I can, Captain ; but he pretends he can't walk."

"Who is it ?"

"Number Eight !"

Ogle at this moment made his appearance with what looked like a huge bundle on his shoulder, and cast it down at the feet of Captain Heron.

———

CHAPTER CLXXXII.

EDITH AND FELIX HERON MEET WITH A FRIEND IN THE EXTREMITY OF THEIR PERIL.

THE object that Ogle cast down at the feet of Captain Heron was most undoubtedly human.

It uttered various half-choked moans and grunts, and rolled about in rather an eccentric fashion.

"Ah !" said Ogle, composedly, "I dare say the noose is rather tight round his neck. He would try to get out of it, and that made it worse."

"Release him," said Heron, "or we shall get no information from him."

Ogle loosened the noose, which in truth was so tight round the neck of that traitorous member of Captain Heron's band that he could not speak.

And even then he was in anything but a good condition to comprehend what was required of him.

"He is half-choked !" said Heron ; "give him some water, Tom Ripon."

"There you are !" said Tom, as he flung a pail full of water, that had been brought to that spot for the use of the horses, right over the half-strangled wretch.

This operation looked rather harsh, but it was effectual.

The shock did more to rouse the half-hanged wretch than probably anything else could have done.

He sat up at once.

He uttered a loud cry of terror and surprise.

Ogle then clapped the muzzle of a pistol to his forehead, just between the eyes, as he said, "Another such cry as that, and you are a dead man!"

"Mercy!"

"That's as it may turn out!"

"Oh, oh! I'm a dead man!"

"Not quite; but you will be in a few minutes, I dare say!"

Then Captain Heron stepped forward, and spoke in deep, earnest tones. that struggled with the natural indignation he felt at the treachery of one whom he had trusted.

"What had I done to you," he said, "or what had I left undone, that you should seek to betray me to my enemies?"

The traitor was silenced.

"You cannot answer either of those questions, I know," added Heron; "but there are others that you can and shall answer."

Still the man did not speak.

"What force has Jonathan Wild in and about the wood?"

Still no reply.

"Very well! Ogle?"

"Yes, Captain!"

"Hang this fellow; it is quieter than a pistol-shot!"

"All's right, Captain!"

Ogle gave the noose a pull, which made it feel disagreeably tight again about the neck of Number Eight; and he saw that if he would save his life he must needs tell all that was required of him.

"Let me go when I have made a clean breast of it, and I will tell you all."

"No," said Heron, "we make no conditions with a fellow like you. Tell all, or die."

"Say on, then. What am I to tell you, Captain?"

"What force has Jonathan Wild in and about the wood?"

"Twenty-five men."

"And are you all traitors—you, I mean, who composed my band?"

"All!"

Heron sighed.

"And what is the plan of operations?"

"Look!"

"Ah!"

A strange light began to show itself in different parts of the old forest. That strange light shone upon the faces and forms of the little party then assembled, and it shone, too, upon the horses, scaring them so that they pricked up their ears and stamped with their fore feet, as though anxious to be gone.

"Look!" again said Number Eight; and there was a tone of triumph in his words.

There needed nothing more to let Felix Heron see at once what was intended.

The forest was on fire!

The light increased each moment.

A sensation of heat even began to be felt, and now and then a rolling column of smoke made its way to where they stood.

"Now you know all," added the treacherous Number Eight. "We all know, and Jonathan Wild knows, that you have hiding-places in the old ruins here that might baffle him, and so he intends to make them too hot to hold you."

"So," said Felix Heron, "that is the plan, is it?"

"It is."

Heron glanced about him for a few seconds, and then he cried out to Ogle, "Mount at once, Ogle—mount at once! We will ride through the great glade."

"Stop a bit," said Number Eight. "The great glade has a strong party of Jonathan Wild's men in it, and there you will be nabbed. I don't advise you to go that way."

"No," said Ogle; "because you want us to be baked alive in the old priory ruins."

"It would be quite a pity," said Number Eight, "certainly, if things did not go on as they were meant."

"So it would," said Heron,—"so it would!"

"What do you mean, Captain?" asked Ogle.

"Just this, Ogle—that I always meant to hang any of the band who turned a traitor, and this one shall not escape the just doom!"

"All right, Captain! Help, Tom!"

"Yes, Ogle!"

"Just take the end of the rope, and run up this tree with it."

Tom saw what Ogle intended, and he went up a chesnut tree with the agility of a monkey, carrying the end of the rope with him.

Then Ogle lifted the man as high as his arms would let him, while Tom fastened the rope round a stout bough of the tree.

Number Eight uttered a yell of fear and despair.

"Help! murder! Oh, help! They are hanging me! They are going to hang me!"

"No," said Ogle, as he let him go, "they are not going to hang you—they have done it!"

With a jerk, the traitor fell to the extremity of the rope, and when there his toes were actually within three inches of the ground.

Those three inches, by the tension of the rope, gradually lessened; but before the cord had given out sufficiently that the toes of Number Eight actually touched the green sward beneath them, he was a dead man.

While this little act of retributive justice was being enacted, Captain Heron had placed Edith upon the back of Daisy.

She held the child in her arms, and Heron himself, as he patted the neck of his gallant steed, spoke to it encouragingly.

"My noble Daisy, you will carry this night your master, whom you love with all your honest heart, and all whom he holds dearest in this world!"

Then Heron mounted on to the back of his noble four-footed friend, and took the reins.

"To horse—to horse!" he cried. "Let them beware who try to stay me!"

The fire in the wood was gaining strength each moment, and the dull, red glare that it gave forth pervaded the whole forest.

The trees, and the shrubs, and the deep green grass looked all very beautiful in that crimson light; but the time was not one in which to take more than a passing glance at the old leafy home where had passed so many happy hours; and Felix Heron at once set Daisy in motion through and over the underwood that led to one of the glades of the forest.

The rest of the party had managed to get mounted as best they could.

Tom Ripon was supremely happy, because he had behind him, with her arms, for safety's sake, round his waist, the young girl whom he had fallen so head over years in love with since she had been rescued from death at Tyburn by Captain Heron.

Ogle rode alone, and Mrs. Ogle was fain to sit behind the Rev. Mortification Ripon, who muttered to himself, "Yea, a man might be safe enough against the bullets that peradventure will soon fly about like hailstones in May, if he had one other such extensive female before him as I have now behind me."

"Get on, do!" said Mrs. Ogle.

It was scarcely to be supposed that Jonathan Wild had not in some measure prepared himself for the contingency of a start of this character on the part of Captain Heron.

He must have known that in all probability the boldest course out of the difficulties that surrounded him would be that which would recommend itself more particularly to Heron.

An encounter, therefore, was to be expected.

Over the brushwood, then, Daisy, guided by the skilful hand of Felix Heron, went: not a moment could be calculated upon that might not bring them face to face with Wild and his party.

Yes, surely now the alarm is given.

The sound, rapid and continuous, of a bugle is in the wood.

At the moment that its echoes are awakened, Daisy, with her precious treble burden, emerges into one of the open glades of the forest.

What a beautiful sight that glade was! One side of it was in flames.

But now there is a shout of triumph from Jonathan Wild!

He is there!

By some fiendish calculation, he has surmised that that would be the route Heron would choose if he attempted to gallop out of the forest.

"Yield—yield!" he shouted. "Not a hair of the head of any one shall be injured, if Felix Heron yields himself a prisoner!"

This had no inducement to any one to stop.

They all dashed onward.

"Fire!" cried Wild.

A rolling discharge of pistols took place.

If any one was hurt, it was not by a cry or a pause that Jonathan Wild had the gratification of knowing it, the little cavalcade swept past like an apparition!

"Fire!"

Again the voice of Wild rose with the murderous command above all other sounds.

Another volley of pistol-shots flew after the fugitives.

Heron thought that some sharp piece of twig from one of the trees had struck his shoulder.

It was a bullet that just furrowed up the skin.

"Edith, Edith!"

"Yes, Felix."

"You are unhurt?"

"Quite!"

"And our child?"

"Safe, safe!"

"Thank heaven! On, Daisy, on! On, for three lives and your own, my gallant Daisy!"

A half-burnt tree fell exactly in the way.

Daisy, with one leap, cleared the obstacle.

The other horses followed, and then Jonathan Wild raised a yell of rage, for he saw that all his schemes for the capture of Felix Heron in Epping Forest had resolved themselves into a mere chase out of it, and along the high road to London.

He was mounted on a powerful black horse, and as he struck the spurs deep into the flanks of the startled animal, he shouted aloud, "My own share of the reward be the man's who captures or kills Felix Heron! Follow! follow!"

With these words Wild dashed onwards in pursuit of Heron and his party, who were now getting rapidly clear of the wood.

Daisy was rather overweighted.

With Heron alone she would have taken the gallop to London, and thought nothing of it.

About a mile from the forest he saw, coming along a cross road, obliquely towards him, a chariot.

A couple of good horses, one of which was ridden by a postilion, drew it.

An idea at once darted into the mind of Heron, "Edith," he said,—"dear Edith, for my sake, and your own, and for the sake of our dear child, I propose that we separate for a short time."

"Oh, Felix, Felix!"

"Nay, dear one, think nothing of it! You see that cariage approaching?"

"Yes, Felix—yes!"

"I will ride up to it, and ask its occupant to afford you and our child a refuge."

There was no time for further parley on the subject. The carriage rapidly approached, and Heron dashed up to the side of it.

"Halt!" he cried to the postilion. "Pull up, I say!"

"Oh, Lord!—a highwayman, as sure as my name is Peter!" cried the postilion.

But he stopped his horses abruptly

Heron looked into the chariot.

"Thank heaven!" he said.

He uttered that ejaculation because he saw a lady alone in the vehicle.

"Madam," he said, in tones of emotion, "will it please you to do an act of charity and goodness to two innocent souls?"

"What do you mean?" asked the lady, who was both young and handsome.

She leant forward as she spoke, and then Edith cried, "It is the Lady Trelawney, the sister of Colonel Trelawney, or I am much mistaken."

"Yes," said the lady, "that is my name; and can it be possible that I see the Earl and the Countess of Whitcombe?"

"Yes!" said Heron; "and the Lord Warringdale."

Edith started at the sound of that name, for it had never yet occurred to her that such was the title which, by courtesy, her own child was entitled to.

The Lady Trelawney, too, had heard quite enough from her brother, the Colonel, of Lord

Warringdale, not to be in any way desirous of his company.

A very few words, however, sufficed to rectify the mistake into which the mere pronunciation of the name of Warringdale had plunged both Edith and Lady Trelawney.

"Ah, yes!" said Edith; "my son is entitled to that name, which has been usurped by one in every way wholly unworthy of it."

"Yes, Edith," added Captain Heron, "you and I will never forget the right that our child has to rank with the nobility of the land."

"No one," said Lady Trelawney, "will willingly forget it, who wishes for justice. My brother, who is so intimate a friend of the Earl of Bridgewater, has told me over and over again of the great injustice and wrong which has been done to the Earl and Countess of Whitcombe."

"Then, madam," said Heron, "you grant my request, and will afford an asylum in your carriage to the Countess and our son?"

"Willingly."

"Edith, you are saved!"

"And you, Felix?"

"I, too!"

"You come with us?"

"Not so, dear Edith. I only meant to say that I, too, was saved, and by the same means. Lady Trelawney, by taking you and the child, will enable me to distance Jonathan Wild and his gang."

As Captain Heron spoke, the sound of a bugle came upon the night air, and he knew that his foes were close at hand.

"Quick, dearest Edith," he said, "if you would save us all!"

Edith at once dismounted, and was instantly safely bestowed in the carriage along with the Lady Trelawney.

"On, on, now," said Heron; "on to London, and take no notice of me!"

Edith waved her hand from the carriage window, and then the vehicle started again, although the postilion was in such a state of bewilderment in regard to what had happened, that he hardly knew whether he was in the clutches of a highwayman or not.

Daisy, then, lightened of the load she carried, made two of her bounds, by which she testified that she was ready for any extraordinary exer-rtion that might be required of her by he master.

Captain Heron felt a sense of security and ease now that for the past half-hour had been a stranger to his breast.

"No, Daisy, no," he said. "Not yet, my own gallant Daisy! We will let the villain Jonathan Wild see us before we start on the road to London again."

The object of Heron was to draw off effectually from all observation of Lady Trelawney, Jonathan Wild and his men.

To do that effectually, it was only necessary that Jonathan should get a fair sight of him.

"Ride on, Ogle!" said Heron to those who were with him. "Ride on, and get to town as quickly as you can. Let me find you in the street that runs from St. James's Street, close to Whitcombe House."

"All right, Captain."

Ogle knew perfectly well that Felix Heron had far better chances of escape from the large party that pursued him if he were left quite alone.

And now that Edith and the child were in safety, there was no further cause for anxiety.

"Come on, Tom," said Ogle. "The deuce take the hindmost! Come on!"

"I don't agree with you there," said Tom. "The hindmost, as far as I am concerned, is the prettiest girl in all the world, and you won't get me to hand her over to the deuce, I can tell you."

Ogle laughed, but all conversation was quickly put an end to by the pace at which they sped onwards to the metropolis.

And so it was that Captain Felix Heron was alone on the high road.

Alone with Daisy.

It was quite like old times revived again; and he felt that he had only to cry "Stand and deliver" to some passenger on the highway, to be as he had been years gone by, when the thought of ever calling Edith his own was but a dream.

Not for long, however, was Captain Heron able to indulge in any fanciful mood.

Jonathan Wild and his party came on at a thundering pace.

They were all pretty well mounted, for Wild had well calculated his chances of success and failure in regard to the enterprise.

Felix Heron stood like the statue of a man and horse, exactly in the centre of the road.

There was a portion of that highway which was raised somewhat like the crown of an arch, and in fact it was so, on account of a watercourse that ran beneath.

It was on the very apex of this raised part of the road that Felix Heron stood with Daisy.

The knight was dark.

But it was not so dark that his figure, and that of his horse, might not be seen against the night shade in sufficient relief to make no doubt of what they were.

And as he waited there for the space of about one minute and a half, a sense of bitterness and irritation came over him that he should be so relentlessly hunted by Jonathan Wild.

Hunted like some wild animal from his beautiful sylvan home in the forest of Epping.

Drawing from the holster of his saddle one of the pistols that Ogle had taken good care should be placed there, properly charged, he presented it at the advancing form of Jonathan Wild.

"Who knows," he said, "but chance or providence may direct this bullet to the destruction of that fiend in human shape, who can be anything but precious in the sight of heaven?"

As the cavalcade, with Wild at their head, turned the corner of the road which would at once bring them into the sight of Captain Heron, he levelled the pistol.

"Ah, I see him!" shouted Jonathan Wild.

Bang!

The pistol was discharged at the same moment, and the report mingled with the echoes of Wild's voice.

Then there was a yell.

A scene of confusion ensued, and Heron thought Wild was down.

Then he gave Daisy the rein, and off he went.

"Hurrah!" he shouted.

Was Jonathan Wild killed by that chance shot?

That was the anxious question that Felix Heron put to himself, and it was one that he would have been glad to get answered one way or the other.

There were no means, however, at that time, of solving it, and he could only gallop on.

"I have tried to hang him," he said, "and I have tried to shoot him; and still, as if he had a charmed life, he lives.

From the clatter of horses' feet in the wood after him, Felix Heron was led to the belief that the pistol-shot had not been effectual as against Jonathan, considering, as he did, that if it had been so the pursuit would have been given up for want of a leader.

Daisy made little of the distance to London.

The house-tops of the City, if it had been daylight, would already have been seen from a little common that had to be passed, when, to the surprise of Heron, Daisy slightly stumbled.

To dismount was the work of an instant to

No. 55.—EDITH.

Heron, and one by one he made a careful examination of the feet of Daisy.

Yes, it was as he fancied.

She had cast a shoe.

Any idea of proceeding on to the stony road, which he well knew almost immediately surrounded the common on which he had made this unwelcome discovery, was out of the question.

Heron stood by the side of Daisy in doubt what to do.

By the dim leaden-coloured light that began to show itself in the eastern sky, he managed to see the face of his watch.

It was half-past four in the morning.

In another half-hour he knew that the dawn would be making rapid progress.

It was necessary, therefore, that whatever he did should be done quickly, or he would not reach London by any hour that would make it safe for him to take refuge at Whitcombe House.

The delays of one kind and another on the road had eaten into the night in an extraordinary manner, and he had not, until he held the face of his watch towards the east to look at it, imagined it to be so late by a good hour.

Mount his disabled horse he would not; and it was with something like a foreboding of danger that he led Daisy along the narrow bridle-way of the common.

From frequently traversing the road, Heron knew that in the hollow immediately past the common there lay a little village of about twenty houses only.

One of those houses had, as a matter of course, at the lower part of it a smithy.

Adjoining that smithy was a mill, so that the miller was a smith likewise, carrying on both the trades, as occasion required.

Heron's idea was to rouse up this man, and get him, by the promise of some unusual payment, to light his forge-fire, and put a new shoe on Daisy.

All this would take time, but there was in reality no other resource, since to gallop Daisy right into London with one shoe off might lame her for months.

That was not to be thought of.

As yet, nothing could be heard of his foes, for Heron had fairly galloped at very nearly the top of Daisy's speed for a few miles, and distanced them completely.

Indeed, he had a hope that the road he had come was not the one which they had chosen.

If so, all would be well.

He took Daisy by the bridle, and led her carefully over the common through the darkness, which seemed just then to be increasing instead of diminishing.

But Heron knew that that was a common phenomenon just before the dawn fairly began to show itself.

CHAPTER CLXXXIII.

CAPTAIN HERON MEETS WITH AN ADVENTURE OF DANGER AT THE OLD SMITHY.

THE distance across the common to the little village in the hollow was something short of a quarter of a mile.

It was an anxious distance, though, to Felix Heron.

As he went, he kept his sense of hearing painfully on the stretch to catch the slightest sound which should be indicative of the approach of his foes.

It was a consolation to hear nothing of them, and in the course of about eight or nine minutes, Heron and his poor half-lamed Daisy reached the little cluster of houses that, by courtesy, were called a village

How still and wrapt in repose they all were!

If that little hamlet had been only inhabited by the dead, it would have been impossible for it to be more profoundly still than it was.

Heron halted.

At some distance off in the track he had come he heard the faint sound of horses' feet.

He knew that those who sought his life were not far from the spot.

He knew that the villain Wild, whose hatred of him had got to that pitch that it transcended even his love of money, was intent upon his murder.

By that time Heron had quite made up his mind

that the pistol shot he had sent on a chance errand among his pursuers had, at all events, whatever other mischief it might have done, not killed Wild.

"No," said Heron to himself, as with the bridle of Daisy upon his arm he looked about him in the quiet village,—"no, the villain is born to suffer on the gallows, whither he has consigned so many persons both innocent and guilty, and by no other mortal means can he be brought to death."

Hark!

A new sound.

New and strange too.

It breaks the stillness of the village, which was so like death.

A sound like the rushing of a cloud on its passage over the quiet spot, by some suddenly sprung up gale of wind.

And yet the air blew but lightly, nevertheless Heron had become aware that for the last few hours a kind of breeze, in a fitful manner, was gradually getting up.

Daisy was startled at the odd sound.

At one moment it was like wind, and then like water, and then like the passage through the air of a flock of huge birds.

What could it be?

A man's voice broke the stillness of the village.

> "Oh, the miller is a jolly wight—
>   A jolly wight is he;
> He lets the wind do all his work,
>   While he is singing free!"

"Hilloa!" cried Heron.

"Hilloa! to you; hilloa!" was the prompt reply.

"Are you the miller?"

"Mayhap I am; and if you were to say 'Are you the smith?' I should make the same answer; for as the old song goes:

> "The smith he is a mighty man—
>   Clank! clank! goes the anvil;
> He drinks deep from the flowing can,
>   And——"

Oh! what's that? Don't! What do you want?"

"I want, my friend, less singing and more work," said Heron, as he caught the smith by the arm; "and I want to know first what is your charge for putting on a shoe?"

"Three groats."

"Three! I will pay you three times three if you will put one on for me at once."

"For you? Do you wear shoes of my make, my friend?"

"Come! come! no trifling. My horse is here, and she does."

"Your horse, and you call him she?"

"Yes, a mare is but a female horse, as you ought to know."

"Then this is a woman but a female man; so I will put on the shoe at once."

"Have it all your own way," said Heron; "only be quick about it, and you shall have a guinea for your pains."

"Then you are one of two things!"

"What things?"

"A lord or a highwayman!"

"Both! both!" cried Felix Heron, as he followed the smith into the smithy by the light of a lantern, which the humourist had lighted hastily.

"Come on, then—I like a frank fellow like you; and if I charge you a single groat for your horse's shoe, why I am not John Brown, the jolly miller and smith of Little Hampton!"

"Tell me," said Heron, "what strange noise is that I hear in the air?"

"Noise?"

"Yes, like the rushing of something through the air."

"Why, don't you know what that is? I have just set loose the sails of my mill."

"Oh! to be sure."

Felix Heron, the moment he heard the simple explanation of the phenomenon, was quite astonished at himself that he had not hit upon it before.

The smithy was of great extent, and an old, picturesque-looking structure it was.

In one corner were heaps of old rusted iron implements of all kinds and descriptions. In another, cart-wheels and old house furniture were piled up almost to the soot-begrimed roof.

The forge and all its appurtenances occupied a considerable space; and the smith, as he held up the lantern to look at Heron, put on a strange expression, and nodded his head.

"Ah," he said, "you are in a hurry?"

"I am."

"The bull-dogs are after you?"

"They are."

"Now, my friend, what would you say to trusting me with your name?"

"I mean to do. I am that Captain Félix Heron who am the rightful Earl of Whitcombe; and this is my mare, Daisy, of whom you may have possibly heard something."

"What—what! Am I to have the honour and credit of putting a shoe on Captain Heron's Daisy, from old Epping Forest?"

"It is so. Look at her."

The smith was too good a judge of horses not to see by a very casual inspection that it could be no other than the veritable Daisy who stood before him in the smithy.

"Beautiful—beautiful!" he cried. "My gracious, what a head and eyes she has! She looks at one like a Christian!"

"Better than many who call themselves by that title," said Heron, bitterly.

The farrier put down his hand to lift Daisy's foot, but it was not until Captain Heron said to her, "Up, Daisy—up, up," that she would allow it to be lifted.

"Now, for the love of Heaven, be quick," said Heron, "for I am pursued by Jonathan Wild, and he will be here in five minutes more."

"Hush! Trust to me."

A horseman came at that moment galloping into the village, and stopped about twenty paces from the smithy.

"Come on, laggards," shouted a harsh voice, which there was no mistaking as belonging to any one but Jonathan Wild. "Come on! I am certain that he has come this way!"

The clatter of other horses' feet in the little quiet street of the village showed that Wild's party had joined him, and that they were in force.

"Hide!" said the smith.

"Take care of Daisy."

"Leave that to me."

"Quiet, Daisy, quiet!"

Heron patted her on the neck, and then taking the hand of the smith, he let Daisy see that he placed it on her neck.

After that Heron was quite sure that she would look upon the smith as a friend and a person to be trusted.

Captain Heron then himself retired to a distant part of the smithy, and was in complete hiding in the darkness of the old, spacious place.

Another moment, and Jonathan Wild and his party rode up to the door of the smithy.

"Hillo, Mr. Farrier," he said, "are you at work early or late?"

"A little of both."

> "'Oh, a can of ale, a can of ale,
>   Is a very good thing in the morning;
> And another can, and another can,
>   Is not a thing to be scorning;'"

especially if somebody else pays for it. Stand still, will you? Anybody would think you were not the parson's quiet old horse, that comes here at four miles an hour on a Sunday afternoon. Do be quiet!"

Tap, tap, tap! went the smith at his work.

"You are a merry fellow," said Wild. "Where's your fire, Mr. Smith?"

"Here."

The farrier stirred up his forge fire, which had been damped down over night with a heap of wet, small coal, and as he gave his bellows two or three puffs, the bright flames began to roar and crackle.

But he took good care to keep between the party of Jonathan Wild and Daisy.

"How long have you been at work?" asked Wild.

"About thirty odd years."

"Tush, tush! I mean this morning."

"Oh, about half an hour."

"Then you can say if a man has ridden through the village?"

"Yes I can; and yes I can say to it."

"Did he go fast?"

"Like mad!"

"Ah!"

"Yes; I was just setting my mill sails to the morning air. Why, fast!—he came on a black, or a very dark bay, horse, that seemed not to touch the ground, but to skim over it like a shadow!"

"Confound him!" muttered Wild.

"Yes," said the smith.

> "'A can of ale—a can of ale!'"

"Hold your row, do!" cried Wild.

"Eh?"

"I say, hold that row. My horse has cast a shoe!"

Wild dismounted as he spoke, and, taking his horse by the bridle, he led it into the smithy, leaving his party in the roadway, on the outside.

That a similar accident should have happened to the horse of Jonathan Wild to that which, for the time being, had disabled Daisy, was one of the most provoking things in the world.

The smith was rather staggered at the coincidence, and could hardly believe it to be true.

"Your horse cast a shoe?" he said.

"Yes, idiot; why not? Did you never hear of such a thing as that happening before?"

"Yes, and believed, too," said the smith, promptly. "I'll soon put that all to rights for you. Dobbin can wait."

The smith pushed Daisy further on into the darkness and shadow of the old smithy, for if the eyes of Wild had only happened to be cast for half a minute upon her he could not have failed to recognise her as the redoubtable Daisy.

But owing to not the remotest suspicion on the subject crossing his mind, he did not pay the least attention to Daisy, further than seeing that it was something in the shape of a horse.

"Now, sir," said the smith, as he lifted the foot of Wild's horse, "we will make the parson's galloway wait, as your worship is in a hurry."

"Rather!" said Wild. "Be quick about it, for I want to be on the road again!"

As he spoke, Jonathan Wild strolled up the old smithy, with that feeling of curiosity and prying which such a man was sure to feel in a strange place.

Quite casually, then, he turned and looked towards the forge fire.

The aspect of things from his present point of view was completely changed. He saw Daisy quite plainly, and knew her at once.

The cry that Wild raised was of the most extraordinary character.

The smith dropped the horse's foot on which he was at work.

Daisy pricked up her ears.

The party of Jonathan Wild in the road crowded round the entrance to the smithy.

And then surely all would have been lost but for that rare presence of mind in moments of extreme peril which was so marked a characteristic of Felix Heron.

Wild was about five long paces only in front of him.

By a single bound Heron reached him, and caught him by the back of the neck.

Wrenching, then, his head back with a violence and suddenness that nearly broke his neck, Heron dashed the muzzle of one of his small pocket-pistols right into his mouth, as he said, "Choose, Jonathan Wild, between death or submission!"

"Did you speak, sir?" asked one of Wild's men, from the road.

CHAPTER CLXXXIV.

JONATHAN WILD HOLDS HIS LIFE AT THE MERCY OF FELIX HERON.—THE DAWN APPROACHES.

THE state of affairs in that old smithy was curious enough.

The smith could not imagine what had happened or what was about to happen.

He had heard the sudden shout from Jonathan Wild, but what was the immediate occasion of it he had no means of knowing.

But he was doomed to be still further astonished.

Captain Heron whispered into Wild's right ear, with a hissing earnestness that admitted of no two opinions about the sincerity of what he said.

"Jonathan Wild, for my own preservation, it is necessary that I should spare your life. If you are tired of that life, you can refuse to do as I bid you, in which case I shall give the alarm of something amiss to your men, by the report of the pistol that will scatter your brains among all this rusty old iron!"

"Don't!" said Wild.

He could only speak at the back of his throat, in an odd sort of way.

"I will, however," added Heron, "make a bargain with you so far, that I can spare you upon your obeying me."

"Agreed!"

"Did you speak, Mr. Wild?" asked the janissary again from the road.

"Say no in your own amiable way," whispered Captain Heron.

"Go to the deuce!" cried Wild.

"That will do."

"Beg pardon, sir," said the janissary, "but we all thought we heard you cry out, and that something was amiss."

"Tell them no," whispered Heron.

"Go and hang yourself!" said Wild.

"That will do."

The farrier began to have a sort of glimmering of the truth of what was going on; and as he pulled up the foot of Jonathan Wild's horse again he said, "What, sir, are you the famous Mr. Wild, the officer, that people do talk about so much, and that everybody is so fond of?"

Wild's men laughed at this.

"Answer them!" said Heron.

Wild growled like a bear.

"Mind your business, and shut up your stupid owl's throat, you idiot!"

"Thank you, sir! Ah, I don't wonder at anybody being quite taken by you.

"'A can of ale, a can of ale,
    Is a good thing in cold weather:
It warms a man, it helps a man,
    And puts him in good feather.'"

Heron whispered to Wild again.

"Send your men off!"

"I can't."

"You must."

"You will murder me."

"Killing, in your case, would be no murder if I were; but I will not."

"Dare I trust you?"

"As you like."

"And if I don't?"

"Death!"

"That will do. While there's life there's hope. Hoy! Atkinson—and you, Devilskin!"

"Yes, Mr. Wild."

"I have a fancy to stay here."

"Very good, Mr. Wild."

"I find myself in such agreeable company, that I intend to wait here awhile. You can all ride on to London, and wait at Little Newgate for me."

"Yes, sir. If we meet Captain Heron, I suppose we are to nab him?"

"Oh, dear, no!"

"No, do you say, Mr. Wild?"

"Yes; I say no. If you do meet him, give him my compliments, and say that I live yet in hopes of a clear stage and no favour."

"Yes, sir."

"Be off with you all!"

The troop clattered away.

"There!" said Wild: "I suppose I shall have my brains blown out for being a fool."

"Not so," said Heron. "When I make a promise, I keep it; but you and I will now ride to town together."

"Indeed!"

"Yes, and in truth. Firstly, however, you will give up your arms."

"There!"

Wild produced two pistols from the deep pockets of his coat.

"Is that all?"

"Yes, Captain Heron, that is all. I am not above knowing and owning that I am beaten."

"Look you here, Jonathan Wild: I warn you! Anything in the shape of treachery, or an attempt to do me an injury, shall meet with, at my hands, but one reception, and that shall be death!"

"I know it."

"Be wary, then, as you wish to live."

CAPTAIN HERON COMES TO AN UNDERSTANDING WITH HIS ANCIENT
ENEMY, JONATHAN WILD.

Presented Gratis with No. 55, of the New Edition of EDITH HERON, the Sequel to Edith the Captive; or, the Robbers of Epping Forest.

Heron then let Wild be perfectly free, and advanced towards the forge.

The smith had put the shoe upon Wild's horse, and Heron said, quite calmly, " Mr. Wild and I intend to ride to London together as soon as my mare is fit for the road."

The smith rapidly glanced from one to the other of the men, but he made no remark.

He set about putting on Daisy's shoe with skill and expedition ; and he sung as he worked—

" ' A man that's wise is not a fool,
    Which every person knows ;
  His head is best upon his neck,
    Because it's there it grows.'

There, sir ! All's right now !"

" And there is your guinea," said Heron.

" Thanks, sir !"

" And there—ha, ha !" growled Wild,—" there is a groat for my shoe !"

" Oh, thank you, sir ! I shall want it to get a standing in a cart at Tyburn to see some one hanged some fine morning."

" Hah !" said Wild, as he sprung to his horse's back ; and then, turning to Heron, he said, " You are a laggard, Captain. What, now, if I rode off ?"

" I should overtake you in half a mile," said Heron quietly as he mounted Daisy.

" You would ?"

" Try it."

" No—no ! What's the use—what's the use ? I wait for you you see !"

Wild and Captain Heron trotted out together upon the high road to London.

A strange assorted pair.

Never in all the changes possible to occur in his relations with Jonathan Wild, could Felix Heron have supposed it within the reasonable bounds of probability that he could be in apparent peace with him on the highway.

But the peace was only apparent.

The thing of all others that staggered Wild, and kept him from some desperate attempt on the life of Captain Heron, was the cool confidence of the latter.

Jonathan thought it simply out of the question that any one could be so calm and careless in his company if they had not had some complete assurance of safety.

The idea then took possession of Wild, that, although he saw them not and heard them not, some of Heron's friends might be close at hand.

In that case, he felt that his life might hang upon a word or look.

Jonathan Wild did not want to die just then, and therefore he was discreet accordingly.

————

CHAPTER CLXXXV.

CAPTAIN HERON AND EDITH COMMENCE A NEW CAREER AFTER AN AWFUL DISCOVERY AT WHITCOMBE HOUSE.

THE dawn of the new day was now quite evident.

Long streaks of sickly-looking light were in the eastern horizon.

It is a popular mistake to suppose that the first approach of daybreak is beautiful. On the contrary, it is raw, and doll, and chilly. It is not until the sun has made such progress that the disc of fire is close to the extreme edge of the horizon,

that any of the warm, beautiful tints are evoked from it.

But that time was speedily approaching.

At about the distance of half a mile from the village, the ground rose again so that Jonathan Wild and Captain Heron reached an eminence which commanded a full view of many miles of country.

Heron drew rein.

Wild did the same.

He was afraid that something was about to happen.

Looking at him calmly in the eyes, Heron spoke to his evil-minded companion.

" Jonathan Wild, wherefore is it that the delight of your life is to persecute me ?"

" It is my duty."

" For which you gain nothing !"

" My pleasure, then."

" Neither is it that, for you suffer far more pain than pleasure in the pursuit."

" My interest."

" Ay, so you fancy it ; but it is not so, for it will be your destruction as sure as you are now a living man, and might be a dead one at my feet this moment if I so willed it."

" What do you want of me ?" growled Wild, with a downcast look.

" You are such a mass of wickedness that the only thing any one with a grain of compassion in his heart could really want of you, would be that that you should repent."

" Repent ?"

" Yes ; repent before it is too late !"

" Ha ! ha !"

The laugh was a horrible one.

" You laugh at the word ?"

" I do."

" And wherefore ?"

" Because it is too late, and has been too late any time this last twenty years."

" I am afraid it is ; but if I thought you had sufficient remains of humanity in your disposition to keep a promise, I would extort one from you."

" What is it ?"

" It is that whatever may be your hostility for me, and whatever may be the attempt you make against my life and liberty, you will never again contrive aught against the Countess of Whitcombe and our child ?"

Wild was silent.

" Do you hear me ?"

" I do. What will be the consequence if I won't promise ?"

" Nothing."

" You don't threaten me with a bullet, then, if I won't ?"

" I do not. I promised you your life at the old smithy if you consented to what I then proposed— namely, to send your men off on a wild-goose chase—and I shall assuredly keep my word."

" Very well. Look you here, Captain Felix Heron, or Earl of Whitcombe, whichever you like best to be called, I will promise ; and so help me ——Hem ! No, it's no use a man like me speaking of heaven—it's a place that is not likely to help me, or that I am in any way to be acquainted with."

" And you will keep faith ?"

" I will."

" Hold up your hand to this fair morning light and say ' I swear it !' "

Jonathan Wild held up his hand, and Felix Heron thought he saw it shake a little in the light air.

The bleared and blood-shot eyes of the thief-taker blinked and winked at the coming daylight like those of some wild predatory animal whose habits were all nocturnal, and who could not bear the presence of the daylight.

"I swear!" he said.

"Then, Jonathan Wild, take back your pistols, and you are free."

"What?"

"I say you are free."

"But—but——"

"But what?"

"My pistols?"

"Oh, yes! Take them!"

"They are well loaded."

"Doubtless! I am not afraid!"

Wild turned of a deathly paleness as he took the pistols from the hand of Felix Heron, or, rather, a strange, cold, yellow tinge spread itself over his face.

As Heron handed him the pistols their muzzles were towards his (Heron's) breast.

A very slight effort on the part of Jonathan would have touched one of the triggers, and Felix Heron might have been a dead man.

The temptation was great.

Never in all his life, perhaps, had Felix Heron tried so hazardous an experiment as that with human nature.

But he was determined to try it.

Wild took the pistols, and, all of a tremble as he did so, he put them into the pocket of his coat that was next to Heron.

"No," he said, "I—I am not quite so bad as all that; and besides——"

He glanced uneasily about him.

His firm impression was that the whole of this scene must be taking place under the eyes of Heron's men—perhaps of Ogle and some others who were still true to him.

In that case, although he might kill Heron, it would only be a life for a life.

"Tell me now, truly, my Lord Whitcombe," he said, "are we not well watched?"

"Yes."

"By Jove, I thought so!"

"No."

"What do you mean?"

"I mean that we are watched, but you have mentioned the name of a heathen divinity instead of the Christian one."

"What do you mean?"

"I told you we were watched. It is not by Jove, but by the Creator of all. You may depend, Wild, that an eye is upon you that never sleeps!"

As he spoke, Heron pointed upwards to where a soft and beautiful white cloud was floating in the air.

Wild shaded his eyes with his huge, coarse hand and looked up.

When he looked down again, Daisy and Captain Heron were far from him, and with that terrific swinging gallop that Daisy was such an adept in, she was going over the ground with the speed of an antelope.

Captain Heron did not trouble to look back at Wild.

On—on to London.

That was his object, and he feared that he should reach there too late to make it safe to enter Whitcombe House as it had been his intention to do.

The great consolation of his mind, however, was that Edith was safe.

That Lady Trelawney would place her in security he did not doubt, and if Wild kept his word, which by some freak he really, for once in his life, might do, she might feel tolerably safe from any further persecutions.

It was nearly five o'clock when Felix Heron galloped into London.

Under an archway in the street that he had appointed them to wait for him, he found Ogle and Tom Ripon, and the rest of the little party.

"Thank the fates!" cried Ogle, "here is the Captain!"

"Any news, Ogle?"

"None; only the watchmen have been a little troublesome, so we have had to do the best we could with them. One of them is in that box."

A watchbox was lying on its face on the pavement.

Heron smiled.

"And another one," added Ogle, "is down this area, I think."

"Come, Ogle," said Heron, "there is but one chance now of making our way into Whitcombe House unobserved, and that will be by the stable."

Captain Heron led the way.

The stable entrance to the old aristocratic mansion was in a neglected state, but the gate was fast.

That was an obstacle that did not long stand in the way of Ogle, who, standing for a moment on the back of his horse, was so enabled to easily clamber over.

Then he undid the small door in one of the large carriage entrance gates, and as Daisy stepped through very adroitly, the other horses followed the example as horses are apt to do.

The wicket was closed and made fast again, so that the party felt themselves to be in something like security.

"Yea," said the Reverend Mortification, "but that my inward man calleth out in audible tone, the word breakfast, I should feel quite delighted."

"Silence!" said Heron. "Ogle, you will see that the horses are well taken care of here, and we will consult afterwards about what had best be done with them for safety's sake. Bestow them for the present in the stalls, and then all of you follow me."

This was soon accomplished by Ogle and Tom Ripon, and then Felix Heron led the way by the secret route from the stables to the house.

Tom took care of the young girl, with whom he had ridden from Epping in such loving companionship, and the Reverend Mortification, with his long body, looking over the head of Tom, brought up the rear of the party.

That suite of chambers, which Edith used to call her own, and where those interviews with her brother, so full of evil to her and to Felix Heron, had taken place, was soon reached.

Then Heron paused.

"Remain here, all of you," he said, "and make yourselves as much at home as you can. This is my house, and I bid you welcome to it, with all my heart. I am on an expedition to explore the premises, and see that all is safe."

"Shall I not go with you Captain?" asked Ogle.

"No, Ogle, this suite of rooms is, I consider, the post of danger. Stay here, in case of any emergency. Tom can come with me."

"Yes, Captain," said Tom Ripon, "I'm your man."

Tom then whispered to the young girl.

"Keep up your spirits, my dear, till I come

back. You see a fellow can't be in two places at once, and the Captain wants me to go and take care of him."

The girl laughed.

"Come, Tom!" cried Heron. "Follow me. Look well about you, Ogle, if you hear any strange noise."

"That will I, Captain!"

It was with rather a heavy heart that Felix Heron traversed the chambers of that mansion.

He had as yet tasted but little of the supposed enjoyment of such a home; and, in fact, all his recollections of it were tinged with some sorrow, or some great peril.

And yet, under all the circumstances he thought it the safest retreat he could have.

It was perfectly true that he might have gone at once to Lady Castleneau's house in Bloomsbury fields, but that would only in all probability have bought danger and trouble upon the old gentlewoman.

And beside, there it was as a refuge at any time, if circumstances compelled him to leave Whitcombe House.

With these feelings, then, Captain Heron commenced his search through the mansion, with only Tom Ripon as a companion.

And Tom was not a little proud of the implied confidence which Felix Heron had in him by selecting him on this duty, although the real truth was that Heron did so in case he should have to send some message to Ogle.

"Captain," said Tom; "may I say a word?"

"What is it?"

"Don't you think we had better see to the priming of our pistols?"

"No."

Tom was, to use a common expression, rather taken aback by this brief reply.

It was evident that the Captain was not talkative just then, and that the wisest thing Tom Ripon could do was to hold his tongue.

And Tom was quite acute enough to see that.

The truth was that the further Felix Heron penetrated into that house, the more sad and powerful became his reflections and recollections.

It was the house in which he had that memorable and terrible interview with his father, the late Earl of Whitcombe, which so strangely preceded the supposed death of that nobleman.

It was the house in which that father had been found murdered by the brother of his own much-loved Edith.

It was the house, too, to which he had first brought Edith as to a home of her own, and to which he had welcomed her with the fond hope that it would be a happy one.

Alas! how fallacious had been all those summer day dreams!

How fleeting had been the dawn of the contentment which he had vainly hoped to find within those walls!

No wonder that Felix Heron found the atmosphere of that mansion pressing like a solid weight upon his heart.

He began to fear that he should never be able even to make it the temporary refuge he had intended.

If he could not, and if Edith felt as he felt towards Whitcombe House, there would be no resource but to trespass upon the hospitality of Lady Castleneau.

Her mansion in Bloomsbury Fields would be always open to him and his.

The upper floor was now left behind them, and

Captain Heron and Tom Ripon reached that first and most costly and important floor of the house where the drawing-rooms were situated.

There they were, in all their magnificence.

Faded, somewhat, by neglect, and assuming that strange appearance of dilapidation which houses so soon put on when deserted by human inhabitants, but still costly and beautiful.

Heron paused in that drawing-room with the green silken hangings, where he had last stood with the Earl of Bridgewater, previous to leaving the mansion, and looked around him with a sigh.

"Hem!" said Tom Ripon.

Tom was anxious for Felix Heron to say something.

But the latter preserved a melancholy and abstracted silence.

The next apartment was one, that if it did not transcend in actual magnificence that in which they were, certainly did so in size.

The shutters of that room were now all closed.

Not the least wandering ray of light found its way into it.

Tom paused on the threshold.

So did Heron.

A feeling of he knew not what came over him, as he stood just one pace within that lordly apartment.

To the great relief of Tom Ripon, then, Felix Heron spoke.

"Tom!"

"Yes, Captain."

"Did you hear anything?"

"Well, Captain, I thought I saw—that I heard something!"

"Pho! pho!"

Tom whistled.

"Silence!"

"Yes, Captain."

Heron made his way right across the room towards the windows, and took down the bar that fastened one set of shutters.

He flung a leaf of the shutters open, which was not a reckless or dangerous thing to do in relation to the outer world, and any observation that might be made of the mansion from the street, for the blinds were closely drawn down, so that the movement of the shutter would not be visible.

A long ray of subdued light fell into the magnificent apartment.

Then Tom Ripon uttered a cry.

He ran towards the door as he did so, for he had followed Captain Heron far into the rooms.

Heron turned sharply from the window.

"What is the matter? What is the matter?"

Tom pointed to the table that stood in the centre of the room.

It needed, then, but one glance on the part of Heron to see the cause of Tom Ripon's alarm.

Seated at the table was a man, on rather a low chair, so that as he slept—for he seemed to sleep—his head rested conveniently on the edge of the table.

A cold, uncomfortable feeling came across the heart of Heron.

"Speak!" he cried; "arouse yourself, be you whom you may!"

All was still.

The figure did not move hand or foot.

Tom Ripon got a pace or two nearer the door.

"Hilloa!" shouted Heron again. "Do you sleep so soundly that no sound can awaken you?"

Tom shook his head.

"Captain," he said with a shudder, "I rather think that's just it."

"What is it?"

"Why, whoever he is, he sleeps so sound that nothing will ever wake him again."

"Ah!"

"That's it."

"Dead?"

"My idea, Captain, is just that. If that is not what may be called a corpus, why I am not the sort of man I took myself to be."

As Tom spoke, he drew himself up to all his height, with a triumphant expression, as if he would have added that he rather thought he had settled the matter.

"Can it be so?" said Heron, as he now approached the table.

Yes.

There could be no possible mistake as to the character of the form that leant its head upon the table.

No sound but that which shall awaken all humanity from the sleep of death could suffice to awaken the spirit that had fled from the cold, still form that there slept

The light of the young day without was increasing each moment, and there was quite sufficient for Felix Heron to see well the general aspect of the dead man.

But nothing but a sight of his face could afford any prospect of identifying him

Heron took hold of the back of his head.

"Oh, don't! don't!" cried Tom.

Heron lifted the head sufficiently to see the face.

Yes; he knew it.

The face was that of Mr. Boom, the attorney, who had, with such singular audacity and assurance, striven to make himself appear to be the heir to the earldom and estates of Whitcombe.

That was the end of his career.

He had died, then, in one of the lordly apartments of the mansion of the family with whom he had no real connexion, but whose honours and properties he had made so infamous an attempt to appropriate.

"I know him!" said Heron.

"Yes!" said Tom.

Tom Ripon was right out on the landing of the staircase now.

He had no sort of ambition to know the dead man.

All that awe and fright of the dead, and at the appearance of death, which is so common to the young, beset Tom Ripon, and nothing but the positive command of Captain Heron could have induced him to come back to that room.

Heron did not, however, issue any such command.

Quickly he stepped out of the apartment, and closed and locked the door.

"Be it so," he said. "Rest in peace! I know not exactly how you have come by your death, but you shall, for the time being at least, have a costly sepulchre.

Heron, then, with a slow and solemn step, went down the great staircase.

Tom followed him so closely, too, that when about two-thirds of the distance down Heron suddenly paused, Tom was nearly as possible on his back.

"Hush!" said Heron.

"Yes, Captain. Oh, dear! is there any more dead un's, or is he coming after us."

"Hush, I say! Listen!"

CHAPTER CLXXXVI.

CAPTAIN HERON AND TOM FIND LORD WARRINGDALE IN A MOST DEPLORABLE CONDITION.

THE sound that had brought Felix Heron to a standstill on the grand staircase of Whitcombe House was an unmistakable groan from some one in the lower part of it.

Tom Ripon had not heard it, although in general his senses were sharp enough; but the fact was, he kept so continually looking over his shoulder for fear the dead Mr. Boom should be coming after him, that he attended to nothing else.

Felix Heron stood listening.

The groan came again.

"Now, Tom, did you hear it?"

"Rather, Captain."

Tom shuddered.

"I can't help thinking one thing, Captain."

"What is that?"

"Why, that the sooner we get out of this house the better."

"I don't know that. Come on."

"But, Captain——"

"What now?"

"It's full of dead people and ghosts. My idea is that the ghosts occupy all the lower part, and the dead folks are the lodgers up-stairs."

"Hush!"

Tom was silent, but, unknown to Heron, he kept a fast hold of the skirt of Heron's coat. There was safety in the thought that he had established such a connexion with so strong a party as Felix Heron.

With the utmost caution now, for Heron could not tell what form danger might take in that house, he slowly descended the remainder of the stairs.

Tom gave him two or three pulls by the skirt of his coat as he went.

"What's that?" asked Heron.

"What, Captain?"

"Something pulled my coat."

"You don't say so, Captain. It's very odd that something has pulled mine, too."

Tom thought that a capital excuse, and as Heron now knew perfectly well what the pulling at his skirt meant, he said no more about it.

And so they reached the hall.

That superb hall, which was, with its statuary and its adornments, quite an apartment in which a feast might have been laid for a king.

The groan came again.

Heron felt convinced that it came from the immediate direction of that room which had been, up to the day of his supposed death, in the occupation of his father, the late Earl.

Was it possible that any of those singular and startling phenomena which both he and Edith had met with in connexion with that part of the mansion were about to renewed.

Ah, no!

That was not possible.

The late Earl slept the sleep of death, and was past all groaning.

Captain Heron kept his hand upon one of his pistols, so that he might make use of it at a moment's notice, and went then directly towards the private study of his father.

The door was fast.

That is to say, the door of the outer room, which served as a kind of vestibule to the apartment with all the mysterious doors and cupboards where the late Earl used to sit so much alone.

Heron tried to find out in what manner the door was fastened, and he felt convinced it was locked on the inside.

The key, too, was in the lock.

If he would make his way in that direction the lock must be forced.

The small side windows of the door of the house had shutters, to each of which was a protecting iron bar lying slantwise across them, and about three feet in length.

More admirable substitutes for crow-bars could not have been found.

With one of them Felix Heron soon forced the lock, that resisted fair means to move it.

The door opened with a crash.

It was just possible that such an act as this might bring him face to face with some foe.

With this idea Heron stepped aside, and held his pistol in his hand ready for action.

No!

No. 56.—EDITH.

No one appeared.

The groans that had, in his estimation, so evidently come from that direction, had ceased.

The room was but dimly lighted, for all the daylight that could make its entry into it had to come through a window of stained glass, that naturally hindered its progress and its brightness.

Heron, then, closely followed by Tom, advanced towards the study of the late Earl.

Then, when close to the threshold of it, the groan came again; and by being much more distinct it came in a much more dismal fashion to their ears.

"Oh, gracious!" exclaimed Tom.

"Hush, Tom! Somebody is in trouble."

"Or their trouble's over," said Tom; "for if that wasn't somebody's last groan, it ought to be!"

Felix Heron placed his hands upon the lock of the door.

It yielded instantly.

He crossed the threshold.

The room was but faintly lighted, for most of the shutters were closed; but as he entered it a voice uttered a cry of despair, and then all was still.

On a couch in one corner lay some one.

"Speak!" he said; "and say who you are that, in sickness and distress, have made a home and a refuge of this house?"

There was no reply.

"Another dead 'un!" said Tom. "Upon my word, Captain, this is like to be a lively sort of place; one won't know what room to go into without finding it occupied by somebody or another who has popped off to be a ghost!"

Heron let Tom go on speaking without stopping him; for he was really too much interested by the object on the couch in the corner of that room to heed what he said.

A glance at the wan and wasted face of that object was enough for recognition.

It was his half-brother, Lord Warringdale, who lay there, apparently with but the thinnest possible shadowy partition between him and death.

Heron looked at him with a feeling that was compounded of loathing and compassion.

There at length, lay the man who had been the cause of such a world of danger and suffering to him and to Edith.

There he lay, still breathing, and completely at his mercy.

With a pressure of his hand.

With a stamp of his foot.

By the use of any weapon that came most ready to hand, he might have killed him, crushing the life out of him as easily as one might tread upon a snail in a garden path.

But Heron was not the man to do that.

Lord Warringdale, in that extremity of his fortunes, was probably more safe in the hands of the man he had most injured of all the world, than as if he had been found by any one else who could have rescued him.

"Tom!" said Heron.

"Yes, Captain!"

"Run down to the kitchen of the house, and find some water."

"Y e-s."

"Run!"

"Oh, dear!"

"What do you mean? Do you not hear me?"

"Yes—oh, yes, Captain! Did you say the—a the kitch—kitch—en?"

"I did"

"Captain, I'm a highwayman."

"Be off."

"A high—way—man! I don't like ghosts and people of that sort; and if the old dark kitchens of this house are not just about as crammed full of that sort of company as any place can be, I'm a Frenchman!"

"Very well. If you are afraid, I will go myself."

"Stop, stop! I am not exactly afraid, only I—I—— On, he's off! I wonder, now, who this dead 'un is. Hilloa!"

Lord Warringdale at this moment opened his eyes, and Tom Ripon knew him.

"What, is it you?"

"Help—oh, help! I am dying!"

"And a capital job, too," said Tom. "If you had thought of that little way of being of no further trouble ever so long ago, it would have been a good job."

"Help me!"

"What's the matter?"

"Badly—badly hurt."

"Oh, indeed!"

"Have some mercy upon me!"

"I shan't."

"Wretch!"

"Wretch, yourself! You see, you have come to a bad end, and worse is to come after. I only wish old Daddy Mortification was here this moment; he would bring you what he calls spiritual consolation, and let you into all about them lakes of burning brimstone and melted lead, and such like little matters that you will soon know all about. Suppose I try to tell you?"

"No, no!"

"Oh, it's all for your good!"

"Mercy!"

"Well, it ain't pleasant, but I can't help it. First of all, you are picked up with a red-hot pitchfork in the small of your back."

"Fiend!"

"Yes, that's the gent as will do it! Then you go on to the gridiron, when the first grilling goes on, and then——"

"What is all this?" asked Heron.

"Oh, I was only telling him what he was agoing to," said Tom. "I've heard old Mortification say so much about it that I am quite a reverend article myself, I am! It's what he calls consolation to sinners in their latter ends, you see!"

"Peace, Tom, peace!"

Captain Heron raised the fainting form of Lord Warringdale with his left arm, and held some water to his lips.

The fevered man drank long and eagerly of the cool draught.

"Life!—life!" he gasped. "That is new life! Oh, what I have suffered transcends the tongue of man to tell!"

"Did you, in the midst of all that suffering," asked Heron, "ever reflect on what you had made others suffer?"

Lord Warringdale looked in Heron's face with a glance of terror.

Perhaps up to that moment he had not had a full and perfect apprehension of who it was that had brought him that draught of water.

If, however, such had been the case it was so no longer.

He knew Heron well!

The last lingering of shame in the sinner's breast were summoned forth then; and Warringdale could not look above one moment into the eyes of that brother to whom he had been so bitter and uncomprising a foe.

He looked askance, and groaned.

The stain of blood was upon his pillow, and his condition was altogether one that, to those who did not know him, would have provoked compassion.

The utmost that any one who did know could feel for him might be comprehended under the head of forbearance.

It was Felix Heron who spoke first; and his deep-toned voice broke the awful stillness of the room, and made Lord Warringdale shudder as he heard it.

"And is it thus," he said, "that we meet again, brother?"

Lord Warringdale only shuddered again.

"Why, oh, why has it been that, making yourself my foe to the extent you have, you likewise have been such a foe to yourself?"

"Yes, that is it!" groaned Warringdale.

"You see that now?"

"Yes, I do!"

"And yet I doubt not but that if all had to be repeated it would be again ever as it has been, would it not?"

"No! oh, no!"

"Tell me—how came you here?"

"I have met with a wound, and I crawled here, I suppose, to die!"

"Do you repent?"

"With all my heart!"

"Of the wound," said Tom Ripon, "which you say, Captain, lays him up so that he is forced to keep in his claws a bit?"

"Peace, Tom—peace!"

"I only spoke the truth, Captain."

Lord Warringdale bent a malignant glance at Tom, and then, in a whining, supplicating tone, he said, "That is the way—that is the way! There have always been people, brother, to fan the flame of discord between us, and make us feel hatred."

"No," said Heron,—"no! There have been no such people. Your own acts have been the cause of all."

"Nay, I——"

"Traitor," said Heron, sternly, "do not attempt to excuse yourself, or to fritter away your wickedness, or you will make me look back to too many proofs of it which it would be well for you if I could forget."

Warringdale was silent.

"Tom," said Heron, "will you stay by this man awhile?"

"Yes, Captain."

"No, no!" said Lord Warringdale; "he will kill me!"

"Oh, don't be frightened," said Tom; "I shan't interfere with you. I can see you are going, and it wouldn't be any good for a man like me to help you on, even with a kick."

"I shall soon be back, Tom," added Heron.

As he spoke, he left the room, without paying any further attention to the remonstrances of Warringdale.

Rapidly Captain Heron made his way to where he had left Ogle, and, touching him on the arm, he led him aside.

"Ogle," he said, "two of our old foes are in the house!"

"Two, Captain?"

Ogle placed his hands upon his pistols.

Heron shook his head.

"There is no occasion, Ogle, for that. One is dead, and the other, I think, is dying."

"Who, in the name of goodness, or badness, Captain, are they?"

"Boom, the lawyer, and Lord Warringdale."

"You don't say that, Captain?"

"I do, Ogle. They must both be removed from Whitcombe House."

"To be sure, Captain!"

"I would recommend that the dead body of Boom be merely taken somewhere and put down, so that the police may find him, and make the most of it."

"All right, Captain!"

"As regards Lord Warringdale, I propose that he be removed at night to one of the London hospitals, and there left."

"Too good for him."

"No, Ogle, let it be done. Mortification Ripon will help you, and so will Tom. We are rather short-handed now, Ogle, but I daresay we shall manage."

"No doubt of that, Captain. Better to have few hands than bad ones, any day in the week."

At this moment both Ogle and Captain Heron were startled by the sudden appearance of Tom Ripon, who called out, "Captain, he's a cutting away as fast as he can, and wants some spirituous consolation!"

"Yea, that will I give him!" cried Mortification.

"Spiritual, I suppose you mean?" said Heron.

"Yes, it is all the same; for, as the Psalmist judiciously remarks, by taking spirits down, you keep the spirits up; and that reminds me, Thomas, that, yea, I gave you a bottle to take care of."

"Yea, you did," said Tom.

"Where is it?"

"Here, daddy."

"Oh, excellent Thomas, you are a good youth! I never did expect to see this bottle again, but yea, here it is——Eh? What? The deuce!"

"As the Psalmist says——" put in Tom.

"The dev——Hem! No! Why, Thomas, the bottle is, I may say, empty of all but air—air, Thomas, I declare! Where is the ancient pineapple rum that was in it?"

"Gone," said Tom. "You told me to take care of the bottle, and I did, but you said not a word of what was in it; so I took some myself, and gave some to Daisy in a pint of water, and there was an end of it."

"Cease this contention," said Heron, "and follow me, both of you. I may need you."

———

CHAPTER CLXXXVII.

LORD WARRINGDALE MYSTERIOUSLY DISAPPEARS, AND HAS AN UNHAPPY MEETING WITH JONATHAN WILD.

THE course which Felix Heron had made up his mind to carry out in regard to Lord Warringdale, was the only one that presented itself to him which would carry the two conditions he required.

To get rid of him from Whitcombe.

To do nothing in so getting rid of him that would be detrimental to his life.

Ogle was desirous of just placing Warringdale in the street, but Captain Heron overruled him, and would not have it so.

"He is hurt," he said, "and should be taken somewhere that he can at once have assistance. Come, Ogle, and you, too, Mortification, we will all go together about this business."

The room in which Lord Warringdale had been lying was soon reached.

What was the surprise of Felix Heron to find it vacant.

During the short time that it had taken Tom Ripon to seek Captain Heron, Lord Warringdale had in some way most mysteriously disappeared.

"You see, Tom," said Ogle, "that when you are left in charge of a prisoner, nothing that that prisoner can say or do should be sufficient to induce you to leave him."

"But," said Tom Ripon, "I thought he was at his last gasp, and that perhaps the Captain would like to see him start?"

Heron shook his head.

"I fear, Ogle," he said, "that my Lord Warringdale was not quite so bad as he made out?"

"Or," replied Ogle, "either shame or fear have given him strength to get away in preference to seeing you again."

"Be it so. He has only saved us the trouble of removing him. Ogle, you will see to the other affair!"

"The dead lawyer?"

"Yes, he is above—Tom will show you."

"Oh, dear me, no!" said Tom. "You can't miss him, Ogle, if you go into one of the big rooms up-stairs. I think, Captain, I ought to, you know, look after the ladies."

Captain Heron was not disposed to submit Tom to the terror of any further personal communication with what he (Tom) called the "dead 'un," so he spoke to Ogle in a low voice.

"You and Mortification manage it between you. The boy is terrified at death."

Ogle nodded.

But while all this was going on in Whitcombe House, Lord Warringdale, who had fled from it, had not exactly exchanged what he thought a bad situation for one much better.

He certainly had had a dread of meeting again with Heron, and when alone with Tom he had simulated that death-like swoon which had alarmed Tom, and induced him to seek Heron.

But the moment Tom turned his back, Lord Warringdale made a desperate effort, and rose from the couch. He struggled into some of his clothes, and wrapping round him a roquelaire cloak, and fixing his hat firmly on his head, he staggered out of the room into the hall, and opening the outer door, left the mansion.

Lord Warringdale felt like an owl, who, by some accident, is forced to face the daylight.

He winked and blinked at the early morning sun, and staggered along St. James's Street like a drunken man.

The hour was yet sufficiently early to make the streets bare of people; and, in fact, the only person who saw and stopped to look at Lord Warringdale, as he made his way in devious fashion down the street, was a very small sweep, who was up early in the practice of his vocation.

And so Warringdale reached Pall Mall, without having any fixed idea of what to do or where to go.

If Captain Heron had chosen to institute the least pursuit of him, he would have come up with him easily.

It was not with any fixed object as regarded any particular direction that Warringdale turned to the left, in the route towards Charing Cross.

He began to feel weaker each moment; for the temporary excitement which had enabled him to leave Whitcombe House was passing away.

He had to stop to support himself by a street post.

Some one approached.

Was it a friend or a foe?

Lord Warringdale was in that frame of mind when a man is apt to think every one who approaches him must bear one or the other of those characters.

He could not imagine that he might meet people who would be perfectly indifferent to him, and only look upon him as some intoxicated man returning from a late revel.

The footsteps came nearer and nearer, and Lord Warringdale was so impressed with the idea that they boded danger to him, that he made an effort to glide into the obscurity of a court that was close at hand.

But he was too late.

Not exactly too late to make his way into the court; but too late to avoid the observation of the person who was approaching.

That person stopped.

Stopped exactly at the mouth of the court.

"Hilloa, there!"

Lord Warringdale uttered a cry of fright.

He knew the voice.

"Hilloa, there!"

The man was Jonathan Wild.

In his present debilitated state, Warringdale had no reason to wish to meet Wild. He always had a dread of him when he was well and able to take care of himself; but now that he was at the mercy of any one, he dreaded to fall into the hands of the man who knew no mercy.

But, as we have said, it was too late.

Wild had seen him.

True, he had not recognised him; but the manner in which Warringdale had turned into the court had excited Wild's curiosity, and he was resolved to know who it was.

"Hilloa!—hilloa, there!"

Warringdale made no reply.

Beyond that first cry of alarm he uttered no sound.

How faint was the hope that Jonathan Wild would pass on.

"Come out!"

Lord Warringdale shrunk down into the shadow of a door-way.

"Come out, I say!"

No answer!

"Very well, then, I must make you, and I am apt to do that in not the gentlest manner in the world. Stay; perhaps if you know who I am. you will come out. I am Jonathan Wild. Ha! ha!"

Wild always pronounced his own name in the harshest and most hideous way he possibly could, and generally added to it a fiendish laugh, such as may be heard upon the stage at times.

No; that did not succeed.

The skulking figure in the court came not out.

Wild drew his hanger, and walked up the court.

He seized Lord Warringdale by the collar of the roquelaire cloak, and dragged him out into the daylight.

One look at the pale, cadaverous face was enough.

Wild started with surprise.

"My Lord Warringdale?"

"Yes—yes—I—I—yes!"

"Why did you avoid me, and how is it that I see you in this plight?"

"I think, Jonathan Wild, you might, by thinking back a little, guess what has put me into such a condition."

"Dear me, no!"

"Yes, yes! You—you——"

"Well?"

"I say no more but to express a desire that you will leave me."

"Leave you?" said Wild, with a sardonic grin. "Leave a friend and a nobleman like you in such a state of distress? Never!"

"I beseech you?"

"Never! never!"

Wild turned round twice as he spoke, and looked up and down Pall Mall.

There was a glare about his eyes that was awful to see.

Did he contemplate at that moment the murder of Lord Warringdale?

It would almost seem like it.

No one was visible.

WARRINGDALE ESCAPES THE VENGEANCE OF JONATHAN WILD.

Presented Gratis with No. 56, of the New Edition of EDITH HERON the Sequel to Edith the Captive ; or, the Robbers of Epping Forest.

"My lord!"

"What? What would you say?"

"I think you will never succeed."

"Succeed in what?"

"In getting the earldom of Whitcombe from Felix Heron."

"Yes — oh, yes, I have good hope, and then——"

"Then, what?"

"I will pay you."

"Indeed!"

"I will, in truth."

"Look you here, my Lord Warringdale. I hold your bonds for a large sum—as large a sum as one hundred thousand pounds; and the only portion of it that is at all secured, consists of a small estate at Hampton Wick, which you have for your lifetime been deprived of, but which, if you were dead, I could take possession of."

"Dead? dead?"

"Yes, dead!"

The hateful look came again to the eyes of Jonathan Wild.

Again he looked up and down Pall Mall. No one was visible.

He looked up at the windows of the opposite houses.

Not one was open, nor was a blind removed at that early hour.

Wild tightened his hold of the hilt of his hanger.

One blow with it at the back of the neck would produce instant death.

"Sweep! sweep!"

Wild started.

The little sweep who had looked at Lord Warringdale in St. James's-street, turned suddenly the corner into Pall Mall.

Wild was foiled.

There was a witness to the deed he meditated, in whose presence he felt that he dared not act.

That little sooty urchin, not above ten years old, was, at that moment, more than a match for the great Jonathan Wild.

He prevented him, by his mere presence, from committing murder.

"Sweep! sweep!"

"Go to the deuce!" said Wild.

"Do yer want ere a chimley sweep, governor?" asked the little sweep.

"No, and be hanged to you!"

"Thank yer, governor. Do yer want a sweep anywheres?"

This last inquiry was addressed to Lord Warringdale, who shook his head in reply to it.

The boy passed on.

Jonathan Wild sheathed his hanger. He gave up the idea of murdering Lord Warringdale in the open street, from the moment that some human eyes, although they were only those of a poor little sweep, had seen him in company with the proposed victim.

Warringdale had not been fully aware of his real danger.

If he had been, he would surely have raised the street with his cries.

"My lord," said Wild, "I can see that you are ill."

"Wounded!"

"Ah, I suppose so. It is both a duty and a pleasure to me to look after you. Take my arm. I will lead you to some place of safety."

"No, no!"

"No?"

"Not there!"

"Not where, my lord?"

"To your house."

"Oh, I did not think of it. Ha! ha! So you don't like Little Newgate? Well, well, I admit that people may be prejudiced against it!"

"Not there, I say—not there."

Wild was thinking where he could best bestow Lord Warringdale, and it occurred to him that the chambers lately in the occupation of Mr. Boom might suit.

Since the death of Boom, Jonathan had taken possession of the suite of chambers, and had succeeded in stifling inquiry about their former tenant, by sticking on the outer doors various announcements and little slips of paper according to the custom in the chambers of the Inns of Court.

"Out of town! Return next week! On professional business in the north!"

Such-like were the little placards which Wild changed from time to time, so that he stilled inquiry, and kept possession of the suite of gloomy rooms.

To a man like Jonathan Wild, such a suite of chambers might at any moment be of the most incalculable use.

It was to them, then, that after a little consideration he resolved to take Lord Warringdale.

"Hark you my lord," he said; "I have a friend in the Temple."

"The Temple?"

"Yes; you know it well, no doubt. I have a friend there who will gladly receive you into his chambers for a time until you get quite well."

This was a proposition that at all events was more agreeable to Warringdale than one that involved a visit to Wild's house.

"Very well," he said; "I consent to that."

He felt quite certain that, say what he would, he should not succeed in shaking Wild off.

"Come on, then. We can find a hackney coach at the corner of the Haymarket, no doubt."

Lord Warringdale was compelled to lean on the arm of Wild.

The coach at the corner of the Haymarket was easily enough found, and in half an hour from the time when Wild had dragged Lord Warringdale out of the court in Pall Mall, they were both at the entrance to the Temple.

Wild tapped at the wicket.

The porter opened it suddenly, for it was before the regular hour.

"What now?"

"To Mr. Boom's chambers."

"Then, you can't come in."

Wild lifted his hat about a couple of inches above his head, and the porter then knew him at once. A look of terror came over him, and he flung open the wicket.

Wild, with a nod, entered the Temple with Lord Warringdale.

Such, at that period, was the reputation of the great thief-taker, and such the terror he inspired, that there was not an official of any description in London, whose

"Conscience with injustice was corrupted,"

who did not feel the possibility of falling into his clutches some day.

It is possible that the man at the wicket-gate of the Temple might have his own reasons for being civil to such a personage as Jonathan Wild.

"Now, my lord," said Wild to Lord Warringdale, as he reached the chambers of the late Mr. Boom, "you will be safe and comfortable here."

"I hope so."

"Be assured you will. You much mistake me if you suppose for a moment that I am your foe: on the contrary, I still entertain the hope of one day seeing you with the earldom of Whitcombe on your brow."

"Alas, I doubt it!"

"Never give up a game, my lord, while there is a remote chance even of wining it."

Wild produced the key of the chambers, and opened the door.

"By the by, my lord," he added, as they crossed the threshold of the gloomy rooms, and Wild closed the outer door with a bang, "where did you come from when I so opportunely saw you in Pall Mall?'

"From Whitcombe House."

"Whitcombe House! Why—why, then——"

"Then, what?"

"Hem! I don't know; but may I ask—did curiosity prompt you to go over it?"

"No. I was too unwell."

"Then you did not see in the first-floor, in one of the drawing-rooms——"

"What? Why do you pause? What did you expect me to see?"

"Nothing, but in what a capital state of preservation the furniture was in."

Wild was quite satisfied in his own mind that Lord Warringdale could not have seen the dead body of Boom in Whitcombe House, and so admirably kept his countenance while questioned.

"Come," he said, "is not this snug? I think you knew Boom."

"You know well I did!"

"Oh, ah! Of course!"

"Where is he?"

"Impossible to say with any certainty; opinions differ so much on that subject."

"What subject?"

"Why, as regard to what is likely to be known of such a man; although, being a lawyer, the general impression will, of course, be that he has gone——"

Wild pointed downwards.

"What on earth do you mean, Wild?" asked Lord Warringdale, almost angrily.

"Why? don't you know that Boom is dead?"

"Dead? No!"

"Oh, I thought you did, and that you referred to his ultimate destination. But it don't matter. What may be the value, now, of that little property at Hampton Wick?"

The hateful expression of Wild's eyes decidedly deepened.

"About eight thousand pounds. It brings me in three hundred a-year, which, in truth, is all I have to live on."

"Ah!"

"Yes—all!"

"Oh! Three hundred a-year, and about eight thousand its saleable value. Let's be jolly!"

"What?"

"Jolly, I said!"

Wild went to a cupboard and took from it a square, Dutch-looking bottle and a couple of glasses, and placed them on the table.

"Let's be jolly!" he said again.

"No!" replied Warringdale. "In my state of health I dare not drink."

"You had better."

"No, no!"

"You must,"

"I cannot."

"Well, 'a willful man must have his way,' as the old saying has it. Will you eat anything?"

"I perhaps could, if it were something simple and fit for a man out of health. I feel weak, and very likely some of it is for want of food."

"No doubt, no doubt! I can give you something which will set you to rights, and you will feel no such want."

Wild got up and went to the cupboard again.

Now, it happened that Mr. Boom had been accustomed in that room to settle his cravat, and otherwise put himself in out-of-doors order, so that he had a small looking-glass hung on the wall.

Lord Warringdale was opposite to the glass, and he saw in it what Wild was about.

He sat fascinated!

———

CHAPTER CLXXXVIII.

JONATHAN WILD CONSIDERS THAT HE HAS GOT RID OF ANOTHER TROUBLESOME ENCUMBRANCE.

Yes! Lord Warringdale was fascinated!

With a kind of horror that took away his breath, and that sat like tons of lead upon all his limbs, depriving him of the power of action, he looked upon the proceedings of Jonathan Wild in the little dressing-glass of Mr Boom.

Like some bird fascinated by the eyes of a snake, Lord Warringdale could only look on in speechless horror.

Wild did go to the cupboard.

But it was not to get something for Lord Warringdale to eat.

On the contrary, he took from it an object that would have been rather hard of digestion.

It was one of those short, heavily-weighted, hideous bludgeons which Wild might have been said to have invented.

Not above three feet in length, and at one end a knob of lead of a good two pounds in weight, the bludgeon was calculated to be a most murderous weapon.

It generally was so in the hands of Jonathan Wild.

That it was to be the instrument of his death Lord Warringdale did not doubt for a moment.

One good downright blow of it would fracture his skull were it as hard as iron.

Wild, with the terrible weapon in his hands, stood behind the chair on which Warringdale sat.

He certainly had not the least idea that his victim saw him in the glass.

The position of that little mirror had escaped the observation of Jonathan, and he attributed the quiescence of Warringdale to exhaustion and a want of suspicion of his terrible peril.

But it so happened that as Wild raised himself on his toes to give the blow of the bludgeon greater force upon the defenceless head of Lord Warringdale, he happened to cast his eyes right on to the little glass.

There he saw his own face.

And there he saw Lord Warringdale's.

A glance was quite sufficient to let him see the terrible expression of concentrated agony that was on the features of Warringdale.

The look!

The stare!

The parted lips!

The protruding eyes!

The bristling hair!

All the tokens and expressions of a man struck dumb, and unnerved by some awful shock which has come over him like the shadow of death.

"Ah!" cried Wild.

It wanted only that.

Some sound, no matter what.

The spell was broken.

Lord Warringdale was able to move.

With a yell that sounded far and near in the Temple, he sprang to his feet.

At the same moment down came the bludgeon.

But it missed its victim.

It only struck the back of the massive old chair on which Warringdale had been seated, and at once smashed it into splinters.

"Help! help!"

"Curses!"

"Help! Murder!"

"Consume you!"

Warringdale fled round the room.

Jonathan Wild pursued him.

"Murder! murder!"

"Perdition! Fury!"

"Help! Oh, mercy!"

Lord Warringdale, in his flight, flung down a chair.

Jonathan Wild could not stop himself in time to avoid it, and he fell sprawling over it.

That was a mercy.

Warringdale reaches the door of the chamber. For a moment the lock baffles him. He cannot open it. He is lost!

No! It yields! He rushes out to the old staircase!

"Help, help! Murder!"

Wild has got to his feet again. He pursues his victim. He sees him half-way down the stairs.

A door opens on the landing below, and a man looks out.

"Bless us all, what is the matter?"

Wild flings his bludgeon after Lord Warringdale, but this man had just put his head out at his chamber door to intercept it.

Crack!

The rap on the side of the man's head was severe, and he staggered back into his own room again.

Wild almost flings himself down the stairs after Lord Warringdale.

But the latter has the start of him.

Revenge and murder may have fleet feet, but fear has wings as well.

Jonathan has no chance of overtaking the maddened fugitive, and yet he keeps up the chase.

Across the large garden of the Temple towards the terrace Lord Warringdale takes his way.

The river is before him.

Jonathan Wild, intent on murder, behind him.

With one desperate leap Warringdale is in the stream.

Wild saw him tossed about in the heaving tide, and then disappear, as he was carried away rapidly down the stream.

"That will do!" said Jonathan. "Good morning to my Lord Warringdale! Ha, ha!"

The alarm in the Temple was great, but Wild took no notice of it. He managed to mingle with a throng of people, who in vain asked each other what it was all about, and then made his way back to Boom's chambers.

He picked up his bludgeon as he went, and carefully put it into the cupboard again.

He took a good draught from the squat-looking Dutch bottle, and then he said, quietly, "I think that's over!"

With his hands, then, in his pockets, Wild left the Temple, after sticking a fresh notice on Mr. Boom's door—"Return next week!"

Wild whistled a tune as he passed out of the Temple into Essex Street, Strand.

"I rather think," he said, "that matter is about as well over in the way it is as in any other. If I had knocked him on the head in the chambers, I should have had the usual bother about the disposal of the body, and now he has kindly disposed of that himself."

While all this was going on at the chambers of Mr. Boom in the Temple, Captain Heron had left Ogle in charge of the house in St. James's Street, and on foot he gently took his way to Castleneau House, where he fully expected to see Edith.

Nor was he disappointed.

Lady Trelawney, at the request of Edith, had driven, with her and the child, direct to her aunt's house.

Oh, with what joy it was that once again, after all the dangers of the night, Edith rested on the heart of her Felix.

From the shadow of one of the deep window recesses now, there stepped forth a gentleman.

It was Colonel Trelawney.

He took Heron by the hand, as he said, "My sister sent for me to see you here, and I have had a long talk with Lady Castleneau about you. Can anything be done to put an end to all the perils that beset you?"

"I fear not," said Heron. "But I am lighter at heart than I was."

"Indeed!"

"Yes. I see you all look at me with some surprise, and wonder what it is that has taken some of the burden from my heart. I will tell you. Edith, I think, for the future, will be safe."

"Safe, Felix," cried Edith. "You speak in riddles. What can you—what do you mean?"

"Simply this, dear Edith: that whatever may be my dangers or persecutions, I do not think that my breast will again be attempted to be reached through you."

"How is that, Felix?" asked Lady Castleneau.

Heron smiled.

"I have made an arrangement with Jonathan Wild."

"With Jonathan Wild?"

"Even so."

Well might such an announcement from the lips of Felix Heron excite the most unqualified surprise at Castleneau House.

But Edith saw that there was a something more in the affair than Heron had yet explained.

"Tell us all, Felix, and let us share with you in the lightness of heart you speak of if we can."

"The explanation, dear Edith, is short and simple. Circumstances placed the life of Wild completely in my power, and he knew it."

"You spared the villain?" said Colonel Trelawney.

"I did!"

"Then more the pity."

"Perhaps so; and yet I never, for the life of me, could take such vengeance upon a foe who so entirely stood at my mercy."

Lady Castleneau nodded her approval.

"I made up my mind," added Heron, "to try if it were possible that even in so degraded and depraved a nature as Jonathan Wild's, every spark of better feeling was extinct; so I gave him his life on condition that whatever might be his hostility to me, and however he might seek to carry it out, he was never again to contrive aught against Edith or our dear child.

"Oh, Felix!" cried Edith.

Lady Castleneau held out both her hands to him, as she said, in a voice of emotion, "Yes; I, too, cry 'Oh, Felix!' but it is with a cry of admiration. You are the best and the bravest soul I ever met with, Felix!"

Edith flung herself into the arms of her husband as she said, sobbingly, "And do you think, Felix, that you save me anything by only directing the baneful hate of that man against your breast?"

"I will hope so, Edith."

"Oh, no! Only let me have the opportunity, and I will make a different bargain with Jonathan Wild!"

"And only let me have the opportunity, and a fair excuse for taking advantage of it," said Colonel Trelawney, "and I will take good care that Jonathan Wild and all his bargains are at an end."

Lady Castleneau smiled through her tears.

"But what is to be done now, Felix?" asked Edith. "Whither are you and I and our little one to go for safety?"

"That," said Lady Castleneau, "is a first consideration; for this house will be suspected at once."

"It will," said Heron. "And I will now explain a plan which I think holds some prospects of success; and none the less so that it looks at first sight a little bold, and perhaps a little extravagant."

They all looked eagerly at Felix Heron to hear him explain what his plan was.

"I propose," he said, "to take up my abode at Whitcombe House."

"At Whitcombe House!" was the general exclamation.

"Even so."

"But, Felix——"

"Yes, dear Edith!"

"The great—the positive danger——"

"Listen to me!"

"With all our ears, my lord," said Colonel Trelawney. "And yet I ought to apologize for saying so, since, perhaps, I am an intruder here upon your family counsels on this occasion."

"Not so, sir," replied Heron. "There are but two persons out of the immediate circle of my family, and apart from some faithful dependents I have, who will form the household at Whitcombe House, that I should like to know all."

"I hope I am one of them?"

"You are, Colonel."

"Then I can guess the other."

"Doubtless you can."

"It is our good friend Bridgewater."

"Even so. And now I will further explain what I think of doing."

The utmost attention was given to Captain Heron, while he spoke in rather a low voice, as though he feared the very walls might carry to some hostile ears the secret of his plans.

"I am quite certain that Whitcombe House will be deserted, because it is well known that either I or my half-brother, Lord Warringdale, must be the owner of it, and no one will interfere between us. He is scared from it by superstitious fears, and I propose to give a written authority in my proper name as Earl of Whitcombe to a Mr. Smith and his wife to occupy the mansion."

"Smith!" said Lady Castleneau.

"Smith!" exclaimed Edith.

"Just so. Mr. Smith."

"But, Felix——"

"Hear me out. I propose that you and I, Edith, should play the parts of Mr. and Mrs. Smith."

"Ah, I see!"

"We will so far disguise ourselves as to appear an elderly couple, and I do not think there will be any difficulty in accomplishing so much, calculating, as I do, that the last place in which any one will look for us will be Whitcombe House."

Edith sighed.

"You are afraid, Edith?"

"I am; and yet I know not why I should be."

"Be of good cheer, dear one. I am confident about the plan. I will take measures that Mr. Smith shall seem to be at the mansion in St James's Street, while Captain Heron, the highwayman, shall be known to be elsewhere."

"Upon my life," said Colonel Trelawney, "I wish you every success; and still hope that something may be done to restore you to all your rights."

"Time may do it. I have such an enemy at Court, that while he lives I have no hope."

"You mean Lord Clackington?"

"I do."

"Yes, he has the ear of the King, from some circumstance to which it is not necessary to allude."

"It is so. And now, Aunt Castleneau, what say you to the plan?"

"I have many fears."

"Do you not think that I can play an elderly gentleman well enough?"

"You may be able, Felix"

"I am sure I can; and that Edith, too, will play her part well."

"I will try, Felix."

"The Earl of Bridgewater," announced old Anthony at this moment.

CHAPTER CLXXXIX.

THE EARL OF BRIDGEWATER SUGGESTS AN IMPORTANT ALTERATION IN THE PLANS OF FELIX HERON.

A MORE welcome visitor to Castleneau House could not possibly have been found than the Earl of Bridgewater; and Felix Heron welcomed him with that silent pressure of the hand which is far more eloquent than words.

The young Earl looked about him inquiringly as he said, in a tone of only half-seriousness, "I can well perceive that some important affair is in progress, and perhaps I ought to retire."

"Not so, my dear friend," said Lady Castleneau. "On the contrary, your presence is most opportune."

"Yes," added Edith; "you will be able to take a calmer and cooler view of affairs than perhaps any of us can."

The impetuous young Earl shook his head.

"Lady Whitcombe," he said, "I am very much afraid you give me credit for qualities I do not possess. Where my feelings are much interested, I am not very cool or calm."

"But your judgment is good. Felix, tell our dear friend, the Earl, what your plan is."

Upon this, Felix Heron related all to the Earl of Bridgewater that is already known to the reader.

"Speak freely, Bridgewater," he said, in conclusion; "and if you seriously object to my plan, say so candidly."

"I do, then."

"I feared so," said Edith.

"I hoped so," said Colonel Trelawney.

"And I expected so," said Lady Castleneau.

Heron smiled, but not gaily.

"Ah," he said, "I can see that you all think my plan a little too romantic, and that I shall have to confine myself more to the regions of commonplace in what I propose."

"May I speak?" said the Earl.

"Assuredly."

"Then I like the plan in some respects, and I don't like it in others."

"Good!" cried Colonel Trelawney.

"I think," added the Earl of Bridgewater, "that it will be well to reside at Whitcombe House; but

EDITH.—No. 57.

how you are to do so may perhaps be modified by news I bring you."

"There has been a meeting of the Privy Council, and it has been resolved, more to gratify a whim of the King than because any of the councillors, except one, think it expedient, to proceed against you, Whitcombe, for high treason."

"High treason?"

"Yes It is pretended that you are an emissary to the exiled royal family; and whether he really thinks so or not, the King insists upon the charge, aided by you all know who!"

"Lord Clackington?"

"Just so."

"Then that ridiculous charge is persevered in," said Heron.

"It is, with this addition; that a proclamation of outlawry will be proclaimed against you."

" Let them do so. I care not."

" But that makes your position more dangerous ; and I should advise that a step be taken which will effectually baffle your foes."

" What step ?"

" Yes," cried Edith,—" what step ?"

They all looked deeply interested.

The Earl lowered his voice so that the words he uttered could only be heard by those in that room, who listened to him so intently.

" It is in my power to adopt a course which will have the effect of at once putting an end to all persecution against you, Whitcombe, and enabling both you and Edith to reside in peace at Whitcombe House."

" A miracle!" cried Colonel Trelawney.

" Tell us—oh, tell us ?" said Edith.

" The impression on the mind of the King, and of Lord Olackington, must be that you are no more."

" Dead ?"

" Just that!"

Edith crept closer to Heron, as if the mere pronunciation of the word "dead," even in so remote a connexion with him, was one step towards such a calamity.

" Fear nothing, Edith," added the Earl of Bridgewater. " I only wish him to seem to die, in order that he may really live."

" Go on!" cried Lady Castleneau. " Let us hear all !"

The Earl proceeded.

" A gamekeeper of mine has, in a contest with some poachers among my pheasants, been shot and killed. An inquest has been held on his body, and a verdict of murder returned. That body lies now in a shell, awaiting interment, at my country-seat, close to the little old town of Edgeware, about eight miles from Tyburn Gate."

Heron nodded.

" It will be easy for me, Heron, if you can let me have a complete suit of your clothes, and the assistance of one or two of your men——"

" I have only two left, and a boy," interrupted Heron.

" Well, they will suffice. What I propose to do, is to dress the dead gamekeeper in a suit of your clothes—and it fortunately happens that he is about your height and size—and then, with the shell in which he now lies, some bricks and stones will take the place of the body which can be placed on the highway to be found."

" But," said Edith, " who will say that is Felix Heron ?"

" I will."

Edith still clung to her husband.

" Dear Edith," said Heron, " you do not like the plan, because death is an element in it; but it is only the death of the already dead."

" Pray go on, my Lord of Bridgewater," interposed old Lady Castleneau; " for I can see that you have more to say."

" I have."

They were all silent.

" I am quite convinced that if it was supposed Felix Heron was no more, no molestation would be offered to Edith taking possession of Whitcombe House, and possibly of some, if not, by degrees, all, of the estates of Whitcombe."

" Dear Edith, what say you to this scheme ?" asked Heron.

" You would still be with me ?"

" As ever."

" You would only have, as in a play, "said the Earl of Bridgewater, " to seem a widow."

" In one disguise and another, as circumstances rendered expedient, Heron could be ever with you in the mansion, and——"

Here the Earl lowered his voice until it only became a whisper.

" The King is so infirm that it is not supposed he can live another year. The young Prince who will succeed him will not inherit his likes or his dislikes, and then the imposture can be openly avowed, and the danger of the time having passed away, Felix Heron can claim his own in the light of day !"

" And, besides," said Colonel Trelawney, " before twelve months are past something else that we shall be able to congratulate ourselves upon is sure to happen."

" What is that ?" asked everybody.

" Jonathan Wild will be hanged !"

They all laughed, for the Colonel uttered the last words with a graphic solemnity that would have made him famous as a fortune-teller.

" It is likely enough," remarked Heron.

" Come, now," cried Bridgewater; " what do you all say to my plan ? Do you consent, Heron ?"

" I do."

" And you, Edith ?"

" Yes."

" And you, Lady Castleneau ?"

" I consent."

" And you, Lady Trelawney ? And you, Colonel ?"

" We both agree."

" Then you will all aid me in carrying it out to the utmost of your several abilities ?"

" We will."

" And nothing that I shall ask will be denied me ?"

" Nothing ! Nothing !"

" Heron, I shall want Daisy."

" Ah !"

" Yes, Daisy, your famous horse. Nothing in all the world would so prove your identity with the dead gamekeeper in your apparel, as the presence of Daisy on that spot."

" My poor Daisy !"

" Pho ! pho ! I will look after her; and Edith, here, must claim her, so that she will soon again be in the stable of Whitcombe House, with the advantage of being there openly, and without any concealment."

" You shall have Daisy !"

" Then leave all the rest to me, Heron, and I feel sure all will be well."

" I feel sure of that likewise," said Lady Castleneau ; " and now, until all this is settled, you stay with me, Edith."

" Yes, dear aunt."

" And you come with me, Heron," said the Earl of Bridgewater. " Only if you can make some change in your outward appearance it would be well."

" That I can help him to," said Colonel Trelawney. " I will provide him with an undress suit of regimentals of the Royal Horse Guards, and in that I almost think he might pass Jonathan Wild himself unsuspected."

The Colonel wrote a note, and sent it by Anthony to the barracks ; and in an hour's time, the suit of regimentals came.

Heron, when he came down stairs to the breakfast-room of Lady Castleneau in this disguise, looked so perfectly the soldier, that no one doubted for a moment the efficacy of the dress to shield him from all eyes.

Follow us, Heron," said the Earl. "Trelawney and I will walk on, and you can keep in well in view."

The plan was adopted; and they made their way to the house of the Earl of Bridgewater without any accident.

From there Heron sent for Ogle, and fully explained to him what was to be done.

The plan, in its details, was that Edith, so soon as the report of the death of Heron was well about, was to take possession of Whitcombe House.

Ogle, Mortification, and Tom Ripon were to be domestics, or play the part of them; and Mrs. Ogle and Mrs. Ripon, if she could be found, along with the young girl who was so tantalizing a flame to Tom, were to be the female servitors at the mansion.

By this plan no strangers were to be allowed in the establishment.

Edith had by this time improved a little upon the plan, for she had persuaded her aunt, Lady Castlenean, to say that she would pass much of her time at Whitcombe House, and bring with her Anthony and Martha, so that the establishment was not to be a very weak one.

Ogle was to explain the whole affair to Tom, and to Mortification, and to his wife, and he was likewise to ride Daisy to Edgeware so soon as the evening of that day fairly set in.

In the meantime, Lord Clackington was using his utmost exertions to do all the harm he could to Felix Heron.

For that purpose he thought he could not do better than call upon Jonathan Wild.

It was about three o'clock in the afternoon, therefore, of that eventful day that the carriage of my Lord Clackington halted at Little Newgate.

The peal upon the knocker that the footman executed soon brought the janissary, who was "on the lock," to his post, for he had been gossiping in the kitchen.

"Is—aw—Mister Wild at—aw—home?" asked the footman, with his nose in the air.

"To be sure he is, stupid!" was the not over-courteous reply.

"His lordship's cawd!"

The footman handed in Lord Clackington's "cawd," as he called it.

Jonathan Wild, however, who was in the house, heard the appeal at the knocker, and now made his appearance. A glance at the "cawd" pretty well opened his eyes in regard to the object of the visit of Lord Clackington, and he went out to the coach door.

"Glad to see your lordship, at Little Newgate. Quite an honour. What can I do for you, my lord?"

"I will come into your house and speak to you, Mr. Wild."

"Certainly, my lord. Make way—make way, you rascals, for my Lord Clackington!"

Wild led Lord Clackington to that room on the first floor where the reader has often seen the great thief-taker, and ceremoniously offered him a chair.

"Hem!" said Clackington. "I am afraid, Mr. Wild, you don't stand very well with the authorities."

"Indeed, my lord."

"No, no! 'Pon soul, no! They have their suspicions of you."

"I am quite surprised."

"Ah!—are you?"

"Yes, my lord; and still more, that your lordship

should have taken the trouble to come here and tell me as much."

"I have not exactly come for that."

"Oh!"

"But to tell you, and show you, how you may by a signal service, set all these very suspicions at rest, and raise yourself to good favour with an exalted personage."

"The King?"

"I said an exalted personage."

"The hangman?"

"Mr. Wild!"

"My lord!"

"You give way to a levity that does not become you; but if you will earn a couple of hundred guineas, in addition to all the other rewards that I hear are offered, and likewise the gratitude of several great people, you will make short work of Captain Felix Heron."

Wild shook his head.

"You will not?"

"I am a long way off from saying I will not, my lord; but what I mean is, that it is easier said than done."

"Confound the scoundrel!"

Wild laughed.

"Well, my lord, I will do my best."

"Do so, and rest satisfied of the favour of those whose favour goes even to the length of life and death, should you ever be in a position to require it."

"Many thanks, my lord. It will not be from the want of will that I shall fail, if I do, in placing Felix Heron in the hands of justice."

Lord Clackington took a pinch of snuff.

He looked with all the sly malice of an old baboon into the face of Wild.

"Pho, pho! What do you care about justice? Kill him!"

"I mean to."

"Very good! A nice day, Mr. Wild. When Felix Heron is dead, bring that to me for my signature, which I will then instantly attach to it."

As he spoke, Lord Clackington placed a piece of paper in the hands of Wild.

It was a cheque filled up all but the actual signature

It read thus :—

"Pay Mr. Jonathan Wild or order the sum of five hundred pounds."

Lord Clackington meant that blank cheque to be the death warrant of Felix Heron.

"I will do my best," said Wild, gloomily. "But your lordship hardly appreciates the difficulties, I have, at times, had strange thoughts about him."

"About Felix Heron?"

"Yes, my lord."

"What thoughts?"

"That he bore a charmed life."

"Pho, pho! Old women's tales. Pho, pho! You—a sensible, practical man, Mr. Wild—to talk such absolute nonsense."

"Well, well, I will do all that man can do."

"That is all that can be expected of you; only I should think that there can be no real practical difficulty in taking a life."

"We shall see!"

"Good day—good day! Wherever I may be, come to me at once when the event happens, and I will sign that cheque."

———

CHAPTER CXC.

DAISY HAS TO PLAY A STRANGE AND STARTLING
PART IN THE DRAMA AT EDGWARE.

THE night has come!

Dark and still, with now and then a dull, far-off sound of thunder.

The air had been too close and preternaturally calm the whole day not to threaten some rather violent change.

The clouds dropped low, and those birds, whose habits were nocturnal, flew lower than usual, and uttered discordant cries.

" Confound you!' cried a horseman who had just got clear of the village of Kilburn, and up the hill beyond leading to the windmill, as a bat flew in his face—"confound you! Can't you look where you are coming to!"

It was Ogle who spoke.

He rode Daisy.

His errand was to a small estate which the Earl of Bridgewater owned close to Edgware.

Daisy was a little startled at the bat, whose leathery wings flapped about her eyes for a few seconds.

" Gently, Daisy, lass—gently!" said Ogle.

Daisy trotted along again composedly.

Ogle, to tell the truth, was not very well pleased with the part he had to play in the drama which was got up for the purpose of impressing upon the enemies of Captain Heron the idea that he was no more.

The mere fact that death and Heron were associated together, was not pleasant to Ogle any more than it had been to Edith.

But he trotted on.

Behind him he had a bundle shaped like a valise, and strapped to the saddle.

That bundle contained a complete suit of Captain Heron's clothes, such as he was wont to wear when he went out openly on the highway, or the common, to cry "Stand and deliver!" to the King's lieges.

To Daisy the trot to Edgware was nothing, although Ogle was not a light weight, and in about half an hour the little dim lights of the still old-fashioned town were visible.

Ogle then drew rein.

"I must not overshoot my mark," he said. "I was to meet somebody here at the milestone, just before getting into the town."

Ogle thought he saw a milestone, but he was not quite sure in the darkness, and he dismounted to see it closer.

He started back!

It was not a milestone, although the object was about the same size, and looked dully white in the darkness.

It was something with life.

"Hilloa!" cried Ogle. "Who, and what are you?"

The sound of sobbing was the only one that met his ears.

Ogle got over his first start, and bent low down, and touched the figure.

"Speak," he said. "Tell me what's the matter with you, and who you are?"

"Nothing! nothing!"

It was the voice of a boy—almost a child—that broke upon the ears of Ogle.

"Come, come, my little man," he said. "I am quite sure something is amiss. Are you hungry?"

" No, no!"

"Thirsty?"

"No! no!"

" What then?"

" They have killed father."

"Who?—who?"

" The cruel keepers. It was all about the pheasants. They shoot 'em, and why shouldn't father? But they shot father, too ; and what is to become of poor little Dick?"

The boy began to cry again bitterly.

" As sure as fate," said Ogle to himself, "this is the son of the gamekeeper that Lord Bridgewater talks about. Hoy, my little man, who was your father?"

" Under-keeper to Lord Bridgewater, he was."

" Ah, I thought so! I'm quite sure the Earl will provide for you, Dick."

" No, he won't."

" But I say he will!"

" And I say he won't."

" Why?"

" Because, though father was an under-keeper, he was out with the lads that take game when they can get it, and so got shot!"

"Ah, I begin to see now! Never mind, you come along with me."

" Are you a keeper?"

" No."

" A poacher?"

" Sometimes."

" Then I don't mind going with you. Is that your horse yonder?"

" Yes, it is. There you are, my little chap! All you have to do is to hold on."

" Yes, I'll hold on. Where be you going to?"

" Not a wedding."

" Where to, then?"

" Perhaps a funeral. Hilloa! this won't do!"

Ogle had all of a sudden bethought him that the expedition he was on, and the part he was to be in the proceedings of that night, were not exactly suitable for the observation of the son of the murdered keeper.

" I can't take you any further, little chap," he said. " Here is half a crown. Get a night's rest somewhere, and in the morning you go and speak to the Earl, and, you may take my word for it, he will do something handsome for you."

" I will."

" Good night."

" Good night, and thank you for the half-crown."

Ogle rode on.

But the boy ran back and whistled.

From the shadow of a hedge a man started up and called to him.

" Come here, Dick. Who was that?"

" I don't know."

" Did you cut away the valise?"

" Yes."

" Come on, then. It's sure to drop on the road, somewhere. Don't you be grieving about your father. Bless you, a sharp little chap like you will find lots of fathers!"

It was quite evident that Dick, the son of the poacher and gamekeeper, was not disposed to grow grey with grief.

What effect his encounter with Ogle was calculated to have upon the fortunes of those persons in whom we are interested, will sufficiently soon be apparent.

.Ogle satisfied himself soon that he was at the mile-stone, where he was to wait for some one from the Earl of Bridgewater, who would conduct him exactly where he was to go.

JONATHAN WILD REJOICES IN THE OVERTHROW OF HIS FOE.

Presented Gratis with No. 57, of the New Edition of EDITH BROWN, the Sequel to Edith the Captive; or, the Robbers of Epping Forest.

It was at that mile-stone that Ogle found out the fastenings of the valise-like shaped bundle, that he had with him on the saddle, had been tampered with.

But Ogle was by far too experienced a traveller to leave any parcel that he valued at the mercy of a leather strap.

A small but strong iron chain of complicated links likewise fastene i the bundle, so that although Dick had cut the straps cleverly enough, it had not fallen.

"So, so!" said Ogle, "that young rascal is one of that sort, is he? Only let me come up with him again, that's all!"

"A nice night!" cried a voice, suddenly.

Ogle started.

It was the first part of the signal agreed upon that would let him know he had met with the right person.

"Yes," replied Ogle, "if the moon was up."

"Sometimes the moon is not wanted!" was the reply.

"All right!" cried Ogle.

"Follow me."

"I will, though it is so plaguy dark I can hardly see you."

"This way!"

There was the flash of a lantern, and Ogle saw that the man he was to follow turned down a narrow lane to the right of the high road.

Ogle followed, putting Daisy to a walk, and keeping the dim and dusky figure of the man in view.

In a few moments they left all traces of a regular road, and trod upon soft turf, which seemed mightly to please Daisy.

"Ah!" said Ogle, in a whisper, "I suppose you think you are back again in old Epping."

"Hush!" said the guide.

"All right!"

"Do not speak again until I address you."

Ogle was silent.

There was a tone of authority about this mysterious guide which made Ogle think that, in all probability, he was some one of consequence.

The dull sound of Daisy's feet upon the grass was now all that broke the intense stillness of the night.

Although, in truth, but seven or eight miles at the utmost from one of the principal thoroughfares of London, the solitude of that rural spot was complete.

"Halt!" said the guide.

Ogle paused.

A gate was opened, which creaked a little upon its hinges, and then Ogle put Daisy into motion again, and rode through.

The ground on the other side of the gate was gravel, and crumbled under the shoes of Daisy.

"He is here!" cried the guide.

"In good time!" said a voice.

Then there was a gleam of a stable lantern, and no other than the Earl of Bridgewater himself appeared.

Ogle touched his hat.

"Glad to see you, my lord."

"And I you, Ogle; for well I know how faithful and brave a follower you are of Felix Heron."

"I try to be so."

"And you succeed."

The lantern flashed upon the person who had guided Ogle to that spot, and he then saw that it was no other than Colonel Trelawney.

Both the Colonel and Lord Bridgewater had seen enough of the world to know that what you want well done you must do yourself, always provided it does not involve the exercise of some special skill or handicraft which can only be acquired by pratice.

The Earl opened a stable door wide.

"Ride in," he said.

In trotted Daisy with Ogle.

"Now," said the Earl again, after a pause, "are you very particular, Ogle, about a job that I cannot take upon myself to say is altogether a pleasant one?"

"Not over so, my lord."

"You can guess what it is?"

"I think I can. This little roll at the back of the saddle contains a full suit of the Captain's clothes."

"Yes, I see that you do guess. Will you do it, Ogle?"

"I will. You mean, will I dress up the dead gamekeeper in these clothes, I take it, my lord?"

"That is it?"

"It's as good as done, then. I can't say I ever met a live man that I was really afraid of, and I don't mean to begin to put myself in fear of a dead one."

"Come this way, then."

The Earl led Ogle into another stable that opened from the first one, and then into a coach-house, where, on some tressels, lay the coffin with the dead body of the gamekeeper.

Ogle placed his hand on the bridle of Daisy, as he said, "It's a pity, my lord, that she has anything to do with it."

"She—who?"

"Daisy."

"Oh, the horse! You quite startled me, Ogle. But why is it a pity?"

"She don't like it."

Daisy evidently hung back, and it was with great reluctance that she would cross the threshold of the coach-house.

"Leave her in the outer stable, Ogle."

"I will, my lord; she will be safe enough, I daresay."

"Quite! quite!"

A footstep was heard approaching.

Colonel Trelawney put his head in at the coach-house door.

"I cannot persuade myself," he said, "that there are not some persons in the meadows."

"Ah! so soon!" said the Earl.

Ogle looked from one to the other of them, as he said, "Soon or late, my lord, I can say that I know there are persons about this spot, for an attempt has been made already to steal this bundle of the Captain's clothes."

The Earl of Bridgewater looked disquieted; but he felt the necessity of immediate action, and he said sharply, "Then the sooner all that we have to do to-night here is done the better it will be. Ogle, there is your man: I will leave you a light."

The Earl and Colonel Trelawney left Ogle alone with the dead gamekeeper.

The screws of the coffin were loose, and a powerful screwdriver was lying on the lid, with which Ogle completed the task.

It was, as Ogle afterwards said, about the ugliest job he ever had in his life; but he did clothe the dead body completely in the dress of Captain Heron he had brought with him.

The coat of scarlet.

The boots.

The waistcoat with its gold lace.

And the cravat, and hat, and gloves.

All complete.

But the dead man looked very ghastly indeed in that brave apparel.

"All right!" said Ogle, as he opened the door of the coach-house.

"Bring him out!"

"How, my lord?"

"Won't Daisy take him?"

"I should say decidedly not."

"Then, Trelawney, let us have out the black horse; he will not be so particular."

Colonel Trelawney brought out of one of the loose stalls of the stable a black horse, and the dressed-up body of the dead man was placed upon it.

"I will lead the way," said the Earl.

"Hush! What is that?"

A clock struck something in the distance.

It was the hour of ten.

"We had need be quick," said the Earl; "for the anonymous letter to Jonathan Wild appointed this hour."

"May I make so bold as to ask what that letter was about?"

"Yes, Ogle."

"Yes," added the Colonel. "I think that whoever is trusted in any part of an affair like this ought to know all about it."

"So do I, Colonel—so do I. Lend me the lantern, and I will read Ogle a copy of the letter."

Ogle was rather glad that he was not asked to read the letter, since, as the reader has had occasion to see before, that was a branch of education in which he was rather deficient.

The letter ran thus:—

"A friend informs Jonathan Wild that Captain Heron, the famous highwayman of Epping Forest, intends to be on the Edgeware Road, not far from the town of Edgeware, to-night, to try his fortune with one of the cross country mails."

"That is all," said the Earl.

"It is enough," responded Ogle. "Wild will be here."

"Yes, and at this time; for written on the outside of the letter were the words, 'Not till ten o'clock.'"

Ogle sighed.

"What affects you, Ogle?" asked the Earl.

"Daisy!"

"What of her?"

"The idea that she is to get into the hands of such a rascal as Jonathan Wild!"

"That she shall not. The Colonel and I intend to ride up as if by accident, after Wild has made what he will no doubt think a wonderful discovery, and we will lay claim to Daisy."

"Do so, my lord, and my mind will be quite at ease."

"It shall be done. On, on, or all our plans may be lost."

"They are lost!" whispered the Colonel.

While thus conversing in low tones, the little party, consisting of Ogle and Daisy, and the Earl and the Colonel, and the black horse with the dead gamekeeper upon it, had reached the lane where road there was none but over the soft green sward.

Just as they did so, there came up to it a party of mounted men.

"Halt!" cried the harsh voice of Jonathan Wild.

The clatter of the horses' hoofs suddenly ceased.

"If this is a hoax," growled Wild, "I only wish I had the author of it in my grip, that is all!"

No one replied to this speech.

"What's o'clock, Swiney?"

"Past ten, Mr. Wild."

"Ah! I'm afraid the rascal will not show himself. How far do you take it to be to Edgeware now?"

"About half a mile, sir."

"Come on, then, gently."

Wild and his party rode on.

"Now," whispered the Earl of Bridgewater,—"now is the time!"

They all emerged into the road, and the dead gamekeeper was let drop from the horse that carried him on to the green sward close to the entrance to the lane.

Daisy's bridle was then brought right over her head, and tied in a knot round the wrist of the dead man.

Daisy did not see very well what was going on, but she planted both her fore feet before her, and got as far off from the dead man as she could.

By little successive jerks, then, she began to drag the body along the roadside.

"Now, Colonel!" said the Earl.

"Shall I fire?"

"Yes."

Bang! went a pistol which the Colonel took from one of his pockets.

A pause of only a couple of seconds was then allowed to take place, when he discharged the companion pistol.

Bang! went the sharp report, and it mingled in the far-off distance with the echoes of the first one.

Then the Earl placed his hands before his mouth in a peculiar manner, and uttered a loud and startling yell that must have spread alarm wherever it was heard.

It certainly spread alarm in the mind of Daisy.

The pistol-shots she paid no attention to, for she was used to them.

But the unearthly cry that the Earl of Bridgewater had thought proper to utter as part of his plan, did the business.

Daisy started off at once.

Towards Edgeware she went at a sharp half-gallop, dragging the dead body at her side by the bridle.

"Halt! hold! Form across the road! Stop whatever and whoever this is!" shouted Jonathan Wild.

At the first pistol-shot he had faced about.

At the second, he had put his party to speed.

At the strange cry that came upon the night air, he drew rein and waited.

Then he heard the rapid approach of a horse.

Of Daisy, although he knew her not.

Unaided by the intelligence of a rider on whom she could depend, and who could bring out all her latent intelligence to meet his, Daisy fell into the kind of ambuscade that Jonathan Wild and his men had prepared hastily across the road.

Half a dozen hands were on her bridle at once.

A couple of dark lanterns were unmasked, and shed two broad gleams of light upon the scene.

It was a strange one.

There was Wild, with a party of horse some half a dozen strong, and armed to the teeth.

And there was Daisy.

Her mane erect.

Her eyes flashing.

Her nostrils quivering with emotion, and still dragging at her bridle the lifeless body of the gamekeeper.

The gamekeeper, in the exact costume of Felix Heron, the highwayman.

Wild raised a shout.

"At last—at last !" he cried. "It is all over at last !"

"What, Mr. Wild ?" asked all his men, in chorus.

Wild raised his hat.

A demoniac smile lit up his face.

His eyes gleamed like those of a decomposing fish by the light of the lantern, as he half-sang, half-shouted, "Good night—a long good night to Felix Heron, Earl of Whitcombe, and some time the king of old Epping Forest !"

"Is that him, Mr. Wild ?" cried several of the janissaries, as they pointed to the body of the gamekeeper which had been dragged half over on to its side.

Wild nodded.

Wild laughed.

"Will you look at him in the face, Mr. Wild, and be sure ?" asked one.

"No !"

Wild laid hold of Daisy by the mane.

"This is my evidence—I am sure. This is his famous mare, Daisy. I have no need to look there, being quite sure about her."

He pointed to the body as he spoke.

But a couple of his janissaries had hastily dismounted and ran to the dead gamekeeper, whom they turned on to his back, and to whose face they held a lantern.

"Dead ?" asked Wild.

"Quite, sir !"

"Ah !"

Wild drew a long breath.

"How ?"

"Shot, sir."

"Of course !"

"Will you come and look at him, Mr. Wild ?"

"Yes—no, no ! Why should I ? I am content. I have seen his face in life—I don't want it to haunt me in death ! No, no ; I won't look at it !"

CHAPTER CXCI.

THE EARL OF BRIDGEWATER RESCUES DAISY FROM JONATHAN WILD, WHO REJOICES EXCEEDINGLY.

THE vein of superstition that formed a part of the mental condition of Jonathan Wild began to come into action.

He had a dread that if he looked into what he supposed to be the dead face of Felix Heron, he should see some impression there he might never be able to forget.

Jonathan was getting rather subject to bad dreams.

That might mingle with them.

"No, no !" he said again ; "I don't want to see him !"

As he spoke, he drew from his pocket a clasped knife and, opening it with his teeth, as was his general habit, he cut the bridle of Daisy, and released her from the enforced connexion with the dead body.

But he took good care that she should not get away, for if he ever succeeded in compassing the death of Felix Heron, Wild looked upon the reversionary interest in Daisy as a matter of no small importance.

But Jonathan was doomed to a little disappointment in that particular.

At the moment that his men had dragged the supposed corpse of Felix Heron on to the grass by the side of the road, the rapid beat of horses' feet upon that road became apparent.

Wild cried out to his men.

"Look sharp, bull-dogs—look sharp ! Some horsemen on the road !"

The janissaries took up a strong position in two parties, one on each side of the way ; and Jonathan Wild stood in the very centre of the road with a lantern in his hand.

"Halt !" he shouted.

"What for ?"

"In the King's name !"

"And who are you with such a word in your mouth on the highway ?"

"I am the King's officer ! Halt, I say ! There has been a highway robbery here, gentlemen."

Wild added the word "gentlemen" on the horsemen—there were but two—coming within the influence of the light of the lantern he carried.

They were both richly dressed and well mounted.

The reader knows them well.

They were the Earl of Bridgewater and Colonel Trelawney, carrying out the next act of the little drama which was so completely confounding and deceiving Jonathan Wild.

"What is amiss here ?" said the Earl, in a cold and haughty tone.

Jonathan Wild then knew him.

"My Lord Bridgewater," he said, "unless I am very much mistaken."

"Well, sir, what then ?"

"Oh, my lord, not much, only that your friend Felix Heron—Captain Heron of Epping Forest—has been up to his old games, and has somehow met with his match."

"Felix Heron ?"

"Just so, my lord."

"Can this news be possible ?"

"I will convince you of it. Do you happen to know his mare Daisy by sight ?"

"Well—well !"

"Behold her !"

Wild held up the lantern so that quite sufficient light shone upon Daisy for the purpose of recognition, and the Earl, with a well-affected start, exclaimed, "That is, indeed, Captain Heron's famous steed, Daisy."

Wild nodded.

"No mistake about that, my lord."

"And he is killed ?"

"Shot !"

"Through the head," added one of Wild's men.

"You hear, my lord ?"

"Good heaven !"

"Amen !" cried Wild, with a hypocritical twang that was not very unlike the tone in which the Reverend Mortification was in the habit of recommending sinners to a certain hot place.

"And the body ?" said the Earl.

"Oh, I have nothing to do with that."

"And the horse ?"

"That, as a constable, I take up. Ha, ha !"

"As a constable ?"

"Yes, my lord."

"Well, it seems to me that a magistrate has surely more power than a constable, and as I happen to be in the commission of the peace, I will take the horse.

"You, my lord?"

"Just so."

Wild looked deeply mortified.

"Not only am I a magistrate," added the Earl of Bridgewater, "but I am lord of the manor here; and the ground on which we now stand is part of the manor."

Wild looked like a fiend.

He still held the bridle of Daisy.

He glanced at his men as though the vague and desperate idea of making a fight of it, and resisting the authority of the Earl of Bridgewater, had come across his mind.

"My Lord Bridgewater," he said with a concentrated bitterness in his tone which he did not take the trouble to conceal, "I know you well, and I know that you have always been the friend and the upholder of Felix Heron, the highwayman!"

"Well?" said the Earl, calmly.

"The law," added Wild, "calls it aiding, and abetting and comforting."

"Well?"

"It would not have run quite so well with you, my lord, had you stood at the bar of a criminal court to answer for such acts even as Edith, the wife of that same Felix Heron, did."

"Perhaps not. But it's possible, Jonathan Wild, that Felix Heron might then have held your life in his hands, and bargained for all future non-molestations of me and mine as he did in regard to Edith."

The Earl of Bridgewater had an object in saying this much.

He wanted Wild fully to comprehend that, although, to all appearance, Felix Heron was no more, the compact that he had made with him, Wild, not to annoy or disturb Edith in any way, was known.

Wild looked pale as the Earl spoke.

"So, my lord," he said, "I see you are deep in the confidence of the highwaymen."

"Not particularly so. Felix Heron was one of those open, generous souls who have no petty secrets!"

"Be it so. Have it your own way."

"I mean to do so."

The Earl laid his hand on the bridle of Daisy.

"Let me, however," added Wild, "say this much—that there is not another magistrate of England who would take from a police-officer the horse of a highwayman whom he had overcome on the King's highway."

"Nor will I."

"Ah!"

"I say, nor will I. Only show me that you did overcome him, and the famous horse Daisy is yours."

Wild bit his lips.

He was wondering how much the Earl knew of the actual circumstances, and how far, consequently, he might have a chance of going to attempt to deceive him.

"Why," he said, "the facts speak for themselves, my lord!"

"They do, Jonathan Wild. You found the horse and the dead rider on the highway—but that is all the fact as regards you!"

Wild let Daisy go.

"Take her," he said; "only I wish another magistrate was present, in which case I feel confident the decision would be in my favour."

"Are you sure of that, Jonathan Wild?" said Colonel Trelawney.

Wild looked at him sharply.

"I am, sir."

"Then you are wrong again. I, too, am in the commission of the peace, and I adhere to what the Earl of Bridgewater says."

Wild uttered a snarling growl; and then, turning to his men, he cried, "To London!—to London! My lord, and you, sir, since you are so mightily smitten with the highwayman's horse, may have the highwayman himself. Ha! ha! I make you a free present of the dead man!"

Jonathan Wild liked to have the last word; and he now set spurs to his horse, and galloped off, so as not to hear any reply that might be made to him

His party of janissaries followed him.

Now this was just what the Earl of Bridgewater and Colonel Trelawney wanted.

Their whole effort was to bring the interview with Wild to exactly this termination.

"That will do!" said the Earl.

"Exactly!" added the Colonel.

They waited awhile, until the sounds of the horses' footsteps belonging to Wild and his party had entirely disappeared, and then the Earl called, "Ogle! Ogle!"

"Here!"

Ogle came out of the shadowy space by the road-side, where, out of the sphere of the rays of Jonathan Wild's lantern, he had been a witness to the whole affair.

"Take possession of Daisy again, Ogle, and ride to London You will find Felix Heron at Whitcombe House."

"With pleasure, my lord; and I don't think I should have had a moment's peace this night if Daisy had remained in the hands of Wild."

"One moment, however," said the Earl, "before you go, Ogle. Will you restore the dead body to the coffin from which you took it?"

"That will I. He was no acquaintance of mine, poor fellow; but I will do my best for him, as I would like to think some kind soul would do for me."

Ogle was as good as his word; and the dead gamekeeper having that night made himself so very useful—perhaps more useful in death than ever he had been in life—was once more consigned to his narrow home, and firmly screwed down

Ogle did not take the trouble to divest the body of the suit of highwayman's apparel belonging to Felix Heron; so that for the future speculation of any one who might get, in the changes and mutations of time, a glimpse of that dead body, the gamekeeper was doomed to go to the grave in the full dress of a knight of the road.

Ogle then started for London.

He took good care, however, as he rode Daisy to take a different route from the ordinary highway, for he did not wish to encounter Jonathan Wild and his party.

Ogle, therefore, went up one of the narrow, verdant lanes that led to Hampstead, and so reached London across those fields for so many years so well known to Londoners, but which now, alas! are shorn of all their beauty, and a prey to the builder.

It was at about half-past twelve o'clock at night that Ogle drew rein at the door of old Whitcombe House, St. James's Street.

Felix Heron was there.

Pacing the hall, he was waiting anxiously for Ogle to tell him how affairs had sped at Edgeware.

Heron was too well acquainted with the sound

THE PRINCESS DEMIDOFF.

No. 58.—EDITH.

of Daisy's footsteps not to recognise them on the moment.

Heron himself opened the massive street door.

It was not prudent; for, although he might have been certain that it was the footstep of Daisy he heard, he could not be so certain of who was on her back.

Ogle had dismounted.

Not a sound was in the street.

It was just that hour at which such a street was likely to be deserted at times for a full five minutes.

"Ogle?"

"Yes Captain."

"All well?"

"Excellent! You are dead, and Jonathan Wild is ready to swear to it!"

"Good!"

"Oh, it was well managed!"

"I do not doubt but it was. Come in and tell me all about it."

"Daisy, Captain?"

"Bring her in."

The hall was large enough to have driven in a coach and pair with ease, so that Daisy, hearing her master's voice, at once stepped across the threshold of Whitcombe House, and stood close to Heron in the hall, rubbing her head upon his shoulder.

"Ah, my gallant Daisy," said Heron, "I am as well pleased to see you again as you can be to see me!"

Ogle carefully closed and barred the door of Whitcombe House before he said another word to Felix Heron.

CHAPTER CXCII.

JONATHAN WILD MEETS WITH A TERRIBLE FRIGHT, AND GOES HOME IN A SAD PLIGHT.

"Now, Ogle, tell me all about it."

"I will, Captain."

Ogle, then, in his short, terse way, related to Felix Heron all that had taken place on the outskirts of the little town of Edgeware.

"It was capitally done!" said Heron.

"Indeed it was, Captain."

"And Jonathan Wild now thoroughly believes that I am no longer in this world?"

"You may depend, Captain, that he will go before the magistrates and make a declaration to that effect the first thing in the morning, taking a wonderful deal of credit to himself in the matter."

"Let him."

A small lamp was burning in the spacious hall of Whitcombe House, and in the great extent of the place, and up the grand staircase, where many of the feeble rays were likewise dissipated, the lamp only produced a very dubious kind of twilight.

By that twilight, however, pale and indistinct as it was, Ogle could see that Captain Heron was full dressed, as if for the road.

"Captain," he said, "you don't surely mean to go out to-night?"

"I do, Ogle."

"And alone?"

"No; I thought of taking you with me, Ogle."

"All's right, then!"

"We must ride to Epping and back before the morning. I have hidden beneath one of the old chesnut trees, close to where, as you have probably seen, there are the ruins of an old lodge, once, no doubt, inhabited by a keeper, when Epping was a royal chase, a small tin box, in which there is a good sum of money in gold."

"We will get it, Captain."

"Yes," added Heron, with a faint smile. "Edith will want it to keep house with here."

Bang!

They both started.

Daisy pricked up her ears.

A loud single knock had come at the door of Whitcombe House.

Who could it be?

Neither Heron nor Ogle ventured to utter a word.

Bang! came the knock again.

Heron whispered to Ogle.

"I suppose it is some idle person who thinks it an amusement to knock at the door of an empty house."

"I will soon see, Captain."

"How?—how?"

"This way."

Ogle was a big, brawny man, but he was strong and active; and with a dexterity that, to look at him, no one would have supposed it possible he possessed, he climbed up by the back of the shut door to the fan-light above it.

The lock.

The bolts.

The fastenings of the two knockers. All afforded Ogle some foothold, and he was soon able to look through the fanlight on to the doorstep.

A glance seemed to be enough.

Ogle rapidly descended.

"Who is it?"

"Jonathan Wild."

"Ah! The villain! What wants he here?"

"He has some deep design upon Whitcombe House, Captain, now that he thinks you are not in the world to thwart him in it."

"No doubt! No doubt!"

Bang went the knock at the door again.

Jonathan Wild had apparently made up his mind to knock three times, and then to feel an assurance that no one was in the house.

In a few seconds more they heard that he was fumbling and rattling at the lock.

Ogle whispered to Heron.

"He is trying his skeleton keys now."

Heron nodded.

"The iron bar, though, will baffle him, Captain."

"Take it down, Ogle."

"What?"

"Take it down, and let him make his way in."

"But, Captain——"

"Hush!"

Jonathan Wild, from without, uttered a series of awful maledictions, for he was both surprised and disappointed that the door did not at once yield to him.

Assuming no one to be in the house, the door could not be bolted, barred, or chained on the inside, so that the pick-lock, which no one in all the world could use with more skill than Wild, ought to clear the way for him easily.

But the bar that Ogle had put up lay close to the panels of the door, and held it fast.

"Fear nothing," said Heron, in a whisper, close to the ear of Ogle. "I intend to give Jonathan Wild such a warning not to show himself in the hall of Whitcombe House again that he will not be likely to forget it were he yet to encumber the earth for a hundred years."

"Yes, Captain, you can."

"Easily."

"Capital! capital! He was always mightily afraid of ghosts. We used to make odd noises in the night-time at Little Newgate on purpose to scare him."

"Indeed!"

"Yes, Captain; and he would come down stairs looking as white as a sheet, with his hanger in one hand and a light in the other, to know what it was."

"Well, Ogle, take down that bar, so that he can open the door and get in, and I promise you he shall have a fright to-night such as he has never yet had the chance of having."

Wild still rattled with the key in the lock of the door.

He still swore fearfully.

Cautiously and slowly Ogle took down the iron bar.

While he was doing so Felix Heron mounted Daisy, and stood with her exactly in the centre of the hall.

There he was in his full costume, just as Jonathan Wild thought he had seen him lying dead by the road-side at Edgeware some two hours before.

And mounted on Daisy, too, about whom there could be no mistake, for he, Wild, had had her actually by the bridle.

Felix Heron always had rather a grave and thoughtful face, but now he composed it to a look of stern dignity, and kept his eyes fixed upon the little lamp, so that there was a brightness from the reflection of it upon those eyes which Jonathan Wild could not fail to be struck with.

Ogle took up such a position that when the door should be fairly opened he would be shielded by it.

And now Jonathan Wild found that whatever had hindered the operation of his skeleton key hindered it no longer.

The lock yielded.

The massive door creaked gently upon its hinges.

Wild stepped lightly into the hall.

Coming from the darkness without, it was very probable that the little lamp in that hall, feeble as were its rays, appeared to him a very tolerable light.

At all events, it was enough to enable him to see all that the hall contained.

And all that he saw was the equestrian figure in the middle of it.

The man and the horse!

Felix Heron and Daisy!

No possible form of words could give a really just idea of the effect upon Jonathan Wild of this apparition.

He stood about five paces within the hall, glaring at it.

His mouth open!

His eyes distended!

His hands stretched out, with every finger as far apart from the other as they could get!

The very agony of fear sat at the heart of the great thief-taker.

He wanted to fly.

But his limbs refused to move.

He wanted to scream.

But his tongue refused its office.

The only sound that, by a great effort, he could utter, was a sort of hiss, such as some rattlesnake in the agonies of dissolution might have produced.

Never in all his life had Jonathan Wild met with a fright so terrible as this.

Ogle enjoyed it immensely.

And so, in truth, did Felix Heron.

It was so easy to play the part of one's own ghost.

But this was a state of things that could not last long.

No mortal could suffer what Jonathan Wild was suffering, and preserve his reason for another half minute.

Felix Heron put an end to it.

"Ho, Daisy!—forward! forward!"

If anything had been wanting to convince Wild of the full reality and identity of the apparition, these words, in the well-known voice of Captain Heron, would have been more than sufficient.

They broke the spell of fear that sat upon his limb and voice.

With a yell that was something terrific, he turned and darted out of the hall.

"Good!" said Ogle.

Wild ran down St. James's Street like a hunted hare.

A watchman, in his watch-box, was at the corner of Pall Mall.

Wild hardly knew what he did, but he seized the man by the throat and tore him out of the watch-box in an instant, and then dashed into it himself.

But the watch-box was old and frail, and did not stand very firmly, so that as soon as Wild got into it, shaking as he was in every limb, it swayed about for a few seconds, and then fell over on to its face.

Wild was a prisoner.

The watchman sat on the flag-stones, and sprung his rattle vigorously.

"Help! help! Watch! watch! A madman—a wild hanimal in the box! Watch! watch!"

*   *   *   *   *

We will now leave Jonathan Wild to his horrors, and the other less important personages of our story to their various devices, while we turn attention specially to the situation of Felix Heron and Edith in the patrimonial mansion of the Whitcombes in St. James's Street.

A week has elapsed.

One short week, and yet the changes in and about the house have been very great.

Edith has, in her own proper character, as the Countess of Whitcombe, taken possession of the mansion.

The hopes and expectations of the friends of her and Felix Heron have been so far justified, that no sort of annoyance or hindrance was even attempted, either by the Court or by the police authorities.

The supposed death of Felix Heron seemed to have put an end to the rancour of hatred by which he had been pursued.

The King ceased to mention his name.

Even that vigorous old foe, the Lord Clackington, was now satisfied.

And Jonathan Wild, although at times he would place himself on the opposite side of the way to Whitcombe House, in St. James's Street, and gaze at it with a strange and horrified look upon his face, did not attempt in any way to interfere with Edith's quiet possession.

The whole household, as had been agreed upon, consisted of Ogle, Mortification Ripon, Tom, Mrs. Ogle, and the young girl to whom Tom had so completely surrendered his affections.

By this plan the officious curiosity of strangers was entirely defeated.

Ogle and Tom both had a horse in the stables.

And Daisy occupied a loose stall to herself, and was specially attended to by Tom.

In the care of her little child Edith found that the hours were far from hanging heavy on her hands.

The glades and deep solemn shadows of old Epping Forest gradually faded from her mind, and she was almost happy.

Almost only, because there was still the deep anxiety, that could never be forgotten, about the peril of Felix Heron.

We will now look into one of the drawing rooms of Whitcombe House in the dusk of the evening, and just before the lights were ordered by Edith.

She is there with her infant son, alone.

It is near the bed-time of the child, but Edith is keeping him up for a purpose.

It is that he may see his father.

The shadows deepen on the walls.

The lights in the street send in faint gleams past the full, rich hangings of the windows.

Still Edith will not call for light in the room.

And the darkness begins to confuse objects.

Then, with that preternatural acuteness of hearing which enables us all to hear the lightest footfall of those whom we love, and even their very breathing, before they appear to our eyes, Edith was sure that Felix Heron was close at hand.

There is a ring at the visitors'-bell of the outer door.

Yes; Edith felt certain it was her husband.

The room door opens, and Tom Ripon appears.

"The Baron Von Peck, my lady!"

Edith could scarcely speak.

"Let him come in."

A stout, elderly man crossed the threshold of the room.

He wore a wig of foreign make, of a dull iron-grey colour.

His huge moustaches were of the shade of wood ashes, and perhaps justly so, as probably that was the substance that was upon them.

His complexion had an aged, saffron sort of hue.

His dress consisted of a blue surtout, with immense skirts; horseman's boots, and a vest, the great flaps of which reached nearly to the tops of those boots.

In one hand he carried a large, heavy walking-cane.

In the other, a rather old, three-cornered hat, without any ornament whatever.

Such was the aspect of the Baron Von Peck, as he made his appearance at the door of that drawing-room in Whitcombe House.

Tom closed the door.

And then any one who could have seen Tom would have been much surprised at what he was about.

He sat down on the first stair of the second flight, and holding his sides, he laughed with a silent chuckle, and with so many convulsive throes and grimaces to keep himself from making a noise, that the wonder was he did not burst outright.

But the Baron Von Peck walked a few paces into the apartment.

He did not speak.

Then Edith, with a cry of joy, sprang forward. She flung her arms about the Baron, as she exclaimed, "Felix! my Felix!"

It was indeed Felix Heron, and that was one of the disguises in which he was accustomed to visit Whitcombe House.

It was a very perfect one.

By its aid he had been able to walk down St. James's Street and defy all recognition.

All traces now of the bent figure of an aged man vanished, as the Baron straitened himself up, and folded his arms about Edith.

"Are we, then, alone, dear one?"

"Yes—oh, yes!"

"Once more, then, in the house of my father— that house which is so truly yours, and my own— am I permitted to hold you to my heart, my Edith!"

"Yes—oh, yes. All is safe now."

"I trust and hope it is. How is our dear little one?"

"Well and happy."

Edith ran to the child, and placed it in its father's arms.

"The little one grows like you, my Edith."

"And you, too, Felix. Oh, if we could only be for ever together!"

"That, Edith, may not be yet, I fear, for a time, but the period will surely come when such shall be the case."

"Yes, yes!"

"Until then, let us bless the happy chances that enable us to see each other, even so often as we do."

"I do bless those happy chances."

"And has there been no alarm—nothing to vex you?"

"None—nothing."

"That is well."

"You have seen my aunt, Lady Castleneau, Felix?"

"I have, and she is well."

Felix Heron sat down by the side of Edith, with a sigh.

"You are unhappy, Felix?"

"No, no! It is only the necessity that I have of leaving you at times. That is all."

"But why do so?"

"Do you not remember, dear Edith, that I am a highwayman?"

"Oh, be one no longer!"

"I cannot yet afford to be so strictly good. You know, Edith, that the tenants of the Whitcombe estate have one and all refused to pay any rent whatever, to anybody, until the question of the succession to the title and properties is settled."

"Yes, I know that, Felix."

"Well, dear one, we must not only have funds to pay our way with, but an ample sum in reserve in case of any reverse of fortune."

"My Aunt Castleneau will help us."

"Alas! she is not rich."

"Not rich?"

It seemed so strange to Edith to think that any one could be in want of money, that she listened to what Felix Heron was saying with an almost childish kind of interest.

CHAPTER CXCII.

EDITH MAKES THE ACQUAINTANCE OF THE PRINCESS DEMIDOFF, AND HERON TAKES TO THE ROAD.

A SILENCE of some few moments' duration ensued between Edith and Felix Heron.

JONATHAN WILD BELIEVES HIMSELF IN THE PRESENCE OF THE
DEPARTED.

Presented Gratis with No. 58, of the New Edition of EDITH HERON, the Sequel to Edith the Captive; or, the Robbers of Epping Forest.

He had a painful communication to make.

And she felt that he had.

Heron was preparing Edith for the necessity that existed for his again going on the road.

To Edith that was a dire and sad necessity, and yet she knew not, in truth, how to combat with it.

Heron held her hand gently in his.

"Be under no apprehension, my Edith; I will seek no danger, as in old times. When I was alone in the world, I was wont to do so for danger's sake; but I will not see you in want of those abundant funds which you ought to possess."

Edith started.

The sound of some tumult in the street came upon their ears.

There was a shrill scream, in a female voice.

A cry, then, of "Watch—watch—watch!" was raised.

Felix Heron went out on to the balcony of the house, and looked down to the street.

A sedan chair was upon its side, and several men were about it; but whether in strife or in amity he could not tell.

The question, however, was soon settled by a loud exclamation in a female voice.

"No—no! Never again—never again! I am free now, and to your tyranny I will never again subject myself!"

"Bring her along!" shouted a man's voice. "Force shall settle that point!"

"Help! oh, help!"

"Oh, what is it all about, Felix?" whispered Edith.

"Some one is in peril."

"Who—who?"

"I know not, Edith; but for your sake, as it is a lady, I must interfere."

"Nay, Felix. What if it be but a snare to draw you from the house to your destruction?"

"If it be a snare, let those beware who lay it!"

The tone in which Felix Heron spoke convinced Edith that opposition would be little heeded even from her, since his feelings were excited on behalf of the lady in distress below.

But still, with a fear that he might be but rushing on his destruction, Edith clung to him.

Heron folded her in his arms for a brief moment.

"Fear nothing! fear nothing, my Edith! I will be doubly, trebly careful of myself, for all our sakes."

Heron then ran down the grand staircase of Whitcombe House.

In the hall was a short ladder that Tom Ripon had left there for some purpose, and as the eyes of Heron fell upon it, an odd idea took possession of him.

What a capital weapon, he thought, would this be for the sudden dispersion of a crowd of people at once.

He seized the ladder.

He opened the outer door, and sallied out into the street.

Some four or five men were about the prostrate sedan chair, the bearers of which had ran off in fright.

It was quite the custom of the chairmen, as they were named, to run off and leave their fare to fight his own battles in case of a fracas of any kind. They knew perfectly well they would find the sedan chair where they had left it.

And in this case the lady who called help had been so deserted.

Felix Heron paused for a moment or two.

He wanted to be quite sure that he was interfering in the right cause.

"Oh, let me be! Oh, let me be!" cried the lady, in imploring accents. "I will not trouble you, and why should you follow me, and seek again to make me your victim?"

"Bring her along," said the harsh voice. "Take her direct to the old stairs at Westminster, and we will have her down the river with the ebb-tide, and on board the sloop for Flushing, quickly enough."

The lady screamed again.

Felix Heron was quite satisfied.

He made up his mind, there and then, that the lady, be she whom she might, should go on board no sloop that night except by her own free will.

Advancing with the ladder, Felix Heron swung it round his head, at a height of about five feet from the ground.

Down went the group of persons who were surrounding the sedan chair, as though struck by a flash of lightning.

The lady and the sedan chair, in the depths of which she still remained, were left in possession of the field.

The sudden disappearance of all her foes seemed to strike the lady with astonishment.

"Ah, sir!" she said, as she looked up from the sedan, "to whom am I indebted for this speedy release?"

"That matters little, madam," replied Heron "in comparison with your making good use of your freedom. If you have anywhere to fly to for refuge from these men, do so before they recover and again molest you."

"Alas! alas!"

The lady began to sob bitterly.

Some chance passengers, too, in the street, although it had happened that when the attack on the sedan chair took place it was singularly quiet and deserted, began to hasten up.

"Decide quickly, madam," cried Heron: "where can you go?"

"Nowhere now; I am helpless."

"Not quite," said Heron.

Before, then, any one could actually reach the place where the fracas, that, in truth, had not occupied a fourth of the time that it has necessarily consumed in the telling, Felix Heron caught the lady in his arms from the wreck of the sedan chair, and at once carried her into Whitcombe House.

He closed the door.

"Here at least, madam, you are safe."

So quickly, so adroitly was this act completed on the part of Felix Heron, that by the time the passengers in the street ran up, and some of the party that had been prostrated by the ladder had recovered from the knock-down blow, and looked about them, the disappearance of the lady was effected, and no one, in the semi-darkness, could say where she had gone.

The sound of angry voices began to be heard in the street.

"Save me! save me!" said the lady, in accents of distress, as she clung to Heron. "Do not let them take me."

"You are quite safe."

"Will they not force an entrance to this house?"

"No. They know not that you are here, and should they suspect it, any force they may raise could be met with a fully sufficient resistance."

"How can I thank you?"

"Do not attempt to do so. The service has been easily rendered. I only hope it is a signal one."

"You have saved me, sir, from worse than death."

"Is that possible?"

"It is, indeed. I am the Princess Demidoff!"

"Demidoff? That is a Russian title, surely; and yet you speak the purest English!"

"I am English. I am the daughter of the Honourable George Clackington."

"You are, then, the niece of the lord of that name?"

"I am."

"I cannot congratulate you, madam, on your uncle."

"Ah, you know him?"

"Too well."

"And I, too—and I, too; for it was by his means, and in consequence of his despicable arts, that I was obliged to wed the Russian Prince, Demidoff, who was about two years since the Ambassador from the Court of St. Petersburgh here. Oh, what sufferings I have gone through since then!"

The lady began to sob and cry at the recollection of what she had endured.

Felix Heron lingered in the hall of Whitcombe House only so long as to feel quite sure that the mob of persons who had assembled about the sedan chair, as well as the men who had sought to capture and carry off the young Princess Demidoff, had dispersed.

Then he spoke to her in a low, gentle tone.

"Follow me, madam, and I will take you to a lady who will be to you a more efficient protector than I can."

Felix Heron was desirous of at once introducing the young Princess to Edith; but he was by no means as yet in the mood of letting her know who he really was.

Preceding her, then, by a few paces, he opened the drawing-room door, and said aloud, "The Baron von Peck has the honour to introduce to the Countess of Whitcombe the Princess Demidoff!"

Heron knew that by shaping the introduction in those words, Edith would know that he meant to keep up his incognito.

Tom Ripon had lit one of the chandeliers, so that there was sufficient light in the room for Edith and Felix Heron to behold in the Princess Demidoff one of the most charming ladies they had ever seen.

Her absence in Russia during the brief period that Felix and Edith had shown themselves at the Court of St. James's had accounted for her not knowing anything about them but by repute.

At the sound of the name of Whitcombe the Princess started.

"Is it possible," she said, "that I am indebted to the lady who has suffered so much from my bad uncle for hospitality this night, when I am so much in want of it?"

"I am the Countess of Whitcombe," replied Edith.

The young Princess took Edith by the hand, and pressed it to her lips as she added, in a voice of emotion, "Grant me your protection, madam, for you see before you one of the most unhappy persons in all the world."

"I freely do so," replied Edith, who was much taken with the beauty and amiable simplicity of manner of the Princess.

"And help me, too, to thank this gentleman, who rescued me from my enemies."

"The Baron von Peck is a gallant gentleman," said Edith, "and only second to my late hus-

band, the Earl of Whitcombe, in his chivalrous devotion to the cause of all who need him."

"Your late husband!" exclaimed the Princess Demidoff.

Edith sighed.

She liked not the deception she was forced to practise; but still, as it was necessary for the safety of Felix Heron, she would not shrink from it.

"Pardon me," added the Princess. "Your loss must be much, and I do wrong to allude to it. For my own part, I found, upon reaching Russia with the Prince Demidoff, that all the restraints of civilized life which he had been compelled to put on in this country, vanished, and I was yoked to a fearful savage."

"But how did you escape?"

"In the dress of a peasant. I made my way through many dangers till I reached England; but on this night, when on my route to a lady whom I am sure will afford me protection, I was met and attacked in the street by the emissaries of the Prince Demidoff, and but for this gentleman, the Baron —Baron——"

"Von Peck!" said Heron.

"Yes, the Baron Von Peck, I should have been carried off to pass a life of long imprisonment."

"You are safe here, Princess, I am sure," said Heron; "for your foes have evidently not the least idea of where you are."

"Thank heaven! thank heaven and you, Baron! I intend to make an immediate appeal to the Queen, who is, in fact, the lady of whom I spoke, whose protection I was this night about to seek."

"Then my advice to you," said Heron, "is to delay seeking it until morning, when in the broad open face of day no one will dare attack you in the streets of London."

As he spoke, Heron rose, and ceremoniously bowed to Edith and the Princess Demidoff.

But he gave Edith a look that let her know he would fain speak with her.

"Princess," said Edith, "may I make so good a friend of you as to leave you alone for a few moments."

"How can I be alone," said the young Princess, "with this charming companion?"

She alluded to the child, who was fast asleep in the depths of one of the chairs in the room.

Edith and Felix Heron now held a short conference in an adjoining apartment, the object of which may be explained in the few words with which Heron commenced the brief conversation.

"Edith, shall we trust this lady?"

That was the idea that took possession of the mind of Felix Heron on this occasion.

He was naturally of so trustful a disposition that he was always inclined to seek the way to the hearts of people by confidence, in preference to any other mode.

But the proposition was one from which Edith shrunk a little.

It was only, however, on one ground that she could urge the shadow of an objection.

Was the lady really what she represented herself to be?

That was the only question.

Poor Edith had suffered so much, and so, in truth, had Felix Heron, by the most elaborate deception, that their honest, trustful natures had received a shock.

"Dare we so rapidly," said Edith, "come to a conclusion in regard to this lady?"

"We ought not."

"That is my feeling, Felix; and yet I may at

the same time say that I am inclined fully to believe every word that she has uttered."

"And I too. But yet, Edith, how shall we prove her truth?"

"I can think of but one test."

"What is that?"

"She is alone with our child. From this room we have an opportunity of looking into that where she is, and of noting her conduct while she thinks herself unobserved. If she is deceiving us, you may depend Felix, she will be in thought, and paying no attention to the little one."

Felix Heron pressed Edith's hand in approval of this plan, which was so essentially feminine and feasible, that he was quite willing to abide by it.

Hand in hand they stepped cautiously to the door of the drawing-room.

They could look in and command a good view of whatever was doing in that apartment.

The Princess Demidoff was standing by the side of the large arm-chair, on which the little one slept.

They heard her speak in a low, plaintive voice.

"May heaven shower on your innocent head its choicest blessings, for your mother's sake!"

Those words were decisive.

Both Edith and Felix Heron felt that they required no other test of the sincerity of the character and motives of the Princess Demidoff.

They did not say a word to each other, but they exchanged looks which fully spoke all they thought.

Another moment, and they were in the room together.

The young and lovely Princess rose hastily.

There was a look of charming candour on her face.

Edith approached her, and took both her hands in hers.

"I am convinced," she said, "you will be my friend."

"Only show me what I can do to make myself worthy of the title!"

"I will show you, dear Princess, that I have faith in you by trusting you with the most important of secrets to me and to mine."

Edith turned round as she spoke, and, taking the hand of Felix Heron, she said, "This is my husband!"

"Your husband, Countess?"

"Even so!"

"The Baron von Peck?"

"Yes; the Baron von Peck to the world, but to me, Felix, the Earl of Whitcombe."

In a moment, Heron had lifted off the wig he wore, and stood at his full height, with a smile upon his face, and his young and handsome head in full relief.

"Is this possible?"

"It is true, Princess," said Heron. "In me you see the proscribed Earl of Whitcombe, who is compelled to assume a disguise, in order to visit his own house."

The Princess held out her hand, which Heron took.

"Ah!" she said, "allow me to say that, if by any means I can prove to you both my feeling of gratitude, that moment will be to me a very, very happy one.

"We feel sure of it," replied Heron. "At present, we are only in a position to wait and hope; and the question is uppermost in our minds as regards what good we can do to you?"

"I am certain of an asylum, and a safe one, too,

so soon as I can get into the presence of the Queen who knows me well, and who, I think, loves me as much as her nature will permit her to love any one."

"That is easily accomplished," said Heron. "I will undertake to convey you in safety to Buckingham House, where, I presume, the Queen will be found."

The young Princess was now thoughtful for a few moments, and then, with a face of animation, she looked up and spoke.

"Out of what looks like evil how often springs good. I shall, in defiance of the Prince Demidoff, remain in the protection of the Queen, and in that position I shall be able faithfully to let you both know all that passes at the Court in which it may be supposed you have any concern, as well as gradually, I hope, influencing the Queen herself in your favour."

Both Felix and Edith felt that it was no slight thing to have such an ally at the Court and about the Queen, so that they, too, were of opinion that out of the attack which the Prince Demidoff and his gang of miscreants had made on the young and charming Princess, much good was likely to arise to them.

Heron now left the room and summoned Ogle.

"Arm yourself well," he said. "I have a lady to escort across the Park to Buckingham House. I think you and I can do so easily."

"All right, Captain. Are we likely to be attacked?"

"It is possible!"

"Then I shall take a hanger with me, which I can easily dispose of under my coat."

"Do so."

In the course of a quarter of an hour there issued forth from Whitcombe House three persons.

Captain Heron, Ogle, and the young Princess Demidoff, to whom Edith had lent a cloak and a hat, which materially helped to disguise her.

They passed into St. James's Park by the side of Marlborough House, and proceeded along one of the side walks to Buckingham House, which stood where the palace of that name now stands.

The Park was very dark, as the night was cloudy, and it was very inefficiently lighted.

Felix Heron spoke to the Princess in a low tone.

"It will be a great solace to my poor Countess, Edith, to see you as often as you will visit her; for the only female friends she has are the Countess of Bridgewater, whom you, doubtless, know, and her dear aunt, the Lady Castleneau."

"Your dear Countess, then, lives under no disguise, and I may visit her frankly and freely?"

"You may indeed."

It might have been the low, murmuring sound of this brief conversation that attracted attention, or else people were on the watch for whoever might be passing along the Mall of the Park; but be the immediate cause what it might, a tall, burly looking man suddenly emerged from behind a tree, and confronted, with more valour than discretion, Felix Heron and his little party.

"Halt!"

"What for?" asked Heron, mildly.

"Just because I say so."

"Indeed!"

"Come here, Jacks, come here!"

"Who is it?" said another man, making his appearance. "Who is it, Wills, my boy?"

"I don't know; but one of this lot is a woman, and it's just as well we should make sure of who she is, as well as who she is not."

The Princess Demidoff shrunk back, as she whispered in alarmed accents to Heron, "I know those voices!"

"You do?"

"Yes. They are the men who attacked me in the street."

"I am right glad to hear it. Do not stir from this place."

"No, no!"

Heron darted forward and caught one of the ruffians by the throat, as he said, in a calm voice, "Well met, Mr. Wil's. I am delighted to see you!"

By an exertion of that great strength that on occasions he could put forth to the surprise of every one, Heron lifted the fellow fairly off his feet and flung him over the iron rails of the Palace garden.

A crash and a yell showed that he had fallen upon some wood-work, most likely some fancy rustic chair, and that he had demolished it as well as himself.

The other ruffian, who had answered to the name of Jacks, made a blow at the back of Heron's head with a bludgeon, but Ogle was by far too wide awake and active to permit such an attack to be effective.

Ogle made a leap right on to the fellow's back, and held the cudgel up above his head in the air just as he had poised it for the blow.

"Not so fast, if you please," said Ogle.

The fellow thought that surely whatever was upon his back had come down from the clouds there, or if his imagination was not equal to so high a flight as that, he thought that from one of the trees the sudden attack had come.

Down he fell with a roar of consternation.

Ogle dealt him two or three heavy kicks, and then standing on his back he said, "I think, Captain, that will do; and we can jog on quietly now."

"Certainly, Ogle."

All this had happened in such a moment that the Princess Demidoff hardly knew which way the conflict had gone, although she had very little doubt which way it was likely to go.

When, however, Heron offered her his arm again she was violently trembling.

"Calm yourself, Princess," he said; "there is nothing to fear, and I think that this is rather a lucky encounter than otherwise, for those two fellows, who I take it are about the boldest of those by whose aid the Prince Demidoff seeks to get you into his possession again, will think twice before they engage in any enterprise against you."

The Princess, however, found it very difficult to get over the nervous agitation that had taken possession of her, and Captain Heron was right glad to see her in safety within the gate of Buckingham House, where her name procured her immediate admission.

CHAPTER CXCIII.

CAPTAIN HERON HOLDS A CONSULTATION WITH OGLE IN THE PARK —AN ADVENTURE.

OGLE and Felix Heron walked slowly along the Mall in St. James's Park, after disposing of the young Princess Demidoff in safety.

"Ogle," said Heron, "I wish to talk to you of what kind of life I mean to lead."

"Yes, Captain."

"I am forced by my foes to be what they will not let me cease to be."

"A highwayman, Captain?"

"Just so."

"Well, I don't know that there is a better thing for a distressed gentleman to do than that."

"I must do it."

"And with Daisy, why who can say nay to you on road or on common?"

"True, Ogle; and since it is from the Court, and the myrmidons and sycophants of the Court, that I have received wrong and neglect, why I intend that they shall find out what it is to exchange the quiet and peaceable Earl of Whitcombe for Captain Heron, the knight of the road."

"Capital, Captain; capital! I rather fancy they will regret the change."

"I will take good care they shall, for I will make the road from here to Windsor, and to the White Lodge at Richmond, and to the Palace at Kew, too hot to hold the minions of the Court."

"Bravo! bravo!"

"It is on that bit of road that I intend to carry on a commerce that will be profitable in purse, and no doubt will in adventure."

"I am delighted to hear it."

"Alone I shall be able to spread terror in the Court, and in the mean hearts of those who live and fatten on its intrigues."

"Alone, Captain?"

"Yes, alone; and yet I ought not to say so, since I shall have with me my gallant Daisy."

"Hem!"

"You are dissatisfied, Ogle."

"Well, Captain, to tell the honest truth, I did hope that I should accompany you."

"No, no! That cannot be, for one good and special reason."

"What is that, Captain?"

"I should never be able to feel my mind at ease in regard to the safety of Edith if I had not the assurance that you were at Whitcombe House while I was absent from it."

There was a reason that Ogle was not able to combat with.

"Be it so, Captain," he said; "I only live to do you service."

"I know it, Ogle—I know it."

Captain Heron, without any special design in so doing, but because he was busy in thought, sat down on one of the benches of the Park, beneath a wide spreading old elm tree.

Ogle sat by him.

The Park was very still, and Heron was about to say something, when they both saw a couple of figures coming slowly up the old Mall.

There was something about the gait and air of these persons that had, to the eyes of Heron, dimly as he could only see them, an aspect of familiarity.

And yet he could not name them.

As the bare, shadowy forms slowly advanced, Heron spoke to Ogle in a whisper.

"Do you know those people?"

"No, Captain."

"Let us get into the shadows of the old tree."

They rose from the bench, and quickly passing behind it they were both hid from observation in the deep, black shadow cast by the huge trunk of the old elm.

The two shadowy-looking figures slowly advanced.

The conversation that was taking place between them was evidently of a very absorbing and interesting character—indeed, so much so that

they took no heed whatever of any one else being in the Park, or of the possibility of listeners.

They paused exactly opposite to the huge old elm tree, behind which Captain Felix Heron and Ogle had found a hiding-place

Then Heron and Ogle at the same time recognised one of those two men.

That one was Jonathan Wild.

Who the other was remained for a short time a mystery.

But it was only for a few minutes that they were in doubt about his identity.

"I am fagged and weary," said Jonathan Wild.

As he spoke he flung himself upon the bench that Ogle and Captain Heron had so recently quitted

Wild was not the most civil or ceremonious individual in the world to any one, and in the pre-

sent instance he treated the person who was with him with but scant consideration.

He put his feet at full length upon the bench, so that there was barely room for that companion to sit down.

When he did, too, it was in close contact with the boots of Jonathan Wild.

But the person who was on that night in the Mall of old St. James's Park with the great thief-taker was humble, and put up with all and everything.

He quietly took possession of the extreme corner of the bench, and rubbed his hands slowly one over the other.

"Well?" said Wild.

"Well, as I was just saying, I cannot make you out."

"Ha, ha!"

"But it is no laughing matter, Mr. Wild."

"Who said it was."

"You laughed."

"Did I?"

"I heard you."

"Well, you are about the first person who ever paid me the compliment of calling that a laugh!"

At this juncture Ogle whispered in the ear of Captain Heron "Do you know the other one, Captain?"

"Too well."

"It is John Tarleton."

"It is, indeed. It is the murderer of my father!"

Captain Heron sighed as he spoke; for the memory of that father, who in his last days had so repented him of the past, and striven to reform the evil he had done, came strongly back to him.

But he had promised Edith that no vengeance from his hand should fall upon that unworthy brother, and he was strong enough to keep his faith and word.

There was now a pause of a few moments' duration in the discourse between Jonathan Wild and John Tarleton.

It was Wild who spoke again the first.

"I tell you what it is, Deuce Ace," he said. "I am sorry to have found you still alive!"

"What?"

"I say I am sorry; for I, in common with every one else who knew you, thought you were dead!"

"Oh, such men as I recover wonderfully!"

"So it seems!"

"You, too, Mr. Wild, have at times narrow escapes!"

"I have," replied Wild, gloomily; "and it makes me think that the fate which is, after all, to be mine, must be some one that the fancy may shrink from aghast!"

Wild suddenly sprung to his feet.

A cold damp was on his brow.

He shook in every limb.

"Way, what's the matter?" asked John Tarleton, alias Deuce Ace.

"Folly! folly is the matter. I am not so strong as I was."

Wild sat down again with a deep groan.

"Why, Mr. Wild, I never expected to see a man with your iron nerves give way so much before."

"Pho! pho! Iron rusts."

"So it seems!"

"Well, what, after all, is that to you? Go on now with what you wanted to say to me."

"Well, then, in my opinion my sister is still fair game!"

"No!"

"No? And why not?"

"Because it is not to be. Look you here, Deuce Ace! That man—that Captain Heron, or Earl of Whitcombe, call him what you will—held my life in the hollow of his hands, and he let me go!"

"Oh!"

"He did, I tell you, but it was on one condition."

"What was that?"

"That henceforth I would never, by act, word, or implication, contrive or seek to contrive aught against his wife, Edith."

"Oh!"

"I promised."

"You—you promised?"

"I did."

"And he—he——?"

"He took my word!"

"Your word! Ha, ha! The word of Jonathan Wild! Your word of honour, I suppose you mean? Well, I hardly supposed that my worthy brother-in-law, Felix Heron, was quite such a fool a-head!"

"You did not?"

"Certainly not!"

"And yet there is a still greater fool not far off me just now."

"Do you mean me?"

"I do!"

"What have I done or said?"

"You have spoken some few words that all but hastened away your worthless life. It is with difficulty that at this moment I keep my hands off your throat."

"Mr. Wild!"

John Tarleton jumped off the bench instantly, and got several paces from Wild.

"Oh, you are safe now!"

"I hope so."

"Having lived through the last few moments, you are safe."

"I did not intend to offend you."

"Pshaw! what care I what such a thing as you can say? I have told you what I promised to Captain Felix Heron, and now I tell you that I mean to keep my word."

"You do?"

"I do!"

"But—but, Jonathan Wild, it is—it is so—so very——"

"Very what?"

"Extraordinary!"

"Perhaps so; but now I will tell you exactly why I intend to keep my word."

"Ah! I see you have some deep and artful dodge in the wind. Ha, ha! I begin to see now."

"I don't think you do. I mean to keep my word, just for the same reason that Felix Heron took it."

John Tarleton was silent. He felt that it might be dangerous to cross such a man as Jonathan Wild on the only bit of sentiment, perhaps, that he was ever, so to speak, guilty of.

"I can imagine you are a little surprised," added Wild, "but that is nothing to me."

"Well, Mr. Wild, you have of course a perfect right to do as you like; but still, I think I may make something out of my sister's fears, for all that."

"Stop!"

"Eh?"

"Stop, I say! Captain Heron is dead."

John Tarleton gave a great leap from the bench on which he had again seated himself.

"Dead! Dead! Captain Heron—the Earl of Whitcombe—my sister Edith's husband—dead?"

"Dead, I said!"

"Are you sure?"

"I saw him!"

Wild shuddered as he spoke, and added, in a low tone, "And I have seen him since!"

John Tarleton uttered a cry of fright.

"No, no!"

"I say yes; I have looked upon the dead body of Felix Heron; and I have looked upon the shade, the ghost, apparition, call it what you will, of that man since; and I know why he stood in my way—it was to put me in mind of my promise."

"Good gracious!"

"But I intended to keep my word, and I will do so."

"The Earl of Whitcombe dead! Why—why, then, my sister, the Countess, is a widow; and—and there is no one to interfere, if I go just to ask her to help her poor brother in distress."

"Yes, there is."

"Who? who?"

"I—Jonathan Wild."

"You?—you?"

"Just so. Now, look you here, Deuce Ace. I promised Captain Heron, when he had me at his mercy, and had nothing to do but to blow out my brains if he so wished, and get rid of me at once, that from that time Edith should be quite free from all assailment, so far as I was concerned. Now, Deuce Ace, I mean not only to keep my word, but to be a little better than it."

"How? how?"

"I don't intend to let you, or any one else, if I can help it—and I think I can—interfere with the Countess of Whitcombe."

"Well, really!"

"Understand me, Deuce Ace; I am not a pleasant man to trifle with; and what I say, I mean. Let your sister alone, and I will let you alone; but if you begin to persecute her, I will wring your neck."

"Oh!"

"That's all."

"And—and where is my Lord Warningdale?"

"Dead!"

Deuce Ace gave another gulp.

"He dead, too?"

"Very dead, indeed."

"Then the—a—the title and the estates of Whitcombe——"

"All go now, without any more dispute, I take it, to the infant son of Felix Heron."

John Tarleton, alias Deuce Ace, drew a long breath.

"And now," said Wild, as he rose from the bench again,—"now you comprehend me, and I advise you to be careful; for if you do interfere with the Countess of Whitcombe, I shall be certain to hear of it, and you will as certainly then hear of me, in a manner that won't at all be pleasant to that part of your back-bone that joins your neck."

John Tarleton felt a sympathetic twinge in that part of his anatomy already.

"I won't go near her," he said. "If you take her under your protection, that is quite enough for me."

"I hope so. Good night! I am hungry, and can't be pagued with you any longer."

As he spoke, Jonathan Wild strode off without waiting to hear anything further from John Tarleton.

The latter then sat down upon the bench again, and soliloquized upon what had passed.

"Here's a pretty go! Jonathan Wild has taken a nice turn, I do think! That fellow Heron out of the way, and my sister left with only a little child! Why, I might have worried her life out, and got as much money out of her as I wanted! If she had been obstinate about it, I might have found some means, too, of getting the child into my hands! Ha, ha! What a game that would have been! What a hostage for fortune! Why, I could have played with Edith as a cat does with a mouse, and put her to as much agony; and is all that to be spoilt on account of Jonathan Wild? Pho, pho!"

Ogle whispered to Heron.

"Captain—Captain!"

"Yes, Ogle!"

"I haven't promised anybody to spare that fellow! Do oblige me for once, as the only favour I will ask of you, to let me crack him on the head!"

"No, Ogle; let him be."

"But really——"

"Hush!"

John Tarleton spoke again.

"Ah! I think that will do it. Let me think it over! If I can get some of those out at-elbows fellows that hang about the gaming-house I know so well to lend a hand, surely I shall be able to get possession of the child; and then even Wild will not be able to hurt me until I make my own price! Why, it is a hostage to fortune, as against him as well as Edith!"

"Now, Captain," whispered Ogle again, "what do you say now?"

"Nothing, yet! Let him go on."

"And the idea, too," added John Tarleton—"the idea of such a man as Jonathan Wild being scared at something that he thought was a ghost! Oh, how absurd! What stuff—what absurd nonsense! Ha, ha!—a ghost, indeed!—ha!"

Captain Heron glided from the shadow of the tree, and sat down on the bank by the side of that false and unkind brother of his Edith.

CHAPTER CXCIV.

JOHN TARLETON TAKES FLIGHT, AND CAPTAIN HERON HAS AN ADVENTURE ON THE ROAD.

In the darkness that was about all objects in the Park, all that John Tarleton could take upon himself to be sure of, was that some one had, in a very sudden and very mysterious manner, come and sat down by his side.

Who the some one was he had not the most distant idea.

But he felt uncomfortable.

He scarcely knew why he did so, but it was perhaps from the consciousness which could not fail to be perpetually present to him that he had committed crimes enough to be always in danger.

He did not like to get up on the moment and go away.

And yet he did not wish to stay.

But he had a desire to find out who his companion on the bench was.

Moreover he felt conscious that he had been, in not the most discreet manner, giving some of his thoughts to the night air.

It was possible, then, that this mysterious stranger, who had come from he knew not where, might have overheard a something that was bad for any one to know but himself, John Tarleton.

"Hum! A cool night," said Tarleton.

The dim and dusky-looking figure on the seat made no reply.

"I said it was a cool night, sir."

Still no answer.

John Tarleton got fidgetty.

He strove in vain to get a look at the stranger's face.

The darkness baffled him.

"Well, sir," he added, "I don't want to force my conversation on you, so will say merely good night, and leave you."

Heron uttered a low, inarticulate sound.

"Eh?" said Taunton.

"Beware!" said Heron.

"Beware of what?—of whom?"

Fortune favoured the trick which Felix Heron was trying to put upon John Tarleton, and helped him at that moment to make it as effective as possible.

One of the windows of St. James's Palace—a window that looked out into the garden and so on to the wall of the Park—was at that moment opened, and a curtain being held aside by some one in the room, a long ray of light from a candelabera came right over the trees and shrubs of the garden of the Palace.

The ray of light happened to have found its way into the Park, between the elm trees.

It then fell upon the bench where was seated Captain Heron and his most unworthy brother-in-law, John Tarleton.

The ray of light rested on the wooden bench, as nearly as might be between them.

But the moment Captain Heron saw it, he made up his mind to take advantage of it before it should disappear, as it no doubt would, quickly.

A slight movement brought him right into the ray.

He then turned his face full towards John Tarleton, and lifted his hat from his brow, so that there should be no mistake about who he was.

Tarleton was transfixed with horror.

Jonathan Wild had told him that Felix Heron was dead—that, in fact, he had seen his body—that afterwards he had had a visitation from the other world in the likeness of Felix Heron.

And there was that likeness looking him in the face on the bench in the park.

The blood paused in the veins of John Tarleton for one fleeting instant of time, and then he uttered a yell of fear and fell forward on his face to the ground.

"Beware!" said Heron.

But John Tarleton had fallen into a swoon, and was then past any more frights or warnings.

Heron turned round and called to Ogle.

"Here, Captain."

"I fancy I have made some impression on the fears of this scoundrel."

"It looks like it, Captain."

"Don't stand on his back, Ogle."

Ogle coughed.

He had pretended, quite by accident, to step on to the back of Tarleton; but now, at the order of Captain Heron, he got off, and only dealt him a hearty kick or two.

"Let him alone, Ogle; let him alone."

"All right, Captain."

"I don't think he will now venture upon the villanous plan that he spoke of a while ago."

"I tell you what it is, Captain," said Ogle. "You don't know what a fellow like this is capable of, after his fright wears off."

"It is true."

"Then let me hang him."

"No, no! But I will go this far, Ogle. If at any time, when I am absent from home, you should find the peace and safety of Edith and our little one assailed by this man, or by any other, I give you free leave to act in their defence as you may think proper."

"Good! I can take on myself to say, Captain, that if he does pay us a visit at Whitcombe House, it will be the last, as well as the first!"

"I have no doubt of it. Come on, Ogle! The shrill, sharp cry of this man may bring the patrol round the Park."

Heron walked rapidly down the Mall, towards Spring Gardens; and he was followed by Ogle, who found it, or thought he found it, the nearest way to walk right over the back of John Tarleton again.

Heron left the Park by that little gate at Spring Gardens; and then he paused, and listened to the clock of St. Martin's Church as it struck the hour of twelve

"Midnight, Ogle."

"Yes, Captain."

"Do you think you could manage to bring Daisy here?"

"Of course I can."

"Take this, then, to Edith; and when you have delivered it to her, get Daisy out of the stable, and ride her to this spot."

"Yes, Captain."

Felix Heron wrote, on a leaf of a pocket-book he had with him, the following words in pencil:—

"My Edith, fear nothing. Rest in peace and security, as it may yet be some hours before I can return to you and our dear little one.

"Felix."

Heron tore the leaf out of his pocket-book that contained these words, and handed it to Ogle.

Then he stood in the depths of a dark doorway, and watched the arrival of Daisy.

Ogle had not ventured to say another word to Captain Heron about accompanying him after what had already passed between them on that subject; but it was a sore disappointment to him that he was not permitted so to do.

In about ten minutes, the sound of a horse's feet announced to Heron the approach of Daisy.

There was something about her light, springing tread that he was always able to recognise.

Another minute, and she was by his side.

But Heron was surprised to see that it was Tom Ripon who rode her.

"Why, Tom, what has become of Ogle? He was to come back."

"Yes, Captain; but he told me to say that there was a suspicious-looking fellow on the other side of the way, in St. James's Street, looking at the house, so he did not like to come away."

"He was right—he was right!"

Heron stood by the side of Daisy, with his arm thrown over her neck, and considering whether he should abandon his intention that night of riding forth in search of adventures or not.

"One person only, was it, Tom?"

"Only one, Captain."

"Did you see him?"

"Oh, yes! I pointed him out to Ogle; but upon our going over the way, he went into one of the houses."

"Probably it is nothing. Some one, out of idle curiosity, owing to the lights in the house so long deserted, I fancy."

"That's about it, Captain! I think so. I fancy one man is enough at the mansion."

"What do you mean, Tom?"

"Oh, I forgot old Daddy Mortification! There's two, after all, without me."

"Tom, I can see what you want?"

"How?"

"You want to come with me?"

"Oh, Captain, if you would only take a fellow!"

"Some other time, Tom! I cannot burden Daisy with us both to-night."

"No need, Captain,—no need!"

"Why so? You cannot keep up with me on foot, Tom. I am bound for the high road to Kew."

BARON VON PECK PERFORMS AN ACT OF SIGNAL SERVICE TO A MEMBER
OF THE ROYAL FAMILY.

Presented Gratis with No. 59, of the New Edition of EDITH HERON, the Sequel to Edith the Captive ; or, the Robbers of Epping Forest.

"No, Captain; I don't say I could. But do you hear nothing?"

"I hear some one; and have heard it for the last few minutes, pertinaciously knocking at a door."

"That's my horse, Captain."

"Your horse?"

"Oh, yes! You see, Captain, when Ogle told me to bring Daisy to you, I brought my own horse too; but, for fear you should not like it, I led him to the knocker of a door, up yonder, close to Spring Gardens; and I suppose he keeps pulling it, and knocking away."

"Take that!" shouted a voice at the moment.

Splash came a quantity of water from an upper window of the house, to the knocker of which Tom Ripon had fastened his horse's bridle.

Captain Heron could not help laughing.

"Come on, Tom," he said—"come on, in the name of heaven, and don't let us have the watch upon us."

Rap! rap! rap! went the knocker.

"Watch! watch!" shouted a voice from the window.

"Get in, stupid!" said Tom, as he flung a good-sized pebble up at the window.

Smash went a pane of glass.

"Come away—come away!" called out Captain Heron.

Tom released the bridle of his horse, and instantly mounting, he was by the side of Heron.

The springing of various rattles in the distance announced that the watch were taking the alarm; but Daisy and Tom's horse trotted off together down Whitehall, perfectly careless of the growing tumult they left behind them.

"Captain," said Tom, "where shall we go just to let the folks have a good taste of our quality?"

"You will be so good Tom," said Heron, "as to ride some fifty paces behind me, for I want to consider a little, and will call to you when I want you."

Tom Ripon let Heron and Daisy trot on a little, and fell back to the distance required.

Heron took his way over Westminster Bridge, and then made for the Kew-road.

The old red brick palace at Kew was then in the regular occupation of the royal family; and on the road from it to London, it was quite a rare thing not to find some of the royal carriages conveying members of the Court.

They were the sort of prey that Captain Heron intended to have.

Increasing, then, the pace of Daisy, the half-way house to Kew was soon reached.

From that hostel to the village of Kew itself the road at that time was very lonely and thinly dotted with houses.

So formidable, indeed, in the preceding reign, had the attacks of the knights of the road been on that small extent of way, that for a long time, a military patrol had traversed it from the hour of eleven at night to the daybreak of the next morning.

But that precaution had of late been discontinued.

Felix Heron thus considered that for a time at all events, he had the road to himself.

There was one spot in particular that was peculiarly adapted for such adventures as those sought by him and Tom.

It was a spot at which the road narrowed preparatory to reaching a turnpike gate.

On each side was a shady lane, that went across the highway.

The facilities for some bold and daring robbery at that spot, and for an immediate escape, were great.

There was but one objection, and that was one that had recently only arisen.

The turnpike-gate was, with its light and its little hut where the pikeman resided, very close at hand.

The fact was, that in order to interrupt vehicles and horsemen crossing the road and make them pay a toll, the gate had been moved a good fifty yards closer to the head of the shady lane.

Captain Heron, when he saw that this arrangement had been effected since he had visited the spot, came to a halt.

"We will ride further on, Tom," he said, "I fancy."

"On account of the gate, Captain?"

"Yes, Tom."

"Well, Captain, what do you say, now, to setting up in a new line altogether; or suppose I do it, Captain?"

"What do you mean, Tom?"

"Why, just this. I should like to keep that gate for to-night I think, and then it would be so handy for you."

Felix Heron saw what Tom meant, and he saw likewise what immense advantage it would be to him to have a confederate at the turnpike-gate instead of an enemy.

"Shall I do it, Captain?"

"Stop a bit."

Felix Heron wanted to see what sort of person was keeping the gate, and whether it was in the possession of more than one.

Telling Tom Ripon to keep close to the end of the lane, in the deep shadow of the trees, Heron himself trotted on towards the gate.

As he approached it, he heard a deep-toned voice, singing in such a low mumbling tone that it sounded like distant thunder.

"Hilloa! hilloa! Gate! gate!" shouted Heron, as he paused at the closed turnpike.

"Here you are—threepence! Do you want a ticket?" cried the pikeman, coming out of the little hut in which he lived.

Heron started.

"Why, Blueskin!" he cried; "is that you?"

"Oh, Lor'!"

"Why, what's the matter?"

The man who came out, on the demand for the gate to be opened, was no other than the redoubtable Blueskin, and the well-known bull-dog and janitor of Jonathan Wild's house in Newgate Street, and then the friend and follower of Felix Heron.

The moment his name was mentioned by Captain Heron, Blueskin retreated into the hut and closed the door.

Well might Heron ask him what was the matter.

"Jog on!" cried Blueskin. "Stop a bit, though; I must know who you are."

"Surely you know me! I am Felix Heron."

"What! The Captain!"

Blueskin ran out of the hut, and held up a lantern to Heron's face.

"Why, so you are, to be sure! Why, what you to this part of the world, Captain?"

"What brings you, Blueskin? I cannot help saying that I took it a little ill of you that you left me at the Forest without a word."

"Don't speak of that," replied Blueskin. "I couldn't abide the trees and the grass, and I couldn't sleep, the place was so precious quiet all night long It was a—what do you call it?—a rural sort o' life; and that never did agree with my constitution."

Heron laughed.

" But what are you doing here, Blueskin ? Can it be possible that keeping a turnpike is the sort of life you like, and that in the country, too ?"

" Lor' bless you, no, Captain; it's only for this one night."

" Then you have taken possession merely on business ?"

" That's it, Captain."

" And where is the real pikeman ?"

" In a bag !"

" In a bag ?"

" Yes, Captain; I brought a flour sack with me, and I put him in, and tied him up comfortable, and he is in the little bit of a crib up agin the wall as happy as a king. Hilloa! Look out! Here's something a-coming "

Blueskin ran into the hut, and in another moment came back with a crape mask on his face, and a broad-brimmed slouched hat on his head.

A carriage was rapidly approaching the gate from Kew.

The lights flashed on the tall hedgerow on each side, and the postilion who drove the carriage cracked his whip loudly, as a signal to the pike-keeper to open the gate.

But Blueskin had no intention of doing anything of the sort He ran over to the other side of the way, and as soon as the carriage stopped at the closed gate, he was at the window of it and shouted, " Your money or your life!"

A scream, in the voice of a lady, testified to the fact that, whatever occupants it had, one of them at least was of the feminine gender.

" Be quick about it, ma'am, will you?" roared Blueskin!

" Help! oh, help !"

The postilion, with more courage than prudence, made a blow at Blueskin with the butt-end of his whip.

" Get out !" cried Blueskin, as he took hold of the postilion, and at once flung him off the horse on to the road.

Captain Heron moved to the side of the carriage, and glanced into it.

One lady only was there.

She had dropped to her knees in the carriage in a state of fright.

It was contrary to all the rules and principles that Heron had laid down for himself, to rob a lady alone, and he did not feel disposed to allow Blueskin to do so.

" Madam," he said, " you shall not want a protector while I can be of service to you."

" Oh, sir, a thousand thanks !"

" Now, ma'am !" cried Blueskin again after he had disposed of the postilion.

" Ruffian !" cried Felix Heron. " This lady is under my protection !"

" What !"

" Be off, lest worse come to you."

Blueskin was thunderstricken He could never have calculated upon any hindrance from Felix Heron, and yet there he was, ordering him off.

" Oh, come, none of that."

" Be off !"

Bang! went Blueskin's pistol right over the kneeling lady, in the coach, at Captain Heron.

The ball, with a whistling rush, went past the face of Heron, who called out, " That shot shall cost you dear."

But Blueskin did not want to give Heron a chance of reprisals. He saw that he had missed him, so off he set at as hard a pace on foot as he could.

But he had to pass Tom Ripon.

Heron called out aloud.

" Fire, Tom—fire !

Tom comprehended what was meant pretty well, and he levelled one of his pistols at Blueskin, as well as he could in the darkness, and fired.

Blueskin fell.

" Hit !" cried Tom.

Blueskin fairly rolled over on the road, and then scrambling to his feet, he ran off again, as if not much, if anything, was the matter.

Felix Heron spoke to the lady in the coach.

" I have rid you of your troublesome assailant," he said. " Is there any other service I can render to you?"

" Oh, yes, sir; will you help the postilion ?"

" All right, your Royal Highness," said the postilion. " I am not hurt, though the rascal did give me a heavy fall."

By these words, Heron found that the lady was of exalted rank.

————

CHAPTER CXCV.

HERON PAYS A VISIT TO THE RED BRICK PALACE AT KEW, AND MAKES A GOOD BOOTY.

THE lady trembled very much, and she could hardly speak from the state of agitation she was in.

She seemed to be equally reluctant to accept or to refuse the proffered service of Felix Heron.

There was an awkward silence for a few moments' duration, which Heron did not like to break, for fear he should be urging her to what was inimical to her feelings in this matter.

But at length she spoke

" I am anxious now to go back to Kew "

" I am at your service, madam, in any direction !" .

" But yet, unless I know who the gentleman is who so kindly proffers his help, I shall hardly feel that I ought to accept it."

" Madam," replied Heron, " I think if I were shipwrecked, I should not stop to assure myself of the maker's name of a boat that offered its friendly shelter to me; but, if you wish it, I will repeat that my name is Baron Von Peck."

" Von Peck ? I don't think I know the name."

Heron slightly inclined his head, as though he would have indicated that it was probable enough she did not know it.

" Nevertheless," added the lady, with quite a generous air, " if you will be so good as to ride by the carriage on its road back to Kew, I shall feel infinitely obliged."

" It shall be done !"

Heron rode a few paces from the window of the carriage, and then he blew the silver whistle which he well knew Tom Ripon would recognise as a call to him.

Tom was close to him in a minute.

" Follow !" said Heron.

" Yes, Captain."

The postilion had now turned his horses' heads in the direction of the village of Kew again, and set off at a good round trot.

Felix Heron rode, like an equerry, at the side of the carriage, but he did not feel exactly well pleased at the manner in which the great lady had received or appreciated his services.

On that feeling, he did not have any great inclination to say anything further to her.

The little drive to Kew thus passed off rather quietly, and it was not until the gates were opened that led directly to the palace that the lady, looking from the window of the carriage, spoke one name.

"Baron?"

"Yes, madam."

"I am not ungrateful for the service you have rendered me, and I hope that you will rest awhile at the palace."

What exactly this invitation implied, Heron was rather at a loss to guess, but his love of adventure prevailed over every other consideration, and he replied cautiously, "I will not deny that myself and my servant are both in need of rest, and I gratefully accept your offer."

"You have, then, a servant with you?"

"I have, madam."

"I did not see him."

"He is but a lad, madam, but he is faithful and brave."

The carriage, while the very short conversation took place between Felix Heron and the lady, was proceeding at a very slow pace towards the principal wing of the palace.

There was a flashing of torches and some commotion as the carriage made its appearance, and Heron saw that there could be no doubt about the rank of the lady, by the guard presenting arms to her.

He began to cast about in his mind to think which member of the royal family she was; and at length he decided that she must be the Princess Mary Sophia of Mecklenburgh, the sister of the King.

"Tom," whispered Heron.

"Yes, Captain."

"Take good care of Daisy."

"I believe you, I will."

"Get her and your own horse under cover, but keep as close as you can to this part of the palace, and don't let any gate or stable-yard be closed upon you."

"I won't, Captain."

"You can easily say, as an excuse, that the Baron is expected to leave for London at any moment."

Heron had dismounted as he spoke to Tom, and then, with that high bred air of courtly grace which was so characteristic of him, he stepped forward and handed the lady from the carriage.

It was quite impossible for her to say no to the act, and she walked by the side of Captain Heron into the hall and vestibule of that old building which had been the lodging of so many of the Hanoverian family.

A blaze of light was in that hall, and for the first time the lady got a fair good look in the face of Captain Heron.

She was disappointed.

The disguise, that had not been sufficient to baffle the keen and most practised eyes of Blueskin, was to her perfect.

All she thought she saw was a man past the middle of life, with a dull, tawny complexion and iron-grey moustache.

Yes, the lady was much disappointed.

Felix Heron had not cared to disguise his voice from her; and the consequence was that he had spoken to her in that rich, soft, musical voice, which so well became him.

That voice which was in itself a charm, and which was the delight of all those who loved him.

The lady sighed.

But she could not well get rid of the man who had performed for her so signal a service merely because he was not young and handsome.

With more ease and self-possession than she had before exhibited, since now she was at home and had nothing to fear, she bowed to Heron, and spoke.

"Baron, his Majesty will, I am sure, himself thank you for your gallantry this evening to his sister."

"Then I have the honour of speaking to the Princess Mary Sophia of Mecklenburgh?"

"Yes," replied the Princess, with a sigh; for it was well known that her union with the Duke of Mecklenburgh was anything but a happy one.

By this time they had reached the head of a short flight of stairs, and a gentleman usher threw open a door and bowed low.

The door opened into a pretty reception-room.

When about half-way through it, the Princess spoke again.

"Baron, be seated, and no doubt his Majesty will thank you."

"One moment, Princess!"

"Baron!"

"I am not what I seem."

"Sir?"

Heron spoke in his low, sweet tones, as he added, "I feel that to deceive you I should need to be formed of very different materials to those which make up my mental condition; and as we may never meet again, let me say that I am not a baron."

"Not even that?"

The title of baron, common as it was on the Continent, had not given the Princess any very exalted ideas of Heron; but now to be told, as she found she was, that he had no pretensions even to that distinction, such as it was, proved quite a shock to her.

Heron smiled.

"I do not mean to say, madam, that no title belongs to the humblest of your servants."

"Ah! I see."

"But the title is not that of baron!"

"I am delighted to hear it. You are really, then, a nobleman?"

"I am."

The Princess smiled as she made towards a door at the further end of the apartment.

"I shall leave his Majesty, my brother, the further unravelling of the riddle of who you are, sir."

Another moment, and she was gone.

Heron had done all he intended just then, which was to awaken an interest combined with a curiosity that would make him welcome him to her presence again.

But what did he intend to do now that he had obtained a good hold, so to speak, in that abode of royalty?

We shall soon see.

Another door opened.

Heron started, and was almost guilty of a bow, for he thought it was the King who came in.

It was only Lord Clackington.

"His Majesty desires me to say, sir, that on the representations of the Princess, his royal sister, that you have been of service to her, he is much obliged."

This was quite a polite dismissal.

But Heron did not intend to take it as such.

In quite an altered voice, which it was quite out of question for Lord Clackington to recognise as that of Felix Heron, he spoke in reply.

"I had hoped to be able to give his Majesty some information of the greatest importance."

"You may safely give it to me, sir."

"Are you my Lord Clackington?"

"I am, sir."

"Then I may say that the information is about a notorious highwayman."

"Ah!"

"One Captain Heron!"

"The dev——I mean, you don't say so. We heard he was dead!"

"So he is, but his ghost!"

"His what?"

"His apparition!"

"Pho!—pho!"

"What can all this mean?" exclaimed a voice, as the door at which Lord Clackington had come into the room was flung open, and the King, who had evidently been listening, made his appearance.

Lord Clackington bowed low.

"What is this, sir, that you say about the apparition of a man who has given us more trouble than any one individual in all England!"

Heron bowed.

"I was about to tell my Lord Clackington what I now feel I ought only to tell to your Majesty."

"What—what is it?"

"A most curious revelation."

"Leave us, Clackington."

"Your Majesty!"

"Leave us! leave us!

"With a perfect stranger? Oh, your Majesty, the interest of England is too much concerned in your royal safety."

"His Majesty is perfectly safe," said Heron, "with the man who, already this night, has endangered his life for the Princess, his Majesty's sister."

"True, true! you can go, Clackington."

Lord Clackington had now no resource but to bow himself out of the room.

The King sat down.

Felix Heron stood a few paces from him, as he spoke.

"Is your Majesty quite sure we are out of earshot of all persons?"

"Quite! quite!"

"Then, your Majesty, Felix Heron, the notorious highwayman, was on the road to Kew this night."

"No?"

"I saw him."

"But we had authentic intelligence that he was dead."

"That it is that makes the fact of his appearance so strange and inexplicable."

"But how was it?"

"The carriage lamps—that carriage in which was her Royal Highness, your Majesty's sister—shone far into the gloom of a shadowy lane, which crosses the highway near a turnpike."

"We know it! we know it!" said the King impatiently.

"Coming up that lane, then, I saw a man on horseback; but what attracted my attention was that they both seemed to move onward without any action of the horse's feet; and what was more——"

"Stop!"

"Your Majesty!"

"Do you mean to tell us that the horses glided along the ground in such a fashion as that?"

"Even so."

"Go on—go on! What then?"

"The next thing that surprised me was, that although the forms of both the man and the horse were quite distinct, as to outline, I could see the trees and the herbage of the lane right through them."

"What?"

"Right though them, your Majesty."

"But—but——"

"And then I remembered that I had once before seen both the man and the horse, and that the one was Felix Heron, and the other his well-known flying steed, Daisy."

"This is incredible, sir."

Heron bowed.

"Well, what next?"

"That which followed is more incredible still!"

"No; that cannot be."

"You shall judge, sir. I was transfixed with surprise at the sight I have described to your Majesty, and did not attempt to get out of the way of it, when the apparition rode up to me, and in a voice which I thought one of singular mildness, spoke. 'Tell the King,' he said, 'that I will be with him to-night, to——'"

"No!"

"'To claim of him the rents of the estates of Whitcombe, which are withheld from me and mine, by his vacillation in not fully acknowledging my claims, and, according to promise, condoning my errors of the past, in consideration of the injustice I have endured.'"

"Appear to me?"

"It said so."

"What then?"

"Then, your Majesty, it disappeared."

The King looked cautiously about him, with an evident appearance of fright.

"But you, Baron," he said—"it is not surely possible that you believe in this—this ghost story?"

Heron shook his head.

"I only tell your Majesty what I saw, and what I know."

"But——"

"Hush!"

"What is it?"

"I hear something."

"What? what?"

"A sort of fumbling, or scratching, as if at a door."

"Which door?"

"That one—no, it is that one—no, now it is that one. Why, it is at all the three doors opening from this apartment in succession!"

The King had started to his feet.

That he was intent upon effecting an escape from the room was quite evident; but the statement of Heron, that a mysterious noise was at all the doors, kept him from any nearer approach to either of them.

"What does it mean?" he cried. "Sir, Baron, or whatever you may be, we shall be obliged by your making an instant examination!"

"Outside one of the doors?"

"Yes—yes!"

Heron wanted a good excuse for that exact act, and he hastened to obey the King.

He darted out of the room by the door that the Princess had left by.

He felt confident that he had awakened too many superstitious fears in the mind of the King for him to move from the apartment, and he knew sufficient of the usages of the Court to be certain that no one would intrude unbidden.

But there was one thing that Heron had quite forgotten.

That was Lord Clackington.

He had left the royal presence, but he had only gone as far as the other side of the door, and he had heard all.

The rapid movement of Felix Heron from the room prevented Lord Clackington from getting out of the way, and Heron very nearly tumbled over him.

Heron felt the immediate necessity of getting rid of such an obstruction as quietly as possible.

"Idiot!" he cried; "what do you here?"

The hearty kick that Heron dealt him made Lord Clackington utter a yell.

EDITH.—No. 60.

"Murder!"

"Peace!"

"Murder! help!"

"Another such cry, and you are a dead man!"

Heron shook him to within an inch of his life.

At some short distance from the landing-place on the outside of that door there was a flight of steps, that had, at the foot of them, one of those velvet-covered doors so profusely dotted over St. James's Palace, to keep the numerous draughts of cold air in subjection.

Down the steps Heron flung the prying Lord Clackington, and when he reached the foot of them, his weight dashed open the door that was there, and he disappeared down a much longer flight of stairs.

The velvet-covered door closed with a spring.

Felix Heron was now fairly rid of Lord Clackington, and he was within the Palace, with the King much at his mercy.

For a few moments only did Felix Heron hesitate as to what he should do.

Then he made up his mind to play his own ghost.

A very few minutes sufficed to effect a remarkable alteration in the exterior of Felix Heron.

The coat he wore he had had made to his own especial order.

On one side it suited well the pretensions and appearance of the Baron Von Peck, but on the other it was a light scarlet edged with gold lace.

It was so made too on that other side that it could be buttoned much more tightly over the slim and graceful figure of Heron.

When he had, therefore, effected this change, he looked not about half the size of the Baron.

The wig was the next thing dispensed with.

Then a good hard rub of a handkerchief upon his face enabled Heron to get rid of the greater part of the false colour he had put on to personate a man much older than himself.

A twist of the hat that the supposed Baron Von Peck had worn changed its aspect most completely.

And all this change he effected so rapidly that to the King, who was in that state of nervous terror that could take no good cognisance of him, it seemed as if the Baron Von Peck had only just passed through the doorway of the room.

And then that door, slowly and in a solemn kind of way, was opened.

The King glanced at it with protruding eyes and bated breath.

The door creaked.

It was a good half-minute before it was wholly opened.

Then the King felt inclined to cry out, but his tongue clove to the roof of his mouth.

He was completely, for the time, paralysed with terror.

Heron, in that full and complete costume of a highwayman, stood on the very threshold of the door.

Slowly, then, and according to the most approved supposed fashion of ghosts, he glided into the room.

He uttered a hollow groan.

The King gasped.

He slid off his chair.

He dropped to his knees.

Heron spoke.

"O King! O King!—you, who while the breath of life animated the mortal frame of Felix, Earl of Whitcombe, list—oh, list!"

"I—I—will."

The King could only speak in choking accents.

"Contrive not, dream not aught that can in any shape or way bring the shadow of unhappiness to the hearth of the widowed Countess of Whitcombe or her infant son."

"We—we will not."

"It is well."

Heron stood in the middle of the apartment, and pointed to an escritoire that was there significantly.

"The time has come," he said, "when this immortal spirit must return to those realms from which, for a brief space, it has been allowed to visit the earth."

"Y-e-s."

The King seemed quite delighted to hear that the ghost of Captain Heron was about so politely to take its departure.

But Heron still pointed to the escritoire, and the King could not understand what the ghost exactly meant.

CHAPTER CXCVI.

CAPTAIN HERON POSSESSES HIMSELF OF SOME ROYAL GEMS, AND THE BARON VON PECK IS IN GOOD FAVOUR WITH MAJESTY.

THE King followed the direction of the eyes and the pointed finger of the supposed apparition; and then, in a deep toned voice, Heron said, "Open! open! open!"

The King began to comprehend.

"Open—the—a—the—cabinet?"

"Open! open!"

Heron put on a stern look.

"Yes, if you wish; but——"

"Peace, oh King! It is not permitted to mortal eyes to see the manner in which spirit mingles with the elements, and disappears from mortal gaze. In that cabinet I can take my leave."

"In—the—a cabinet?"

"In it. Open! open!"

Heron had heard that the King had a large cabinet, of which he himself always kept the key, and wherein it was believed he kept a goodly share of gold and jewels.

Upon the speculation that this might be that very cabinet, Heron made the deadset at it that he did.

The King fumbled in his pockets.

He produced a key.

The impression of Heron that the cabinet or escritoire was the very one of which he had heard approached to a certainty.

"But—but," said the King, shaking as he spoke,—"if—if you go there, I shall be afraid to open the door again."

"I will knock there when I have passed away."

The King opened the cabinet.

It was capacious enough on the inside for Heron to walk into it very well, only slightly stooping.

He pulled the door shut after him.

Then he uttered a strange, unearthly cry from the inside.

It only wanted something of that sort to increase the terror of the King to such a height that he could no longer remain without some human companionship.

With a shout of despair and fright, he fled from the room.

That was exactly what Felix Heron wanted him to do.

He stepped out of the cabinet at once, and taking a wax candle from the candelabrum on the table that was nearest to him, he commenced an examination of the cabinet.

The inside was peculiar.

There were two tall nests of drawers, and between them an open space, in which Felix Heron had stood.

Feeling, then, that he might not have many moments to spare, Heron proceeded at once to attack the drawers.

They were not locked.

The sight that met his eyes most abundantly satisfied him.

In the first drawer that he opened he saw a quantity of unset jewels which looked to be of great value.

Heron took possession of some eight or ten.

"Thus much," he said, "in earnest of compensation for the loss of the rents of the Whitcombe estates."

He closed the drawer again on the instant, and darted out of the room by the same door through which he had previously gone, on the occasion of his encounter with Lord Clackington.

That was not, however, the door at which the King had made his hurried and frightened exit.

Heron ran down the short flight of steps, where he had precipitated Lord Clackington so short a time before.

At the foot of these, he pushed open the velvet covered door.

No Lord Clackington was to be seen, however, and so dim was the light that came from a corridor below, to that part of the Palace, that Heron was very nearly falling down the next and longer flight of steps himself.

Then he paused, and asked himself what he had better do.

"Escape" was the word that came uppermost to his lips.

In all likelihood he would be able to make good his exit from the Palace by that route.

Heron began to descend the stairs.

He paused.

The flash of more light came from below.

The clash of arms

The murmur of voices

"This way—this way—Yeomen of the Guard!" cried a voice "Up these stairs—I will follow you!"

The voice was Lord Clackington's.

Heron hesitated.

Should he make a rush, and trust to his address and carriage, to force a way through the body of the Yeomen of the Guard, who were in the vestibule below?

No.

With all his contempt of danger, Felix Heron felt that that would be too hazardous an attempt

There was no resource but to retrace his steps.

And why not return to the room in which, as Baron Von Peck, he had had an interview with the King?

The work of a few moments would suffice to make him look like the Baron again.

To be sure, he had rubbed off his face some of that skilfully arranged paint and colour that had given age to it, but he could pull his wig low down, and that might not be noticed.

The King was not exactly in a state of mind to notice nice distinctions

The idea no sooner found a home in the mind of Heron than it was carried out.

He changed the coat again, and in a few seconds he was in the apartment as the Baron Von Peck, looking much as he had before looked.

"Save the King!" cried Lord Clackington as he followed the Yeomen of the Guard into the room.

"Treason! treason!" shouted another voice, and another of the doors opened, disclosing another party of the Yeomen of the Guard, in whose midst was the King himself, with a drawn sword in his hand.

The Baron von Peck stood between these two forms.

They all came to a standstill.

"Baron!" cried the King.

"Your Majesty!"

"The—the ghost!"

Felix Heron got up a well-acted shudder.

"I saw it, your Majesty! In vain I tried to interpose, but it seemed to pass me like a cloud of vapour!"

"Gracious heaven!"

"I feel chilled to the marrow of my bones, on account of the promise I have made!"

"Promise! What promise?"

"The spectre came out of that cabinet!"

"Ah!"

"And it spoke to me in a hollow, awful voice!"

"What? what?"

"'If,' it said, 'you would save the King from further visitation from me, you must yourself consent to see me each month whenever the moon is in the same position as now!"

"And—and—you——"

"Consented!"

"Oh, Baron!"

"I feel that I could not possibly do less than encounter even the terrors of the unsubstantial world in your Majesty's service!"

The King looked gracious.

"May I humbly represent," said Lord Clackington, "that something much more substantial than a ghost met me, and flung me from top to bottom of a flight of steps! I have not a square inch of me that is not a bruise!"

"Where was that, my lord?" asked Felix Heron.

"Exactly outside that door?"

Heron shook his head.

"Impossible, my lord!"

"But, I tell you, it was so; and, if I am not mad, it was you who——"

"Hold!"

"And why hold, sir?"

"I will prove to you that it was not so!"

"How? how?"

"Because you were somewhere else!"

"I was not! I was——"

"Not outside that door, surely, when the King was holding a private conference, my lord! That is impossible!"

"I—I——"

"Exactly! No one could have been there at the time I left this room, considering that you, my lord, had left it ten good minutes before, unless with the one object of listening!"

"I listen!"

"Certainly not, my lord; and, therefore, you were not there!"

Lord Clackington shrank back.

A quiet smile passed over the face of the King.

Lord Clackington had the fate of all sycophants and parasites. He was heartily despised, and but that he was of use in his vocation, the King would have heard, without the least emotion that he had broken his neck.

From that moment, Lord Clackington hated the Baron Von Peck.

The King sat down, with a sigh.

"My Lord Clackington!"

"Your Majesty!"

"It seems to me that it is singularly remiss in the first gentleman of our household to be attacked by apparitions!"

"But, your Majesty——"

"We have no further need of your services to-night, my lord."

Lord Clackington bowed

"And to-morrow," added the King, with a wave of his hand, while he half closed his eyes, as if the sight of Lord Clackington was painful to him,—"and to-morrow we hope and expect a fuller and better explanation of your conduct."

"Your gracious Majesty, I——"

"No! Know, my lord, we will hear no more

o-night.   Baron, you will oblige us by stay-ing."

Heron bowed.

The discomfited Lord Clackington retired with the Yeomen of the Guard.

"Baron," said the King, "I would fain ask you to what noble family you belong?"

"The Von Pecks of Darmstadt, your Majesty."

"Oh, well, we never heard of them, but it is evident you are a brave man, Baron."

"I hope so, your Majesty!"

"And you have the manners and the appear-ance of a gentleman, likewise."

Heron bowed.

"Baron, it so happens that we, at this present time, require the services of a bold and devoted gentleman."

Heron bowed again.

"There is a lady——Well, Baron—ha, ha!—you are a man of the world, and therefore I need not excuse myself to you——a lady, who, to our eyes, contains many charms in her own person. We wish some devoted friend of ours to be so good as to take upon himself to be upon such friendly terms with her, that—that——In fact, we want the help of a man of courage and address."

Heron bit his lips.

Was it possible that he could sink so low as to be employed on such a matter?

But he dissembled.

"Your Majesty makes a half-confidence," he said.

"You want to know more?"

"All—if I am to be of any service to the lady," Heron added to himself.

"You are right."

"I hope so, your Majesty."

"The lady is young, and an orphan. It is in our hands to appoint a guardian to her, and if that guardian is a friend of ours, we should feel that we were on the road to success."

"Success?"

"Yes; we love the lady, Baron."

"And she is so young as to need a guardian?"

"She is of the poetical age of seventeen."

"Indeed!"

"Even so, Baron. In a word, will you accept the office of guardian to the young lady, and occupy a suite of apartments at Hampton Court?"

"Your Majesty, I really——"

"Stop, Baron; I ought to ask if you are a married man?"

"Yes."

"Oh, that's a pity."

"Indeed, sire?"

"Yes; your wife will be an obstruction. Women are such dragons of virtue in regard to any one but themselves."

"My wife is not with me, sire."

"Ah! At Darmstadt?"

Heron inclined his head.

"That will do—that will do! Come, Baron; I see we shall be able to arrange this matter satis-factorily. You will call on us to-morrow at the general audience at one o'clock."

Heron understood this to be his conge, and bowed low.

"And as regards this apparition of the late Earl of Whitcombe," added the King, with a shudder, "you take that on yourself."

"It is as I have had the honour of reporting to your Majesty."

"The whole affair bewilders me, Baron; and I know not what to think. I saw him, and only his day I had the most authentic news of his

death. It is more than strange; but now good night, and do not forget that you are in the ser-vice of the King!"

Felix Heron could not help feeling in some degree surprised at this sudden confidence of the King in him; but, upon reflection, he could not consider that it was a very flattering distinction.

Had the service which the King wanted been of an honourable description, he would not have turned to a stranger to render it to him.

Heron paused at the door of the apartment, and then he bethought himself that it would be well to make the most of the present opportunity.

He tapped at the door again, and re-entered the room.

"Your Majesty forgets that I am a stranger here in the palace. I may even be questioned as I leave it."

"That is true," replied the King. "Wait one moment."

Felix Heron was left alone for about a couple of minutes, and then the King returned to him and handed him a small strip of parchment, on which was a freshly impressed seal in red wax.

The word "Pass" was written on the parch-ment just above the seal.

"This will clear a way for you, Baron, in the palace whenever you please. It will be recognised by my servants as the pass I give to those who are in my private and confidential service."

Heron could not but feel the full importance of such a document, and he eagerly possessed himself of it.

"I thank your Majesty, and will take care to make good use of this."

"Good night, Baron."

"I have the honour again to wish your Majesty good night."

In five minutes more Felix Heron was free of the palace.

Tom Ripon had been in a great state of alarm, but the sight of his Captain, safe and sound, soon restored his spirits.

A short, sharp gallop took them to London, and Felix Heron drew a long breath of relief as he crossed once more the threshold of Whitcombe House.

"Felix—Felix!"

It was Edith's voice.

She was sitting up waiting his return, and she was pale and anxious.

"Edith, this must not be!"

Heron looked in her face with an air of gentle reproach.

"Nay, think nothing of it," replied Edith. "Since you are returned, all is well again!"

Felix Heron then related to Edith the full par-ticulars of his night's adventure, and it was deter-mined that he should still keep up his delusive connexion with the King, and seem to coincide with him in his views for the sole purpose of thwarting them, and saving the young lady who had excited the royal admiration from the other-wise wretched fate that awaited her.

Heron was breakfasting with Edith in the little dressing-room connected with the suite of rooms on the second floor, which she, Edith, called her own, when Ogle tapped at the door and put on a look of puzzled half-alarm when he was told to come in.

"What is amiss, Ogle?" said Heron.

"I hardly know, Captain, whether to say it is anything amiss or not; but Jonathan Wild is below."

"Jonathan Wild?"

THE KING INTRODUCES MARIANNA TO HER NEW GUARDIAN, THE BARON VON PECK.

"Just so!"

"Oh, heaven, save us!" ejaculated Edith, as she flew to the side of the cot on which her child was sleeping.

"Be under no apprehension," said Heron; "his visit I do not look upon as hostile."

"And besides," said Ogle, "we can soon dispose of him if it is"

"Who has seen him?" asked Heron.

"Tom Ripon!"

"Did he know Tom?"

"Immediately!"

"And what passed?"

"Oh, he only gave him a knock on the top of the head, and said he was a fine boy, and that he, Jonathan Wild, would attend his execution."

"What is to be done, Felix?" asked Edith.

"Who did he ask for, Ogle?"

"The Countess of Whitcombe."

Heron was silent for a few moments, and then he took Edith's hand, as he said, "My Edith, have you any great objection to see this man, and ascertain what his errand is here?"

"None, Felix—none! It is the best thing to do, I am sure!"

"Then show him, Ogle, into the green drawing-room. I will occupy a place in the adjoining one, and Edith will come to him"

It was not without a little shrinking and trembling that Edith made her way down stairs for the purpose of meeting the man who it appeared must either be killed or conciliated.

Felix Heron took up a position in the adjoining room, where he could conveniently overhear all that passed.

Jonathan Wild was in the middle of the floor, with his back to the window of the green drawing-room when Edith entered.

"Sarvent, madam," said Wild, with an awkward attempt at a bow.

Edith looked calm and rigid.

She did not speak.

"I don't wonder," added Wild, "that your ladyship is rather surprised to see me: but the fact is, I want to set your mind at ease about me."

Edith was still silent.

"You might fancy that because I thought it my duty to follow up your husband, the late Earl, that I might be an enemy to you and your son; but it is not so. I am rather a bad enemy, and it generally happens that those who are such can, if they please, be a good friend."

"I am content," replied Edith, "that the rancour with which you pursued the father will not be carried out against the son."

"It will not, my lady. I promised as much to the late Earl, and although there is nothing in life that Jonathan Wild can be said to fear, yet a promise to the dead he holds sacred."

Edith made a movement of assent.

"But," added Wild, "as there should be always two sides to a bargain, perhaps you, in your turn, will have no objection to oblige Jonathan Wild?"

CHAPTER CXCVII.

FELIX HERON GOES TO A COURT BALL, AND IS INTRODUCED TO THE KING'S FAIR WARD.

AT these words from Jonathan Wild, Edith shrunk back and trembled.

What could he possibly wish of her?

"A very few words, madam," added Wild, "will suffice to let you know what I want. Lord Warringdale——"

"Ah, it is from that bad man you come!"

"No. I should be very sorry to come from him, considering where he is likely to be, madam."

"What do you mean?"

"Lord Warringdale is dead!"

"Dead? Can that be really the truth?"

"It is indeed. The particulars of his exit from this world are of very little consequence."

"He has made some terrible end!"

"Well, madam, that is neither here nor there. My Lord Warringdale was not an angel in life, and he was not likely to be afflicted with much piety on his taking leave of it. He is dead, and he owes me money!"

Edith was about to ask what could that possibly concern her, but she thought it better, as Felix Heron was listening, to let Jonathan Wild say all he chose.

"Yes, he owes me money, and the only surety I have for it is on a small estate which belonged to him, and which was apart from the rest of the properties of the earldom. Now, if I take possession of that estate, will you abstain from setting up any claim to it on behalf of your son, the present Lord Warringdale?"

It sounded so strange to Edith to hear any one speak of her little child as Lord Warringdale, and yet that was the title of courtesy which was his, as being the eldest son of the Earl of Whitcombe.

The question, however, which Jonathan Wild asked was one that she knew not how to reply to.

Without some consultation with Heron she neither liked to say yes or no.

"Give me until this time to-morrow," she said, "and you shall have your answer."

Wild bit his lips.

"Hark you, my lady," he said; "there are other persons still alive in whom you feel an interest. Say yes to my request, and I will not meddle with any of those who have been the comrades of Felix Heron."

Edith hesitated.

"I will name them to you," said Wild.

He counted them off upon his fingers.

"Ogle, Tom Ripon, his mother, and Mortification, his father-in-law. I will hang them all next sessions. Let me see. Yes, I will get up a good plate robbery, and hang them all next sessions if you refuse me."

Edith was thoroughly alarmed.

"So long, then," she said, "as you abstain from interference with the persons you have named, there will be no disposition on my part to interfere with you or whatever means you may adopt to get your money on account of Lord Warringdale."

"That will do."

It was strange how perfect a reliance Jonathan Wild had upon the word of Edith.

That men like Wild know what honour, and honesty, and virtue are, is made evident by the fact that they are sharp in discerning such qualities in other persons, and are always ready to give them every weight.

"It is a bargain, Lady Whitcombe," he said; "and so now I will take my leave of you, and you will have no more trouble from Jonathan Wild."

These were welcome enough words to Edith; and she thought the sacrifice of some, perhaps, doubtfully legal claim which her son might have to the property in question, well bartered for the peace and security promised by Jonathan Wild.

Edith was delighted to see him leave the room,

and from the windows she saw him likewise leave the house.

"Felix, Felix!"

"I am here, Edith."

"You heard all?"

"I did."

"And have I done right?"

"Quite right, Edith—quite right! The time will come when that little estate can easily be wrested from such hands as Jonathan Wild's. At present let him possess it as the bribe for your security and peace."

"That, Felix, was in truth the light in which I viewed it."

"And the proper one, too."

Felix Heron remained at home at Whitcombe House for the greater part of the morning, during which the young Earl of Bridgewater called, and they had a long conversation in regard to what had happened between Heron and the King.

"I am at a loss," said the Earl of Bridgewater, "to think who the young lady can be to whom the King has become guardian; but it is a most fortunate thing for her that he has met with you in your assumed character of the Baron Von Peck."

There was an air of sadness and chagrin about the Earl, the cause of which Edith inquired.

"Shall I confess," he replied, "that I am sorry for the death of Lord Warringdale, since I had not given up the hope of bringing him to justice for the murder of my father?"

"Do not," said Edith, "nourish such an idea. Leave him now to the justice of heaven."

"I must fain do so."

The impetuous young Earl of Bridgewater could not reconcile himself to the fact that Lord Warringdale had, so to speak, slipped through his revengeful fingers.

But there was no help for it.

He left Whitcombe House with the promise of calling again in the evening to hear what had happened to Heron with the King.

With greater care than he had used on the day previous, Felix Heron painted and disguised his features so as to look considerably older than his real age.

He got himself up, as the theatrical phrase is, excellently; and with the slight stoop that he assumed, he looked a man of, at the least, five-and-forty years of age.

At one o'clock he took his way on foot to the Palace of St. James's.

The King had slept at Kew, but had come to town early in the morning, for the private audiences at the hour of one.

Those private audiences were held every other day, and all persons, in any way connected with the various households of the King, had the liberty of attending them, and communicating personally with the Sovereign.

Heron presented himself at a door in the Colour Court, where he saw various persons going in.

He was stopped instantly.

"No admittance here, sir."

"I am the Baron Von Peck."

The Groom in Waiting shook his head as he replied, "We have no orders, sir, about you?"

"Will this suffice?"

Heron exhibited the pass which the King had given him.

It did suffice.

"Pass on, sir."

An open book was in the small vestibule to which that door in the Colour Court of St. James's led, and in that Heron was requested to write his name.

He wrote, in a large, bold hand, "The Baron von Peck."

"Pass on, Baron."

Up a short flight of stairs, covered with scarlet cloth, Heron took his way; and then, pushing open a door at the top of it, he found himself in a long gallery, or waiting-room, which was tolerably full of people of all sorts and conditions.

Pages — Grooms of the Chamber — favourite tradespeople—officers of the Guard—retired members of the household, who had favours to ask either for themselves or their relatives, and not a few of those men who picked up a living at that period by the pretended discovery of Jacobite plots.

These persons were for the most part the real and only plotters themselves, but were quite willing to sell either party to the other at any moment.

But perhaps there was no Court in all Europe at that time so strangely assorted and attended as that of Great Britain.

The change of dynasty was as yet very fresh as a disagreeable fact in many people's minds, and in effect it took quite another generation before the exiled Stuarts, with all the special interest connected with them, were quite forgotten.

It was no part of Felix Heron's wish to mingle with the corrupt society about him, so he retired into the deep shadow of a bay-window until his name should be called.

In about half an hour one of the royal pages shouted out the name—

"The Baron Von Peck!"

All the names of the persons who were to have, by previous arrangement, special audience of the King, were entered in a book kept by the Groom in Waiting, and as they were one by one wanted in the royal closet, the name was called out by one of the pages in waiting.

"The Baron Von Peck!"

"Here!"

Heron saw that he was regarded with no small amount of curiosity by the throng of persons in the ante-room, for the name of Von Peck was a new one at Court.

"This way, sir."

Heron followed the page.

In another moment he was in the presence of the King.

"Well, Baron!"

"I have the honour to wait your Majesty's commands."

"You shall hear them, and I will not doubt but that you will study to entitle yourself to our royal gratitude."

What difference there was between royal gratitude and any other, the King did not condescend to explain, but perhaps he meant that kind of gratitude which contents itself with promises only.

Heron paused.

"Alone!" said the King.

The page who lingered by one of the doors, immediately retired, and let fall over the door a very heavy velvet curtain.

The King and the supposed Baron Von Peck were alone.

"You see, Baron, I trust you implicitly, notwithstanding this is an age when we may look with suspicion upon strange faces."

"I was wondering," replied Heron, "how it was, when it is well known the land is full of plots and plotters, you could place such confidence in me."

"I have tried you."

"Tried me?"

"Yes Last night you had a far better opportunity of assassinating us than you have this evening."

"Assassination! I an assassin?"

"Certainly not, Baron We have one faculty which it is said belongs to kings. We think we can detect who to trust and who to be on our guard against."

"Your Majesty does me but justice. If no hand but mine were to be ever lifted against you, you might live in peace."

"We are sure of it."

"And I hate plots and plotters."

"We are sure of that, too."

"Then I wait your royal orders."

"Baron!"

The King paused, and Heron bent on him an expectant look.

"Baron, the young lady is—is, we may say, obstinate."

"Indeed!"

"Yes, Baron. We have had one interview with her, and she does not exactly—that is to say, she rather, in effect, repels——"

"Your Majesty's advances?"

"Well, yes."

"It was to be expected."

"She is very young, too; and one would have thought might, from inexperience, have found the attentions of a king rather flattering."

"And she did not?"

"Well, no."

Heron was delighted to find that the young lady, whoever she was, had repulsed the advances of the King.

"Your Majesty must have noticed," he said, "in your many experiences, that there are some natures in which there is an inherent sense of virtue that nothing will tempt to transgress the bounds of modest prudence and reserve."

"Oh, stuff!"

"I merely meant to say that that was the way in which some people would put the case."

The King curled his lip.

"Baron, we have nothing to do with what you call some people. If, in plain language, you are not the unscrupulous man we take you for, say so, and our confidence is at an end."

Felix Heron felt very much inclined, at that moment, to rise from his chair, and throw his Majesty of England out at the window.

It was only the thought that he might be instrumental in saving the young girl in question from the royal clutches that lent him the power of forbearance.

He had to bow, however, to conceal the flush of indignation on his face.

"Well," added the King, "is it to be a bargain, Baron?"

"A bargain, your Majesty."

"Good. You will receive from the keeper of our Privy Purse the sum of fifty pounds per month; and of course, as I before mentioned, you will have free quarters at Hampton Court Palace."

"Your Majesty is very good."

"Well, Baron, if you are quite satisfied, so are we. Come to-night to Buckingham House, and will be introduced to the young lady, who, with her governess, will accompany you to Hampton Court."

"Her governess?"

"The King smiled."

"Yes, her governess."

"May I ask is the governess devoted to your Majesty?"

"She is eighty seven, half-blind, three-quarters deaf, and generally infirm; so it don't matter to whom she is devoted."

"I see! Not in the least! Your Majesty chose her?"

"We did."

Heron could not but see how cruelly ensnared, by the base and villanous intrigues which the King sought to fasten on her, this young girl was.

He resolved that, let it cost him what effort over his natural feelings it might, he would so far dissemble as to be the mortal saviour of the young girl in question.

"May I venture to ask the name of the young lady?" he said.

"Marianna"

"Marianna something?"

"Let that suffice. We shall expect you at Buckingham House at the hour of seven."

The King inclined his head, and Felix Heron left the royal presence, passing through the anteroom the observed of all observers, and the envy of many who for weeks had waited there hours in attendance, without being able to procure an interview with the King.

Some one touched Heron on the arm.

It was the Earl of Bridgewater.

"Follow me; but do not seem to know me. You are well watched."

The Earl glided away among the crowd.

But Heron managed to keep him well in view, and slowly made his way after him.

They entered a small club-room, and then they went down a short flight of steps that led down to the old deserted guard chambers, the walls of which were fancifully covered with arms and armour of all dates and styles.

There the Earl paused.

"Felix!"

"Yes, Bridgewater!"

"We can safely speak here, and I have an important question to ask of you. Do you know the name of the young lady of whom the King wanted you to take charge?"

"Yes. Marianna!"

CHAPTER CXCVIII.

THE EARL OF BRIDGEWATER CONCERTS MEASURES WITH FELIX HERON TO SAVE MARIANNA.

THE moment Heron uttered the name of Marianna, the young Earl of Bridgewater clapped his hands together, and exclaimed, "Good heavens! can it be possible?"

"What possible?"

The girl is the orphan child of an officer who has fought and bled in the service of the ungrateful King"

"You know him?"

"Well."

"And you know his daughter?"

"I saw her when about six or seven years of age, and a more lovely child could not exist. She gave promise of possessing beauty of no common order. Both myself and Lady Bridgewater know her well enough to have been delighted to have charge of her."

"How comes it, then, that she is so cast into the hands of the King?"

"She is what is called 'a king's orphan'—that is the child of one who has died in the service of the Crown."

"Well, Bridgewater, she is safe, as you well know."

"Thank heaven! yes."

Felix Heron then detailed to the Earl all that had passed between him and the King: and it was resolved between them that he, Bridgewater, should likewise be at Hampton Court on that night, to aid and assist Heron, if necessary, against the King.

Much disturbed in mind on the whole subject, Felix Heron, in a thoughtful mood, went home to Whitcombe House.

When Edith heard all that he had to tell her, she made an instant resolve.

"Felix, I will go to Hampton."

"You, Edith?"

"Yes, Felix, I will help you, too, to save that young girl from the danger that awaits her."

"But our little one?"

"The distance is short, and I will take him. Nay, Heron, do not shake your head, and look grave at me. I cannot endure to remain here on such an occasion; and moreover, you know, I am acquainted with old Lady Dewar, who is a friend of my dear aunt, Lady Castleneau, and who has rooms in the old Palace."

"Dear Edith, the only difficulty that presented itself to my mind thus vanishes. I wondered on what pretence you were to make your way into a place so jealously cared for and guarded as Hampton Court; but as the visitor of Lady Dewar, you are safe."

Edith was delighted that Felix Heron had no objection to her presence at the old Palace. And when he left Whitcombe House to keep his appointment with the King, Edith went to Hampton in her own coach, with her child, the real Lord Warringdale.

The clock of the Horse Guards sounded the hour of seven as Felix Heron, still satisfactorily keeping up the character and appearance of the Baron Von Peck, crossed the threshold of old Buckingham House.

He was shown into a small drawing-room, the same that soon after that time became well known as the common sitting-room of the unhappy Caroline, Princess of Wales, and wife to George the Fourth.

In a few moments a door opened at one end of the room, and the King appeared, leading two ladies by the hands.

One was a little, old, infirm woman, who fully, in looks, came up to the description that the King had given of the governess he had appointed to the young Marianna.

The other was Marianna herself.

Felix Heron was charmed.

He was not what the world calls a "gallant" man, and all his best affections belonged to his Edith; but he was not, on that account, blind to all other beauty.

In Marianna he saw such a delicate, exquisite loveliness, that he could hardly wonder at the King admiring her, although the dove-like manner that sat upon her face should have kept her from any unholy thought.

"Baron Von Peck," said the King, "allow me to introduce you to one of our royal orphans."

Heron bowed.

"Marianna, this is a noble gentleman to whom you will look as our representative, and who will only be too happy to grant you any possible indulgence."

Marianna bowed, as she spoke in low, gentle tones.

"I hope soon to be no trouble either to this gentleman or any one else, as the few accomplishments my poor father was able to get me taught may get me a subsistence."

"Perish the thought!" said the King.

"Nay; if your Majesty will forgive me for saying so," interposed Heron, "I think the young lady is right."

Marianna looked for the first time approvingly at Felix Heron.

She had no occasion to hold the King in high esteem, and she was, therefore, the more inclined to think well of any one who differed from him.

The King himself was far from resenting this apparent boldness on the part of the supposed Baron Von Peck.

All he saw in it was, an admirable piece of finesse on the Baron's part, for the purpose of winning the confidence of the young and beautiful Marianna.

"Well, Baron," he said, "we are not used to contradiction, but we can admire the independent spirit that dictates your words."

Heron bowed.

The young girl seemed to feel instinctively that he would be a friend to her, and a protector.

Imperceptibly she crept across the room, almost to the side of Felix Heron.

"It seems, Marianna," said the King, "that you will be quite content with the Baron Von Peck."

"I hope so, sir."

"Then, Baron, I relinquish the charge of this most dear and interesting young lady to you for the present, convinced that you will do all you can for her happiness at the old palace of Hampton Court."

"I shall strive so to do, your Majesty."

The old governess during this brief colloquy had fallen fast asleep.

She had not sat down in the presence of royalty, but settling herself on her feet in some odd way, she had gone to sleep as a horse would do without lying down.

The old governess was a decayed lady in waiting, and long habit of standing in the presence of the King or Queen, in the last reign, had enabled her to do so without trouble or fatigue.

The King touched her on the arm.

The old governess, with a slight start, awakened, as fully as she would ever again do on this side of the grave.

Nobody spoke to her, and she slowly followed the fair and innocent Marianna from the apartment.

The King stood by the door, and as Heron passed him, he whispered, "Baron."

"Your Majesty!"

"You will not retire to rest on this night?"

Heron made a slight inclination of his head to signify that he fully comprehended what those words meant.

The signification was that the King would be at Hampton Court some time before dawn.

But Heron did not tremble for that beautiful young girl.

He knew that she was safe.

Safe in his keeping, although twenty kings were to try their utmost to destroy her.

He held out his hand to Marianna.

"Come," he said; "I am sure we shall be good friends."

"And I, too, am sure," said the girl, as she placed her hand confidingly in his.

They left Buckingham House in this way, and at the gate was a carriage with four horses, and a couple of postilions.

Heron handed in Marianna, and then with a feeling of the most profound pity that the infirmities of old age in the ancient governess should be played upon by the King for his own base purposes he handed her into the carriage likewise.

Heron, as he seated himself opposite to Marianna and the old governess, was curious to know if the ancient lady could really hear a word he had to say, or was quite deaf.

He addressed the question to Marianna,

"Your governess is rather infirm?"

"Yes," replied the young girl; "and I cannot imagine of what service she is to be to me. I cannot talk to her. She mistakes all I say; and for the day and a-half that I have had her about me, I have been her nurse, but she has not been to me a governess."

"I should think not," thought Heron; and then he added, "Is she quite deaf?"

The girl laughed.

"If you bawl very loud into her ear, she can make out something of what you say."

"I will try."

Heron made a sign to the old lady that he wanted to speak to her; and she took a curiously shaped ear-trumpet from her pocket, and placed it at her ear.

"Madam!" bawled Heron.

"Eh?"

"Madam!"

"A madman?   You don't say so?"

"I am afraid she is a hopeless case," said Heron.

Marianna laughed like a happy child.

"That is the odd way in which she always answers me."

Heron was resolved to make another effort.

"I—have—not—the honour—to know—your —name."

"That's all the same," replied the old governess.

"That will do," said Heron, in a quiet tone. "I shall say no more."

He nodded to the old lady, who, with a nod of satisfaction in return, put her ear-trumpet into her pocket again.

"A very pleasant, conversible sort of man," she said, as she did so.

Heron could not help laughing in spite of himself.

"You see, Baron," said Marianna, "that I am not likely to benefit much from my governess."

"I think not.   But now, my dear girl, tell me one thing."

"Oh, yes!   What is it?"

"Have you no relations living?"

"Not one."

The eyes of poor Marianna filled with tears.

"I am," she added, "what they term a king's orphan; but—but I would rather be the poorest girl that ever worked for her livelihood than— than——"

"Than what, dear?"

"Oh, do not—do not!"

"Do not call me dear. He did so, and he wanted me to love him; but I do not love him, and I will not!"

Marianna, to the surprise of Heron, began scrubbing at one of her fair cheeks with her handkerchief as she spoke.

"Why do you do that, Marianna?"

"It is where he would kiss me."

"The King?"

"Yes. I feel as if I could never get it quite off."

Heron laughed.

"I don't think, my dear Marianna, that you need be under any further apprehension from the King."

"Why so?"

"You are now under my care."

"And will you protect me?"

"I will."

"On your word, on your honour, and as you love heaven?"

"On my word, on my honour, and as I love, and have hopes of, heaven, I will protect you from all possible injury, were he who would harm you the emperor of all the earth."

Marianna held out her hand to Heron, as, with the glow of joy upon her face, she said, "I am sure you will—I am quite sure you will, and I will let you, call me dear Marianna!"

"It is a privilege that I shall avail myself of," said Heron.

The old governess had gone fast asleep again.

With the motion of the carriage upon the rather unequal road, she jerked her head to and fro, something after the fashion of a mandarin of China.

The royal carriage had by this time performed about one-half of the journey to Hampton Court, and the four horses were just beginning the ascent of a hill when a pistol-shot startled Marianna.

She uttered a slight scream.

But the sound was too familiar a one to have much effect upon the well-drilled nerves of Felix Heron.

"Do not be alarmed," he said, as he took from his pocket a pair of pistols, and gave a hasty glance at the priming.

"Oh, what is it?"

Before Heron could make any reply the horses in the carriage came to a standstill, and a loud, harsh voice shouted, "Stand, at your peril!"

"What can this mean?" Heron asked of himself.   "Can it be possible that I am stopped by a highwayman?"

"What's the use of shooting a poor fellow like me?" cried one of the postilions.

"Keep your cattle still, or I will scatter your brains on the road-side!   Now, your money, or your life!   I am a desperate man!"

The windows of the carriage were up, but the "desperate man," as he called himself, broke away the glass instantly with the butt-end of a large horse-pistol, and then projected it into the coach.

"Your money, or your life!"

By the light from the carriage-lamp on that side, Heron could see that there was a mounted man, with a half-black crape visor on his face.

"Well, sir," said Heron, "and who are you?"

"Your money, watches, and jewellery! Quick, I say; for your lives, be ye whom ye may, hang upon a thread!"

"Stop a bit!" said Heron. "Who are you, sir?"

"I am Felix Heron, the well-known highwayman of Epping Forest!"

"Indeed!"

"Yes, and I say again that I have no time and no patience!"

"Nonsense," replied Heron, quietly. "This is the first time you have said any such thing."

"Quick—quick!"

"What for?"

"You will have it, then?"

"No."

Heron, with his left hand, coolly grasped the barrel of the pistol that was projected into the coach, and, with his right, he held one of his own pistols to the head of the highwayman.

The huge horse-pistol, that Heron held by the barrel, he turned so that, if it had been discharged, the bullet, or bullets, would have gone through the roof of the coach.

"Now, sir," he said, "it is my turn. What have you to say for your worthless life, liar as well as coward?"

The highwayman pulled the trigger of his pistol.

Fluff!

The powder in the pan only exploded, but the pistol itself missed fire.

"Just so," said Heron.   "Those great, ugly weapons are never to be depended upon   and now, sir, if you do not take off that mask, and let me see who you are, for I fancy I know your name, I will fire; and my pistols never miss, I can assure you."

The highwayman shook in every limb.

"Help me, gallant comrades!" he cried. "Come forward, and avenge me!"

"Well," said Heron, "I will wait a little for the gallant comrades; but I will shoot you all the same, if you do not lift your mask!"

Heron had slipped his hold from the barrel of the pistol that had missed fire to the cuff of the highwayman's coat, which, being very thick and ample, afforded him a capital grip.

Slowly the highwayman raised the half-crape mask.

Pale, haggard, and with his face livid, and seamed by care and by suffering, Heron, to his surprise, saw before him the features of Lord Warringdale!

CHAPTER CXCIX.

FELIX HERON CONQUERS LORD WARRINGDALE, AND PROCEEDS ON HIS JOURNEY TO HAMPTON COURT.

NOTHING in that way could probably have been a greater surprise to Felix Heron than the appearance of his bad half-brother, Lord Warringdale.

The statement of Jonathan Wild, on the occasion that he had called at Whitcombe House, that Warringdale was dead, had been so explicit that Heron had given perfect and complete credence to it.

It was something of a shock, however, to find him there, at the door of that carriage, with his pale, wan face full of alarm, and at the same time full of suspense.

"Do you know me?" said Warringdale, with an eager look.

"I do."

"Ah!"

"And you me, or you have lost your reason."

Felix Heron quite forgot, at the moment, what pains he had taken to disguise himself as the Baron Von Peck.

Warringdale looked at him anxiously, and then shook his head.

"No! no! I know you not! Let me go, and take your way in peace."

"But for one thing, I would."

"What is that, sir!"

"You say you are Felix Heron, of Epping Forest."

Warringdale was silent.

"How dare you assume the name of a brave man?"

"Let me go!"

"No, not till you have in as loud a voice as you made that lying assertion disclaimed it, and stated who you really are."

"Would you have me destroy myself?"

"I insist, without further argument, upon what I say, or I will lay you dead at your horse's feet."

There was a terrible earnestness about the manner of Heron, which let the terrified Lord Warringdale see that there was no escape.

In a high, cracked voice he called out, "I am not Felix Heron of Epping Forest, but I am——"

He paused there.

"Go on," said Heron.

"You say you know me."

"I do."

"Who am I, then? Do you really know that I am the highwayman called the Flying Captain?"

"I know no such thing; but I do know that you are to be recognised as Lord Warringdale, the half brother of the Earl of Whitcombe."

Warringdale groaned.

"Speak up man, or I fire."

"I am not Felix Heron, but I am Lord Warringdale, his half-brother."

"Now you may go," said Heron.

Warringdale galloped off to about a hundred feet from the coach, and then he drew the second pistol from the holster of his saddle, and fired it at the vehicle.

It was a chance shot, and the pistol did not miss fire.

The slugs with which it was loaded rattled about the roof of the coach.

Warringdale had levelled just a little too high.

"That was a foul and dastardly shot," said Heron.

Marianna looked very pale, but she neither swooned nor did she faint, as many young ladies of the present day would have done.

The ancient governess, thinking she heard some faint noise, put her ear-trumpet to her ear, and assumed an attitude of listening.

"Let him go!" said Heron, more to himself than to Marianna. "He is on the high road to destruction. Let him go!"

"Oh, I am so glad," said Marianna.

"Glad, my dear girl? At what?"

"That you did not kill that wretched man."

"You think him a wretched man?"

"Oh, yes—do not you? Did you not see his face?"

"I did, indeed, Marianna, and I agree with you that he is a wretched man. Postilions, drive on!"

"Yes, sir."

The four horses, who had had a rest, and who had just taken that sort of half-alarm that horses are so subject to on anything out of the way happening, started at a good hard trot up the hill.

Hampton Court was gained in another half-hour.

"Tell me, Marianna," said Heron, "do you know this place?"

"Not well; I have seen it. Do you live here, sir?"

"I am to do so, it seems. The King assigned me a suite of rooms in the Palace, and I suppose some one will be here to receive us, and tell us exactly where to go."

The royal carriage entered the precincts of Hampton Court by the route usually taken, where the cavalry barracks are situated, and it went on without opposition or question of any kind until it reached one of the old quadrangular court-yards of the palatial edifice.

Then the postilions came to a standstill with their horses.

A man stepped up to the side of the carriage, with a lantern in his hand.

"Do I address the Baron Von Peck?" he asked.

"Yes, I am that person."

"Then, sir, if you will alight with your party, and follow me, I will conduct you to your rooms."

Felix Heron sprung from the carriage, and assisted Marianna and the old deaf governess to alight, and then, with one on each arm, he followed the man with the lantern.

Up a broad flight of stone steps, across an ample corridor, and then through a suite of nobly proportioned rooms, their conductor led them, until he reached a door, in the lock of which was an ancient gilt key.

"This is the place, sir," he said.

He opened the door, and disclosed a room that, from the character of its appointments, and the profuse gilding that was upon its walls and ceiling, must have been the special abode of royalty at some time when the old Palace was in all its splendour and popularity.

A bright fire of logs burnt on the hearth.

A couple of tall candelabra, each with half-a-dozen wax lights, lit up the room, which, take it for all-in-all, was a very handsome sitting-room

"This, sir, is your room," said the guide; "and your bedroom is here."

He opened a gilt door, and disclosed a bed-chamber that looked as richly adorned as the sitting-room.

"Where is the accommodation for the two ladies?" asked Heron, somewhat impatiently.

"Their apartments sir, are three in number and they are further on."

"Pray lead the way."

The guide did so; and, after crossing two large rooms and a corridor, he ushered them into a pretty suite of three rooms, which were to be Marianna's and her governess's.

In one of those rooms sat a young woman reading by the light of a table-lamp.

She rose at the entrance of the visitors, and curtsied profoundly.

"This is the servant who will attend to the ladies," said the guide.

As the light fell upon the face of the young woman, Felix Heron thought he had seldom seen an expression of countenance that he liked less.

He had a strong feeling to her prejudice on the instant.

And it was well deserved.

Experience had told Felix Heron that these predilections of the mind for or against particular people were seldom wrong.

But it was evident the pure and unsophisticated mind of Marianna was well disposed to be pleased and charmed with all she saw.

To her, the old palatial home of the great Cardinal Wolsey was a place full of romantic and interesting associations.

She looked around her with the pleased expectation of each moment seeing a something more interesting still, and Heron sighed as he saw the young, ingenuous face lighted up with gratification.

"Oh!" she said; "I shall be so happy now."

"It is my earnest hope that you may be," replied Heron.

"I am sure," said the forbidding-looking young woman, "it will be the young lady's own fault if she is not."

Heron did not think it politic to make any reply to this too familiar speech; but lifting one of the sockets of the wax candelabrum that was nearest to him from its place along with its lighted candle, he said, "I will accompany you, Marianna, to the door of your room, if you please."

"Yes, sir."

The servant-girl looked rather sharply at Heron for a moment, as though she could not exactly make out what that was for; but then she nodded her head, as much as to say, "Oh, yes, that is all right."

She led the way.

Heron's object was to find out exactly where the chamber allotted to the young girl was situated, and to fix in his mind the precise route from his own apartments to it.

"This is the young lady's room," said the servant.

They had paused at the door that we have before mentioned, and now Marianna turned to Felix Heron, and, with a charming simplicity, held out her hand to him as she spoke.

"Good night, dear friend. I shall, I think, be up with the dawn, to take a walk in the dear, beautiful garden."

"Good night, Marianna," responded Heron, "and may happy dreams attend you."

The old, deaf governess trotted into the room after Marianna, and the servant followed them.

She gave Felix Heron what she intended should be a meaning look, as she so closed the door.

It was a look, however, to which he did not respond.

Heron's object now was to find out if Edith had reached Hampton Court in safety.

The evening was yet sufficiently young that he might, without exciting any particular surprise, walk about the old courts of the Palace.

In one of them he met one of the regular staff of domestics of the place, from whom he made the inquiry for the apartments of the old lady to whom Edith was to pay a visit.

He found that he was quite close to the part of the Palace he sought for under the cloisters, where he was directed to a brass-plate on a door, with the identical lady's name upon it.

In five minutes more Felix Heron was with Edith, who, without any cross accident, had reached the old Palace, and was received by Lady Castlenean's old friend with great joy and cordiality.

Edith took Heron aside for a moment.

"Felix, shall we make a confidant of my friend here?"

"Decide for yourself, dear Edith."

"Then I wish to do so."

"Let it be done, then, at once. But to what extent?"

"All! Tell her all!"

The old lady was quite delighted to find that the supposed Baron Von Peck was no other than the real Earl of Whitcombe; but when they both came to tell her the occasion, strange as it was, of their presence at Hampton Court, she trembled excessively.

"Alas! alas!" she exclaimed. "Another?"

"Another what?" asked Heron, anxiously.

"Another tragedy!"

"Tragedy?"

"Yes. This is not the first young creature who has been brought here with such intentions!"

"Is that possible?"

"It is. I will tell you. Come to the window, which looks out into the court with what is called the Cardinal's Fountain in the centre."

From the window of the old lady's sitting-room they could just dimly see the outline of the fountain in the court.

The pipes and apparatus, that at one time had kept it in action, had long since gone to decay.

The fountain no longer sent up

"It's loosened silver to the sun."

Rank weeds and mosses had made their home in its beautifully-sculptured basin, and the whole court-yard was indeed a picture of decay and neglect.

The old lady put out the light in the room, and they then saw into the court-yard better, and avoided themselves the observation of any busy-bodies who might be about the building.

"You see," she said, "that window up above the bust of the Roman Emperor?"

"Yes," responded Edith and Heron.

"Well, one night, at about the hour of twelve, when, from severe indisposition, I was unable to sleep, I came to this casement where we are now, and my eyes fell on that window there."

Both Heron and Edith regarded the window with a feeling of great interest that they could not well define.

THE BARON VON PECK MAKES A FORTUNATE DISCOVERY IN THE OLD
PALACE OF HAMPTON COURT.

Presented Gratis with No. 61, of the New Edition of EDITH HERON, the Sequel to Edith the Captive; or, the Robbers of Epping Forest.

The old lady continued.

"You see that it is quite dark now; and, though upwards of four years have expired since that night, I have never seen again a light there!"

"The circumstance," said Heron, "whatever it is, affects you much. Do not, if it creates distress, tell it to us."

"Yes, yes; I feel that I ought. As I looked at it on that night, there came suddenly a light reflected from it!"

As if the old lady's words had been the magic spell to conjure up the light she had mentioned, there spread at that moment over the window from within a faint light!

The old lady started.

"Good heavens! What does that mean? A light?"

"It is a light!" said Edith.

The light slowly increased in brilliancy, until it was tolerably evident that the room to which that casement belonged must be well illuminated from within.

It seemed as if this gradual lighting up of the apartment had been the result of one candle after another being ignited, until there was a sufficiency for any purpose.

While the process was evidently going on the old lady was silent.

Edith and Heron, too, looked on with great interest and curiosity.

The blind of the window was down, but still the lights from within shone through it, making a dim sort of twilight in the court beneath where the reflection fell.

In a few seconds the shadow of a head and face was projected on the surface of the blind.

CHAPTER CO.

THE INTEREST OF THE NIGHT AT HAMPTON COURT BECOMES DEEP AND INTENSE.

THIS most unexpected appearance of a light in the window of the room to which the old lady had alluded, so overcame her that it was doubtful if she would be able to continue her story.

"Can it be—can it be," she cried, "that the past is coming back again?"

"Compose yourself, I pray you," said Heron, "and let us know what that past was."

"I will try."

"Yes," said Edith, "I feel now that I would fain know that; if I do not, curiosity will keep me wakeful this night more than fear or hope."

"Oh, Edith, look!" cried Heron.

"What?—what?"

"The shadow on the blind! I know it well now."

"You do, Felix?"

"Yes, it is the beautiful likeness in outline of Marianna!"

The seeming mystery of the light was explained.

That chamber from which it showed was the one allotted to Marianna and her governess.

In the complications and intricacies of the vast building, Felix Heron was not aware until then that he had reached the court into which that chamber looked.

But now he had no doubt of it.

The shadowy and beautiful outline of the fair girl was before him on the blind.

"Look, Edith—look!"

"Yes, Felix."

"That is the dear Marianna!"

Edith did look with interest, and she could guess, from the graceful curve of the head and neck, that the description Heron had briefly given her of the young "king's orphan" was by no means overdrawn.

The old lady then spoke faintly.

"This is a coincidence that is terrible to think of!"

"Then what you have to relate has reference to some such an affair as the present?"

"It has, indeed!"

"There is all the more reason, then," said Edith, "that we should know it at once."

"You shall—you shall. It was, as I have said, about the hour of midnight; and even as we all see it now, there came a light into that room, but it was a faint one, and only such as might be produced by some person entering it with a lighted candle."

"On the blind, too, as we see it now, was the shadowy reflection of a face and head."

"Like that?" asked Edith.

"No; it was the face and head of a man."

"Did you know it, as I know the shadowy likeness of that young girl?" asked Heron.

The old lady was silent for a few seconds, and then she said, "As I may have been mistaken, I pray that you will not ask me who I thought the shadow on the window-blind represented."

From his experience, however, of the last four-and-twenty hours, Felix Heron had no real difficulty in guessing who the shadow on the blind of that room in Hampton Court Palace had exhibited.

He felt, however, that it would be unfair to press the question, and he forbore from doing so.

The old lady, with a deep sigh, added the following words:—"I would that I had at that moment left this window and sought my rest—rest which it was many a long night before I again knew in its unbroken serenity."

"There!" cried Edith; "the light has gone!"

"Not wholly," said Heron.

It had not, indeed, gone wholly, but it seemed as if a number of the wax-lights that had illuminated the room were suddenly put out.

But a faint radiance remained.

"It was some such a light as is there now," added the old lady, "that I was looking at from this window, when I heard one fearful shriek from some one in yonder room, and in another moment the casement was dashed open, and right out, head foremost, into the court-yard below, a figure in white drapery precipitated itself!"

"Good heaven!" ejaculated Edith.

"I heard the fall—the sickening crash with which the figure fell upon the stone pavement!"

"Oh, horrible!"

"I shall never forgot it!"

The old lady shook as if in an ague.

"Tell us no more," said Felix Heron; "the recollection is too much for you."

"Nay, I have told the worst. Let me now tell all. There was a general alarm through the whole Palace, for the one shriek that had been uttered previous to the window being flung open was echoed by my screams, which, had I had all the inclination in the world so to do, I could not control!"

"And—and—the figure?"

"When lights were brought it was found that a dead body lay in the court!

"Killed!

"By that terrible sickening fall. It was a young and beautiful girl, not above sixteen years of age, in her night-dress, who lay there with her blood about her!"

"And the man?"

"What man?"

"The shadow that you saw."

"No one was ever found. The room in which the young girl had slept was carefully searched, and nothing was found that could implicate any one."

"There was surely an inquiry?"

"Yes; but nothing came of it further than the supposition that in her sleep, or in some paroxysm of fear from some dream, the young creature had opened the window and cast herself out."

"But you——"

"I know what you would say—I knew that a man was in the chamber. I did, but the shock of the occurrence laid me on a bed of sickness for many weeks; and, when I recovered, the whole affair was past and over, and the poor young thing rested in peace in the little churchyard of the village."

Heron paced the room twice.

It was an action he was in the habit of doing when much moved.

"This is, indeed," said Edith, "a terrible story!"

"So terrible a one," added Heron, "that I will stake my life it shall not occur again to-night!"

"Do not take from me the short space of life that remains to me," cried the old lady, "by such a supposition as the possibility of such another tragedy!"

"No, madam; rest in peace. Such another tragedy I am here for the express purpose of preventing; and, with the help of heaven, I will prevent it!"

"And I, too," said Edith. "I must and will help you, Felix!"

"Remain, then, here, Edith, and you will be on the alert to offer a shelter to Marianna. Hark! What hour is that?"

It was ten o'clock only.

But Marianna had retired to rest, and Felix Heron felt the necessity of being in the rooms that had been appropriated to his use, for fear the King, or some one from him, should arrive at the old Palace.

"Fear nothing, dear Edith," he said; "nor you, madam. I will protect Marianna. By the by, did you ever discover who the poor girl was who perished so tragically?"

"I forget the name; but she was what is called a 'king's orphan.'"

It sent a cold chill to the heart of Heron to find so strong a similarity between the case of the dead victim and Marianna.

Heron was apt to turn pale when his feelings were strongly acted upon, and he did so now, as he left a kiss upon the brow of Edith.

"You will hear of me to-night, Edith," he said.

"Be cautious, Felix."

"Yes, and resolute!"

Felix Heron left the suite of apartments in which this conversation had taken place, and made his way across the court-yard towards his own rooms; but he was not yet sufficiently well acquainted with all the intricacies of Hampton Court to find the route easily.

He got bewildered among the courts, and cloisters, and corridors.

And as he got bewildered, he became terribly anxious about Marianna.

He feared that there would be no one to ask to guide him, and he was about to try to make his way to the court-yard with the silent fountain, when he saw a moving shadow on the wall that was nearest to him.

The presence of the shadow argued that of the substance not far off.

Heron called out aloud, "Who goes there?"

"I, the King's servant," replied a voice hastily, and a man emerged from one of the old gateways.

"Can you direct me to the rooms of the Baron Von Peck?"

"You are the Baron, sir?"

"I am."

"And you have lost your way, sir, among all these old courts and cloisters?"

"I have."

"That is easily done now; but fortunately, it is easy for me to put you right, as I know every nook and corner of the place."

"I shall be obliged to you."

"Follow me, Baron."

Felix Heron kept tolerably close to this man, and in a very few minutes he found himself at the doorway which would lead him to his rooms.

"Now," he said, "I know where I am."

"Exactly, Baron. Hem!"

The man lingered.

It was evident that he wished to say something, and Heron, under all the circumstances that surrounded him, was anxious to know what it was.

"You wish to speak?"

"Yes, Baron."

"Say on. What is it?"

"I am aware, sir, you are in the confidence of a certain person."

"You mean the K——"

"Hush! We always call him a certain person here. I, too, am in his confidence; and what I wanted to make bold to ask you, Baron, was, if you could tell me at what hour he would be here to-night?"

The sensation that came over Felix Heron at this complete confirmation of his supposition that even that night would not be allowed to pass over without the presence of the King at Hampton Court, in pursuit of the destruction of Marianna, was sickening.

For a few moments he did not reply.

"I beg your pardon, Baron," added the man, "if my question seems to you to be indiscreet."

"No, no!"

"Then I should be glad to know."

"I cannot tell you."

"It will be at about twelve, then, sir."

"Perhaps."

It was with the greatest difficulty that Heron could keep his hands off this fellow. He would have enjoyed much throwing him into the lake that was close at hand.

But such a course was not to be thought of.

If anything in the world more than another would be calculated to prevent him, Heron, from being of service to Marianna, it would be a premature exhibition of his state of feeling on the subject.

So Felix Heron was decided, and said no more.

He was soon in his own apartments, as they might be called, and there he strove to think what course, now that he knew the localities and the position of the room in the occupation of Marianna, it would be best to adopt.

But he could come to no safe conclusion.

He wanted more information.

Would the King come to him?

Or would he try to obtain access to the chamber of the young orphan first?

That was the question.

In his own mind, Heron decided it on the first supposition; for, otherwise, what would have been the benefit of having him as an assumed accomplice down there, at Hampton Court, at all.

But Heron could feel certain of nothing, situated as he was, and he passed an hour of feverish anxiety.

Then he took one of the wax-lights, and bethought him that he would reconnoitre the route between his rooms and those in the occupation of Marianna.

His intention was to reach the door through which he had seen the young girl go, and there listen for awhile, to be sure that all was still and serene.

Treading as lightly as foot could fall, he sallied out into the long corridor.

He held the light above his head, so as to avail himself of the greatest portion of illumination from it he could.

And so, in that old and memory-haunted Palace of the haughty Wolsey, Felix Heron softly trod.

Hush!

What is that?

A confused rumbling noise, as if something, or some one, had fallen down a staircase.

Heron paused to listen.

Could it be that that place was haunted with the spirits of those who, in old times, had played so busy a part in the ancient halls and apartments of the great prelate's Palace.

A strange, cold shudder came across Felix Heron as he mentally asked himself such a question.

But he was not superstitious.

Soon the prejudices of early life, which, for a moment, had gained an ascendancy over him, gave way before the light of reason.

Heron could then have smiled at the idea of diznal, who had once called that royal pile haunting it by

" The glimpses of the pale moon."

But there could be no question about the noise he had heard. The only query was, what caused it?

And as Heron stopped to listen if it should be repeated, he heard again a strange sound.

This time it was like the clash of arms, and it sounded as if not further off than the foot of a dim old flight of oaken stairs, on the top of which he, Heron, stood.

His curiosity was greatly excited, but he would not allow its gratification to interfere with the object of his migration from his own rooms.

That object was to seek the chamber-door of Marianna.

But an unexpected difficulty presented itself.

The appearance of the various corridors, doors, and staircases seemed to have altered since he last observed them, and Heron was compelled to admit to himself that he had taken some wrong route.

This was both provoking and perplexing in the extreme.

Hastily retracing his steps, he crossed two rooms, one of which was an ancient bed-chamber, with one of those old, tall, four-post bedsteads of polished oak in which our ancestors delighted, and in which, notwithstanding changes of fashion have proscribed them, one thing is quite clear, which is, that they slept well.

Heron then felt certain he had left one of those rooms by a wrong door.

He was puzzled, however, to find the only other door fast locked.

And yet he was quite certain that that fast-locked door was the identical one through which he had passed with the young girl when she went to her own rooms.

What did it mean?

Was that door locked on purpose?

On purpose to baffle him?

It looked like it.

Felix Heron, however, was not exactly the man to allow a locked door to stand in his way.

He had with him a weapon which he never used either for offence or defence; it was a dagger, with a long triangular-shaped blade of exquisite steel, and of amazing strength and tenacity.

That it would answer all the purposes of a formidable crowbar Heron was well aware.

It would be a strong lock, indeed, that could resist the force he was able to bring to bear upon it with that pionard.

The locks in the interior of the old Palace were large and showy, but not strong.

One wrench with the triangular-shaped poniard, and a portion of the gilt lock flew off.

Crash went the remainder.

Heron paused to let the noise that he had necessarily made subside.

Then another effort opened the door, and he was able, without further opposition, to step lightly and quietly through to a passage beyond.

CHAPTER CCI.

FELIX HERON MEETS WITH SINGULAR ADVENTURES AT HAMPTON COURT.

Yes, he was right now.

He saw before him the direct route to the rooms in the occupation of Marianna.

He heard a clock strike eleven.

If the King's hour was twelve, he, Heron, had plenty of time yet before him for his explorations in the ancient building.

From what that, no doubt, confidential servant, who was in so suspicious a manner lurking about the Palace had said, Heron had every reason to suppose that the midnight hour was the one pitched upon for the arrival of the King.

But still Heron felt full of anxiety.

He got into that most uncomfortable, nervous condition when the sense of hearing seems to be preternaturally acute, and every sound, far and near, strikes with a jar upon the senses.

A very few steps now took him to the door of Marianna's room.

There he listened.

No! All was still!

No alarm!

Not even the slightest sound, indicative of a disturbed rest on the part of the fair sleeper.

That chamber might have been the chamber of

the dead, so far as regarded any sound coming from it indicative of breathing, living existence.

"Rest in peace," said Heron.

He turned away from the door.

As he did so, he started back, and nearly struck heavily against its panels.

The sudden flash of a beam or pencil of light, such as the children produce with a looking-glass, and call "Jack o' Dandy," came across his eyes.

It was gone as soon as seen.

Like lightning.

Ere you could say, "Behold!" it vanished.

But Heron was quite certain such a phenomenon had presented itself, and was no delusion of the imagination.

What could it be?

And where could it be?

He kept profoundly still in the position he occupied close to Marianna's door, and he listened with all that painful acuteness we have remarked upon.

He heard something.

It was like a footstep.

A footstep marching with a slow, measured step, but where it was he could not by any means determine.

Then, as he still listened, and still heard it, he was tolerably sure that it approached him.

The sound, however, was muffled, as though some wall or door intervened between him and the full expression of it; and from the peculiarity of it now, Heron thought that it proceeded from some one ascending the stairs.

Just before him—that is to say, about twelve paces from the door of Marianna's chamber—there was a flight of steps that conducted to one of the corridors below.

Now the sound that came upon the attentive ears of Felix Heron was exactly as if some one was ascending those steps within his observation.

A large window that looked clear out into the open air in day-time shed abundance of light on to that staircase, and even at that hour of the night sufficient reflected light from the night sky came in by that window to let Heron see that, most incontestably, the stairs were vacant.

No form could be ascending them towards where he stood without looking more black and bulky than the mere night air.

And yet he heard the foot-falls plainly enough.

Nearer and nearer!

Plainer and plainer!

Here was food for superstition.

But Heron only kept on his guard, and strained his eyes into the darkness.

Possibly that very straining of the vision might, in a short time, have conjured up some seeming form on those dim stairs, had it continued much longer.

But it did not.

Heron was instantly startled from his attitude of looking and listening by the perceptible shaking of a panel of the wall, not three feet from where he stood.

To and fro!

To and fro, with an impatient, tottering sound, the panel shook!

Then he thought he heard, and he was pretty sure he did hear it, and it was not a mere thought, a voice mutter something on the other side of the panel.

What the voice said he could not gather.

Gently, though, and quietly, the footsteps on the staircase began to retreat and fade away.

Heron, by, as the saying is, "putting this and that together," came now to something like a rational opinion on the whole matter.

There was behind the panelling of the wall of the staircase another secret staircase, which no doubt formed, in substance, the end in that direction of the steps that were open and visible to all eyes.

The panel which had been shaken from the other side was some mode of exit on to the landing, which the person who had ascended the secret flight of stairs had not found the way to open, and so had retreated.

The human voice which had struck inarticulately on his, Heron's, ears was no doubt an expression of disappointment on that occasion.

Such was the theory, in regard to the whole transaction, that Felix Heron got up in his own mind.

It was a rational one.

A very few moments decided him as to the course he would like to pursue.

He would try the panel on the side he was on, and discover the secret stairs, which might be exceedingly useful both to him and to the fair Marianna.

The panel which had been shaken was not above two feet wide, but it was upwards of twelve feet in height. Indeed, it looked so narrow, on account of its height, that Heron almost doubted if any one, of ordinary dimensions, could pass through it.

That, however, was merely a delusion of the eyes.

There was, in reality, ample space.

Heron felt the panel carefully.

No!

Not the vestige of any fastening or spring could be found.

His triangular-bladed poniard would be wanted again.

Stop!

What is this?

A moulding runs the whole height of the panel, which is so contrived that it affords a good hold to the fingers.

Heron presses laterally upon it.

With ease the panel glides open.

It runs in a parallel fashion with the thickness of the wall, of which it seems to form a part.

There is no fastening.

The panel wholly depends for its security on the fact of its existence being kept secret.

How dark!

How absolutely black appears the space immediately beyond it!

Well might Heron hesitate before he adventures a step farther in that direction.

And yet he feels certain there is a staircase there, and that it runs down by the side of the open steps, with only the wainscot-wall between them.

He makes a cautious move.

Yes, he finds something to stand upon, but it feels soft.

Involuntarily Felix Heron recoils.

It is but for a moment.

The soft substance on which he has trodden is dust.

The accumulated dust of many years; and now he feels that he is breathing it—that it is attacking his eyes—his nostrils—that, in fact, that secret staircase possesses a complete atmosphere of it.

Heron draws back.

He waits until the cloud of dust has, in some degree, subsided; then, with his handkerchief tied

over his mouth, to keep it out so far as possible, and to filter the air as he breathes it, he commences the descent of the secret stairs.

They are narrow.

The walls on each side are scarcely at half-arm's length; but the supposition that this secret flight of steps is formed from the actual ends of the open staircase, merely cut off by the wall partition, is in Heron's mind confirmed.

He counted the steps.

There were twenty-four.

Then he came to a stand-still.

At the foot of them was nothing but plain, abrupt woodwork, in the manner of a panelled wall.

It took Heron some time before he could find an opening, and then he found it all at once.

Another sliding panel—only in this case it sunk right down perpendicularly—yielded to an accidental touch.

EDITH.—No. 62.

Beyond was what appeared to be a vast open space.

But Heron felt quite certain it was not the open air into which he looked.

The stillness of the atmosphere, as well as its temperature, forbade that notion.

But, as he looked, the darkness seemed to be dissipating; and, but that it was by far too soon to expect such a thing to happen, Heron would have thought that it was the rapidly approaching dawn of a new day he was watching.

Slowly and gradually the soft light increased, and he could see into a hall of large dimensions.

Tall, stained glass windows were let into the walls at regular intervals, and upon the spaces between hung arms and armour of all sorts and ages.

In niches, too, and on pedestals, were the effigies of men-at-arms and knights of the me-d several times, bearing pole-axes, or spears, as their rank required.

Then Heron knew that he was in Wolsey's banqueting hall, where the great Lord Cardinal feasted like a king.

But, as he looked, the light grew stronger.

One of the stained-glass windows was projected in a symmetrical shadow on the floor.

Heron then saw that it was to a newly-risen moon that he was indebted for the light around him.

He was about to step forth into the old hall.

He pauses.

The blood seems, for a moment, to stop about his heart.

Can he believe his eyes?

One of the effigies of the men-at-arms moves.

One of those false representations of old times is actually in motion.

The long halberd shakes. The cold moonbeams shift upon the helmet with its iron-barred visor.

The figure slowly steps from a short kind of pedestal, on which it had stood grim and still, and slowly walks across the reflection of the painted window on the floor of the great hall.

Felix Heron feels no terror.

He is not perplexed with alarm, but he owns to himself at the moment that he has never been so surprised in all his life before.

He can make nothing of it!

No rational supposition can aid him at the moment in coming to any conclusion in regard to the phenomenon, except that it is supernatural.

Slowly—very slowly—the figure moves on.

Heron is half in the mind to sally forth and question it.

To sally forth, and intercept it in its slow and stately march across that moon-lighted floor.

But a new phenomenon, and one that causes him to shrink back, presents itself.

As the figure passes over the reflected appearance of the painted window on the old oaken floor, he has a good opportunity of looking at it.

Of looking at it well.

What does he see?

The figure is tall.

Tall above the ordinary height of men.

The helmet, and the face, and the head are there.

But there is no neck!

Something—he cannot tell what it is—but it is something stern and rigid—holds up the head at a height of about two feet from the body!

And in this manner the figure takes its way slowly over the floor of the hall!

Heron watched it with his eyes.

It disappeared in the gloom at the further end of the hall, and the last he saw of it was the faint gleam of the moonlight upon the elevated helmet upon the elevated head.

Then Heron rushed into the hall.

"Hold! hold!" he cried. "If you be mortal, turn and face me! If immortal, say why it is that you haunt these bygone halls! Speak—oh, speak!"

His own voice echoing among the dust-covered banners overhead was the only response.

He had, to all appearance, Wolsey's great banqueting hall solely to himself.

But Heron could not help now looking with equal suspicion upon the other effigies of men-at-arms and knights of the period of King Henry the Eighth by which he was surrounded.

Were they, too, capable of stepping from their niches and their pedestals, and moving, in slow and stately fashion, across the ancient hall?

He stepped up to one of them.

He felt the face.

All wood!

Nothing but wood!

The feet—the hands.

All wood!

And yet had he not seen one of them step down and walk away?

And was there not the empty pedestal from which he had stepped?

It would be a curious thing to revisit that hall in the open daylight, and see if that one had returned to its pedestal.

Heron made up his mind, come what come might, to do so without fail.

But now he hears the Palace clock.

It chimes the three-quarters past eleven.

A feeling of anxiety takes possession of Heron's mind to get back to the rooms that had been assigned to him as the Baron Von Peck.

The King might come at twelve.

Hark!

The rattle—the roll of carriage wheels sounds on the old stones of one of the court-yards.

It might be the King!

Heron hastily left the haunted banqueting hall—for such must be the character it bears in his mind—and made the best of his way back to the rooms he had so recently left.

He went by the secret doors and the secret stairs, closing both the doors after him.

Only for one passing moment he paused at the door of Marianna's chamber to listen.

All was still.

Then he passed on, and reached his own sitting-room.

It was a relief to him, after what he had since heard in Wolsey's Hall, to seat himself in peace by the log fire that burnt cheerfully on the hearth.

But Heron was not left long to himself, or to his own reflection. A tap came at his door.

"Come in."

The man who had directed him from the garden to his rooms appeared.

"A gentleman, Baron, will call to see you."

Heron rose.

A figure in a camlet-cloak entered the room, and the man who had announced the "gentleman" softly closed the door behind it.

The figure cast off the cloak.

"Well, Baron, you are snugly housed here!"

It was the King.

"I am, your Majesty."

"And your fair charge? Is she quite well?"

"I hope so."

"Ah! and so do we—and so do we. Well, Baron, we are always grateful for good service."

Heron bowed.

The King flung himself into a chair by the fireside, and rubbed his hands together, as though he were cold.

"I had some thought, Baron, of making a royal residence of Hampton Court again, but it is far from town."

"It is."

"And Kew is handier."

"I should presume so."

"Yes, this place is so immense, that it would require a little army of domestics to people it; and our Parliament might grudge the few hundred thousands required to make it habitable for us, so we give it up."

"Yes, your Majesty."

The King gave a kick to some of the half-consumed wood on the hearth.

A bright flame shot up.

"Well, Baron, and what is your opinion of our royal orphan?"

"She is very beautiful."

"Ah!"

"She is very good, too, I think."

"Eh?"

"I said good. I mean virtuous and pure-minded,—one of those gentle English girls into whose innocent mind no thought of evil has ever strayed."

"Oh!"

The King kicked another bit of wood.

"And so that is your opinion, Baron?"

"It is, your Majesty."

"Well, it is ours, too."

"And yet——"

"Eh?"

The King turned half-round upon his chair, and looked at Heron in suspense.

"Pray, go on, Baron. What extraordinary thing was it you were about to say to us, with such a tone and such a look?"

"I was about to say, that if your Majesty thought of the destruction of one so innocent——"

"Baron, are you mad?"

"I hope not."

"Well, we will condescend to explain. Do you think that we would take one tithe of the trouble, or that it would be necessary to take it, for any one who was not innocent? Why, what on earth do I want with those who are in *my way* at all hours of the day? No, Baron. You have mentioned the one charm that Marianna possesses above even her wondrous beauty, and that is her innocence!"

A glow of indignation was upon the cheek of Heron as he bowed, for he could not trust himself to speak in reply to those degrading and despicable words of the King.

"Well, Baron, I am disappointed in you!"

"In me?"

"Yes."

"And may I ask why?"

"You are not such a man of the world as I thought you, Baron."

"Perhaps I did not quite comprehend your Majesty?"

"Oh, pho, pho!"

The King rose.

Felix Heron felt his breath come short and thick as he looked at the King, and wondered what would be the events of the next half-hour.

The King took a small key from his pocket.

"Baron, I am about to let you into one of the secrets of the old Palace of Hampton Court."

———

CHAPTER CCII.

THE MYSTERY OF THE APPARITION IN WOLSEY'S BANQUETING HALL IS SOLVED TO FELIX HERON.

HERON could only hope to preserve his temper and equanimity during the conversation with royalty from reminding himself that it was for a purpose that he endured it

But for that purpose which, in good truth, comprised the safety of the innocent and fair Marianna, he must have broken forth and declared his true opinion of the atrocious principles set forth by his Majesty.

But he kept his thoughts to himself.

It required an effort of self-control, but yet he succeeded.

"You see, Baron," added the King, "I have a small key here."

"I do see."

"Well, it is the passport to the arms of Marianna."

"Her arms?"

"Yes. I admit that she is not well disposed to my suit; but what then? This Palace is large, and I flatter myself that a scream will reach no other ears but yours."

Heron could not speak.

He felt as though his heart was swelling nigh to bursting.

"And that," added the King, "will, of course, be of no consequence. Now, Baron, you are tall, and you look strong. I daresay you are a tolerable master of fence?"

"I can use a sword."

"I thought so; and, although you are past the prime of life, one can see no symptoms of decrepitude in you."

"I am happy to say I feel none."

"Good—good!"

Heron was still rather at a loss to imagine what was the kind of service the King expected of him; but he was not for long left to conjecture.

"You will then, Baron, take your station outside the door of Marianna's chamber:"

"I?—I?"

"Yes. And you will have no scruple—for men like you have none—in taking the life of any one who may be rash enough to interfere with us."

"When? How?"

"Baron!"

"Your Majesty!"

The King spoke drily.

"I was about to remark, Baron, that your manner and tone towards us was not quite respectful."

"I have never changed in the feelings I entertain for your Majesty, I assure you."

"Well, well, let it pass. We have no objection to a little genuine bluntness. You will, then, Baron, be so good as to make free use of your sword upon any one who shall attempt to force your post to-night."

"Which post is at the chamber-door of Marianna?"

"You have said it."

As he spoke, the King took from a pocket of his coat a rolled up mask of black silk.

This mask was so well contrived that, by means of some elastic bands that went behind the head, it could be fitted very accurately to the face—fitting, in fact, into the features, so as to be a most perfect and complete disguise to any one who might wear it.

Heron looked upon it with a shudder!

The King fitted it on.

He looked hideous!

"When the fair Marianna makes her complaint in the morning," he said, "we think she will have some difficulty in giving a name to her assailant. Ha, ha!"

The laugh was infernal.

"Baron!"

"Yes."

"Well, you are a blunt fellow, I must say; but now you will be so good as to go by the regular route, and take up your post at Marianna's door."

"And your Majesty?"

The King laughed again.

"We have our own route to that chamber."

As he spoke, he held up the little key.

Heron then felt convinced of what he had already surmised; namely, that the King knew of some secret route to the sleeping-room of Marianna.

It was equally evident, too, that that secret route was not about to be communicated to him, Heron; for the King, although he held up the key, turned neither to the right nor to the left, but still faced the wood fire.

Heron could do nothing but obey.

Or, rather, he had no resource but to seem to obey.

"Your Majesty," he said, "will allow me a few minutes' time to find the way?"

"Oh, take your time."

"I ask it for a reason."

"Ah! a reason?"

"Yes, your Majesty. A mysterious occurrence has taken place in the Palace since my arrival!"

"What?—what?"

"I do not know if it forebodes danger or not."

"For the love of heaven, Baron, out with it! What is it?"

"As I was crossing one of the court-yards in which there is a fountain—which, however, is silent——"

"Ah!"

The King shook a little.

Heron continued.

"A shadowy form came out of the cloistered walk that was round the court-yard. It looked feminine in its aspect; and, as far as I could judge, I should say it had the appearance of a young girl——"

"No, no!"

"Yes, your Majesty; in her night-clothes!"

"Impossible!"

"So I am inclined to think, because I am not one who is ever over-hasty in referring appearances that may, after all, be natural, to the supernatural."

"Well, well? What—what next?"

"I approached the figure, and, as the moon at that moment shone out, I saw it plainly."

"Plainly?"

"Too plainly!"

Felix Heron was resolved, by this made-up story, to see what effect he could produce upon the imagination and the fears of the bad King.

The reader will see that Heron based his pretended narrative upon that terrible episode of the court-yard, that had been related by the old lady with whom Edith was staying.

And the King was really alarmed.

He took off the black mask, and looked with terrified eyes in the face of Heron.

"What—what then?"

"What surprised me, your Majesty, was that the figure was so transparent I could see through it the old groined arches of the court, and yet at the same time the figure had a sufficiently palpable outline."

"What did it do? What did it say—if—if anything?"

"It said nothing."

The King was evidently glad to hear that, for he drew a long breath of relief.

"It moved from out of the shadow of the cloistered walk, and it pointed to a particular slab on the paved court; and then it slowly, as though it had done all it wished to do. and had performed its mission on earth, faded away, and appeared to mingle with the moonbeams."

The King was visibly disturbed.

With the black mask crumpled up in his hand along with the small key he had produced, he paced the chamber to and fro twice in its entire length.

As he so paced it, Heron heard him muttering to himself disjointed sentences.

"No, no! It cannot be—it is not possible; and, besides, it can never happen again, for the gilt bars that I have had put to the inside of that particular window. It is no warning on that account; and yet—yet it disturbs me. Baron!"

"Your Majesty."

"Have you mentioned this to any one but us?"

"Not to a soul!"

"That is well—that is well!"

There was wine upon the table; although, how it came there, Heron knew not. unless it were there placed while he was pursuing his explorations in the old banqueting hall of the Cardinal.

There it was, however, and the King poured himself out a good bumper, and drank it off.

"My own prime Burgundy," he said.

No doubt the attendant, who was on the alert in and about the Palace, had placed the King's favourite wine on that table specially for him.

The colour came back to the pallid face of the King.

"Baron," he said, "a thousand ghosts shall not deter me from the expedition of to-night! Marianna's beauty is a something for the fancy to run riot upon! I never, in all my life, looked upon her like."

"She is, in truth, most beautiful!"

"Oh, lovely, lovely; and in the first fresh bloom, too, of her radiant youth! Baron, to your duty. Love invites us, and we obey the call!"

"I am but strange to this place," said Heron, "will your Majesty give me five minutes to find Marianna's chamber door?"

"Ten—ten!"

Heron left the room.

"This way, sir!"

Heron started.

Exactly on the threshold was that troublesome and obsequious servant.

"What way?"

"This is the way to the young lady's chamber door, sir."

"I know it."

"But I will keep you company, sir."

"I think not, unless I come down stairs and stay with you, scoundrel!"

Heron, with one straightforward blow, sent the fellow right down the staircase to the corridor below, and the fall was so rapid that it made very little noise, and there lay the man like a corpse.

Perhaps he was one.

That little action was a great relief to Heron, as it allowed him to feel that he had got rid by it of the pent-up wrath in his bosom.

Without bestowing another glance at the discomfited King's confidential servant, he made his way, as fast as he could go, to Marianna's chamber door.

"Ten minutes," he said to himself. "The King said ten minutes."

He rapped at the door.

Tap, tap, tap!"

THE BARON VON PECK RESCUES MARIANNA FROM A POSITION OF
GREAT DANGER.

Presented Gratis with No. 62, of the New Edition of EDITH HERON, the Sequel to Edith the Captive; or, the Robbers of Epping Forest.

"Marianna! Marianna! It is I! Open! Open! What shall I say to you, to make you know that I come to save you? Open, open, open!"

There was no reply.

No movement in the room.

Heron got desperate.

He shook the door.

"Marianna! Marianna!"

This time he had placed his lips close to the key-hole, and had called in a shriller voice.

The young sleep sound; but the girl was awakened from her innocent slumbers.

Heron heard her cry out.

It was a cry of alarm.

"Marianna," he added, "open the door, and you will be saved! Quick—quick! I am your friend—your only one now!"

The door was flung open.

The young and beautiful Marianna appeared in her night-dress.

"Oh! what is it?"

"Fling some garment over you, and come with me, or you are lost!"

"Is it fire?"

"No. Worse!"

"Murder?"

"Worse—worse!"

"Oh, heaven, protect me!"

Marianna hastily slipped her arms into the sleeves of a velvet cloak trimmed with sable, and ran out of the chamber, and clung to the arm of, as she thought, the Baron Von Peck.

"Will you trust me, Marianna?"

"With all my heart!"

"Come, then; and if I deceive you, may heaven in my utmost need desert me!"

Heron at once turned to the secret sliding panel in the wall, at the top of the staircase, that he had so recently and so providentially discovered, and dashed it aside.

"This way, Marianna—this way, and fear nothing. Oh, what is this?"

Marianna uttered a cry.

Felix Heron was astonished.

The moment he slid aside the secret panel, there fell headlong to his feet the very apparition of the armed man he had seen in Wolsey's banqueting hall!

The man-at-arms, with the head and helmet perched on the top of some slender apology for a neck, two feet or more in length!

A night light, that burnt on a gilt bracket in Marianna's room, lent sufficient light for Heron to recognise the terrible apparition.

The head now rolled off!

It was only on the iron spike at the end of a lance!

The body, without a head, and with a half coat of mail and huge buff boots, rolled on the floor, and the legs kicked vigorously!

The thing was a mystery; but that it was a thing of flesh, and blood, and bone, Felix Heron felt assured from a couple of smart kicks he got.

"Speak!" he cried. "Who and what are you?"

"It's me, Captain!"

"Eh?"

"Me!"

"Who is me?"

"Tom—Tom! Oh, gracious, Captain! don't you know Tom Ripon? That will do! I thought my ears would be left behind me! Oh, dear! oh, dear!"

Tom Ripon succeeded in thrusting his head out, like a tortoise from his shell, at the top of the cuirass which, up to that moment, he had let rest on the top of his head.

Above that, again, with the lance he had held up one of the wooden heads of the effigies of the men-at-arms in Wolsey's Hall—in fact, the head of the one whose dress and equipments he had appropriated!

It was Tom's voice!

It was Tom's face!

And yet Heron was so completely surprised at finding Tom there, when he thought him at Whitcombe House, that he looked at him more as if he were in truth an apparition than a living person.

"Why, Captain, don't you know me!"

"I ought!"

"In course you ought! Oh! oh! oh! I give up the other—I give 'em all up!"

"What, on earth——"

"Oh! oh! oh!"

Tom had caught sight of Marianna, and had lost his heart at once to the fair girl; and that was what he meant by "giving up all the others."

Heron seized him by the hair of his head, and shook him to and fro.

"Speak, wretch, and say how you came here, and what for?"

"Don't—don't! You are as bad as Daisy, Captain: she always pretends to be taking off my cap for me, and gets hold of half a peck of a fellow's hair! Oh, don't!"

"Speak!"

"I am speaking!"

"But to the purpose! How came you here?"

"I came to look after you and Miss Edith——I begs pardon, I ought not to call her Miss Edith! But do you think that Tom Ripon was a going to let you both get into no end of trouble here, and not be close at hand to help you out of it? No!"

"But this disguise?"

"Oh, this?"

"Yes, why put it on?"

"Well, I thought it would be a nice way of going about the old crib, you see, to look about me, and see all that was going on; and so I have found, for whoever I met have cut away like mad!"

"Tom!"

"Yes, Captain?"

"Go into that room."

"That—room?"

"Yes; you are quite at liberty to frighten as much as you like some one who will come to you."

"Well, but——"

"It is this young lady's room."

"Oh, the love, I will! It's her room, is it, the darling? Miss, if you please, I give 'em all up in a heap for you; and I will say that never—no, never——"

"Go along!"

Felix Heron pushed Tom Ripon into Marianna's room, and closed the door.

"Now come with me," said Heron, "and I will at once place you under the protection of a lady who expects you, and who will be delighted to befriend you."

"What lady, Baron?"

"My wife!"

"Your wife, Baron? Oh, if she is as good as you, I know I shall love her!"

Hand in hand with Felix Heron, Marianna went down the secret stairs and they both

emerged through the other door in the panel into
the banqueting hall of the Cardinal.

Heron could not but smile to himself as he
saw the empty pedestal which Tom Ripon had
just stepped from on the occasion of his last visit
to that hall.

And but for the discovery he had just made of
the identity of Tom, what a capital ghost story in
connexion with Hampton Court he might have
told!

An eye-witness, too, of it!

But Heron had no inclination to pause in his
route to where he should find Edith, to whom he
wished to give the charge of Marianna.

The young girl clung to Heron confidingly as
she said, with an air of candid simplicity, "Dear
sir, what is it all about?"

"Danger!"

"What danger?"

"Do not ask further, but rest satisfied that
heaven and myself, as its humble instrument,
have rescued you from it, and that it will not
occur again."

"Ah, Baron, then I have indeed found a true
friend in you!"

"It is so; but I am not what I seem."

"Indeed!"

"I am not a baron."

"Not a baron?"

"No; I am the Earl of Whitcombe, sometimes
called Felix Heron, of whom you may have
heard; and the lady into whose care I am about
to place you, is Edith, my own true, and gentle,
and loving Countess!"

CHAPTER CCIII.

TOM RIPON ASTONISHES AND TERRIFIES THE KING, AND HALF KILLS LORD CLACKINGTON.

TOM RIPON was a true lover of adventure.

He was without fear likewise, so that he was
just the person to enjoy with infinite zest whatever
fortune threw in his way of the strange and the
wonderful.

Now, when Felix Heron pushed Tom into the
chamber of the fair Marianna, he felt certain that
some service was required of him in that direction, which it would be on his part a duty and a
satisfaction to render.

Tom therefore made no opposition to the arrangement.

To be sure, he was rather encumbered with
that Henry the Eighth cuirass that he wore, and
with those immense boots in which he had encased his legs.

But those were minor considerations.

There he was, in the chamber of the young girl
who had at one glance taken his heart captive,
and, as he himself expressed it, induced him to
"give up all the others," be they whom they
might.

She was not there.

Of course, that was a drawback, but still it was
her room; and Tom looked about him well
pleased, but wondering, after all, what he was
there for.

The small night-light, with its tiny flame, sent
a faint kind of twilight over the apartment.

He saw various articles of feminine apparel
about, and on the toilet table a pair of ear-rings
and a small finger-ring with a turquoise in it.

But still, why was he there?

That was the ever recurring question that Tom
Ripon put to himself.

He was soon to find out.

As Tom stood close by the little night-light he
heard a singular noise behind the wainscot of one
part of the room.

"Mice!" said Tom.

And indeed that seemed to be the most practical
as well as the most rational supposition, if it were
the most common-place.

The odd noise continued.

Click went something like a lock.

"It isn't mice," said Tom.

The next idea of Tom Ripon was to put out the
light, so that whoever was making a way into the
room should not have the advantage of knowing
he was there; but his own curiosity to know and
see who it was overcame that impulse, and he left
the light alone.

But Tom darted behind the curtains of the bed,
and drew them close.

Indeed, he jumped on to the bed itself, and
covered himself over with a satin counterpane
that had belonged to one of the old state beds of
Hampton Court.

Then Tom waited.

He heard a door gently creak upon its hinges.

He heard a footstep.

A slow and stealthy one.

Tom was armed.

His right hand strayed to the butt of a pistol
that he had in a pocket he could just get at, in
spite of the encumbrance of that abominable old
cuirass.

The King did not know his danger.

He was the intruder; and if Tom Ripon had
taken such a thing into his head, he was just as
likely to fire the pistol and then ask, "Who are
you?" afterwards, as not.

But it was the total absence of fear on the occasion that made Tom forbearing.

Cowards only are hasty with violence.

The stealthy footstep approached.

"Hem!" said a voice.

"What does that mean?" thought Tom.

"Hem!" said the voice again.

"Well," thought Tom, "I may as well say
'Hem!' too, whatever that may mean."

"Hem!"

Tom spoke, with the satin counterpane muffled
over his face a good deal.

"Beautiful being," said the voice, "are you
awake?"

"The deuce!" thought Tom. "Who does he
take me for?"

"Fair girl, are your rosy slumbers broken?"

"Oh, that's it!" thought Tom.

He replied in a little, low, squeaking voice, that
was as unlike that of Marianna as anything could
be; but the King was not disposed to be at that
moment critical in voices.

"Yes, I'm awake."

"Oh, dear one!"

"Get out, do!"

"Eh?"

"Go along!"

"Oh, Marianna, can it be possible that you do
not, after all, view with great alarm my presence
here?"

"Oh, gammon!"

"Oh, what?"

The King was fast lapsing into a state of blank
amazement.

He began to doubt if he were in his right
senses.

Or if he were, certainly the fair and gentle Marianna had bidden adieu to hers.

"Dear girl," he said, "you so greatly astonish me that know not what to say to you!"

"Walker!" said Tom.

"Who?"

"Get away, bad man! Don't come here trying to deceive a respectable young woman!"

"Good gracious!"

"Amen! If you want to say your prayers, be off somewhere else, and let me go to sleep!"

"Marianna!"

"Well, what now?"

"Are you talking in your sleep, or is it possible that, after all, the seeming gentleness and innocence of your tone and manner was but a sable cloak to cover what you really are!"

"A what?"

"A sable cloak!"

"I never heard of such a thing!"

"Oh, Marianna! Marianna! I love you! I love you with all my heart—with all my soul! Accept the adoration of one who——"

The King had, while speaking in this enamoured strain, approached the side of the bed.

Tom thought the joke might just as well come to an end.

Suddenly jumping up in the bed with the pillow in his hand, he uttered a loud yell that struck terror into the heart of the King.

Accompanying the yell, the pillow was dashed into the royal countenance with a bewildering effect.

The King fell.

Tom leaped out of bed with the tall boots, and alighted exactly on the royal chest.

The King shouted for help.

"Take that!" said Tom, as he dealt him several hearty kicks.

"Help! help! murder!"

"And take that, too!" added Tom.

He danced a sort of *pas seul* on the King, to the great detriment of his animal economy; and then, darting towards the door, Tom made his escape, and ran down the staircase.

As he went, Tom made efforts to rid himself of the cuirass, and succeeded in getting it off him.

"Bother you!" he said, as he apostrophised the awkward piece of metal; "I wonder the fellows in those old times ever put on such a weight of old iron! I would rather have gone into one of the jolly fights without it fifty times over!"

The boots Tom easily got rid of.

He sat down on the stairs, and thrust the huge feet of them through the balustrades, and so extracted his legs from them.

The boots had rather a comical appearance, stuck, soles outwards, through those balustrades.

And Tom had his own shoes on independently of those ancient boots, so that he felt, now that he had got rid of those encumbrances, light and active as a harlequin.

His object was to find out Captain Heron and Edith as soon as possible, and in that he succeeded more quickly than he could well have hoped.

Turning abruptly into one of the courts of the Palace, Tom heard a voice pronounce his name.

"Tom! Tom! Tom!"

"Here you are!"

"This way! Up here!"

Tom looked up in the direction the sound came from, and he saw a dim and dusky form at a window; but dim and dusky as it was, Tom Ripon had no difficulty in recognising it as Captain Heron.

"Captain!"

"Yes, Tom—come up here!"

"All right, Captain!"

Tom began to climb up to the window by the door-post, and any little projections he could find, with the agility of a squirrel.

"I did not intend that," said Heron. "If you had rung the bell, you would be admitted."

"All right, Captain! Here I am."

And there indeed was Tom at the window, when Felix Heron helped him in.

Three ladies were in the room.

Edith, her friend (who resided in the Palace of Hampton Court) and Marianna.

The moment Tom looked upon Marianna again he assumed an attitude of the most intense adoration, but Captain Heron checked him by saying, "This is no time, Tom, for gallantry. You must remain here, and protect these ladies."

"Yes, Captain!"

"I have important business in another part of the Palace."

Felix Heron felt the necessity of as soon as possible seeing the King, and putting the best complexion he could upon the royal disappointment.

It felt now much easier to Heron to play a part in regard to the King and Marianna than it was before.

He was now the victor.

Before, all was vague uncertainty, and he could not tell how things would turn out.

"Edith," he said, "and you, Marianna, remain here at peace, and be assured that all danger is now over"

"Yes, Felix," replied Edith; "it is all over, and most happily over, too; and with this dear girl as a companion and friend for the time to come, I shall learn to think of the events of this night without regret."

"And I, too!" said Marianna.

The tears gathered in her eyes as she spoke, and she took the hand of Felix Heron in both her own.

"Nay," said Heron, "you owe me few thanks, Marianna; for if I had not done what I have, I should have been the most unhappy wretch beneath the sun to-morrow!"

Heron then hastily left the apartments of the lady who had so kindly obliged Edith with a shelter, and made the best of his way back to the place of contest between Tom Ripon and the King.

Captain Heron was by so very frequently traversing the same route tolerably well acquainted with it

The consequence was that he reached the door of Marianna's chamber in a very short space of time indeed.

At first, Heron was of opinion that the King had fled.

But such was not the case; and Heron heard some one uttering doleful moans and groans from the chamber.

He felt certain that some one could be no other than the King.

Secretly delighted at his full and complete discomfiture, Heron entered the chamber.

"Murder!" cried the King.

At the sound of Captain Heron's footsteps, he thought it possible enough that whoever had assailed him before was now coming back to finish the business.

"Murder! murder!"

"What do I hear?" cried Heron.

"Eh? what? The Baron!"

"His Majesty!"

The King sat up.

"Oh! oh! oh!"

"What has happened? Is it possible that your Majesty, too, has been a sufferer?"

"Too?—too? What do you mean?"

"I mean that I have hardly a whole bone in my body! I was attacked by a strong party!"

"A party!"

"Yes, your Majesty! I was attacked and flung down one of the steep flight of stairs!"

"Indeed!"

"I regret to say that it was so; but still, bruised and grievously hurt as I was, I consoled myself with the idea of your Majesty's great happiness in the society of the fair and exquisite Marianna!"

"Bah! Bo!"

"What do I hear? Has your Majesty, then, altered your opinion of the charms of that beautiful girl?"

"Baron, you will oblige us much by holding your tongue."

"Certainly."

"Now help us to get up."

The kicks with which Tom Ripon had saluted royalty, and the maniacal kind of dance that Tom had executed upon the very body of the King, as he lay on the chamber floor, had not been at all beneficial.

"Oh! oh! Gently, Baron. Confound it, how has all this happened? I will take the life of somebody for this!"

———

CHAPTER CCIV.

CAPTAIN HERON RETAINS THE KING'S CONFIDENCE, AND REMAINS AT HAMPTON COURT.

IF anything could be more amusing than another to Captain Heron, it would certainly be this impotent rage of the King.

Knowing that Marianna was so perfectly safe from even a semblance of any further danger, he could well afford to smile at any threats the King might deliver himself of.

"Do you mean to tell me, Baron, that you, too, have been a sufferer by this night's adventures?"

"I find a difficulty, your Majesty, in moving one arm and both my legs."

"Ah! and we find a difficulty not only in moving our arms and legs, but our body likewise Had it been but two or thee persons who attacked us, we might have rought a good fight, and protected ourselves; but give me leave to assure you, Baron, that we have been set upon by a multitude of traitors, and nearly pommelled to death."

Felix Heron had great difficulty in preserving his countenance while the King thus spoke, knowing, as he did so well, that it was Tom Ripon alone who had produced all the mischief.

The King was evidently badly bruised, and made many wry faces as Felix Heron helped him to a chair, from which he was able to look about him by that dim night-light which still burnt in the chamber of the fair and innocent Marianna.

That chamber that would never again be lighted up by the fair beauty of that incomparable girl.

"Yes," said the King, "there is the couch on which she slept, or was to have slept; and there is the secret door in the panelling, exactly behind the state bedstead, by which I, and I alone, could approach this room.

"Your Majesty momentarily forgets," said Felix Heron, "that that was a secret with which I was not entrusted."

The King looked vexed. He had certainly, at the instant, forgotten how sedulously he had kept from Heron a knowledge of the means by which he could make his way to that sleeping chamber of youth, innocence, and beauty.

He strove now to make a virtue of necessity.

"You see, Baron, how entirely we trust you, by speaking thus freely to you."

"I do see it, your Majesty, and am grateful accordingly."

At this moment, to tell the truth, Heron started as much as the King, for a slight continuous rapping came at the chamber door, which was partially closed.

It was not etiquette of the King to take any notice of this demand for admission. Felix Heron had no such scruples, and while he laid his hand upon his sword, he cried aloud, "Come in."

The person who presented himself was that useful servant of his Majesty, who had been such an annoyance to Heron, by prowling about the precincts of Hampton Court during the whole proceedings of that night.

The appearance of this man was lugubrious in the extreme, for the tumble he had had down the staircase had by no means improved his general appearance.

At the sight of Felix Heron and the King, he raised a cry of indignation and rage.

"Justice! justice! Help! Consume him! Confound him! He pretends to be in your Majesty's confidential service, and pitches me headlong down the staircase fit to break one's neck."

"Eh? What, Baron? What is this?"

Heron feigned a look of perfect amazement.

"I think we are attacked by fiends to-night, who assume each other's likeness, for I could have sworn that this man, who represents himself to be a servant of your Majesty, was one of the rascals who set upon me and half killed me, at the moment thought I heard your Majesty's voice in this room calling for assistance."

"And I am ready to take my oath at any moment," said the man, advancing into the apartment, and glaring at Heron like an enraged hyena, "that you pitched me from top to bottom of the staircase, with no more ceremony than as though I had been a sack of coals."

"All this transcends belief," said the King, "and puzzles and confounds us."

Felix Heron shrugged his shoulders, and put on a look of innocent candour, as much as to say, "Well, I cannot explain all this, but so it is."

The King looked from him to the servant, and from the servant back to him again, and was evidently at a loss to come to any reasonable conclusion upon the subject.

There was one point, however, upon which he soon became anxious.

"Baron," he said, "where is Marianna all this time? Has she disappeared amid all the confusion of people and ideas?"

"That is not at all likely, your Majesty. My firm impression still is that she is within the precincts of the Palace."

"Go!" said the King, with a wave of his hand that at once dismissed the serving-man.

"Baron Von Peck?"

"I attend your Majesty."

"There is evidently more in all this than meets the eye."

"A great deal more," replied Heron.

"You are a brave man, and you are well armed. Will you search this portion of the Palace with a scrupulous attention which will convince us the girl is here or not here?"

"I will do your Majesty's behests," said Heron, as he drew his sword; "but upon the possibility of a second attack being made upon your royal person, I grieve to leave you in this chamber."

"Did you suppose, Baron, for a single moment," cried the King, springing to his feet with much more alacrity, considering the damage he had received, than could have been expected,—"did you suppose for a moment that we were going to expose ourselves to such a contingency? No, Baron, we have had enough of it for this night, and we shall return to town immediately. Make what

EDITH—No. 68.

discoveries you can, and present yourself to us at the morning reception."

"I shall not fail to do so."

"We shall be at St. James's. Good night, Baron!"

There was a bitterness of expression about the manner of the King that showed he deeply felt his disappointment; but it was especially gratifying to Felix Heron to hear him express his intention of immediately leaving Hampton Court.

Such an event, so immediately taking place after the escape of Marianna from that chamber of guilt and misery, would afford an opportunity for more permanent measures being taken for her safety.

The King walked with difficulty, and leant heavily upon the arm of Felix Heron as they proceeded together down the staircase that led to the lower part of the Palace.

The obsequious and useful servant was there

and, in truth, that man seemed to have the faculty of always making his appearance at the exact moment he was wanted.

It must have been a special talent, and had no doubt recommended him to a high place in the favour of his royal master.

"The carriage," said the King.

The serving-man immediately disappeared without a word.

"My curses alight upon the rascals who have assailed me to-night, Baron! I am full of aches and bruises."

Felix Heron could scarcely prevent a covert smile from playing upon his lips as he heard the King thus speak in the plural of his assailants, knowing, as he did so well, that Tom Ripon was answerable for all the damage the royal person had sustained.

The ubiquitous servant, who made himself so useful, must have had a suspicion that, after what had happened, the King would take his route to London with all possible speed, or the carriage with its four horses and two postilions that had brought him down to Hampton Court could never have been ready in so short a space of time as had elapsed before they were again at his Majesty's disposal.

"Baron, once more, good night! I leave you to unravel as best you may this tangled web of mystery and suspicion which attaches to the proceedings of Marianna."

"I have the honour to bid your Majesty good night, and to say that I will do the best I can," responded Heron.

The carriage drove off.

Felix Heron drew a long breath of relief, for he saw that, at a sign from the King, the troublesome and useful servant had mounted into a sort of rumble behind, and had gone to town with his iniquitous master.

"So far, all is well," said Heron. "Edith and Marianna shall rest to-night at Hampton Court, and, by the earliest and faintest streak of dawn to-morrow, they shall start for Whitcombe House, which will probably be the last place in all London which will suggest itself to the mind of the King as the retreat of the fair fugitive, whose destruction he aims at."

Felix Heron did not consider that any caution was now necessary; for, so to speak, armed as he was with an express authority from the King, he might consider himself the most important personage at Hampton Court.

He by no means, however, abandoned his disguise of the Baron Von Peck; but, without any special caution as regarded his movements, he crossed the court-yard which led to the lodgings of the lady with whom Edith and Marianna had found a refuge.

"All is well," he said. "We are safe, and there is no royalty in Hampton Court!"

Edith took Heron aside, and spoke to him earnestly.

"I feel, Felix, that by remaining another moment here in these apartments, we are endangering the subsistence and safety of the kind friend who has opened them to us."

"Has she said as much, Edith?"

"No, Felix; but I can gather it; and it would be ungenerous."

"Yes, Edith," interrupted Heron; "and unjust likewise for us to remain here, to the detriment of any one."

"I knew you would say so."

"Let us, then, thank this lady warmly and

kindly for what she has already done, and leave her for the present, perhaps to see her again in happier times."

"But whither shall we go, Felix?"

"Let me think a moment."

One — two — sounded the clock at Hampton Court.

The hour was late.

"At half-past four the dawn will begin to show itself."

"My advice," said Heron, "is that we rest for two hours, or more, in the old Palace. The rooms that have been assigned to me as the Baron Von Peck are still at my disposal. The King has gone to town, and has taken with him the only man who would be inclined to be troublesome."

There was a slight reluctance on the part of Edith, which almost took the character of a foreboding of evil, on account of their staying even for so short a time beneath the roof of the great Cardinal's old Palace.

But she forbore to urge her fears.

They did not stand the test of a few moments' mental examination, and therefore she dismissed them.

"Marianna," said Heron, as he turned to the young girl, "shall you now be content to be the friend and guest of the Countess of Whitcombe?"

"Oh, yes," replied Marianna, "for all my life!"

Heron then, after due acknowledgments had been made to the old lady, led the way across the court-yard with Edith and Marianna towards the staircase, which led to that part of the Palace assigned as his residence.

Tom Ripon followed them.

"Captain," he said, "what am I to do? Hadn't I better prowl about here, and pounce upon anybody who shows himself?"

"You may prowl about as much as you like, Tom—but beware who you pounce upon; for I do not think there are any persons here inclined to interfere with us, if we have the prudence to leave them alone."

"All right, Captain," said Tom. "You can always depend upon a man like me being a model of discretion."

Felix Heron was not at all uneasy as to what might become of Tom Ripon, since the Palace abounded with places of shelter, in any one of which he could make himself quite comfortable for the two or three hours they were all likely to remain beneath its roof.

There was only one thought that occurred to him as worthy of a little reflection, and he wondered that that had not struck him before; but, amid the turmoil of events that had taken place during the last two hours, the subject had entirely escaped him.

What had become of Marianna's deaf and purblind governess?

That was the question he now put to himself.

It was one, however, which Marianna would be herself able to answer accurately; and when they had reached the sitting-room allotted to him by the arrangements of the King, and he had stirred the logs upon the hearth until they sent forth a cheerful flame, he spoke to the young girl upon the subject.

"Your governess, Marianna—what has become of her?"

"I was going to speak to you of her."

"Indeed!"

"Yes. I am convinced she is neither so blind nor so deaf as she assumed to be "

A sudden pang of alarm—not on his own account, but on that of Marianna—shot across the heart of Felix Heron at those words.

"Tell me all you know, Marianna," he said; "and what has given rise to this idea "

"After we had retired for the night into that apartment from which you took me, she turned sharply towards me, shaking off very much the appearance of age and decrepitude, and in a voice very different from any I had ever heard her speak in before, she told me it was my own fault if I were not a duchess within a month."

"And you, Marianna—what reply did you make?"

"I was alarmed and surprised, and said something—I know not what—to which she replied as promptly and as quickly as any one could with a full sense of hearing about them."

"There is danger!" cried Felix Heron; "and we will not stay another hour in Hampton Court."

———

CHAPTER CCV.

CAPTAIN HERON MEETS WITH A GREAT SURPRISE, AND EDITH AND MARIANNA ARE IN PERIL.

THE danger that menaced the little party in that suite of rooms in the old Palace was none the less that it was undefined.

But its presence, or its probable presence, was to the mind of Felix Heron so palpable a fact that he could not rest without taking some immediate step to arrest it.

"Edith, dear Edith, and you, Marianna, make what preparations you can on the moment to leave this place."

"I am ready, Felix "

"And I," said Marianna, as she clung to the arm of Edith.

"I will call to Tom Ripon," said Captain Heron: "he is, no doubt, close at hand "

Looks of alarm now passed between Edith and Marianna, for they could not doubt the existence of real danger since it was so evident to Felix Heron.

He stepped on to the corridor at the commencement of the suite of rooms, to call to Tom Ripon.

"Tom! Tom!"

There was no reply.

With an undefined feeling of apprehension at his heart, Heron ran down the flight of stairs to the court-yard.

"Tom! Tom!"

Still no reply.

If Tom Ripon did not answer to a call from his much-loved master, Felix Heron, it was quite clear either that it did not reach his ears, or, if it did, he was not in a position to speak.

That something had taken place that was significant of danger, and that still more might ensue, Heron felt convinced.

He ran up the staircase again, and reached the door of the outer room of the suite that had been assigned to him in the Palace.

He had only a few minutes before passed through that door, and left it half closed.

Of that he was certain.

But now it was fast, and no power that he was capable of exerting at the moment was able to stir it.

A feeling of intense alarm came over the heart of Heron.

It was not on his own account that he felt it, but on account of Marianna and on account of Edith.

What it would be most advisable to do under the circumstances he could not on the spur of that instant decide.

But he made one vigorous attempt to force the door, which even the sturdy oak of which it was composed, and the massive lock that held it, felt the force of.

Hampton Court Palace, however, was built at a time when the art of running up structures with the least possible quantity of material was not recognised.

It still resisted him.

Then a thought occurred to Heron, which he resolved at once to put into practice.

The door of the chamber so recently in the occupation of the beautiful Marianna might still be open; and if so, the secret route in the thickness of the wall, between that room and the one where he had left Edith and Marianna, might be available.

Heron did not pause to reason further upon this idea.

He flew, rather than ran, to carry it into execution.

Yes, the door of Marianna's room was on the latch; no inducement had presented itself to any one to close it.

With a bound, Heron was in the apartment.

His feelings were wrought up to the highest pitch of anxiety, for he heard, or he thought he heard, at the moment that he reached the sleeping apartment of Marianna a scream.

A muffled scream, as though it only came to his ears through the intervention of many doors.

It might have been only fancy.

Or it might have been the night wind among the old weather vanes of the Palace.

But still it might be reality; and if so, it was suggestive of some great peril to those whom he loved.

To Edith.

And to Marianna.

With frenzied eagerness Heron felt for the secret panel in the wall by which the King had made his way on the unhallowed errand that brought him there into that room.

His haste, as haste always will when it degenerates into hurry, defeated his intentions.

It was two minutes before he found the panel, and opened it.

Then Heron darted along the narrow secret passage with a speed that, at various turnings, brought him into rude contact with the walls.

He reached the corresponding opening in the wall of his own sitting-room, and without caring what damage he did, he dashed it open.

Edith!

Marianna!

Both those names were on his lips as he looked around him in blank amazement.

The room was empty.

Completely deserted of human occupation.

The wood fire still burnt in the low-lying iron supports of the logs.

A couple of wax candles were still alight on the table.

A glove lay upon the floor.

And that was all that remained of Edith and of Marianna.

Heron clasped his head with his hands.

A burning, hot feel was about his brow.

Was he mad?

That was the terrible question he put to himself.

And then, by a powerful effort of that will which he had on so many occasions of danger and difficulty appealed to, and not in vain, he forced himself to be calm.

"No, no!" he said. "Let what may have happened, I will keep a heart and brain to meet it!"

He held up one of the candles, and made a more minute examination of the apartment.

There was nothing there to remind him of the so late presence of Edith but that glove.

It was a glove of Edith's.

With the wax-light in his hand, Felix Heron went into the next room, which was that assigned to him in his character of the Baron Von Peck, as a sleeping chamber.

That was quite undisturbed.

The quietude of the suite of rooms grew painful.

They began to have the feel and the aspect of a prison.

Edith, Marianna, Tom Ripon—where could they be?

Spirited away, as it appeared, by some power able to work in silence and safety.

But he, Heron, had heard the tramp of horses' feet in the Cardinal's Court.

He had heard the roll of carriage wheels. There could be no doubt whatever on those points.

Was that carriage and its horses still there?

Heron made his way back to the chamber of Marianna, and he looked as well as he could through the barred-up casement.

The cold moonbeams fell placidly and calmly upon the old, silent fountain, but no appearance of either carriage or horses presented itself.

To look at that silent court, one would hardly have supposed that any footstep either of horse or man had disturbed it since the days of the great Cardinal, who no doubt had looked with pleasure upon the sparkling waters of its now silent fountain.

Heron felt a positive pain now at his heart, and every nerve in his body seemed jangled and out of tune.

It was the dreadful feeling of want of power of action that came over him so depressingly.

He was about to turn from the window, when he saw a shadow close to the fountain.

A slowly-moving shadow, that had the outline of a human form unmistakably.

That some one was stealthily creeping along the cloisters on one side of the court-yard, Heron did not doubt for a passing instant.

He watched the shadow to see in which direction it went.

To the right.

That was enough.

In the shortest possible space of time that aught human could pass through the space to be traversed, Felix Heron was at the doorway that led into the court-yard at the foot of the staircase.

He saw the shadow still.

Slowly it passed over the fountain; and, by the direction it took, he felt certain that the substance that projected it would pass exactly where he stood.

He was not disappointed.

Not only did the form that cast the shadow come in that direction, but it turned in at the very doorway where Felix Heron stood, concealed in the deep night gloom.

Indeed, the person, whoever it was, dropped gently upon Heron, and he had only to stretch forth his arms to hold it tightly.

From the touch of the clothing, the form was feminine.

The slight scream that came from the person so surprised was further proof of that fact.

"Oh, are you Cosmo?"

"Yes."

"What a fright you gave me!"

"Did I?"

"To be sure you did. Who would have thought of your being just inside this doorway?"

"Ah, to be sure!"

"Eh?"

"I said, 'Ah, to be sure!'"

"Well, your cold is worse, I will believe now, for it has quite affected your voice."

By this, Felix Heron found how nearly he was betraying the fact that he was not the person named Cosmo, for whom the woman mistook him.

He pretended to cough.

"Yes, my cold is bad."

"It's a shame, as I have often said, for Crown to keep you waiting about staircases so much. You are always in draughts; and if you don't catch your death of cold, I will say it is no fault of Crown's."

"None in the least."

Did the woman mean the King by that nickname of Crown?

It was more than probable that she did.

Felix Heron was exceedingly desirous that she should say something of more importance than mere chat about his cold.

And she soon did so.

"Now, Cosmo," she said, "tell me who the pretended Baron Von Peck really is?"

"I don't know."

"Oh, you must know. I confess that he puzzles me; but, in my own mind, I never had a doubt, from the first moment I saw him, that he was playing a part."

"So much for my disguise!" thought Heron.

"Yes," he replied; "that was my own idea, too."

"But," added the woman, "he never suspected that in the old, deaf, and half-blind governess, he had me to contend with."

Here was a revelation!

This woman, then, was that very governess who, from her infirmities, had seemed to be so entirely unfit for the service of the fair Marianna. She was in reality, then, nothing in the world but a spy!

This was news to Felix Heron—news that almost induced him to stretch forth his hand and hold her as a prisoner.

But he abstained; for he thought, and no doubt rightly, too, that she was likely to give him more valuable information still.

"He never once suspected you?" said Heron.

"Of course not. I flatter myself I can play my part rather too well for that."

"Of course—of course."

"And I took good care to keep such an eye upon the Baron Von Peck that I was able to open Crown's eyes a little."

"Yes, yes."

"And so he is off?"

"Oh, yes. The Baron, do you mean?"

CAPTAIN HERON RESCUES EDITH FROM THE HANDS OF HER GAOLERS,
AND TOM RIPON AMUSES HIMSELF AT THE EXPENSE OF THE SAME.

Presented Gratis with No. 63, of the New Edition of EDITH HERON, the Sequel to Edith the Captive; or, the Robbers of Epping Forest.

"No. How stupid you are, Cosmo, to-night!"

"Well, I am. It's my cold."

"I suppose it is Crown is off—I mean with the girl?"

"Oh, yes, of course; and—and—the other persons are off, too."

"Well, you may call them off, if you like; but I should not exactly like their lodging."

"No, no!"

The heart of Heron beat fast and thickly, as he longed to ask that woman what lodging it was she alluded to, and who were the other persons of whom she spoke.

Were they Edith and Tom Ripon?

It was but too likely.

He hazarded a direct inquiry.

"I don't think that boy," he said, "is a likely person to put up with more than he can help?"

"No; he is a strange young scamp!"

This was a nice character of Tom Ripon—if it were Tom that was spoken of.

"And the—a—a—lady?"

"She says she is the Countess of Whitcombe, and I must confess she looks like a lady; but she won't say who the Baron really is."

CHAPTER CCVI.

CAPTAIN HERON RESCUES EDITH AND TOM RIPON, AND PLACES A PRISONER IN THEIR STEAD.

FELIX HERON was anxious and willing to prolong this dialogue as far as he could, with the conviction that each moment of it gave him some valuable information.

He fully expected, however, that, should he emerge more into the faint light of the court, he would be discovered.

"And so," he said, "you are inclined to think that the lady is really the Countess of Whitcombe?"

"I am. You know I ought to be a tolerable judge of such persons by this time."

Captain Heron, of course, knew no such thing, but he felt that it was quite politic to say that he did.

"Oh, yes; I am, as you say, well aware of that."

"Of course, you are!"

"And—and—you think that, in a short time, the girl may be reconciled to her fate?"

"Oh, yes; obstinate as she is now, she will be like all the rest of them, pleased enough to make the best of matters when they see there is no help for it."

"No doubt!—no doubt! But do you think those two prisoners are safe?"

"What two!"

"The Countess, as she calls herself, and that troublesome imp of a boy!"

"Oh, the young wretch! I shall never forget him as long as I live!"

Captain Heron was rather curious to know how it was that Tom Ripon had succeeded in making so great an impression upon the mock deaf and blind governess.

"Why what did he do?"

"I am black and blue all through him. When his hands were tied, what do you think he took to doing?"

"Kicking?"

"Just so! If you had known him before, you could not have guessed more truly."

Little did she think that probably no one in in the world knew Tom Ripon, and what he was likely to do under any given set of circumstances, so well as the person she was speaking to.

But still Heron had not the exact information he anxiously sought.

Where was Edith?

And where was Tom Ripon?

These were the two questions he wanted answered in a colloquial manner.

But he almost decided to ask them in a more direct way, for fear the information was what, in his assumed character, he ought to know.

"Come now," suddenly said the governess; "if C own is as liberal as he ought to be for this affair. I do not think you and I need wait!"

"Wait?" thought Heron; "wait for what? What on earth does she mean?"

"Ah!" added the sham governess; "you don't reply to that; and I cannot help suspecting you wish, after all, to deceive me, or fly from your word!"

"No; believe me."

What the word was that he was accused of flying from, Captain Heron had not the least notion.

As long as he could, however, he made up his mind to keep up the delusion which the woman had brought most certainly and most deservedly upon herself.

"Well," she added, "when shall it be?"

"When you like."

"You mean that?"

"Of course I do."

"Then tell me exactly how much money you really and truly have saved."

"A good sum."

"Indeed!"

"Yes; a very good sum."

"Oh, you gay and charming fellow!"

"Hem!"

Felix Heron began to perceive the drift of all this; and that it was, after all, a matrimonial speculation that the pretended governess was thinking of.

"I, too," she said with a sigh, as she slid her arm with an air of fond familiarity under Felix Heron's,—"I, too, have been prudent!"

"You have?"

"Yes; I have money!"

"I am delighted to hear it!"

"I thought you would be; and here comes Peter."

"The deuce!"

"Eh?"

"Oh, nothing! Did you say Peter was coming?"

"I did. Don't you see the glimmer of his lantern? There he comes, up the secret steps in the fountain that we know so well."

Felix Heron was full of surprise and curiosity, for, as he now looked towards the old, decayed fountain in the middle of the Cardinal's Court, he saw the fluttering gleams of some artificial light playing upon it.

The light shifted about among the old stone figures and ornaments of the fountain, bringing them occasionally in broad relief, and making them assume all sorts of strange grotesque shapes.

Heron wondered much who Peter was.

He spoke more for the purpose of breaking a rather awkward pause than that he had anything really to say.

"And so that is Peter?"

"To be sure. Who else could it be?"

"Oh, of course—of course!"

The light at and about the old fountain each moment increased.

Felix Heron kept his eye upon it, and as he did so, he clasped the arm of the pretended governess tighter and tighter still beneath his own.

"Oh, how you squeeze!"

"Do I?"

"You know you do."

"I am afraid of Peter."

"Of Peter! Ho! ho! ho!"

"You know he might take you from me, since he is such an Adonis!"

"He? he? Oh, you are joking! Why, he is fifty if he is a day!"

"Is he?"

"Is he, yes; and here he is."

A gleam of light, stronger than had yet shown itself, came from the very basin, as it appeared, of the old fountain.

At the same moment, Felix Heron saw the outline of the figure of a man.

There was no longer any time for procrastination, or farther amusement with the mistaken governess.

Felix Heron clasped her arm so tight beneath his, that her escape from him was impossible, and he bent down his head to her, as he said, "One word, and I scatter your brains beneath the columns of this court! The slightest struggle —the slightest cry, and it is your last! I am the Earl of Whitcombe!"

So completely taken by surprise was the woman, that although, from the mere pain of the excessive pressure that Felix Heron subjected her arm to beneath his, she might well have cried out—not a word escaped her lips.

It suited Captain Heron much better on the present occasion to announce himself by his own proper name than as the Baron Von Peck; for, disguised as the latter personage, he might still be of service to Marianna.

The pretended governess in a few seconds found her voice, however.

"Gracious heaven! have I been deceived?"

"Yes, and not the proper fate of all deceivers!"

"Let me go."

"No—I am firm and resolute! Your life hangs upon the events of the next few seconds! I know that you value it, and it depends upon yourself that you preserve it. Be still and submit, or you cast it away past recall."

The tone in which Felix Heron uttered these words was one eminently calculated to have an effect upon the nervous system of whoever might hear them.

He felt the woman's arm tremble beneath his own.

He felt that but for the support of that arm she would have fallen to the stone floor.

The superiority of his own strong will over hers was manifested; and certainly so far as she was concerned he stood a conqueror.

How far he might succeed in gaining a like ascendancy over Peter, who was approaching, remained to be seen.

That was a problem, however, which would be quickly solved; for with a slow and lounging gait, the man, who had emerged apparently from the very basin of the fountain, came towards the arched doorway, where Felix Heron and she who may be called his prisoner were waiting.

The man shaded the lantern he carried with one hand, so that its rays fell full upon his face.

Captain Heron looked upon him with some degree of curiosity, but he felt quite confident he had never seen him before.

The lantern sent a sufficient halo of light about it, to make the two figures in the arched doorway, faintly visible; and Peter—as the woman had named him—never doubting but what they were his accomplices, at once strode forward.

"All's right!" he said: "they won't get out of that in a hurry!"

It was under his left arms, that Felix Heron held the woman a prisoner, so that his right was free.

The hand of that right arm, as the man approached, was plunged into the breast of his apparel; and by the time Peter actually got within a couple of yards of those in whom he expected to find companionship and commendation, he was horrified to find that the gleam from his lantern fell upon the barrel of a long suspicious-looking pistol, the muzzle of which was pointed in a direct line to his breast.

"Peter," said Felix Heron, "if you have any desire to feel the hot and sickening sensation of a bullet in your heart or lungs, you will resist my orders; if not, you will obey them, and save your life, worthless as it is."

Peter stood aghast.

His mouth opened.

His eyes dilated.

The woman made a vigorous attempt to free herself from the left arm of Heron; but, as he pressed and shook her to the ground, he said, almost fiercely, "Not yet. I spare you, although I should not do so. Beware how you rouse a feeling in my heart which is struggling into existence and which will overwhelm you in destruction."

With a faint shriek, the woman half fell, crouching down to his feet on the pavement.

The moral ascendancy of Felix Heron over her was complete.

These few little incidents happened with such rapidity that it seemed to the bewildered Peter as if, the moment he had appeared, some one had flown at him and grasped him by the throat.

"Wretch!" said Captain Heron, as he held him with a grip that threatened suffocation,—"wretch! dispute with me, or contest in any way with me my will, and you rouse a spirit you cannot quell!"

Peter was by no means the sort of person to rouse any such spirit; for cowardice was written legibly by the hand of Nature in every lineament of his countenance.

He submitted at once.

Indeed, he put on such a look of faint and sickly degradation, that Captain Heron's anger ran a good chance of giving way to a feeling of utter contempt; and, probably, he might have cast this man from him as utterly unworthy of regard, but for the certainty that from him or from the woman who crouched at his feet, or probably from both, he would come at the secret of what had become of Edith and of Tom Ripon.

The abject fear, however, that possessed these two people was just the kind of feeling to breed treachery

Heron felt that they were not to be trusted for a single moment with the power of evil.

While holding the singular conversation we have recorded with the meek governess in the dark, Felix Heron had been able to make sufficient changes in his appearance and apparel to destroy his identity as the Baron Von Peck.

He had taken the wig from off his head which gave him an elderly appearance.

He had dashed away from his moustache some of those wood ashes which had imparted the greyness of age.

A tolerably hard rub with his handkerchief had likewise effaced some of those simulated hues upon the face, which had given him the appearance of a man past even the middle of life.

And now Felix Heron completed the transformation from the Baron Von Peck to the Earl of Whitcombe in a manner that made the last change available for other purposes.

He took off the very voluminous neckcloth which he wore in his character as the Baron, and with it so firmly tied the right arm of Peter to the left arm of the governess, that if they ran at all it must certainly be in couples, and that was to the great impediment of each other.

They were perfectly passive in his hands.

Downright fright deprived them of all power of resistance; and, to keep up this feeling in their minds, Captain Heron every now and then pointed the gleaming barrel of that pistol in their faces, as though he were half repenting of his clemency, and much inclined to scatter their brains in the Cardinal's Court.

When he did this, they made mute signs of horror and consternation, for they were afraid to speak, unless he asked them a question.

"Now, Mr. Peter," said Heron, " since that is your name,, where did you come from just now in so mysterious a manner, through the decayed fountain ?"

Peter gasped like a fish several times before he spoke.

"From—from the Cardinal's Kitchen."

"Where is that ?"

Peter pointed to the flag-stones of the courtyard, as if to intimate that the Cardinal's Kitchen, to which he alluded, was somewhere beneath.

Probably a look of impatience passed across the countenance of Felix Heron, for the woman spoke hastily.

"It is a vaulted room beneath this court, having one opening to the private garden, by an iron grating, and another into the basin of the old fountain."

Peter seemed now desirous of taking the initiative in the way of giving information, and he chimed in at once with the word.

"Yes, sir, that is it ; and there, I think you will find the two persons you want — the lady and the most horrid ruffian of a boy I ever met with."

Felix Heron had no doubt whatever but that he alluded to Edith and to Tom Ripon, although he could not conceive it possible that Tom had allowed himself to be made prisoner by such a person as Peter.

Nor had Tom done so, as we shall presently perceive.

Felix Heron considered for a few seconds as to what he should do with his prisoners, and then he made up his mind that they should both accompany him to the Cardinal's Kitchen they mentioned.

"Show me this gloomy prison-house," he said ; " and, by your alacrity in doing so, show me that you wish to preserve your worthless lives."

They almost tumbled over each other in their eagerness to precede him to the fountain in the court.

——

CHAPTER CCVII.

TOM RIPON ASTONISHES PETER, AND EDITH REACHES HOME IN SAFETY.

THE distance was short, and it was well that a time of night had arrived that rendered it improbable any persons should be at the windows looking into that court of the old Palace of Hampton.

At all events, Felix Heron thought these a fortunate conjunction of circumstances—although, perhaps, mysterious proceedings in and about that portion of the Cardinal's ancient Palace were sufficiently common to make those who were prudent enough to consult their own interests to shut their eyes to them.

But, be this as it may, Felix Heron was right glad when the little party stepped over the margin of the old fountain.

"Here," said Peter, as, among the weed and rubbish which in process of time had collected in the basin of the basin, he pointed to a grating certainly not three feet square.

Heron was too eager to rescue Edith to wait for the tardy operations either of Peter or the mock governess, although they both, no doubt, knew well how to raise that grating.

Stooping himself to it, he raised the rusty bars of which it was composed, and found that it turned over with ease upon a pair of hinges.

The light of Peter's lantern disclosed a flight of stone steps, the sides of which were thickly coated with green moss.

There could be no doubt but that the politic and wary Cardinal Wolsey, at the time he built the magnificent mansion of Hampton Court, was not unmindful of one very prevalent idea at that period.

The idea of having places of concealment and modes of secret transit from one part of the Palace to another.

The well-contrived way from the fountain was doubtless one of them, and it would have been no very difficult matter even to the mechanical genius of the age in which Hampton Court Palace was built, to contrive some mode by which the basin of the fountain might hold water, and yet in a few moments be available as a secret mode of exit from the principal dwelling-rooms of the building.

Or probably the wily Cardinal never had that fountain in working order, as it would have been by no means difficult to keep it constantly under repair.

Felix Heron hesitated only a moment, and that was to consider wither he should descend first, or force Peter and the governess to do so.

His impatience to reach Edith prevailed over all other considerations.

He descended first, but as he did so he held up the lantern, and darted at them a look which almost paralyzed them with fear.

"Follow!" he said ; "or your blood be upon your own heads."

It was by no means an easy matter for two persons yoked together as Peter and the governess were to descend so narrow an opening, and how they accomplished it was little short of miraculous.

The body bends itself, however, to the supremacy of strong passions ; and fear enabled them to do what otherwise they would have declared impossible.

They followed Heron.

Heron counted sixteen steps until he arrived at

a vaulted passage beneath the pavement of the court.

Then he shouted out the name that was uppermost upon his lips.

"Edith! Edith!"

There was an answering cry which shaped itself to the name of "Felix!"

There were two answering cries; and if there could have been any possible mistake about the first, there was none about the second.

It was a ringing cheer from Tom Ripon.

"Hip—hip—hip! Hurrah!"

"That's Tom!" cried Captain Heron; and dashing forward, he shook violently a door which impeded his progress.

A series of kicks upon the other side of the door, which were inflicted upon it with wonderful rapidity, let Heron know that he was upon the right track.

"The key of this door at once!" he shouted, as he hurried to the trembling prisoners he had brought with him.

Peter fell on his knees immediately, and dragged the sham governess after him.

"Mercy! Have mercy upon us!"

"The key!"

"Here it is!—here it is! I intended to come and pay them every attention; and I've no doubt I should have let them go, for I was beginning to get quite fond of them; and I am now, and wish them all manner of luck, and you, too, sir, if you please!"

Felix paid not the slightest attention to these asseverations from Peter, but snatching from his hands an old-fashioned and rather ponderous key, he applied it to the lock of the door.

"Out of the way, Tom—the door opens inwards!"

"All right, Captain!"

The door was opened; and in another moment Felix Heron forgot, not only his prisoners, but Tom Ripon likewise, as he clasped Edith to his heart.

"Safe and well, Edith?"

"Both, Felix! What of Marianna?"

"Yes," cried Tom; "what of the lovely Marianna? A pretty thing it is for a fellow to be pushed into a black hole like this, just as a fellow had made up his mind to give up all the rest of the girls, and stick to that one for ever, and a whole week after! But I'll be off, and ferret her out, if she is above ground!"

Tom made a rush from the dungeon-like place he was in, and not noticing the two kneeling figures of the sham governess and Peter, he went sprawling over them, to their great detriment and his own utter astonishment.

Tom Ripon had a habit of kicking whenever he got into a difficulty. He used to say it was Daisy who taught it him.

Whether or no, he on this occasion liberally carried it out, and the scuffle that ensued between him, and Peter, and the mock governess, would have been something ludicrous if Captain Heron had not been too seriously inclined to view it in that light.

"Peace, Tom—peace!" he cried. "Let us leave this place at once. The night is flying fast, and we have far to go."

"All right!" said Tom. "I didn't see the two images! Bless us and save us! Why, they're live people, after all; and one of them is a very old rascal, and told me and Lady Edith that if we happened to feel hungry in the night we might eat each other."

"No, no!" cried Peter, in a paroxysm of rage; "I didn't say it!"

"You know you did!" added Tom.

"It was only a joke, then—a little joke. I didn't mean it."

"It was a very bad joke, then," said Tom. "But never mind, Captain; on we go again. What are we to do next?"

"Get out of this place as quickly as we can!"

"Tom, lead the way. You will see a flight of stairs."

"I hope I shall," said Tom; "for coming down them, nobody told me to look for them, and I only made one long step of it from top to bottom!"

"How came you, Tom, to allow yourself to be made a prisoner by such a thing as this?" asked Felix Heron, pointing to Peter.

"Why, Captain, that wasn't the thing at all. I was sitting down as comfortably as possible in the court-yard, pitching little stones into the fountain, just to pass the time, when a what-do-you-call-it all of a sudden took place—it's when the sun gets behind a cloud, or behind the moon, or behind a something—what is it, Lady Edith?"

"An eclipse, Tom."

"Yes, that's it; and it came upon me in the shape of a bag that some fellow popped over me, and tied round my head and waist from behind before I could move hand or foot; and that's how I came here, Captain."

"I could have sworn it was some such trick!"

"But what's to be done with these folks?"

"Let us have even-handed justice," added Heron. "As you, Edith, and Tom Ripon leave this dungeon-like place, let these people occupy it."

"Hurrah!" cried Tom: "that's it! In you go, both of you!"

Peter protested.

The mock governess got up some faint screams.

Tom Ripon, with very little ceremony, thrust them both into the vaulted chamber from which he and Edith had just emerged, and locked the door upon them.

"Come, Tom, come," cried Captain Heron.

"One moment, Captain."

Tom dealt the door a vigorous kick or two, and shouted, "Hallo!"

"Yes, yes," faintly responded Peter from within.

"Are you hungry?"

"Yes, yes."

"Eat each other, then! Now, Captain, my mind's easy. Let's be off."

Tom Ripon, no doubt, would have been quite unhappy if he had been denied the opportunity of retaliating upon the persons who had made such a speech that he had just repeated to him and to Edith.

But Captain Heron had his own opinion in regard to the nature of the imprisonment that he was to all appearance inflicting upon the sham governess and her associate, Peter.

They took the matter with by far too much ease and equanimity, for it to be serious.

That they knew of some mode of speedily and effectually releasing themselves, he had no doubt.

That was a consideration that made it all the more necessary that he and Edith and Tom Ripon should get clear of Hampton Court as soon as possible.

The basin of the old fountain was soon reached, and as Edith emerged from that gloomy and underground place into the night air, she thought that it had never before felt so fresh, or so grateful to the senses.

"Free—free once again!" she said. "Oh, what a joy it is to feel that there is no roof above us but the canopy of heaven!"

Felix Heron pressed the hand of Edith, and that mute reply was as eloquent to her as any form of words could possibly have been.

"I suppose, Tom," said Captain Heron, "that there is no chance of getting hold of any conveyance to London?'

"I don't know that, Captain."

"What horses have you?"

"Why you see, Captain, I have been prowling about this fine old crib, till I know pretty well all about it, and there is a capital stable, with a good half-dozen horses in it."

"If we could get three of them, Tom!"

"Why not, Captain? This is the way."

Tom took the lead now, and keeping much in the shadow of the building on its garden front, so

as to avoid even the chance of any observation, he led them to a small door in one of the wings of the immense edifice.

"This is the way, Captain."

"To the stable?"

"To one of them, I take it, for there are no end of such places. Only the most of them have got nothing in them but old gardener's tools and broken flower-pots. This one only has some horses in it."

"Doubtless the King's."

"All the better, Captain."

"So say I. Ah! the door is fast."

"It won't be so long, Captain."

Tom was an adept at unfastening doors, and as this one was only locked, he soon flung it open.

A horse slightly coughed.

"We are right," said Edith. "There are horses here."

"Tom, I do not like to leave Edith for a single moment in this place," said Heron. "Do you go, and get out, if you can, three horses."

"All right, Captain."

Tom entered the stable, and Edith, with Felix, remained just within its doorway, or rather the doorway of the paved yard across which the stable might be reached.

"Oh, Felix!" whispered Edith; "what is the fate of that poor girl, Marianna?"

"Let us hope for the best, Edith; and that she will still be protected by heaven!"

"Amen to that prayer, Felix."

"Come on, will you?" they heard the voice of Tom say.

He was leading out some horse that, perhaps, was a little unwilling.

At that moment the attentive ears of Edith caught the sound of advancing footsteps, some distance off, on the gravel path of the garden.

"Listen, Felix," she said; "do you hear nothing?"

The sounds were more plain.

There could be no doubt, too, of what they were. The measured tread was that of the guard, which, no doubt, was about to be changed in and about the old Palace.

Edith and Captain Heron retreated within the doorway, and Heron held the door close, so that it should still have the appearance of remaining fastened, in the event of any one being so over-suspicious or cautious as to think proper to try it.

As at present, a cavalry guard was always on duty at Hampton Court; and the dismounted troopers kept watch and ward at the various posts.

It was a fortunate circumstance that one of those posts was not very close at hand to the stable door, so that there was no difficulty except to preserve silence while the guard passed.

"We are fortunate," whispered Felix Heron; "for if we had issued forth but a few minutes earlier, we must have inevitably encountered the relief guard."

"Let them pass again on their return," replied Edith.

"That is well thought of. Tom, are you there?"

"Yes, Captain. All's right."

"Keep close with the horses; we must not issue forth yet."

It was about ten minutes before the guard passed again that way with the sentinels who had been relieved from their posts.

As they did so, the non-commissioned officer who led them spoke in anything but a cautious one of voice.

"There's something amiss, men," he said; "or there would never have been a change of pass-word at this time of night. You will all remember that no one is to be allowed to leave the precincts of the Palace except they use the words 'King's service!'"

As the Sergeant spoke, the guard passed on.

Felix Heron smiled, as he whispered to Edith, "We shall not be likely to forget so simple a pass-word as that."

"No, Felix; nor the simplicity of the man who has furnished us with it."

"Indeed, not; but I am willing to believe it is one of those little circumstances that favour us, because we are battling for the right."

"Now, Captain," said Tom; "isn't it time to come out of this?"

"I think so. Lead the horses out."

Felix Heron opened the door of the stable-yard, and with, no doubt, a look of great pride and satisfaction upon his countenance, if it could only have been seen in the darkness, Tom Ripon led forth a horse thoroughly equipped with a side-saddle.

"There, Captain!" said Tom; "what do you think of that?"

"This is most fortunate, Tom," he said; "and I have no doubt this side-saddle has been for the special accommodation of that very unfeminine female whom we have left in what Peter called the 'Cardinal's Kitchen.'"

"It will be all right, Captain," said Tom; "you and I must manage in the best way we can. I cannot find any saddles for us; but there are halters on both the horses, and I dare say we can contrive to get along."

"Doubtless—doubtless. If any one is authorized to borrow the King's horses to-night, I certainly consider myself that man."

Captain Heron assisted Edith to mount, and then he and Tom quickly possessed themselves of the other two horses.

It was not an agreeable idea to ride fourteen miles to London without a saddle, but it had to be done, and in the course of five minutes they had given the password and issued forth from Hampton Court in perfect safety and security.

CHAPTER CCVIII.

FELIX HERON RESCUES MARIANNA, AND MAKES ROYALTY PAY THE EXPENSES.

Felix Heron was anxious to procure from Edith a full and detailed account of all that had happened to her since he had left her with Marianna in the apartments allotted to him in his character of Baron Von Peck at Hampton Court.

It was not, however, until they were in safety at Whitcombe House, and Tom Ripon had turned the three horses adrift along Pall Mall, that Felix Heron felt inclined to ask any questions upon the subject.

What Edith had to tell was brief in the extreme.

"You had hardly left the apartment three minutes," she said, "when two persons appeared in it, coming from I know not where, although of course there must have been some secret panel or entrance in addition to that we already know of."

"Was one of those persons the King?"

"No; the man Peter was one of them, and the other a stranger. So sudden was the appearance, and, I might almost say, the attack upon us, that we had no means of resistance, and were hurried through a doorway which I should scarcely be able even now to identify, before the first surprise of the transaction had subsided. I was soon separated from Marianna; and whither she was taken I know not, but I was myself conducted with a rapidity which set resistance and remonstrance at defiance, to that gloomy chamber beneath the court-yard, where, I must confess, it was a satisfaction to me to find Tom Ripon was already a prisoner."

Felix Heron looked thoughtful, and paced the room for some seconds in silence.

"I must and will, Edith," he said, "make an effort to rescue that girl from the power of the King; but I am greatly in doubt whether he suspects me or not."

"And I, too, Felix; and yet we cannot abandon that young creature to her fate."

"Certainly not, Edith. Something must be given to chance. The King may still have faith in me as the Baron Von Peck, or he may suspect me, and be playing a double game. That, however, I will endeavour to understand; for I will make my way to the Palace as soon as twilight confounds a little the shadows, and lends me the assistance to my disguise which is so essential."

Felix Heron thought it prudent to remain in Whitcombe House for the remainder of the day, and, indeed, he felt the necessity of rest after the many fatigues he had undergone.

It was between seven and eight o'clock in the evening, that in his full costume of the Baron Von Peck, and more carefully disguised than ever, in order to represent that personage, he made his way to St. James's Palace.

It was quite possible the King might not be there, for it was well known he had a fancy for passing with great rapidity from one to another of the three royal residences in London.

St. James's Palace, Buckingham House, and Warwick House, or Warwick Lodge, as it was frequently called, were equally kept up as royal residences, although St. James's was the proper official residence of the monarch and his Court.

From one of the pages of the back-stairs Felix Heron easily got the information of where the King was to be found.

Warwick Lodge was the place.

It was but a short walk across the Park, and Felix Heron made his way through the somewhat fanciful iron gates of that then well-known residence of royalty, which has long since been swept away.

Heron found no difficulty in penetrating to one of the ante-chambers, by virtue of that written pass had from the King, and which he had carefully preserved.

It was something of a mortification, however, to encounter Lord Clackington alone in that apartment, and looking so smiling and contented, that he was quite a caricature of the courtier in favour.

This self-satisfaction upon the countenance of Lord Clackington was suggestive of bad fortune both to Felix Heron in his assumed character of Baron Von Peck, and to Marianna.

But he resolved to put the best face upon the matter that he could, and however repugnant it might be to his general principles, he felt the necessity of meeting villany and duplicity by finesse.

"A fair morning, my lord," he said. "Is his Majesty stirring?"

Lord Clackington deliberately drew forth a gold snuff box before he replied, and regaled himself with a pinch of the then favourite snuff, which went by the name of Macabaw.

"Yes, Baron, his Majesty is stirring."

"Then," replied Felix Heron, scarcely able to restrain his impatience, for he had an earnest desire to kick my Lord Clackington—"then I shall have the honour of paying my respects to him."

"I think not, Baron."

"Indeed, my lord!"

"I repeat, I think not. In fact I am rather inclined to state that his Majesty will have no further occasion for the services of the Baron Von Peck."

"Is that, my lord, a message from the King, or merely a little bit of private pique and malevolence on the part of my Lord Clackington?"

"Pique—malevolence, Baron?"

"Those are certainly the words I used, my lord!"

"It seems to me that you wish to quarrel!"

"Not at all; but I'm ready to do so, if necessary, in the service of his Majesty!"

"But, I assure you, Baron, his Majesty no longer desires your services, and, there the quarrel ends; and, therefore, if you please, I will order one of pages to the show you with all possible respect to the vestibule, which you need never cross again!"

"From his Majesty's own lips I will accept my dismissal, but from none other."

"Impossible, Baron!"

"And yet it must be so. Who shall deprive me of the pass given to me by his Majesty's own hands, which admits me to his presence?"

"But, Baron——"

"Not another word, sir. Here is one of the pages, to whose good care I commit myself. Be pleased, sir, to conduct me to his Majesty's cabinet, and announce that the Baron Von Peck, on business of importance, presents himself."

"I dare not, sir," was the page's reply, as he adroitly backed through a narrow pair of folding doors, and was about to close them, when Felix Heron put his foot in the entrance in such a manner that it was impossible to do so.

"I will take the responsibility upon myself," he said, "of any blame that may attach to you."

The page was timid, and made but a slight show of resistance; but seeing Lord Clackington, he ran out into the ante-chamber, calling, as he did so, in a voice of alarm, "Guard—guard!"

The page was accustomed to the life at St James's, where the interior of the Palace was well looked to by the Yeomen of the Guard; but in that private residence of the King, although a couple of sentinels held their posts at the gates, there was nothing of the strength and state of royalty within.

Lord Clackington half-drew his sword, but he took care to keep the other half in the scabbard.

Felix Heron cared little whether he drew it wholly or not, but passing completely through the narrow folding doors, he closed them behind him, and shot into its socket a brass ornamental bolt which was beneath the lock.

The room was but a small one.

On a table, with a large cover of crimson velvet edged with bullion, stood a hand lamp, and that was the only light in the apartment.

Felix Heron, with the conviction on his mind that he was on the eve of some adventure which would test perhaps all his resolution and all his courage, lifted the lamp from the table, and casting his eyes about him, perceived another pair of doors similar to those he had entered by, immediately opposite.

The panels were richly gilt in high relief, and as Heron placed his hand upon the lock, he fancied he heard a faint cry, but from what direction it proceeded he was at a loss to conjecture.

It was more like some wandering echo in and about the precincts of Warwick House, than any cry from one of its apartments.

But it made the blood run cold about the heart of Felix Heron.

Without any particular aim or purpose about the route he took, but leaving himself to be guided either by instinct or by heaven, he strode onwards.

Two apartments were passed through, the soft carpeting of which felt like untrodden snow beneath his feet.

Then Felix Heron paused abruptly, for most unmistakably he heard a voice which he knew well.

It was the voice of the King.

"Pooh, pooh, girl! You know not what you say! This is all childish nonsense. The preferment that I offer you is such that there is not another person in all these dominions who would not shout for joy at the chance of accepting. As soon as you are of age, letters patent shall pass the great seal, making you a peeress in your own right; and that, with an adequate allowance from the privy purse, places you in a position far beyond anything you have a right to expect."

The reply was in the voice of Marianna.

That voice thrilled through the nervous system of Felix Heron like a shot of electricity.

"No, no!" she half-shrieked; "I reject all—I despise all! There is but one now whom I can love in this world, for my dearest affections are with the dead. Be great, and just, and merciful; and let me reside with that Countess of Whitcombe who, although I have seen but once, I feel that I can love for ever!"

"Childish nonsense!" exclaimed the King, in a voice of irritation."

"And that noble and gallant Earl of Whitcombe, too!" added Marianna.

"What?" shouted the King. "Who do you say?"

"The Earl of Whitcombe—so good, so noble, and so brave!"

"Why, the girl's mad!—the fellow's dead!"

"Dead!" screamed Marianna. "Have you killed him?"

"Killed him? I? Not I! But he has met with his deserts, as a highwayman. Do you not know that this Earl of Whitcombe you speak of took to the road, and became a well-known highwayman, by the name of Captain Heron? He was shot some time ago, near Edgeware. How did you ever become acquainted with him, brought up, as you have been, in strict seclusion and privacy?"

"Last night."

"Last what?"

"Last night I saw him."

"You dream, girl—you dream; or some impostor has imposed upon you."

"No, no! I saw him; he took me by the hand, and promised to aid and save me. I have faith in him that he will do so still. I do not think that even these walls and all these doors, and even all the guards and attendants that can surround your Majesty, will keep him from me."

Before Marianna had begun to utter these last words, Captain Heron had made up his mind what course to adopt.

No longer as the Baron Von Peck would he present himself before the King, but in his more proper character of Felix Heron, the highwayman of Epping Forest.

The coat that he wore was that which he had to meet emergencies of this character.

He had but to slip it off and reverse it, when it presented the bright scarlet horseman's surtout which assimilated well with his character of a knight of the road.

The wig of the Baron Von Peck was dispensed with in an instant.

A slight alteration in the hat he wore, and the addition of a half crape mask, which only left the moustache, the mouth, and the chin visible, made up altogether a complete change in the person and appearance of Captain Heron

With the butt-end of a pistol he struck three heavy blows upon the panel of the door that separated him from the King and from Marianna.

An exclamation of surprise came from the lips of the King.

Marianna uttered a shriek of joy and hope.

Any interruption of the terrible scenes in which she bore a part was welcome to her.

Bang! bang! bang!

Heron struck three more blows on the panel.

It was not etiquette for the King to cry, "Come in," had he been ever so much inclined to do so, and certainly he was not at all so inclined; but Marianna had no such scruples.

"Come in! Come in! Whoever you are, come in, and save me!"

"No!" shouted the King.

Heron opened the door, and slowly stalked into the apartment.

The King retreated backward until he could get no further. The wall stopped him, and then he paused, with such an expression of fright upon his face, that Heron saw resistance was quite out of the question.

The looks of gratitude and joy which poor Marianna bent upon Felix Heron required to be seen to be appreciated. No words could, in any degree, do justice to them.

She clung to his left arm—the arm next to his heart — as she would have clung confidingly to a father.

All doubt—all fear—all anxiety had vanished.

The only words she uttered were, "I knew that you would come!"

"And you know me?" whispered Heron.

"At once!"

The perception of the young girl, that this masked figure in the scarlet coat was, indeed and in truth, that same Felix Heron, the Earl of Whitcombe, who had been so true a friend to her at Hampton Court, was too strong on the mind of Marianna to be questioned for a moment.

But Felix Heron felt that he had to arrange matters with the King, whose first fright might soon pass away, and then the situation would be one of some peril.

And, in fact, this seemed to be exactly the case, for the King hastily approached a bell-rope that hung close to one of the windows of the room, and grasped it with a nervous clutch.

"Hold!" cried Heron. "On your life, hold!"

As he spoke, he presented that same long, bright-barrelled pistol which had bred such consternation in the mind of Peter at Hampton Court, full at the head of the King.

The royal countenance blanched with fear.

The bell-cord was dropped.

"That is well," said Heron; "and now, your Majesty, I have but two requests to make to you."

"Stop!"

Felix Heron paused.

"You live! You are no ghost!"

"Beware!"

"No, no! Tell me only that you are a living man, and I will forgive and forget."

"Can she forgive and forget?"

Heron, as he spoke, pointed to the girl, who clung to him with such a confiding energy, as her only support and hope.

The King was silenced.

"I demand of your Majesty that jewel-casket.

"Oh, no, no!" cried Marianna. "He tried to make me think that those jewels were worth

CAPTAIN HERON, WITH EDITH AND TOM RIPON, EFFECT THEIR ESCAPE FROM HAMPTON COURT PALACE.

Presented Gratis with No. 84, of the New Edition of EDITH HERON, the Sequel to Edith the Captive ; or, the Robbers of Epping Forest.

honour—virtue—all the world! Do not take them!"

"They will no longer corrupt any one now," said Heron, as he lifted a casket that was upon the table, and coolly put it in his pocket.

The King looked aghast.

"And now, your Majesty," added Heron, "I make no doubt but there is some mode of egress from this place different from that I have entered by."

The King was silent. A look of dogged, stolid obstinacy settled upon his face.

"I insist upon an answer," said Heron.

Heron strode up to him, and placed the cold threatening muzzle of the pistol to his ear.

"Once—twice——"

"Hold!"

"It is twice. If I say thrice, I fire!"

"Take this key."

The King handed to Felix Heron a gilt key.

"Take this key. You will see a key-hole that it will just fit close to the frame of yonder mirror."

"That will suffice."

Heron opened a long door, that brought the whole of the mirror with it, and disclosed beyond it a black and dismal opening.

CHAPTER CCIX.

CAPTAIN HERON REVISITS HIS OLD HAUNT AT EPPING FOREST, AND MEETS WITH A SURPRISE.

THE King uttered a cry.

He was on the point of escaping from the room when Felix Heron darted after him, and caught him just in time by the skirt of his coat.

"Not so fast!"

"Treason—treason!"

Lord Clackington put his head in at the door of the room, and Felix Heron at once flung at it the casket of jewels.

The crack that the casket came against Lord Clackington's head was alarming to hear, and the casket itself flew open, scattering its bright and glittering contents on the floor.

Then Felix Heron grasped the King by the arm as he spoke in a tone the sincerity of which could not be doubted.

"Is it worth while to cast away a life and a crown for this folly? I must and will escape, and carry with me this young girl, whom you would have betrayed to destruction."

"You shall."

The King was thoroughly alarmed.

"You shall—I promise it."

"Then speak aloud, and dismiss yon meddling fool."

"Meddling—fool! Who?"

"Clackington."

"Oh!"

The King called out aloud—"Tell my Lord Clackington not to interfere with what does not concern him."

A confused murmuring noise was heard in the next apartment, and then a door was closed.

"Not that way," added the King, as he pointed into the black space behind the mirror, which had been disclosed by the agency of the gilt key. "Not there. It has no outlet."

"I surmised as much."

"Follow me."

Heron hastily picked up the casket, and thrust back into it all but two or three of the jewels.

The King crossed the room, and entered another, the window of which looked into the garden of Warwick House, and from which window down to the garden there was access by a flight of stone steps.

"Go," said the King. "Your way lies plainly before you. Here is a key to the private gate of the garden. I only ask one thing."

"What is that?"

"Simply that all the proceedings of this night shall be buried in oblivion."

Heron was silent.

He looked at Marianna.

"Oh, yes! yes!"

"Then be it so. The proper person has replied to that question, and so, your Majesty, good night; and may the next adventure in which you engage your royal leisure be a something more worthy of a king."

No answer was returned to this biting reproof; and as Captain Heron no longer entertained a doubt but that he really and truly saw the way before him to leave Warwick House, he took Marianna by the hand, and led her at once down the flight of steps.

The King then called after him, and in rather an undignified tone of voice. "Cast the key," he said, "over the garden wall. One of our household will find it."

To this Heron made no reply, for he intended to do no such thing; and thus was it that neither of those observations made by either of these parties met with any direct answer from the other.

The garden of Warwick House in that direction was but of limited extent; and as Felix Heron felt the necessity of leaving the precincts of the royal residence as quickly as possible, he hurried Marianna with him.

For once in a way the King had spoken the truth, and the key he had handed to Heron did its duty at the little gate which was the private entrance to the garden.

Far from casting the key over the garden again, as he had been particularly requested to do, Heron put it cautiously into his pocket for future service.

There was a narrow pathway by the side of Warwick House that led towards the western end of Pall Mall; and as Felix Heron with rapid footsteps conducted Marianna along it, he congratulated her upon her escape.

"You will be safe now, at least for a time," he said, "with the Countess of Whitcombe; and it may be that you may be so altogether for an unlimited period. And at all events, if danger should threaten from any quarter, we shall probably have sufficient notice of it to guard against it, or to fly at its approach."

"Can it be possible," said Marianna, "that after all, I should be so happy as to reside with the Countess of Whitcombe?"

"We will hope so; and I feel assured she will be equally pleased to have you as an inmate."

Felix Heron began to feel quite conscious that Marianna was suffering greatly from fatigue. He could hear that it was quite with an effort she spoke, and she was compelled to lean almost her entire weight upon his protecting arm.

Marianna was like many persons with courageous impulses. She was able to support herself well while the excitement of the events that made a call on her energies lasted, but when that was over her strength forsook her, and she was scarcely able to feel that she existed.

The distance however, was very short to Whitcombe House.

And yet how full of risks it was to Felix Heron!

He had to cross St. James's Street at a tolerably early hour of the evening—not in the disguise of the Baron Von Peck, which gave him a certain assurance of safety, but in his own proper person, and as nearly as he could assimilate himself to it, in the costume of Heron, the highwayman of Epping Forest.

Five minutes, however, would place him upon the doorstep of Whitcombe House.

Surely no evil destiny would pursue him for that short space of time, and bring an atmosphere of danger about him.

"Courage, courage, Marianna," he cried. "We shall be at home in a few brief seconds."

"I am faint and weak."

"I know—I feel you are; but let the same spirit that has hitherto supported you hold you up still. In the hall of Whitcombe House you are safe."

"Oh, yes, quite safe!"

"There, lean upon me: you see your weight is nothing, and your feet need do little more than merely touch the ground."

Felix Heron had his head bent down towards Marianna as he spoke, but when he looked up again he staggered back as if her light weight had been too much for him.

In the dusky twilight of the rapidly approaching night he saw dimly a figure upon the doorstep of Whitcombe House, and from its attitude there could not be a moment's doubt that it was some one trying to make observations in the hall by peeping through the key-hole of the outer door.

The darkness of the evening was too far advanced, and the distance, short as it was, was yet too great, for Heron by ocular demonstration to convince himself of the identity of this person.

And it was not at this time, that brilliant gas lighted the streets, but miserable oil lamps, which were sure to be blown out by a gust of wind, or, as was more frequently the case, extinguished purposely by the depredators of the night, in order to carry on more securely their deeds of darkness. Such, indeed, was the case on the evening of which we are writing: the oil lamps, few and far between, and some of them extinguished, left Whitcombe House in deep shadow.

It was rather, then, a perception on the part of Felix Heron that he knew this person, than any evidence from his own eyesight of the fact.

He paused and spoke to the young girl softly, who hung upon his arm.

"Marianna!"

"Yes—oh, yes! What would you say?"

"Do not be alarmed—but it is necessary that for a few seconds you should conceal yourself in this doorway, which, you perceive, is only a short remove from Whitcombe House."

"There is danger, then! We are pursued!"

"Not so! But there stands a person on the doorstep of Whitcombe House who may or may not be a foe to you, but who certainly has been a bitter one to me!"

"Yes! yes! I will do anything you wish! It is for my sake you run all these risks, and that the very air you breathe is full of peril!"

"Not so!—not so! All will be well! Speak to no one—remove not from this spot on any persuasion until I return to you!"

The doorway into which Felix Heron conducted Marianna was one of a house about fifty paces distant from Whitcombe mansion. It was in such deep gloom that half-a-dozen persons might there with ease have ensconced themselves, and mingling with the black shadows cast by some massive columns supporting a heavy portico, completely escape observation.

Heron, then, without the slightest hesitation, walked towards the doorstep of Whitcombe House.

As he did so he spoke to himself in the faintest possible whisper, saying, "If that is not Jonathan Wild spying into the gate of the mansion, it is his ghost!"

But it was Jonathan Wild himself.

Quietly and noiselessly, Felix Heron stood on the step immediately behind him.

Wild was stooping low, so that his back was completely at right angles with the door, and he was so intently engaged with looking into the hall at Whitcombe House, that if Felix Heron had made much more noise than he did, it is doubtful if he would have been heard.

"I can't make it out," muttered Jonathan. "There is something mysterious here still, and I am deceived in some way. I can't make it out at all, but I shall, or I will know the reason why."

Jonathan Wild drew a long breath as he straightened himself up, and faced about.

By that movement he was so close to Felix Heron, so absolutely face to face with him—for Heron had taken off the half crape mask, and held it in his hand—that Wild saw into his very eyes.

There could be no doubt of his identity.

It was not that which caused the look of terror which spread itself over the face of Jonathan Wild.

It was of the mortality of Felix Heron that he doubted; for one of the few things that Jonathan Wild believed in was death; and that Felix Heron was no more was to his mind a truth so firmly impressed upon his understanding, that the sight of him then and there before him, apparently as a being of flesh and blood, could not be eradicated.

If it were indeed an apparition that he looked upon, its close proximity to him was anything but pleasant.

"Beware!" said Heron, in a deep, solemn voice.

That was enough for Wild.

Mortal man he feared not, but a being of another world, armed with unknown powers, and invested with unknown terrors, was too much for his organisation.

He bent down his head, and dashed off the door-step.

As Heron stepped adroitly aside, it was Jonathan Wild's full impression he had gone right through the supposed apparition.

Felix Heron could not imagine what Wild's object could be in turning neither to the right nor to the left, in each of which directions the pavement was perfectly clear; but it seemed as if a straightforward course over the roadway of St. James's Street was the only thing that suited him.

A sedan-chair was passing at the moment, and Jonathan Wild, as if for some great wager he was to keep a straight line, despite all obstacles, actually scrambled over the roof of it, to the great dismay of its bearers and a passenger who was in it.

Felix Heron had ample time to make his way to the deep doorway where he had left Marianna; and before Wild had disencumbered himself of the entanglement of the sedan-chair, he had flung his arm about her waist, and fairly carried her into the hall of Whitcombe House, the door of which he opened with a key which he always had in his possession.

If Heron then had been in a position to watch Jonathan Wild, he would have found a clue to the mystery of that headlong progress.

Jonathan had taken possession of the old chambers belonging to Lord Warringdale immediately opposite to Whitcombe House.

Believing that he had disposed of Lord Warringdale at the bottom of the Thames, Wild had thought it as well that he should have a West-end place of abode; and picking the lock of the chambers, he had quietly taken possession of them, along with all the goods and chattels of Lord Warringdale.

Felix Heron thought he was alone in the hall of his house with Marianna, but an exclamation from her made him aware of the fact that Tom Ripon was fast asleep in an arm-chair.

"Tom, Tom!" cried Heron. "Look alive! Jonathan Wild has been upon the doorstep!"

Tom Ripon sprung to his feet.

"The deuce he has, Captain! Oh, there she is!—there she is! I give them all up from this moment!"

"What do you mean? Are you asleep, or mad?"

"Neither, Captain; but when a fellow has eyes in his head, and sees Venus and all the Graces, aged sixteen, what's he to do?"

"He is not to fall asleep in the hall, under pretence that he is waiting for his master," replied Heron.

Tom was rather, as he explained it to Ogle when relating the circumstance to him, taken "a-back" by this speech; and before he recovered, Felix Heron had escorted Marianna to that well-known green drawing-room where Edith was anxiously expecting his return.

There was joy in that little household on that night; and if Edith could but have prevailed upon Captain Heron to forsake, at once and for ever, his perilous adventures on the road, she would scarce have had a wish unfulfilled upon earth.

Heron sighed deeply.

"It is my fate," he said. "You know well, Edith, what exertions I have made to assume the position that in truth belongs to me."

"Yes; but, as the Baron Von Peck, surely you may be a constant and a safe visitor here to me as the supposed widowed Countess of Whitcombe."

"I scarcely know how long that would last, but there is one expedition upon which I wish to start as early as may be."

"Ah! what is that?"

"It is unattended with danger, and I hope will be profitable. In one of the deepest recesses of old Epping Forest I have hidden some gold, and it is far better in our possession than that it should remain to test the chances of time, and fall into the hands of strangers."

"Deep in the forest?"

"Nay, Edith, look not scared at a visit to those green old haunts where we have passed some happy days. The owl, the bat, and the timid hare alone inhabit the darksome recesses of our beautiful and sylvan home."

Edith sighed.

A feeling of unknown peril took possession of her, and she would fain have cried to him, "Go not forth to night."

She saw, however, that he was bent upon the enterprise, and she would rather he went with her prayers to accompany him, than detain him until perhaps some more unpropitious time.

"Go, Felix," she said, "but take Ogle with you."

"Nay, rather let me leave him here, as your protector in my absence. Tom Ripon will accompany me; he is well mounted, fearless, and agile as a squirrel. The distance, after all, is but short, and we shall be back by the dawn."

Edith was fain to consent; and after again assuming his full disguise, as the Baron Von Peck, Heron started from the stable entrance of Whitcombe House, mounted on Daisy, and accompanied by Tom, who was quite delighted at the enterprise.

It was a great object with Heron to get out of London as soon as possible, and he put Daisy to such speed that it was rather difficult for Tom's horse even with his light weight to keep up with him.

When once, however, fairly on a good country road, Captain Heron let Tom come up to him, and restrained Daisy to a considerably easier trot.

"Captain," said Tom, "it's one of the fairest nights for us that ever I saw or expect to see."

"For us, Tom? What do you mean?"

"Why, of course, Captain, I mean for our little affairs on the road."

"But you don't suppose that I am out on any such expedition, do you?"

"Not out? And Daisy too! Oh, won't she be just a little disappointed!"

Heron laughed.

"No, Tom, I am bound for Epping Forest, to see if some gold that I hid in its depths is still to be found there."

"Well, Captain, that comes to much the same thing; but you don't mind me doing a little in the stand and deliver line on the road, do you?"

"On the way back, Tom, but not now."

CHAPTER CCX.

CAPTAIN HERON AND TOM RIPON FIND EPPING FOREST IN THE OCCUPATION OF OLD ENEMIES.

TOM RIPON was rather dull after this half-and-half sort of permission to play the part of a highwayman, that Captain Heron had given him.

The last thing, however, that would ever have struck the mind of Tom Ripon would be to dispute any positive orders of Heron.

They rode on, therefore, for some miles in silence, and it was not until the old trees on the outskirts of the forest became visible that Tom again spoke cheerfully.

"Ah, Captain, there's the old crib!"

"Yes, Tom, but it is sadly deserted now."

"I almost wish we were back to it, Captain."

Perhaps at the bottom of his heart there lingered a wish that was very near akin indeed to that which Tom had just given utterance to.

Both he and his faithful follower were, however, soon diverted from all other thoughts and considerations by a circumstance that struck them as decidedly singular.

They had believed Epping Forest to be entirely deserted, but such was evidently not the case.

A low, clear whistle sounded among the first clump of trees on its outskirts.

This whistle was followed by a hooting noise, very similar to that which used to be the private signal at the time that Heron and his band occupied the recesses of the verdant and picturesque wood

Daisy pricked up her ears, as though she, too, recognised the old well-known sounds.

Tom Ripon looked astonished.

"Why, Captain, what does all that mean?"

"I cannot imagine, Tom."

"We don't hold the forest now!"

"Hush!"

"To-whoo! to-whoo! Whoot! whoot!"

The cries came clearly upon the night air, echoing from glade to glade.

It was quite clear that Epping Forest was not in the lonely and deserted condition that Felix Heron thought it.

He paused to consider what course it would be most advisable to pursue.

"Tom," he said, "I think I will not risk anything in the wood to-night!"

"How do you mean, Captain?"

"I mean that I will take care of you and of Daisy, as the two most valuable things I have with me!"

Tom looked both pleased and alarmed.

He had no objection to be classed with Daisy, as of similar value, but he dreaded being left behind while Felix Heron sought adventures in the old forest.

"I hope you don't mean, Captain, that I am not to go with you into the wood?"

"How can you take care of Daisy, if you do?"

Tom was silent.

"And how can Daisy take care of you?"

"Well, Captain, I suppose it can't be helped."

"All is for the best, Tom. I have with me my silver whistle. You will comprehend that, if you hear three loud calls on it, you are to make your way with Daisy to that part of the wood where the large old sycamore tree was one night struck by lightning."

"I know it, Captain."

"Be wary, then, and vigilant."

"All's right. I will keep close. There is a capital cover here, by those nut-bushes that have grown up wonderfully since I last saw them."

Captain Heron dismounted, and handed the bridle of Daisy to Tom Ripon.

On foot, then, with a cautious step, but with his hand upon the hilt of his sword, he made his way into the wood.

Again the hooting noise echoed from copse to glade.

Heron fancied that he was seen.

That circumstance, however, did not in any way discourage him, and he walked on until he saw a light moving among the trees.

The light evidently approached him.

"Hilloa!" cried a voice.

"Who is there?" asked Heron.

"Hoy!"

Heron stood still, and the person who bore the light, and who had called out to him, came forward among the bushes.

Heron could see but little of him, except that he was a man about the middle height, and that the light he carried consisted of a lantern at the end of a short stick or pole.

He so held the lantern that he was very much cast into shadow himself.

But Heron had a suspicion that he knew him, and that it was none other than that John Tarleton, the bad brother of Edith, whom he had once sworn to kill, but had allowed yet to live for her sake.

When this man with the lantern spoke again Felix Heron felt quite certain of his identity.

"Hilloa, friend!" he said, "you are late in the old wood!"

"I have lost my way," replied Heron.

"Oh, indeed; and who may you be?"

"A gentleman!"

"Hem! Well, so am I. I suppose you want to find the nearest route out of the wood?"

"I do."

"You have only to follow me then, and I will soon show it to you."

"I am much obliged. Pray lead the way."

Felix Heron, whose real name and identity were effectually concealed by his disguise as the Baron Von Peck, heard John Tarleton laugh to himself, as he preceded him towards one of the forest glades, that was perfectly well known to him, Heron.

"Do you live in the wood?" asked Heron.

"Sometimes—just for a change, you see."

"A rough life, and I should almost think a hazardous one, from what I have heard."

"What have you heard?"

"Why, that Epping Forest was the haunt of a band of robbers, at the head of which was one Captain Felix Heron."

"Ha, ha!"

"You laugh at that?"

"I do. Perhaps you will in good time find out why I laugh at it. Come on, my good sir. This is the way, if you please. You are quite fortunate in having met with me in the forest, as otherwise you might have come across some bad characters."

"Indeed!"

"Oh, yes; the whole wood is alive with such desperadoes, I assure you."

By this time they had reached the glade, which by the route they took it was evident to Felix Heron they were approaching.

The quiet, easy manner of Heron had impressed upon the mind of John Tarleton that he had lit upon some very easy prey.

"Now see," he said, "if you look to the right, so far as you can be expected to do so in this darkness, I shall be able to point out to you exactly the route you should take to get clear of the forest."

"I am infinitely obliged to you," said Heron.

The moment he spoke John Tarleton laid the lantern he carried on the ground, and placing his hands to his lips he executed what no doubt Tom Ripon, who was an adept in such matters, would have declared to be an exceedingly clumsy adaptation of the hooting of an owl.

Felix Heron stood perfectly calm and composed, but he kept upon his guard, and looked warily about him.

It was quite evident, from what followed, that, though he, Heron, had deserted Epping Forest, and no longer held it with that band so devoted to his service, other persons had taken possession of it, and were quite prepared to carry out a similar career to that which had characterized Captain Heron.

From the bushes and thick-growing trees on each side of that forest glade there issued forth about a dozen desperate looking men, who, not without some skill and strategy, took up various positions, so that any attempt to escape on the part of the supposed strange gentleman who had lost his way in the wood was tolerably well provided against.

"Now, sir," said John Tarleton, altering his tone, and assuming one of brutal ferocity, "we are desperate men, and the less you say to us is the

soonest mended. We want your money, watch, jewellery, and, in fact, anything that is worth taking you may happen to have about you."

"Then you are thieves," said Heron, quietly.

"Call us what you will; we won't quarrel about terms, but hand over the booty."

"To your leader, probably, I may."

"I am the leader."

"Oh, no! I am quite sure the captain of so respectable an assemblage would never himself be prowling about, as a scout, with a lantern."

The thieves who had so hastily collected about Felix Heron in the Forest laughed at this observation, and one of their number called out, in a voice of ferocity, "Put a bullet into him, and have done with it at once."

"Hold, there!" cried a voice, as a tall man emerged from among the bushes. "What is all this? and whom have you here a prisoner?"

Heron too well knew that voice.

It was Lord Warringdale, who, notwithstanding all the dangers he had gone through, and the ferocious attempt that had been made upon his life by Jonathan Wild, still existed, and had taken up his abode in the forest as a last resource from the many dangers, both legal and personal, that assailed him.

"The Captain!—the Captain!" was now the general cry, and it was evident that the lawless men in that dense and shadowy wood looked upon Warringdale as their leader.

A strange feeling came over the mind of Felix Heron.

More than once, twice—ay, even more than thrice, he had spared Lord Warringdale, and made him a present so to speak, of his life.

The question that Heron asked himself was this.

Was there a sufficient feeling of humanity shame, or gratitude in the heart of that bad man which would induce him to act similarly to him, Heron?

It was not that Heron actually felt that his life was in the hands of his half-brother; but, no doubt, under the present circumstances, Lord Warringdale would be inclined to think such was really the case.

Upon that thought Heron wanted to test him.

He still kept up the assumed voice in which he had spoken from the first; and, with the same calmness of demeanour which had characterized him throughout, he said, "I may as well state now, at once, that my presence here is not accidental. I have sought Epping Forest for a special purpose, and it is to make an important communication to your leader in regard to a certain earldom and its contingent properties and estates!"

Lord Warringdale uttered an exclamation.

Such a communication could only be addressed to him or to Felix Heron; and he, in common with all the world, was impressed with the idea that Heron was no more.

"Speak," he cried, "and speak truly. What is it you have to say to me?—for I, of all here present, am the only person interested in such a subject."

"Is it your pleasure that I speak aloud what I have to say," added Heron, "or will you receive it yourself alone?"

Lord Warringdale hesitated a moment, for he was constitutionally cowardly; and even in the depths of Epping Forest, with a band of desperadoes about him willing to do his behests, he was still full of fears.

The reflection of a few moments, however, was sufficient to convince him that no man in his senses would attack him with the slightest prospect of escape, and his death was not so important a matter to any one that they would sacrifice their own lives to compass it.

He stepped aside with Felix Heron.

"Now, sir," he said, "what is it you have to say of the Earldom of Whitcombe, for it is that you came to speak about?"

"I have simply to ask you," said Heron, at once assuming his natural voice, "if you know me?"

Surprise and consternation kept Lord Warringdale silent for a short time.

The course he then adopted was at once startling and unexpected to Heron.

"Fire, all of you," he shouted, "and heed me not!"

Simultaneously with the utterance of these words, he suffered himself to drop completely to the greensward of the forest glade, so that the rattling discharge of pistol shots that immediately succeeded brought no danger to him.

Captain Heron, however, was a fair target, and at that moment he ran a greater risk of his life probably than he had ever ran before.

One bullet struck him on the shoulder.

Another grazed his neck.

Neither could be said to have absolutely wounded him, so slight in truth were the injuries they produced, but it was a great risk, for all that.

And so sudden and so totally unexpected was the action on the part of Lord Warringdale, that Heron, for once in his life, was sufficiently taken by surprise to be irresolute.

The sound of fire-arms, however broke the spell which the sudden act of treachery on the part of Warringdale had cast about Heron.

With one leap he cleared the crouching form of his half-brother.

"Warringdale," he shouted, "we shall meet yet again, when you will bitterly repent this act."

Heron was so well acquainted with Epping Forest, in all its intricacies, that it was much the same to him by night as by day.

A few minutes sufficed to take him quite clear of all danger and all pursuit.

Then he paused, and asked himself if he should still carry out, or not, his projected search for the gold he had hidden about the ruins of the old Priory.

"No," he said. "There let it still abide. If the time should come when any one dear to me requires it, still I shall have the power to seek it."

A glance about him at the well-known trees enabled Felix Heron to know in what direction to go in search of Tom Ripon and Daisy.

In five minutes he had rejoined them.

"Come, Tom," he said "I have seen and heard quite enough in Epping Forest for to-night."

"And I too much, Captain," said Tom.

"What, then, have you seen?"

"I hardly know what to call it; but the old wood is pretty well surrounded by men, who, if they are not 'Robins,' I am not Tom Ripon."

A "Robin" was a familiar term frequently used to signify police-officers, on account of the red waistcoats they all at that time wore.

"Constables, Tom?"

"Yes, Captain."

"Who leads them?"

"I don't know; but I do know that it is not Jonathan Wild."

"Then let us be off as quickly as we can, Tom, for this is no place for us."

Felix Heron mounted Daisy, and at a trot he and Tom Ripon left the forest.

It was not until they got about five miles on the road to London that Heron pulled up, on hearing the clear, loud notes of a horn on the night-air.

"A mail coach, Tom," he cried.

"Ah! yes, Captain. Oh, dear me!"

"What's the matter?"

"Not much, Captain; but I feel rather bad. Don't you think you could ride on and wait for a fellow at the next mile-stone?"

"What for?"

"The coach. Stand and deliver! Your money or your life! That's the dodge!"

Heron laughed

"You are too late, Tom! You are too late!"

Felix Heron and Tom Ripon had only just time to draw aside on the road, as a horseman, closely followed by another one, came at a gallop past them.

That bit of the road happened to be extraordinarily light, for an opening in the night clouds sent down a good strong moonlight reflection, and by that light Heron saw, to his great surprise, that the two horsemen were fully equipped as perfect highwaymen.

They were well mounted, too, and went past him and Tom Ripon at a good speed.

"Hilloa, Captain!" cried Tom, as soon as these two men had galloped on so far as to be well out of earshot,—"hilloa, Captain! Who may they be?"

"I cannot imagine, Tom!"

"Gentlemen in our line, Captain?"

"I must and will ascertain who they are! You trot on gently by the road, Tom: I will, with Daisy, take to the meadows and have no doubt but I shall soon overtake them."

"All right, Captain!"

"Don't you pass them, Tom."

"Oh, no ; I will keep on this side of them till you blow that whistle for me."

"That will do."

CHAPTER CCXI.

CAPTAIN HERON DISPOSSESSES LORD WARRINGDALE OF HIS FOREST HOME, AND STOPS THE SHAM MAIL COACH.

CAPTAIN HERON rode on about fifty paces, till he came to a gate on the left-hand side of the road that led into the fields.

Perhaps the gate might have been opened with some trouble, but it was the easier and shorter mode of operations for Daisy to leap it.

Heron backed the gallant creature as far across the road as the hedge on the other side would permit, and then cried out, "Leap, Daisy—leap!"

Daisy was over the gate as if she had had wings with which to do such feats at pleasure.

Turning, then, to the right, Heron set off at a swift racing pace along the meadows in a parallel line with the hedgerow.

The two horsemen, who bore so completely all the outward semblance of highwaymen, had, as they were well mounted, made, by this time, considerable progress.

But Heron knew that he should soon be able to overtake them, as, at the pace he now went, it is no exaggeration to say that Daisy went two feet while the horsemen on the road went one.

The sound of the horses' feet on the road came plainly to Heron's ears.

Daisy's progress, being on the soft turf of the fields, was muffled as to sound, and could not have been heard unless specially listened for.

But just as Heron came abreast of the two highwaymen, they ceased the hard trot at which they had been going, and subsided into a very quiet walk.

The long, prolonged notes of a horn came again on the night air.

Heron guessed that the coach which was so evidently upon the road had been stopped to change horses, and was now starting again.

So close to the hedgerow as he was now with Daisy, he could hear distinctly what the two highwaymen said to each other.

Their discourse was rather mysterious.

"Well, my lord," said one, "I think we shall soon test the nerves of our party in the stage coach."

"I think so, too, Colonel," replied the other.

Heron was puzzled.

Were these two fellows only giving themselves the titles respectively of "lord" and "colonel" from some absurd fancy so to do, or were they really what they implied they were?

That was a question.

But as Heron kept pace with them, he resolved to pay every possible attention to what they said, that he might come to some correct conclusion on the subject.

The horn of what no doubt was a coach advancing sounded again

"There they come, my lord!" said the one of the highwaymen who was called "Colonel" by the other.

"Yes, Colonel. I wonder if the Marquis is driving himself to-night?"

"I rather think his Grace the Duke will take the reins."

Heron listened to all this incredulously; but from the next few words they uttered, he was better able to come to some opinion, whether right or wrong, on the matter.

"Your lordship actually means to rob them?" asked the Colonel.

"Oh, undoubtedly!"

"It will be capital sport!"

"Excellent, I expect ; and I intend to produce the watches and purses at the Duchess's entertainment to-morrow night!"

"Capital! capital!"

"Yes ; I flatter myself that the little affair will make a sensation, and be the best part of the fete that her Grace has taken so much trouble and spent so much money to make attractive, at Ranelagh."

Heron considered.

It was just possible that these two persons were really members of the aristocracy, and were a lord and a colonel.

If so, the object of their present disguise was a practical joke.

But there was one difficulty.

They projected stopping a public mail coach on the King's highway !

There was no joke in that.

First of all, some one might resist, and the conflict, began as a joke, might end as a tragedy

Secondly, it would be no answer to a charge of felony to say that the matter was only a practical piece of pleasantry.

But Heron heard more.

"What an odd fancy it is, Colonel," said he who was called my lord, "for such a man as the Duke to set up and drive a stage coach!"

"Very, but yet common enough."

"Yes! yes!"

"Do you know, my lord, that I have an idea on that subject?"

"What is it."

"Just this. When I find a young nob'eman take to such matters, I always fancy that at some time or another there has been a handsome groom in the family, and a frail ladyship."

"Ha! ha! Capital; you have hit it, Colonel!"

By this time Heron began to have a better notion still of the state of affairs.

The coach which was approaching was one of those vehicles started by some nobleman whose lordly ambition was to be a stage coachman, and these two mock highwaymen were two of his acquaintances, who intended that he should have the practical joke played upon him of being stopped by knights of the road.

Heron smiled as he patted the neck of his noble and sagacious Daisy.

"It may be," he said in a low tone,—"it may be, Daisy, that we shall be able to turn this joke into a reality."

Heron paused then, and let the two sham highwaymen pass him, for he wished to intercept Tom Ripon, who by this time was likely to be near at hand.

In a few seconds Heron heard the sound of the horse's feet Tom Ripon rode, and he looked over the hedgerow to call to him.

"Tom! Tom!"

"Yes, Captain."

"Stop now ; I will come over to you. Out of the way of Daisy's leap!"

"All right, Captain!"

Another moment, and Daisy was in the roadway

by the side of Tom Ripon and the other horse, and then Heron possessed Tom with the story that he had heard, and his own impressions in regard to the whole affair.

"It will be capital fun, Captain."

"It will, and capital sport too, no doubt. I propose that we watch the whole affair, Tom, and then rob the robbers."

"That's it! that's it, Captain!"

"It will be so very obliging for them to take the trouble of bringing the coach with their own intimate friends in it to a stand-still, and then to give up to us all they take."

"Excellent! excellent, Captain! Let us give them a good fright, Captain, while we are about it."

"We will so. Come on; keep very quiet and close to the hedgerow. Ah! this is just the very thing—a double hedge, where we can see and hear all that passes."

Captain Heron and Tom Ripon had noticed one of those double hedgerows so common in England, where, in addition to a regular road, with its bank and luxuriant hedgerow on each side, there was a little supplementary way, as if an extra half-mile or so of hedge and tree had been made on the side about four or five feet into the highway.

These little extra shadowy pathways no doubt have some special origin, and at one time had some special use which is now forgotten; but there in country districts they remain, beautifully cool and verdant even in the midday heat.

It was in such a place as this, occurring in such an opportune juncture, that Tom Ripon and Captain Heron were able to await the progress of events in connexion with the stage coach and its aristocratic occupants.

A more eligible spot for the species of observation which they wished to bring upon the whole transaction could not possibly be found; and as the extent of the narrow sort of lane in which they were was at least three quarters of a mile, the collision between the two amateur highwaymen and the sham stage coach was certain to take place within that space.

Tom Ripon was about to make some observation, but as the two horsemen who respectively denominated themselves a lord and a colonel at that moment rode up, and actually halted opposite to where Heron and his follower were in hiding, Tom's Captain checked him with a low hush, and they remained profoundly silent.

"This is the very place, Colonel," remarked that one of the mock highwaymen who was called my lord,—"this is the very place for our operations."

"It is as excellent, my lord, as if we had contrived it ourselves."

"Yes, only look at its capabilities. The moment we have frightened them half out of their lives and taken from them their watches and purses, we can ride into this little lane by the roadside, and I warrant me they'll be in too great a fright to know where we have gone."

The horn blown by some one on the coach top sounded again, and it was quite evident that the coach was very near at hand.

The tramp of its four horses was plainly to be heard.

The gleaming of its side-lamps came gliding along the hedgerows.

"It seems to me, Tom," whispered Heron, "that we have now nothing to do but to wait the course of events."

"That's all, Captain."

In about a minute and a half the coach reached the spot where the conflict, if there was to be one at all, was sure to take place.

The two mock highwaymen had separated, placing themselves respectively on each side of the road; and as the stage coach was not going at any very great speed, as soon as the reflection from the lamps fell upon them they must have been well seen by all its passengers.

And, in fact, Felix Heron had a better view of these two personages now than he had ever had before. And he could not but smile at the ferocious manner in which they were got up to play the part of highwaymen.

Scarlet coats, with the lappets thrown open at the breast, to exhibit the stocks of a pair of pistols.

Crape masks nearly down to the chin, and low-crowned hats, pulled as far down over the brow as possible.

"Halt!" cried one of the mock highwaymen. "Your lives be on your own heads!"

"Halt!" shouted the other: "my noble friend, Captain Blood, means your deaths on your own heads."

"So I do, Captain Gore," responded the other. "Fire!"

The report of two pistols, one from each of the mock highwaymen, had all the effect they intended upon the coach and its occupants.

"Egad!" said the person who was driving, and who had an eye-glass at his eye—"egad! this looks serious. We're stopped by highwaymen, by Jove!"

"Sink me, your Grace!" said a supercilious looking personage, who sat next him on the box seat. "Sink me, if we shall not be all robbed and murdered in the regular way."

"Stir another inch," shouted one of the pretended highwaymen, "and we will shatter everybody's skull to atoms."

"Stir half an inch, or even a quarter, and I will do it!"

"Egad! this looks serious. Woa! woa, leaders! Ned Rocket, where are you?"

"Here, your Grace," said a weak, timid voice from the back portion of the coach.

"Well, egad! it strikes me you ought to fire the blunderbuss, Ned Rocket!"

"So I would, your Grace, but it won't go off."

"Egad! you told me you had loaded it."

"Yes, your Grace; but it was with the sweetmeats that Lady Betty Blueacre gave us at May Fair."

"Then, egad! we're in for it."

The two sham highwaymen had by this time ridden up respectively to each window of the coach, and putting on the most bullying and ferocious voice they could command, they each dashed the barrel of a pistol on to the window ledge, as they both shouted in chorus, "Your watches, money and valuables; or your lives, or altogether, if you like better. Quick, for we have no time to lose!"

The coach was occupied by some private friends of his Grace the Duke who drove it, and whose little eccentricity was to take the rather disreputable set that called themselves his intimates, some ten or twelve miles out of town and back again, as if they had gone a regular stage coach journey, and he the accredited driver.

A couple of ladies, called so by courtesy, were in the vehicle, and they, as a matter of course, began screaming with all their might.

It was not that they had anything to lose, or

CAPTAIN HERON TURNS THE TABLES ON THE MOCK HIGHWAYMAN.

Presented Gratis with No. 65, of the New Edition of EDITH HERON, the Sequel to Edith the Captive; or, the Robbers of Epping Forest.

were in the slightest degree afraid, but the opportunity of making a noise was not to be disregarded.

The two gentlemen who were with them, likewise so called by courtesy, were genuine poltroons, and shook with fear.

"Spare our lives," said one, "and take all we have."

"Fire and fury!" cried one of the sham highwaymen. "I don't know that we shall, unless you are quick about it!"

"Thunder and crackers!" said the other, "I feel half a mind to blow the roof off the coach! What do you say, Captain Gore, to flinging our powder flasks into the concern, and then show a light? Puff, flare, bang! Away everything would go, and everybody with it!"

"Murder! Have mercy upon us!" shouted the other gentlemen from the coach.

With nervous eagerness, they divested themselves of their rings and watches, and likewise handed, each of them, a well-filled purse to the mock highwaymen.

"Will that do, Captain Gore?"

"Not quite, Captain Blood; we must attend to the ladies."

"Oh, certainly! Now, ladies, if you please. I see you have handsome earrings; and if you cannot get them out quickly, we have a shorthand way of taking them, with a bit of the ear along with them!"

"Brutes!"

"Monsters!"

"Look sharp—look sharp! Time flies, and so must we!"

"Here, Jeremiah," said one of the gentlemen, still shaking with fear; "do give them everything, or they'll be the death of us all!"

"You'll make it up to me double?"

"We will—we will!"

"There then! There, Mr. Highwayman; and I can only say I never came near such a wretch in my life! Pull a bit of my ear off, indeed! You ought to have your own boxed!"

"Ladies," said the mock highwayman, who was called my lord, "we have now the distinguished pleasure of bidding you good night, and hope sincerely you will enjoy yourself at the Duchess's ball to-morrow."

The two gentlemen, as well as the two ladies who were within the coach, appeared to be very much surprised at this remark from a highwayman on a lonely road some six or eight miles away from London.

"Egad!" cried the Duke—and he was really a Duke who drove the vehicle—"have you settled everything with the insides?"

"Yes," cried the two highwaymen, in chorus; "and we are now going to begin upon the outs."

"Well, egad! you see, I am the coachman; and little Ned Rocket, there, with the blunderbuss that won't go off, is the guard."

"We don't interfere with you, but that gentleman sitting by your side looks as if he had something in his pocket!"

"No, no!" cried the personage alluded to. "I have not!"

"Egad!" said the Duke,—"you mustn't say that! It never struck me when I set up a coach that to make things regular it ought to be stopped on the highway; and now that it is so, why it's all right and proper that you should be robbed!"

With a very bad grace, this person surrendered a watch and seals and a pocket-book.

By this time the two mock highwaymen had

their pockets pretty well stuffed with booty, and were satisfied that they had carried that part of the joke far enough.

"You may drive on now, coachman," said the one who was called Colonel; "and I hope you and your passengers will remember as long as you live the two notorious and celebrated highwaymen, Captain Gore and Captain Blood!"

CHAPTER CCXII.

FELIX HERON MAKES A GOOD BOOTY, AND REACHES HOME IN SAFETY.

WITH these words, the two gentlemen—for such, no doubt, they were, both by birth and fortune—who had carried out the practical joke of stopping their friends' coach on the highway, rode off.

They took the route towards town.

"Well, Captain," said Tom, "I call all that rather a cool affair!"

"Hush! Let the stage coach go!"

"Egad, friends all!" said the noble Duke who drove the coach, "I would not have missed this little affair for the best horse in my racing stables!"

"It's all very well for your Grace, who has lost nothing!" responded the personage who sat by his side.

"Egad, yes! Ha, ha! Well, never mind; it's all a part of the scuffle! Ya! Hip! hip! Come up!"

The four horses were set in motion again, and off went the stage coach.

"Now, Tom," said Captain Heron, "you may speak as much as you like; and I don't see why we shouldn't come in for our share in this night's work."

"Nor I, Captain. It will be a better joke still to rob the robbers, won't it?"

"I think it will. Come on as quick as you can. A stern chase, as they say at sea, is a long chase; and we may have a good gallop before we come up with our men, who are not badly mounted."

"Hoy! hoy! Stop, Captain! It will be ever so much better to let me go first, or else Daisy will leave me a mile behind!"

Captain Heron was of a different opinion on that point, and merely waved his arm to Tom as he put Daisy to speed and galloped on.

Tom Ripon had, then, no resource but to make the best speed he could, which was good speed, although the horse he rode had no pretensions to the fleetness of such a racer as Daisy.

In about ten minutes, Captain Heron came to the foot of rather a steep hill; and as he drew rein a little, in order to prevent Daisy from going at full speed up the steep incline, which she otherwise would, he saw a couple of mounted men some half-way up the hill, going at a gentle walk.

That they were the two sham knights of the road whom he wished to come up with he saw at a second glance; for they were high enough up the hill for their heads and hats to be reflected well against the rather light patch of sky that seemed to crown its summit, and which looked towards the east, where the first faint effulgence of morning light was beginning to be seen.

Tom Ripon was about a mile behind.

But that was not much on a good road, with a tolerable horse.

Captain Heron, however, had no idea of waiting

for Tom Ripon when only two men were in question ; and he at once rode up to the Colonel and "my lord," whoever he might really be in regard to actual title.

The two horsemen who had perpetrated so capital a joke, as no doubt they thought it, on the stage coach of their friend the Duke, only casually glanced back as they heard the rapid trot of a horse's feet on the road behind them.

The next moment Heron had passed them ; and then, wheeling Daisy round. he faced them both.

This action on the part of Felix Heron took the two gentlemen by surprise ; and for the first moment they began, as the Americans say, to "realize" the fact that this single strange horseman had something to say to them.

What that something was, they were not long left in doubt concerning.

Captain Heron, as he reined in Daisy till she stood as still as a statue, spoke calmly.

"My lord, and you, Colonel, allow me to state a proposition which I think neither of you will feel inclined to dispute. A joke, however capital it may be in conception, is nothing unless carried out. You did your parts well in robbing his Grace and the stage coach ; it is now my turn to cry 'Stand, and deliver !'"

The two sham highwaymen looked at each other in mute surprise ; and then Captain Heron, who kept his eyes firmly fixed upon them, saw that he who was called the Colonel slowly and furtively moved his hand towards the holster of his saddle, where, possibly, he might be provided with loaded pistols, notwithstanding that he and his friend had sallied forth merely to perpetrate a jest.

Heron at once dropped his reins upon the neck of Daisy, who he knew would not move an inch.

Rapidly, then, snatching from his saddle his own pistols, he held one in each hand, covering the two horsemen, as he said, in a voice that had about it a tone of stern determination that was not to be trifled with, "I warn you, gentlemen ! The affairs of to-night have had a farcical character ; beware that they do not end in a tragedy !"

The hand of the Colonel slowly came away again from the butt of the pistol he intended to grasp

A look of blank dismay sat upon the faces of both the mock highwaymen ; and then it was the one called "my lord," who spoke in a tone of vexation.

"What is that you want? or is this, after all, only a joke ?"

"That is all, my lord ! It is but a similar joke to that which you have yourself practised ; but it would be a poor one without its termination. And therefore, gentlemen, I tell you I not only want your own watches, jewellery, and money, but the whole of the booty you have taken from his Grace's visitors in the stage coach !"

My lord and the Colonel looked rather blank at these words.

Whether the assault of Captain Heron upon them was a mere jest or a piece of serious business, it was equally evident that the laugh would be against them.

The Colonel was more irate of the two.

His anger and mortification almost lent him courage enough to engage in a contest with Captain Heron.

"Do you think, sir," he said, "be you whom you may, that we will, being two of us, calmly surrender to one ?"

"Yes, I do think so !"

"Then you will find yourself mistaken !"

"Hold !" cried Heron. "I dislike bloodshed for its own sake ; and if you have any real scruples about yielding to one man, I can dispel them !"

"How ?"

"Listen !"

The clatter of horses' feet that came now plainly enough upon the night air, showed that some one was approaching. Who it was, the two personages had no means of knowing ; but from the looks they exchanged, it was tolerably evident they hoped it might be some one whose accidental presence would turn the tide of affairs entirely in their favour.

Felix Heron knew well that it was Tom Ripon, and that although his appearance was not absolutely wanted, yet that it would materially change the aspect of affairs.

Willing, however, to try what might be the feeling of the Colonel and the noble lord provided they really had any advantage in the shape of numbers, he put on an air of mock candour, as he said, "Well, gentlemen, I cannot pretend to say, but that three to one would be long odds ; and I suppose my best plan would be to go off, wishing myself better fortune in the time to come ?"

"Go off with you, in the fiend's name !" said his lordship, "so that you don't spoil the capital joke we've been at some pains to carry out to-night !"

"I don't know that, my lord !" cried the Colonel. "It seems to me we ought to apprehend this fellow !"

Heron smiled, for at this moment Tom Ripon galloped up, and, touching his hat, he cried out, "Any orders, Captain ?"

My lord whistled rather ruefully.

The Colonel made a movement as though he would have shot past Heron, if he could, and trusted to the heels of his horse.

"No, sir !" cried Heron,—"that will not do ! My horse would outstrip yours in a half-mile run ; and, moreover, I might feel inclined to send something after you swifter still !"

Captain Heron looked significantly at his pistols as he spoke.

It was quite evident now to the two aristocratic jesters on the road that their sport was at an end. They looked particularly crest-fallen, and Felix Heron enjoyed their discomfiture exceedingly, as he put on a look of unconcern, saying to Tom Ripon, "You will be so good as to take care of what these gentlemen will hand over to you: and now, sirs, I beg that you will be quick about it, for we have other business on the road to-night !"

A very few minutes sufficed to place in the possession of Tom Ripon the whole of the booty that had been taken from the coach, while Felix Heron looked on as though he had been the most uninterested spectator in the world.

"Now, gentlemen, I have the honour to bid you good night !" he said ; "and when we meet again it will probably be in the saloons of the Duchess !"

This expression Heron had borrowed from the brief conversation he had overheard between the aristocratic highwaymen, and he merely made use of it now for the purpose of adding to their discomfiture ; not that he had any real intention of attempting to encounter them again at any duchess's, nor had he, in fact, the least notion of which duchess was alluded to.

But Felix Heron, like the rest of the world, was carried hither and thither by the force of circumstances ; and it was his fate, ultimately, not only o discover who the Duchess in question was, but actually to make one at the brilliant assemblage where his lordship and the Colonel had hoped that the relation of their practical joke upon the Duke and his stage coach would be the grand jest of the evening.

We will not anticipate, however.

Sufficient were the events which that night surrounded Captain Heron.

Tom Ripon's pockets were tolerably capacious, but they were tolerably well filled, not only with the booty which my lord and the Colonel had possessed themselves of, but likewise with a quantity of articles which, in their vexation, they handed over to him from their own pockets.

"All's right, Captain!" cried Tom.

"Gentlemen," said Captain Heron, "I advise you to pass on!"

"I suppose we may do that, or not, at our pleasure!" said the Colonel. "It is a poor privilege to those who are robbed on the highway to please themselves as to which route they take!"

"Beware!" said Heron. "I am the most patient man alive for ten minutes, but at the end of that time I will not answer for what may happen!"

"Come on, 'Colonel," cried he who was called "my lord." "What is the use of chaffering now that the mischief is done?"

His lordship struck spurs into his horse, and started off at a gallop.

The Colonel thought it was too much to be left alone in such suspicious company as Tom Ripon and Captain Heron, so he even followed his lordship as quickly as he could.

Heron paused until the last sounds of their horses' feet had died away.

"Come, Tom," he said. "Let us make our way through Woodford to town, and we shall not encounter these men again."

"This way, then, Captain; there is the narrowest lane in all the country side close at hand!"

"I know it—I know it! It is more like a footpath than a bridle road."

"Yes, Captain, and it leads direct through Woodford to town. And what a lucky thing it is that, after all, we've not had our journey for nothing, but have actually found the gold we came to Epping to look for!"

"Found it, Tom?"

"Yes, surely; it's in my pocket, isn't it? Where it comes from is of very little consequence, so that we take it home!"

"True—true! You lead the way, Tom, and I shall not outstrip you with Daisy!"

"All's right, Captain! We need not look to the right nor to the left, for the lane is a mile and a half in length, and the hedges on each side are a good fifteen feet in height!"

This lane was well known to Captain Heron as being one of the most dismal thoroughfares in the neighbourhood of Epping.

It had all the appearance of a long, narrow tube, and, moreover, had the reputation of being haunted.

This evil repute doubtless arose from the fact that about the middle of it there was a strange echo, which repeated, first at one end and then at the other, any sound that might be there made.

Tom Ripon was by no means so delighted with this lane as ever to go down it by himself, but his faith in Captain Heron was so great that he would have gone anywhere could he only be quite sure

that he was followed closely by, or was permitted to follow, that redoubtable personage.

But, on this occasion, the lane was passed through without any adventure of any kind or description.

But both Heron and Tom Ripon, upon emerging from it, full in the face of the eastern sky, were not a little surprised at the progress which the dawn had made.

A pale yellow light—but still one which made every object visible—shone upon the vegetation and upon their faces — their horses and their dress.

A little hillock, at a short distance in front of them, had the effect of hiding the adjacent country, but Felix Heron felt certain that he heard the sound of voices immediately on the other side of it.

He made a sign to Tom Ripon to be silent.

They both listened attentively.

A high voice was speaking.

A voice, not unpleasant in its intonation, but borrowing its high character evidently from the excited feelings of the speaker.

"Be it so, then, my Lord Clackington," said the voice. "I know not, and cannot conjecture, what misadventure has befallen the young officer who was to have seconded me in this encounter; but, assuming that the gentleman you have brought with you is a man of honour, I am content that he should do duty for both sides!"

If Captain Heron was surprised to hear these words in so lovely a spot, at such an hour in the morning, he was still more so when they were replied to in the undoubted accents of Lord Clackington.

"Marquis, you have forced me to this meeting, and most reluctantly have I come into the field to fight with one who has not yet attained his majority!"

"Peace, sir, peace! This is idle nonsense! Your character is well known, and it will be well if I succeed in ridding the English Court of one of its ancient and hoary-headed disgraces!"

"Your second, Marquis, is of a different opinion, since he comes not!"

"At that I marvel much; but, since I agree to accept yours, we need not wait!"

"As you please—as you please! What say you, Major Jarvis?"

"Oh," cried a shrill voice, "I am but a soldier of fortune, and am willing to be the friend of any gentleman who is a gentleman!"

"Then, be mine, sir, as well as my Lord Clackington's, on this occasion, at least! I do not see how we can go wrong! You have but to load the pistols, and stand by and give the signal to fire!"

"True, Marquis, true; nothing can be plainer!"

The Major coughed ominously as he uttered these words.

"Stop one moment!" said Lord Clokington. "I am far from satisfied with this arrangement!"

"Craven!" shouted the young man who was called Marquis.

"Not so hasty, my young sir—not so hasty! If you kill me, it will be all very well, because the Major is my second and my friend; but if I kill you, the case is altered!"

"How so? how so?"

"Oh, the world is not so good-natured!"

"What is the world to us, sir? One of us should bid it good-bye this morning!"

"Simply this, Marquis: that if you happen to

be the one to bid it good-bye, gossip will say that I and my friend Major Jarvis got you out here to a lonely place and killed you!"

"No, no!"

"I say, yes!"

"And I say 'no' again, and insist upon the contest commencing at once!"

"Indeed," added Lord Clackington, in a peculiarly dry tone of voice, "the censorious, ill-natured world might go so far as to say I had taken some steps to prevent your second being here!"

Major Jarvis, upon hearing Lord Clackington say this, was taken with quite a violent fit of coughing.

Tom Ripon slightly nudged Captain Heron on the elbow.

"Captain, Captain!"

"Yes, Tom—speak low!"

"Those are two rascals, and they mean to kill that young fellow!"

"I know it!"

"Hurrah!"

The hurrah that Tom gave was in so silent a manner that it could scarcely have disturbed a grasshopper out for a morning walk among the tall luxuriant weeds of the hedg-row.

"What do you desire? what can I do?" cried the young Marquis.

Lord Clackington was silent for a moment, and then he said, in the same peculiar voice in which he had last spoken, "Write a few words on a leaf of your pocket-book or tablets, to the effect that you consent that Major Jarvis should act as your friend on this occasion!"

"Ah, that would do!" cried the Major.

"It is easily done," cried the young Marquis, "if that will facilitate matters; for, declaring upon my conscience, I believe you guilty of all I impute to you, I have dared you here to the field, and, by the heaven above us, you shall not escape me!"

"Write, then—write!"

"With pleasure!"

There was a pause, during which Captain Heron slowly and carefully dismounted from Daisy.

"Tom Ripon!"

"Yes, Captain!"

"Take care of Daisy: I am going to be that young gentleman's second!"

"Bravo! bravo!"

"Hush!—not a word! Keep out of sight, for it is against the etiquette of these transactions that there should be any spectators but the principals and their seconds."

"There, Major Jarvis," cried the young Marquis at this moment,—"there is a full and complete memorandum written upon a leaf of my tablets, and signed by me, constituting you my second. Take it, sir!"

"No!" cried Felix Heron, stepping forward,—"there is no occasion!"

CHAPTER CCXIII.

FELIX HERON SAVES THE YOUNG MARQUIS, AND AVENGES MARIANNA.

IF some one had suddenly dropped from the moon, and offered to take the place of the missing second of the young Marquis, the surprise depicted on the countenances of the three persons among whom Felix Heron suddenly made his appearance could scarcely have been greater than it was.

Lord Clackington uttered a cry of fear.

Major Jarvis showed a strong inclination to run away.

The young Marquis, who was a slightly-built, fair-haired youth, but with a strikingly handsome and singularly intellectual-looking countenance, was the very picture of surprise.

Heron lifted his hat a few inches above his head, and in those courteous tones which bespoke him the well-bred gentleman, he spoke again.

"Chance has made me a listener to a chance dialogue, which has informed me of a difficulty that among gentlemen ought not to exist. It appears that a duel is in progress, and feeling bound to believe that the quarrel is a good one, I offer you my services, Marquis, as frankly as I hope you will accept them."

"Perdition seize you!" shrieked Lord Clackington.

Major Jarvis looked scared and pale.

But a bright light shone from the eyes of the young Marquis, and he held out his hand at once to Felix Heron.

"I accept with pleasure!"

Lord Clackington and Major Jarvis exchanged glances.

"By Jove!" cried the Major, assuming a bullying tone, "I should like to know who you are?"

"Jove has nothing to do with it: I am a gentleman!"

"Ah!" cried Lord Clackington. "Now I know him!"

"You know him?"

"Yes; that odious Baron——"

"Von Peck!" interrupted Heron, as he slightly raised his hat again,—"the Baron Von Peck, at your service, who will do himself the honour of seeing fair play to all parties, and that bullets are in both the pistols!"

Major Jarvis again made the movement to run away.

Lord Clackington looked so ghastly pale, that his thin, wrinkled physiognomy presented the aspect of some hideous waxen image rather than anything human.

Felix Heron had by mere accident hit upon the very plan which they had concocted for the purpose of murdering the young Marquis, which was that the Major was to load both the pistols, but only to put a bullet into that one which he handed to Lord Clackington.

A look of suspicion darted across the face of the young Marquis.

"Gracious heaven!" he cried. "Can it be possible that——"

"Hush!" said Heron. "Let us proceed; we will speak of all this afterwards, for I don't think that same 'gracious heaven' you mentioned will allow you to fall a victim to such a man as my Lord Clackington."

The business-like way in which Captain Heron turned to Major Jarvis was evidently perplexing.

"Gentlemen," said the Major, while the only particle of colour that his face exhibited settled itself in the end of his nose,—"gentlemen, cannot this little affair be arranged?"

"Certainly," replied Heron.

The countenance of the Major brightened up, and he now exchanged encouraging glances with Lord Clackington.

But the young Marquis interposed.

"No, no!—no arrangement!"

"I beg your pardon," said Heron; "as your second, I act for you in this matter!"

"But——"

"One moment. I fancy that more than half of the disputes in the world are about words merely; and it seems that we all take different views about this word arrangement."

The Major looked doubtful.

Lord Clackington's visage fell again.

"In my opinion," added Heron, "the affair, whatever it is, is being arranged in the only way which offers itself to the feelings of a gentleman."

"Good!" cried the young Marquis.

Heron smiled.

"Come, Major," he said, "you look for your principal, and I will do the same for mine."

"One moment," said Lord Clackington.

"Well, my lord?"

"The young Marquis of Ormond here has challenged me, because he will have it that I have had some hand in the—the—a—abduction—or

call it what you will—of a young lady to whom he is attached."

"I am sure of it!" said the Marquis of Ormond, whose title Felix Heron had just heard for the first time,—"I am quite sure of it!"

"You think so," added Lord Clackington. "But as we are, I hope, all gentlemen, and may speak freely here, I beg to say that this person, the Baron Von Peck, whom you are so ready to take as a second, was actually employed by a great personage in the matter of which you complain, because I was too scrupulous."

"Infamous slanderer!" cried Heron.

"It is true!"

"One moment!" said the Marquis of Ormond. "I have a letter here which will resolve my doubts."

The young nobleman took a small folded note from his pocket, and having first lightly pressed it to his lips, he opened it

He read half aloud:—

"And, dear Arthur, should you ever encounter a gentleman who names himself the Baron Von Peck, know him to be one of the dearest friends of your Marianna!"

"Marianna!" exclaimed Heron.

"Yes, Marianna!"

"A king's orphan?"

"The same, sir."

"Then I am the same Baron Von Peck she speaks of!"

The young Marquis turned with a triumphant look to Lord Clackington.

"My lord, I am quite satisfied with my second."

"And I with my principal," said Heron, who was much pleased to hear it, as he hoped soon to have it in his power to take the Marquis of Ormond home with him to Whitcombe House and to Marianna.

"Now, sir," said Heron, "the pistols!"

"Here!"

The Major shook visibly.

Heron looked at the pistol that was handed to him by the Major, and then said, "Marquis, did you bring no weapons with you?"

"I expected my second with them."

"Oh, true, true! I am your second, and here they are."

As he spoke, Felix Heron took from the pocket in the breast of his coat, where he always kept them, those long, bright-barrelled, highly-finished pistols, on which he knew he could so well depend.

Lord Clackington seemed ready to sink into the very earth with fear.

That he meditated flight Heron could see; and he was not altogether indisposed to indulge my Lord Clackington in such a course.

Felix knew well that a coward turned at bay might probably prove as dangerous to others as to himself, and he had already seen enough of the young and gallant Marquis of Ormond to feel a great interest in whatever might befall him.

But the truth was, my Lord Clackington was getting paralyzed with fear; and although he would gladly have fled from, to him, the terrible Baron Von Peck, and had every disposition in the world to do so, he was fast losing the power.

The Major, too, as he looked at his principal, and saw the deadly fear that was coming over him, seemed to add all that shrinking terror to his own, until the sum of it was too much for his endurance.

"My lords, and you, Baron," he said, in a trembling voice, "I'm afraid I don't feel very well."

"I am certain of it!" said Heron, sarcastically.

"Then, sir, for a sick man to be a second in a duel, you know, is one of those things that ought not to be."

"Oh, sir," added Heron, "we will excuse a great deal in a gentleman, who, so short a time ago, was willing to do that service for both parties. Come, sir, place your principal, for my time is short, and I have none to waste."

"And my patience is exhausted!" said the Marquis.

Lord Clackington glanced from the face of one to the other with a look of deep distress.

He evidently made two or three weak and imbecile attempts at flight, but his ancient legs, however nimble they might be on occasions in the carrying him about to the perpetration of various iniquities, failed him now, and he could not move.

"Quick, my lord!" cried Heron. "Time presses!"

Heron handed one of the pistols to the Marquis of Ormond.

"Hold—hold!" cried Lord Clackington. "One moment!"

The Major looked grim and ghastly.

"One moment!" added Clackington. "Life is sweet to all, and doubly so to the young Marquis. You are yet but on the threshold of existence, and surely do not wish to bid the world good-bye!"

"He has no such intention," interposed Heron. "It is you, my Lord Clackington, who may either bid it good-bye or leave it without any ceremony, as it may please you on this occasion."

"But, Baron——"

"Tush, tush! My lord, this is trifling!"

"A moment more!"

"Marquis," cried Heron, in a loud tone, "if your opponent will not move from where he is, you may suppose that is the spot upon which he chooses to stand and be shot!"

"No, no!"

"Yes, I say! And, since I happen to be here accidentally, and there are two pairs of pistols on the ground, I will engage with the Major here while you settle matters with his lordship."

"Not for worlds!" shrieked the Major.

"But I say yes, sir; for I feel that I must have offended you deeply."

"Not at all—not at all! I never had such a high respect for any gentleman in all my life!"

"Then you have offended me, so that it comes to the same thing."

"I will apologize, Baron—I will apologize!"

"I never accept apologies."

"Then run, my lord—run!" shouted the Major; "for this bloodthirsty Baron is evidently bent upon our destruction! Run, my lord—run!"

Lord Clackington seemed to be roused to a sudden energy by these words.

He turned and fled.

The Major took an opposite direction, and Heron spoke rapidly to the young Marquis.

"Fire after him, but don't hit him! He is not worth your vengeance; and the mere report of a pistol will go nigh to kill him. I will send a bullet after my Lord Clackington, for I've old scores to settle with him, although I will not kill him."

The two pistols were discharged almost simultaneously.

The effect was curious.

Both Lord Clackington and the Major fully believed themselves to be hit, and fell to the ground as if they had been so, rolling over, when there, in the most ludicrous manner.

Indeed, so complete was the downfall of each of these persons, that the Marquis of Ormond and Felix Heron looked at each other in doubt for a few seconds as to whether their pistol-shots had not really taken effect.

But Lord Clackington and the gallant Major scrambled to their feet again, and set off, each with increased speed, and, as before, in opposite directions.

The Major got clear off, and soon disappeared behind a clump of trees.

Lord Clackington was not so lucky.

Skirting the little hillock where Tom Ripon lay concealed, his lordship, without the least suspicion that an enemy was in that direction, came right upon Tom and the two horses.

Heron's faithful young follower had been a delighted and attentive spectator of the whole scene.

Leaving the two horses to take care of each other, which he knew they would do very well, or, rather, with a perfect confidence that Daisy would not stray from the spot, nor permit her four-footed companion to do so, Tom Ripon, by lying flat upon the ground, had succeeded in just projecting his head over the brow of the hillock so as to see everything, and yet be himself hidden by the low shrubs and brushwood with which it abounded.

"Where are you coming to?" cried Tom, as he set himself rolling so as to intercept the unfortunate Lord Clackington.

The latter was at speed, and could not stop himself.

He encountered Tom Ripon, and over he went.

"Now, stupid," cried Tom, "can't you look afore you? Oh, you needn't try that dodge; there's nobody else a comin'!"

The "dodge" Tom alluded to was the same rolling process down the side of the hillock which had enabled him so cleverly to intercept Lord Clackington.

But there was an essential difference.

Tom rolled down the hillock on purpose.

Lord Clackington's was an involuntary action, and only ended in a sedgy ditch covered with green slime that ran at the foot of the little eminence.

While this dramatic scene was going on between Tom Ripon and Lord Clackington, Felix Heron had addressed a few words to the surprised and indignant Marquis of Ormond.

"My Lord Ormond," he said, "I presume by this time you can have no doubt of the character of the two persons whom you so unsuspiciously met to-day."

"The cowards!"

"Worse than cowards! Call them assassins!"

"You really think, Baron, they contemplated my murder?"

"I am certain of it! And when you reach town you will discover that your second, who should have been here to-day, has been by some act of force or fraud prevented from keeping his appointment."

"Alas! all this must be too true, Baron! Believe me, sir, I do not forget or under-estimate the service you have rendered me, but my heart is still full of grief and indignation!"

"I doubt it not."

"Grief for the loss of her whom I love, and indignation that I have come here and not succeeded in avenging myself upon her greatest foe!"

"Not her greatest," said Heron, significantly.

"Ah! What would you say, Baron?"

"I would say that that wretched Lord Clackington, who, with old age, has not one of the qualities which should render it respected, is but the tool of one greater than himself."

"Alas, then, I despair!"

"Not so. Your visit to this spot has been far from fruitless; and had your vengeance been sated to its utmost, it would not have advanced the objects of your heart so much as a few casual words with the Baron Von Peck!"

Heron lifted his hat slightly as he spoke.

"Yes, yes!" cried the young Marquis, with an air of enthusiastic vehemence. "Why do I forget that Marianna gave me that name as belonging to one whom I might trust?"

"Never forget it, Marquis, but trust me still, and accompany me to London."

"With pleasure! Dispose of me as you will; I am at your service, Baron!"

"It is wisely resolved."

Heron blew a shrill note upon his silver whistle, and Tom Ripon stood up upon the brow of the hill as he shouted out, "Here, Captain, here! All's right! The old 'un is still kicking in the ditch down there below. He seems to be the wrong end uppermost; but it don't matter!"

"The boy calls you Captain," said the Marquis.

"Yes. An old familiar habit," cried Heron, as he smiled. "He and I have been in the wars together."

"Then you have seen service, Baron?"

"Yes. But that is a point we will not discuss at present. Tom, bring the horses down."

"Yes, Captain."

Tom Ripon led down Daisy and his own horse to the spot where the duel was to have taken place.

"My lord," said Heron, "I presume you have no steed at hand?"

"Yes. I trotted down here from London, and left my horse at a roadside inn, named 'The Wheatsheaf.'"

Tom Ripon's countenance brightened at this announcement, for he had began to suspect that the next proposition of Captain Heron would be that he should lend his horse to the young Marquis of Ormond, and find his own way to London in the best manner he could.

There was no necessity, however, for any such proceeding, and the little party trotted into London without meeting any other adventure worthy of record.

Tom took charge of the horses.

CHAPTER CCXIV.

THE MARQUIS OF ORMOND MEETS WITH AN AGREEABLE SURPRISE, AND BECOMES AN ATTACHED FRIEND OF CAPTAIN HERON'S.

It was at the corner of Pall Mall that Felix Heron dismounted; and, patting the neck of Daisy, gave her into the charge of Tom Ripon to take round with his own steed, and that of the young Marquis of Ormond, to the stables of Whitcombe House.

That there was some great mystery about the Baron Von Peck the Marquis was not at all slow to perceive, but what it was he could not at the present moment divine.

The manner of Captain Heron, however, was quite sufficient to convince him that that mystery was one the solution of which he had no cause to dread.

Already was the name of the Baron Von Peck favourably associated in his mind with that of Marianna; and he implicitly followed Heron wherever it might please him to lead.

It was now broad daylight; and Felix Heron felt the necessity of housing himself as soon as possible.

The confidence he felt in his disguise as the Baron Von Peck was tolerably perfect; but still there was a possibility, however remote, of it being penetrated by some of those lynx-eyed individuals who would only have been too glad to recognise in the so-called Baron the dashing and daring highwayman, Captain Heron.

Arm-in-arm with the young nobleman whose acquaintance he had so singularly made, Heron walked up St. James's Street.

The broad threshold of Whitcombe House was reached without any interruption of any kind or description.

"Do you reside here, sir?" asked the Marquis of Ormond.

"I am permitted to make use of this house as a home," was the somewhat ambiguous reply of Captain Heron.

"Then," added the Marquis, "you are doubtless acquainted with the noble lady who inhabits it?"

"I rejoice to say I am, Marquis; but have you too any knowledge of the Countess of Whitcombe?"

"Nothing further, Baron, than that a friend of mine, Colonel Trelawney, pointed out the house to me as in the occupation of such a lady, of whom he spoke in the highest terms."

"Indeed!"

"Yes; and I understand she is the widow of that famous Captain Heron, undoubtedly claiming to be Earl of Whitcombe, and who, they say, led as adventurous a life in Epping Forest as ever did Robin Hood in the nomadic glades of Sherwood long ago."

Heron could scarcely forbear from smiling as he knocked at the door of Whitcombe House.

That door was immediately opened by Ogle, who was so rejoiced to see Captain Heron safe and sound, that he was almost on the point of uttering an exclamation which would at once have let the Marquis know who he really was, but a glance from Heron stopped the words upon Ogle's lips.

"Is the Countess within?" asked Heron.

"Yes, Baron," replied Ogle, with a half grimace, for he never liked that title.

"Will you present my compliments to her, and request for me the favour of an interview?"

"Certainly, Baron. Will you be so good, Baron, as to walk up-stairs, Baron, if you please, Baron?"

"There," thought Ogle to himself, "I hope I've said Baron often enough to convince him that I'm not likely to make any mistake."

"Be so good as to follow me, Marquis," said Felix Heron, "and I will introduce you to this noble lady, from whom, I feel convinced, you will hear some news of your Marianna."

"On the invocation of that name, Baron, I would follow you to death itself!"

The Marquis of Ormond followed Felix Heron up the grand staircase of Whitcombe House, and into that same green drawing-room which has been so frequently presented to the reader as the scene of some of the most curious episodes in this narrative.

Felix Heron knew perfectly well that Edith was not likely to be in that apartment, or he would scarcely have so abruptly introduced the Marquis of Ormond into it; and, indeed, had Edith been there, Ogle would, by some means, have contrived to let him know.

The magnificent and costly room, however, was vacant; and then, with that courtly grace which was inbred in him, Captain Heron invited the young Marquis to be seated.

"Do not, my lord," he said, "think it strange or wanting in politeness on my part that I leave you alone for a few minutes: the time will speedily come when the mysteries which surround both you and myself, and which likewise implicate the Countess of Whitcombe, will be fully explained."

"I am quite at your service, Baron. I owe you already the obligation of a life: dispose of me as you please, and be assured I shall ever put the best construction upon all your acts and all your words."

The young nobleman was left alone in the green drawing-room; and it is no impeachment of his charitable disposition to presume that his impression certainly was favourable to the idea of a projected union between the Baron Von Peck and the, as he supposed, widowed Countess of Whitcombe.

He had heard that the Countess was young and handsome; and certainly Felix Heron, in his disguise as the Baron, looked neither the one nor the other.

With all the disposition in the world to be perfectly confidential and trustful in the extreme as regarded the young Marquis of Ormond, Heron yet wished to take the opinion of Edith before confiding to him what may now be called the secret of their lives.

In that suite of rooms on the second floor of the mansion, which communicated by the secret passages to the stables of Whitcombe House, Edith was waiting, with no small anxiety, the arrival of Heron.

The sound of his footstep, light as it was, upon the staircase reached her attentive ears.

She flew to meet him.

"Safe—safe again from more perils! Oh, Felix, Felix, when will this life of danger to you abroad, and anxiety to me at home, cease?"

"Be not anxious, Edith, but be ever assured that all is well! I bring a visitor with me who is welcome to me, and will be more welcome to you when you know him, but still more welcome to one in whom you feel a friendly interest."

"What riddle is all this?" said Edith, with a smile, as she hung upon Felix Heron's arm.

"It is a riddle easily read, dear Edith! Where is Marianna?"

"With me in yonder apartment; and the more I see of that dear girl the more fondly I am attached to her!"

FELIX HERON SAVES THE YOUNG MARQUIS OF ORMOND FROM THE
TREACHERY OF LORD CLACKINGTON.

Presented Gratis with No. 66, of the New Edition of EDITH HERON, the Sequel to Edith the Captive; or, the Robbers of Epping Forest.

"I was sure of it."

"Yes, Felix; and if no action in all your life but that one were to come to your remembrance in the midst of disaster or of sorrow, it would be sufficient to bring with it a consolation, for you have saved her from worse than death!"

Heron smiled upon Edith as he replied.

"And now I bring her something better than life!"

"Again enigmatical, Felix. What can that something be?"

"A lover!"

"A lover; and to Marianna! I fancy he will be scarcely welcome, for she is heart-whole."

"Which only proves that she has not made you a confidante, Edith, and that I know more of her affections than you do. But come into the deep shadow of this window, and I will tell you all."

Felix Heron then related to Edith the whole particulars of the adventure in which the young Marquis of Ormond had borne so conspicuous a part, and concluded by the expression of an opinion that the Marquis should be included in the small circle of intimate friends acquainted with the secret of his (Heron's) existence.

Edith hesitated, and shrunk a little from the extension of this confidence, which, at first sight, seemed more and more to endanger the safety of Heron.

"It shall be as you wish, Felix," she said. "I will not, and do not, question for a moment the honour and secrecy of this young man; but by your own account of him he is fiery and impetuous, and therefore it is I ask you can you trust his discretion as much as you would trust his loyalty and honour?"

"I think so, Edith, and counsel that he be implicitly relied upon."

"Be it so, then; and there is one safeguard at least which we will not forget, and that is his love for Marianna. I ask but one thing of you, Felix, and that is that you allow me to prepare her for his approach."

"Be it as you please. I will remain with him in the green drawing-room, where I have left him full of wonder and impatience at the mysteries that surround the Baron Von Peck. Come to us with Marianna when you will."

That Edith intended, in some manner peculiar to herself, to prepare Marianna for the interview with the Marquis of Ormond, Felix Heron could well perceive; but he was not perfectly aware that Edith felt in the slightest possible degree aggrieved that Marianna had not communicated so important an episode in her young life as her love for the Marquis of Ormond.

And Edith was resolved that she would extract the secret from her before permitting her to meet her lover.

"Dear Marianna," she said, "my husband, the Earl, has come home, but has met with a most strange adventure, which delayed him past the time he calculated upon."

"Indeed!" remarked Marianna, with all the calmness imaginable, and little suspecting that any one so interesting to her was beneath that roof as the young Marquis.

"Yes; he came upon a group of persons who were fighting a duel."

"Oh, Lady Whitcombe! how barbarous is that custom which places a weapon of death in the hands of, perhaps, the basest of men, because he may have have injured the noblest and the best!"

"It is so; and, in this case, I fear that was precisely the state of affairs. A man grown old in iniquity, a man full of many crimes, and whose name is the very antagonism of virtue, had been summoned to the field of honour by a mere youth, who, although we know nothing of him but his name, may still have those who love him dearly, and to whom his death may be the greatest calamity under heaven."

A very faint flush came over the features of Marianna.

Far, very far, was she at that moment from identifying herself in any way in the occurrence of which the Countess of Whitcombe spoke; but all the elements of a similar case existed in her own heart, and she mentally asked herself, with a sigh, how she would be able to endure such a calamity if it happened to one dear to her.

It was scarcely with a feeling of curiosity that she spoke, asking who the parties were in that barbarous duel.

"Both were gentlemen," replied Edith,—"gentlemen and noblemen; that is to say, one by courtesy, if those words really possess their real meaning, and one in reality. Old Lord Clackington can, in truth, have nothing in common with the young Marquis of Ormond."

The moment these words passed the lips of Edith they were bitterly repented of.

She felt all the heedless cruelty of which she had been guilty when she cast her eyes upon Marianna.

The young girl became as pale as death itself, her lips even were bloodless, and the look of reproach and anguish with which she regarded Edith was one that the Countess of Whitcombe felt that she should never forget.

Marianna did not scream, but with a deep-drawn sigh she half slid, half fell, from the chair upon which she had been sitting.

Who so anxious, then, as Edith to repair, as far as it lay in her power so to do, the unintentional mischief she had created?

"Look up, look up, Marianna!" she cried. "He lives! he lives! All is well, and he lives! Forgive me for thus cruelly playing upon your feelings. It was done without a thought, and only because I knew that all was well."

But Marianna heard her not.

Without having absolutely fainted, she was past the consolation of words.

Edith flew rather than ran to the head of the stairs and called out aloud.

"Felix, Felix! Here—here at once, with your friend, the Marquis! It is his voice alone that will now reach the dull ears of Marianna; no other sound in all this world can charm her back to life."

Felix Heron came up the staircase three steps at a time. He was closely followed by the Marquis of Ormond, who, when he reached the entrance of that suite of apartments, looked scarcely less pale than Marianna herself.

"What is it, Edith? what has happened?" cried Heron.

"Nothing but what two words may set to rights. Sir, I know you; you are the Marquis of Ormond. Do not pause for formal introductions or ceremonies, but press onward quickly, for there is one whom you wish to see in the adjoining apartment—one who requires a physician, and you are the only one in all the world who can be of the slightest service."

The Marquis of Ormond looked in a confused, bewildered manner from Edith to Captain Heron, as though he would have said, "Is this some unfortunate lunatic, or the Countess of Whitcombe?"

"Pass on, sir," added Edith, "and waste not in hesitation or remark, moments which, in five minutes from now, you will call the most precious of your life."

Thus adjured, the young noblemen paused no longer, but with rapid steps entered the apartment where Marianna still remained, hovering almost between life and death.

There was a faint cry—an exclamation—and then Edith gently closed the door of communication.

"Let them be, Felix," she said. "Let a short time be sacred to them both, and tell me if you have informed this young nobleman who you really are?"

"Yes, Edith; and he has given me a piece of information in return, which renders double caution on my part necessary."

"More peril?"

"I know not if it may be called peril, but he tells me that our arch foe, Jonathan Wild, has actually taken possession of the chambers opposite, formerly in the possession of Lord Warringdale, and that when not engaged in some of his nefarious enterprises, he sleeps there."

"Oh, indeed!" said a voice on the staircase at this moment.

"Who is there?" cried Heron, looking over the balustrades.

"It's only me, Captain," cried Tom Ripon. "All's right—it's only me. I've come to say that Daisy is as comfortable as possible, and if you don't want me any more, we'll just go to bed."

"To bed, Tom, in the morning?"

"Yes, Captain; you see when a fellow's been up all night, the best way is to get something to eat and drink, and persuade himself it is his supper, and then turn in."

"As you please, Tom. I don't think I shall leave the house for the next four-and-twenty hours."

"That'll just suit me," said Tom Ripon to himself as he slowly descended the staircase. "Four and-twenty hours, the Captain says, and Jonathan Wild in the house opposite; up to some mischief, of course, which I'll try and thwart him in, or my name's not Tom Ripon."

What particular scheme Tom Ripon had in his mind with respect to Jonathan Wild we shall quickly see; but be it what it may, it was one which evidently required darkness to carry it out; so Tom, with that charming facility of going to sleep, which he always enjoyed, settled himself down for a long rest; and it was not until the day had passed away, and the twilight had deepened into night, that he might have been seen standing in the deep doorway of Whitcombe House, with his eyes fixed upon the chambers of Lord Warringdale opposite.

No light was visible in those chambers.

The centre blind of the three windows that faced the street was up, so that Tom must have seen if the chambers were tenanted by any one.

But Tom Ripon was persevering, and with occasional walks up and down St. James's Street, he kept a tolerable watch upon Lord Warringdale's rooms until the clock of St. James's Palace struck the hour of one in the morning.

He then saw a flash of light from the window of which the blind was drawn up.

The outline of a dim and dusky form stood close to the window for a few seconds, as if contemplating Whitcombe House.

Then the blind was drawn down with an impatient gesture, and Tom Ripon saw no more.

But he had seen quite enough for his purpose.

His sharp young eyes had immediately detected, in that dim and dusky form which appeared at the window, the coarse and rugged outline of Jonathan Wild.

"All's right!" said Tom; "that's the wretch—he's there, and he's there for no good. If I don't find out what harm he has in his head, why I'm—what shall I say? Why, a Frenchman; and I'm sure I shouldn't like to be that for a trifle."

Tom was resolved upon some course of action, but what it was exactly to be he had not made up his mind, so he still lingered for a time in the deep shadows of Whitcombe House, and kept his gaze upon the windows of the house opposite.

"Now," said Tom, "if I could only make my way into that room without Jonathan being the wiser for it, I would find out the old rascal's schemes. Hilloa! What's that? Here's a row!"

The row that Tom Ripon noticed was rapidly approaching, and consisted of a throng of watchmen who had some one then in custody.

The some one evidently would not walk, so the watchmen were carrying him in a very undignified fashion—neck and heels.

CHAPTER CCXV

JONATHAN WILD BELIEVES HIMSELF THE VICTIM OF SPIRITUAL DELUSIONS.

TOM RIPON shrunk back deeper still into the old doorway as the tumult approached him; not that he supposed it could in any manner concern him, either in advancing or retarding the object he had in view; but Tom Ripon's life had been of that adventurous character that it had inclined him always to take as much observation of any unusual circumstance as possible.

The tumult rapidly approached.

The watchmen, of course, used the worse possible language; and in proportion as they loaded the person whom they had in custody with opprobrious epithets, that person seemed to enjoy his situation.

In a high, and not altogether unmusical voice, the prisoner almost overpowered the imprecations of the watchmen by singing.

The song was what may be called a flash one, and was perfectly familiar to Tom Ripon.

In fact, so delighted was he to hear it, that he felt quite inclined to join in the chorus which usually belongs to that class of minstrelsy.

He looked out from behind the column where he was ensconced, with a broad grin of delight upon his countenance.

But Tom had not yet recognised whom the watchman had in custody.

He was soon to do so.

The prisoner, however, be he whom he might, seemed to be seized with a sudden desire of giving a little more trouble than usual immediately opposite to the doorstep of Whitcombe House.

It is perfectly true that two watchmen had hold of each leg, and two hold of each arm, while two more had passed their staves under the back of the refractory prisoner, and so assisted to carry him on in rather an uneasy extemporised couch, but which seemed to have about it all the elements of security.

Despite all this, however, the prisoner managed, by a vigorous effort, to reach the ground.

"Now, cripples all!" he shouted, "let's have a rest!"

"Come on, will yer?" yelled the watchmen in chorus.

"Wait a bit. What's the charge?"

"Didn't we see you beginning to get into the skylight of Sir James Thornhill's house in Pall Mall?"

"To be sure you did!"

"Then come to the roundhouse like a Christian, and don't give any more trouble."

"But I explained."

"Oh, come along, do!"

"I told you Sir James had invited me to drink a dish of chocolate."

"What, at one o'clock in the morning?"

"Yes; he's an early riser; and I don't mean to go any further till you send for him."

Tom Ripon was delighted.

Long before the dialogue had got thus far between the watchmen and their captive, Tom had recognised who that captive was.

His old friend and associate, Jack Sheppard, was the person who had been apprehended by so strong a force of the guardians of the night, while making an attempt at burglary at the house of Sir James Thornhill, the celebrated painter.

Now Tom Ripon always imagined that Jack Sheppard had served him rather a scurvy trick the last time they were together; but it was not in the nature of Tom to nurse up grievances for long, and he was delighted now at the opportunity of being of some assistance to his old associate, or pal, as he called him.

The watchmen were no less than eight in number, so that Tom Ripon thought some sudden surprise would be the best way of aiding or assisting Jack Sheppard.

Situated as he was, he was just in a position to execute such a manœuvre.

He took a flying leap on to the shoulders of one of the watchmen, shouting out, as he did so, "Come on, my merry men, and each tackle his man! Hurrah!—hurrah!"

The effect of this sudden charge from Tom Ripon was decisive. The watchmen thought themselves completely beleaguered by a host of new foes, and they immediately took to flight in all directions.

Jack Sheppard was left sprawling on the pavement.

But he was free.

"Now, Jack," said Tom, "up with you, and be off."

"Not if I know it," said Jack Sheppard, as with the agility of a harlequin he bounded to his feet,—"not if I know it, Tom Ripon! But how, in the name of all that's wonderful, came you to be here at such a lucky moment?"

"I live here," said Tom; "and this is my house."

As he spoke, he gave Jack Sheppard a pull into the shadowy doorway of Whitcombe House; for, happening to cast his eyes to the opposite side of the way, he saw that one of the blinds was partially pulled aside at a window of Lord Warringdale's late chambers, and that a face was close to the glass with a pair of fiery-looking eyes, endeavouring to look out.

It was but an endeavour.

St. James's Street, at that period, was only lit by half-a-dozen oil lamps, and four of them were out.

The dubious kind of twilight, therefore, that reigned in the place rather confused than assisted the vision.

And yet no doubt Jonathan Wild had heard the disturbance without, and was endeavouring to see what occasioned it.

"Keep close, Jack!" whispered Tom.

"What for? Any sneak about?"

"Yes. Look opposite. That's Jonathan Wild at the window!"

Jack Sheppard whistled a long, low note.

"I see him, Tom; but I can't make all this out. You say this is your house, and ugly Johnny seems to live opposite. Why, what will Newgate Street do without the beauty?"

"This isn't my house," said Tom, "and yet it is, if you understand that, Jack."

"It's difficult."

"Let it alone, then; but I suppose you're free to admit I got you out of that little scrape with the watch?"

"All's right, Tom; and I'll do as much for you another time."

"You can do something now a great deal better than I can. I want to get into that house opposite; for come of it what may, I want to find out what Jonathan Wild is about. It's like enough that the doors are only on the lock, and if so, I suppose you can manage to let me in?"

"Of course I can, Tom, if you wish it; but I would just as soon go into a wolf's den as into any house with Jonathan Wild."

"Never mind, Jack, I'll take care of myself. He's gone now; so let's set about it."

Tom Ripon and Jack Sheppard walked right down to Pall Mall, and then up St. James's Street again on the other side of the way, until they came to the house where Jonathan Wild was unquestionably passing the night.

Jack Sheppard was the most skilful picklock in all London, although at that period he had not obtained the celebrity which has made him almost an historical character.

"We'll soon see, Tom, how the matter stands," whispered Jack.

There was a slight rattle in the key-hole of the door, and then the lock yielded.

"Come in!"

Tom was quite delighted with the success of Jack Sheppard, and rather surprised at the same time that the door should have been left without any fastening from within.

Jack explained in a whisper how that arose.

"It's one of these big houses, Tom, all let out in separate chambers; and as everybody has a key to the outer door, and nobody knows who's out and who's in, you see, it's never more than on the lock. But what are you going to do?"

"Take a look at Jonathan."

Jack Sheppard shook his head.

"Rather you than I, Tom. But still, if you want a fellow to help you, and don't mind going my way to work, I'm your man!"

"What way is that, Jack?"

"Why, if you want a comfortable interview with Jonathan Wild, you should have a knife at his throat and a pistol barrel at his ear."

"No, Jack, I don't like that. We, that is Captain Heron and I, might have settled Jonathan over and over again, if we had liked, and I'm afraid some day we may have to do it, though we don't want to cheat Tyburn tree. I've made up my mind, however, to find out what he's about here, and I'll take care of myself, you may depend."

"Good night, then, Tom. I've two cribs to crack yet before morning."

Jack Sheppard went his way, leaving Tom in the hall of the house which contained Jonathan Wild.

It could scarcely be said that Tom had any very defined idea of what he was about, except that he felt there was great danger to Captain Heron and to Edith by this close proximity of Wild to Whitcombe House, and he was willing to run considerable risk to find out exactly what the great thief-taker meant by it.

Creeping softly up the stairs, Tom Ripon stood by the outer door of the chambers, and then he regretted that he had not detained Jack Sheppard for a short period in order that he might use his picklock on that door as well.

But fortune favoured Tom.

He had scarcely well established himself on the landing when the door, close to which he was abruptly opened.

Jonathan Wild thrust his head out on to the dark staircase.

"I thought I heard a noise," he growled.

The door very nearly struck Tom Ripon as it opened, and he had to shrink back as far as he could get to avoid the probability of observation.

"I'm pretty sure I heard a noise," growled Jonathan Wild again.

Now Tom Ripon executed a very daring and clever feat at this moment.

As Jonathan Wild leant out at the doorway, Tom ran his hand up the edge of the door until he came to the lock.

The key was in it.

Noiselessly and adroitly Tom drew it forth, and felt that he had the means, at all events, of letting himself into the chambers, provided Wild did not secure the door by any other means on the inside.

"Bah!" said Wild, after listening for a few moments; "I suppose it was only fancy, but what have I to do with fancy? Bah! Bo!"

After uttering this semi-defiance into the darkness of the staircase, Wild withdrew his head again and banged shut the door.

Tom Ripon heard him fumbling with the lock.

Then there could be no mistake about what he had done.

The sharp click of some well-hung bolt into its socket proclaimed to Tom Ripon that his possession of the key was of very little service.

"Done again!" said Tom. "This won't answer."

The night was passing away, and he felt that if he did not by some means compass his object quickly he would have to leave the house and give it up, at all events, for the present.

Fertile, however, in resources, Tom was not without another "dodge," as he called it, to get the better of Jonathan Wild.

He suddenly stamped violently upon the staircase, and then lurched up heavily against the door, so that Wild could not be off hearing him.

Then Tom waited the result.

That result was just what he wished and expected it to be.

Wild was aggravated past discretion, for he had just laid down in bed again, and composed himself to rest.

Dashing open the door, he made a rush out on to the landing, exclaiming, as he did so, "Fool—beast! Who are you? Drunk, I suppose; but if you live here, why don't you go to your own rooms?"

Jonathan Wild's impetuosity had carried him right to the head of the stairs.

That was Tom Ripon's opportunity.

Rapidly, upon all-fours, he made his way into Wild's rooms, and never halted until he had got into a far corner, where he squeezed himself into an incredibly small space, almost between a large old wardrobe and the wall.

Wild came back with a growl.

"I hate these houses," he said, "that are everybody's and nobody's. You don't know what you're doing and where you are. All night long some fool or another is coming home and making a disturbance. Ah! I don't feel well to-night."

Jonathan sat down upon a chair, which creaked under him.

"I'm cold, too," he said; "and that night-light won't burn; at least, it only burns enough to make darkness visible, and to people the room with all sorts of shadows. What's that—eh? What's that? Oh, I see; only the clothes-horse. The corner of it just looked like the face of Jerry, the magsman, who was hung at Tyburn last Monday. Well, how could I help it? Why didn't he pay me my dues, and he wouldn't have gone there at all?"

The night-light to which Jonathan Wild alluded was a little floating wick in a saucer of oil, and certainly the miserable illumination that proceeded from it was, as he said, only sufficient to make darkness visible.

And this light, such as it was, was in an adjoining apartment, so that it was no wonder Jonathan Wild saw many shadows floating about him.

Tom Ripon began to think he saw them likewise.

The superstitious fears of Jonathan Wild were to a certain extent contagious.

"Confound him!" said Tom. "Why don't he go to bed and have done with all this?"

That was exactly what Wild would have liked to do if he could, but he had already been to bed, and while there some

" Dreams had come "—

dreams that had shaken even the iron nerves of the king of the thief-takers.

Resting his head upon his hands as he sat in the dark room, Wild still muttered to himself, "I cannot make it out. What was it the man said in the play the other night? That his eyes were something wrong, or else worth all the rest of his senses put together. Yes, that was it. Well, that is just the case with my eyes. I have either seen Felix Heron or I have not. If I have not, why, then, I am a little mad; and if I have, my eyes are worth all my other senses. But he is dead—dead! Am I not well aware that he is dead?"

Wild now uttered a series of most dismal groans that Tom Ripon was delighted to hear.

"Well, well," he added after a long pause, "it is useless to think of such things. But they thicken around me, I say—they thicken around me: for if I am not much mistaken, I have likewise

EDITH.—No. 67.

seen Lord Warringdale to-day, and he, I think, in reality lies, or ought to lie, at the bottom of the tide of the old Thames."

"So, so!" thought Tom Ripon. "You meant to settle him too, Johnny, did you? Well, I can forgive you that."

"And what is the meaning of it all?" added Jonathan Wild, after a few moments' silence. "What is the meaning of it all? Can it be possible that when they are near their own—departure"—Jonathan Wild had a great dislike to use the word death, in relation to himself,—"can it be possible that they then begin to have glimpses of that world beyond the grave, to which they are hastening?"

"Well," thought Tom, "Johnny is coming it to-night! He beats Mortification all into fits, for that's something the sort of way that old boy used to go on in."

"I seem," added Jonathan, "as if I were impelled to live in this house, so that from its windows I may see the ghost of Felix Heron upon the doorstep of the ancient abode of his race; and here, in these chambers, surely is the best possible chance that I may be visited by the apparition of Lord Warringdale. I'll go to bed."

"Ah, do!" whispered Tom.

"I will go to bed, but I will put my pistols under my pillow handy, and woe be to any one of mortal mould who disturbs me! To-morrow morning I will make my way into Whitcombe House, and I will know who this mysterious man, who calls himself the Baron Von Peck, really is, or the widowed Countess shall rue it."

"Oh, that's the little game, is it?" thought Tom.

Jonathan Wild, groaning and sighing as he went, repaired to the inner room, and cast himself on the bed.

Tom Ripon quietly crept out of his hiding-place.

On tip-toe he went towards the door of communication, and listened.

Jonathan Wild was breathing heavily.

Tom peeped in at the door.

The night light surely burnt a little brighter than ordinary, for Tom Ripon was able to see pretty well about him in that apartment, which had been luxuriously furnished by Lord Warringdale as his own bedchamber.

Wild lay huddled up in the bed, and unless he were actually counterfeiting a deep sleep, which there seemed no inducement whatever for him to do, he certainly had fallen into one.

"All's right!" said Tom.

With the noiseless, stealthy step of a cat, Tom Ripon made his way to the bedside of Jonathan Wild.

Now, had Tom Ripon suddenly come in from the light of a well-illuminated room into that darksome chamber, he would probably have not been able to distinguish one object from another; but as it was, his eyes had become accustomed to the semi-twilight, and he saw everything distinctly.

He crept close up to the bed head.

With his hand to his ear he listened again.

Yes, there could be no doubt about it—Jonathan Wild, the man of many crimes, who was hastening to the end of his career, slept!

CHAPTER CCXVI.

TOM RIPON BARGAINS WITH WILD FOR THE SAFETY OF THE BARON VON PECK.

TOM was not unmindful of the declaration of Jonathan that he had put his pistols under the pillow.

The possession of them, therefore, became a matter of the first necessity.

That they were there, as Wild had stated, Tom did not doubt for a moment; but although he looked down as closely as he dared, yet he did not see them.

He suspected that, although Wild breathed heavily, he slept lightly.

But while Tom was considering what to do, he was, certainly, with all his coolness and nonchalance, terrified at the fact of Wild suddenly

opening his eyes and looking him full in the face.

Tom did not speak, but, mentally, he gave himself up for lost; and he bitterly regretted he had not brought fire-arms with him, so that, at the worst, it might be a life for a life.

Jonathan Wild must have been only half awake, and in that dreamy condition which only confounds realities with the visions of sleep.

He did not seem greatly surprised at seeing Tom Ripon by his bedside, but rather gazed at him with a look of half-sleeping curiosity.

"Another of them!" he said in a low, moaning voice. "I suppose something's happened to that boy, and he's dead, too, or he wouldn't be here—he couldn't be."

Tom Ripon took the hint in a moment.

He was to play his own ghost.

Jonathan Wild having seen, as he supposed, the apparitions of persons whom he thought he knew to be dead, was content to believe that the living, breathing Tom Ripon must be a ghost likewise.

Tom kept up the delusion very well.

He had an impression on his mind that ghosts ought to disappear, as he had seen theatrical ones do at the theatre in Lincoln's Inn Fields, merely by going through a trapdoor perpendicularly.

He managed this very well.

Doubling up his legs under him, Tom slowly sunk lower and lower by the bedside of Jonathan Wild, until he got right down to the floor, and then, as quietly as he could, he crept under the bed.

Jonathan followed the descent of Tom with wondering eyes; and when he disappeared below the edge of the bed, Wild slowly raised himself up so as to catch the last glimpse of him.

"Gone!" said Wild.

He leant his head and face over the edge of the bed completely; but, of course, nothing was to be seen of Tom Ripon.

"Yes," added Wild, "that's another of them. I suppose by degrees I shall see everybody that I've known in life looking into my eyes in death, and trying to scare me from my senses. What does he want here? I didn't kill him, nor did I stir hand or foot to contrive his death!"

A dim sort of suspicion seemed to come across the mind of Jonathan Wild that, after all, he might be the victim of some trick or delusion.

He crept softly out of bed.

But Tom Ripon heard him.

The possibility that the appearance he had seen might be real, and that his tormenting enemy, Tom Ripon, be really present, presented itself to Wild's mind.

In fact, unless he had been quite insane, it could scarcely fail to do so.

Jonathan Wild stooped down and looked under the bed.

But Tom was not to be caught so easily as that, for he had crawled out at the other side, and was round the foot of it by that time.

If any one could have looked into that chamber with but a slight sense of the ludicrous, the manœuvres of Tom Ripon and Jonathan Wild certainly must have excited laughter.

Wild crept right under the bed and out at the other side, even as Tom had done; but by that time Tom was round the bedstead again, and making his way under it for the second time, so that Wild missed him.

"No," muttered Wild, "there is no one here; and perhaps, after all, it was merely fancy."

He crept into bed again.

"Bother it!" whispered Tom to himself. "Why can't he go to sleep quietly, and let a fellow get his pistols."

Tom waited for some time before he again ventured to rise up again in a ghost-like fashion by the bedside.

Wild slept again.

This getting in and out of bed, however, had had the effect of displacing the pillows; so that, to his great satisfaction, Tom Ripon saw the heavy, brass-mounted butt-ends of a pair of pistols fully in view.

"That will do!" he whispered.

Very cautiously he drew out the pistols one after another.

Wild did not stir.

Tom took a glance at the weapons, and saw that they were fully loaded, with plenty of powder in the pans, and good sharp flints.

Carefully moving a chair, then, to a distance of about two feet from the bedside, Tom knelt upon it, and resting the pistols upon its back, the muzzles were both conveniently presented towards Jonathan Wild.

"I rather think that'll do," said Tom. "If Jonathan is tired of the world, he has only to say so, and bang, pop, and away he goes!"

Tom Ripon did not think it at all necessary to be cautious as to the tone of voice he used now; and there could be no doubt that Wild did partially hear him in his sleep.

The great thief-taker moved uneasily.

One—two—three! struck the Palace clock at St. James's.

"It's getting late," said Tom. "I must wake him up."

Tom gathered a long breath, and then shouted out, "Hoy, hoy! Johnny! Lots o' ghosts, and to spare!"

Wild sprung up to a sitting posture in the bed with a yell of dismay.

"That'll do!" cried Tom. "Now, how do you feel, old 'un? Just open both eyes as wide as you can."

Wild uttered an imprecation.

He thrust one hand beneath the pillow for the pistols.

"Oh, you must look a little further for them," said Tom. "Here they are."

He rattled the barrels of the pistols on the back of the chair as he spoke, to the imminent danger of their explosion; for those old flint and steel fire-arms either would never go off at all, or did so with an alarming facility.

Wild began to get wide awake.

He began to comprehend his situation.

"You young villain!" he cried. "What do you want here?"

"Don't speak in that way to a respectable ghost," said Tom.

"Ghost?"

"Yes. Don't I look like one? But however that may be, Johnny, you'll be one in a brace of shakes if you don't mind? What's in these pistols? Bullets, buttons, old nails, or slugs, or what?"

"Scoundrel!"

"Now, don't be calling yourself names, Johnny!"

Wild showed a disposition to get out of the bed.

"Stop a bit!" cried Tom. "If you move another inch, over you go! I'm a fellow of my word, and mean what I say!"

Wild suspected that such was the case.

"What do you want?" he growled.

"That's just what I want to know of you. What do you want, Johnny, and why do you come prying about here, and peeping and spying at Whitcombe House, as though you'd like to eat up our Edith, eh?"

"Oh, that's it!" said Wild. "You're sent over to question me, are you?"

"No, I ain't!"

"But here you are!"

"I wasn't sent; I came of my own accord!"

"Bah!"

"What do you want, Johnny? Out with it at once; and if I don't like it, over you go!"

"You're a charming youth!"

"That's what all the gals say. But I don't want any compliments from you, because, you see, of the difficulty of returning them! Come, Johnny, what's your little game here?"

"Put down those pistols."

"Oh, dear, no! My old master, Captain Heron, used to count three when a fellow was obstinate and wouldn't answer him a civil question; and if he went on being obstinate after that, over he went! Now, Johnny, what do you want here? One!"

"What's that to you?"

"Two!"

"Stop! What is the use of throwing away a life upon a heedless wretch such as you are? I want to know who and what that Baron Von Peck is, and why he's so continually going in and out Whitcombe House."

"Is that all?" said Tom.

"It is, for the present."

"Well, then, you must know, Johnny, missus is a widow, and the Baron ain't bad-looking."

"Oh, that's it, is it? Ah! I might have suspected it! But still there's a mystery about the fellow which I must fathom. I cannot take my Lord Clackington's gold for nothing."

"Now, look you here, Johnny," said Tom. "I like the Baron, and so do we all. Now, if you won't promise to let him alone, I won't leave this room without sending the contents of these pistols into your head! It's nothing to you who or what he is, so don't you interfere! Come, now, is it a bargain?"

"Tom Ripon!"

"Here you are, Johnny!"

"I once made to you a proposal to come into my service; I make it you again."

"Don't; it's a waste of time! I've got ten pound a year and my victuals with the Countess of Whitcombe; and the Baron Von Peck says that if everything goes right, and he marries her, he'll make it guineas. What do you say to that, Johnny?"

"I say that you shall have from me ten guineas a month, and whatever you can pick up besides."

"It's of no use. I've told you what I want

and what I mean. Come, Johnny, make up your mind, and don't let's have any more fuss about it! Will you promise never in any way to interfere with the Baron Von Peck, or will you rather that I should pull the triggers of these two pistols, and so do the job completely?"

"Very well, I promise!"

"Now, Johnny, I've heard you say you'll do things, and I believe, then, you always try to do them; so I think, when you say you won't do a thing, you ought to stick by that; and I'll trust you for once, though I suppose I'm about the first that ever really did. There's your pistols, Johnny."

To the surprise of Wild, Tom Ripon got off the chair and handed him his two pistols with the butt-ends towards him.

"Is this possible," said Wild, "that, threatening me so recently as you have done, you now place your life in my hands?"

"Oh, dear, no!" said Tom. "Haven't you promised?"

"And you will take my word?"

"I have!"

Wild was silent for a few seconds.

A struggle between the faint and long since trodden-down good that might be even in his nature, and the thoughts of evil and treachery that were familiar to him, was taking place.

Tom Ripon was in great danger.

Almost a feather's weight, either way, would turn the scale for life or for death.

The fearless, open look that Tom bent upon Wild's face, had, however, its effect.

The thief-taker handed back the pistols to Tom.

"Put them on that table over there," he said. "I shan't want them to-night."

"All's right, Johnny!"

"Bah! bo! Be off!"

"You'll keep your word?"

"I will, and as you got in here you can get out. But look ye here, Tom Ripon, join me, and I'll make it twenty guineas a month, and I'll promise that you shall name who you like never to be interfered with by me, come what may."

"Not for twenty thousand, Johnny! So good night!"

Jonathan Wild, with a growl, pulled the bed-clothes over him; and Tom Ripon, very well satisfied with the night's adventure, left the chambers and went over to Whitcombe House.

Tom slept, as usual, in the stable with Daisy, and he debated with himself long and anxiously whether or not he should inform Captain Heron of the little adventure he had had with Jonathan Wild. After debating the matter *pro* and *con* for some time in his own mind, he determined not to do so.

Tom was so extremely fond of engaging in these little personal adventures, and he was, at the same time, so reluctant to do anything opposed to the orders of Captain Heron, that he feared a general prohibition might issue against his engaging in any such matters.

"No," he said, as the bright sunlight came into his eyes and wakened him in the morning,—"no, I won't say anything to the Captain about it; and if Jonathan Wild only keeps his word, it will be a job well done; and so——Eh? what's this? What do you want? Who's this?"

Tom Ripon was only half awake, but he became conscious that two figures were in the stable, one on each side of him.

"Hilloa!" he cried, "what are you bringing in now?"

"Oh, Tom, are you really awake?" said Mrs. Ripon,—for she was one of the persons there present.

"Why, it's the old gal!" said Tom.

"Yea," said the other figure, "as the Psalmist says, let the sluggard arise. Yea, we have something to communicate; and as, further on, the Psalmist justly remarks, if you have any swag to sell—no, I don't mean that—but even the Psalmist himself promised if he had half-a-dozen silver spoons or a candlestick, he would feel it his duty to deal with his relations."

"What the deuce are you driving at?" said Tom to Mortification. "What do you mean by coming and waking a fellow up about Psalmists, and candlesticks, and silver spoons."

"Oh! my dear Tom," said Mrs. Ripon, patting her eyes with her handkerchief,—"we are all sinful."

"I believe you, old gal!—only some of us is a little worse than others. What's up now, old gal, eh?"

"Yea, I will explain," said Mortification,—"I will explain to Thomas. Your sainted and respectable parent, Thomas, along with the humble individual who stands in the relation of father-in-law to you, thinks of going into the old line of business.

"Oh, I see!" said Tom Ripon—"set up a fence again."

"Yea, you may call it a fence."

"Oh, Tom!" added Mrs. Ripon; "in this vale of tears we're all bound to be useful as far as we can; and as the Captain goes on the road again now, and you with him, we thought you might as well deal with us as with any other thie——"

Mortification coughed.

"Thieves, you mean," said Tom.

"And so," added Mrs. Ripon, taking no notice whatever of the interruption,—"and so, my dear boy, we have taken a little shop in Wardour Street, Soho, where we sell needles and tape."

"And thimbles and stay-laces," said Mortification.

"And buttons, and hooks and eyes," added Mrs. Ripon.

"Yea, and tracts," said Mortification.

"That'll do," cried Tom; "I know all about it: the shop's a blind, the back parlour's a fence, and there's a melting pot in the kitchen."

"Yea, as the Psalmist says, wisdom's head groweth on young shoulders. That is just it. Ready money and no favours."

"It's a pity," said Mrs. Ripon as she settled her cap, "to stagnate in this world; and if the Captain sticks to business, why shouldn't we?"

"Why, look ye here," said Tom; "there's not a soul, old gal, in this great old Whitcombe House but is an old friend or acquaintance of the Captain and Edith's, and there ain't too many of us now. There's Ogle and Mrs. Ogle, and that young girl, who was never so pretty till the other one came; and then there's myself and you two; and now you want to be off."

"Yea, all will be well," said Mortification, "and your sainted mother will call occasionally, Thomas,

TOM RIPON EXTORTS A PROMISE FROM JONATHAN WILD.

Presented Gratis with No. 67, of the New Edition of EDITH HERON, the Sequel to Edith the Captive; or, the Robbers of Epping Forest.

just to look after any trifles, and pick up—yea, I mean clean up anything she can."

"Go it, Mortification!" said Tom. "That's about it, I expect; but, however, I suppose you must have your own way. But, I tell you what, old 'un, I won't consent, except on one condition."

"Eh?" said Mrs. Ripon. "What do you mean by calling me old 'un, you wretched little badger."

"Is a man to be insulted," said Tom, "and be called a badger?"

"You odious boy; you think nothing of breaking your mother's head and heart, both."

"Peace, peace!" cried Mortification, waving his hands up and down, as though he were trying to mesmerise both Tom and his mother. "Peace, peace! Let me pour oil upon the troubled waters; yea——"

"If you pour any oil on me," said Tom, "I'll pretty soon settle you. And I tell you what it is, mother; I'll not only consent to you opening a crib such as you speak off, but I'll deal with you, on one condition; and that is, that you take good care that, night and day, there shall be good accommodation for me, for Daisy, and the Captain, if we are hard pressed."

"Yea," said Mortification, "we have the whole house; and we pretend to let it out in lodgings, but we don't, so that the accommodation is ample; and you, and Daisy, and the Captain are welcome at any time to come and get up the chimney of any of the rooms."

This was too much for Tom's patience.

He scrambled to his feet, and seized a hay-fork, on which the Rev. Mortification and his mother precipitately retreated.

Probably they had attained all their object by letting Tom Ripon know that they were tired of the inactive life at Whitcombe House, and were going into the old line of business as fencekeepers again.

"Well," soliloquised Tom, as he performed a hasty toilet, "let them go—we don't want them, Daisy; but I must tell the Captain all about it. And who knows but what it's all for the best?—for since we do go out on the road again, we may have the Philistines after us, hard and fast, some night, and be glad to take refuge at the crib in Wardour Street, though not in the chimney."

Felix Heron did not stir from Whitcombe House for the whole of that day, so Tom easily had an opportunity of communicating to him the defection of his mother and Mortification from the household.

"Let them go, Tom," he said. "We shall do well enough; and I've some idea that the young Marquis of Ormond will take up his abode in this house, for he is much alone in the world, and has scarcely a friend or relation living. Next week he will be united to Marianna."

Tom staggered back till he stumbled over a chair, and then sat on the floor with it in his lap, looking in speechless horror at Heron.

"Ma-r-ried?"

"Yes, Tom."

"To Ma-ri-an-na?"

"Exactly so; and a charming young couple they will make!"

"Brimstone and blazes!"

"Why, what's the matter?"

"I wanted her myself."

"Oh, that's it!" said Heron, coolly. Well,

you see, Tom, you can't have her, so there's an end of it; and remember to have Daisy saddled, and your own horse likewise, ready at eight o'clock to-night. I have a desire to visit that old mansion that belonged to my dear old friend and protector of my early days, Sir Dominick Browne; and we may possibly meet with some adventures by the way."

CHAPTER CCXVII.

CAPTAIN HERON AND TOM MEET WITH A REAL GHOST ADVENTURE.

IT was eight o'clock.

Flying showers and a blustering wind pervaded London.

Tom Ripon had been forced to get over his love disappointment as best he might.

But his feelings, lacerated as they might be, did not prevent him from being quite ready with Daisy and his own horse, at the corner of Pall Mall, precisely as the Palace clock struck the hour named by Felix Heron.

Tom Ripon fell in love very easily, and such a facility for the tender passion generally brings with it an equal facility of falling out of love again.

If any one had remarked Tom particularly, as, mounted on his own horse, and leading Daisy by the bridle, he slowly moved up and down by Marlborough House, they might have recognised the air that Tom was whistling.

It was a remarkably consolatory one for a disappointed lover:—

"What care I how fair she be,
If she smile not upon me."

"Yes," said Tom, in a low tone, "she is a pretty girl; but it's no use making a fuss about it, and I think I'll go back to the t'other one now, for fear she should break her heart, poor thing! Oh, there's the Captain!"

Felix Heron, in his costume as the Baron Von Peck, approached, and lightly vaulted into Daisy's saddle.

"Come on, Tom," he said. "The night is clearing, and the roads will be in capital condition."

"All's right, Captain."

Felix Heron, closely followed by Tom Ripon, trotted up St. James's Street, and, turning sharp to the left, took their course towards the Western Road.

They were far from being wholly unobserved, for Jonathan Wild had left one of his men as a spy in St. James's Street, who was to bring him information of the outgoings and incomings of the Baron Von Peck.

This man ran off at once to Newgate Street with his information; and, in half an hour's time, Wild was knocking at the door of Whitcombe House.

It was a strange business for such a man as Jonathan Wild to come to Whitcombe House upon; but the fact is, he had resolved to warn Edith of the sort of man he believed the Baron to be.

It would be difficult to analyze the kind of

friendly feeling that Jonathan Wild had towards Edith since the supposed death of Felix Heron.

He was, as we have frequently said, eminently superstitious.

It is possible enough, then, that an element of fear entered into the feeling, and that by holding a protecting hand ove Edith he might suppose he was in some manner propitiating the spirit of Felix Heron.

Certain it is that he had a very bad opinion of the Baron Von Peck; and his errand, on this occasion, to Whitcombe House was to let Edith know it.

Wild gave a brief nod to Ogle, who opened the door.

"Is the Countess within?" he asked.

"Mr. Wild, what do you want here?" said Ogle. "This is no place for you and me at the same time!"

"Pooh, pooh! With the death of Felix Heron let our animosities cease. I am willing to forget the past so long as you keep your present position as a faithful servant of the Countess of Whitcombe, whom I now want to see upon as friendly an errand as even you coul think of!"

Ogle was somewhat surprised at this altered tone on the part of Jonathan Wild; but there was only one of two things to do with such a man.

Either to kill him or to temporise with him.

Ogle felt, too, that the conservation of the secret of Felix Heron's continued existence was of the first importance.

He spoke fairly to Wild.

"I'm as willing to forget as you are; and any service you can render to the Countess of Whitcombe will lay up in my mind gratitude instead of animosity. Tell me what you want to say to her, Mr. Wild, and, as a living man, I will repeat it!"

"No. I must see her, if it be but for a moment.

Ogle hesitated.

That hesitation, however, was cut short by Edith herself, who happened to be in one of the rooms upon the ground floor of the mansion, and overheard all that had passed.

She stepped out into the hall, and presented herself abruptly to Wild.

"What is it, Jonathan Wild, you have to say to me?"

Wild took off his hat with involuntary respect, and presented his round, bullet-looking head, with its short cropped hair, and various ugly seams and patches upon it, arising from the many deadly encounters he had been engaged in.

"I would speak with you, madam, and alone."

"No," replied Edith. "You can say nothing that I would wish to keep from so faithful a friend and servant as Ogle."

"Very well," said Wild. "Look here!"

He placed his finger upon a deep scar upon his brow.

"This was given to me by your late husband, Felix Heron, the Earl of Whitcombe; but it was in fair fight, and I bear no animosity to him or to his now!"

"It's of little use," said Ogle, "bearing animosity to a man who is dead and gone; but if you have any quarrel still with the Captain, and choose to fight it out with me——"

"Bah!" cried Wild; "be quiet. And as for you, madam, since you will have it that I should speak out, I tell you that I've heard something of you that vexes me!"

"Of me?"

"Yes; your husband was a brave and noble gentleman, though he and I were generally at loggerheads! He was not a man to forget! But yet it seems you're about to change your state, and marry a certain Baron Von Peck."

Edith and Ogle exchanged glances.

"Yes," added Wild; "I'm told as much, upon very good authority. Now, I tell you the fellow is a rascal; one of those scamps in the pay of the biggest rogue of all, something after the fashion of my Lord Clackington; and what you can see in him all of you I can't imagine, for he seems to have bewitched you all alike!"

"No, no," cried Edith; "he is but a friend."

"I know better! You have even let him have Felix Heron's mare Daisy; and he is off with that scamp Tom Ripon on the road to-night. Cast him off, I say, Countess of Whitcombe!"

Edith and Ogle again exchanged glances.

These odd looks of intelligence did not escape Jonathan Wild.

"What can all this mean?" he asked himself. "There is something going on that I don't at all comprehend, but that I ought.——Well," he added, after the pause of a few seconds, "I can do no more than warn you. If the saying is a good and a true one, that a wilful man will have his own way, it is a great deal more true of a woman!"

With this speech, which Jonathan Wild thought to be, and meant to be, a particularly sharp one, he turned, and left the house.

Then Ogle laughed.

But the heart of Edith was too heavy to permit her to do so.

"Ah, Ogle!" she said, "I don't know where all these alarms and mysteries are to end!"

"They will all end well, you may depend, my lady," said Ogle; "for I would back the Captain and Daisy against the world!"

With a sigh, Edith made her way to her own rooms.

Jonathan Wild stood for a few minutes at the corner of Pall Mall, and considered.

"What shall I do?" he said.

He clasped his hands behind him, and sauntered to and fro.

His brows were knit, and he was evidently in a state of deep cogitation about something that interested him much.

"Yes," he said, at length,—"yes, I will be after him!"

He took a small whistle from his waistcoat pocket, and blew upon it shrilly.

A man darted out of a deep, shadowy doorway, just at the corner of St. James's Street.

"Is that you, Wilkins?"

"Yes, Mr. Wild."

"Run on as fast as you can to Volckman's stables, and get ready the dark bay mare."

"Yes, Mr. Wild."

The janissary, for such he was, of Jonathan Wild ran on up St. James's Street.

Wild slowly followed him, and as he went he muttered to himself, "There is a something in all this that I don't yet quite comprehend, but I will do my best to do so to-night. The fellow has gone out upon the Western Road; and whether he is a highwayman or a Court spy, it is my business, as well as my pleasure, to find out."

The horses that Jonathan Wild was in the habit of riding were always kept, for convenience of getting at readily, at various places in London.

Indeed, there was hardly a thoroughfare out of the City where, at some stable or another, Jonathan Wild had not a horse waiting for him.

It is said in contemporary history that he was not a good horseman, and that he was always tumbling off his steed.

But, if that was the case, he contrived to tumble on again quickly, and be none the worse.

There is a kind of luck in riding.

One man will ride all his life and be thrown fifty times, and will hunt in the most difficult counties and come to no harm.

Another will break his neck in a trot round his own lawn.

It is fate!

By the time Wild reached the stables he had made mention of, a dark brown, tall, long-legged vicious-looking brute of a mare was ready saddled and bridled for him at the gate.

"That will do," he said.

"Shall I follow you, Mr. Wild?" asked the janissary.

"No."

The man walked away at once.

Jonathan Wild scrambled on to the back of the vicious-looking mare, and then, holding the bridle loosely on his arm, he took his pistols from his pockets and carefully examined the primings.

"All's right!"

He thrust them into the vacant holster-cases on each side of the saddle.

"That will do," he muttered. "We shall see if the Baron, who is, no doubt, some rascally German, is proof against a good British bullet!"

That Jonathan Wild was now, in his odd and strange way, actually, as he thought, in the interests of Edith, there can be no doubt.

He had since the death, as he supposed, of Captain Heron, taken Edith, so to speak, under his protection.

He had always admired her.

Her beauty!

Her courage!

Her unflinching endurance of misfortune; and the wonderful manner in which, through good report and bad report, she had clung to her husband, had extorted the admiration of the great thief-taker, Wild.

And he had made up his mind that if he could possibly help it, she should not throw herself away upon such a man as the Baron Von Peck.

But Edith seemed to be obstinate.

"Women always are," said Wild.

The only way, then, to settle the whole affair was to forbid the marriage in a way that would be certainly effectual.

A pistol shot would do it.

And it was with the express idea of this that Wild now sought the Western Road, mounted on that wiry, vicious-looking horse, which he knew, with all its apparent ill-condition, would carry him well and safely almost any distance he required.

Jonathan turned sharp round to the left upon reaching the top of St. James's Street, and then

put his horse to a half gallop until he reached a turnpike gate.

That gate, which has now been abolished for many years, was within a few hundred paces of the commencement of the Green Park.

"Hilloa! Gate—gate!" cried Wild.

The night was by no means far advanced, but the gate was closed, for the traffic along Piccadilly after sunset was not above one in a thousand carriages and horsemen that are now to be seen, up to long past midnight, in that populous thoroughfare.

"Gate—gate!"

The gate-keeper flung the bar open.

"Threepence. Threepence for a horse."

"Stuff!" said Wild. "Hold up your lantern, man, and look at me!"

"Oh, Mr. Wild, I beg your pardon, sir! I didn't know you! It's so precious dark here since they've moved the street lamp to the corner of Albemarle Street, that I can seldom see anybody!"

"Who has passed through the gate lately?"

"Let me see! A man and a boy, both well mounted."

"Ah! that will do! Good night!"

"Good night, Mr. Wild; and when you're hung, which I hope will be soon, may I be there to see!" added the gatekeeper, so soon as he thought Wild was fairly out of hearing.

Jonathan knew perfectly well that the dread of his name would be quite sufficient to procure him every information as to the road the Baron Von Peck and Tom Ripon had taken.

His only dread was to overshoot his mark, and pass them upon the road, in consequence of their taking some turning of which he was not aware.

He went, therefore, at an easy trot, pulling up at intervals to question either some stray watchman, or to shout out his inquiries at some roadside hostel.

But we must leave Jonathan Wild on what may be termed the trail of Captain Heron and Tom Ripon, while we rejoin those two important personages of our story as they make their way towards the Western Road.

It was necessary to go considerably to the right in order to reach the part of the country to which they were bound.

Upon reaching the environs of Knightsbridge, Captain Heron slackened the pace of Daisy in order that Tom might come up to him.

"I think, Tom," he said, "that if we ride on we shall find a bridle-path by the side of Holland House that will lead us to the high road we wish to be upon."

"To be sure, Captain! It's called the Haunted Path."

"Is it so?"

"Oh, yes, Captain! You know Holland House is deserted now; and they do say that there's a ghost on horseback who rides up and down that path, and that everybody he passes is sure to meet with some ill luck!"

"What nonsense, Tom!"

"Well, it may be, Captain; and at all events you and I, I'm thinking, are a match for a single ghost!"

"I presume so, Tom; and if the ghost should cross our path, perhaps we may try what power a bullet has in laying the spectre!"

"That'll do it, Captain! I know the entrance to the shadowy path well enough; it leads us right out close to the foot of Notting Hill, and we shall come upon it now in about three or four minutes at the pace we're going."

"All right, Tom!"

Captain Heron could not but observe, though, that Tom Ripon kept sedulously in the rear as they neared the bridle-path by the side of Holland House.

And, indeed, but for the presence of Heron, of whose capacity to fight and conquer anything, either mortal or immortal, Tom had the highest opinion, he would certainly have been shy of passing down that reputedly haunted grove after sunset.

The suburb of London in which Captain Heron and his faithful follower now were was much more rural than at present.

The tide of fashion had not yet set in that direction.

Before they reached Holland House, therefore, instead of the rows of trim residences that are to be seen at present lining each side of the way with their unpicturesque frontages, there were tall trees and hedgerows, with here and there a garden wall.

"Here we are!" cried Tom. "I know the spot by these immense elm trees that grow on each side and meet overhead, making such a thick canopy that you may take shelter under it in the smartest summer shower you can ever meet with."

———

CHAPTER CCXVIII

JONATHAN WILD PURSUES THE BARON VON PECK ON THE WESTERN ROAD.

BLACK, dreary, and indistinct as the mouth of a cavern, was this bridle-road by the side of Holland House, which had existed doubtless ever since the palatial abode had been built.

Tom shrunk back a little.

"Hem! Captain!" he said.

"Well, Tom?"

"It has just struck me that if we ride half a mile further on there is a better road still."

"Oh, this will do very well," said Heron.

He turned Daisy's head towards the shadowy entrance of the lane, if lane, indeed, it could be called; for although three horsemen might possibly, by riding close together, have passed down it abreast, no carriage of ordinary width of wheels could possibly have made its way between the tall, banked-up hedgerow on one side, and the massive substantial wall of the garden of Holland House on the other.

That wall, too, was so overgrown with ivy that its actual construction was completely hidden.

It looked like a mass of vegetation.

And here and there trees, which had been planted as young saplings, and no doubt intended to be trimmed into some comely shape on the garden side of the wall, had outgrown all control.

Stretching their limbs and branches for light, air, and warmth, right over the roadway, they added largely to the gloom of the bridle-path.

Captain Heron reduced the pace of Daisy to a quiet walk.

Tom Ripon followed him close at hand, and for a few minutes not a word was spoken.

But the silence was irksome to Tom.

It seemed rather to increase the gloomy and suspicious character of the place.

"Captain," he said, "did you ever come down here before?"

"I think I must have done so; but I don't quite recollect."

"Well, Captain, of course a fellow isn't afraid; but I don't mind saying that the sooner I get out of this place the better I shall be pleased."

"Hush, Tom!"

"Goodness gracious! You don't hear anything, Captain?"

"I thought I did."

"What was it?"

"Be quiet, and we may hear it again."

Captain Heron brought Daisy to a standstill, and Tom Ripon with his horse followed the example.

The stillness of the bridle-path in which they were was so profound, that it would seem that even the fall of a leaf would have been heard.

"It's nothing," said Heron.

"Oh, dear no!" responded Tom, "it's nothing. Let's push on, Captain; or, if you think it's nearer to go back, I should say that's the best way."

"No; hush! There it is again."

Tom, as well as Captain Heron, this time heard a strange, low, wailing sound, that they could compare to nothing human, although it was quite possible it might have been artificially produced by human lips.

"Captain! Captain! What is it?" whispered Tom.

"I don't know yet."

"Let's go! Let's go!"

"Quite the contrary, Tom. You ask me what this sound is, and I cannot tell you; but I'm quite sure I know its object."

"What? What?"

To scare us out of this bridle-path, and implant in our minds a fixed determination never to come into it again."

"I don't want to come into it again," said Tom.

"Be quiet, and follow me. I think we are about half-way through it by this time."

Captain Heron put Daisy to a walk, and nothing was heard for some minutes but the soft hollow tread of the horses' feet upon the damp, ill-made and ill-kept bridle-path, where the fallen leaves of many an autumn were allowed to lie and decompose, forming an elastic, spongy surface, which, being never visited by the most wandering ray of sunlight, retained its moisture all the year round.

"Halt!" cried a voice, suddenly.

Captain Heron pulled up at once.

Tom Ripon uttered an exclamation of dismay.

They both looked about them—if the useless attempt to penetrate with human eyesight the darkness of that place could be called looking about—but not the smallest indication of the presence of any one could be observed.

"Halt!" cried the voice again.

When Captain Heron had first heard this summons to come to a stand-still, he had been puzzled to know in which direction to look for it.

Now he felt certain it came from towards the left.

That was in the direction of Holland House.

But all doubt—not only as regarded the direction from whence the sound came, but also in respect of the person who uttered it—seemed about to be put to an end.

A faint, spectral-looking light shone among the thick ivy that came over, in immense trailing masses, the top of the wall.

The light itself—that is, the source of the light—could not be seen.

But its reflection in the dim, dark atmosphere spread for some yards around a particular spot.

That particular spot seemed to be about three feet above the top of the wall bounding the garden of Holland House.

Tom Ripon involuntarily laid his hand upon the neck of Daisy.

The two horses shrunk closely together as if for companionship; and as Captain Heron and Tom Ripon both looked up at the reflected light above the garden wall, they saw that it revealed the outlines of a human figure.

What costume the figure wore—or, indeed, whether it were male or female—could not be observed; but the same voice that had cried "Halt!" called out in high, wailing accents, "Sacred to the memory of the murdered! Pass on, nor desecrate hallowed dust! Pass on! or woe, woe unutterable, and evil fortune, be the consequence!"

Bang! went one of Captain Heron's pistols.

The report of the pistol in that solitary spot, so quiet and full of peace and serenity, and apparently so completely abandoned to repose, was startling in the extreme.

And the noise was so much greater there than it would have been in a more open situation, that it sounded more like the discharge of

EDITH.—No. 68.

a small piece of ordnance than a mere pocket-pistol.

And Tom Ripon, whose eyes and whole attention were directed to the mysterious figure on the wall, was so startled by the unexpected report, that he echoed it with a shout.

And whether it was Tom's shout or Captain Heron's pistol that produced the effect might be a matter of doubt, but the ghost certainly, if it were a ghost, abruptly disappeared.

The faint light on the top of the wall vanished, and all was darkness again.

"I think that will do," said Heron.

"Goodness gracious!" said Tom.

"Amen!"

"Did you fire, Captain?"

"I did."

"I thought the world had blown up."

"Why, Tom, I thought you knew by this time the sound of the report of a pistol!"

"Yes, Captain, but I was not thinking of it."

"Hush, Tom!"

"Oh, you don't mean to say, Captain, that it is coming again?"

"Silence!"

Tom was still.

The same strange wailing sound that had at first attracted the attention of Felix Heron in that lane now met his ears.

It was a sound so altogether unlike any other that ever he had heard, that Captain Heron could not but listen to it with a great deal of curiosity.

But it was nothing but curiosity with which Captain Heron listened to those sounds.

Not the least particle of the smallest idea that they were supernatural crossed his mind.

Upon Tom Ripon, however, they had a very different effect, and he was fully prepared to believe that they came from beings of another world, armed, possibly, with powers of mischief against which human weapons would be of no avail.

But the tone in which Captain Heron had commanded him to be silent was one which he did not choose to disobey.

Much inclined, therefore, as Tom Ripon was to urge an immediate departure from that gloomy spot, he held his peace, and he suffered many pangs in silence.

The sounds ceased.

But Captain Heron was by no means inclined to give up the adventure that had been so strangely commenced.

He spoke to Tom Ripon in a low voice.

"You may depend, Tom, there is some door in the wall close at hand, which, no doubt, could be easily enough opened from the inside."

"I shouldn't wonder, Captain."

"Very well, I'll help you over, and you can creep along and feel your way till you find a door at which you can let Daisy and me in; I will bring in your horse likewise."

"Did you say help me over, Captain?"

"Yes; the wall is not so high but that, hanging to it with your hands, you can drop lightly and easily on to the other side."

"Yes," said Tom, "and into the arms of a dozen ghosts, at least."

"Nonsense, Tom!"

"I couldn't do it. I would if I could, but I can't. It's out of the question, Captain: don't ask me."

"Very well," said Heron; "it shall never be said of me that I asked another to do that which I shrunk from myself. I will do it; but for your life's sake, Tom, be careful of Daisy; for there is no adventure in all the world, let it end how it may, that could compensate me for the loss of that faithful friend."

"Am I likely, Captain, not to be careful of Daisy?"

"No, Tom, but I could not help giving you this caution, since something like fear has taken possession of you by the mysteries of this bridle-road."

"Come away—come away!" urged Tom; "it isn't worth staying."

"I don't know that; let us see what is to be seen."

Heron, as he spoke, rode with Daisy so close to the wall that he and she were both completely entangled and covered up by the ivy.

By standing then upon the saddle, Heron was just able to look over into the garden of Holland House.

He might as well have looked down a well.

The darkness was profound and excessive.

But Heron was resolved to come at the root of the mystery, which had only gathered darkness and obscurity by the little he had seen of it.

"Tom," he said, "keep your pistols well in hand, and use them freely enough if you see cause."

"I will, Captain—I will."

Heron drew himself softly up to the top of the wall.

He felt all the hazard of his position; for if any one had been there, it would have been easy enough to pick him off by a pistol-shot, and so at once put an end to his career.

But these were considerations which never influenced Felix Heron.

If he had always stopped upon any enterprise to consider what might happen, he would soon have abandoned all that adventurous life which possessed for him so many charms, and at home he would only have sought peace and serenity.

It was precisely at that moment that Heron reflected upon one piece of forgetfulness that had come over him.

It was easy enough to reach the top of the wall when mounted on the back of Daisy, but how was he readily, if it were necessary, to surmount it from the inside?

This was a consideration that was worth attending to, so Felix Heron carried out the instruction he had given to Tom Ripon—namely, to creep along the inner side of the wall until he should find a door, by which a more ready access to the bridle-road could be got than by scaling it.

It was not a particularly easy process.

The thick ivy so completely impeded him, and sent down such showers of moisture upon him from the recent rains, that he could hardly make his way at all.

Moreover, he walked upon some soft bed of earth that had been a flower-border.

But these little difficulties soon ceased.

Captain Heron came to firmer footing.

He trod upon a gravelled path which termimated close to the wall, and at a door, as he had suspected.

But that door was locked.

Age, however, had done its work with both its iron and wood work.

Heron had very little difficulty with his sword in wrenching the lock completely off.

The door then was only held close by one old rusty bolt which he shot in to its socket on the inner side, and which he guessed had not been used for many a long year.

Having thus, like a prudent general, secured his retreat in case of accidents, Felix Heron felt much more at ease in his mind as regarded the adventure he was upon.

He made his way, as nearly as he could guess in the darkness, at right angles from the wall.

His route was impeded by shrubs and bushes, and occasionally by a tree.

But at length he emerged upon an open lawn.

Directly in front of him was the mansion.

He could see it but dimly, and it looked of much greater extent than it really was; although Holland House is by no means one of the smallest of those palatial half-baronial residences of the old nobility of England, so few of which survive in the neighbourhood of the metropolis.

Not a leaf seemed to be stirring in the gardens.

Not a human soul in the house.

But as Heron carefully ran his gaze over the ample front, he was certain that at one of the windows he saw a long, thin streak of light.

It was very faint.

But light it was.

It looked like just such a thin perpendicular reflection as might come through an ill-fitting shutter in the room beyond which was an illumination.

This was quite sufficient for Captain Heron.

The adventure was working itself out.

Cautiously and slowly he made his way towards the house.

He recollected hearing that, in consequence of two sudden deaths in the Holland family, that beautiful and ancient home of their race had been for a time deserted, and that for a time it had become the haunt of persons who found it their interest to surround it with a halo of superstition, he did not doubt.

He was exceedingly curious to know who those persons were.

So carefully and so cautiously, that it was impossible his approach should be detected, Heron made his way onwards until he stood close to the porch of the ancient residence.

To the right of where he stood, so far as he could see it by straining his eyes in the darkness, the house seemed very much broken up into gable-ends and circular corners, but to the left there was a long range of windows.

Heron concluded that they must belong to one of the principal rooms of the place.

He thought it would be hard indeed if at some one or other of those windows he could not make his way into the house.

He crept along them, touching their frameworks gently.

All were fast but one.

That one, however, was enough for him.

He opened the sash gently, and stepped into the picture gallery of Holland House.

Heron did not know the apartment, however,

by that name; and it was only by feeling along the wall, and finding the frames of pictures as close as they would go together, that he was able to come to the conclusion of where he was.

Thus feeling his way, of course, he naturally came to a door.

It was slightly closed, but yielded to a touch.

And Heron was very careful now in his progress.

Careful for two reasons.

First, not to make a noise.

Secondly, not to precipitate himself down some staircase which, in the darkness, he could not take the least cognizance of.

He was certain that the thin streak of light he had seen coming from one of the rooms of Holland House was on the upper floor.

Therefore he had to seek for some staircase by which he could ascend.

Suddenly he pauses.

He hears confused voices.

A flash of light, faint, but yet, amid the intense darkness that had surrounded him, sufficiently noticeable, streamed down upon him.

"Hilloa!" cried a voice. "Is that you, Jennings?"

Of course Heron made no reply.

But the light, faint as it was, was quite sufficient to let him see his whereabouts.

He was in the hall of the mansion.

Statuary and pictures were about him on every side, and he had no difficulty in hiding himself behind one of the former, which he did as a precautionary measure, in case the person from above should come down to look for the "Jennings" he spoke of.

But he did not come.

And from the position he occupied Felix Heron was able to see the exact position of the grand staircase, with its gilt balustrades and the rich carpeting that covered it.

CHAPTER CCXIX.

CAPTAIN HERON DIVES STILL DEEPER INTO THE MYSTERIES OF HOLLAND HOUSE.

"I THOUGHT I heard Jennings," said the voice again, in tones of suspicion.

Then another voice spoke; and, from the indistinct manner in which Felix Heron heard it, the person who spoke was evidently in a room on the first floor of the mansion, the door of which might be only slightly open.

"Come back!—come back!" cried this voice. "Let Jennings alone."

"But the pistol-shot? You heard it as well as I."

"Well, well! It's likely enough he's given an ounce of lead to somebody in the bridle-road; and a good job too!"

The light disappeared.

The man who had come to the head of the stairs with it had gone back again.

The darkness seemed to come down upon Heron in that hall with double blackness.

But he had noted well the position of the staircase, and was able to make his way to it with certainty, although with prudence and caution.

He reached it.

He touched the balustrades.

As gently as foot could fall he commenced the ascent.

And, as he did so, Heron asked himself where, and under what circumstances, he had heard the voice of the man who had spoken from the room to the other one at the head of the stairs.

There was a familiar accent about the tones which Captain Heron felt quite certain he had heard before.

But where, he could not exactly define

Heron paused at the head of the stairs, having lifted his foot once too often, and so brought it down with more force than he had intended.

In the intense silence of that house this sound was enough to give an alarm.

"Come in, Jennings!" cried a voice; "and don't be playing the fool out there!"

At the same moment a flash of light came over the landing-place to which Heron had attained.

He saw several doors about him, some open and some closed.

He chose one of the former, and made his way at once into a room which was in darkness, with one singular exception.

That exception was a little oval spot of light upon one of its walls.

Heron guessed in a moment from whence it proceeded. It came from some room adjoining in which there was a light, and that was the ray that made its way through the keyhole of a door of communication.

It was singular, too, considering the small portion of light that thus penetrated the darkness, what an effect it had.

A faint, a very faint twilight, seemed to permeate that apartment, and to chase away completely that intense blackness which had appeared in the atmosphere of the hall.

Heron approached the door of communication quite easily.

Stooping down, he applied his eye to the keyhole, and saw a sight which filled him with surprise.

At a table, on which were some bottles and glasses, and on which were a couple of hand lanterns, the slides of which were thrown back, sat three men.

Two were complete strangers to him.

The third he knew full well.

In the brutalized, intemperate features he recognised John Tarleton.

His, then, was the voice that had struck with familiar cadences upon the ears of Captain Heron.

John Tarleton was speaking.

"Stuff!" he cried; "don't talk to me of ghosts; Haven't I slept here for a week, and seen none of them?"

"Yes; but I can't make this out," growled one of the other men.

"Make what out?"

"The foot upon the stair."

"The fiddlestick upon the stair, my good friend! Pass the bottle."

"You're a reckless fellow, as you always were; but I wonder we've not his lordship here by this time."

"Oh, he'll come, safe enough, he's sick of the forest, and so am I. He don't like to hear the wind among the trees at night, nor do I; and it's dull work, too. They may say what they like of the beauty of the green glades, but give me the green cloth that covers a faro table above them all."

"Well," said the third man, who had not yet spoken, "I must say that I, too, prefer to crack cribs in London, to crying 'Stand and deliver!' on the highway."

"To be sure—to be sure!" cried John Tarleton; "and the one I was speaking to you about is the best crib you can get into."

"Whitcombe House, you mean?"

"To be sure I do!"

"What can have become of Jennings?" said the man who had spoken before, and who seemed the most nervous and anxious of the three.

"Oh, he is shot, or shot somebody."

"No."

"Why, didn't you say you heard it yourself? Didn't he go out and play the ghost of the murdered Captain as usual? And haven't you heard some fire-arms in the bridle-road? So if you put this and that together, what can you make of it?"

"You are careless, but I don't feel quite at ease."

A shrill whistle from the outside of the house at this moment attracted the attention of all parties.

"That's my lord," cried John Tarleton. "Take one of the lanterns, and show him in."

The man who had expressed his fears and apprehensions so freely, hesitated; so the other, who seemed a stolid sort of ruffian, took one of the lanterns, and growling out some oaths as he went, left the room.

In a few minutes he returned, bringing with him two persons.

One of them was no other than Lord Warringdale, who, from what Captain Heron had heard, he fully expected.

The other was shorter than Warringdale by a head, and was both cloaked and masked, so that no one could recognise him.

"A friend of mine," said Warringdale, with a wave of the hand.

"Ah!" cried John Tarleton; "one of our sort?"

"Not exactly; but a gentleman, who has something to propose to us more profitable than anything we have yet attempted."

"Pray be seated, Mr. Gentleman; you're the man for our money. Pray be seated."

The stranger in the cloak and mask turned to Lord Warringdale, and pointing as he did so to the flasks and glasses on the table, he said in an evidently feigned voice, "Intemperance is fatal!"

Lord Warringdale put on an air of veration.

"Be assured, your Grace, it shall not be."

"Fool!" cried the man with the mask and the cloak, with a stamp of his foot. "Why apply such a title to me?"

John Tarleton and his two companions exchanged glances.

They felt quite certain, from that moment, that they were in the presence of one who was entitled by his rank to the prefix to his name that Lord Warringdale had incautiously given utterance to.

TOM RIPON DOES A LITTLE BIT OF BUSINESS ON HIS OWN ACCOUNT.

Presented Gratis with No. 68, of the New Edition of EDITH RIPON, the Sequel to Edith the Captive; or, the Robbers of Epping Forest.

"I crave pardon," said Warringdale; "but, being accustomed to call you that in jest, I did it inadvertently."

"Quite inadvertently," said John Tarleton, with a sneer.

"Business—to business," said the man with the mask and the cloak.

"Then, sir," said Warringdale, "I can only say, that I and these worthy gentlemen are quite willing to be of use in any way you may suggest."

The man in the cloak seemed to consider a few minutes before he spoke again, and then speaking from behind the mask, and evidently at the same time making an effort to conceal his natural voice, he murmured out his words rather than uttered them aloud.

But Heron was sharp of hearing.

Every word, however lightly uttered, reached his ears.

"There is a society of gentlemen who each pay five hundred guineas for certain service that may be rendered to them. The service is easy, but it requires three things."

"Please to name them," said John Tarleton.

"Address, for one."

"Well, sir?"

"Courage."

"And the third?"

"Utter unscrupulousness."

John Tarleton laughed.

"Then, sir, whether you're a Grace or not, you have come to the right shop for that article, for here we have it in abundance. I think, my Lord Warringdale, you and I are about the two most unscrupulous rascals in existence!"

"Speak for yourself!" said Warringdale, with a frown.

"Oh, it's true—it's true!"

"Peace! I like not this levity!"

"Well, sir, what are we to do?"

"Of that you shall be informed to-morrow night, and the next day you will commence your operations."

"For five hundred guineas?"

"That is the sum."

"And quickly and easily earned?"

"Probably in an hour or two."

"I'm game for that!"

"Listen," added the stranger with the cloak and mask. "Near to Pall Mall, and some fifty paces past the gate of the old Palace of St. James's, there is a tall house, the lower part of which is of stone in its frontage. The windows of its ground floor have crimson blinds. Come there to-morrow night at the midnight hour. Knock four times, not loudly, but so as to be distinctly heard—one steady, light blow of the knocker at each time—and you will be admitted and receive your instructions, and half your money in advance for your next day's work."

This was all very mysterious; and Captain Heron, while he could not imagine what kind of service was required by the person in the cloak and the mask, was resolved that he would know.

"I agree, for one," said John Tarleton.

"Then be true to the appointed time."

"Never fear me."

The man in the cloak and mask at once moved to the door of the room, and made a sign to Lord Warringdale that he intended to leave.

"We shall meet again shortly," said Lord Warringdale to John Tarleton and his two rascally companions.

"Oh!" said Tarleton, as he pointed in a significant way to the flasks of liquor and the glasses on the table—"we can wait very well."

Captain Heron was puzzled to know exactly what to do for the best.

Nothing to him could be easier than to intercept the man in the cloak and mask, and force from him the secret of his midnight machinations; or, if he, Heron, did not think proper to adopt that course, another was open to him.

He could let Lord Warringdale and his mysterious companion go, and then make his way into the room in the occupation of John Tarleton and his rascally companions, and from them insist upon a full disclosure of the truth.

But, upon reflection, Felix Heron determined upon adopting neither of those courses.

He made up his mind to come at the heart of the mystery in another fashion.

Was he not in possession of the means of admission to that house in town, whither John Tarleton and his associates had been invited?

What, then, was to prevent him taking advantage of the accidental information he had obtained, and so counteracting some iniquitous plot or proceeding which it would give him pleasure to foil.

Acting upon this idea, therefore, Captain Heron was desirous of leaving the house as speedily as possible.

There was no real difficulty in taking that step.

So soon as John Tarleton and his associates were left to themselves, they began to pay so much attention to the flasks of wine and spirits on the table before them, that they were quickly oblivious of all sounds but what they themselves made.

Heron glided out of the room where he had been so attentive a spectator of the singular scene we have related, and making his way down the grand staircase of Holland House, he left it by the hall door, which he now found open.

No doubt Lord Warringdale, and the mysterious person in the cloak and mask, had so left it.

Heron crossed the threshold, and was in the garden, when some one ran up to him and touched him on the arm.

"Is it you?" he said. "Is it you? Tell me if it is you, Deuce Ace?"

Captain Heron remembered well that that was the name by which John Tarleton went at the gaming-houses, and among the disreputable companions of his ill-spent hours.

There was a peculiarity of John Tarleton which it was not difficult to imitate, and Captain Heron, now that he was challenged with being that person, essayed to keep up the delusion.

"What's the matter?" he said.

"Oh, yes, it's you, Deuce Ace, I hear now; for it's so precious dark I can't see you; and when I came up to you I thought you looked ever so much taller."

"What's the matter?" said Heron again.

"Well, you see, I was on the watch, as usual, and I was quite sure I heard some people in the lane, so I tried to frighten them off in the old fashion by playing the ghost. I got on the ladder, as usual, and hoisted myself up above the old ivy on the wall."

"Indeed!"

"Oh, yes! But whoever it was wouldn't be frightened at all; but, without saying so much as by your leave, fired a pistol-shot at me, and the bullet took off the corner of my ear."

"You don't say so!"

"Yes. You must have heard the shot. I have been hiding in one of the old, dilapidated summer-houses ever since, and have only just now ventured to creep out."

Captain Heron could not but smile to himself at this rational account of the ghostly phenomenon that had had such an effect upon the nervous system of Tom Ripon.

That this was the man who had been called to by the name of Jennings there could be no doubt whatever; and now, having heard all he had to say, Captain Heron was anxious to get rid of him.

"You'd better go in," he said. "You'll get something to drink."

"That's just what'll suit me. All's right! It might have been worse."

Mr. Jennings brushed past Captain Heron, and made his way into Holland House.

"Now for Tom Ripon and the horses!" said Heron to himself, as he made his way as quickly as he could to the door in the wall of the garden, which he had so arranged that he could open quickly and make an immediate exit.

That door was soon found, and Heron emerged into the bridle-road, calling out as he did so, "Tom! Tom! where are you?"

"Here, Captain, here! Why, you've been away a week!"

"I think scarcely an hour, Tom; although the time doubtless has seemed long to you. Let us ride on, for the night is still young, and as we go I will tell you what I've heard and seen in Holland House."

Tom Ripon was very much interested at the brief account Captain Heron gave him of John Tarleton and his associates.

"Of course, Captain," said Tom, "it's some villany or another, and we're not the sort of men to see it go on and not try to put an end to it."

"Certainly not, Tom; but here we are, on the Western Road, and I am not sorry, for one, to leave that gloomy bridle-road behind us."

The rapid galloping of horses' feet coming from London put a check to further conversation between Tom Ripon and Captain Heron.

They both involuntarily drew aside into the shadow of that portion of the wall of Holland House garden which directly fronted the Western Road.

The horseman approached at good speed, but before he reached the spot where they might be said to be in hiding he slackened his pace, the cause of which seemed to be that from the opposite direction some vehicle was approaching.

It was a light chaise, and in which one man was seated, and in front of which a small lamp was burning, which shed sufficient rays of light about it to enable Heron and Tom Ripon to make tolerably accurate observation of what was going on.

"Hilloa!" cried the horseman, who came from from the direction of London. "Halt, there! I want to ask you a question."

The man in the chaise cart pulled up abruptly.

CHAPTER CCXX.

TOM RIPON TRIES HIS FORTUNE ON THE ROAD, AND TAKES SOME VALUABLE BOOTY.

TOM RIPON and Captain Heron spoke both at the same moment.

"Jonathan Wild!" was the exclamation that burst from each of their lips.

Yes, it was no other than Wild, who, on that night expedition in search of the Baron Von Peck, had got on to the Western Road.

"Hilloa!" he shouted. "Who are you?"

"A poor man, sir!"

"Bah! I don't care whether you are poor or rich! What are you, and what is your name?"

"John Dobkins, sir, and a market gardener."

"Very well! Now tell me if you have seen a man on horseback on the road, and a boy?"

"No, sir!"

"You are quite sure?"

"Oh, quite, sir!"

"Confusion!" muttered Jonathan Wild; "I have missed them! You can pass on!"

The man in the chaise-cart seemed glad to get past so imperious a questioner on the road, and he drove off as quickly as he well could.

"Captain!" whispered Tom.

"Well?"

"What on earth does anybody mean by calling me a boy?"

"Because you are not a girl, I suppose, Tom!"

This was anything but a satisfactory reply to Tom Ripon; and he felt inclined to relapse into silence for some time.

That was just what Felix Heron liked; for he was at that moment busy with his own thoughts.

He could scarcely guess how Jonathan Wild could so readily have come upon his track.

But the fact was that Wild had reached the immediate neighbourhood of the bridle-path by Holland House a very short time after Felix Heron and Tom Ripon.

From a chance passenger he heard that two such persons had gone down the narrow thoroughfare.

Wild knew it well.

It led nowhere but to the Western Road; and he at once adopted a course that he thought would enable him to watch well the proceedings of Tom and the supposed Baron Von Peck.

Wild had some special objection to passing down the bridle-road at the side of old Holland House.

Perhaps that objection bore some special reference to the bad name the lane had.

But be that as it may, he avoided it.

Galloping on, therefore, to that road which Tom had mentioned to Heron, and which was about half a mile further on, Jonathan Wild felt that he was losing no ground.

On emerging from it into the Western Road, his impression decidedly was that he was lower down the road than Baron Von Peck and Tom Ripon.

At a walk, therefore, Jonathan took his horse townwards.

He paused as he passed the bridle-road, and listened.

But he heard no sound.

It happened that that was just the time when Heron was in the mansion, and Tom was, although in the lane with both the horses, as quiet as a mouse.

Jonathan Wild was puzzled.

He could not make out how it was he had missed, or apparently missed, the Baron Von Peck and Tom Ripon.

After lingering a little on the roadway, he still pursued his route towards London, for the conviction on his mind was still so strong that they had not passed him towards the country, that he could look for them nowhere but in that direction.

Still, however, his mind misgave him after he had trotted about half a mile, and he returned again.

It was upon that return that Tom Ripon and Felix Heron saw him so plainly.

What were they to do?

Were they to be content with the adventures of that night, and return home in peace?

Should they determine to do that, they might defy Jonathan Wild, who would have no excuse then for interfering in any way with the Baron Von Peck.

Felix Heron felt all the hazard he ran.

But the spirit of adventure was strong within him.

Was he to be baulked in what he had undertaken just because Jonathan Wild was on the road?

Certainly not.

"Tom!" he whispered.

"Yes, Captain."

"We must wait a few moments until Wild is gone."

"We might do better, Captain."

"As how?"

"Why not take the Kensington Road instead of the Western? The one's as good as the other."

"True; but you have rather a disinclination, I fancy, to pass down the bridle-road again."

"Not with you, Captain."

"Be it so, then. Keep close!"

Foiled and enraged, Jonathan Wild paced his horse slowly westward, and when he had got about a hundred yards past the hiding-place of Heron and Tom Ripon, the former gave the word to move on.

"Follow me, Tom," he said, "but walk your horse, so that its footsteps shall make as light a sound as possible."

Noiselessly they reached the bridle-road again by the side of Holland House; and then, as they were quite sufficiently distant from Jonathan Wild to be out of hearing, they both set out at a hard trot.

And the bridle-road was so soft and humid, that even at that pace their horses' feet scarcely made a sound.

A very few minutes sufficed for them to traverse the whole of that road; and to the great relief of Tom Ripon, they emerged again in the immediate neighbourhood of Kensington.

In the south-east there was a rapidly brightening sky.

A young moon was rising over the tree-tops. Tom shook his head.

"I'm afraid, Captain, it'll be too light for us."

"No, Tom. A moonlight night and a cloudy sky is a highwayman's delight."

"Then we shall have it," said Tom, "for I see the clouds are breaking away; and, young as the moon is, it will shine like silver."

They paused, and turned their attention to the beautiful luminary which rose majestically over a clump of trees in a garden of some estate close at hand.

"This is very beautiful," said Heron.

"It's stunning," said Tom.

"Who would not rather enjoy this," added Heron, "in preference to the crowded saloons of the Court?"

"Hurrah!" said Tom.

"What's the matter?"

"Don't you hear, Captain, the crunching and grinding of carriage wheels?"

"I fancy I do."

"Yes, Captain, and there come the carriage-lights. Don't you see a pair-horse chaise, driven by a postilion, and nobody in the dicky behind?"

"Very well, Tom; this shall be your adventure."

"You don't mean that, Captain?"

"Yes; but if you should happen to be over-matched, whistle for me, or fire one of your pistols, and I'll soon be by your side. But always remember, Tom, no violence : it is quite as easy to rob on the highway gently as roughly."

Tom Ripon was so well pleased that Captain Heron had left this adventure to him, that waving his hand without speaking a word, he dashed forward into the road to intercept the chaise.

"Halt! halt!" he cried to the postilion. "Halt! or you're a dead man!"

The only reply of the postilion was to make a slash at Tom with his whip, and then to urge his horses forward.

The situation of Tom Ripon was a little critical, and if he had not, in consequence of his frequent expeditions with Captain Heron, become by this time a pretty good horse rider, he might have got the worst of the encounter, from the pure weight of the pair of horses and the chaise.

As it was, Tom trotted by the side of the horses, and seized the check-rein of the one nearest him.

"Hands off, you rascal!" cried the postilion. "Hands off!"

"Halt!" cried Tom, "or it will be worse for you!"

The postilion lashed at him furiously with his long-thonged whip.

Tom got some smarting cuts about the head and shoulders.

Slowly and surely, however, he was succeeding in his object, which was to turn the horses' heads from the direct road towards the hedge-row.

"You'll upset us, you vagabond, as sure as fate!" cried the postilion. "You'll upset Mr. Brydges, his Majesty's jeweller, and you'll be hung as sure as fate!"

"That'll do!" cried Tom.

He relinquished his hold of the horses' heads.

The fore wheels of the chaise lurched into the hollow of the road, close to the pathway, and the horses, finding a blackthorn hedge opposed to their further progress, came to an abrupt halt

"That'll do!" cried Tom.

"Yes, I hope that'll do!" said the postilion.

As he spoke, he reversed his whip, and coiling the thong round his wrist, he made a heavy and savage blow at Tom's head with the butt-end of it.

Tom saw the blow coming, and backed his horse suddenly at least a dozen paces beyond its influence.

But the patience and the discretion of Tom Ripon were both exhausted.

"Take that!" he said.

As he spoke, he drew one of his holster pistols, and fired it direct at the head of the postilion.

In the midst of the smoke and the flash Tom Ripon certainly saw the white hat of the postilion flying through the air, but whether it contained his head or not likewise he could not determine.

Certainly the saddle of the horse was empty.

"That'll do!" said Tom. "A mighty obstinate fellow that was, but he would have it!"

Tom dashed his heels against his horse's flanks, and was at the side of the coach in an instant.

"Now, sir!" cried Tom, as he looked in.

The moon shone tolerably brightly in at the other window.

Then a very blank look came over Tom Ripon's countenance.

The coach was empty.

"Confound the fellow!" said Tom. "All this trouble about nothing!"

He looked again more carefully.

There could be no mistake about it.

For all he knew, a passenger might have been in the chaise, but he was not there then.

And what made it more puzzling still was, that Tom felt perfectly sure neither door of the coach had been opened during the brief but decisive contest he had had with the postilion.

What to do Tom knew not.

It was just one of those emergencies in which he required the advice of Captain Heron.

Now, the pistol-shot had reached Heron's ears quite plainly, and almost at the moment that Tom was wishing for the appearance of his friend and master, Heron trotted up.

"What's amiss, Tom?"

"Oh, Captain, I am so glad you're here! The only booty I seem likely to get is a chaise and pair."

"What do you mean?"

"Why, it's empty, Captain; although the postilion fought like a lion, as if the wealth of the Indies were inside it; and now I think of it, he did say that Mr. Brydges, the King's jeweller, was here."

Heron looked into the coach.

"It's empty, Tom! Who did you fire at?"

"Oh, I was forced to settle the postilion!"

"I hope not."

"Well, I couldn't help it, Captain."

Heron raised his voice.

"Speak up, if any one is hurt. There will be no more harm done, and some help given!"

There was no response to this polite invitation.

Heron knew not what to do exactly.

He felt in the position of some naval commander who has captured a ship at sea too heavy for him to bring along.

"We cannot encumber ourselves, Tom, with a chaise and pair!"

"Then what are we to do with it, Captain?"

"Just nothing; and yet, when I think of it, the horses will get into mischief. Cut these traces, Tom, and let them go whither they will; in all probability they will find their way to their own stables, wherever they may be."

"I'll do it," said Tom, "but it's rather disappointing. I see the chaise is only hung upon leather springs, so I'll just let that down, and see if I can't get it into the ditch by the road-side."

"Stop, stop, Tom! On second thoughts, a novel idea strikes me. I will get into the chaise, and you shall lead Daisy, and I will contrive to drive it with the reins through the front window. It will be something new in the history of life on the road to cry 'Stand and deliver!' from the interior of a coach!"

Captain Heron might or might not have been serious in this proposition; but he certainly dismounted and leaped into the open coach.

Almost as he did so, Tom Ripon was nearly startled out of his senses by a voice crying out, in loud yelling tones, "Mercy, mercy! I'm a dead man!—I'm a dead man!"

The voice unquestionably came from the chaise.

For a moment Tom could almost have imagined the vehicle itself was endowed with some miraculous voice, and was giving utterance to its complaints.

But a few words from Captain Heron soon put things to rights in Tom's mind.

"All's right!" said Heron. "Here's your man, Tom."

"Good gracious, Captain!"

Tom looked through the window of the chaise; and, to his intense surprise, saw a small, frightened-looking being, in a full Court suit, trembling in the grasp of Captain Heron.

"Why, where did he come from, Captain?"

"From under one of the seats, that's all."

"Oh, idiot, idiot!" said Tom.

"Yes," gasped the little man in the Court suit; "I am an idiot—a poor idiot gentleman going to an asylum."

"I meant myself," said Tom, "for not guessing where you were."

CHAPTER CCXXI.

CAPTAIN HERON AND TOM RIPON ARE WATCHED AND PURSUED BY JONATHAN WILD.

HERON had about as much power over this person in the coach as if he had been a mere child, and he made him sit down on the seat opposite to him with all the ease in the world.

"You need not be frightened, sir," he said. "No one will harm you."

"Certainly not," said Tom. "All we want is your money, your watch, jewellery, and, in fact, everything of value you have about you! We don't want any dead bodies just now, because we have supplied all our regular customers with them, and so you're safe!"

"Mercy upon us!" said the little man.

"Come, come," said Tom, "hand out."

"Yes, my good sir, with great pleasure. There's my watch. You'll find it a good one to go."

"I should say it was," said Tom. "And now it's gone altogether!"

"Jewellery, my good sirs, I have none; but my money you are welcome to. Here it is, amounting to one and ninepence, which I put in my pocket to pay the turnpikes between Kew and London."

"One and what?" cried Tom.

"Ninepence."

"Stop," said Heron. "What were you doing at Kew?"

"I—I went to visit a friend."

"In a Court dress, with diamond buckles in your shoes?"

"Paste, paste, my dear sir—nothing but paste, as I am a jeweller and a Christian man!"

"Oh, then, you are a jeweller?"

"Well, I—a—I—a—think I am."

"And your name is Brydges?"

No. 69.—EDITH.

"You may call me Brydges."

"And the friend you went to visit at Kew, in a Court dress, was no other than the King?"

"Mercy upon us! What put that into your head?"

"And your visit could only be professional. Come, sir, you have jewels of value about you, and we must have them."

"I declare, by all the saints——"

"Stuff! You don't believe in saints, so it's no oath."

"But, my good sir——"

"Tom!"

"Yes, Captain."

"Take this man out of the coach, and pick him to pieces!"

"All's right!"

Mr. Brydges fell at once to the bottom of the coach as though he had been shot; and, driving his hand under the seat, he produced a small black leather packet, which he handed to Heron.

"There," he said, "are the jewels I took to show to the King, and if you take them from me I'm a ruined man."

"That we've nothing to do with," said Tom. "We are ruined if we don't take them!"

"Alas! alas!" said the little jeweller, as he sank back upon the seat opposite to Heron, in the coach, with a look of profound despair— "alas! alas! I am lost—I am ruined! I am ——Murder! What's that?"

He sprang to his feet again with great celerity.

"It seems to me," said Heron, "that you've something in your pocket, on which you have inadvertently sat down."

The little jeweller looked perfectly aghast.

"Come, sir, hand it forth!"

With a groan, he took from his pocket an exquisitely-fashioned gold cup, round the rim of which was an entire circle of Oriental jewels, while the stem and foot were thickly encrusted with brilliants.

As the moonbeams fell upon this article of goldsmith's work, the brilliants shot forth a thousand beautiful rays.

There could be no doubt of their great value.

The jeweller did not seem to have breath enough now to speak with; and it was only in a spasmodic manner that he contrived to jerk out, "The King—his Majesty—entrusted me with that cup to take out the brilliants from it, and set them in a bracelet, for a present to the Duchess of Oldenburg! If you take it from me, I'm a ruined man!"

"Nonsense!" said Heron; "you're as liable to be stopped on the highway as anybody! How are you to keep it? You have done your best; and the King cannot blame you for that which is inevitable."

As Heron spoke, he sprang from the coach.

It was possible enough that the jeweller might have other booty of value; but still Heron felt that he ought to be very well satisfied with the issue of the adventure.

"Take care of that black case, Tom," he said. "I have the King's cup. Let us mount, and away!"

"Which way, Captain?"

"By a circuitous route homeward."

"All's right!"

Heron sprang to the back of Daisy, and, instead of turning townwards, he trotted down the sloping country in the direction of the Thames.

Tom followed him speedily.

Heron then took the first turning he could to the right, and came out through the eastern suburbs of Hammersmith; after which, he turned his face towards London.

"Tom!"

"Yes, Captain."

"It seems we have carried through that adventure without the slightest peril."

"I hope so, Captain."

"I don't hear a single person upon the road! Let us see what the time is."

Heron held up his watch to the moonbeams, which were just sufficiently powerful to enable him to see that the hour was three in the morning.

Tom slightly touched Heron's arm at this moment; and the touch was so evidently one of warning, that, without speaking a word, he turned, and looked in Tom's face to know what it meant.

They were just in that bit of country between the little village of Brook Green and Shepherd's Bush.

There is there still a large triangular piece of common ground dividing the two roads, one of which leads to Acton and Ealing, and the other to Hammersmith.

A rather broad turning to the right, as Felix Heron and Tom Ripon stood with their faces towards London, led to Brook Green.

That turning, at the period of our story, was so little frequented, that it was completely grass-grown, with the exception of a few cart-tracks; and a row of tall poplars on each side of the way shadowed it, as well as narrowed it, completely.

It was towards these poplars that Tom silently pointed.

Captain Heron followed the direction indicated with his eyes, and there he certainly saw a horseman looking as motionless as a statue, and who might have been mistaken for one, but for the improbability of such an object in such a spot.

"Who is that?" said Tom in a whisper.

"I don't know?"

"What shall we do, Captain?"

"Nothing but ride on."

"But haven't you an idea about him?"

"Only one, Tom, that seems at all reasonable, at this time in the morning."

"What do you think he is, then, Captain?"

"A highwayman."

"Oh, if that's the case," said Tom, with a long breath of relief, "it's all right. What used we to say at the forest?—'hawks don't pick hawks' eyes out.' Come on, Captain!"

It seemed to Heron—but he was not quite sure upon that point—that as they passed the road leading to Brook Green, where this horseman was stationed, he gradually receded so as to be more in the gloom and shadow of the trees.

It was certainly not Heron's policy, however, to take any notice of him, be he whom he might.

Passing on quickly with Tom, they soon left the suspicious object behind them, and mounting the rise of Notting Hill, they paused for a few seconds within a hundred yards of the turnpike-gate to listen.

The sound made by their own horse's feet had, up to that moment, prevented them from hearing the regular tramp of another horse behind them.

"We are pursued, Tom. Let me think a moment."

"I'll go back and shoot him," said Tom.

"No, no! I think we might make a gallop for it, and so distance him. And yet, after all, that might not succeed; for although I could match Daisy easily against any horse, our enemy may be quite as well mounted as you are, Tom."

"Then you ride on, Captain, and leave me to shift for myself."

"Would it be like me to do so?"

Tom was silent.

He knew it would be useless to urge that plan any farther.

It was evident that the horseman in their rear had a pursuit of them for his object, for now that they had come to a standstill, the sound of his horse's feet stopped abruptly.

"It is Jonathan Wild," said Heron.

"Of course it is," said Tom; "and I tell you what it is, Captain—we shall know no peace till we get rid of him!"

"How?"

"A bullet!"

"No, Tom; there is one consideration which will induce me never to lift my hand against Jonathan Wild's life, if I can help it."

"Indeed!"

"Yes, he believes me dead; and since then, in his rough, careless way, he has shown a disposition to befriend Edith. And, at all events, he has no longer been an enemy of hers, or of what he considers her fatherless child; and, bad as he is, that trait in his nature commends him to my consideration."

"But he's after us now, Captain!"

"You forget, Tom, that it is the Baron Von Peck he is after, and not Felix Heron."

"Oh, ah! to be sure! Well, I don't want to shoot Johnny, but it's very awkward."

"It is, and I am thinking what to do. He may find a means of following us to town, I do not doubt, so I shall not go direct to Whitcombe House. What is that, Tom, you were telling me about Mortification and your mother taking some shop in their old trade?"

"Why, you see, Captain, 'what's bred in the bone will never grow out of the flesh,' as the old proverb says; and they have taken an old tumble-down sort of crib in Wardour Street, Soho."

"I recollect, Tom, your mentioning some such circumstance; and I thought it hard at the time that Mortification and your mother, to both of whom I have at times been a good friend, should desert my household at Whitcombe House, which as you know, Tom, I can only people with those who know the secret of my existence."

Tom made a wry face.

"It's wrong enough, Captain, of the old gal as well as of old Mortification; but it can't be helped; and who shall say now that it don't serve us at a pinch?"

"True—true!"

"And as, Captain, you have a particular objection to settling matters with Jonathan Wild by means of a bullet, and an equal objection to his dodging us home to Whitcombe House, what do you say to a visit to the new 'fence?'"

"Be it so, Tom! Let us get on, in the name of heaven, for I do not wish to be the death of that man!"

"All's right, Captain; and I'm sure we neither of us intend he should be the death of us!"

The tramp of Jonathan Wild's horse was still upon the road.

Neither to the right nor to the left was any turning down which Tom Ripon and Captain Heron could make their way without being pretty sure to be dogged and traced.

But Captain Heron was not the sort of man to be foiled by even the rather uncomfortable train of circumstances surrounding him.

"Tom," he said, "we must do one thing, and do that effectually."

"Anything, Captain! I'm game for it, whatever it is!"

"We must get through this turnpike gate ourselves, and, at least for a time, prevent Jonathan Wild from doing so."

Tom felt that this was rather a difficult proposition.

Indeed, it would have been an impossible one had Wild really been in pursuit of Heron and Tom Ripon; but the fact was, his progress on the road was speculative, and he was making such speed as he might.

Had he been on the gallop instead of still entertaining a suspicion that those he sought might after all be behind him, Captain Heron would not have been able to carry out in time the little scheme which his fertile brain suggested.

Daisy, he knew perfectly well, could carry him over the turnpike gate at a flying leap.

But Tom's horse was unequal to such a feat.

Moreover, that would not exactly have answered his purpose.

"Tom," he said, "the gate is no doubt locked."

"You may make sure of that, Captain. All these old pikes are, after sunset; and, bother the fellow, his little crib of a house is on the other side."

"All the better, Tom. Hold Daisy a moment."

"Bless you, Captain, she don't want holding. All you've got to say is to tell her where you want her to stand, and what you want her to do, and she'll do it like a Christian, and a great deal better than many of them."

"I believe you, Tom. Wait a bit, and I'll soon let you through the pike."

Captain Heron hastily dismounted, and made his way through the little wicket gate for foot passengers on the pathway by the side of the road.

That small thoroughfare was cunningly contrived, so that nothing on four legs should be able to pass through it.

The little wooden hut in which the turnpike-keeper resided was closely shut up; and, no doubt, its occupant was in profound repose.

The usual shout of "Gate, gate!" would, in probability, have aroused him, since it was a thing of habit at such a cry to get up and issue forth, take his toll, and open the gate, closing and locking it again, and retiring again to rest, all in a mechanical kind of way only to be acquired by custom.

But it is doubtful if any other sound whatever except that cry of "Gate, gate!" would have affected the repose of the pike-keeper.

Felix Heron found no difficulty in opening the door of the little hut by one vigorous kick.

The pike-keeper sprang from his pallet-bed, and confronted the intruder.

"Silence!" said Heron, as he let the man see the bright barrel of a pistol.

"Thieves! Mur——"

"Another such a word, and you are a dead man! Be prudent and silent, and no harm will come to you! Give me the key of the gate."

"The—the key—of the—the——"

"Quick, I say! No paltering with me! Give me the key of the turnpike-gate; and then, if you are a prudent man, lie down to rest again, or worse will come of it!"

"I daren't."

Heron dived his hand into his pocket, and flung several guineas upon a rough table that was in the hut.

"Take your choice," he said ; "which will you prefer—gold or lead ?"

"Gold or lead, sir ?"

"Yes, guineas or a bullet !"

"Stop ! stop ! Ha, ha ! I see it all now !"

"What do you mean ?"

"You're a highwayman, and there's somebody after you."

"A bright guess !"

"Lord bless you ! I footed the pad myself once, though I couldn't come the high-flying toby business, because, you see, I never took to horseback. Some do, and some don't. I think it's born with people. But I keeps a pike now, because a stray bullet was sent after me one fine night, and touched me on the heel ; so that spoilt my galivanting, though I've a fellow-feeling for 'the family' still."

"All's right, then !" said Heron. "Keep the guineas, and give me the key."

"Here you are !"

"Thanks."

"I know your game. But who is after you ?"

"Jonathan Wild !"

"Ah !"

A look of consternation came upon the face of the pikeman, and he half repented that his attachment to "the family" carried him so far, on that occasion, as to place him in antagonism to the great thief-taker.

Captain Heron, however, left him no time for repentance.

Provided now with the great key of the turnpike gate, which from constant use was clear and bright, Heron dashed out of the hut, and opening the gate, called out in a subdued tone.

"Tom ! Tom ! Quick ! quick ! The horses ! Come through !"

Tom Ripon did not want for a second invitation, but was through the turnpike gate in a moment.

Heron then locked it and, placed the key in his pocket.

"My good fellow," he said to the pikeman, "you can't be blamed now, for, you see, I take the key from you by force ; and, when Jonathan Wild comes up, you had better advise him to climb the gate, horse and all—or else he will find it rather a difficult matter to keep up with us."

"Stop ! stop !"

Heron did not stop, however, but giving a hasty direction to Tom to gallop forward at his utmost speed, he himself followed with Daisy, for if Heron had gone first, Tom would soon have been distanced, and they would necessarily have parted company.

Some slight indication of a confusion at the turnpike gate had met the ears of Jonathan Wild, as he came up the long slope of hill from Holland Park ; and by the time he reached within a hundred horse paces of the gate, he felt confident something interesting to him was taking place.

"Gate ! gate !" he yelled as he leant from his horse, and shook it violently.

The gatekeeper, with a wholesome terror of Jonathan Wild, had hastily adopted a ruse he thought best on this occasion.

He flung himself flat in the middle of the road on his own side of the gate, so that he was safe from any assault on the part of Jonathan Wild, and began to utter the most awful groans.

"Gate, gate, I say !" cried Wild. "Hilloa ! Pike, pike ! I'll have you hanged, you scoundrel, if you keep me waiting another moment !"

Jonathan's eyes then fell upon the prostrate form of the gate-keeper.

"What's this ? what's all this ?" he shouted. "Drunk, I suppose ! I'll rouse you up with a vengeance !"

Wild tied the bridle of his horse to the topmost bar of the turnpike gate, and was quickly on his feet on the other side.

"Mercy upon me !" said the gate-keeper. "Two ruffians have just come through the pike, and after I'd locked the gate again, instead of the toll, they knocked me down, and I think they've stove in my skull, as well as took the key away."

"The key—the key of the pike ?"

"Just so."

"A man and a boy ?—the man on a dark bay mare, the like of which you will never see again on the longest summer night you may live ?"

"Yes ; and he called the boy Tom."

Wild gave a howl of rage.

"The Baron—the Baron !" he shouted,—"the Baron, and the Earl of Whitcombe's horse, and that young villain, Ripon, with him !"

"The who, sir ?"

"Get out, idiot ! A hatchet—a sledge-hammer —anything that'll break down the gate !"

"It's felony, sir, by Act of Parliament, to break down a turnpike gate."

CHAPTER CCXXII.

JONATHAN WILD SUCCEEDS IN HIS PURSUIT OF HERON.—MRS. RIPON'S NEW "FENCE."

JONATHAN WILD was so enraged at the cool manner in which the turnpike keeper obstructed his progress, that, drawing hastily one of his pistols, he levelled it at the man's head, as he cried in a voice that was hoarse with rage, "Wretch ! villain ! you shall hang for this, as sure as my name is Jonathan Wild !"

The man was terrified at the looks and gestures of the great thief-taker, whom he knew perfectly well, and who he knew was quite capable of carrying out any threat in which he might think proper to indulge.

"There's an axe just inside the pike-house, sir," he said, "if you go in and turn to the left——"

Jonathan Wild did not wait for the man to finish his sentence, but rushing into the little wooden habitation of the pike-keeper, he glared about him with the utmost ferocity.

"Ah !" he cried, as his eyes fell upon a short, bright-bladed axe ; "this is the very thing."

Wild felt now utterly hopeless. He was, without his horse, hopeless of the capture of the Baron Von Peck, and of Tom Ripon, which he had set his heart upon.

A few vigorous strokes with the axe soon

knocked off the rather dilapidated lock of the turnpike gate.

"That's done!" cried Wild.

"Murder!" shouted the gate-keeper.

Jonathan had flung the axe carelessly at him, and although, luckily for him, it only struck flatwise, it levelled the pike-keeper, who was just scrambling to his feet, to the ground again.

Utterly heedless of whatever damage he might have done, Jonathan Wild now led his horse through the dilapidated pike, and springing on to its back he started off at a gallop.

But he could see nothing of the Baron Von Peck or of Tom Ripon.

Then he drew rein, and began to think.

"Let me see," he said. "What will they do now, and where will they go? Certainly not home to Whitcombe House, for by this time they must have an idea that some one is on their track."

One of Wild's great ingenuities, and upon which he prided himself, was in that strange kind of identification with the thoughts and opinions of the criminal population, which enabled him, although at a distance, to decide almost prophetically what they would do next.

And now, as he halted his horse, and pressed his hand upon his brow, he asked himself where the Baron Von Peck and Tom Ripon, presuming them to be in possession of the booty they were, would be likely to take it.

"Yes!" he cried suddenly; "that's it! I recollect now, Mrs. Ripon has taken a new 'fence' in Wardour Street, Soho, along with that old canting rascal, Mortification, and there I shall find them."

Like most men of action, Jonathan Wild had not many ideas.

But those he had, he quickly carried out.

In another half-hour he was in London.

A private watchman who had a box constructed in the doorway of a jeweller's shop, was looking dreamily out of it, and wondering if the night had passed away, as Wild stopped abruptly and dismounted.

The place was Coventry Street, a few paces from the top of the Haymarket, and close to the old, dingy, disreputable thoroughfare then known as Swallow Street; but which has in more modern times given place to the aristocratic Regent Street.

"Come out!" cried Wild to the watchman.

"Eh?—what did you say?"

"Come out, I say!"

"If I do come out, I'll take you up. Come out, indeed! You're a nice article, to cry out to a respectable watchman, who is always wide awake, except when he's having a little nap like any other Christian!"

"Silence! Listen to me, and obey my orders!"

The watchman looked amazed.

"You will take this horse, and lead him at once to the Mitre Inn, East Smithfield. Say he's mine, and put him up."

"Anything else?" said the watchman, with an ironical tone.

"No; that is sufficient."

"And who may you be when you're at home? Because it's just as well I should know, as I intend to lodge you in the Round-house, and send your horse to the green-yard."

"Oh! you want to know who I am?"

"Rather."

"Jonathan Wild."

The watchman had unhooked the little front wicket of his watch-box, and at the mention of this dreaded name he fell right out of it on his hands and knees, as he gasped out, "Jonathan—that is, Wild—Mr.——"

"Well?"

"I asks your honour's worship's pardon. I'll take the horse."

"Of course you will."

Wild strode off without deigning to bestow another look upon either horse or watchman.

He kept in the shadow of the houses as he strolled slowly up Princes Street, walking in that odd manner habitual to him, with his body bent slightly forward, and his legs wide apart.

Wild, when on foot, always seemed as though ready to spring on some one, or to be alert and on the look-out lest some one should spring upon him unexpectedly.

"Yes," he muttered, "that will be the game. This rascal Von Peck is, after all, only some foreign highwayman; but since he has crept into favour with the Countess of Whitcombe he is initiated into the old ways of Captain Heron by that young scamp, Tom Ripon. But I'll hang him! Ha, ha! I'll hang him! and, by so doing, I shall save the Countess the commission of an indiscretion; for, on my faith, I believe she would marry the rascal!"

Wild reached the commencement of Wardour Street.

Then he ensconced himself in a doorway, and peered about him right and left, to make sure that no one was watching him.

The street was quite deserted.

A couple of low-looking, villanous public-houses that were in it were, by that time, closely shut.

"All's still," said Wild; "but I wouldn't mind taking my oath—not that I mind that much at most times—that I shall find the birds I want to cage at old Mother Ripon's."

Wild knew perfectly well everything of that kind that happened in what might be called the "family" world of London, as the thieves' slang had it; and Mrs. Ripon and Mortification were not four-and-twenty hours in their new establishment before a report of the circumstance was duly made to Jonathan.

He knew exactly the number of their house, and halted before it now with certainty and precision.

It was a little, old, wretched, broken-down abode of only one storey in height, and yet it occupied more space laterally than many a flaunting, fashionable modern house of the present day.

Very rudely over the shop-front appeared painted the words, "Ripon, Dealer in Marine Stores."

"Yes," said Wild; "this is the crib. She's a clever woman that old Mother Ripon; but I wonder if old Mortification finds all that praying answer?"

Wild placed his ear flat against the shutters of the shop window.

He heard, or thought he heard, a confused murmur of voices from within.

At a few paces off one of the wretched oil-lamps with which London was then pretended to be lighted was fluttering, and flickering, and sending some dubious rays about it.

Wild stepped up to it; and standing as much as possible within the sphere of its illuminating power, he looked carefully to the priming of his pistols.

"Who knows?" he muttered; "this Baron Von Peck may show fight!"

He replaced his pistols in his pocket, and in quite an easy way strolled back to Mrs. Ripon's shop.

He had quite made up his mind what to do.

Close under the window was a flat iron grating, about three feet in length and two in width.

Wild stooped down, and exerting all the strength he possessed, which was still considerable, when we consider the life of intemperance and riot he had led, he tugged at the old dilapidated iron until it came away from its supports bodily in his hands.

"That'll do!" he said.

The orifice beneath looked blank and fathomless.

In reality, however, it was only about eight feet deep; and Wild dropped into it with ease, bringing the grating into its place after him, and adjusting it so that to any casual passer-by it did not appear to have been disturbed.

The hollow area in which Wild found himself communicated with the dilapidated old house by a sort of kitchen window.

It was fastened, and there was a shutter within.

But no burglar in all London, however accomplished he might be at his business, could at all compete with Jonathan Wild in overcoming such obstacles to an entrance into a house where he wished to make his way.

In six or seven minutes Wild was in the kitchen.

It was damp and dismal.

Indeed, it was a matter of courtesy to call it a kitchen, since probably many a long year had passed without it ever being used in that capacity, or any cheerful blaze illuminating its grate, or dismal, damp precincts.

It was intensely dark, likewise.

But that was nothing to Wild.

Of course he knew there was a door somewhere, and he crept round the walls, feeling them with his hands, damp and clammy as they were, till he came to it.

Then he crept out into a dismal passage, and commenced the ascent of a flight of stairs that creaked so under his tread, and seemed so bodily to move beneath his footsteps, that he had a not ill-grounded apprehension they would all come down together, and bury him in their ruins.

There was a door at the top of these stairs, and that for a time appeared to be the most serious obstruction that Wild had yet met with.

It was a provoking obstruction, too, because he certainly heard voices, and one of them he knew to be that of Mortification by its long drawling tones.

Wild was not in a position, however, to hear exactly what was said, and that made the matter more perplexing.

The conviction, however, grew upon him, bit by bit, that there he should find the Baron Von Peck, against whom he had conceived a terrible hatred.

And so he bethought him of a means of overcoming the obstruction of the door at the top of the stairs.

His experiences soon enabled him to ascertain how it was fastened.

"A couple of bolts!" he muttered.

Had it been a hook, the work would have been much easier; but still Wild adopted a mode of action which was tolerably successful, and the only drawback to which was, that it necessarily made some slight noise.

He set to work, with the assistance of his hanger, removing the lower panel of the door.

It took him ten minutes.

But he fully succeeded; and, for a man of his bulk, he crept through an exceedingly small space.

He was fairly in the passage of the house.

A faint light came through a half-glass door, which, no doubt, communicated with a back room adjoining the shop.

He heard a voice.

He knew it was that of the Baron Von Peck; and it was a thousand wonders that Felix Heron, who was indeed there, and speaking, still kept up the assumed tones by which he personated the Baron.

Had he not laid it down as a matter of principle that, while he wore the disguise, he would in no particular depart from the means of keeping it perfect, he would there and then have been tempted to converse in his natural tones, and Wild would have been stricken with wonder and astonishment, to hear that the Baron Von Peck spoke in the accents of the supposed deceased Felix Heron.

"Then that is understood, Mrs. Ripon," were the words Wild overheard. "Tom will be your frequent visitor?"

"Yea," cried Mortification, "as the Psalmist says, always keep the melting pot ready for the spoons of the Egyptians."

"Oh, indeed!" muttered Wild, as he dived his hand deep into one of the ample pockets of his coat, and slowly drew forth a pair of handcuffs. "Oh, indeed! Well, it will go hard but I shall spoil your sport, Mr. Baron Von Peck."

"I'll get out the horses," said Tom Ripon, "and we'll be off."

"No," replied what Wild thought was the Baron Von Peck; "let them stay here a couple of hours. It will be safest for me to go home on foot."

"Home, indeed!" thought Wild. "Why, the rascal's actually taken up his abode at Whitcombe House! Can it be that she has been infatuated with him enough to marry him already?"

"Then I'll run out and see how Daisy is," said Tom.

Tom Ripon was very quick in his movements, and Jonathan Wild had only just time to dart away to the further end of the passage, where he half tumbled down three or four steps, and found himself in another room, the floor of which was littered with straw.

Wild came to the conclusion at once that this was an extemporised stable for Daisy when hard pressed, but as Tom Ripon was really coming there, it was by no means an advisable place for him.

Ignorant, however, as he was of the topography of the place, Jonathan Wild had no recourse but to hide himself as best he could.

He had no wish to interfere with Tom Ripon, for, in fact, as the reader is aware, he had made a sort of compact with him to let him alone, so Wild felt along the walls of this temporary stable until he found a long coat or cloak—he knew not which at the moment exactly—hanging on a nail from one of the walls.

He slipped behind it as not a good hiding-place, but the best that offered.

Another moment, and Tom came in with a lantern.

"Now, Daisy, my beauty!" said Tom; "I don't ask you if you like your quarters, but I do hope you've eaten up that quartern loaf I crumbled down for you, and that you liked that pail of water with the pint of old ale in it. I haven't neglected you either, Charley; and you know you've had something worth eating and drinking."

These last words Tom Ripon addressed to the other horse, for they were both there.

He then whistled for a few seconds, and was evidently patting Daisy on the neck.

But Wild could not see him.

The coat—for it was a coat, and one of Mortification's—was thick and opaque, and Wild was afraid to move either it or himself, lest the sharp young ears or eyes of Tom Ripon should catch some indication of his presence.

"Well, that's all right!" said Tom. "Good-bye to both of you. I'll soon be back. Don't quarrel."

Tom left the stable, and Jonathan Wild heard him whistling as he went back to the room in which he had left Felix Heron, his mother, and Mortification.

Wild thought it prudent to remain for a few minutes where he was, but he little suspected that during those few minutes something very important was taking place in the back room of the "fence."

So soon as Tom fairly got into that room he closed the door, and as noiselessly as possible shot a bolt into its socket.

"What's the matter, Tom?" said Heron.

He turned from bolting the door, and then they all saw that his face had a flush of excitement upon it; and he spoke in a low tone, saying, "There's somebody we know in the stable along with Daisy and the other horse."

"Ah!" cried Heron, as he sprang to his feet.

Tom nodded.

"Who is it?"

"Wild!"

"Impossible! You dream, Tom!"

"No; I saw his boots!"

"Yea, the Philistines are upon us!" said Mortification.

"I am a dead woman!" said Mrs. Ripon. "Get into the melting-pot, Mortification, at once! Do!"

"Yea," as the Psalmist says, 'that will be out of fire into the frying-pan!'"

"Silence!" said Felix Heron. "This is perplexing!"

Tinkle, tinkle, came a sharp ring at the shop door bell at this moment, and the little party looked at each other in doubt to know what they should do, or what was about to happen next.

CHAPTER CCXXIII.

THE UNEXPECTED VISITOR.—A SURPRISE.—FELIX HERON IN DANGER.

THE impression on the mind of Felix Heron—and it was, under the circumstances, a most natural one—was that this appeal to the bell indicated the arrival of some of Jonathan Wild's janissaries.

Tom Ripon thought so likewise.

But the Rev. Mortification, with an eye to business, was of a different opinion.

"Yea," he said, "some individual who has been spoiling the Egyptians wanteth to dispose of the swag!"

Mrs. Ripon caught at the idea in a moment.

"Goodness gracious, yes!" she cried. "I never thought of that. Of course it is!"

Mrs. Ripon made a rush at the door leading into the shop, but Tom, who had no idea of allowing his mother to let in any one so precipitately, and felt how hopeless it would be to recall her by words, suddenly flung himself down in her way, so that Mrs. Ripon came to an abrupt pause in consequence of tumbling over him.

"There you go, old gal!" said Tom. "You shouldn't be in such a hurry."

"Oh, you odious little wretch!" cried Mrs. Ripon; "what do you mean?"

"Get up—all's right. "Now, Captain, give your orders. What's to be done?"

"Yea," interposed the Rev. Mortification, "if some individual has accidentally become possessed of some other individual's spoons, it is wrong to keep him waiting. Amen!"

Captain Heron glanced about him, and seeing a very capacious cupboard in the room with double doors, he pointed to it.

"Get in there, Tom, and I will follow you. If this arrival should be one or more of the bull-dogs of Jonathan Wild, we must just fight the matter out; but if it be, as Mortification thinks, some customer to the 'fence,' we will adopt another course."

"Yea," said Mortification, "I feel a presentiment that it is an individual who has a propensity towards silver candlesticks; and verily he goeth by the unsavoury name of Mangy Dick. Susannah Sarah Amelia, my dove, open the door."

"Good gracious!" said Tom, "who are all they?"

"Ungrateful monster!" said Mrs. Ripon; "you ought long ago to have found out where your mother was christened, and gone down on your knees and got the certificate, and then you'd have seen that those were my proper names."

"Oh, Lor'!" said Tom, "I never knowed it. I always thought the old gal's name was Tabby."

"What?"

"T-a-b-b-y."

Mrs. Ripon made a dart at Tom, who adroitly fled behind the Rev. Mortification, so that that individual came in for a scratch and a bump of his head against the wainscot of the room, that seemed for a moment or two to bewilder his faculties, for he sat down again, muttering something about men of wrath and the Canaanites being rumpagious.

Felix Heron stepped into the deep recess with the folding-doors.

Tom Ripon followed him.

Mrs. Ripon, carrying the candle in her hand, crept through the front shop and took down a wooden bar that was across the door.

"Is it business?" she said.

"Yes," replied a voice, "if this is Mrs. Ripon's."

"To be sure," said Mrs. Ripon. "I hope it's something worth having; but money's so scarce we can't give much; and there's a great fall in the price of silver. It's only worth two shillings and three halfpence an ounce, so we can't give more than ninepence halfpenny and expect to live."

The personage who had rung at the bell of Mrs. Ripon's "fence" crossed its threshold, and exhibited himself to the delighted eyes of that lady in the costume of a highwayman.

The hat was pulled down low over the brows, and a roquelaire cloak hid a good deal of the dress, although sufficient of it could still be seen to leave no doubt that this personage was in verity a knight of the road.

"Bless you," said Mrs. Ripon, "you go upon the high toby, I see; and I hope you've had plenty of luck. Times are hard in Wardour Street; but for ready money this is the place to come."

"I have had a dream!" said the stranger.

"A what?"

"A dream; and it is the strange impression which it has made upon me which has brought me here."

"Gracious powers!" said Mrs. Ripon, putting the candle down upon the counter with a great jerk and a bang; "what's the use of a dream? It's neither spangles, glitter, nor rags!"

Mrs. Ripon meant gold, coin, jewels, and banknotes by these three slang expressions.

"Tell me, woman!" said the stranger, "have you seen aught to-night of one who calls himself the Baron Von Peck?"

"Woman!" cried Mrs. Ripon; "woman to yourself! Who's a woman, I should like to know? Marry come up, and fiddlededee! My young spark, I'd have you to know——"

"Hush!" said the highwayman.

He pushed the hat higher above his brow, and removed the collar of the roquelaire from his chin.

Mrs. Ripon uttered a scream, and upset the candle.

At that moment Jonathan Wild tried the door leading into the passage, and which Tom had prudently bolted.

Captain Heron stepped a pace out of the recess with a pistol in his hand; and the Rev. Mortification, upon hearing the scream, darted at once under the table and hid himself.

Then all was still.

Had Mrs. Ripon fainted?

Was it possible that she had seen the countenance of any one that could have such an effect upon her?

It seemed probable.

But Felix Heron was not the kind of person to remain in doubt much longer about such a state of affairs.

He made his way at once into the shop, which was very dark, although the candle was not actually extinguished by its fall, but lay upon the floor guttering and glimmering, and threatening momentary extinction.

Heron's first movement was to raise it and relight its wick.

Then holding it above his head, he glanced about him, as he said, "What is the meaning of all this, and who have we here?"

"Felix!" cried a voice, "can you forgive me?"

Heron faintly staggered back with astonishment.

It was the voice of Edith.

"Edith! Edith!" he exclaimed; "surely it is I who dream now!"

"No, Felix!" she cried, as she flew forward and rested her hands upon his shoulders. "No, Felix, it is I who have dreamt. Twice to-night vividly there came before me a vision of danger to you. I thought I saw you seated in a wretched room, and that a small circular orifice was opened in the top panel of a door, through which appeared the face of Jonathan Wild; and then so plainly did I see, in my sleep, that he presented a pistol at you with a full intent to take your life, that the terror awakened me, and a voice seemed to cry in my ears, 'Seek him at Mrs. Ripon's, in Wardour-street.' Twice, Felix, was this vision repeated. I could not rest, and you behold me here."

"It is something more than strange, Edith."

"Have I saved you?"

"Hush! Let me explain to you. Wild is here, and with my feelings towards him I know not how to extricate myself. Doubtless I could kill him with ease, but I can never now raise my hand against that man's life!"

"Never, Felix—not even in self-defence."

"No, my Edith; for well you know, in his rough, coarse manner, he is friendly and protective as regards you and our little one. It is the one touch of human feeling which redeems the monster, and I believe he would risk his own life at any moment for her whom he considers the widow of Felix Heron and her child."

Edith pressed the hand of her husband fondly.

"Yes," she said, "I well know that it is for my sake you forget and forgive all the offences of Jonathan Wild."

"And for whose sake, in all this world, my Edith, should I do such an act, if not for you?"

By this time, Mrs. Ripon had recovered sufficiently from her downright fright at the sight of Edith, to make her way into the back room again.

"Mortification! Mortification! You hardened wretch!" she cried, "where is the cherry brandy?"

"Yea, here!" exclaimed Mortification, as he made a sudden dart from under the table; and for the third time, by coming into alarming contact with Mrs. Ripon's feet, he brought her to the floor.

"Murder!"

"Fire!" cried Mortification.

Jonathan Wild tapped at the door again that led into the passage.

"Hush, all of you," said Tom Ripon. "Don't you know who that is?"

Edith trembled.

Felix Heron was perplexed.

"Edith," he asked, "did you see any one in the street who had the appearance of a janissary of Wild's, for I cannot well conceive that he came here alone?"

"No, Felix, no!"

"Look here, Captain," said Tom Ripon, stepping forward, and speaking in low tones,—"look here, Captain; and you, Lady Edith. That's Jonathan Wild tapping at the door; and as we don't want to kill him—because, as you say, Captain, there seems to be some good in him, after all,—let's play him a trick!"

"A trick, Tom! What trick?"

"Look ye here, Captain. You've been disguising yourself as the Baron Von Peck; but if

No. 70.—EDITH.

Jonathan should come here, and have a row with us in this room, it's odds but he'd find out who you were really!"

"He certainly would!"

"Then let's puzzle him, Captain! Let him find out that the Baron Von Peck is not the Baron Von Peck, but somebody he knows a great deal better."

"Myself?"

"No; the Lady Edith! Give her the hat and that cravat. Let her sit down here, along with the old gal and Mortification; and while you hide in that bit of a cupboard, I'll let Jonathan come in; and if he isn't so puzzled that he won't know whether he's on his head or his heels, my name is not Tom Ripon, that's all!"

Felix Heron glanced at Edith.

"Can I—dare I—expose you to this risk?" he said.

"It is no risk, Felix! I feel in no danger from Jonathan Wild."

It was evident that Heron shrunk from thus substituting Edith for himself; but the circumstances were so peculiar, that it was no discredit to his manhood so to do.

In truth and reality, it was for the purpose of saving the life of Jonathan Wild; for, situated as he was, nothing would have been easier for Heron than to have sacrificed the great thief-taker to his own safety and the exigencies of that night of adventure.

How singularly changed were all the circumstances connected with Heron and Wild!

The latter sought the life of the supposed Baron Von Peck from sheer respect and consideration for the memory, as he called it, of the late Earl of Whitcombe.

And Felix Heron skulked from Wild like a timid criminal, not from any fear of him, but from the dread of being forced to kill or injure him in self-defence.

A moment's consideration convinced Edith that Tom's plan of operations was the very best that, under the circumstances, could be pursued.

"Consent to this, Felix," she said, "and all may yet be well."

"You wish it, Edith?"

"With all my heart. And you will be at hand, too, in case any change comes over the spirit of this man. Two steps will bring you to my side."

"It is so," said Heron, as he hastily laid down the hat, and took the cravat from his own neck "Let us try this plan further to mystify Jonathan Wild."

The hat was a peculiar one. It was looped up on one side with an ornament of jet, and had a long, drooping feather, which partly shaded the countenance of the wearer.

And now, when Edith had folded the cravat round her neck, hiding her chin and the lower part of her face likewise in its thick folds, and when she seated herself at the table, with the hat upon her head, and rested her cheek upon her hand, she bore a very tolerable resemblance to the supposed Baron Von Peck.

Captain Heron retreated into the recess, pulling the door after him.

"Now, Tom," he whispered, "let in Wild."

"There's no occasion, Captain; he's at work; let him come in his own way."

"Be it so."

It would seem that Edith's dream was about to be fulfilled to the letter, for a strange grating noise was heard upon one of the panels of the door.

If Edith had been as well acquainted with the tools and weapons of housebreakers as Mrs. Ripon and the Rev. Mortification were, she would have come to the conclusion that Wild was using a well-known implement among the fraternity, by which a circular piece of panel from any door or wall could be removed with great ease in a few seconds.

The machinery was simple.

A little thumb-screw, the end of which was shaped like a gimlet, was easily inserted into the woodwork.

Round that a loop of cat-gut of great strength, and about four inches in length, was placed, carrying at its other extremity a small, sharp, exquisitely tempered short cutting blade.

A rapid motion round the gimlet as a centre, would, in a few seconds, suffice to take out a circular piece of woodwork of an inch in thickness.

This was just what Wild was about.

The grinding motion was like the humming of a bee, and as it proceeded, Mrs Ripon looked at Mortification, and kept his garrulity in check.

As for herself, the necessity for silence produced as much effect upon her, and induced her to keep her lips so closely compressed, that her very breathing occasioned a noticeable sound.

Edith's heart beat strangely, as she thus felt that her dream was coming true in its minutest particular.

Tom Ripon stood looking on, a pleased and observant spectator of all that was taking place in that miserable little apartment at the back of the fence.

The strange noise continued on the upper panel of the door.

Jonathan Wild was evidently making progress, and probably he was as surprised as any one that no immediate notice was taken of what he was about, and that he was permitted to work so easily at that door without remark or interruption.

Suddenly there was a slight creaking sound, followed by a light blow.

The circular piece of the panel had come out.

Jonathan Wild at once projected a pistol through the opening into the room.

He spoke in a loud, harsh voice.

"Baron Von Peck, you are my prisoner! Stir hand or foot, and I will blow out your brains."

"Ah!" cried Edith, as if taken by surprise.

"Yes," added Jonathan, "your little career has come to an end; and I will not only rid society of you, but likewise save the Countess of Whitcombe from the commission of a folly; for I verily believe she would make you, otherwise, the unworthy successor of Felix Heron."

Edith did not answer this speech, but she still sat by the table, as though transfixed with fear at the threat that Jonathan Wild had uttered.

"Tom Ripon," cried Wild, "where are you? The game's up. Open this door. I have nothing to say to you; but your new master must pass the remainder of this night in Newgate."

Tom made his appearance.

"You're mistaken, Jonathan Wild," he said, "and will be sorry for what you are doing."

"Not at all," said Wild. "I am only sorry I've not sent a bullet at once into the thick skull of the Baron Von Peck. We've enough to do with our English high-flyers and knights of the road, without having any foreign ones among us."

"Open the door," said Edith, in a low tone.

"That's the most sensible speech you've made yet, Baron," added Wild.

Tom Ripon stepped up to the door, and shot back the bolt.

Jonathan Wild strode into the apartment, and laid his hand heavily upon the shoulders of the supposed Baron, as he said in his harshest and most grating tones, "You are my prisoner! Resistance will be madness and folly! Be so good as to hold up your hands, and I will fit you with a pair of bracelets, such as probably you never wore before."

"And is this from you?" said Edith, in her natural tones, as she lifted off the hat, and let the cloak fall away from her face.

Wild staggered back as though he had been shot.

"Is this from you," added Edith, "whom I took to be my friend?"

"Edith!" he gasped; "the Countess!"

"Look at her again, Johnny," said Tom Ripon, "and make sure."

Wild turned round twice, and fairly staggered about the room, until he came to a chair, upon which he sat down, with a concussion that nearly started all its joints.

"Stop a bit!" he cried; "stop a bit! It's either a dream, or I'm mad!"

CHAPTER CCXXIV.

JONATHAN WILD PERPLEXED.—TOM'S ENJOYMENT AT HIS CONFUSION.

Tom Ripon enjoyed immensely the perplexity of Jonathan Wild, and looked at him with unaffected delight, as he sat upon the ricketty old chair into which he had staggered, pressing his hands over his eyes, to try to convince himself he was not awake.

"Speak to me—speak to me!" cried Wild,—"some one speak to me, or do something to assure me that this is not a dream!"

Tom Ripon stepped up to him, and inflicted a sharp kick upon his shin.

"Will that do, Johnny?"

"Villain!"

"Try that, then!" said Tom.

An old, empty tin candlestick was close at hand, and, by reversing it, Tom was able to hit Wild a sharp crack on the head.

Jonathan sprung to his feet, and made a grasp at Tom, who dodged him, however, and got in safety round the table.

"Hold!" cried Edith. "What is the meaning of all this? Tell me, Jonathan Wild, what you want with me; and why, contrary to all promises and expectations, you hunt me down to-night?"

"I don't know," said Wild. "But I will ask of you but one question; and without saying that it will be far better for you to give me a truthful answer, I warn you that, if you do not, I must find one for myself."

"What is it? I will give you a truthful answer."

"Is there such a person as the Baron Von Peck?"

"There is."

"That's a relief," said Jonathan. "Now for another question,—Do you intend to marry him?"

"Perhaps."

"That means 'Yes' from a woman. Now, listen to me, Countess! That rascally old Von Peck shall never be father-in-law to Felix Heron's child while there is such a place as Tyburn Gate, and such a person as Jonathan Wild! Good night, Mrs. Ripon; I wish you all sorts of luck in your new establishment. Now and then, to be sure, I may 'want' some of your customers, and then you may depend upon it I shall come and get them; but live and let live is my motto,—ha, ha!"

"Get away with you," cried Mrs. Ripon; "you're uglier than ever!"

"Yea, he is," said Mortification. "Nevertheless, Jonathan Wild, we will bestow upon thee thy share of the plunder, because thou knowest as well as we do that if there were no fences——"

"There would be no thieves," shouted Wild. "Ha! ha!"

"Yea, thou hast said it; and if there were no thieves——"

"There would be no officers," added Wild.

"Amen!" said Mortification.

Wild crossed the shop, and banged the outer door after him as he left the premises.

"Follow," said Felix Heron, in a low voice, from the recess; "follow him, Tom—he's up to some trick."

"All's right, Captain. Mother, where are you?"

"I am here, you unnatural wretch!"

"Lend us one of those mob caps of yours, and the bundle of rags you call a gown."

"Oh, the villain!" cried Mrs. Ripon; "he wants to personate a respectable female, and bring the sex into disrepute."

"Yea, he is a villain!" added Mortification; "and the day will not be far distant when he will execute what profane people call a dance upon nothing; for, as the Psalmist truly observes——"

"Murder! Help! Murder!"

Mrs. Ripon had made active use of the same candlestick with which Tom had aroused Wild to a consciousness of his wakening existence; and the unfortunate Mortification experienced such an assault and battery, first on one side of his head, and then on the other, with the tin weapon, that he thought himself in a kind of pillory, where he was continually pelted by old candlesticks.

"Take that!" said Mrs. Ripon. "And I'll have you to know that if Tom thinks proper to put on a mob cap and one of my dresses, who has a greater right? Eh, you thin wretch?"

Tom was immensely amused at this *fracas*, and, as far as he was concerned, put an end to it, by snatching the cap off his mother's head, and then rushing into the shop and helping himself to one of the dresses there ostensibly hanging for sale; and so, rapidly attiring himself in a costume that might in the dark pass muster as a feminine one, he left the fence as a spy upon the actions of Jonathan Wild.

Tom was gone about a quarter of an hour; but when he returned it was with the information that Wild had got into a hackney coach, and actually gone home.

"He's done up for to-night, Captain," said Tom; "so we can bring out Daisy, and make our way to Whitcombe House."

"At once—at once!" cried Heron; "for, after all, he may only be going to Newgate Street to get assistance."

Tom Ripon, with the assistance of Mortification, got out the horses, and Felix Heron assisted Edith to mount Daisy.

The distance was but short to Whitcombe

House, and it was a great relief to Heron when its massive doors closed upon him and Edith, and Tom had taken the horses round to the stable.

"Thus, Edith," said Heron, "end the adventures of this night; and I hope no other will ever arise that will necessitate your appearance in this character."

It was on the following morning then, at rather a late hour, that Edith and Felix Heron held a long consultation upon the state of affairs as regarded the supposed Baron Von Peck.

Edith was of opinion that the disguise should be completely abandoned, so that the Baron, as an individuality, should disappear from the face of the earth.

"Then, Edith," he said, " I should have to appear in some new disguise immediately, and which I might find it more difficult to maintain than this."

" Not more difficult, Felix, and yet with far greater safety. Jonathan Wild has now a great spite at the supposed Baron Von Peck, and I would counsel that he be so far disarmed of that hatred, that he should be convinced of the permanent departure of Von Peck from England."

" Yes," said Heron, "if we could but manage that."

"It may be done. I am quite convinced that, let him once think I have given up all hopes of marrying the Baron Von Peck, and one half of his spite and indignation will vanish."

"It can be tried. What say you to this, Edith, as a plan for carrying out your ideas? Suppose I, as the Baron Von Peck, make a communication that I am willing to leave England at once and for ever, if permitted to do so by him, without hindrance or interruption?"

" Yes, that will do."

" I can then be back here in the course of twelve hours, in another character."

"And what character will you assume, Felix?"

" I was once acquainted with an old officer in the navy, of the name of Fantome, and so marked were his peculiarities, that I do not think I should have the slightest difficulty in successfully personating such a man."

" Be it so—be it so, Felix. This supposed Captain Fantome, then, Jonathan Wild could have no charge against; and at the risk even of some loss of reputation, and some remarks upon my supposed folly, why should I not publicly marry Captain Fantome, so that you might be here at all times, without question, remark, or suspicion?"

" It shall be so, Edith, and I will set about this plan of operations at once."

Heron was well pleased to effect this change in his condition, and during the day he wrote the following letter to Jonathan Wild:—

"To Mr. Wild, at his house in Newgate Street.

"The Baron Von Peck cannot but feel how useless it is to enter into a prolonged contest with the great Jonathan Wild.

"The Baron, therefore, is willing to compromise matters, so far as to give up all pretensions to the hand of the Countess of Whitcombe, if Jonathan Wild will abstain from all persecution

of the Baron, on account of certain little transactions on the road.

" The Baron will likewise quit England at once, as Mr. Wild may convince himself of, by seeing him off in the Hamburgh packet, which starts next Monday, and in which the Baron purposes taking a passage.

"If Mr. Wild should accept these terms, and signify the same in writing, addressed to the Baron, at Whitcombe House, to the care of the Countess of Whitcombe, he, the Baron, will be found on board the said Hamburgh packet, with bag and baggage, off Gravesend, on next Monday."

This letter was despatched to Wild's house, and in the course of two hours an answer came back, addressed to the Baron.

It was as brief as possible :—

"Go, and be hanged! If you stay, I will see to that process. So no more at present from

"JONATHAN WILD."

This was satisfactory as far as it went, but Edith was not quite well pleased at the tone of the reply, and dreaded some treachery on the part of Wild.

She wrote him a note in the following words :—

" If Jonathan Wild at all values the good opinion which, in one solitary respect, the Countess of Whitcombe has of him, he will let the Baron Von Peck depart from England in peace, since she, the Countess, is quite certain that he never intends to return."

Wild called at Whitcombe House within an hour, and saw Edith.

"Let him go," he said; "but let this be the last I shall ever hear of such a rascal aspiring to the hand of the widow of Felix Heron."

All this being arranged on the Monday morning in question, Felix Heron rode down to Gravesend, accompanied by Tom Ripon.

They put up at a little hostel about half a mile from the town, and there Heron left Tom with the horses and a well filled valise, which contained the new disguise that Heron intended to adopt.

The Hamburgh packet lay about half a mile out in the stream, a little below Tilbury Fort; and as Captain Heron stepped into a wherry to be taken on board, carefully disguised still as the Baron Von Peck, he saw Jonathan Wild leaning against a post on the little quay from whence the boat took its departure.

Not a word was exchanged between them, but Wild kept his eyes on the supposed Baron until he gained the deck of the packet, which, in another quarter of an hour, lifted its anchor and set its sails to a breeze which carried it rapidly down the river.

Heron dived down to the chief cabin of the packet, and after the bustle of getting the little vessel under weigh was over, he requested an audience of the captain.

"Circumstances," he said, " render it necessary that I should return to London; therefore, on consideration that I pay you for my full passage, and likewise for any delay that may be occasioned in putting me on shore, I trust there will be no difficulty in landing me quickly."

The captain demurred a little, but as Heron threw upon the table between them some gold pieces that covered at least three times over all that he could reasonably be charged, the difficulties vanished.

At the dusk of evening, Heron was put on shore at Southend, to make his way back to Gravesend and to Tom Ripon as best he might.

He hired a little fishing vessel, and about half-past ten o'clock on that night he was with Tom Ripon at the small suburban hostel where that faithful follower, with no small anxiety, awaited him.

"Now, Tom," said Heron, "this disguise must be more perfect than the last, and must differ from it as largely as possible."

"Yes, Captain, but it can't be much better; for sometimes when I looked at you, while you used to call yourself the Baron von Peck, I hardly knew you myself."

Heron smiled; for, in his own estimation, he considered the disguise that he was now about to attempt would be a much more perfect and artistic thing than the former one.

At the period of which we write the different professions, military, naval, lay, and clerical, were much more accurately distinguished the one from the other by even the costumes of ordinary life than they are at present.

A man in the army or navy never, under any circumstances, entirely laid aside his uniform.

He might not wear it with all the exactitude of actual service, but still there it was, something after the fashion of our clergy of the present day, who carry into private life a clerical costume, by which they may always be distinguished.

From the valise, then, that he brought with him, Captain Heron took such a complete suit as would entirely change his outward appearance.

He succeeded likewise in imparting a totally different colour to his complexion, by the use of an extract from the Spanish chesnut, which had been taught him by a tribe of gipsies with whom at one time he had sojourned for a few weeks.

This, in addition to a wig, which concealed every fragment of his natural hair, made him look so very different that it would have required great intimacy with him to know him.

By affecting a stoop, then, in his gait, and an awkward, difficult walk, as though he were balancing himself on the unsteady planks of a vessel's deck, Heron very well sustained the character he had assumed.

"Now, what do you think of it, Tom?" he said.

"It's capital! I shouldn't know you myself, Captain."

"And yet," said Heron, "I feel that the principal security I have in these disguises from the keen, scrutinising eyes of Jonathan Wild consists in the fact that he never expects under any circumstances whatever to discover Felix Heron beneath them."

"You think so, Captain."

"I am certain of it, Tom. Wild believes I am dead, and, therefore, never looks out for me; and if he saw anything even in the Baron Von Peck, or were to see anything in the Captain Fantome I now mean to call myself, that reminded him of Felix Heron, he would only look upon it as one of those accidental resemblances that are in no way to be accounted for."

"But, Captain!"

"Well, Tom?"

"What are we to do as regards our little affairs on the road? You don't mean, I hope, to give up business altogether?"

"Certainly not, Tom."

"Then who are we to be, and what are we to be, when we cry 'Stand and deliver?'"

"Look at me, Tom, and then I shall be able to explain to you my intentions. You know that as the Baron Von Peck I wore a suit of clothes that were thickened and padded so as to make me appear half as bulky again as I am in reality."

"Yes, Captain, you looked about twice the weight and size of yourself."

"Well, you see, Tom, I am not depending upon any such plan in my disguise as Captain Fantome, of the royal navy; so I shall have no difficulty in putting on at any moment over this dress the whole of the costume of the Baron Von Peck, previously divesting it of its padding, which will not be required when its goes over another complete suit."

"I begin to see—I begin to understand," said Tom.

Heron laughed.

"I think you do, Tom. I shall still cry 'Stand and deliver!' on the highway, as the Baron Von Peck, but I shall trot quietly home as Captain Fantome."

"Capital!" said Tom; "we shall have some fun, and, if we don't drive Jonathan Wild mad, it will be no fault of ours!"

CHAPTER CCXXV.

CAPTAIN FANTOME AND HIS BOY, PETER, ENCOUNTER JONATHAN WILD ON THE ROAD TO LONDON.

FELIX HERON had no intention of remaining a moment longer at Gravesend then necessary.

But still it was requisite to proceed to town with some amount of caution, inasmuch that Jonathan Wild was of so crafty and suspicious a nature, that there was every probability of encountering him on the road.

"It is necessary, Tom," said Captain Heron, "that you likewise should be disguised, or your presence with me will beget a thousand conjectures and suspicions in the mind of Wild, which it would be well to avoid!"

"I don't know how I'm to manage that, Captain!"

"Look further into the valise, Tom, and you'll see that I have not forgotten you!"

Felix Heron had carefully packed this travelling receptacle himself, so that Tom Ripon had no knowledge of what was in it.

Upon diving into its inmost recesses, however, in obedience to the order of Heron, Tom fished out a complete suit of clothes, suitable for himself, and such as might be worn by a boy-groom of the period, somewhat answering to the description of the modern "tiger."

Tom Ripon shook his head.

"It's all very well, Captain," he said, "but Jonathan Wild will know me!"

"Look a little further, Tom, and you will find a small parcel!"

Tom Ripon did so, and discovered that it contained a light flaxen-looking wig, which would convert him at once into a thorough specimen of a Saxon youth.

Tom's hair was naturally dark, and he wore it cropped close.

He said he did that in order to save trouble in case he was captured by Wild, and sent to prison, where he knew that the first operation would be to cut his hair.

He was just arriving, too, at that time of life when the colour of early youth was deserting his cheeks.

In fact, Tom Ripon was getting decidedly sallow, which would continue to be his natural complexion.

In a small glass that was in the dressing-room at the hostel, Tom admired himself exceedingly with the flaxen wig.

But still he felt that there was a something wanting, for the artificial hair did not look as if it naturally belonged to his complexion.

"Look a little further, Tom," said Heron, "and you'll see a small earthenware jar, and in it you'll find your new face. It will do you no harm, as it is but some powdered earth of the requisite colour."

Tom Ripon was delighted.

In the little jar or gallipot that Felix Heron pointed out to him, he found some finely powdered, reddish-looking earth; and when he had rubbed that over his face it gave him a complexion that exactly assimilated with the flaxen wig.

The change in Tom Ripon was very complete, and it is doubtful if either his mother or the Rev. Mortification, even knowing him so well as they did, could possibly have recognised him.

"Now, Tom," said Heron, "we won't go to town on horseback, because both our horses might be well known to Jonathan Wild and his janissaries."

"How then? Good gracious, Captain, you don't mean to leave Daisy here?"

"Certainly not. You will wait here for me, and I will go into the town of Gravesend, and manage to hire a pair-horse carriage of some sort. We will then dispense with the horses that may be already in it, and let Daisy and your horse take us to London."

"That's the thing, Captain! Why, we may give Jonathan Wild a lift if we should happen to meet him, and he would be none the wiser."

"That would be a hazardous experiment, Tom; although, on my faith, I think it might be done."

Heron left Tom at the hostel, and walked rapidly to Gravesend, where he easily succeeded in hiring an open carriage by paying handsomely for the use of it, and promising to leave it at a particular livery stables in London that was in constant communication with Gravesend.

A boy drove him back to the hostel, and by his assistance Daisy and Tom's horse were easily accommodated in the harness of the two rather miserable hacks usually in the habit of drawing the open chaise.

The saddles and bridles were disposed snugly inside, and the boy trotted back to Gravesend with his horses, well pleased with the crown piece Heron gave to him.

"Now, Tom, for London!"

"All's right, Captain."

Off they went.

Heron had paid his score liberally at the little hostel, but the landlord and his wife stood at the door gazing after him and Tom Ripon in undisguised astonishment.

They had taken but a cursory glance at their guests on their arrival, but the impression on their minds that the two people who had started away in the open chaise were not the same two who had arrived on horseback, was too strong to admit of contradiction.

This was just one of those incidents that Felix Heron expected; but he saw no easy way to guard against it, so he let it take its chance.

He knew well that no human arrangement could be quite perfect in all its particulars.

The two horses carried them on swiftly, and about one-half of the distance from Gravesend to London—that is to say, something over ten miles—was traversed before they became aware of a horseman in advance of them, who suddenly drew up, and dismounted by the road-side.

The horseman lifted a fore foot of his horse, and, by the hammering sound that he made, it was evident that he was knocking out a stone which the horse had picked up, and which, probably, had lamed him.

"Caution, Tom!" whispered Heron.

Tom, with his mouth open, looked at Heron, and, in a whisper, pronounced the name of Jonathan Wild.

"Yes," added Heron, "it is he, and there could not be possibly a better opportunity of testing our disguises."

"But, Captain!"

"Well, what is it?"

"If the worst should come to the worst, and Jonathan Wild should be particularly disagreeable, you've no objection, I suppose, to me giving him a bullet?"

"Self-preservation, Tom, is the first law of nature; but let us hope it will not come to that. And mind, when you speak, do so as a country boy."

"I will."

"If you play your part well, it is impossible he can suspect you."

Heron had by no means relaxed in the pace at which he was driving, which was ordinarily fast, but not so fast as to give the impression of any hurry.

He thought it better to pass Wild without taking any notice of him, and was about doing so, when the thief-taker looked up and called out.

"I don't know who you may be, sir, but you may do me a favour."

Heron pulled up.

"What is it?" he said.

"My horse has fallen dead lame. He picked up a stone in his foot, and it has cut him. I don't like to ride the beast; so, if you are going towards London, and can give me a cast, I will tie my horse's rein to the back of your chaise, and he won't hurt half so much with no weight upon him as if I were to ride him."

Heron considered for a moment.

Should he, or should he not, run the fearful risk of taking Wild as a companion actually into the chaise?

No, it was too much.

So close a proximity would give the disguises, the wigs, and the false colour on their faces no fair chance.

"I am an officer in his Majesty's service," said Heron; "and strike my topsails if I can pick up every chance fellow on the road with a lame horse."

"I, too, am an officer in his Majesty's service," added Wild, with a sneer; "and birds of a feather you know, my good sir, ought to flock together."

"I don't understand your shore-going lingo," said Heron, keeping up his character as a naval officer. "Peter, what do you think of this fellow?"

"Why, maister," said Tom, "I've been more used to cows; and he do rather mind me of our black bull at home, as was named Vicious, and tossed old Mother Crumpet, 'cos she would go across the common in her red cloak."

"Then you don't like him, Peter?"

"No, maister."

"Nor more do I! So on we sail again!"

"Confound you," muttered Wild, "for a sea bear!"

Heron gave the rein to the two horses, and trotted on.

He and Tom both thought that they had got effectually rid of Jonathan Wild; but in that they were reckoning without their host, for such was very far indeed from being the fact.

They had hardly gone three miles further when he came up to them again at a sharp trot.

This time he was mounted on a grey horse, whereas the one that had fallen lame was a dark bay.

"Well, Mr. Officer," cried Wild, as he reined in abreast of the chaise; "I am able to get on without being indebted to your courtesy!"

Heron made no reply.

But Jonathan, for once in a way, was inclined to be garrulous, and he kept exact pace with the chaise, as he added, "I was able to leave my lame horse at the King's Head Inn, by the wayside, and borrow this one. So now, Captain, if you are a Captain, I'd like to know your name!"

"You're an insolent ruffian!" said Heron.

"Shiver my timbers! if I don't believe you're a highwayman!"

"Perhaps I am!"

"Oh, very well! Peter!"

"Yes, maister!"

"Prepare for action! Run out the guns!"

"Here ye are, maister!"

Tom Ripon handed to Captain Heron his pistols, which had been placed at the bottom of the chaise ready for use.

"Now, Mr. Highwayman, clear your decks," added Heron, "and let's have it out yard-arm to yard-arm."

"Nonsense!" said Wild; "I was but jesting."

"I don't understand jokes on the high seas—I mean, in the highways."

"Well, well, sir! I will soon satisfy you that I am no highwayman, by telling you who I really am."

"Hoist your colours, then. What ship ahoy?"

"My name is Jonathan Wild."

According to custom, Wild, when he uttered his own name, always made one of his hideous demoniac faces.

But in this case he was greatly disappointed, for neither the name nor the face had the slightest effect upon the supposed sea captain and his agricultural boy, Peter.

"Jonathan who did you say?" asked Heron.

"Wild—Wild."

"Oh, very well; I can't help it."

"He do look main wild," said Tom,—"for all the world loike our black bull, as tossed Mrs. Crump, on the common, 'cos——"

"Bah! Bo!" roared Wild. "Idiot, who wants to hear about you and your black bull. Can it be possible that you have never heard of Jonathan Wild?"

Heron shook his head.

"No," said Tom; "never heard o' he, and don't want."

"Well," said Wild, as he drew a long breath, "this beats everything. I am much obliged to you, sir; and it may be that you and Jonathan Wild will become better acquainted some day."

"I doubt it."

"And for your information, I tell you that I am the great Jonathan Wild—the well-known thief-taker and officer—the terror of evil-doers—and a man as well known in London as the Monument."

"Can't help it," said Heron. "Nothing to do with it. Never sailed in my ship. Come on, Peter."

Heron jerked the reins, and the two horses set off at increased speed.

Jonathan Wild did not make any positive attempt to follow the chaise, although they heard that he was on the road behind them, coming on at a good pace.

"We have baffled him for the present, Tom," said Heron.

"Rather," replied Tom Ripon.

"I am glad we have met him," added Heron; "inasmuch as it affords a good test to our disguises, which have been singularly successful."

"But what are we to do next, Captain?"

"We shall proceed directly home, whether Jonathan Wild watches us or not. And yet a thought strikes me that I should like to puzzle him a little further to-day, and send him to London, more full of doubt and wonderment than he has ever been."

"I should like to do that, too," said Tom, "but I don't see how."

Captain Heron was driving the chaise and pair, and as Tom spoke, he turned the horses' heads down a shadowy lane to the left.

"Open the valise, Tom," said Heron, "and I will put over this costume the rather capacious clothes of the Baron Von Peck; and as for you, you can hide yourself in the lane."

Tom was quite delighted at one part of this arrangement, but not at the other.

That Captain Heron meant to mystify and enrage Jonathan Wild by committing a highway robbery in the dress of the Baron Von Peck, he considered a capital thing.

But what vexed him was that he should be out of it.

There was no resource, however, but to do just as Captain Heron required, and in a few seconds Daisy was released from the traces; and Heron having slipped on, over his dress as Captain Fantome, the rather remarkable and capacious suit of clothes that distinguished the Baron Von Peck, mounted, and was ready for the road.

"You remain here, Tom," he said, "just as you are, and take care of the chaise."

"All right, Captain, I'll do it; but I hope on the next occasion you'll manage that I shall be with you!"

"I will try to do so."

Heron at a hand gallop reached the road again.

Scarcely had he done so, when he heard the sound of wheels, and he saw an ordinary hack post-chaise coming along in the direction towards London.

Heron was not disposed to pick and choose his adventures, and this one, for aught he knew, might be as desirable as any.

It was broad daylight; and probably the persons in the chaise had about as little idea of being stopped by a highwayman, as of any one dropping from the moon upon them.

The spot, however, at which Heron appeared was a romantic one, and, in that respect, was in every way adapted for an adventure.

Some chalk hills, through which a cutting had been made, rose up on one side to a height of some eighty to a hundred feet—the fissures in the chalk, and little plateaux accidentally left, being filled and crowded with coarse vegetation.

The road itself was but a rough and uneven one, so that it was a matter of necessity that anything upon wheels should make but slow progress.

"Halt!" cried Heron, as he reached the side of the chaise.

"Goodness gracious! What's the matter?" said the postilion.

"There's a highwayman on the road!"

"Is there, sir? Where is he?"

"Here!" added Heron, as he presented a pistol at the head of the postilion; "and he advises you to keep perfectly quiet if you value your life."

"Murder!"

"You may call what you like, so that you hold in your horses."

"What is all this?" cried a voice from the inside of the chaise, as one of the windows was let down violently, and to Heron's surprise—for the voice was decidedly masculine in its tones—a woman's face appeared.

"What is the meaning of all this? Drive on, fellow, or I will soon teach you what it is to trifle with me."

There was no difficulty in seeing the kind of lady it was who uttered these words.

She was one of those females who, from their size and physical proportions, are received by the great mass of society as fine women—the terms fine and coarse always being completely transposed when applied to feminine humanity.

The face was large, fat, and insolent.

The eyes were bold and staring.

And the costume of this lady was as unladylike as it possibly could be, and seemed a compound of a female horse-jockey and an amazon.

It was either her natural voice or an assumed one in which she spoke, but it was masculine in the extreme.

Take her for all in all, she was just the kind of female that Felix Heron had a perfect abhorrence of.

And yet he had a disinclination to stop and rob on the highway anything in the shape of a woman, let her be as unfeminine as she might be; and he hesitated for a few seconds, as the lady glared at him from the coach window, and then cried out, "Hilloa, you sir! what do you mean by stopping my postilion? I've half a mind to come out and lay my riding whip over your shoulders."

"That might be a hazardous experiment, madam," replied Heron, "for human patience has its limits; and, moreover, example is contagious."

"What do you mean, insolent?"

"I mean that since you have evidently forgotten that you are a lady, I might forget it likewise, and then you would fare but badly."

"Wait a moment—we'll soon see about that."

—

CHAPTER CCXXVI.

THE STRONG-MINDED WOMAN MEETS HER MATCH.—THE BILLET DOUX.

THE masculine woman made an effort to open the door of the post-chaise, and might doubtless have done so but that she was partially prevented by some one within, who remonstrated with her in low, timid tones.

"Amelia, my love!—really, now, Amelia my love! do not give way to your fine high spirits to such a degree. Remember how precious and valuable you are!"

Heron was quite delighted to find that some one else was in the post-chaise as well as the masculine lady.

He rode up to the door in a moment, and looking in, he saw that her companion was a small, light, sandy-looking man, with such immense whiskers, that scarcely more than the tip of his nose and two ferret-looking eyes were visible between them.

That this was man and wife Heron at once concluded, but his attention was quickly drawn off from all other subjects by the lady making several slashes at him with a small riding whip through the open window.

"Amelia, my love!" remonstrated the gentleman with the whiskers—"now, really, Amelia, my love, you are too delicate and tender for all this! Do not let your high spirits run away with you."

Felix Heron had to watch his opportunity to snatch hold of the riding-whip, and wrench it from the hands of Amelia.

"Come, come, madam," he said, "enough of this. You have already exhibited yourself in such colours that the name of Amelia will ever be one abhorrent to me, since it will remind me of you."

The fine woman uttered a scream of rage.

The gentleman with the whiskers remonstrated.

"Really, sir," he said, "whether you are a highwayman or not, I must say that I am perfectly astonished at your words. This is the most amiable and lovely of her sex, and universally acknowledged to be the finest woman in all——The deuce!"

The amiable and lovely Amelia having been summarily deprived of her riding-whip by Felix Heron, dealt the gentleman with the whiskers such a box on the ear with her right hand that it seemed half enough to take his head off.

"Take that!" she said; "and speak when you're spoken to! Who told you to interfere?"

"Oh, oh, oh, dear Amelia, you are at times really a little violent and hasty!"

"Do you want another?"

"No, my love, no; certainly not!"

Heron could scarcely be amused at this appear-

No. 71.—EDITH.

ance of servility on one side and tyranny on the other.

His pity for the abject and forlorn condition of the gentleman with the whiskers was almost lost in contempt that any man could put up with the freaks of such a virago.

"Quick, sir!" he cried, impatiently. "I want your money!"

"Then you are a highwayman?" said the gentleman with the whiskers, timidly, as he still rubbed his ear.

"As you please, sir, at your service! I want your purse, watch, and jewellery! Quick, quick!"

"Bless you, Mr. Highwayman, I never have any purse, watch, nor jewellery! Amelia keeps everything, and gives me eighteenpence now and then to spend!"

"And now and then something else," said

Amelia, as she raised her other hand to inflict a box on the other ear of the wretched personage she so completely triumphed over.

That hand, however, happened to be nearest the carriage window where Felix Heron was, and by stretching forward his right arm he caught it by the wrist.

"Shame, madam!" he said,—"shame and disgrace to your sex! What devil has possession of you, that you can thus act?"

The lady made vigorous efforts to release her wrist from Heron's grasp, but she might just as well have attempted to have got out of an iron vice.

She screamed and shrieked with rage, and drummed on the bottom of the coach with her feet with frantic violence.

The unhappy wretch with the whiskers was thoroughly alarmed.

"Oh, dear—oh, dear! If you please, Mr. Highwayman," he said, "let her do what she likes! I don't want anybody to interfere! She's the best and most amiable of persons, and the finest woman in all Paddington!"

Heron began to regret that he had interfered with these people at all, but it was a principle with him always to carry out an adventure when he began it.

"Well, madam," he said; "since it appears you keep the purse, it is from you I must get it!"

"Never, wretch, never!—and I shall only live in hopes of seeing you hanged."

"I live in hopes of disappointing you. Now, sir, what is your name?"

"Broom—my name is Broom—it's always Broom—and was my father's before me!"

"And is this your wife?"

"Certainly; and she's the finest woman in all Paddington!"

"Silence!" cried Amelia. "I thought I had told you over and over again, and that at last, idiot though you are, you fully understood you were not to presume to call me your wife! You are my husband, if you please—that is, my property; and surely a lady may do what she likes with her own!"

"Well, my dear," said Mr. Broom, humbly; "I don't mean to contradict you!"

"You'd better not!"

"I know it—I know it! and I never do!"

"Well, madam," said Heron; "where is this purse?"

"In my pocket—and where you won't get it."

Heron leant forward upon Daisy, letting the bridle hang upon her neck, so that both his hands were at liberty, and catching the right wrist of Mrs. Broom as well as the left, he held her securely, as he said, "Now, Mr. Broom, you will take the purse from her pocket, and this coarse, detestable woman cannot help herself!"

"Coarse?" shrieked Mrs. Broom.

"Exactly so!"

"Detestable?"

"More so than tongue can tell!"

"I daren't do it!—I daren't do it!" said Mr. Broom.

"If you don't," said Heron, "I shall have no resource but to hand her over to some of my men, who are close at hand, who will make short work of her!"

"Then I must, Amelia!"

"Wait till we get home!" said Mrs. Broom.

"There, that's it!" said Broom. "That's what I expected. "She'll shut me up in the back kitchen, on bread and water, for three days for this!"

"Never mind," said Heron. "You know she's the finest woman in all Paddington."

"Yes, she is—she is. Oh, Amelia! You see I can't help it! This highwayman is peremptory. I must give him the purse!"

"If you were half a third of a man," said Mrs. Broom, "you would fight him, while you had a drop of blood in your veins!"

"But don't you hear, my dear, he talks of his companions? And if there are only two of them. I had need to be three men to fight them."

"But you might fight them all, and distinguish yourself!"

"Extinguish myself, you mean, Amelia. There, my good sir—there's the purse. Dear me! What's this? A note to Mrs. Amelia Broom—with Wiggins in the corner! Why, that's the great fishmonger on the Green!"

Mrs. Broom uttered a shriek.

"Read it," said Heron, "now you have it."

"On your life, I dare you to do so!" said Mrs. Broom.

"Then I will for you," said Heron.

He released Mrs. Broom's hands as he spoke, and snatched the letter that her husband had taken from her pocket, from his hesitating grasp.

Heron opened it, and read it aloud :—

"MOST CHARMING AMELIA,—
"Get rid of the wretch you call your husband to-morrow night, and I will come to sup with you. A lobster will arrive at ten o'clock, and you, charming Amelia, will find the trimmings.
"This is from your own
"ADOLPHUS WIGGINS."

Mr. Broom, with a deep groan, sunk to the bottom of the coach.

Heron laughed.

"Now, sir," he said, "I leave you to your own reflections; and if, as the charming Amelia says, you are half a third of a man, you will have something to say to Mr. Wiggins and the finest woman in Paddington."

Heron turned his horse's head, and at the moment he did so, a loud, harsh voice cried out, "And I shall have something to say to the Baron Von Peck, who should be on his road to Hamburgh, but who is on the highway, stopping his Majesty's lieges in the broad, open face of day."

Heron looked in the direction of the sounds, and beheld Jonathan Wild mounted on the grey horse with which he had trotted on towards London, and on which he had unaccountably turned and come back again to the Gravesend road.

Heron was astonished.

A grim smile of satisfaction sat upon the face of Wild.

"So, Baron," he added, "we meet at last, face to face, and I catch you in the very fact of highway robbery!"

"Indeed!" said Heron.

"Yes, indeed! Newgate yearns for you—the prisoner's dock at the Old Bailey yearns for you—and, last of all, Tyburn Tree only waits the good time of the law to bear as one of its choicest pieces of fruit, the criminal and robber, the Baron Von Peck."

"It appears to me," said Heron, "that you are premature."

"Ah! As how?"

"You have not caught me yet!"

"I have! Yield, or you're a dead man!"

Jonathan Wild pulled both his holster-pistols out from the saddle, and presented them full at Felix Heron.

"Blaze away!" said Heron.

Wild was surprised.

"By heaven and earth!" he said, "you're a brave fellow; and, were it not for one thing, I should feel inclined to make terms with you for a sessions or two, and let you have your swing out on the road, before you took your final swing out on Tyburn Tree."

"To what consideration," said Heron, quietly, "am I indebted for your rankest animosity?"

"You aspire to the hand of the widowed Countess of Whitcombe!"

"Oh, is that it?"

"That is it!"

"Then, Jonathan Wild, you are mistaken, for the Countess of Whitcombe has already accepted a proposal of marriage from a certain Captain Fantome, an officer in the royal navy, to whom she will be married, probably, to-morrow!"

"I don't believe a word of it!"

"As you please!"

"I give you half a minute to yield yourself a prisoner! Let that time elapse, and I fire!"

"Shoot him — shoot him!" screamed Mrs. Broom, from the post-chaise. "Kill him—kill him, at once! I hate the wretch!"

This unexpected cry saved, probably, Felix Heron's life, for Jonathan Wild, not expecting it, involuntarily turned his eyes in the direction from whence it came.

Captain Heron was watching him with the keenness of a man who felt that his life depended upon the issues of the next few minutes.

He could not but feel that the time had come which had been slightly hinted at by Tom Ripon, when all other considerations would have to be forgotten, and where that self-preservation which is indeed the first law of nature would come into operation, as between him and Jonathan Wild.

The moment, therefore, that he saw Wild's eyes distracted from the steady contemplation of him, Heron drew forth one of his own pistols and fired.

Wild's hat flew off his head.

Believing himself shot, Jonathan at once discharged both his own pistols, but in the hurry of the moment his aim was lost, and the pair of slugs with which each of them was loaded flew harmlessly past Felix Heron.

"Forward, Daisy!" cried Heron.

Then Daisy took one of those terrific leaps she was accustomed to, and so unrivalled at.

The leap brought her and her rider full against Jonathan Wild and his horse, and Heron reversing the pistol in his hand so that he held it by the barrel, dealt Wild on the instant of the encounter such a blow with the butt end of it on the head, that horse and man went down together, rolling amid the chalky dust of the road.

It was not part of Heron's plan to linger for a moment after this victory.

He took no notice whatever of the occupants of the post-chaise, but wheeling Daisy abruptly round, he made off at a gallop towards the shadowy lane where he had left Tom Ripon.

Even as he went, and riding fast as he was, Heron began to loosen the dress of the Baron Von Peck, which he wore over the naval costume of Captain Fantome.

The shadowy lane was reached.

"Tom, Tom!" shouted Heron, "are you there?"

"Here, Captain—here! Is all well?"

"Quite so. But this has been an adventure more eventful than I expected."

"What has happened, Captain?"

"I have had an encounter with Jonathan Wild."

Tom Ripon's eyes opened amazingly wide, and he looked anxiously in the face of Captain Heron, as though he would ascertain by so doing, without further questioning words, what had been the result of that encounter.

Heron knew perfectly well that that was Tom wanted to know, so he added, hastily, "I have left Wild and his horse both sprawling in the roadway, Tom."

"Hurrah!" shouted Tom. "There's an end of him!"

"Do not make too sure of that. The fellow has more lives than a cat, and that they say has nine; and of late I am very much inclined to be of old Lady Castlenau's opinion, which is that Wild, being born to be hanged, no other fate can possibly overtake him."

By this time Felix Heron had succeeded in divesting himself entirely of the over-clothing which represented the Baron Von Peck, and in restoring himself to the outward appearance of Captain Fantome, of the royal navy.

"What's to be the next move, Captain?" asked Tom.

"To town with what speed we may; and if Jonathan Wild is not seriously injured, I feel quite confident that we shall yet hear something of him before reaching London."

Felix Heron drove out of the lane with Daisy again in harness, and all the arrangements as complete as they had been in the first instance, when he started from the little hotel at Gravesend, in his new disguise.

The road seemed perfectly clear, and although Heron looked back for a considerable distance, so as to command a view of the spot of his encounter with Mr. and Mrs. Broom, the post-chaise which had conveyed that singular couple was not to be seen.

Jonathan Wild too had disappeared along with his horse.

"Well, Tom," said Heron, "there is just a possibility now that we may get to London without further interruption."

"Unless we interrupt somebody ourselves," said Tom.

"True, true; but it is the Court, the King, and their adviser, who have driven me to this course; but after to-day, I mean to make up my mind to one proceeding, and one proceeding only."

"What may that be, Captain? Not to go off the road, I hope?"

"No; but I intend to be the special scourge and terror of all persons connected with the

Court. My sphere of action henceforth shall lie between London and Windsor, London and Kew, and the White Lodge in Richmond Park. Those shall be the places which I will render at once dangerous and famous. And since the Court and its minions deprive me of the legitimate property which should keep me as a gentleman and a nobleman, I will make them pay the penalty, and with interest to boot."

"Yes, Captain," cried Tom Ripon, "that's the plan. It will be fine sport; and if we should happen to get a little more than we want, why, you know, we can be charitable; and that will be making those selfish rascals who only look to themselves, distribute some of their money among the poor, whether they like it or not."

"Hush, Tom!—do you hear nothing?"

Captain Heron, as he spoke, slackened the speed of the two horses, so that the sound of their hoofs upon the ground, and the grinding of the chaise wheels, were not sufficiently loud to obliterate any other sound.

An approaching horse at a fast trot was heard.

In two or three minutes more Jonathan Wild himself rode up to the side of the chaise.

He presented a grotesque and wretched appearance.

His hat was far back upon his head, for he had taken off his cravat, and wound it twice over his brow, so that his hat was not large enough to cover it.

His fall, too, upon the chalky and dusty road had disordered and begrimed his apparel.

But otherwise, with his usual good luck, Wild did not seem to have sustained any particular injury.

He glanced savagely into the chaise, as he cried out, "Well, sir, as an officer in his Majesty's service, I cannot help thinking you might have lent some little assistance to me in the performance of my duty."

"What's your duty to me?" said Heron. "I know nothing about you or your duty either. Strike my topsails, man! whatever do you mean?"

"You must have heard a disturbance on the road; and, in fact, now I come to think of it, I can't make out how you're here in advance of me, when I never met you as I rode back again. That's suspicious."

CHAPTER CCXXVII.

THE PERILOUS POSITION OF FELIX HERON.—THE FAMILY COUNCIL AT WHITCOMBE HOUSE.

THE keen, hawk-like glance that Jonathan Wild bent upon Felix Heron and Tom Ripon, impressed them both with a sense of danger.

They could not help feeling that if their disguises stood the test of that critical and practised examination, they might rely upon them in any emergency.

"It's very strange," said Wild, half-communing with himself and half addressing Heron,—"it's very strange, but I can't help thinking I've seen both of you before!"

"In course you have, stupid!" said Tom; "and it bean't strange at all! Why, you met us awhile

agone down the road! You're as bad as our black bull as tossed Mrs. Crumpet!"

"Bah! Stop your fool's tongue!" said Wild. "There is some mystery here which I shall find out sooner or later."

"In the meantime," said Felix Heron, "I look upon you as the most impertinent rascal I have met with for a long time!"

"My service to you," laughed Wild; "that's just what I am! I live, eat, drink, and sleep by my impertinence; and I've an impression upon my mind that you and I some day will be better acquainted!"

"We may be," said Heron; "but I don't like crowds, and seldom attend executions."

Wild made a gesture of impatience, and shook the bridle of his horse.

He seemed in the act of riding off, when a sudden thought made him pause; and turning abruptly, he said, "Your name is Fantome—Captain Fantome, of the royal navy?"

"Well, what then?"

"By all that's infernal, I thought as much! And what that rascal Von Peck said is true! You're going to London, and your destination is Whitcombe House, in St. James's Street?"

"Peter!" said Felix Heron.

"Yees, maister."

"This fellow grows more impertinent every moment. I shall certainly complain of him to his superiors, and get him discharged. I only wish I had him on the main-deck of my ship, I should know then what to do with him."

"Yees, maister; and if our black bull had he on a common, he'd know what to do with him!"

Without then making any further reply to Jonathan Wild, Heron drove on.

It was a strange thing to see Felix Heron and Tom Ripon driving to London, with Jonathan Wild following a few paces in the rear, totally unconscious that they were the two persons, of all living beings, in whom he felt the greatest interest.

But so it was; and his conviction of the death of Heron was so strong, nothing having at all occurred to shake it, that, had he seen him actually in his ordinary costume, and totally undisguised, he must have taken him for a spirit.

The remainder of the distance to London was soon achieved; and, as Wild seemed thoroughly resolved to follow them, to make certain of their destination, Heron found that there was no resource but to put a bold face upon the matter, and drive at once to Whitcombe House.

This seemed all that Wild wanted to see, for he drew up at the corner of Pall Mall; and then, uttering an exclamation or two, he rode off to the City.

The only remarkable thing as regarded Jonathan Wild in the whole of this transaction was that he had failed to detect Daisy as one of the horses in the chaise.

That was the weak point of the whole arrangement; and if Jonathan Wild had seen it, it must have awakened a thousand strange thoughts and suspicions in his mind, which would have been full of danger and turmoil to Heron and Tom Ripon.

But happily that danger was avoided.

The chaise was taken by Tom to the inn,

where it was to be left, and the two horses were snugly ensconced in the stable of Whitcombe House.

It was late in the afternoon, then, that a small party was assembled in the well-known green drawing-room of Whitcombe House to debate and decide upon certain important matters connected with the welfare of Edith and of Felix Heron.

The party consisted only of those few persons who were aware of the existence of Felix Heron, and of all the circumstances connected with his position.

The young Earl of Bridgewater and Lady Bridgewater.

Colonel Trelawney, and his sister.

And last, though not least, in everybody's estimation, the old Lady Castleneau.

The young and gallant Marquis of Ormond, too, was expected.

The party, therefore, was a strong one in rank, intelligence, and beauty.

Felix Heron spoke in those low, gentle accents, which, in the privacy of his own house, he was wont to assume; or rather, we may say, they were natural to him, and only exchanged for different accents and tones, as the circumstances and collisions of the great world around him enforced particular lines of action.

"The prejudice against me, it appears," he said, "is still so strong in the mind of the King and of his principal counsellors, that, until some change takes place—which can scarce be at present hoped for—it is as well that I should still be supposed among the dead than among the living."

"Yes," said the Earl of Bridgewater. "I have tried in vain all the influence I could bring to bear among those Privy Councillors whom I thought the most reasonable, and I find there was a fixed determination to adopt a proceeding, in regard to the Earldom of Whitcombe, of the most calamitous character!"

"More peril and more grief!" exclaimed Edith.

"It is proper," added the Earl of Bridgewater, "that I should inform you there was some scruple about bringing scandal to the peerage, by accusing Felix Heron of highway robbery; but it was intended to construe some of his acts into high treason, so as to establish an attainder against the title."

A flash of anger came across the face of Heron.

"I see—I understand," he said; "my innocent child would have been made to suffer for the prejudices against his father!"

"Yes," added the Earl of Bridgewater; "and the attainder, once established, the estates of the earldom would, as you all know, have been forfeited to the Crown; and they would have constituted now a nice little bit of plunder, to divide among some of the poverty-stricken minions of the Court!'"

"Well, it is then," said Heron, "that I should be considered with the dead!"

"It is well," said Colonel Trelawney, "for it saves both the estates and the title; but this is a state of things which we hope will not endure for ever. You are still a young man, Whitcombe, and may outlive all your enemies!"

"That is more than probable," said the Earl of Bridgewater; "and I may mention here, without the risk of it being carried further, or even whispered into adverse ears, that the King is ailing, and that his physicians do not give him a year of life!"

"Indeed!" was the general exclamation.

"Yes; and I have it upon good authority that Lord Bute, the Duke of Portland, and some others of the Privy Council, have had long and secret interviews with the illustrious personage who will be his successor on the throne of England."

"The demise of the King," said Colonel Trelawney, "would change the whole aspect of affairs, and his successor could not commence a reign with the persecution of any of the old nobility. Moreover, it is well known that he has a special dislike to one of your great enemies, Whitcombe—if not the greatest—at the Court."

"You allude to Lord Clackington?"

"I do."

"He is thoroughly contemptible."

"Truly so, personally; but having the ear of the King, is like some dangerous serpent on such vantage ground that he can sting his enemies without fear of retaliation."

"Unless one chooses to put one's heel upon his head," said Heron, "and crush him."

"I have had serious thoughts," said Colonel Trelawney, "of calling him out, and giving him six inches of cold steel in Bloomsbury Fields."

"You would lose your commission to a certainty," said the Earl of Bridgewater. "I advise that you let him alone."

"Well, gentlemen," said Lady Castleneau, "this is all very interesting, but I want to hear what Felix has to say about a domestic proposition that I, for one, should be glad to see carried out."

"Thanks, dear Lady Castleneau!" said Heron. "I will come to the proposition at once, and it is simply this. This house wants a master—and Edith——"

Edith smiled as she said, "You would say, Felix, that I want one likewise!"

"No, Edith, you want a protector; and am I not one ever?"

"You are indeed, my Felix!"

"Yes; but it is in secret! You and our little one want such a protector as can stand by you in the open face of day, and shield you with a strong hand from all peril. The proposition, then, which I make, and which I hope will meet with the concurrence of all here present, is that Edith shall marry Captain Fantome, of the royal navy, represented by me; and then I shall be able to show myself here at Whitcombe House as its master, and defy all comers!"

"But how," said Lady Castleneau, "would that effect Edith's position, when all these things come to be known, and Felix Heron is declared to be still in life?"

"I don't think," said Colonel Trelawney, "that any bad effect can ensue. The thing will only need to be explained, and there will be an end of it."

"And I think the proposition a good one," said the Earl of Bridgewater.

"It shall be decided by the votes of the ladies," added Heron. "And I would ask—is it not better that I should be here openly as Edith's husband and the master of this house, than here secretly, subject to all manner of suspicion, and likewise incurring the possibility of casting a slur upon her fair name."

"I vote for the marriage!" said Colonel Trelawney's sister.

"And I!" said the Countess of Bridgewater.

"And I!" said Lady Castleneau, "upon one condition."

"What condition, dear aunt?" asked Edith.

"Simply this, my dear. This marriage is a kind of mockery to deceive the world. You are, if I may be allowed the expression, a mock bride, and Felix Heron a mock bridegroom. It will be to my mind, therefore, a kind of desecration of so solemn a service of the Church to allow a marriage to be celebrated under such circumstances."

"What would you do, aunt?" asked Heron.

"It must be an apparent marriage, but not a real one. Let the necessary license be got and the marriage performed, or said to be performed, at my house, but not by a clergyman; so that, as the thing is unreal in the beginning, it shall be unreal to the end."

"In that case," said Edith, "there need be no ceremony at all; and, if we can persuade the world that there has been one, it will be sufficient."

"Now hear me," said the Earl of Bridgewater. "I cannot see the danger and the difficulty in this matter, and I advise that the union be public. Nothing can come of it in the end in the shape of disaster; and you may depend upon one thing, which is, that there are too many eyes bent upon Whitcombe House, and upon the proceedings of the Countess, to make any other course a safe one."

This strong opinion on the part of the Earl of Bridgewater had all its effect upon the persons present.

All eyes were bent upon Edith; for, after all, it was upon her decision that the whole matter rested.

"Let this mock union, then, be public," she said; "but let that publicity not outrage an ordinance of the Church—for that is a thing I can never consent to."

"But, Edith!" said Heron, in a tone of remonstrance.

"Nay, Felix," interrupted Edith, imploringly, "do not urge me to this. The more I look at it; the more repugnant it is to my feelings. I have once stood at the altar with you as your wife, and I cannot bear to repeat those vows again, even in mockery, to another."

"But it is not to another, Countess!" said the Earl of Bridgewater.

"I know it is not, and I feel that I have expressed myself badly. Dear Aunt Castleneau, you know what I mean. Can you not suggest some mode of relief from this difficulty?"

"I think I can, my child. Everything in this world is a compromise, and why may not this take the same conditions?"

"How, Lady Castleneau?" asked Bridgewater.

"Just this way. Let a special license be procured for the marriage of Captain Fantome, of the royal navy, with Edith, Countess of Whitcombe. It is not at all an unusual thing, then, for some country clergyman—who is, perhaps, a special friend of the family—to be entrusted with the performance of the ceremony. Let that clergyman be personated by some one who is truly a friend of the family, but yet no clergyman."

They all looked at Edith, to see how she received this proposal.

It was repugnant to her, but yet it was a compromise, since it really stopped her pretended marriage with Captain Fantome of all real egality.

"I consent!" she said.

"Then this conference is over," remarked Felix Heron.

"It is," said the Earl of Bridgewater, "and I charge myself with the duty of carrying out this plan, feeling a conviction that it is the only mode of securing the estates of Whitcombe from confiscation and the title from attainder."

This being all arranged, it was a great relief to Edith to feel that in the disguise he so well assumed, Felix Heron would be able to take his proper place as master of Whitcombe House.

The secret was one to be well kept, inasmuch as the only persons who would know it were those then and there present at the conference, together with those faithful dependants of Felix Heron who made up the household of Whitcombe House.

The Earl of Bridgewater was impetuous and quick in all his transactions, and on the very next day he set about procuring the necessary license for the marriage of the mock Captain Fantome with the real Countess of Whitcombe.

Felix Heron communicated what was about to occur to Tom Ripon and to Ogle.

The former he cautioned most particularly not to communicate in any shape or way to his mother or to the Rev. Mortification the secret of the real identity of Captain Fantome.

"You'll have a rest, Tom," he said, "and so will Daisy, for during the next fortnight I shall not seek adventures on the road; and when I do it will be in a new character, which probably will somewhat surprise the agents of the police."

It was with a secret satisfaction that Tom heard these words.

He had plans of his own.

The temptation to try his fortune on the road, unaccompanied by Felix Heron, was too great for him, and since his last disappointment in love affairs, a feeling of misanthropy had come over him.

For the next few days Tom cogitated deeply with himself.

The result was that he came to a determination, the particulars of which we shall proceed to lay before our readers.

CHAPTER CCXXVIII.

TOM MAKES A HALF CONFIDENCE WITH OGLE.— HE GOES ON THE ROAD.

"OGLE," said Tom, as they both stood in the stable admiring Daisy, "what do you think of Bright Eyes?"

"Of who?"

"She," added Tom, with a jerk of his head. "You know who I mean. That young girl—the idol of my heart, and the pearl of St. James's Street!"

"Which of them?" said Ogle.

"Why, the original."

"Oh, you've gone back to her, have you? I thought you gave her up, and placed all your affections on that young lady who went by the name of the King's Ward."

"So I did," said Tom; "but she had the bad taste to prefer that thin, lanky young fellow, the Marquis of Ormond; so, you see, Ogle, I let him have her!"

"How much obliged he must have been, Tom! Woa, Daisy!—woa! Don't stamp upon my foot, lass."

"Then, don't you pull her ears, Ogle, for she don't like it."

"Very good. But what is it you want to do or say, Tom?"

"Why, just this, Ogle. I want you to do what I know you can do quite well, and that is to keep a great secret."

Ogle looked rather grave.

"I can't say I like secrets, Tom; and till I know what this one exactly is, I should not like to promise to keep it."

"It won't hurt you. Look you here, Ogle; the Captain is not going on the road for some time, since I rather fancy he has an adventure on hand that he keeps all to himself."

"What is that?"

"Why, you know, Ogle, I told you all about that ghost we saw in the lane leading to Holland House over by Kensington."

"You did, Tom—but it turned out to be no ghost at all."

"I'm not quite so sure of that!"

"Why, the Captain fired at it!"

"Yes; and you know as well as I do, Ogle, that he wouldn't mind firing at anything that was in his way, ghost or no ghost! But that's not the question. I know he found out something in Holland House that has set him to work ever since. I asked him to let me have a hand in it, but he said it wasn't the sort of thing for a man like me."

Ogle shook his head again.

"What do you mean, Ogle, by all those antics? You keep on shaking your head, as if you did not believe a fellow!"

"Are you quite sure, Tom, the Captain said a man like you?"

"How particular you are! Perhaps he did, and perhaps he didn't! But that's not the question either."

"Good gracious, Tom, then what is the question? What do you want to do, and what do you want me to do?"

"Only to keep my secret, that's all! I want to try my own fortune on the road, and that alone, too! But I don't seem to like the idea of going without anybody having an idea of what I'm about! I might want some help, or I might want to send some message home here, and I shouldn't like, then, that there wasn't a soul in Whitcombe House who knew anything about me."

"Very well, Tom, I can't help it! If you like to go, you can! A wilful boy must have his own way at times; and I'm sure neither I, nor the Captain, nor the Lady Edith, could wish to baulk you, however we might all of us advise you to the contrary."

"Very good, Ogle; so that when I'm missed you will know what has become of me?"

"Oh, certainly! Is that all you have to say?"

Tom was silent for a few seconds, and then he replied, "Yes, I think that is all I feel inclined to say."

"Very well; I seek for nobody's secrets. I can see you have one beyond what you've told me; and I only hope you're not going to get into any mischief you will find it difficult to extricate yourself from."

"Oh, no! Trust me for that."

"Very well, then; please yourself."

Ogle strolled out of the stable, and left Tom in companionship with Daisy.

Tom sighed, as he flung his arm round Daisy's neck.

"I should have liked to have told him, Daisy," he said, "that I meant to take you with me; but I was afraid, when it came to the last moment, that he would say ' No;' and if I went on saying ' Yes,' he might speak to the Captain himself, and then there would be an order against it, and it would be all up with my dashing career on the road."

Tom caressed Daisy as he spoke.

"As it is, you know, Daisy, the Captain expressly ordered me to take you out for exercise, and he did not say a word whether the exercise was to be in the night or the day, nor does that matter much to you, Daisy. Eh? Does it?"

Daisy was very fond of Tom, and rubbed her head affectionately upon his shoulder.

"That's right!" added Tom. "That means that you don't care a bit. So we will take ourselves off this very night, and see what we can do; and who knows but Tom Ripon may yet make a name on the road that may be almost equal to that of Captain Heron?"

With all the secrecy and despatch in his power, Tom, at about eight o'clock on that evening, when it had become thoroughly dark, made his way to Daisy's stable.

Silently and swiftly he saddled and bridled the docile and beautiful creature; and then, carefully examining his pistols, or, rather, Captain Heron's pistols, which were kept in the holsters of the saddle, he took Daisy by the bridle, and led her to the door of the stable.

"There's a good deal yet to do," he said, "before I can please myself, and go on the road as I ought to go; but I think the old gal ought to manage all that, so I'll just trot down to Wardour Street first, and see what she's got in that mouldy old crib that she and Mortification live in."

There was no difficulty in leaving the stables of Whitcombe House without observation.

We had have before occasion to remark that those stables were very extensive, and went far back to a quiet, dull street, into which opened some capacious gates.

Under ordinary circumstances it would have been necessary to open one of those gates to take out a horse.

But Daisy was as docile as a cat or a dog; and when Tom Ripon opened the small wicket, which was intended only for human ingress and egress, Daisy stooped low down, and followed him out through it with the greatest ease and dexterity.

"That's right, Daisy," cried Tom; "now we

can fasten up the stable nicely, and there will be no danger."

The wicket door closed with a strong latch, which could only be opened on the outside by a key, so that Tom left that portion of Whitcombe House in as complete a state of security as it ordinarily was.

A feeling of great exultation and triumph came over Tom as he now felt himself fairly in the open street, well armed and accompanied by Daisy.

He muttered to himself as he went the self-deception by which he strove to persuade himself Captain Heron could not visit him with much blame.

"The Captain told me to take Daisy out for exercise, and here we are; so that's all right, ain't it, Daisy?"

Daisy knew very well when Tom addressed her, and gave him a sort of friendly push with her head when he did so, which Tom was always ready to translate into yes or no as the occasion suited.

Indeed, Tom put so many words into Daisy's mouth, that to hear him speak to her, one would imagine that, in addition to all her other qualities and rare instincts, she was actually endowed with the power of speech.

Tom did not venture to pass the front of Whitcombe House, but he led Daisy by several circuitous back streets, towards Charing Cross.

Close, then, to the old dilapidated pile of buildings known as the King's Mews, he mounted.

It was but a short trot then to Wardour Street, Soho, where his mother and Mortification conducted that fence which, no doubt, was a sufficiently profitable undertaking.

As usual, at sunset, the shop, which ostensibly was one for the sale of second-hand wearing apparel, was closed.

Mrs. Ripon's customers preferred darkness.

They had no particular predilection either for being looked at through the shop windows.

The business of the establishment then fairly commenced only after nightfall.

Indeed, it is very doubtful if any one ever crossed the threshold except the Reverend Mortification himself during daylight.

Tom rapped at the shutters with the butt of one of Captain Heron's pistols without dismounting from Daisy.

"Yea," said a voice, "who knocketh?"

"Is the old gal at home?"

"Yea, it is Thomas. As the Psalmist remarks, talk of the ——, and he's sure to appear. Your respected maternal relative, Thomas, was conversing of misdeeds; and yea, we were both wondering if thou wert hanged or not."

"Thank you," said Tom—"much obliged; but that little affair has not come off yet."

"Yea, I rejoice."

"Well, don't stand palavering there, but open the door."

"Thomas—yea, Thomas——"

"Well, what now, old boy?"

"Is it business or pleasure?"

"I don't know what you mean."

"Yea, dost thou come to bring spoons, or perchance forks, or mayhap a silver dish-cover?—for those things verily are business. But if thou comest here, Thomas, to eat and drink of our substance, and to sing profane songs in the back parlour—yea, as the Psalmist says——"

"Bother you and the Psalmist too!" interrupted Tom. "Open the door! Can't a dutiful son come and see the old gal, without his pockets full of swag for the melting pot?"

"Then thou hast brought nothing, Tom?"

"That's the amount of it."

"Yea, then, as the Psalmist says, and says most wisely, 'he who bringeth nothing, commonly cometh on an errand to take something away.'"

"Just so, old Corruption."

"Old what?"

"Oh, it's the same thing, Mortification, you know."

"Thou art irreverent, Thomas; and as the Psalmist remarks, brimstone will be thy daily food."

"Look here, old Mortification," said Tom, whose patience was almost exhausted, "I have something to say to the old gal, and I mean to come in and say it. Now, are you going to open the door or not?"

"Yea, I decline!"

"You do?"

"Yea, she whom you call the old gal is in a state of repose, for rum punch is an inviting liquor."

"I don't believe it," said Tom. "So if you won't open the door, I will."

"Ha, ha, Thomas! Ha, ha! Thou mayest try!"

"I mean to!"

The Reverend Mortification no doubt underrated Tom's ability to effect an entrance into the fence, and the means by which Tom intended to carry out that intention never for a moment entered into his imagination.

The little colloquy that had taken place between them had been carried on by Mortification through a small orifice at the top of the door, from whence either he or Mrs. Ripon were in the habit of reconnoitring their customers, and deciding whether, in the thieves' language of London, the person applying was a "plant," that is to say, a spy, or really a "family man," with something to dispose of as the produce of a robbery.

The Reverend Mortification thought himself secure as in a fortress.

But Tom was of a different opinion.

The street was quite deserted, and the only watchman at the corner of it was taking his first nap, snugly ensconced in his box.

Tom, therefore, was in a condition to carry on the siege of the fence, and to take it by assault, which he fully intended to do, without much fear of interruption.

Once more Tom asked Mortification if he intended to admit him, or whether he preferred leaving him to effect an entrance, to which Mortification replied. "Yea, Thomas, verily thy mother is dozing sweetly in an easy chair by the fire, and I will not disturb her slumbers for so unprofitable a sinner as thou art."

"Very well," said Tom; "here goes!"

To the surprise of Mortification, Tom wheeled Daisy round in such a manner that Mortification thought he was about to take his departure—but no such thing entered Tom's head   for giving

Daisy a peculiar touch, he made her throw out her hind legs, when crash, crash went the door of the fence, and Tom had the inexpressible amusement of seeing Mortification sprawling his length on the floor of the fence.

"Hilloa, old boy! hope you're not hurt much," he said, as he dismounted from Daisy, and gave the stool upon which Mortification had been standing a kick with his foot, which again upset his father-in-law.

Mrs. Ripon could not but be conscious of some disturbance in the front of the premises.

During the first part of the cannonade which Daisy's heels had made against the door of the fence, she had only responded to the tumult by a series of sympathetic starts.

But upon the door actually giving way, and the reverend Mortification coming to grief with the stock, Mrs. Ripon was fully aroused.

No. 72.—EDITH.

She started up with a shrill scream.

"That's the old gal!" said Tom.

"Thieves!—thieves!"

"All's right!" said Tom. "Here we both are."

"Murder!" cried Mortification. "Yea, Thomas, it is thy duty to assist thy paternal relative-in-law. This stool hath three legs and I have two, and yea we have become entangled together, so that I know not which are mine and which are the stool's."

"Come on Daisy," said Tom. "Don't tread on the old boy."

Daisy, with great care, stepped over Mortification and the stool; and then Tom backed her into a snug corner of the shop, and, patting her on the neck, he said, "Just wait there a bit, my lass, and I'll soon come back to you."

Tom, then, at once made his way into the par-law, where Mrs. Ripon was sitting on the floor in a very undignified way, with a full conviction that an earthquake, or some other natural phenomenon, was taking place, to the destruction of Wardour Street.

"Why, what's the matter?" cried Tom.

"Gracious powers! is it you?"

"To be sure it is. Is this the way you receive your customers?"

"Customers, Tom? Is it candlesticks or spoons?"

"Neither, just at present, old gal; but listen to me—I'm going on the road on my own hook."

"A hook, Tom? We don't take them in. We profess to buy old iron, but don't."

"Oh, bother!—you know what I mean. I'm going on the road, and the Captain has lent me Daisy, and I expect to get no end of swag."

"Oh, Tom, the very best price, I assure you. Always remember you've an affectionate mother, and a melting-pot in the kitchen."

"Yea, and a paternal relative-in-law," said Mortification, putting his head into the room, "who is always ready to come forward as a witness in a case of *alibi* or some such trifle; for, as the Psalmist says, go on swearing, if you get anything by it."

"Oh! you're a precious old buck," said Tom; "but I tell you what it is, old gal. I want to know if, among all your old traps in the shop, you can fit me out as a real, right down, genuine, high-flying highwayman?"

"Captain Buster!" screamed Mrs. Ripon.

The exclamation was so sudden, and so completely unexpected by Tom, that he fully believed an individual of that name had really made his appearance.

"No nonsense!" shouted Tom. "Keep off, old Buster, whoever you are."

"It isn't that," added Mrs. Ripon.

"But you said Buster."

"I mean his clothes. He came here and sold himself, for one pound twelve and six; and it's a sweet suit, all gold lace and gimcracks, and just the thing for you, Tom."

"Yea," said the Rev. Mortification, "he shall have it for three-ten and six: it's a bargain, for it was the last suit of Buster, and yea, he hath not another."

"Yea," said Tom, "and what did he do after he had sold it, then?"

"Tom," said Mrs. Ripon, "you're getting improper. He went home in a watchman's great coat, of course. But you shall see the suit. Get it at once, Bumblebee."

"Hilloa!" cried Tom. "Keep off, Bumblebee. Who the deuce are you?"

"Yea," said Mortification, "it is a little affectionate name which your respected and sainted mother hath invented for me. She calleth me Bumblebee out of shortness, instead of Mortification!"

"Well," said Tom, "I don't see that much is gained by it. So look alive, old Bumble, and get the Captain's clothes."

"Yea, I will."

"Was he a good-looking chap, old gal, like me, eh? Are the things likely to fit?"

"Where there's a will there's a way!" said Mrs. Ripon. "They may be a little too long and a little too wide; but those are good faults, Tom, as I dare say you're growing still."

"Plague take it!" said Tom. "Am I to wear old Buster's things till I've grown big enough for them? However, let's see 'em. Oh, well, I must say this is the sort of thing. Mother, get up the chimney; Bumble, look out of window, while I put on Buster's clothes!"

CHAPTER CCXXIX.

TOM RIPON PAYS A VISIT TO WARDOUR-STREET.—
HIS FIRST ADVENTURE ON THE ROAD.

TOM RIPON looked smart and handsome in the costume of the Captain, who, from dire necessity, had been compelled to part with his regimentals to Mrs. Ripon.

The costume was not strictly a military one.

That is to say, it did not belong to the regular service, but was the sort of fancy dress adopted by some country yeomanry.

It answered Tom Ripon's purpose, however, admirably.—for the coat was of scarlet, and richly bedizened with gold lace.

The smallclothes were of buff leather, and there were boots of black morocco, which reached up to the knee.

To be sure, the whole of this dress was a little too large for Tom, as his mother had predicted; but somehow or another, he did not look very bad in it; and the probability was that, on horseback, no one would be able to notice that it did not fit him quite so accurately as it might do.

"Old gal!" cried Tom, "you may come out of the chimney—all's right!"

"Gracious powers!" cried Mrs. Ripon; "he looks like the celebrated Richard Turpin, Esquire, or that very gentlemanly young man, Claude Duval."

"Yea," said Mortification, "and he will come to the same end, if he mindeth what he's about."

Tom put himself in an attitude, and began to sing—

"Hurrah for the road, and a starlight night,
A nag so fresh and free;
Hurrah for a life on the open heath,
A life on the road for me!"

"That's divine!" said Mrs. Ripon. "The dear boy takes after me. If I had not been a delicate and sensitive female I should have gone on the road myself; but whatever becomes of you, Tom, never forget your mother. Honour your parent, and always remember she gives the best price for everything in the shape of——"

"Yea, swag!" said Mortification.

"Take that," said Mrs. Ripon, "for saying your say when it wasn't wanted."

The handiest article that Mrs. Ripon got hold of to throw at Mortification was a flour dredger, and as upon coming in contact with his head the lid came off, the white spectacle he presented amused Tom mightily.

"Well, well," he said, "I can't wait any longer. And now, old gal, I want something else."

"We never pay beforehand," said Mrs. Ripon. "It's a great accommodation to let you have

Captain Buster's smart things; but as for any money——"

"Yea, it is out of the question!" said Mortification.

"Who told you it was out of the question?" replied Mrs. Ripon, with the most charming inconsistency.

"Yea, I——"

"Hold your tongue, will you, and allow the tenderest of mothers to settle with her own infant!"

The Rev. Mortification evidently expected something else at his head, and by way of giving it the least possible chance of hitting him, he kept bobbing down in the most extraordinary fashion, as if some trap-door were beneath his feet, which kept letting him down a foot or two, and then popping him up again to his full height.

"Come, come," said Tom, "don't trouble about me. What I want, old gal, is a riding habit!"

"A what?" screamed Mrs. Ripon.

"A what?" cried Mortification, as he bobbed down again.

"A riding habit!"

"Yea. Mrs. Mountweazel!"

"Confound her!" cried Tom; "don't let her see me. Who and what the deuce is she?"

"Yea, her riding habit, I mean! Sarah Jane Jemima, my love,—don't you recollect Mrs. Mountweazel's habit? Yea, Thomas, her habits are immense!"

"Gracious powers!" said Mrs. Ripon, "it's the very thing. I divine everything—I divine everything. I saw all this in the grouts of my tea, yesterday, not very clearly, but now I understand what it meant. You want to put on a riding habit over Captain Buster's dress, and take it off when it's convenient; which fully accounts for that singular piece of coal that popped out of the fire and went into your pocket, Mortification, red hot."

"Yea, and it would not come out. I became a martyr to fire. Yea!"

"Well, be quick about it," said Tom. "You have guessed it, mother; and so are as good as a witch, in addition to looking like one."

"You wretched boy, how dare you? A witch, indeed! I a witch?"

"Never mind—never mind! Come, old Bumble, the riding-habit; and I tell you what I want beside. A small portmanteau, or round valise, that will strap on the saddle at the back of Daisy, and then I'm all right. And if I'm not here before daylight with plenty of booty, call me a Dutchman, or a Frenchman, or any other outlandish stupid you like. Good-bye, old gal! Good-bye, Mortification!

"'Hurrah, hurrah for the road!
Something, I hear, approaches!
Hurrah, hurrah for the road!
It's a sound that's just like coaches!
And that suits me!'"

Tom was very well provided, now, from the miscellaneous stores of the fence in Wardour Street, with all he wanted; and as he had consumed an hour there, and nine o'clock had pealed forth from the church-steeples in the metropolis for some time, he hastily mounted Daisy, and took his way, at a smart pace, towards the Western Road.

The riding habit he had in the valise that Mortification had found him, so that, as yet he appeared in the scarlet regimentals of Captain Buster.

The sense of exultation in Tom's mind was very great.

Here he was, fairly launched upon the world upon his own responsibility.

He bestrode one of the best—if not the best—horse that was to be found in the three kingdoms.

He was light-hearted and brave.

And he was well armed.

He knew that he could perfectly depend upon Captain Heron's holster pistols, and he had with him a powder flask well filled, with a separate receptacle containing a dozen bullets.

Tom was quite resolved, if it were possible, to render a good account of his night's adventures, and to inaugurate his career as a highwayman by some exploit that should excite the admiration of every one who knew him.

What that exploit was to be, Tom of necessity left entirely to the chapter of accidents.

And so he trotted on.

He was soon clear of the houses in what was then called the Oxford Road, and the open country beyond Tyburn Gate lay before him.

Perhaps, Tom, in common with many knights of the road, who took that route out of town, felt a slight misgiving as to what might be his ultimate fate, as he passed the celebrated and well-known spot where for so many years criminals had expiated their offences with their lives.

Tom reined in his horse.

But it was not to look at Tyburn tree, but it was in curiosity to see who it was that, mounted on a tall, strong-looking horse, seemed to have stopped on the precise spot where executions took place.

That part of the Oxford Road was not lighted, for there being no houses, there were no inhabitants to pay for the necessary tax.

But at the turnpike gate, a little in advance, there were two hanging lanterns, and they cast a lurid glare up and down the road.

Tom fixed his eyes on the strange horseman, and as he did so, he began to regret that he had not trotted on at a hard gallop, and minded his own business.

It did not take a second glance from the keen, youthful eyes of Tom Ripon to recognise in this horseman Jonathan Wild.

Wild's horse was standing still as a statue.

But Jonathan himself seemed to be muttering something which seemed almost like an invocation to the spirits of the many persons who had suffered death on that identical spot.

Wild took no notice of Tom Ripon.

He was in such a state of absorbed abstraction that he had not heard the light footsteps of Daisy; and Tom was able to approach close to the great thief-taker without being observed.

Tom Ripon was sharp of hearing, as well as sharp of sight.

The muttered sentences of Wild came sufficiently clearly to his ears for him to understand them.

"This is the 14th of September," said Wild, "and here I am; but I have not suffered! The prediction is false; but yet, when I heard it, it seemed to sink deep into my soul, and to be there acknowledged as an incontrovertible truth! I was to suffer death at Tyburn tree, so ran the prophecy, on the 14th day of September, but the year was not named; and therefore, as this is that date, and it wants now but two hours of midnight, even if my fortune has been read aright, I have another year's lease of life!"

Wild laughed hideously as he spoke.

Tom Ripon shrunk back, and would gladly have left the thief-taker to his meditations, but as Wild suddenly turned his horse's head he saw that he was not alone.

"Who are you?" he cried, fiercely.

Tom made no answer.

"I say, who are you? and I tell you, at the same time, that it is not the safest thing in the world to intrude upon my privacy."

Tom was bewildered for a moment to know what to do.

But that indecision only lasted for a moment.

He then recollected that he was mounted on Daisy, who was so matchless in speed that if he chose to start off at a racing gallop, Jonathan Wild would have no chance, on the heavy horse he bestrode, of coming up with him.

There was but one objection to this course.

The turnpike-gate.

At that time of night it was closed.

But fortune favoured Tom.

A carriage coming from the country to town came rapidly up.

There was a shout of "Gate, gate!" and it was swung open.

But the gate-keeper was wary, and only opened the barrier sufficiently wide for the carriage to pass through.

Tom had given Daisy the impulse to rush forward, hoping to find space enough through which to make his way, but the gate slammed shut exactly in the face of himself and Daisy.

"Halt!" cried Wild,—"halt, I say, or I will send a messenger after you that will bring you to a standstill somewhat unpleasantly."

Tom Ripon knew perfectly well what the character of this messenger was likely to be.

"A bullet," he said to himself.

But with all his recklessness Jonathan Wild was not so reckless as that.

It was no offence at law for any one to ride on and refuse to stop at the bidding of Jonathan Wild.

Tom, however, thought it just possible that, in his usual angry impatience, Wild might commit such an act.

The possibility of being brought up at the commencement of his career by a pistol bullet was not a pleasant one.

The gate was closed, but that seemed to be no obstruction, for Daisy, with a perfect consciousness that Tom Ripon wanted to be on the other side of it, made one of her daring leaps, and cleared it in fine style.

Tom was a light weight, and there was nothing in reason, or even what might appear to be somewhat out of it, that Daisy would not have cleared with him on her back.

"Hurrah!" shouted Tom.

It was an imprudent shout, for in the exultation of the moment, he uttered it in his natural tones.

Those tones that were so well known to Jonathan Wild.

Too frequently had he had opportunities of hearing them under all circumstances.

"By Jove, it's Tom Ripon!" he cried.

From the fact of ascertaining Tom's identity, Wild easily jumped to another conclusion.

"Yes," he added, "it is Tom Ripon; and there is not another horse in all England could take that leap but Daisy."

The anxiety of Wild to capture both Tom and the gallant animal he bestrode, became for a few moments intense.

He shouted to the man at the gate to open it in a most frantic manner, and showered down expressions of abuse upon his head at a rate that so terrified the gate-keeper that he had hardly sense enough to fling open the bar and allow Jonathan Wild to pass through.

The delay was not altogether above a minute and a half.

Then Jonathan was on the other side of the gate.

But what could not Daisy accomplish when put to her full speed, even in that short space of time?

Swift as the wind, she had galloped onward.

But the road was an unfortunate one, apparently, for Tom, since there were no turnings from it of any importance down which he could make his way.

The darkness, however, favoured him immensely.

The only lights that glimmered on the roadway after passing Tyburn Gate and the corner of the Edgware Road, were twinkling among the few houses which then constituted the little village of Bayswater, then composed altogether of about fifty houses.

The long, dull, dead wall, now removed, of Kensington Gardens, was to the left, and to the right, long market gardens, but no roadway or even lane down which Tom could make his way.

Still, a stern chase, as sailors have it, is a long chase; and Tom Ripon had not the slightest apprehension of being overtaken by Jonathan Wild.

It was no part, however, of Tom's intention on that night to be hunted far away into the country with the great thief-taker at his heels.

And so, as well as the darkness would permit him, he looked anxiously right and left for some spot where he could come to a halt and allow Wild to pass him.

Some large, overhanging trees from Kensington Gardens so completely overshadowed a portion of the road at one place, that the appearance it presented was most black and cavernous.

Tom heard the heavy beat of the horse's hoofs on the road behind him, and he knew that Wild was making as good progress as he could in pursuit.

He turned the head of Daisy towards this shadowy portion of the road, and brought her to a standstill, as he bent low in the saddle to escape any blow from the overhanging branches of the trees.

Tom then found that it was at a little iron gate he had paused, which was one of the entrances to the gardens from the Bayswater Road.

It was quite accident that made him lay his hand on this gate.

He was surprised to find it yield to his touch.

"Capital!" said Tom. "This is the very thing!"

He dismounted immediately, and pushed the gate open.

"Come on, Daisy."

She followed him with all the docility of a dog.

"Now," added Tom, "if Jonathan don't find the gate open as well as I, it's all right, and he'll either go blundering on, or give the affair up as a bad job, and take his way back to town."

The darkness was so excessive that it was impossible to see even the outline of the iron gate, but Tom ran his hand down the side of it, in the hope of finding some latch, or temporary means of fastening it.

His hand struck against a projection.

Tom uttered a sound of gratification.

It was a key, which, by some carelessness, had been left in the gate.

In another moment Tom had locked himself into Kensington Gardens, and felt that, for the time being, he was perfectly secure from Jonathan Wild.

Whether he was so in reality or not we shall presently see; but it is necessary that we should leave Tom for awhile, in order to accompany Felix Heron on that remarkable adventure, the first particulars of which he had ascertained at Holland House from no other lips than those of Lord Warringdale and the reprobate John Tarleton.

CHAPTER CCXXX.

FELIX HERON CONFIDES TO EDITH HIS PLAN FOR FRUSTRATING LORD WARRINGDALE'S AND JOHN TARLETON'S PLOT.

HAVING come to a decision with the concurrence of Edith, and by the advice of those friends who were near and dear to him, that the semblance of a marriage should take place between him and Edith in his assumed name of Captain Fantome, Felix Heron felt his mind more disengaged and at ease than it had been for some time.

He was determined to ferret out and discover, and if possible thwart, the mysterious schemes which Lord Warringdale and John Tarleton were concocting.

Whether those schemes concerned him or not, he had no exact means of saying.

But of one thing he felt assured.

That was, that there could be nothing but evil in any scheme or plan of operations whatever which was to be carried out by such persons.

Fortunately accident had provided him with the means of, at all events, attempting to make some discoveries in regard to the nefarious transactions which the nobleman who had come to Holland House was willing to pay so largely for.

Heron was specially anxious to discover who this person was who had been so "inadvertently" called your grace.

The title implied that he belonged to the highest nobility of the kingdom; and the price that he agreed to pay to John Tarleton and his rascally associates, was quite sufficient to prove that the business they were to be engaged upon was of a highly criminal and villanous character.

It was the good-will and pleasure of Felix Heron to do all in his power to foil these men in what they were about.

He held a long debate with himself whether to communicate to Edith or not the particulars of his adventure at Holland House.

Of course, the only point which made him pause in making that communication was that her brother, John Tarleton, made a reappearance in the midst of those mysterious circumstances, which would be sure to give pain to Edith.

The result, however, of the reflections of Heron was that Edith had better know all.

The hour of midnight was the one at which he had to go to the mysterious house near Pall Mall, at which, as he had overheard, four knocks, given with deliberation, would admit him.

It was eleven on that evening when Heron, with the hand of Edith in his own, communicated to her gently and kindly that John Tarleton still lived, and that, undeterred by the dangers and the retributions of the past, he was still engaged in villanous complications with Lord Warringdale.

Edith was deeply affected.

"Felix, Felix," she cried, "I know the thought is a foolish one, and you will blame me for it; but there is a kind of reflected disgrace upon me in consequence of these actions of one so nearly allied to me."

"It is a foolish thought, Edith; for what earthly power, or what earthly logic, can in any manner connect you to a single act or word of John Tarleton?"

"I feel and know that you are right, Felix; but still it is a grief."

"Granted that it is so; there is another reason why you should dismiss from your mind all such thoughts upon this subject."

"What is that, Felix?"

"Is not this man who calls himself Warringdale my brother; and is there anything that John Tarleton can do or conceive that can be worse than we have endured at the hands of Warringdale?"

"Alas, alas! it is so! But do not court danger, Felix, even for the sake of foiling and confounding these men! Let those whom they are about to assail by fraud or by violence find their natural protectors!"

"I have thought of that, Edith, and what I am about to say in reply to it will sound to you superstitious."

"No, Felix, for I know that that is not your nature."

"Then I cannot help thinking that Providence threw me in the way of acquiring the knowledge I have of their proceedings, in order that I might follow up the clue so obtained, and protect those perhaps unable to protect themselves from some terrible complication of disasters."

"I cannot combat such a feeling as that."

"Nor can I, Edith. It clings to me."

"Then I can only say go, Felix, and heaven go with you! It is some satisfaction to me to know that in carrying out this adventure you are close at hand, and I am sure that for my sake, as well as for the sake of that other one who is so dear to both of us, you will be careful and mindful of your safety."

"In truth, I will, Edith. The impetuosity which marked my early career has passed away. I feel that I have given hostages to fortune now, and will be as careful of myself as you could wish me."

Felix Heron by no means regretted that he had made this confidence with Edith, and he went about the adventure with a lighter heart.

Upon consideration, he determined to go in his assumed character of Captain Fantome.

He made himself up most carefully.

Arming himself with a pair of pistols, and a short hanger, he wrapped about him a dark brown roquelaire cloak, and putting on a hat destitute of ornament or trimming, he started on his enterprise.

It wanted ten minutes to twelve o'clock when he left Whitcombe House.

The description of the mansion to which he was to make his way, had been quite sufficiently explicit and distinct to afford no chance of missing it.

Heron passed the gate of old St. James's Palace, and, pacing slowly onward, he soon reached the house with the identical blinds which had been described as that to which John Tarleton was to make his way, to be possessed with the particulars of the special villany he was to be paid so largely for engaging in.

Felix Heron could not but feel he ran a risk, even of his life, on the very threshold of this adventure.

But that did not deter him.

He stood upon the doorstep.

He placed his hand on the knocker.

And then he paused for a few seconds while he counted the strokes indicating twelve o'clock, as they pealed forth from the old turret of St. James's Palace.

The period of action had arrived.

Felix Heron raised the knocker, and was on the point of executing one of those raps, four of which would make up the preconcerted signal, when a shadowy looking figure passed directly over from the other side of the way, and stepped on to the doorstep by his side.

A glance at this figure sufficed to assure Felix Heron that it was not his half brother, Lord Warringdale.

But he was by no means so certain that it was not John Tarleton.

The new arrival spoke, and then Felix Heron was aware that whoever he was, he was a perfect stranger to him, and that he was in all probability one of the ruffians who had been present with John Tarleton at Holland House.

Heron did not speak, but the new arrival questioned him.

"I suppose it's you, Quiver?"

For a few seconds Heron hesitated what to do, and then a sudden impulse came over him, and with one well-directed blow he sent this man prostrate into the kenel, where he lay in a state of semi-insensibility.

Heron then dragged him by his shoulders into a neigbouring doorway, and there left him.

His idea was just this.

Probably four persons were expected.

That is to say, Lord Warringdale, John Tarleton, and the two ruffianly fellows who had been drinking with the latter at Holland House.

Under the circumstances, the arrival of a fifth person would be sure to create the greatest amount of suspicion; but as one was now, at all events, temporally disposed of, Heron thought there would be a good chance of his coming at the heart of the mystery without discovery.

There was one reflection, however, which gave him some uneasiness.

He feared that after he had knocked at the door, some watch-word might be necessary in order to ensure undisputed admittance.

But, as in all such adventurous circumstances as the present something must be risked, he did not allow that consideration to stop his progress.

One—two—three—four!

He knocked four times clearly and distinctly.

The door was immediately opened.

"You are one?" said a voice.

"I am," replied Heron at random.

He took care as he spoke to keep his hand upon the butt of a pistol; but there was no occasion for any such precaution.

"You come from Holland House?" added the voice.

"I do."

"Come in, and turn to the left when you get to the end of the passage."

The door was immediately closed behind him, and the passage was in intense darkness.

It was rather a nervous thing to traverse a long gloomy avenue like that without having the least idea of where it led to, and with some suspicions that the pathway itself might be of a treacherous character.

But Heron did not hesitate.

He slowly advanced, and had proceeded about six paces, when four more distinct blows at the knocker of the door proclaimed the arrival of some other visitor in pursuance of the instructions given at Holland House.

Heron paused.

Some one passed him swiftly, brushing against him in the narrow passage.

The door was opened.

"A light!" cried the new visitor. "I enter no such place as this unless I see my way! A light, I say!"

The voice was that of Lord Warringdale.

"Wait there a moment," said the man who opened the door; "wait a moment, and I will light my lantern."

Felix Heron drew his hat farther down upon his brow, and muffled up the lower part of his face closely in his roquelaire cloak.

Lord Warringdale, with the natural timidity belonging to him, would not cross the threshold of the house until he saw the glimmer of the porter's lantern.

Assuming, then, a swaggering air of audacity, he strolled in, speaking as he came.

"Who has arrived?" he asked.

"One," replied the porter.

"Oh! Is it Deuce Ace?"

"No, my lord," replied Felix Heron, in so capitally assumed a voice, and in tones so strangely different from his own, that Warringdale could not have the least suspicion of who he really was.

"Oh, then, you are one of those worthy gentlemen who were making so free with the bottle at Holland House?"

"My lord," said Heron, still speaking in the same assumed voice, "I like my glass, and my lass, and a jolly companion!"

"Oh, no doubt—no doubt!" laughed Warringdale. "Ah! there is another!"

Bang! bang! came four more knocks at the door, and while it was being opened Felix Heron took the opportunity of obeying the instructions which had previously been given to him of going to the extreme end of the passage and then turning to the left.

He pushed open a door covered with green baize, and found himself in a large and what might have been a handsome room, but that it was in a state of great dilapidation and decay.

A table of unusually large dimensions occupied its centre.

On this table was a small hand-lantern, the blinding slide of which was partially withdrawn, so that one half of the room was dimly lighted while the other half remained almost in perfect obscurity.

Felix Heron preferred to take up his station in the darkest portion of this apartment.

He had hardly done so when the green baize door was flung open, and three persons entered.

Two were conversing, and preceded the third, who followed them with a show and appearance of respect.

Heron had no difficulty in at once detecting, by their voices, that the two who were conversing were Lord Warringdale and John Tarleton.

The third person was, without doubt, the companion of the man who had been so summarily disposed of by Felix Heron on the doorstep of the mysterious house, in an apartment of which he now found himself.

"Of course, my lord, of course," said John Tarleton; "there can be no difficulties in the matter, and I think from the few hints you have given me I fully comprehend it."

"Do not say I give you hints," remarked Warringdale: "it is not for me to explain what you and your two comrades have to do. That you will hear from another person."

"All's well, then; but I am inclined to think——"

"Hush! think nothing, but keep all your faculties about you for what you will have to listen to."

The third man, who was the subordinate, seemed quite delighted to see Felix Heron, who in the dark he no doubt took for his companion in iniquity.

He stepped up to him at once.

"That's you, Rufus?" he said.

"Yes; be quiet!" replied Heron, in a low tone.

"Oh, all's right!—but how odd you speak!"

"A cold."

"Ah! I told you you'd catch it. You would sleep out in the garden, to keep your head cool, you said, and now you see you can hardly speak."

"Silence!" cried Lord Warringdale; "you come here to listen, not to speak."

A door at the further end of the room, where the principal light fell from the lantern, was abruptly opened, and a man stepped in.

The man was masked.

He spoke in a hollow, strange voice, that was evidently assumed.

But, notwithstanding that assumption, Felix Heron felt perfectly sure that the voice was the same as that of the man who had been called "his grace" so inadvertently at Holland House.

He commenced speaking abruptly.

"Since you are all here, gentlemen," he said, "it is only necessary that I should explain to you, without descending to minute particulars, the sort of service that is required of you."

"Ay, ay! that's it," whispered the man who stood next to Heron in his ear.

"Be quiet, Quiver," said Heron, in as low a tone, and making a good guess that that was the very personage for who he himself had been mistaken on the doorstep.

"Silence!" cried Lord Warringdale, in an angry tone.

The individual with the mask continued.

"The service that you will be called upon to perform is easy if it be conducted with boldness and address; and for the exercise of those two qualities, the reward, you may depend, will be commensurate."

"A high reward—a high reward!" said John Tarleton. "I call the reward which has already been mentioned munificent—that is to say as regards you two, Rufus and Quiver."

"What are we to get?" said Quiver, sulkily.

"Fifty guineas each," said the man with the mask, "on each occasion that your services are required."

"And what are we to do?"

"Simply this. A certain person will be pointed out to you in the streets of London, whom it will be your duty never to lose sight of if possible, but to follow about from place to place, house to house, and street to street, accompanied as you will be by either a sedan chair or a hackney coach; and then at some opportune moment, in some bye place, where no human eyes can scan your conduct, you are to seize this person, blindfold them, gag them, and convey them in safety and secrecy to this house."

"In the open daylight?" asked Quiver.

"Probably."

"Humph!"

"You are at liberty to retire at once from the task; and there is no doubt that some one will be found who will gladly take your place."

"Rufus!"

"Well, Quiver?" replied Heron.

"What do you say?"

"I'll do it?"

"Well, then, so will I."

The man with the mask spoke again, and as he did so he pointed to John Tarleton.

"This gentleman will point out to you the particular person whom you are to seize."

He then pointed to Lord Warringdale, and added, "And this gentleman will always be near at hand to superintend the proceedings, and to lend you any assistance, either with his purse or with his sword, as may be required."

"Certainly!" said Lord Warringdale.

Quiver then asked a question which was quite uppermost on the lips of Felix Heron.

"When do we begin?" he said.

"To-morrow morning!" replied the man with the mask; and even as he spoke he turned and abruptly left the apartment, casting upon all the persons within it a glance of supercilious haughtiness that was absolutely insulting.

Lord Warringdale then strode to the door at which he had entered, and imitating pretty accurately the manner of the personage who had just left, he, too, strode out, leaving the others behind him as though they were beneath his notice.

He said something, however, in a few words, to John Tarleton, who, turning round, repeated them to Quiver and the supposed Rufus.

"You will both of you be at the railings of King Charles's statue, at Charing Cross, to-morrow morning, at one o'clock."

"All's right!" said Quiver.

John Tarleton then left the room.

"Well, Rufus," said Quiver, "it seems to me we'd better go, too. What do you say to something to drink? There's the 'Magpie and Stump,' down by Hungerford—as good a house as we can go to."

"I'll follow you there in half an hour," said Heron.

"All's right—all's right! But you don't seem half like yourself to-night, Rufus; and if I didn't know you so well as I do, I seem as if I should hardly know you at all."

While this brief dialogue was going on, Felix Heron and Quiver had reached the street door of the house.

It was a great object with Heron to get rid of his companion as quickly, now, as possible; and it was a great relief to him when Quiver strode off, crying out, as he did so, "Don't be long, and I'll have a good jorum of punch brewed by the time you get there."

"Good!" said Heron. "That will do!"

As soon as Quiver was out of sight, Heron darted off to the doorway where he had left the man who, no doubt, was the genuine Rufus, whose name he, Heron, had so successfully assumed.

CHAPTER CCXXXI.

FELIX HERON MAKES A PRISONER AND A COMPACT.

THE man lay just where Heron had left him.

Probably, in his fall, he had struck his head against the pavement, which had done more to confuse his faculties than the blow which Heron had given him.

It was not likely, however, that he was much hurt; and Heron at once raised him to his feet, holding him up with a strong arm, as he spoke to him.

"What's the matter?" he said. "Who and what are you, and what has happened to you?"

Heron asked these questions in order to ascertain the mental condition of the fellow, and to enable him to come to some conclusion in regard to his state.

"I don't know—I scarcely know," replied Rufus. "I rather think somebody knocked me down, or else I've had a drop too much."

"Oh, indeed!"

"Are you the watch?"

"No; I am a gentleman."

"Oh! that's a comfort! Just look out for a doorway here where there's some blinds in the window of the house, of—of—what the plague is the colour? I suppose my brains are wool-gathering still."

"I fancy I know the house you want," said Heron, "and can lead you to it."

"Can you? That's the very thing I want, and you're the very best friend I've got."

"Can you walk?"

"Oh, yes, I think so."

"Try."

Quiver did try but he staggered against the railings, and it was evident he had not the power to proceed.

This was just what Felix Heron wanted.

"Take my arm," he said, "and I will lead you where you want to go. I happen to know all about it."

"Do you? Perhaps you're one of the gentlemen themselves?"

"To be sure I am; and we want your services, Quiver."

"Ah! you know my name too?"

"I named you in order that you might have confidence in me. Come on—this is the way; you need give yourself no trouble, and can lean on me as heavily as you like."

Quiver, in his confused condition, was quite pleased to meet with such a guide and support; and leaning heavily, as he had been told, upon the arm of Felix Heron, he allowed himself, without the least suspicion of where he was really going, to be led across the road into St. James's Street, and to the door of Whitcombe House.

Felix Heron had made up his mind to take this man home, and by fair means or foul, make use of him as a means of aiding in the discovery and frustration of the villanies contemplated by "his grace," aided by Lord Warringdale and John Tarleton.

"Is this the place?" said Quiver, in a confused manner.

"Yes," replied Heron, as he knocked sharply at the door of Whitcombe House.

Ogle, who knew Heron's knock perfectly well, replied to the summons.

"Take this man, Ogle," said Heron. "Treat him well, but on no account allow him to leave Whitcombe House."

"Certainly, Captain."

With a bewildered look, Mr. Quiver allowed himself to be conducted over the threshold of the family mansion of the Whitcombes.

"Is he wounded, Captain?" asked Ogle.

He had seen that something was amiss with the person who came with Captain Heron.

"No; he is hurt, but not much. Look to him well; I shall want to speak to him to-morrow."

The hour was now about one in the morning, and as Felix Heron went up-stairs rapidly, he met Edith, who had been anxiously waiting for him.

She had in her hand an open letter.

A smile was on her face.

"You have heard good news, Edith," said

Heron, as he reflected on his own face the smile that lit up hers.

"It is always good news to hear your voice, Felix; but you allude to this letter. It is from our good and kind friend, the Earl of Bridgewater."

"Then, Edith, I guess its import."

"Yes; it relates to our marriage."

Felix Heron, on reaching that suite of rooms on the second floor of Whitcombe House which was especiallly devoted to the domestic privacy of himself and Edith, read the letter.

It ran as follows:—

"MY DEAR WHITCOMBE,—

"All is arranged. I have procured a license, without the slightest difficulty, for the union of George Fantome, a captain in his Majesty's navy, with Edith, Countess of Whitcombe."

"A young brother of Colonel Trelawney's,

EDITH.—No. 73.

who is studying at Oxford, but who happens to be in town at present, will perform the ceremony, so that the scruples of Lady Whitcombe on that point will be properly met.

"You and Edith—and, probably, you will bring Lady Castleneau with you—should be at the little old church at Willesden at eleven o'clock.

"The village is so small, and so quiet, and the place so rarely visited, that we need fear no interruption.

"The rector, who performs the service twice each Sunday, fortunately resides some eight or ten miles off, and is not at all likely to make his appearance.

"Be punctual, and believe me,

"Ever your sincere friend,

"BRIDGEWATER."

"Then, Edith," said Heron, "these new nuptials take place to-morrow"

"Yes, Felix: and I do hope from my heart that there will be no longer any occasion for a further disguise than that which you have now assumed as Captain Fantome of the royal navy. But you are thoughtful. Does the sense of any danger oppress you?"

"No, Edith; but I was thinking of how soon I could get to town after the ceremony to-morrow; for I have an appointment at one o'clock, at King Charles's statue, Charing Cross."

Felix Heron then detailed to Edith all that had passed at the mysterious house close to St. James's Palace.

But they could neither of them come to any definite conclusion in regard to what was really meant by the whole proceedings.

That some person or persons were to be kidnapped in the streets of London was but too apparent; but who they were, and for what purpose this encroachment on public liberty was to take place, they could not divine.

Speculation on such a point was useless; and Felix Heron, therefore, put off the subject until the morning, when he intended to submit the man Quiver to the test of a severe cross-examination.

It was very doubtful, though, if he knew anything more about it than Heron himself.

At an early hour, then, on that following morning Heron met Ogle in the hall of the mansion, and was conducted by him to a strong room in Whitcombe House, which was originally constructed for the purpose of holding the deeds and muniments of the family.

"Here's the prisoner, Captain," said Ogle. "I have given him some breakfast, and he's quite lively this morning."

"That is well."

Ogle opened the iron door of the muniment-room, and exhibited Mr. Quiver enjoying an excellent morning repast.

At the sight of Heron, however, he rose, looking somewhat confused and apprehensive.

There was that in the appearance of Felix Heron, which always at once bespoke the gentleman, and commanded respect.

Ogle was about to leave the room but Heron made him a sign to remain.

Bending, then, a stern glance upon the prisoner, he spoke in tones of calm deliberation, which had a much more terrible significance than as if he had imported any passion into them.

"Your name is Quiver," he said, "and I am quite well aware that you are associated with three men in carrying out an enterprise which will bring them probably to the gallows, and you along with them."

"Three men!" said Quiver, in doubtful tones.

"Yes. Is it necessary that I should name them to you? for, if so, I will do it. One of them is a low fellow, of no account, like yourself, and his name is Rufus. The other two call themselves respectively Warringdale and Deuce Ace."

Mr. Quiver could have no longer any doubt but that the personage who was speaking to him was well informed.

"You and your companion, Rufus," added Heron, "are promised fifty guineas each for assisting in a piece of work which is to be done in the streets of London."

"That's true, sir."

"That piece of work will be discovered, and, as I have said already, bring you all to the gallows."

"If I thought that, sir, I'd have nothing to do with it, for I'm about as careful of my neck as most men."

"You can do better than be careful of your neck by having nothing to say to this transaction."

"Indeed, sir!"

"Yes. You shall receive from me the same amount of money that would have brought you into danger, difficulty, and death, and with it you shall have safety and consideration."

"Is this possible?"

"Yes; think of it. I will speak to you again in a few hours; in the meantime remain here as my prisoner—not to be treated with severity, but for your own safety's sake, and because it is absolutely necessary you should do so."

Felix Heron did not wait for any further parley with Mr. Quiver, but at once left the muniment-room.

Ogle followed him, and carefully relocked the door.

"I am still to look close after him, Captain?"

"Most certainly! But now I come to look at him in daylight, I do not altogether so much dislike his looks. Nevertheless, be careful of him, for I am sorry to say I have lived long enough in the world not to trust altogether to appearances."

Felix Heron brought this interview with Quiver to a rapid conclusion, because he felt that there was little time to spare between that time and the period when he must start for Willesden, in order to contract the mock marriage of Captain Fantome with Edith.

He had to visit Lady Castleneau, and, if possible, bring her with him.

On foot, then, and carefully disguised still as Captain Fantome, Heron rapidly walked towards Bloomsbury.

He was quite aware, though, after leaving St. James's Street, that he was dogged by a man who had been leaning against a post.

That this was one of Jonathan Wild's emissaries, Felix Heron did not entertain a doubt.

But he thought it far better to take no notice of him.

Secure in his disguise, which, if it baffled the acute eyes of Jonathan Wild himself, might well be considered as proof against the scrutiny of any of his janissaries or bull-dogs, Heron took his way rapidly towards Castleneau House.

The ancient gentlewoman was of course at home, and only too happy to see Heron, whom she looked upon with all the confidence and affection as though he had been a child of her own.

With her characteristic energy, Lady Castleneau at once entered into the spirit of the day's proceedings.

Old Anthony was summoned to get out that remarkably ancient carriage, which no doubt was the pink of fashion half a century before.

The old lady herself made her appearance in one of those stiff old brocade gowns, which certainly, without exaggeration, would have stood up of itself, if required to do so.

Edith was ready and waiting at Whitcombe

House; and within another hour, as the three quarters past ten o'clock sounded lightly upon the morning air, chimed forth from various village steeples in the verdant neighbourhood of Willesden, the little party arrived at the church.

At the porch appeared the Earl of Bridgewater, with Lady Bridgewater.

Colonel Trelawney and his sister were likewise there.

The young man from Oxford, looking quite clerical enough for the occasion, was holding what looked like a very confidential discourse with the sexton.

The whole party entered the church at once.

A few of the villagers hastened to the door of the sacred edifice to see what was going on.

And then, as the sun shone brightly through the little gothic windows, the mock marriage ceremony was hastily concluded.

It seemed strange indeed to Edith to be standing there at the altar along with Felix Heron again, to whom she had already been a wife for some years.

"Mine again, my beloved!" whispered Heron, as he tenderly drew Edith's hand through his arm.

"Yes, Felix—but I feel as though I had been committing some crime in even allowing myself to be married to Captain Fantome—I who could never bear the thought of——"

"Hush, dear child!" interrupted Lady Castlenean. "Think no more of it! It was necessary, both for your safety and comfort, to give Felix the right to be always near you!"

"Exactly!" replied Bridgewater. "A truce to regrets! Let us hope that from this day will date a period of much happiness to you both! But now let us leave this sacred building; the sooner we can get clear of the village now the better."

"Yes," said Felix; "and I, too, have an important appointment, which will now occupy my time for some few hours. Let us hasten to town, dearest!" he added, turning to Edith.

At this moment Edith gave a start, and turned deathly pale as she clung to the arm of Felix for support.

"What is it, my Edith?" asked Heron, as he cast his eyes in the same direction, and saw, glaring through one of the gothic windows at the upper portion of the church, the hideous countenance of Jonathan Wild!

CHAPTER CCXXXII.

JONATHAN WILD GIVES EDITH A WORD OF ADVICE.

FOR a few seconds the eyes of all the little party in that venerable suburban edifice, which for more than five hundred years had been devoted to heaven, were fixed upon the face of Wild.

Amid the quietude of the scene, and the ecclesiastical serenity of the little church, that hideous countenance, which seemed a complete map of every human passion which could deform and degrade humanity, was the one blot and marring influence which should not have been there.

"Jonathan Wild!" exclaimed Felix Heron.

It was well that he spoke in a low tone, for, at the moment, he was thrown off his guard, and did not assume the kind of voice which, with singular skill, he usually kept up in his character of Captain Fantome.

The name was repeated by every one

And Wild, making one of his hideous grimaces, seemed to be acknowledging, in that fashion, the sensation he had created.

With a blow of his fist he broke one of the diamond-shaped panes of glass in the little Gothic window.

But still the orifice was not quite sufficient for him to project his head and face through right into the church.

Another blow demolished the next pane, and likewise a portion of the leaden framework between them.

Then Wild was able to put his head right into the church.

In his harshest and most grating tones he spoke.

"Edith, Countess of Whitcombe, you disgrace yourself, and the memory of Felix Heron, by this marriage! If he could, but for one single hour, start up from his lonely grave, he would not recognise that Edith to whom he had clung so fondly while she leans upon the arm of Captain Fantome; having been, by the force of circumstances, only recently separated from the Baron Von Peck!"

No doubt Jonathan Wild thought this a very severe speech.

It was Colonel Trelawney who replied to it.

"You scoundrel!" he cried out; "how dare you interfere with what does not concern you? I will speak to the Secretary of State, and have your staff and constable's warrant taken away from you!"

"Try it!" said Wild, as he smashed another pane of glass,—"try it; and you may discover that Jonathan Wild can do better without the Secretary of State than the Secretary of State without Jonathan Wild! It is to you, Edith, Countess of Whitcombe, I speak, and not to any of the jackdaw friends about you!"

"I desire to hear nothing," said Edith. "You may mean well, Jonathan Wild; and if you do, the best way to show it is, not to interfere with my actions!"

"Perhaps you think so; but I have a proposition to make, and I have taken some trouble to climb up here to make it!"

Heron was about to speak, but he was checked by Edith, who touched him lightly on the arm, whispering, as she did so, "Say nothing; it will be better. I cannot but feel that I owe this man, bad as he is, a certain kind of respect on this occasion."

"Look here, Edith, Countess of Whitcombe," added Wild—"look here, and listen to me. You have a son—the son of Felix Heron—son of a brave and gallant father. Captain Fantome won't like him—step-fathers never do—and he won't like Captain Fantome. Now, give the boy to me, and I'll take care of him, and bring him up respectably."

"Villain!" cried Felix Heron.

"Ha, ha!"

"Hush—oh, hush!" said Edith. "No, Jonathan Wild; if you have the slightest regard for me, or teeling for the child of Felix Heron, you will not indulge in these insulting propositions."

Edith did not wait for a reply from Wild, but taking the arm of Felix Heron, she hastily left the church, accompanied by the whole of the little party.

A few paces from the door there was a horse with its bridle attached to a cross surmounting a tomb.

That horse had evidently been ridden hard, for there was foam upon its coat, and there could be no doubt that it was the steed that had brought Jonathan Wild down to Willesden.

Before the wedding party could get well clear of the porch of the church, Wild appeared.

"Farewell!" he cried. "Farewell, Edith, Countess of Whitcombe. I pity as well as blame you. And as for you, Captain Fantome, you may be quite sure that I shall keep an eye on your movements, so look to yourself."

"Wreck me on a lee shore," said Heron, "if I'm not half inclined to put an end to your movements at once, for this impertinent interference in my affairs."

"Ha, ha!" laughed Wild, as he sprung to the back of his horse. "We shall see—we shall see; and those that live the longest will see the most."

Wild once more bent a glance of anger at the whole party, and then galloped off.

"We shall never see the last of that fellow," said the Earl of Bridgewater.

"Until he is hanged," remarked Colonel Trelawney; "which I am quite sure will be his fate, for he has already become notorious for dealing in stolen goods, and compounding felonies. The rascal is a disgrace to the age in which we live; and when he is once disposed of, were the world to last another twenty thousand years, society will not again look upon such a man as Jonathan Wild."

The Earl of Bridgewater had brought down his own carriage, which was at a little inn on Willesden Green, so that three quarters of an hour more sufficed to bring them all back to Whitcombe House, where Captain Heron, in his assumed name of Captain Fantome, intended openly to show himself as its proprietor and master.

It was half-past twelve o'clock, however, so that he had little time to spare before attending to the mysterious appointment at King Charles's statue.

It was necessary, however, before proceeding on that errand, that Felix Heron should have another interview with the man Quiver, who was still a prisoner at Whitcombe House.

That this man was in the possession of valuable information, although he professed to know so little of the enterprise in which he was engaged, Felix Heron had a strong suspicion.

He summoned Ogle, and procured from him the key of the muniment-room.

"I will visit this man myself," he said; "there are some people who will speak out more freely to one person than to two."

"Keep a bright look-out, Captain," said Ogle; "these kind of fellows are not to be trusted."

"Be assured of that, Ogle. My interview with him must likewise be a brief one, for I am engaged at one o'clock, and would not be late on any consideration."

There was a small grating in the door of the muniment-room, by which air could be admitted to it by sliding back a panel about the size of a man's hand, that covered it.

Very carefully—for he heard no sound within the room—Felix Heron removed this panel.

He looked in at his prisoner.

The man was seated at the only table in the place, resting his head upon his hands in a disconsolate attitude.

He seemed to be in a state of affliction.

Deep sighs came from his labouring breast.

Heron, by placing his ear to the little grating, could just detect the words he uttered.

"All lost—all lost!" he said. "A youth of frivolity, devoted to false pleasure; a manhood of disgrace; and after that what have I to look forward to?"

Heron was well pleased to find his prisoner in this frame of mind.

He opened the door of the muniment-room, and entered at once.

The man started to his feet, and looked as if he anticipated some immediate danger, but Felix Heron quickly calmed him on that score.

"It is not too late," he said; "the opportunity still presents itself to you of changing your mode of life, and of inaugurating a new career, by an act which will go far towards obliterating the past."

"Who and what are you?"

"I am, as far as you are concerned, Captain Fantome; what I may further be, it will depend upon your conduct for you to learn."

"But what do your words imply? Those words, I mean, which I have just now heard you utter?"

"Take them at their full meaning," replied Felix Heron, "and I will find a means of carrying them out for you into action."

"Is it possible," said Quiver, "that the opportunity presents itself to me of once more retracing the fearful path I have trodden so long, and seek another of peace and serenity?"

"It is possible! You have but to be sincere with me—and let me tell you, it will be somewhat dangerous to be otherwise—and all may yet be well with you."

"Direct me what I have to do," replied Quiver, with fervour, "and I will most assuredly do it."

"There is an appointment, then, at the statue of King Charles, at Charing Cross?"

"There is. I recollect it now; but my brain has been somewhat confused."

Felix Heron did not care at that precise moment to explain to Quiver that that confusion of the brain arose principally from the knockdown blow he had given him.

"It is sufficient that you recollect the appointment," he said. "It is for one o'clock, and that hour rapidly approaches."

"Yes, one was the hour."

Heron was well enough pleased to see that Quiver had sufficiently recovered his senses fully to recollect the appointment, as well as the precise hour at which it was to come off.

"Listen to me, now," he said. "I am perfectly aware that some unexampled piece of villany is in agitation."

"And I, too."

"Give me, then, a test of your sincerity by explaining what it is?"

CAPTAIN FANTOME KEEPS A WATCH ON THE MYSTERIOUS PROCEEDINGS
OF THE CONSPIRATORS.

Presented Gratis with No. 73, of the New Edition of EDITH FITON, the Sequel to Edith the Captive; or, the Robbers of Epping Forest.

"I cannot, for I do not know; Lord Warringdale and the man who calls himself Deuce Ace, no doubt, know all about it; but Rufus and I, who are merely considered as paid underlings, know nothing of the particulars."

"I will believe you."

"You may, sir, for I speak the truth."

"Go, and keep your appointment, then. I shall be there, likewise; but I shall keep myself sufficiently far off, that while I do not absolutely lose sight of you and your party, they will not suspect that I am watching them. If I see cause for interference, I shall interfere; but if not, I require that you come back to this house, and bring me such particulars of what is intended as you can gather."

"I will. I swear it!"

"I am better contented with your mere assurance than with your oath."

It wanted but six or seven minutes to one o'clock; but the distance from Whitcombe House to Charing Cross was so short, that it could easily be passed over in that period of time.

Heron took one side of the way and Quiver the other.

Heron hid himself in a doorway, and he saw his late prisoner join a man who, doubtless, was Rufus, and who was leaning against the railings which were then around the base of the statue.

From the direction of Whitehall two figures approached.

Felix Heron had no difficulty in recognising them as Lord Warringdale and John Tarleton.

They joined the two men at the base of the statue.

The whole four stood closely together for a few seconds, discoursing with great earnestness.

Their conduct then became most mysterious.

John Tarleton went up to the stand of hackney-coaches close to Northumberland House, and brought back to the immediate vicinity of the statue one of those old lumbering vehicles, with its driver and its two worn-out wretched horses.

Some proposition was evidently made to the driver of the coach, which, for some reasons, he strenuously objected to.

Then Felix Heron, who was particularly sharp-sighted, saw Lord Warringdale slip some pieces of gold into his hand.

Those powerful arguments removed the man's scruples in regard to what was proposed to him, and gathering his coat of many capes about him, he left his coach and horses in the hands of the party by the statue, and crossed over the way to the neighbourhood of Hungerford, where, no doubt, in some one of the numerous public-houses of that locality, he intended to enjoy himself until his coach was brought back.

John Tarleton mounted the coach-box.

Lord Warringdale walked on some distance in advance, up the Strand.

Rufus and Quiver strolled along just a few paces in advance of the vehicle, as if they had nothing whatever to do with it.

What could this mean?

What mystery was enshrouded in all these proceedings?

Heron was puzzled.

But he was determined that that bewilderment should not last longer than necessary, and he carefully followed the coach.

It was quite evident that Lord Warringdale was the guide of the whole proceeding.

Rufus and Quiver kept their eyes upon him as the person whom they were to follow.

And John Tarleton with the coach brought up the rear.

The feelings of the parties, however, engaged in that nefarious transaction would probably have been of a very different character from what they were, could they have suspected for a moment that the well-known Captain Felix Heron, Earl of Whitcombe, was actually on their track.

Warringdale turned up a by-street in the Strand, which led towards the neighbourhood of Covent Garden.

Rufus Quiver and the coach followed him.

And Heron followed them.

Warringdale made a signal.

The coach stopped.

Rufus and Quiver hid themselves on the side of it, nearest to the pavement on the side where they were.

Lord Warringdale then paced slowly down the street, and as he did so, he cast his eyes up at a particular house.

The house was evidently some place of business, and by some patterns that hung in the window, Heron considered it to be a dressmaker's.

A small fruiterer's shop was immediately opposite; and into that, without exciting any observation, Heron made his way.

He purchased some fruit, and affecting to eat it, he looked through the window carefully.

The station he occupied was an excellent one for observing the whole proceedings of Lord Warringdale and his party.

And to tell the truth, those proceedings were singular enough.

It was now half-past one o'clock, and scarcely had the hour been pealed forth by the ancient church of St. Paul's, Covent Garden, which preceded by many years the present structure, when the door of the house towards which Lord Warringdale had cast several observant glances opened.

Two young girls came forth.

Heron thought that now something was about to happen which would let him into the heart of the mystery.

But he was disappointed.

Not the slightest notice was taken of these girls by Lord Warringdale and his associates.

Then several more young women, all evidently belonging to the class of workers for their daily bread, came out of that house.

They went to the right or to the left, as their different routes required, and Heron came to the the not unnatural conclusion that this was the dinner-hour of a number of young women whose place of work was within that house.

But without the slightest molestation, and only the merest passing regard, Lord Warringdale, as he passed to and fro, let them all disappear.

The door opened again.

One young girl came forth.

Heron involuntarily sprung to his feet.

He felt quite certain that now he began to understand what was intended.

This young girl was plainly attired, and her

general appearance betokened that painful struggle with poverty which respectability and fallen fortunes have so often to make.

But no plainness of attire.

No shabby or well-worn garments.

Not even the old cloak she wore, darned in many places, could conceal the native grace and beauty of this girl.

A few wandering locks of beautiful hair escaped from her head-dress, resting like sunlight upon her neck and shoulders.

Heron told himself at once that this was the girl sought by Lord Warringdale, in the interest of his infamous employers, of that mysterious house near St. James's Palace, and he determined to act accordingly, and to thwart their designs, let them be what they might.

CHAPTER CCXXXIII.

THE CONSPIRATORS MEET WITH AN OBSTACLE AND A CANE.

It needed not that Heron should observe the prompt signal made by Lord Warringdale to John Tarleton, and the two men Rufus and Quiver to convince him that he was perfectly correct in his conjectures.

From the moment that that young girl appeared it seemed to him as if a cloud or filmy vapour had been suddenly dashed aside from before the whole proceedings, and he understood their scope and import perfectly.

This young girl had excited the admiration, no doubt, of the person called "his Grace;" and the duty of Warringdale, John Tarleton, and their two associates was to seize her, even in the public streets of London, and convey her to the house by the Palace.

Little did she know her danger.

As little, too, did she know her safety.

How could she suspect that four men were intently watching her, leagued together for her destruction?

And how could she suspect that there was a fifth man, of whose eventful life and history she might probably have heard something, who was as determined to save her?

But such was the case.

This young creature paused for a few seconds on the doorstep, and looked about her.

It seemed as if she enjoyed the sight of the open daylight, and was grateful that she could breathe the free air of heaven, even for a short time, unrestrained by labour.

She looked upward.

She seemed to be watching for a few seconds the fleecy vapours that careered over the sky.

And as she so looked upward, Felix Heron had an opportunity of seeing her face well.

It was very beautiful.

It was one of those faces that carry with them a charming childlike look, as though under no circumstances whatever could the purity and innocence of the soul within be really soiled or destroyed.

The sympathies of Heron were strongly excited, and more than ever was he convinced that it was not all accident that had taken him to Holland House, and enabled him to overhear so much of the plot in progress as had brought him to the spot he now occupied, to foil it and protect the innocent.

Then the young girl stepped lightly down from the steps of the house to the pavement.

She drew her old faded cloak more closely around her.

Heron was too far off to hear it, but he fancied he could see by her actions that a sigh was on her lips.

Some painful thought may have crossed her mind.

Perhaps she was hastening home with the scant earnings of her hard toil to some near and dear to her, who depended even upon her exertions for support.

Warringdale made another sign.

He followed the girl.

The coach moved on.

Rufus and Quiver kept close to it; and, little suspecting that such a cavalcade was at her heels, this fair young creature went lightly, though sadly, on her way.

Felix Heron only paused for a few seconds, and then he left the fruit shop.

On the other side of the way to that which was occupied by Lord Warringdale he paced slowly along.

But he kept a sufficient distance not to give the villanous party any alarm; while at the same time he was not so far off but that at a bound or two he could have reached the scene of action.

The girl went on.

She turned down another street.

The whole party followed her.

And yet another turning was taken.

That led rather suddenly into a large open space, which Felix Heron recognised as Soho Square.

The houses even then in that square were dull and dreary-looking, and the place was silent and nearly deserted.

The girl crossed the square, and went down one of those long, narrow streets, the tall houses in which, no doubt once fashionable, had long since given up the idea of even keeping up appearances.

There was not a soul in that street.

Warringdale made another sign.

The coach went quicker.

Rufus and Quiver accelerated their pace.

He who was called Rufus even ran round the coach, and assumed a place upon the pavement of the street, about twenty paces in advance of the young girl.

A crisis seemed approaching.

Heron loosened his sword in its scabbard.

Warringdale went into a doorway, leaving his subordinates to carry out the special rascality on hand.

And all unconscious of danger, the girl went on her way.

She was within about four or five paces of Rufus, and Quiver was not much more than that distance behind her.

The coach stopped.

Felix Heron felt that the moment of action had come.

He was on the very point of crossing over the

way and actively interfering in the transaction, when the door of the house exactly opposite to where the young girl was opened, and an elderly gentleman, with a remarkably stout bamboo walking cane, came out.

This was exceedingly *mal apropos* for the conspirators who were so intent upon their capture.

The position of affairs, but for the seriousness of the circumstances, would have been perfectly ludicrous.

The coach had stopped.

Lord Warringdale was in hiding.

The man Rufus had one arm outstretched for the purpose of grasping the arm of the young girl.

Quiver occupied a similar attitude on the other side of her.

John Tarleton was bending down from the coach-box, looking pale and terrified, as his coward disposition shrunk from what was about to happen.

And last, although not least in the consideration of all these circumstances, there was Felix Heron, with his eyes placed upon the principal parties and his hand on the hilt of his sword, ready to dash forward at a moment's notice, and rescue the girl from her persecutors.

But he soon saw that there was no occasion for him to interfere.

The old gentleman who had emerged from the house was of an exceedingly irascible temperament.

He had that expression upon his face of being constantly in a passion, and on this occasion was quite delighted to encounter quickly circumstances which apparently called forth all his indignation.

The young girl could hardly be said to know her own danger; but she uttered a natural cry of alarm at finding herself so suddenly hemmed in and surrounded.

A coach on one side.

A house on the other.

A man before and a man behind her, each seemingly intent upon obstructing her progress, were circumstances which might well create an undefined alarm in the breast of this girl.

She cried out, then, for help.

Help from she knew not what.

But still from seeming danger.

The old gentleman was delighted.

Here was something that called for his interference.

Something that enabled him to be in as great a rage about as he pleased.

The thick walking-cane descended in a blow upon the back of Rufus, that sounded quite alarming.

Quiver came in for the next application.

"Rascals! thieves! vagabonds!" shouted the old gentleman, while his face from red became of a purple tinge, and he darted about on the pavement with extraordinary agility.

Nothing in the world would have been easier than for Quiver and Rufus at once to have got the better of their elderly assailant.

But that would have made a disturbance.

The mission they were on must be conducted with silence, secrecy, and despatch, unobserved by any human eye, or it must be for that time, at all events, abandoned.

The interference or the presence of a child would have been sufficient to protect the young girl from the abduction with which she was threatened.

From the doorway in which he was hidden, Lord Warringdale clapped his hands.

That was a preconcerted signal.

Rufus and Quiver scrambled up on to the coach.

John Tarleton urged the horses to speed by vigorous applications of the whip, and in a few seconds the vehicle had got clear of the narrow, dingy street, and had turned a corner.

The enterprise was frustrated, but Felix Heron scarcely knew whether to be pleased or otherwise, since it might be carried out on another occasion, when no one was present to interfere, and he himself might not be on the spot.

It was strange, then, to see these two men, Felix Heron and Lord Warringdale, half brothers as they were, left alone in that street.

The one knowing the other so well, but the other in utter ignorance of the proximity of the person whom he had injured so deeply.

Heron felt quite confident in his disguise, and walked slowly down the street, actually past Lord Warringdale.

Perhaps the look that Heron was enabled to give his half-brother on that occasion was the most steady and observant one that he had cast upon him for years.

He saw the ravages that crime and dissipation had made on his countenance.

He saw the shifting eyes and the twitching muscles of that face, which was constantly the index of some hidden fears.

And Heron felt tempted to speak to him.

He even paused for a moment, and half opened his lips.

But he resisted the impulse.

He passed on.

Of all men living, was he to entrust Warringdale with the secret of his identity, so carefully kept from all the world beside?

They passed each other, and Heron made the best of his way back to Whitcombe House.

He fully expected that Quiver would make his appearance shortly; nor was he disappointed, for in the course of an hour after he had returned home, Ogle came to him to say that Quiver had arrived.

At first glance of this man, now, Heron fancied that there was a peculiar look about his eyes that he ought to distrust.

But he did not allow that altogether to sway him, since he had no real reason for doubting his good faith.

"Well, sir," said Quiver, "I suppose we now know all about it?"

"I fancy so."

"That young girl, you see, sir, is to be kidnapped quietly and silently, and taken to the house by the Palace."

"That is evident enough."

"Yes, sir; and you saw how it failed."

"I did; but I presume it will be tried again?"

"Oh, yes, sir, to-morrow, at the same hour. The girl works at the house she came out of. She is very poor, and an artificial flower-maker. She goes home to dinner between one and two;

and it was thought she might be easily nabbed in some bye-street about Soho."

"And what is further arranged?"

"It's to be tried again to-morrow, sir."

"At the same hour?"

"Oh, no; an attempt will be made when she leaves work at night. It will be dark then, and all the safer and easier, they think."

"For those substantial reasons, then," asked Felix Heron, "why was the attempt of to-day made in daylight?"

"That's just what I asked Rufus, sir, and he said it was because she was quite certain to come out between one and two in the day; but when she left work in the evening it might be any time between eight and ten, or even eleven."

"Then, to-morrow call for me here, and I will accompany you again; and be assured that I shall keep my word with you, and that far from losing anything, you shall immensely gain by acting with me, and against your former associates."

"I'm only too happy, sir," said Quiver. "I never did like the life I was leading; only, unless I happen to meet a gentleman like you, who will take me out of it, what chance had I?"

"Well, well, be faithful."

"You may make sure of that, sir."

Quiver left Whitcombe House, and Captain Heron called to Ogle.

"Follow that man," he said, "and see where he goes."

"He knows me too well, Captain; but here's Mrs. Ogle just going out, and she'll do it capitally."

Mrs. Ogle did follow Quiver, and her report when she came back was, that he met another man at the corner of Pall Mall, whom he slapped familiarly on the back, and then that, with much laughing together, they went down towards Westminster.

Heron was dubious what to do.

He had a suspicion that all was not right.

Under such circumstances, he did the wisest thing by immediately consulting with Edith.

Her opinion was immediately pronounced, to the effect that Quiver was not to be trusted.

She was firmly convinced, from a review of all the circumstances, that the next attempt at the capture of the young girl would be on that night, instead of the night following, and that Heron was only told otherwise to throw him completely off his guard.

This opinion coincided very much with his own; and he resolved that, come what might, he would keep watch about the house from which the young artificial flower-maker had emerged in the morning, and still save her, if any attempt were made in the evening to carry her off.

——

CHAPTER CCXXXIV.

TOM MEETS WITH A ROMANTIC ADVENTURE IN KENSINGTON GARDENS.

LEAVING Felix Heron to make his arrangements to frustrate the villany of Lord Warringdale and his infamous employers, we once more repair to the Bayswater Road.

Through a small gate in that long, dreary wall of Kensington Gardens, which, until quite recently, was familiar to the inhabitants of the metropolis, Tom Ripon had made his way, escaping, by that simple manœuvre, the pursuit of Jonathan Wild.

Tom took the precaution of possessing himself of the key, which being inadvertently, as it appeared, left by some one in the gate, had enabled him to pass through it.

Wild came to a halt, for his attentive ears missed the tread of Daisy on the roadway.

He felt confident that Tom had hidden somewhere, but where that could be completely puzzled him.

The market gardens to the right were, to be sure, accessible to such a steed as Daisy, because she could have leaped the ditch, which, black, fetid, and stagnant, had flowed by the roadside for many a long year.

She likewise could have cleared the railings on the other side of that ditch.

But Jonathan felt confident that no such manœuvre had been practised, since, even at that hour, there was sufficient light over the open space occupied by the gardens to enable him to see any such feat, if it had been performed.

Then where had Tom gone?

To the left there was nothing but that immense wall, at least twelve feet high, with the heavy brick abutments, over which no mortal steed could ever make its way.

Wild muttered to himself.

"Was it real, or a matter of imagination? Did I see him, or did I not? Or was it some phantom in the likeness of the horse and its rider, known to me so well? Ah! here is a gate; if it be open now, it solves the difficulty."

Wild halted at the very gate through which Tom had passed with Daisy.

He tried it carefully, and then more forcibly.

It resisted him, because Tom had securely locked it on the inner side.

"No," said Wild, "he couldn't get in here. I'll ride down the road a little way, and see what comes of it."

Tom was just on the inner side of the gate, and heard what Wild said very well.

"Plague take you!" whispered Tom. "Why don't you go home, and leave a fellow to find his own adventures on the highway?"

Tom was much nearer an adventure than he imagined.

Wild had trotted onward, and Tom had just turned the key in the lock of the gate, preparatory to emerging again into the high road from the gardens, when a slight push from without thrust it open a short distance, and a female voice said in accents of alarm, "Alfred—Alfred, is it you? Are you there? for I cannot stay a moment."

There was something pleasant about this voice.

So pleasant, indeed, that Tom had a great desire to look in the face of its owner.

"Yes, I'm here," he said.

"Oh, I thought you would be. I left the key in the lock, and it has not been missed; but I cannot stay, Alfred; my uncle, Sir William, is at home; and you know what he is."

"Rather!" said Tom.

"What did you say, Alfred?"

"I said 'Come in,' my dear. You'll catch cold in the chink of the door."

"Why, Alfred, I should say that is just what you have done; for your voice is not at all like what it usually is."

"Never mind a fellow's voice," said Tom, "so long as his heart's in the right place."

"Why, what odd things you do say to-night, Alfred!"

The young lady—for such, indeed, she was—came through the little gate into the gardens.

Tom adroitly closed the gate, and turned the key in it.

"Keep close, Daisy," he said.

"Daisy!" cried the young lady. "Is that a new name you have got for me? Why, the last time you were here you said you would call me the forlorn Sophonisba!"

"The forlorn who?" said Tom.

"Sophonisba."

"It's long for Sophy, I suppose."

"Now, really, Alfred!"

No. 74. EDITH.

"Oh, well, my dear, I'll call you what you like."

"Ah me!" sighed the young lady, as she took Tom's arm. "What a life we lead! loving in secret, and only meeting now and then in stealth, through the kindness and connivance of Cleopatra."

Tom began to have his suspicions that the young lady was not quite right in the upper storey.

"Oh, yes," he said: "that's all true, Cleopatra, as you say. It's an odd name though, isn't it? and I'm quite sure I never heard it before."

"What, Alfred? Never heard the name of the great Cleopatra, Queen of Egypt?"

"Ah!" thought Tom; "that's a settler. It's quite clear that this young lady is a little out of her mind, and I hardly know what to say to her."

But the voice of the young lady was sweet,

and soft, and clear; and Tom Ripon, with his usual susceptibility in such matters, began to feel already half smitten by the charms of his accidental companion.

The fear of committing himself by some expression that would at once let her know he was a stranger both to her and to the Alfred for whom she mistook him, kept him very silent.

And Alfred, probably, was of the loquacious order of beings, for the young lady complained of the silence.

"You scarcely say a word to the forlorn Sophonisba to-night."

"Oh, don't I?"

"Certainly you do not. What is amiss?"

"It's my bad cold, I suppose."

"How very unromantic, Alfred, to take cold! But I suppose it cannot be helped."

"No," said Tom, "it can't be helped."

"And all our arrangements continue as before?"

"Oh, yes," replied Tom; "every one of them."

"How surprised my uncle will be!"

"I should think he would," replied Tom; "but we don't care about that."

"Oh, not in the least! And, here, Alfred, is another little packet; so that bit by bit, and in degrees this way, I shall get away all my jewels, which Sir William, I am sure, would never let me have, if I ran away with you, and married without his consent."

The young lady placed in Tom's hands a small packet, which, from its weight, and from what she had said, he concluded contained gold and precious stones.

Here was an adventure!

It was better than crying "Stand and deliver!" on the highway.

"My dear," said Tom, "I will take all the care in the world of these jewels; only there is one thing more I should like to have."

"What's that?"

"A kiss."

"Oh, Alfred! I don't know what has come over you. Time was when you never asked for such a thing."

"Oh, very well," said Tom, "if you've any particular objection——"

The young lady uttered a small, faint scream.

"Bless us! what's the matter?" said Tom.

"You're a wretch, Alfred! All men are wretches; but you are the worst of all!"

"Why, what have I done?"

"Nothing."

"Then how could I help it?"

"That's just it. You used to take a kiss, and not ask for it; but now, I suppose, you are becoming unfaithful to your forlorn Sophonisba."

"Oh, that's it!" thought Tom. "Here you are!"

The forlorn Sophonisba had certainly then no reason to complain of any particular backwardness on Tom's part in kissing, and probably she became rather surprised at the unusual ardour of the supposed Alfred.

This was all very pleasant.

Tom Ripon had the packet of gold and jewels in his pocket; and he was enjoying an interview with a very pretty girl amid the shadows of the old trees in Kensington Gardens.

But that state of felicity did not last long.

Envious fate interfered.

A strange sound came upon the night air, which, if they had been in the back woods of some primitive region, might have filled them with dread at the approach of some wild animal seeking its prey.

It was a concentrated kind of howl, accompanied by a battering noise at the gate through which Tom and the young lady had entered the gardens.

"Gracious heavens!" cried the forlorn Sophonisba. "What's that?"

"I've not the least idea!" said Tom.

Then a voice in accents of rage shouted out, "Sophy! Sophy! Sophy, you reprobate girl! is it possible that you are here? Answer me directly!"

"My uncle!" cried the forlorn Sophonisba, as she turned half round and fell backward into Tom's arms.

"My uncle!"

"What a noisy old pump!" said Tom.

"We are lost!"

"Found, I think!"

"Oh! oh! oh! What will become of us? We must fly at once, Alfred—we must fly at once to some sweet isle of the ocean, where it is always summer, and peaches and apricots grow wild—there we can live in bliss and security!

"'And love alone shall be our lot,
The world forgetting, and the world forgot!'"

"But I don't see it!" said Tom. "How are we to get there?"

"On the wings of our mutual affection!"

"Sophy! Sophy!" roared the voice again. "I am quite sure you are here, you wretched girl; and as soon as I catch you, you shall be locked up in the attic for the remainder of your days, and fed on bread and water."

"Yes, it is my uncle," sobbed Sophonisba. "It is Sir William. There has been some fearful treachery. Alfred, what is to be done? Is it to be an attic in Bayswater, or the soft seclusion of a paradise in the Pacific Ocean?"

"I hardly know!" said Tom. "Let's hear what the old buffer says next."

"Bring the ladder here, Pompey!"

"What does he mean by that? Who's Pompey?"

"Cleopatra's husband. She is faithful, but he is not. We are discovered, and your Sophonisba casts herself upon your faithful heart for safety and for succour."

"Oh, I comprehend!" said Tom. "The old chap's going to get over the wall by a ladder. Now, I tell you what you do, my dear. He'll come into the garden like a mad bull, and take a rush forward, and that'll be your opportunity of slipping out at the gate, and going quietly home."

"And we are not to fly?"

"I think not, yet."

"Alfred!"

"Sophonisba!"

"You are a wretch!"

"Perhaps I am. But as we don't happen exactly to have those wings of love, it's better to wait a little."

"I go. But never—never more shall we meet in this mortal sphere. I tear you from my heart, and like rocks which have been rent asunder, we part never to meet again."

Sophonisba began to cry, but Tom Ripon led her to the little gate, of which he still retained the key, and carefully opened it.

It was at a very opportune moment that he did so, for the ladder had just been placed against the wall, and as the door opened outwards, it struck against that ladder, and down it came, bringing with it the irascible Sir William with a grand crash.

"Murder! murder! You villain, Pompey! why didn't you hold the ladder? You have let it go now, and I am half smashed!"

"Oh, massa, massa!" cried a voice in the evident accents of a negro, "it's Pompey be half smash, with massa and de ladder on de top ob his back!"

"Get along as quick as you can," whispered Tom to Sophonisba.

The young lady fled, anything but impressed with the real romantic affection of her admirer, and wondering what had come over Alfred, that he should turn out so common-place a personage.

Tom closed and locked the gate again, and then he was much amused at a colloquy that took place between Sir William and Pompey, his black servant.

"You villain!" cried the irascible uncle; "you ebony villain! I'll have you taken back again to Barbadoes, and made acquainted with the cowhide every day of your life."

"Lor', massa, it were not Pompey!"

"You knocked down the ladder, you clumsy wretch."

"Me, massa?"

"Yes, you; you know you did it; and I fully believe you are as bad as your wife, Cleopatra. But I'll send you both back to the plantation, and see how you like that."

"Oh, massa, me tell you all; but Cleopatra— she *serimpitise* wid de young lady."

"She what?"

"*Serimpitise.*"

"Speak plainer, you rascal, or I'll break every bone in your skin! What do you mean?"

"Oh, don't, massa. Pompey means she tink de same as Miss Sophy, and help her—and dat's *serimpetising.*"

"Hang me, if I don't think you mean sympathising! But if you don't put up this ladder again directly, and hold it tight, you will have to sympathise with your own back; for, as sure as your name is Pompey, I'll lay a stick over it as soon as we get home."

"Dere, massa—dere is de ladder. Pompey will hold him tight!"

"Take care you do."

Sir William got up the ladder on to the top of the wall; and then, with some difficulty, dragged it over, and placed it on the other side.

"Ha, ha!" he said. "Now we shall see what we shall see!"

Diving his hand into the capacious pocket of his broad-skirted coat, the old gentleman produced a lantern, and withdrawing the slide of it, showed that it was lighted.

Slowly and carefully he got down the ladder; and then, turning round, he was in the act of holding up the lantern so as to cast its rays as widely about him as possible, when its tin case struck with a clanking sound against some metallic substance.

The old gentleman started.

He was struck dumb with terror and amazement.

The obstacle that the lantern had struck against was the barrel of a pistol, presented full at his head by Tom Ripon.

By the light of the lantern, likewise, Sir William could easily see his opponent in the scarlet and gold military costume which Tom had procured from Wardour Street.

"Now, Sir William," said Tom, "your money or your life!"

"What?"

"Your money or your life! I perceive you have a watch too. I will trouble you for it."

"A highwayman?"

"Exactly so. If I mistake not, that's a diamond ring on your finger. Take your last look of it, old gentleman, for it will soon be on mine."

"You villain!"

"Come, come—no hard words. A slight pressure of my fore-finger, Sir William, on the trigger of this pistol, and you're a dead man. All your niggers in Barbadoes would make a bonfire and rejoice, when they hear that, like a dead dog, you lie here with a brace of bullets in your skull!"

"But—but——"

"Nonsense, sir — nonsense — no parleying! Your money, watch, diamond ring, and—let me see! I think that's a ruby set in that brooch you have in your neck-cloth. I'll trouble you for that too; and be quick about it."

"Then I am in the hands of a robber and a murder——"

"Not at all; only if you've a particular desire to be shot, you'd better say so at once, as it will save time. I'd just as soon rifle your dead body as a living one."

The old gentleman turned pale and trembled.

"Who are you?" he said.

"A gentleman who lives by his wits on the road."

"Then this is all a trick?"

"What is?"

"About Sophy. She is not here; and this is merely a plan to get me into the gardens to rob me."

"Upon my life," said Tom, "you're not such an old fool as you look!"

"You admit that it is so?"

"Most certainly. The young lady you call Sophy has nothing whatever to do with it; and, I dare say, is at this present moment fast asleep in bed, dreaming of bread and butter and little cherubs!"

"The villain Pompey!"

"No; he's only a fool!"

"The black scoundrel!"

"Yes, he's black; but in this case he's been done brown. But be quick; my time is valuable, as you may easily guess by the few minutes I shall take in possessing myself of all that you have about you worth my carrying away."

The old gentleman, with a sigh, surrendered his watch.

With a groan, he placed in Tom's hands a well-filled purse.

With a sigh and a groan mingled together, he took off his diamond ring.

Tom put that on his own finger.

The ruby brooch was next surrendered.

Tom stuck that rather ostentatiously in his own cravat.

"Now old 'un," said Tom, "the sooner you go the better. There's the ladder—you know the way, and by the time you're half-way home, I shall be out of the gardens by another gate, where my horse is waiting for me, and you will never see me more."

"I hope I shall," said the old gentleman.

"Well, if you've another purse, another watch, another diamond ring, and another ruby brooch to hand to me, I don't care how soon I favour you with another interview."

"You are an audacious scoundrel, and I hope some fine day to see you dancing."

"I like a dance!",

"But upon nothing, I mean—at Tyburn."

Tom laughed.

The old gentleman ascended the ladder, but the little incident that had taken place in the gardens had shaken his nerves, and he was not able to draw it up after him and place it on the other side.

Tom saw the difficulty.

"Let me," he said; "I'll give you a helping hand. Hilloa! Below there, Pompey!"

Tom seized the ladder, and, with one impulse, canted it over the wall.

Pompey raised a shout of dismay, for it came full upon him, and prostrated him at once.

The old gentleman roared and swore immensely, and it was full five minutes before the terrified and bruised Pompey could assist his master down from the wall and homewards.

Tom was alone again in Kensington Gardens. He was intensely amused by the events of the evening, and when he came to think over its results, he fully expected that kind fortune had placed in his hands accidentally a far better booty than as if he had gone in the regular way of the high road.

CHAPTER CCXXXV.

TOM RIPON MEETS WITH STILL FURTHER ADVENTURES IN KENSINGTON GARDENS.

DAISY had kept perfectly quiet during the whole of these transactions.

And now that Tom thought of immediately leaving the gardens, he made his way to the little clump of bushes near to which she was waiting, and patted her neck.

"Bravo Daisy!" he said; "we've made a good night's work; and I have half a mind to mount, and gallop off to the old gal's crib in Wardour Street, and see what the swag is worth."

Tom had hardly half made up his mind to this conclusion when a low, rapping sound came at the gate.

Tom was silent in a moment.

Who could that be?

He took Daisy by the bridle, and withdrew about half a dozen paces.

Indeed, he did not feel quite sure but it would be the best policy to mount and ride through the entire width of the garden until he came to one of the porter's lodges, where, by fair means or foul, he could insist on being let out.

But curiosity was a much stronger element in Tom's character than alarm.

He paused, therefore, to ascertain what the low, mysterious knocking at the gate portended.

The knocking was repeated three times.

Then some one spoke.

The voice was a piping sort of treble, and the tones were in singing accents.

> "Arise, arise—
> Sophonisba, arise,
> And let your true lover
> Look into your eyes."

The knocking was repeated, and Tom almost laughed aloud, as he said to himself, "If that isn't Alfred, I'm a Frenchman!"

The voice continued.

> "Sweet love, I am here,
> By the fair star-light,
> Your Alfred so dear,
> 'Mid the shadows of night.
> Then, dear Sophonisba,
> Breathe but one sigh
> To the heart of your Alfred,
> Who for Sophy could die."

"Well, I never!" thought Tom; "I've heard lots of songs in all sorts of cribs, but nothing so bad as that! I suppose he's made it out of his own head!"

The tapping at the gate continued.

Tom very slowly and gently inserted the key in the lock, and opened the gate.

The moment it was free of its fastening it was flung wide, and some one evidently fell into the gardens on all fours.

"Gracious heavens, Miss Sophonisba, the gate has opened precipitately, and your Alfred is at your feet!"

"Sweet love, arise," said Tom. "Where's your eyes? This is the night, and it's not very bright. Get on to your feet; ain't it a treat?"

"Blessed vision!" exclaimed Alfred. "My forlorn Sophonisba speaks in music! Where are you, loved one? I am late, but I thought I saw a disturbance close to this spot. Speak to me—oh, speak to me, light of the eyes of your Alfred! Where are you, my Sophonisba?"

"Here," said Tom.

"Eh?"

"Alfred" had advanced into the garden about a dozen steps, so that Tom was able to step between him and the door, and suddenly seizing him by the back of the neck, he held him tightly.

"What? what? Help! Murder! It is not —no, it cannot be my Sophonisba!"

"Certainly not," said Tom.

"Mercy! mercy! Is it Sir William? or is it some dreaded rival, with sanguinary intentions?"

"A little of both," said Tom.

"Mercy! mercy! I give her up. I'll give you all her letters, her lock of hair, the white bow and the soiled gloves, the sprig of mignonette, and everything else that this fond heart has cherished—only let me go in peace and comfort, and don't be violent—oh, don't!"

"You're a pretty fellow," said Tom, "to come out at night and meet a charming girl! I only wish she heard you. But come now to business.

TOM RIPON TAKES THE SHINE OUT OF JONATHAN WILD.

Presented Gratis with No. 74, of the New Edition of EDITH HERON, the Sequel to Edith the Captive; or, the Robbers of Epping Forest.

Have you any objection to a couple of slugs in your brain?"

"Slugs! Gracious! I'm a dead man!"

Alfred let his legs slip from under him, and, as Tom found a difficulty in holding him up entirely by the back of his neck, he was forced to let him go; and Alfred fell in a huddled-up fashion at his conqueror's feet.

Tom was puzzled to know what to do with Alfred, but as he made no attempt to escape, his lying on the ground was about as convenient a position as any other.

"Come, now!" said Tom, "I can't waste all my time upon you. Have you got any money?"

"I? I, money?"

"Yes; surely you have some?"

"Why, I'm a poet!"

"A what?"

"A poet—and did you ever hear of a poet having any money."

"Well, I don't know about that," said Tom; "but what business have you coming here after Sophonisba?"

"Gracious heavens! you know her?"

"I do; and now I come to think of it, she told me she had been in the habit for some time past of handing you little parcels of jewellery and trinkets, so that when you and she eloped from old Sir William, her uncle, you might, I suppose, have something to live upon."

"Heavens above us!" cried Alfred, "he knows all."

"I do; and as I consider you quite unworthy of so pretty a girl, I mean to blow the few brains you've got out, and leave you here, in the old gardens as food for the crows, and hawks, they like pecking a bone."

"Spare my life," said Alfred, "and take all I have. I'm a poor wretch, without a farthing; but as Sophonisba had wealthy friends, and a good stock of jewellery, I thought that as I intended first of all to run away with her and live upon her jewels and trinkets until her friends became reconciled to us, and then I meant to live with, and on, them for the remainder of my life.

"That's candid, at all events," said Tom; "and now tell me where are the trinkets and jewels you've already had from her."

"In my—that is to say, they're at home, where it is impossible to get them."

"Permit me to doubt that," said Tom. "I don't like a man to begin to say a thing, and not carry it out. You said in my——, and then stopped short. Now, just be so good as to go on, and tell me what you meant by that?"

"Nothing—oh, nothing."

"You won't tell me?"

"I cannot—it is nothing."

"Then I will. It means 'in my pocket,' and from there they will soon be in mine. Keep quiet, or it will be worse for you."

In spite of a partial resistance from Alfred, Tom Ripon in the most scientific manner, emptied his pocket of sundry little parcels, which no doubt contained portions of the jewellery and trinkets, mention by the deluded Sophinisba.

"That'll do," said Tom. "I wouldn't have done this, but I feel that you are quite unworthy of the girl, because you are a coward and a donkey."

Tom did not wait to hear what remonstrances might flow from the lips of Alfred; but with a full conviction that Kensington Gardens would soon be, metaphorically speaking, too hot to hold him, he made his way towards Daisy.

Opening again that small gate in the wall, he led out Daisy into the Bayswater Road.

But he retained the key in his possession after locking Alfred in the gardens.

"This may be useful another time," said Tom, as he thrust the key deep into his pocket.

Tom was curious then to know what the time was, and he took out old Sir William's watch from his pocket to look.

But the darkness was too great to enable him to do so.

Tom guessed, however, that it was some time past midnight, and he debated in his own mind what he had best do.

No ordinary success upon the road could possibly have brought him the amount of plunder he really possessed; and after due consideration of all the *pros* and *cons* of the matter, he made up his mind at once to ride to Wardour Street and lodge his booty with Mortification and his mother.

Acting upon this impulse, Tom turned Daisy's head towards London.

He saw no occasion for anything in the shape of speed, and he let Daisy go at her own pace.

Tyburn Gate was in sight, and Tom was thinking of other matters, when from out a stable yard close to the market gardens that were now on his left hand, there came a horseman.

"Stand, on your life!" shouted a voice.

"Jonathan Wild!" cried Tom, on the impulse of the moment.

"Stand, or I fire!"

"Fire, and be hanged!" cried Tom. "You don't catch me quite so easy, Johnny!"

Bang went one of Wild's pistols.

"That'll do," shouted Tom. "A miss is as good as a mile."

As he spoke, he turned Daisy's head again towards the country, and gallopped off.

Wild was well mounted and on a fresh horse, to which he set spurs, and followed hard and fast upon Tom's track.

He shouted as he came on, and Tom could just catch the words he uttered.

"I will follow you, if it's half round the world, till I nab you."

Now Tom Ripon knew perfectly well that on a gallop there was no horse that Jonathan Wild could possibly procure capable of beating Daisy.

But there were such things as accidents on the road.

A lost shoe.

An accidental stumble.

The meeting of other persons coming from the contrary direction, to whom Wild might call for assistance.

All these were contingencies which Tom had to look to as against him in a long chase.

And, moreover, he had no desire to get far into the country with Jonathan Wild at his heels.

All these considerations induced Tom to think that under the circumstances a little cunning would be better than speed.

"If I can only house myself," he thought, "for five minutes, I am safe."

So close to town as they both now were, of course many villas and cottages presented themselves, but it was not a time of night to find any of them open, and even if they had been so, how could Tom take upon himself to say that he could trust any of their inhabitants.

At all events, his policy was to place in the meantime as great a distance between himself and Jonathan Wild as possible.

"On, Daisy, on!" he cried, after the manner in which he had heard Felix Heron so often speak to the noble creature.

Daisy flew like the wind.

But even assuming that she could gallop three miles to two that Jonathan Wild could accomplish, it would take a long time to place anything like some miles between them, since they had started from the Bayswater Road almost at the same instant.

As Daisy ascended a slight eminence, Wild exerted his stentorian powers of voice, and made himself heard again.

"Halt, and I promise no harm shall come to you."

"Don't you wish you may get it?" said Tom. "I fancy I would rather take care of myself."

"Halt, or I fire again, and I don't miss twice."

"Try it!" shouted Tom.

Wild did try, and discharged his second pistol in pursuit of Tom Ripon.

"Now for it!" said Tom. "You've had two shots at me, and its my turn, old Johnny."

Tom was dexterous and agile as a harlequin, and drawing the two holster pistols from the saddle of Daisy, he fairly turned round, sitting for a few seconds with his back to Daisy's head.

In this ludicrous attitude, Tom fired at Jonathan Wild.

The two pistols were discharged in such rapid succession that the smoke for a few seconds made the darkness about the spot doubly obscure.

But so it happened that Wild had reached the top of an eminence, and such light as still lingered in the sky formed a background to him and his horse, against which they were tolerably clearly discernible.

Tom saw him fall.

He saw, though, at the same time, that he kept his hold of the bridle.

The horse was dragging him along slantways across the road.

"That'll do," said Tom. "I think I've hit him. He's not killed, of course, because I look upon it as a settled thing that Jonathan Wild is to be hanged, but I rather think I've stopped his little career for to-night."

"Murder! thieves! fire!" screamed a female voice.

Tom looked hastily in the direction from whence it came, and he saw that embowered among some trees there was a little white-washed cottage, from the door of which a woman had suddenly rushed out, in rather an alarming state of *deshabille*, no doubt thoroughly alarmed by the firing.

"Murder! murder! thieves! watch!"

"What's the matter?" said Tom.

"I heard something."

"Whatever you heard, it's not half so bad as the noise you're making."

"But what was it, and who are you?"

"Oh, I—I'm Jonathan Wild."

"What! You Jonathan Wild? You that horrid wretch who——"

"Come, come! don't be abusive! I want to go into the cottage for a few seconds, and you'd better mind what you're saying and doing, or I'll burn it down to a cinder, and you in it."

The woman fled into the cottage again with a scream of dismay.

"Stoop, Daisy!" said Tom; "stoop down, lass —down, and crawl in like a mouse!"

Daisy understood what Tom meant, and lowering her head, while Tom himself lay quite flat back on the saddle, she made her way right into the cottage by its open door.

"That'll do," cried Tom. "Now get a light and take a good look at me; and you will see I'm no more like Jonathan Wild than Blue Beard. Get the light quick, and take a good look at me, and fasten up the door if you can."

CHAPTER CCXXXVI.

TOM RIPON MEETS WITH AN EXCITING ADVENTURE.

THE relation between Tom Ripon and Jonathan Wild was, as the reader is well aware, very similar to that between the latter and Felix Heron.

That is to say, while Wild thought Heron was in life.

Tom had made a sort of compact with the great thief-taker that the one was not to injure the other.

There was no understanding, though, that if Tom went upon the road, Wild was not to do what Wild would have called his duty, and strive to apprehend him.

Tom felt a confidence in the fact that he could on that night, if he pleased, put an end to all difficulty with regard to Jonathan Wild.

To lie in ambush by the side of the road and shoot him would have been the readiest method of putting an end to all trouble on his account.

But Tom never thought of such a thing for a moment.

To outwit Wild he would try with all the ingenuity in his power.

And, possibly, if it came to close quarters, there might be, between them, an interchange of shots.

Chance shots, only, though.

The deliberate act of lying in wait to assassinate him, Tom would have shrunk from as downright cowardly.

And such, indeed, was the usual relation, at period, between what were called the knights of the road and the police officers.

Each lived by the exertions of the other.

The officers found their most lucrative occupation in running after such gentry.

The highwaymen felt and knew that they were tolerated by the officers, who might, any day they pleased, have made a clean sweep of the whole tribe of them.

It was rather a trial of wits, then, between these two apparently opposing parties, than one of life and death.

Hence was it that Tom made his way into this little cottage by the road-side.

He had no fear of Wild.

But he wanted to avoid him.

"Look at me!" he cried to the woman, again. "Get the light and look at me, and don't stand squalling there!"

The woman had had a light, but the opening and shutting of the cottage door had extinguished it.

That was the period of old tinder-boxes, when, in case of any alarm, it took a good twenty minutes to procure a light.

"Stop a bit—stop a bit!" said the woman; "I don't think your voice is at all like Jonathan Wlid's."

"I should rather think not," said Tom.

Click, click went the flint against the steel, as the woman strove to ignite the tinder which was to give her a light.

But the tinder was obstinate.

Or the flint had lost its fine edge.

No light came.

Tom thought of a trick he had often played his mother, and throwing up the pan of one of his pistols, he took a pinch of powder from it.

Leaning over the shoulder of the woman of the cottage, it was an easy thing to drop that pinch of powder into the tinder-box.

Fluff!

"Murder!"

The tinder was thoroughly alight.

"What's the matter?" said Tom.

"The tinder is bewitched."

"Hush!—be quiet! What's that?"

A heavy knocking came at the cottage door.

"I'm a lost woman—I'm a lost woman! Thieves!—thieves!"

"Hold your row!" said Tom, in a whisper. "I am not Jonathan Wild, but that is!"

"Then, indeed, I am lost, since he comes again!"

"Again?"

"Yes; and he said he would kill me!"

"Nonsense!"

"He swore it; and he's a man who will keep his word in any wickedness, although in any good it would be quite another matter."

"You're about right there," said Tom. "But be quick, and get a light."

"I cannot; my hand shakes."

"Give me the match."

Tom's nerves were pretty well strung; and, notwithstanding Jonathan Wild kept banging and hammering at the door of the cottage, there was soon a small blue flame at the end of the brimstone match.

Tom lit the rushlight which was upon the little round table close at hand.

He took one glance into the face of the woman, and he saw an expression of the most abject fear and despair upon it.

"Open! Open!" cried the voice of Wild from without.

The woman wrung her hands.

"Open! Open!"

"Yes," she moaned; "that is his voice. I know it too well! He said he would come again, and he is here. You are one of his men, and between you I am a dead woman. I tell you, as I have told him, that, by all my hopes of heaven, I swear I do not know where poor Andrew left the silver plate!"

"I don't know what you're talking about," said Tom.

"I'm afraid you know too well."

"I'll be hanged if I do!"

"That lets me know that you are one of Jonathan Wild's men, since you mention the fate of my poor boy Andrew."

"Open, I say!" cried Wild. "Am I to be kept here all night?—or do you want me to break down the door? Open the door, I say—open!"

The woman resigned herself to the most abject fear; and it was almost doubtful if she understood what Tom said, as he spoke to her in a whisper.

"You're very much mistaken. I am no man of Jonathan Wild's, but trying to get out of his way. I will stay here, however; and if, as you suspect, he should try to murder you, you may make up your mind that he will be foiled at that."

"You will save me?"

"Hush! Don't speak so loud. I will."

Tom was glancing eagerly around the little cottage, in the hope of seeing some hiding-place for himself and Daisy.

None presented itself in that room; but there was a small door at the back which seemed to lead into some outhouse or scullery, and which further communicated with the front apartment by a narrow slip of a window, filled with diamond-shaped panes of glass.

"Where does that go to?" said Tom.

The woman was far too bewildered to answer him.

Tom, therefore, looked for himself; and he was very much gratified to find that there was a mode of exit from the little back scullery to a cabbage and potato-garden, no doubt reclaimed from the waste land around, since the paling that enclosed it was of the most primitive and insecure character.

"That'll do," said Tom.

He led Daisy right out into the cabbage-garden; and then, returning himself to the little scullery, he looked through the lattice-window just at the moment when Wild, by a powerful effort, had burst the wooden latch of the cottage-door, and appeared with a pistol in each hand upon its threshold.

The woman sunk to her knees, and held up her hands imploringly.

Wild stepped back one pace, as if in surprise.

"Is this possible?" he said. "Do I see Mrs. Mears?"

The woman uttered a half-shriek.

"Well, this is a slice of luck!" added Wild. "I was told, at the old cottage where you used to live, near Ealing, that you had entirely disappeared; and here I find you, by accident, as snug as possible!"

"No, no!"

"But I say yes, yes; and I am quite delighted to see you!"

Wild glanced out at the cottage door, in order, no doubt, to see that his horse was in safety, the bridle of which he had tied to a little cherry-tree that grew close to the humble porch.

"All's right!" he said.

He closed the door of the cottage.

"Now, Mrs. Mears," he said, "I want to ask

you one question before we proceed to other business."

"I know nothing! I cannot tell you!"

"Don't be in such a hurry. I have not asked you yet. I am in pursuit of a fellow who is on the road to-night; and, by the by, that puts me in mind that he has left his mark upon me."

Wild took off his hat and wig; for he occasionally indulged in the wear of the latter article.

When he did so, he exhibited what appeared to be a very serious and ghastly wound in the head.

In reality, though, it was but a trifle.

The bullet from one of Tom's pistols had merely furrowed up the skin of the scalp, which had not bled very profusely, but still sufficient to give the appearance of an ugly gash.

The woman of the cottage uttered a half-scream.

"What are you squalling at now?" cried Wild. "Give me a basin, or a tub, with some cold water."

Mrs. Mears was in such a state of agitation, that it was with the greatest difficulty she could comply with this request of Jonathan Wild.

"A towel!" he shouted

She handed him one.

He dashed the cold water over his head; and then, soaking the towel in it, he wound it round the wound.

Over that, again, he placed his wig.

Then he put on his hat.

Wild looked a more hideous object than ever.

The towel raised the wig and the hat to an unusual height, making him look at once brutal and grotesque.

"Now, marm," he said, "since you appear to be up and quite lively at this time of night, just tell me if you heard a horseman pass your door, and which way he went; for I see there's a lane close by the side of your cottage."

"I know nothing!"

"Oh, you know nothing?"

"Nothing, as I live!"

"Nothing, as you live? Ha, ha! Perhaps that won't be for long; for I hold that people who know nothing are not of much use in this world."

Jonathan flung himself into an old arm-chair as he spoke; and looked at the shrinking and trembling woman with a most diabolical expression of countenance.

He lowered his tone, and spoke in a deep, growling voice.

"Mrs. Mears—Mrs. Mears, I say!"

"Yes—oh, yes!"

"You recollect?"

She wrung her hands and wept.

"Can I ever forget?—can I ever forget?"

"Well, I should think not! You had a son, and his name was Andrew?"

"It was—it was!"

"Like many a better man before him, and as many a better man still will do, he tried his luck upon the road!"

"It was bad company!—it was the ale-house! it was the poachers!"

"Pshaw! What do I care what it was? I nabbed him!"

"And you brought him to death!"

"Not I! I saw that he was a clean-limbed likely fellow, thin and slippery as an eel, and a good horseman! Was that the sort of a fellow for me to bring to death?"

"But you did—you did!"

"Ah, Mrs. Mears, you never understood that little affair! Women are bad hands at business. He was hanged, I admit—hanged at Tyburn, with all the usual formalities; and now, as an old acquaintance of all parties, I'll just tell you how it happened."

"Wretch!"

"Hilloa!—hilloa!"

"Fiend!"

"Come, come, Mrs. Mears, you are getting abusive! This was how it took place. I told your son that if he brought me my regulars I would be as good as a father to him, and he promised he would do so. He did for a little while, till at last—you know as well as I—that, along with Blueskin and Quilt Arnold, he cracked a crib on Wandsworth Common."

"Oh, spare me!—spare me!"

"We shall see about that. His share of the swag was a good bagful of plate, of which he said nothing to me. I never saw any of it; so you see, Mrs. Mears, he brought his death upon himself."

"Alas! alas!!!"

"Ah, you may well cry that! I told him the night before he took his ride down Holborn Hill in the cart for Tyburn, that I could still save him if he told me where the swag was. But he wouldn't. He said he had given it away; but I didn't believe him. I do believe, though, that you know where it is!"

"No!—no!"

"Yes! yes!—and I don't intend to leave this cottage till I know!"

"I cannot tell you! Do you think that all the silver plate in the world would have stood between my boy Andrew and death?"

"I don't know that! It's somewhere; and if you don't know, who is to know?"

"I cannot tell you. Take yourself hence, man of many crimes!—take yourself hence! The judgment of heaven will one day overtake you, and the hour of your own death may be nearer at hand than you imagine! Take yourself hence, I say, Jonathan Wild! and no longer afflict one who is a mourner, and to whom even death has no terrors!"

"Oh, that's it, is it? Very well, Mrs. Mears, I'm not a sort of man to stand upon half-measures; and since you are so independent of life, I shall just give you the option of telling me within the next minute and a half where the swag is, or a pistol-bullet will send you to kingdom come!"

Wild, as he spoke, faced about upon the chair, so that he sat astride upon it as though on his horse, with the back of it in front of him.

On that back he balanced one of his pistols, and presented it full at the unfortunate woman.

"Now decide," he said. "Give me the information I want, or in another minute you are a dead woman!"

"I cannot—I do not know! Heaven have mercy upon me!"

"I shall count six, and if that goes over without the information, I fire."

"Save me! save me!" cried Mrs. Mears.

Tom Ripon was quite certain that this was meant as an appeal to him, although no such appeal was required, since the reader knows quite enough of Tom to feel certain that he was not likely to remain perfectly quiescent while Jonathan Wild committed such a murder.

"One!" said Wild.

"Help! help!"

"Two!"

"Murder! murder!"

"Three!"

"I cannot tell you—I do not know!"

"Four!"

"Save me! save me!"

"Five! I don't see the use of saying six, so keep still, and I'll fire! It's better to get a bullet plump in the brain, than a side shot that may not kill at once."

"No, no, you cannot—you dare not!"

"Indeed! Then here goes!"

"Not yet, Johnny!" said Tom Ripon

As he spoke, he dashed the barrel of one o his pistols through a diamond-shaped pane of glass in the lattice window, and resting it on the little leaden frame-work, he presented it full at the head of Jonathan Wild.

———

CHAPTER CCXXXVIII.

TOM RIPON GETS THE BETTER OF WILD.—HE VISITS HIS MOTHER'S FENCE IN WARDOUR STREET.

If the roof of the cottage had fallen in, perhaps Wild would not have been so very much surprised, since it was rather a frail little building.

But this sudden appearance of Tom Ripon on

the scene of action seemed at once to astonish and bewilder him.

He no doubt, in his own mind, had given up all thoughts of encountering Tom again on that night; but now to meet him in this cottage, and to know that he had been a listener to the fearful conversation which had just ensued between him and the unhappy Mrs. Mears, was a most perplexing circumstance.

"Blaze away, Johnny!" cried Tom; "why don't you say six, and do it?"

"Confusion take you!"

"Oh, dear, no, it's taken you, I think!"

"I know you."

"Who said you didn't? It's quite of as much consequence that I know you."

"Tom Ripon."

"Johnny Wild."

"Be thankful that I do not turn this weapon against you; but I have promised not to do so, and I will keep my word, on one condition."

"That's kind!" said Tom.

"Surrender to me Daisy, the late Felix Heron's horse, and I give you a new lease of life."

"Well," said Tom, "that's what I call reasonable and moderate!"

"You consent?" cried Wild eagerly.

"Certainly. But as we all have our little conditions, I must make one."

"I agree to it beforehand."

"Well, that saves trouble—it's a very simple one."

"Name it."

"It's just this. You shall have Daisy——"

"Yes?"

"When you can get her!"

Wild raised his pistol and fired at once.

There was a great crash of glass in the lattice window.

Mrs. Mears screamed loudly.

Tom then fired.

The cottage was full of the smoke of gunpowder, and the concussion of the air had extinguished the light.

Wild fell backward entangled in the chair on which he was seated in so eccentric a fashion.

Tom flung the door open that led from the scullery, and strode into the cottage.

"I'm not hit, Johnny!" he said. "How have you come off?" Oh, there you are!"

Jonathan Wild lay upon the floor, and Tom had good reason to suppose that at last he had done for the great thief-taker, and sent him out of the world to which he had been a vexation so long.

"Mrs. Mears! Mrs. Mears!" cried Tom; "get another light, and let us have a look at the rascal!"

The affrighted woman, however, had fled, and Tom found himself alone in the darkness, with what might or might not be the dead body of Jonathan Wild.

This was not a pleasant state of things, and Tom hastened to bring it to a conclusion.

"I'll be off to town," he said to himself. "This has been a pretty night of adventures for a beginning. But if I've settled Jonathan Wild, it's nobody's fault but his own."

Tom made his way into the scullery, and then into the cabbage garden where Daisy waited for him.

He mounted hastily, and left Daisy in the darkness to pick her way as best she could through a gap in the palings of the little reclaimed bit of land.

Daisy saw her way very much better in the dark than Tom Ripon, and she soon reached the high road again.

Tom cast one glance back at the cottage, and then set off at speed.

"On, Daisy, on!"

She knew that expression well.

Fleet as the wind she carried her light rider to London.

She leaped Tyburn-gate, a feat which there were not six horses in the United Kingdom capable of.

In an incredibly short space of time Tom drew rein at the door of his mother's house in Wardour Street.

It was two o'clock in the morning, as Tom, leaning from his saddle, rapped at the upper panel of the door.

There was no risk of finding the little family in Wardour Street otherwise than in a fit state to receive visitors.

The peculiar business carried on by Mrs. Ripon was in its greatest state of activity between about two o'clock in the morning and daybreak.

It was then that the midnight burglar came to rid himself of his spoil, in the continued possession of which lay his chiefest danger.

It was then that the highwayman, riding to London upon his clever, serviceable hackney, delivered at some such establishment as Mrs. Ripon's the watches, purses, and jewels he had succeeded in appropriating on the road.

Tom's appeal, then, to the upper panel of the outer door, was a welcome sound to Mrs. Ripon and Mortification.

The sounds betokened the arrival of a customer.

But that that customer was Tom Ripon probably would have been the last idea to occur to either his mother or Mortification.

It was just possible, though, that some party of officers of the police, intent upon the capture of some gentleman who mistook other people's property for his own, might be visiting the fences of London.

Or it might be that some individual Bow Street runner was taking a round for the purpose of collecting what he called his "vails."

Those were the perquisites—the kind of black mail which was levied upon the keepers of the fences, by the officers, for leave to carry on the nefarious trade.

Therefore was it that a reconnoitre was always taken through some loop-hole, for the purpose of ascertaining who the visitor really was.

Tom Ripon knew perfectly well the existence of this loop-hole above the outer door of the fence in Wardour street.

Pulling his hat down upon his brow, Tom altered his voice to a gruff sound, as he cried out, "House, here!—house! What do you mean by keeping a gentleman waiting here on the threshold?"

Mortification had mounted the little stool which enabled him to reach, with ease, the place of espial.

Tom's assumed voice was quite strange to him.

"Yea," he said, "who art thou?"

"Don't you know me?"

"Verily, no!"

"Then I know you! Can you take in a service of gold plate, and two or three bags of diamonds and rubies?"

"What?" exclaimed Mortification, in undisguised astonishment.

"Because, if you can," added Tom, "I've got a donkey round the corner loaded with all the swag."

"Young man," said Mortification, "thy jokes are ill-timed; and as the Psalmist says, 'Go about thy business, and allow other folks to go about theirs.'"

"But this is business."

"Yea, I have but to pull a string, and the respectable Mrs. Ripon, who is on the floor above, will cast something down upon thy head which will make thee remember us."

Tom laughed.

He spoke in his natural voice.

"Don't pull it then, old Mortfication, or you'll spoil Captain what's his name's red coat."

"Gracious powers!" cried Mortification, "yea, it is Thomas!"

In the surprise of the moment, Mortification stepped on one side, and fell from the stool into the passage.

"Yea, where are you now?" said Tom.

"Verily, I have had a fall; but yea, here am I again!"

"Open the door."

"One moment, Thomas."

"Well, what is it?"

"I sincerely hope that thou hast not forgotten the wonderful principles of honesty implanted in thy young heart by the tender Mrs. Ripon that was, but Mrs. Mortification that is."

"Oh, bother!" said Tom.

"But," pursued Mortification, thrusting his arm through the aperture above the door, and waiving it about in an oratorical fashion—"but, Thomas, if thou hast so far forgotten those sublime precepts as to take to thyself the watches, the pocket-books, the purses, the rings, and other jewellery of persons unknown, yea, thou art welcome here; and although we shall not kill the fatted calf, we shall give the best price for swag—yea!"

"Ah, now," said Tom, "that's rather unkind."

"Eh?"

"One can't be always lucky."

"Oh!"

"And you know a fellow may go on the road and lose his pistols, and even his hat, as well as what little money he has in his pocket."

"Oh! is that thy case, Thomas?"

"Rather."

"Then I have no hesitation in saying that thou art the most hardened, impudent, ugly ruffian I ever heard of."

"Hilloa! hilloa!" cried Tom; "no abuse. Just tell the old gal I'm here."

"Yea, I will not; and yea, I will pull the string, and thou shalt have on thy head——"

"Stop! stop! No nonsense, Mortification. Open the door, man. I have made a famous night's work of it. I wouldn't fall into the hands of Jonathan Wild or any of his crew for the best hundred guineas the world ever saw."

"Thou hast booty, Thomas?"

"Lots."

The Rev. Mortification heaved a great sigh.

"Yea, I always said thou wert a charming youth; and verily, Thomas, I will open the door to thee."

The door was opened instantly.

"Come in—come in; for yea, as the Psalmist says——"

"Plague take the Psalmist!" cried Tom. "We shall have some of the night patrols upon us soon. What did you mean by pulling a string, and something coming on a fellow's head?"

"Yea, here is the string; and thy sainted mother, Thomas, is above. We are occasionally visited by disreputable characters, who have nothing to sell, but want some money; and yea, this is the mode by which we let them know they are not welcome."

"A capital mode, too," said Tom. "Just step outside a minute, and fetch in that bundle."

"Bundle?"

"Yes, just on the threshold."

"Is it swag, Thomas?"

"To be sure it is.

"Lovely youth!"

The Rev. Mortification stepped over the threshold at once.

Tom pulled the string that had been pointed out to him instantly.

Down came a perfect cataract from the second floor window, and the voice of Mrs. Ripon called out, "Take that, whoever you are! We don't want such customers as you! Bring something for the melting-pot, like a gentleman, or you'd best be jogging from this house."

"Murder!" cried the Reverend Mortification.

Tom laughed immensely.

"Murder! I am drowned! Yea, I do not like cold water!"

"It serves you right," said Tom. "Now, come in, for my time's precious."

The Reverend Mortification re-entered the house, presenting rather a melancholy spectacle of saturated apparel.

Tom had led Daisy right into the shop, and when the outer door was made fast, he called out in his loudest tones, "Hoy! hoy! Old gal, where are you? I want some money! I've been nabbed and grabbed, but the traps will let me go for a hundred guineas."

"You vile little scamp!" said Mrs. Ripon, as she flew into the back parlour, with her mob cap put on the wrong side foremost. "You horrid reprobate! The gallows is groaning for you!"

"Do you mean to say," said Tom, "that you won't give a hundred guineas?"

"What?"

"A hundred guineas, I say, to save me from the traps."

"Do I live, or am I a delusion and a snare? Am I a lone widow, or am I not? A hundred guineas, did you say."

"Yes."

"And for what?"

"To save me from the traps."

Mrs. Ripon drew herself up with dignity.

"Tom, there have been times when you were

an obedient and dutiful son to your poor mother; be so now, and go and be hanged at once."

"Well, that's kind!" said Tom. "However, things are not so bad as they look. Here are two gold watches, with good bunches of seals; here are some diamond finger-rings, a couple of purses, and a packet here of jewellery that, by its weight, ought to be worth something."

"My child!" cried Mrs. Ripon; "my own Tommy!"

"Get away!" cried Tom. "Do you want to smother a fellow?"

"My child—my child!"

"Be off, I say! Botheration take you! let a fellow breathe, won't you?"

Mrs. Ripon had folded Tom in such a voluminous embrace that he could not possibly extricate himself.

"Yea," cried Mortification, as he stood upon a chair, and waved his long arms over them both like an insane windmill,—"yea, this is affecting. Thomas, take your paternal relative-in-law's blessing."

"But I'm smothered!" cried Tom.

"Yea, never mind; we shall have the swag all the same."

Tom found that the only way to extricate himself from his mother's embrace was to drop to the floor, and then crawl backwards.

Tom executed this operation with his usual impetuosity, and, as a natural consequence, he upset the chair upon which the Reverend Mortification was standing.

"Go it!" cried Tom, as Mortification fell over upon Mrs. Ripon. "Fight it out between you, and you both have my blessing."

It was some few moments before peace and order was restored.

"Oh, Tom, Tom!" said Mrs. Ripon; "the sight of you is like—like——"

"Manna in the wilderness," said Mortification.

"None of your abuse," cried Mrs. Ripon, "but let us proceed to business."

Tom, with a pardonable ostentation under the circumstances, laid out his booty upon the table, which was in the centre of the room.

Mrs. Ripon and Mortification took a rapid survey of it, and then glanced at each other.

"Twenty guineas' worth, as I'm a sinner!" said Mrs. Ripon.

"Yea," said Mortification.

Then, to Tom's intense surprise—for he was not yet half up to the tricks of receivers of stolen property—a small orifice opened in the centre of the table, and the purses, the watches, the little parcel of jewellery, and the rings, all shot down this hole as though they had been endowed with life.

The little trap in the table then closed, and Mortification and Mrs. Ripon both looked up at the ceiling, as though they saw something there peculiarly interesting.

Tom looked under the table.

It was a round one, with an unusually thick, straight pillar in the centre.

"Well," he said, "this is a queer start."

"Twenty guineas!" said Mrs. Ripon.

"Yea, twenty!" added Mortification.

"But you don't mean to say, both of you, that all that swag's only worth twenty guineas?"

"Hush!" said Mrs. Ripon.

"Hush!" echoed Mortification.

"Whist!" said Mrs. Ripon.

"Whist!" said Mortification.

"What the deuce are you both about," said Tom, "with your hushing and whisting? Have you gone mad?"

Mrs. Ripon placed her finger on her lips and shook her head.

Mortification did the same.

"Not a word!"

"No, not one!"

Tom looked from one to the other of them in undisguised amazement.

"He's coming," said Mrs. Ripon.

"Yea," said Mortification.

"From the next house."

"Yea."

"It's Sylvester, the officer. He must have tracked you, Tom."

"Yes, he must have tracked you, Thomas. Give him the twenty guineas, and let him run."

"Oh," said Tom, "that's the game, is it? Ha, ha! That's the way you manage business! You offer a fellow one half of what he ought to have, and then try and scare him off with the grabs; but that won't do for me! I shall be glad to see Sylvester, the officer, if he's up-stairs! Hoy, Sylvester! Come down, old chap! I want to give these two people into charge for receiving stolen goods! I'll turn King's evidence and tell you all about it!"

"Take your money, and be off!" said Mrs. Ripon; "you're an unnatural son!"

"An unnatural son-in-law," said Mortification; "but still we shall be glad to see you, whenever you've got anything to dispose of."

"Yes," said Mrs. Ripon; "and if you come to grief, I shall cry my eyes out, for I never can forget the feelings of a mother. There's your twenty guineas, Tom, and it's the last farthing we have got in the world, and we fully expect to be taken up and hanged, and ruined for buying these things of you at all."

"What a pity," said Tom; "but I suppose it can't be helped. Just give me the bundle with my other clothes. That's all right. Come on, Daisy. What's that o'clock striking?"

One—two—three—four struck the clock of St. Martin's Church.

"Good!" said Tom. "I shall get to the stables of Whitcombe House in capital time, and have a fine snooze before morning in the stable along with Daisy. Good night, old gal!" Good night, Corruption!"

Tom, with the bridle of Daisy over his arm, moved towards the outer door, and then, turning suddenly, as if struck with an alarm, he said, "Hush!"

Mrs. Ripon and Mortification ran against each other.

"Whist!" said Tom.

"Gracious powers!" said Mrs. Ripon; "what is it?"

Tom placed his finger on his lips, and nodded mysteriously.

He let go the bridle of Daisy, and beckoned them both back to the parlour behind the shop.

"The chimney!" said Tom.

"The what?"

"The chimney! I'm sure of it! I'd stake my life on it!"

TOM RIPON MEETS WITH A MOST AFFECTIONATE GREETING FROM THE
OLD FOLKS IN TALLOW STREET.

"What—what?"

"It wants sweeping, and now it's done."

Tom had adroitly taken the two holster pistols from Daisy's saddle; and, as he spoke, he fired them both up the chimney of the back parlour.

Being fully aware of what would be the effect, Tom was able to beat a hasty retreat, and catching Daisy hurriedly by the bridle, he dashed out into Wardour Street, leaving Mortification and his mother amid such an avalanche of soot, that they might as well, actually, have taken up their abode in the flue.

In a quarter of an hour more, Tom was fast asleep in the stables of Whitcombe House.

CHAPTER CCXXXVIII.

FELIX HERON DETERMINES TO RESCUE AND PROTECT THE ARTIFICIAL FLOWER MAKER.

WHILE Tom Ripon was thus engaged in seeking adventures on his own account, Felix Heron, Earl of Whitcombe, still continued to reside at Whitcombe House, in his accustomed character of Captain Fantome, of the royal navy, who had married the Countess of Whitcombe.

That this disguise of Heron's had been complete, and was likely to answer all its purpose, was sufficiently exemplified by the fact that it eluded the vigilance even of Jonathan Wild.

But, as we have more than once intimated, no disguise that Heron could possibly have assumed would have been sufficient to screen him from the hawk-like glance of Wild, but from one fact.

That was the thorough conviction on the part of the thief-taker that Felix Heron was no more.

There lay the safety of the whole proceeding.

If once, by any accident, Jonathan should become aware that the supposed death of Felix Heron were a delusion, there would be an end to all secrecy on the subject.

He would naturally look to Whitcombe House to discover its master.

Five minutes' investigation, then, would convince him that that master was to be found in Captain Fantome, so called.

But, with the sort of feeling that Wild had for Felix Heron, it did not follow that there would be any absolute danger, so far as he was concerned, in trusting him with the secret.

But it was necessary to keep it, for other reasons.

Those reasons have been hinted at by the Earl of Bridgewater.

The enemies of Felix Heron would seek his attainder, and so deprive his infant son of his inheritance.

Such was the reason, then, which actuated Heron in the preservation of his disguise.

His activity both of mind and body, however, was such that, although he had abandoned the road for a fortnight, which gave Tom Ripon the unexpected opportunity of mounting Daisy, and seeking adventures on his own account, he, Heron was well pleased that chance or providence had permitted him to interpose for the protection of that young girl who was sought to be kidnapped in the streets of London.

He was determined to save her.

It will be recollected that the man Quiver, who had been taken prisoner by Heron, and then pretended to be so very contrite, had stated that the attempt was to be renewed on the night after the next succeeding that on which it had failed.

And Heron had had his suspicions aroused that this pretended arrangement was for the express purpose of throwing him off his guard.

Mrs. Ogle's account of how this man had met one of his associates, and gone with him to one of the thieves' houses which then infested the wharfs about Hungerford, increased this suspicion.

Heron determined not to let that night pass away without action.

He had really communicated all that had passed to Edith, and her opinion was strongly expressed in favour of losing no time.

"Go, Felix," she said; "perform this act of mercy and consideration, and I shall still further believe that your destiny, in the hands of Providence, is to succour distress and protect the innocent!"

"I will do my best," said Heron.

He smiled as he spoke.

"I shall have a debtor and creditor account with that providence you speak of, Edith; and my misdeeds on the road, when I held command in Epping Forest, may perhaps be blotted out by some of these transactions in which I foil villany and profligacy in their worst aspects."

The night came.

Or rather the evening, dim and dark, with a cloudy sky.

Heron wrapped a cloak about him, which concealed the trusty sword he wore.

Edith followed him down the grand staircase of Whitcombe House.

She clung to him for a moment in the hall.

She was evidently suffering from some emotion.

"Even now, Edith," he said, "you have something to say."

"I have—I have!"

"And is it possible that you shrink to utter it?"

"I do, Felix; but yet it must be uttered before you leave this house."

"Am I, then, so undeserving your confidence that you hesitate?"

"No, Felix; but what I am about to say is neither right nor just."

"Is that possible?"

"It is true."

"Then, my Edith, indeed, shows herself in a new character."

Edith still hesitated; and then it was in a tone struggling with an amount of feeling that almost deprived her of the power of utterance, that she spoke.

"All men, Felix," said Edith, "stand or fall by their actions without favour or affection, but in this affair my brother John is concerned."

Felix interrupted her at once.

"And can you imagine, Edith, that I am unmindful of that fact? I will foil John Tarleton and his infamous employers, but it will be by accident if a single hair of his head is injured by any act of mine; and now farewell! Rest in peace Edith, and rely on me!"

Heron left the house; and taking his way towards the narrow, gloomy street where the young and beautiful artificial flower-maker worked, he kept carefully in the shadow of the houses and looked narrowly about him.

The street was anything but a populous one for passing passengers.

The few little gloomy shops that were in it had only been extemporized out of the parlour windows of the houses; and as the street led to nowhere in particular, and was no very short cut to anybody's destination, sometimes a quarter of an hour would elapse without the footfall of a passenger awakening its dreary echoes.

It was quite deserted when Heron reached it.

The little shop in which he had taken refuge on the former occasion was closed.

But three miserable oil lamps lit the whole of the thoroughfare.

One was at each end of the street, the other about midway between them.

And the light they shed about them was of that gloomy, dubious description that only might be said to confuse the darkness, and render it more perplexing.

Heron stepped into a doorway, and looked warily about him.

He began almost to suspect that Quiver was right, and that no attempt would be made until the following night to carry off the fair young creature, whose beauty seemed to be the most perilous gift she could possess.

But Heron was not left for many moments to speculate upon this idea.

He heard a footfall in the street.

Shrinking closer into his hiding place, Heron let this person pass the doorway, and only saw that he was a tallish man, wearing a hat with a peculiarly broad brim, and a roquelaire cloak, with a collar of fur of rather a noticeable character.

He might be only a chance passenger in the street.

But still there was a something about the lounging manner in which he proceeded which forbade that idea.

After he had passed the doorway, Heron stepped out a pace on to the step, and although still shrouded from observation himself, by the iron railing of the area, he managed to keep the man in view.

Under the lamp, which was in the middle of the street, this man paused.

He either made the sound with his own lips, or with an artificial whistle, but three times he produced a rather faint but sufficiently shrill sound to be easily heard by any one listening for it.

This was conclusive.

Felix Heron felt quite certain, now, that an attempt would be made on that night to carry out the villanous project.

Situated as the man was within the sphere of the oil lamp, Heron could just manage to take in the outlines of his figure.

It was not Quiver.

But it bore a striking resemblance to the other man, named Rufus, who was his companion in iniquity.

No answer came to the whistling sounds.

Rufus, if it were he, paused for about five minutes, and then whistled again.

During that five minutes Heron had made a determination.

It was to return the signal.

He did so faintly, as though he were desirous of using extreme caution.

The man with the roquelaire cloak started at the sound; and, after listening for a few seconds to assure himself from which direction it came, he walked hastily towards the doorway in which Felix Heron was concealed.

And now Heron stood sufficiently forward to let himself be seen faintly.

"Is that you, Quiver?"

Heron had heard Quiver speak often enough to be able to imitate his voice.

"Yes," he said; "and that's you, Rufus?"

"To be sure it is. But what are you stuck there for?"

"I thought I was to wait."

"Nonsense! Come on! The coach will be here directly. I only wonder it's so late as it is. The girl may come out and go home, and all our trouble to-night will be for nothing."

"Come here," said Heron.

"What is it?"

"I have something particular to say to you."

Rufus stepped on to the doorstep; and, at the same moment, Heron grasped him by the throat with one of those terrible, vice-like pressures which were at once sufficient to convince any one subjected to them that escape was out of the question.

"Villain!" said Heron.

"Help! Murder!"

Heron shook him to and fro.

"Another word, and you are a dead man!"

"What?—what? Who?—who? Have mercy upon me!"

"Dare you ask for mercy, engaged as you are in this infamous transaction? You are worse than your employers; for, poor as the excuse may be, they can, at least, say that they are seduced by human passion and frailty."

This remark was, probably, thrown away upon Mr. Rufus, who only felt that he was in a dangerous position, and that somebody had hold of him who was highly qualified to keep that hold.

"Come this way," said Heron.

"Where to?" gasped Rufus.

"That is my business just now; for you are at my mercy. Either accompany me quietly, or I will fling you over the area rails here, and leave you to your fate!"

"Mercy! Don't do that!"

"Come on, then."

Heron knew perfectly well that two streets off there was a watch-house, or Round-house, as they were then called, belonging to the parish of St. Ann's, Soho.

Not wishing to take this man's life, and yet feeling the necessity of disposing of him for the remainder of the night, Heron thought that it would be a good plan to give him in charge, on some fictitious grounds, so as to ensure his being locked up until the morning.

It would not take many seconds to do this.

Still holding Rufus by the throat, Heron conducted him with rapidity to the door of the Round-house.

Without giving him any explanation, then, he

why he did so, Heron took off his hat and roque-laire cloak, and put them both on himself.

He then tapped at the Round-house door.

"Hilloa!" cried a voice from within. "Is that you, Barney? Have you brought the purl?"

Heron tapped again.

A small wicket in the upper portion of the door was angrily opened.

One of the night watch, with a nightcap, early as it was in the evening, drawn down over his ears, thrust out his head.

"What is it? What do you want here?"

"I am the Marquis of Hastings, and I wish to give this man into custody for robbery."

The magic of a title never fails of its effect in England.

The Round-house door was flung ostentatiously open, and the night watch crowded one upon another, to get sight of a real, live nobleman.

"Certainly, your honour's worship. Certainly, my lord, we'll take care of the rascal."

"But I've done nothing," said Rufus.

"The villain!" cried all the watch in chorus. "He dares to say he's done nothing, when he's given in charge by a real *markis*."

Heron drew himself up to his full height, and in commanding tones spoke.

"It does not suit me, as a nobleman in close attendance upon his Majesty, to say what this rascal has done."

"Certainly not, my lord—certainly not, my lord!"

"But I desire he be kept in close custody."

"We'll knock him down, my lord, and then take him up."

"There is no occasion; all you have to do is to place him in one of your most secure cells, and there leave him."

"We will—we will, my lord. Come on, you villain!"

"But I protest!" cried Rufus.

"He protests!" shouted the night constable on duty. "The villain protests against a *markis*!"

"Of course I do. What have I done? What's the charge?"

Rufus was getting bold, now that he found himself surrounded by the watch.

"Knock him down, Dennis!" cried the night constable.

"There you go!" said Denis. "Be jabers, my illegant darlint, there you goes!"

Dennis, with his lantern, struck Rufus such a crack on the top of the head, that he certainly knocked him down, and demolished the lantern by the same operation.

"That will do," said the night constable. "The charge now is for obstructing Dennis, one of the watch, in the execution of his duty, and breaking one lantern, the property of the parish of St. Ann's, Soho."

"Exactly," said Heron; "that will do capitally. Look him up, and be sure you keep him securely till the morning; and here are five guineas to drink the health of the Marquis of Hastings."

"Hurrah! Hurrah! Hurrah! Long life to your Majesty!"

Heron hastily left the Round-house, with a full conviction that Mr. Rufus was comfortably disposed of, most probably for the next four-and-twenty hours.

As he crossed its threshold, he heard the sententious remark of the night constable, most probably in reply to some remonstrance from Mr. Rufus.

"If a markis who stands five guineas to drink can't do what he likes I should like to know who can?"

CHAPTER CCXXXIX.

FELIX HERON PERMITS THE CAPTURE OF THE ARTIFICIAL FLOWER MAKER.

HERON made the best of his way back to the bye street where the young girl was to be attacked by her bitter foes.

The manner of the disposal of Mr. Rufus has naturally taken much time in the telling; but in reality the whole affair was transacted and concluded within seven or eight minutes of the period when Felix Heron first grasped him by the throat on the dim and dusky doorstep of the bye street.

But the heart of Felix Heron beat rapidly as he turned into that street and saw that a coach was in it.

He feared he was too late.

Yet the coach was stationary, and he had hardly taken six paces down the pavement when from a doorway out darted a man and caught him by the arm.

"A pretty fellow you are, Rufus, to be so late!"

It was Quiver who spoke.

"Am I late?" said Heron

"Yes, to be sure you are; and you were to have been here first!"

"Well, I'm here now!"

"Here now! Of course you are. But what do you mean by it? Am I to do all the work, besides having all the trouble and bother of deceiving that fellow at Whitcombe House, and making him think I'm a sort of saint, only gone astray a little?"

"Ah, yes!" said Heron.

"Come on—we expect the girl out every minute."

"All right!"

"Yes, all right! if I hadn't been as clever as I am, it would have been all wrong; and that gentleman—for he is a gentleman, and no mistake—who nabbed me, and walked me off to an iron room in Whitcombe House, would have been about our ears; and I can tell you we should have had just about as much chance with him as half a dozen mice with a tom-cat dropped among them."

"But how did you manage?"

"I told you."

"Oh, did you?"

"Why, what the deuce are you at? Didn't I tell you I'd put him off till to-morrow night? and then it will be just four-and-twenty hours too late, for this little baby-faced chit of a girl that his Grace is so fond of will be in snug quarters by that time."

"Oh, yes, his Grace—you mean the Duke of—of——"

"No, I don't. I wish I did. I heard him called your Grace, but that's all. However, old

Rufus, if you and I can only find out who he is, we shall make a better thing of it than now. That Deuce Ace and Lord Warringdale know well enough, and of course they are well paid."

"Oh, no doubt—no doubt."

"Well, now, come on. You see the coach?"

"Yes—who is on the box?"

"Deuce Ace."

"And where is Warringdale?"

"Inside."

"Oh, that's it!"

"Yes, but he'll come out and lend us a helping hand. We're not half a dozen doors from the house now, so I'll run on to the end of the street and seem to be coming one way, while you come the other. You can nab her then, if she runs your way, and I'll do the business if she comes my way."

"Of course—of course," said Heron. "But I say, Quiver?"

"Well, what now?"

"What a pair of rascals we are!"

"What of that? We get well paid, and we always were a pair of rascals, if we come to that."

"True! Run on—run on, and depend upon me to do my part of the work."

Quiver ran on, although Felix Heron was very loath to let him go after the treachery that had characterized his conduct.

The coach was drawn up close to the kerbstone of the pavement, about the distance of two houses from that where, in consequence of previous observation, it was known the young artificial flower-maker worked.

The conspiracy was complete in its details, and but for the presence of Heron, the young girl must have fallen into the toils which were laid for her destruction.

Rapidly, however, various ideas passed through the mind of Heron in regard to this transaction.

The painful one of those ideas was this. Would it not be far better that this young girl should be put to some trifling inconvenience—he, Heron, being always at hand to protect her—than that the attempt to abduct her should altogether be frustrated, providing that trifling inconvenience had the effect of enabling him, Heron, to discover who the "Grace" was who was at the bottom of the whole transaction?

But still Felix Heron hesitated before he could make up his mind to such a course as this.

It was one that might entail suffering, although in a limited degree, upon the young girl he wished to save.

It might be productive of the most intense anxiety at her home.

These were considerations which had their full weight with Felix Heron, and he would have given much for a few minutes' conversation with that young girl, in order not only to warn her of her danger, but to suggest to her the expediency of the course he thought of pursuing.

What he would have liked to say to her was just this.

"Will you, with a consciousness that a protecting arm is over you, put up with some temporary inconvenience?"

He had a kind of assurance upon his own mind that the reply would be in the affirmative.

But events were hurrying on, and there was scarcely time even for these few reflections to pass through the mind of Felix Heron.

Quiver had left him, and taken up the post he had indicated.

Peering from the coach window, Felix Heron saw the saturnine-looking countenance of his half brother, Lord Warringdale.

And from the coach-box there leant forward, in an unmistakable attitude of apprehension, as well as of interest, John Tarleton.

That man, of all others, who was ever regarded with a shuder by Felix Heron.

In him, he saw the person who in all the world he looked upon with special feelings of horror and dislike.

The murderer of his father.

The assassin who had deprived the late Earl of Whitcombe of the few precious years that might have remained to him of peace and repentance in this world.

Heron's hand involuntarily sought the hilt of his sword, and it required all his recollection of the sacred promise he had made to Edith to keep him from drawing his sword from its scabbard, and at once sacrificing John Tarleton to the memory of his murdered father.

But he restrained the impulse.

Lord Warringdale spoke.

It was but a word.

"Now!"

That was the word spoken.

It indicated that the period of action had arrived.

The door of the house in which the young artificial flower-maker worked, opened.

The young girl herself stood upon the threshold.

She was perfectly unconscious of danger.

The sort of half attempt that had been made on the day previous at her capture, was so confused and uncertain, that it had scarcely had given her an alarm.

The possibility or probability of any one attempting to seize her in the streets of London had never entered her imagination; and although she could not but be aware that some sort of scuffle had taken place around and about her on the previous occasion, yet she by no means associated that with an attempt to take her prisoner.

She turned and closed the door after her.

It took two efforts to do it, for the lock was rough and rusty.

Then, as she turned her face towards the open street, and as a faint gleam from the oil lamp fell upon it, Felix Heron could not but tell himself that she was radiantly beautiful.

She was one whose affection might well have been sought fairly and legitimately by the noblest or proudest, but the nefarious attempt that was about to be made for her destruction was as villanous as Heron was determined it should be futile.

A slight smile wavered upon the lips of the young girl.

Perhaps she was well pleased that her day's toil was over.

Perhaps she was thinking of her home.

Or it might be that the sunlight of some affection warmed her young heart, and in memory she was looking upon the face of a loved one.

The smile, however, was extremely sweet and gentle; and all unconscious of danger, she stepped forward on to the pavement, and within a very few paces of her foes.

Unconscious of her peril.

Unconscious, too, of the protecting influence that was about her.

Had the coach been close to the door, she might have taken an alarm; but its distance, although short from the house she had just quitted, did not in any way associate it with her or with that establishment.

"Now!" said Lord Warringdale again.

The word was evidently addressed to Felix Heron, who no doubt he fully believed to be the man Rufus.

Heron stepped forward.

Quiver had turned at the end of the street, and was now, in a slow, sauntering kind of manner, approaching the girl so as to meet her.

No. 76.—EDITH.

Heron was a few paces behind her, and could well see by the rate of progression of all parties that the encounter would take place nearly opposite the coach door.

He was still undetermined what to do.

He longed for a few seconds' conversation with the girl, which would have decided him at once one way or the other.

And he had now but those few seconds for reflection.

He came to a decision, but it was a kind of compromise of the question.

He made up his mind that she should be taken into the coach, and that he would enter it likewise, and ascertain from her if the result of her absence from home for another hour would be of consequence or not, she being assured all that time that she was in perfect safety.

But there was one difficulty.

Lord Warringdale was in the coach.

He must be removed at all hazards; and Heron took the opportunity of the few seconds still to spare to dart to the coach window and whisper, "My lord, you are known; I've had private information you'll be hunted to death."

"Ah!" cried Warringdale, in undisguised accents of alarm.

"It is certain!"

"Your name is Rufus?"

"Just so, my lord. Leave it to me, and I'll bring the girl in safety to you know where!"

"Certainly."

"Get out at the other side, my lord."

The fears of Warringdale were all painfully awakened.

Putting his hand out at the coach window on the side next the road, he hastily turned the door handle, and sprung out.

"Stop, stop!" said John Tarleton; "don't leave me!"

"All's right!" said Warringdale. "Desert your post at your peril!"

Heron had just time to effect this arrangement, and then to make his way back to the pavement, as a sharp, shrill cry broke upon his ears.

It was the first alarm of the young girl, upon finding her progress arrested by Quiver.

He had reached her, and seized her by the arm.

"Now, Rufus!" he cried; "quick! quick!"

"Here!" said Heron.

"Help! help!" cried the young girl. "What is it? What does it mean?"

Felix Heron, having made up his mind to a certain course, felt that the truest policy was to carry it out quickly.

He flung an arm round the slender waist of the girl, and taking advantage of his unusual height, he lifted her with ease from the pavement.

"Bravo!" cried Quiver.

Heron did not speak, but in three strides reached the coach door.

He sprung in with his astonished and terrified burden.

"Drive on, Deuce Ace!" he cried.

"Confound you!" muttered John Tarleton; "why do you name me?"

The girl uttered a shrill scream.

"Peace!" muttered Heron. "You are as safe as though in heaven!"

It was probably the tone of gentleness and kindness which had more effect upon her than the words.

She was silent, although she trembled excessively.

Heron closed the coach door himself; and Quiver, with no doubt a full conviction on his own mind that Lord Warringdale was within the vehicle, scrambled up behind.

John Tarleton was in a fright.

The evasion of Warringdale, and the sudden capture of the girl, had all happened so quickly, that his faculties were rather confused.

It was just as much as he could do to feel conscious that now he ought to drive off at once to that dreary house close to St. James's Palace where his "Grace" by courtesy, but not by nature, contemplated so much wickedness.

The coach moved off.

At its first motion, the alarm of the girl came back again; and she uttered two shrieks, which Heron could not suppress.

"Peace! peace! I implore you!" he said.

"Listen to me as calmly as you can; and I will, in a few words, inform you of the meaning of all this, and at the same time convince you of your own absolute safety."

"No, no!"

"Let me say yes! I am a gentleman—a nobleman of unstained honour! My life for your safety! Nothing but my absolute destruction can pave the way for injury to a single hair of those tresses which have awakened unholy wishes in the heart of the destroyer!"

The tones of Heron were eminently calculated to soothe the alarm of the young girl; and, although her tears flowed, and she uttered suppressed sobs, she was comparatively silent.

The coach rumbled on.

CHAPTER CCXL.

FELIX HERON ACCOMPANIES AMELIA TO THE HOUSE IN PALL MALL.

A CONFUSED bumping noise on the roof of the vehicle convinced Heron that Quiver was scrambling over it from behind, to enjoy a conversation with John Tarleton on the coach-box.

The distance was so short from the scene of the abduction to the house in Pall Mall, that Heron felt it necessary to compress into the smallest possible space what he had to say.

He thought it far better to tell the girl, plainly and clearly, what was the meaning of the whole transaction, than to leave her imagination to suggest a thousand doubts and fears.

"There are men in London," he said,—"men of wealth, rank, and influence, who, when they see a fair girl like yourself, whose beauty and innocence attract them—for innocence is in itself a charm even to the most depraved hearts—will seek any means of being enabled to whisper the fact of their odious passion in their ears."

"Oh, kill me—kill me! Rather kill me!" said the girl.

"Hush! Again and again let me tell you that you are perfectly safe. A plan was laid to seize you in the street, and convey you to a house in Pall Mall, where you would have been without help, and where mercy is unknown. That plan came to my ears, and I determined to frustrate it."

"But I am here—I am seized—I am carried off!"

"To appearance—yes; but you shall go no further than to the end of this street, except with your own fair and free will."

"Oh, let me go now!"

"In one moment. Hear me first, however, before you make your irrevocable decision. You are not the only fair young innocent girl who will be exposed to this daring outrage. You yourself are ? , for I am prepared to see you in safety to your own home; but if you would save others who, unlike you, may fall into the hands of the destroyer with no protecting arm near, you will hesitate before you reject the proposition I make to you."

"What proposition?" asked the girl, timidly.

"These people who have seized you believe me to be one of their number, because I personate one whom I have disposed of for the present. What I want you to do, then, is simply this. Suffer yourself to be taken wherever they please, I of course accompanying you and assuring you of safety; the object being to discover who is the prime mover in these transactions, and so, by fears of exposure or more active measures, put an end to them at once and for ever."

The girl hesitated.

"Do not say no," added Heron; "but feeling that you yourself are safe, join with me in the protection of many an unknown and innocent girl, who may else fall a victim when there is no one to stretch out a hand to save her."

"I will."

"That is brave! You trust me?"

"I do—I will."

"Your name?"

"Amelia Travers."

"You have parents, brothers, sisters, and dear friends?"

"Alas! no, I am alone in all the world. There is no one to expect me—no one to mourn for me —no one to——"

The girl paused.

Felix Heron felt perfectly conscious that she could not say there was no one to love her.

But that was not a subject upon which he wished to converse at so critical a moment.

He wished rather to say something more that would give her confidence; and although he could not entrust her with his real name and rank, he said, "It is proper that I should return your confidence by telling you that I reside in St. James's Street. I am the husband of the Countess of Whitcombe, who is well aware of my proceedings this night, and of the determination I made, not only to rescue you, but to ask you to be the means of rescuing others, whom I might not be so fortunate to be able to save as I have you."

"If you are the husband of the Countess of Whitcombe," said the girl, "you should be the Earl of Whitcombe."

This was a shrewd guess, and but that on principle Heron could not entrust her with the secret of his existence, he would have at once assented to the proposition.

"We will talk further on that subject with the Countess herself," he said. "All that I want you to feel is that you are now absolutely safe. I am armed, and well able to use those arms; and I do not believe there is any power that can be arrayed against you with which I shall not be able fully to cope."

"I trust you, sir."

"Freely and implicitly?"

"I do so, indeed; and it is not so much from what you say, as from the way in which you say it. And now that this thing has happened, I can think back, and understand that it has been attempted more than once before."

"There can be no doubt about that."

As Heron uttered these words the coach stopped.

He glanced from the window, and saw that they were at the door of the house where the wicked project had been concocted, and where,

no doubt, his "Grace" was waiting the result of the villany.

Heron whispered to the girl.

"Seem to be reluctant, and call faintly for help; but, trust me, all is well!"

The coach door was opened.

"This way, quick!" said a voice.

"Is she there?" said another.

"Here," replied Heron.

"Bring her in—bring her in! Is it you, Rufus?"

"Yes."

Heron again flung his arm round the young girl, and carried her into the house.

The outer door was instantly slammed shut.

A faint light was at the further end of the passage, and as Heron looked at it he saw it slowly ascending as its bearer went up some staircase in that direction.

"Follow him!" said a voice; "follow the light! Has the girl fainted?"

"Help—oh, help!" said Amelia.

"No!" replied Heron. "All's well!"

He strode forward, following the light; and reaching the landing on the first floor, he passed into a spacious apartment, which was dimly illuminated by a few of the wax-lights in a chandelier, which carried in reality about forty, being lit.

Even by that faint light it was quite possible to see that the room was gorgeously furnished:

Silken hangings, mirrors, rich velvet carpeting, and a profusion of gilding in all directions, testified to the costly character of the apartment.

Heron glanced about him, and was somewhat surprised to see that he and the young girl were alone.

The person who had preceded him with the light had certainly gone into that room, but apparently had found some means of leaving it by another door.

Heron then was about to speak to Amelia, when he was startled by a voice, from whence he knew not, saying, "It is done! Leave the saloon, and lock the door on the outer side!"

Amelia clung to Heron,

"No, no!" she whispered; "not for worlds! I cannot stay here alone! You promised to protect me! Stay with me—stay!"

"I will come back instantly."

"On your word? In the name of heaven, you promise me?"

"I do, in the name of heaven!"

It was a hazardous expedient that suggested itself to Heron, but he seated the young girl on a large settee, the crimson silk back of which was unusually large; he then strode to the door, and opening it suddenly, dashed it shut again, at the same moment sinking quite to the floor, so that if even any casual observation were directed towards him, it would appear that he was gone.

The sort of twilight in which the room was, favoured a manœuvre of this kind, if boldly and rapidly executed.

It was successful.

No notice was taken of Heron's presence, and the room was so full of miscellaneous articles of costly furniture, that he had no difficulty in crawling successfully along the floor to the back of the settee, on which was Amelia.

"I am here," he said.

"Thank heaven!"

"Be at peace, for all is well."

"But what will happen?"

"I know not; but you are safe. I will not leave you again beyond the width of this room."

The stillness in the house was something remarkable, and Heron could not divest his mind from a certain feeling of superstition in regard to the whole affair.

It seemed to him so unreal and so absolutely strange, that he would scarcely have been surprised suddenly to have awakened, and find it but a dream.

This state of affairs, however, lasted but a very few minutes.

A faint confused murmuring sound, as of conversation taking place between several persons, came upon the ears of Heron and Amelia.

After listening attentively for some few minutes, Heron was able to localise those sounds, so to speak, and to feel convinced that they came from a room adjoining the further end of the magnificent apartment in which he was.

"Amelia!"

"Yes—yes?"

"Do you hear those sounds, and will you permit me to cross the room in order to listen to them more closely?"

The girl hesitated.

Nervously she clung to the sleeve of Heron's coat, and he could feel that she trembled with a thousand undefined apprehensions.

"You are a brave girl, Amelia," he said, "and I feel confident you can protect yourself; as confident, indeed, as that I feel there is no one in this house unfriendly to you, who can boast of a real spark of courage. Take my sword—hold it firmly by the hilt, and scruple not to use it freely if necessary, while I go and listen to these sounds."

Amelia took the sword tremblingly; but there must have been an innate spirit of chivalry and courage about her, to induce her to take it at all.

Felix Heron at once crossed the apartment towards a door, the upper panels of which were of looking-glass.

He felt confident that in that direction he was to look for the persons, the murmuring sound of whose conversation had come so plainly upon his ears.

The door yielded to his touch, but before he passed through it, he looked back, and through the twilight obscurity of the room, he saw Amelia.

She sat like some beautiful statue upon that settee, with a drawn sword in her hand.

The faint light from the wax candles shone upon the glittering blade.

That again sent a reflection upon the face of the young girl.

Felix Heron thought he had never seen any one look so truly beautiful.

He would fain have spoken to her.

He would fain have said one word for the purpose of assuring her that all was safe, and that she was still watched over by a hand and heart that would not fail her.

But it would not have been prudent to do so, and leaving that word unspoken, he passed out of the gorgeous apartment into a narrow passage.

That passage was in perfect darkness, and he only saw its limited extent by the faint gleam of light that shone into it from the room he quitted.

But he felt he was on the right track.

The murmur of conversation came more fully upon his ears.

He followed the mysterious passage for a considerable distance, feeling the walls carefully on each side in the hope of finding some door that might lead from it to the room where the mysterious persons were conversing.

At length he felt confident that he had passed the confines of that apartment, for the murmurs of the voices began to die away.

Heron retraced his steps in perplexity.

Once more he reached the door of the room he had recently left; and glancing into it, he still saw Amelia on the settee, with that bright and glistening sword in her hand.

She evidently saw him, for she made a slight movement of the sword blade.

And Heron waved his hand to her to give her assurance that all was well.

He then resumed his search in the narrow passage, and this time it was not without a result.

He had felt before that the walls were covered with a rough kind of cloth, but now he accidentally placed his hand upon a portion of it which was loose and limp to the touch.

That portion of the cloth formed a kind of curtain over a small window composed of but one pane of glass.

The moment he removed the curtain, a broad, but faint gleam of artificial light came through the glass into the passage.

Heron shrunk back; for the natural idea at the moment was that he must of necessity be seen.

A few seconds' reflection, however, dissipated this notion.

He was in darkness in the passage, and the room was lighted.

Looking, therefore, from the shadowy obscurity of where he was into the partially illuminated apartment, it was impossible he could be seen, while, so far as the amount of light would permit him, he might, with ease, be a spectator of everything and everybody that was on the other side of the pane of glass.

It was a singular scene that met his gaze.

The room seemed to be a perfectly square one, and in the middle of the floor was a table covered with a heavy cloth of green velvet.

Around that table sat eleven persons.

One chair was vacant; and on the table immediately in front of it lay an embroidered pocket-handkerchief and a snuffbox, so richly set with jewels, that they kept shooting forth rays of prismatic light in the most beautiful profusion.

Hardly had Heron time to reckon the number of these persons, and take a glance round the mysterious apartment, when a door opened at the further end of the room, and an individual entered, at whose appearance the eleven persons who were sitting round the table immediately rose.

The new comer bowed with something like hauteur, and then took his place on that twelfth chair which had evidently been reserved for him.

CAPTAIN HERON SAVES AMELA FROM AN IGNOMINIOUS FATE.

Presented Gratis with No. 76, of the New Edition of EDITH HERON, the Sequel to Edith the Captive ; or, the Robbers of Epping Forest.

Heron could hardly believe his eyes.

It was the King himself!

It was too evident now that that mysterious house was not in such close proximity to the Palace of St. James's for nothing.

That some secret route existed between it and the abode of royalty was now a matter past dispute.

The plot was thickening.

The King himself was evidently taking a part in it.

Heron felt certain that it was but a new phase of that kind of life in which the King was encouraged by such despicable creatures as my Lord Clackington.

The eleven persons round the table reseated themselves without a word.

The King then spoke.

"Well, gentlemen, I am here! Who is the fortunate individual who is to be blessed by the accomplishment of his wishes this night?"

"His Grace of Harlington!" said a voice.

The voice grated upon the ear of Felix Heron.

It was that of the hateful Lord Clackington, who, since the disappearance of the imaginary Baron Von Peck, had crept again into favour with the King.

"Ah! I recollect the lot fell upon his Grace, and I rejoice to see him present!"

"I humbly thank your Majesty!" said a voice, which Heron now recognised as the same as that he had heard at Holland House.

"Yes," said another speaker; "the ballot was duly taken at our last meeting; and inasmuch as we all take it by turns, without respect of rank, to name some fair and apparently inaccessibly beautiful girl, who may have attracted our individual fancy, and who is to be brought to the house by the agents of this society, let the cost, the trouble, and the risk be what they may, his Grace availed himself of his privilege, and named the fair one whom he adored!"

"I did," said the Duke of Harlington. "Chance —the mere accident of a moment—gave me a glance at the fairest face and sweetest figure these mortal eyes ever gazed upon."

"Stop!" said the King. "Is she of rank?"

"Certainly not, your Majesty. We only prey upon the common people. The middle classes of England present to the eyes of the nobility fair forms and beautiful faces, and I am sure there is no gentleman of this society who for a moment would think of interfering with the honour of a noble or patrician beauty."

"That is well," said the King; "the common people are of no consequence."

"Not the least—not the least," was murmured round the table, from mouth to mouth.

Felix Heron was indignant, but he smiled to himself.

"We shall see—we shall see," he said gently.

"And," said the King, "my lord marquis, you have named your beauty."

"I have, your Majesty. She is but a poor working girl, although I think, by her air and manner that her origin has been something higher in the social scale."

"And her name," said Lord Clackington, in croaking accents, as he opened a book that was before him—"her name is Amelia Travers."

"It is so," said the Duke.

"Then," said the King, "my Lord Clackington will report proceedings, after which it will be the turn of the next on the list to make his choice by giving the name of the—the victim."

The King evidently said victim because he was at a loss for another word.

A slight murmur of disapproval ran round the table.

A community of vice had familiarized those persons too much with the monarch to make them particular in the expression of their disapprobation.

CHAPTER CCXLII

THE COUNCIL CHAMBER IN THE MYSTERIOUS HOUSE IN PALL-MALL.

THE King was there only as an individual—an important one truly—inasmuch as he could throw the shield of his own invulnerability over any of the society who fell into the meshes of the law, but still he did not appear in that room in his character of King of England.

"I should not have said victim," he added; "but a better word did not come to my aid at the moment."

The various members of the villanous society bowed their heads in acknowledgment of this slight apology.

"We will have the report, my Lord Clackington," said the King.

Lord Clackington, in his grating tones, read from the book he had opened :—

"The name of Amelia Travers, an artificial flower-maker, supposed to be about the age of sixteen, having been placed in the urn by his Grace of Harlington, the agents of the society were duly instructed in the work they had to do.

"It was discovered that she resided in Moorfields, from whence, daily, she proceeded to her employment in Queen Street, Soho.

"From careful and numerous inquiries, it was ascertained that the girl's character was irreproachable; but as nothing is so fallacious as such characters given by third parties, the elderly gentlewoman who is in the employment of this society sought an interview with her.

"We have that person's report, which is exceedingly unsatisfactory, since the girl listened to nothing, but repelled all overtures with scorn.

"It became necessary to adopt the other plan of proceedings hitherto found successful in similar cases.

"The order was given to the agents of the society to spare neither time, trouble, nor expense in securing the girl and conducting her to this house."

My Lord Clackington closed the book.

There was a silence of some seconds' duration.

Then the King spoke.

"Let the principal agent make his report."

A bell was rung.

A door, thickly covered with velvet, opened in one of the walls, and Lord Warringdale appeared.

He bowed low and cringingly to the twelve persons there assembled, and it was evident that he had a pretty good knowledge of who it was that occupied the chair of honour, since towards the King he made so low an obeisance, that it seemed doubtful if he would ever assume his perpendicularity again.

"The report," said the King, sharply.

"I have the honour to present it," said Warringdale.

As he spoke, he produced a folded paper, about the size of a note, which he handed to Lord Clackington.

That most obnoxious and profligate individual opened the note, and read in his most croaking tones :—

"Amelia Travers is secured, and waits in the tapestried drawing-room the pleasure of his Grace of Harlington."

The Duke immediately rose to his feet.

"It is well done, by Jove!" he cried; "it is well and promptly done!"

Lord Clackington replied to him, drily.

"This society never fails. An error would be destruction!"

The King waved his hand, and the Duke resumed his seat.

"To business!" he said. "Who stands next upon our list?"

"The Marquis of Morecliffe," said Lord Clackington.

"Whom names he?"

A slim, boyish-looking personage spoke in a piping tone of voice.

"Since it is my turn to name a candidate for the polite attentions of this society, I beg to say that there is a tradesman's daughter at Islington, so dazzlingly beautiful, and yet withal so carefully tended and so narrowly watched, that the voice of adoration can never reach her ears."

"You choose her?" said Clackington.

"I do!"

"Her name?"

"Amabelle Tracy."

"Good! It is enough! Her special residence need only be given, and this day week, Marquis, she will be at your disposal."

"Her father keeps a cutler's shop in the High Street, Islington. I know not the number; but with the name and those indications there can be no mistake."

"None whatever," said Clackington.

The assembled persons slightly inclined their heads, as though they would intimate that that was enough, and that no further particulars need be required for the purpose of decoying or forcing the young girl named to her destruction.

Another of the infamous assembly then loudly spoke.

His voice was eager, and he half rose from his chair, as he said, "When my turn comes, I shall propose the capture of——"

"Hold!" cried the King, sternly. "You strangely forget, my lord, one of the primary conditions of the association—which is, that no more than one name at a sitting shall be given in, and that, until that name is disposed of, another shall nor be mentioned."

"That is so," interposed Lord Clackington; "and I should have thought that the illustrious person who has just spoken, and who has been so

well rebuked by a more illustrious person still, knew well that regulation."

A flush of angry pride was upon the face of the man who had thus interrupted the proceedings.

"Enough—enough, gentlemen," he said; "I had forgotten."

"That is sufficient," said the King.

"Thank heaven for so much mercy!" said the Duke of Harlington, with a forced laugh.

But he was deathly pale.

There must have been at the bottom of his heart some lingering sensation of the villany he contemplated.

The shadow of coming remorse was upon his soul.

It was too evident that a battle was raging in his breast, between the better principles of his nature, and the wild, lawless passion which had induced him to make one of that assemblage.

Felix Heron heard all this with great indignation.

But he was troubled how to act.

Even were he to go back to that magnificent apartment in which he had left Amelia, and procure from her his sword again, it would be for him far too hazardous an enterprise to attack so large a number of no doubt well-armed men.

It was just possible, however, that even yet he might fling an arm around that young girl, and with his trusty sword in the other hand, rescue her from the dim shadows and the polluted atmosphere in that house.

The desire to do so grew strongly upon him.

It was a desire that he would in all probability have carried out, but that as he paused and hesitated for a few seconds, a change took place in the posture of affairs in what might be called the council room.

The King spoke.

"My Lord Clackington."

Clackington bowed.

"Humbly, Mr. President, at your gracious service," he said.

"Is there aught else to bring before this meeting?"

"Nothing, sir."

"Then it is dissolved until to-morrow night at the same hour."

The King rose as he spoke.

Every one present likewise gained his feet, and bowed low towards the King, who, after a slight inclination of the head, left the apartment.

Then a few murmured sentences were exchanged between those who remained.

After that, one by one they left the room, until only the Duke of Harlington and Lord Clackington remained.

"Joy, your Grace," said Clackington,—"I wish you joy!"

"Reptile!" was the brief reply.

Clackington recoiled as though he had been struck.

"Did I hear aright?"

"I said reptile!"

"Then your Grace shall dearly rue that word!"

"I will meet you, my Lord Clackington, when and where you will!"

"And this," said Lord Clackington, in high, croaking accents,—"this is the reward of all my exertions in the formation of this little society! These are the thanks I get for——"

"Peace!" cried the Duke of Harlington. "One may have an object, and use certain despicable tools to carve one's way towards it, but we despise those tools, let them do their work never so well!"

The Duke turned, and began pacing the apartment to and fro with agitated steps.

Lord Clackington clenched his hands and shook them threateningly behind his back.

Then he, too, left the room.

His Grace of Harlington was alone.

Alone in that dim light which had only sufficed to let the assemblage see each other's faces with sufficient clearness to be certain that no intruder had found his way to that secret conclave.

Slowly he wheeled round upon his heels, and cast his gaze into every corner of the apartment.

He drew a long breath, and then he spoke.

"Alone—I am alone, and in the adjoining room is the victim! This has been my first chance, and shall I now shrink from it? Pshaw! Courage, Harlington—courage!"

He took two steps towards that identical door through the half-glazed upper panel of which Felix Heron had been so deeply an interested spectator of the secret meeting.

Heron retreated.

He did not retreat because his Grace of Harlington was advancing, but he felt that his proper place was by the side of that young girl for whose safety he had pledged his honour.

Pledged even his life!

Heron rapidly sped along the narrow passage, and made his appearance again in the magnificent drawing-room.

The speed with which he entered it alarmed Amelia.

For a moment, she scarcely recognised him as her friend and deliverer.

She uttered a slight cry, and dropped the sword at her feet.

"Is this the way," said Heron, "you would have defended yourself?"

She knew his voice, although she could hardly be said to see well the outlines of his face and form, for the single wax-light in that room had burnt lower, and its direct beams were intercepted by the glittering pendants of the chandelier in which it was ensconced.

"Courage!" said Heron. "Remember, I shall be with you! Fear nothing, but be bold and resolute!"

"I am full of fears! My heart beats rapidly, and my brain throbs! I cannot endure this trial! I promised that I would, because I thought I could! Take me hence!—oh, save me, I implore you!"

She trembled excessively.

"One word," said Heron, "and you shall judge for yourself. A man will come here to seek you, whom I should call an unmitigated villain, and who I would not permit to breathe the same air with you, but that from some words I heard him utter, I believe that his better angel is struggling with his evil passions."

"Save me! Save me!"

"Hush! hear me out. I shall be at hand—almost within arm's length of you."

"Are you certain?"

"Certain as that I live that I shall not be further distant from you than I can reach with my sword's point. Will you, then, be patient for a few brief minutes?"

"I will—I will; my trust is in you."

"It shall not be betrayed."

"And in heaven!"

"That will never fail you."

Felix Heron picked up the sword, and had just time to step behind one of the massive silken window curtains, when the door of the magnificent saloon opened, and the Duke of Harlington appeared.

———

CHAPTER CCXLIII.

THE DUKE OF HARLINGTON'S INTERVIEW WITH AMELIA TRAVERS.—THE COMBAT.

DIM as the light was in that gorgeous apartment it seemed to shine specially upon the white face and glistening eyes of the Duke.

Heron heard him speak.

"She is there!"

Amelia uttered a shuddering half shriek, as with slow steps the Duke advanced.

The purposed victim and the purposed betrayer gazed at each other then in silence.

It was the Duke who first broke that terrible stillness by speaking in a low, hoarse voice, as though he feared the very spirits of the air—if there be such things—should overhear him.

"You are Amelia Travers?"

The words were spoken interrogatively; and with a great effort, feeling her safety in the contiguity of Heron, the girl replied to them.

"My name is Amelia Travers."

The Duke advanced another step.

"Did you ever love?"

This time there was no reply.

But Amelia clutched convulsively the back of the couch with one hand, while the other was stretched imploringly towards the hiding-place of Felix Heron.

"Girl," said the Duke, "I have eyes, and I have seen that you are beautiful. I have ears, and they have drank in the melody of your voice. I am rich, great, and noble. There is not a pleasure which gold can purchase which may not be yours. You have but to say the word—promising at the same time to meet me with a smile and leave me with a smile."

"I know not what you mean," said Amelia, faintly. "By violence I have been brought hither. I know you not; and I demand my liberty."

"I will explain. Had I—great, noble, and wealthy as I am—sought you at your own humble home, or in any place where you could have been surrounded by a hundred babbling tongues—each of whom, while probably envying you your lot, would have declaimed against it—I should have pleaded my passion in vain."

"It is in vain now."

"Say not so—oh, say not so! You do but enchant me more by that amiable simplicity of voice and manner."

"Oh, save me!"

These words were addressed to Felix Heron; but the Duke, in his utter ignorance of the presence of a third person there, took them to imply how completely he was a victor upon the occasion, and the arbiter of the fate of Amelia.

"You should be proud and happy," he said. "It is my dearest wish to make you mine."

"That is scarcely possible," said Amelia. "You say that you are great and noble; and how would a poor work-girl grace your lofty state?"

"The brightest gem in my coronet pales before the lustre of your eyes!"

"Ah, no! It is not for the dove to mate into the eagle's nest. The lady-wife of such as you are should be sought for in the Court, and not among the humble workers and toilers of the city."

"But the lady-love," said the Duke, "may be sought anywhere, so that beauty ratify the choice."

"I will not affect to misunderstand you," said Amelia; "and in reply, with all the scorn that I can express, I loathe and reject your offers!"

"Beware!"

"I will not beware; but I repeat my words!"

"Girl, you know not where you are."

"I am on earth!"

"Ay, are you?"

"And there is a heaven above us!"

"There may be. But that same heaven will not interfere to baulk me of my beautiful prey."

"It will—it will! I have faith!"

"Well, fair one, and so have I. Faith in your beauty—faith in myself—in the secrecy and privacy of this house, through the dense walls of which your loudest shrieks will scarce find an echo. I tell you, girl, you are mine, helplessly mine; and it were well you reflected upon the fact."

"No; I despise you still! Your walls are not strong enough to hold me! All your plans and machinations will fail you yet!"

"We shall see."

The Duke dashed the door, through which he had entered, shut, and then turning to Amelia, he cried, "I tell you, girl, your beauty has maddened me! My thoughts by day, and my dreams by night, have been of you; and do you think that now I have you here in safety, seclusion, and secrecy, I will let you escape me?"

"One moment!" cried Amelia.

"What would you say? Ah! you relent?"

"No! But for your own sake I implore you——"

The Duke stamped angrily.

"This is madness, folly! Precious moments fly over our heads like unheeded autumn clouds."

"One moment more!" cried Amelia. "Is there no one whom you really love—not as you love me, with lawless passion—but whom, in the open face of day, you could make your own by the sacred altar, and with words of blessing?"

"Peace—peace! Such is not the question!"

"Have you no sister whose honour is dear to you as life itself?"

The Duke drew himself up proudly.

"Girl, you know not what you say. It is not for you to speak of the high and noble, the pure of blood, whose honour is without a stain, in such a fashion!"

"And think you," said Amelia, "that there is no honour, no purity without a stain, except in what you call your high nobility?"

"Peace! peace!"

"Oh, sir, how strangely you mistake! The honour and the purity of the poor work-girl are dearer possessions to her than to the sisters of a noble, for what has she beside, if those lights of her existence are lost for ever?"

The Duke of Harlington took refuge in great anger.

A common expedient when it is difficult to reply.

"You do but turn me from you," he said, "not as regards my admiration for your beauty, but in respect to any gentler emotions which might be awakened in my heart."

"Have you no mercy?"

"None. I disclaim the word. With toil, trouble, and some mental agony, I have sought you, and consented to the means which have placed you in my power. I will not be baulked of my reward."

"Will not my contempt stir you?"

"Not even that; but still I say to you again, girl, beware; or mingling with my admiration will come a sentiment of hatred, and then, when you are the supplicant, and when you feel that you can have no friend but me in all the world, I shall cast you off to destruction and despair."

"Then," said Amelia, "I echo that one word. I say to you, despair!"

"To me?"

"Yes, great and noble as you boast yourself to be—I say 'despair' to you."

"You speak in riddles."

"No. I said I had faith, and I have faith still, that even here, amid the apparent silence and desolation of this house, heaven will raise me up a protector."

The Duke laughed hoarsely.

"Call upon him now," he said; "for if ever such a shadowy protector were required, now is the time!"

"Not yet!"

"Ha, ha! Not yet?"

"No, not yet, because I wish to give you time for repentance!"

"Repentance! I scorn the word!"

"Oh, do not scorn it, for it brings with it perchance life itself!"

"Life?"

"Yes. I wish to give you time to retreat in safety and in honour. Utter but one word of regret for the ignoble part you have played to-night—summon up from the depths of your heart some better feeling, and—and——"

"And what?"

"Save yourself!"

"Save myself? The girl is mad! If any one has need of saving it is surely you, beautiful Amelia! But we waste precious moments. You are mine, and mine only; and were all the world arrayed against me, I swear by this fond embrace——"

"Help! The time has come!"

"I am here!" said Heron.

He stepped out from behind the silken curtain.

His voice was like a trumpet blast.

In the dim light of that apartment his sword flashed like a meteor, as glittering in the eyes of

the Duke of Harlington, the bright blade interposed between him and Amelia Travers.

He shrunk back, and would have fallen but that a chair intercepted his backward progress.

"Now, sir," said Heron, coldly and sternly, "do you believe, or do you not, that heaven in its own good time can raise up a defender to the helpless and the innocent?"

"Confusion!"

"Yes, my lord Duke, that is the word—confusion! You have well named it."

"There is another word!" half-shrieked the Duke, in accents of rage.

"Doubtless!"

"You know it not! It is death! Death to him who steps in between me and my heart's passion!"

There was a bright flash!

A sharp report!

A ring and shatter of glass, as some of the

No. 77.— EDITH.

window panes gave way to the sudden concussion of the air.

The Duke had drawn a pistol from a concealed pocket, and fired it full at the head of Heron.

Had his intent been not quite so murderous, he might have succeeded in disabling the noble and gallant defender of Amelia Travers.

But owing to the height of Heron, and to the crouching attitude which the consciousness of guilt had given to the Duke of Harlington, he was compelled to fire in a slant line upward.

All the world knows how easy it is to miss such a shot.

The bullet flew at least six inches over the head of Heron.

It struck the centre of a large pier-glass, starring it into fragments.

Amelia, with a shriek of dismay, fell senseless on the couch.

Heron spoke as calmly as he had done before.

"Now, your Grace," he said, "you have added the crime of attempted murder to the outrage which you contemplated against this poor helpless girl, and be assured the time of retribution has arrived for you."

"Help—help!" cried the Duke.

"Shame upon that cry!" said Heron; "and yet it must needs be useless; for was it not your boast but a short time previously that even the shrieks of outraged innocence would scarcely penetrate with the faintest echo through these walls?"

The Duke shrunk back step by step, feeling his way past the various articles of furniture in the saloon until he reached one of its walls.

There he stood at bay.

With flashing energy he drew his sword from its scabbard, and stood upon his guard.

"Be it so," he said. "I will not be murdered in cold blood by any bully. Come on, and let me see if this vaunted courage and generosity will stand the test of cold steel."

"There have been no vaunts," said Heron; "but be assured that the courage which has brought me here, alone and unaided, to stand between an innocent, gentle girl and her destruction, will not desert me now."

Heron strode forward.

"Stop!" cried the Duke.

Heron paused.

A feeling of great dejection began to take possession of him, for he felt in all probability he should kill this man.

"Stop," added the Duke: "this is a duel of life or death!"

"You have said it."

"But I am noble."

"By courtesy and birth."

"And so," added the Duke, "it is not fit that I should cross swords with, perchance, some insolent artizan, who himself, probably, is enamoured of the fair face which has lured me here to so much danger."

"Banish your scruples," said Heron, mournfully; "and learn from me that in the gradations of rank which distinguish the nobility of England, I stand but one step below you."

"An earl?"

"You have said it."

"Impossible! I know you not?"

"And yet many know me. To you, who stand upon the brink of eternity, I will reveal myself; and for once trusting to your word, that no intelligible sound can pass these walls, I tell you, false, faithless Duke of Harlington as you are, that I am the proscribed, persecuted Earl of Whitcombe."

The Duke uttered a strange cry.

"You will fight me now?" said Heron.

"No. I fight not with the dead, or with an impostor living. The Earl of Whitcombe is no more. His death is well authenticated."

"I have spoken," said Heron, "and you shall fight."

The swords clashed together.

"Help! Help!" cried the Duke again.

A rapping knocking came at the door which he himself had slammed so closely shut.

Some concealed spring kept it secure, and whoever was without had no force sufficient to master it.

A feeling of desperation then came over the Duke of Harlington.

"Be it so!" he cried. "One or both of us shall lie in death in this room."

The swords flashed and circled around each other like fiery serpents.

But the combat was brief.

Heron's strength and skill at his weapon soon asserted their supremacy.

The Duke fell with a half stifled shriek.

Heron's sword had passed through his breast

Then Heron turned hastily to the couch upon which lay the still insensible Amelia, and encircling her slight form with his left arm, he raised her with ease.

The furious knocking continued at the door which led to the narrow passage.

But that was not the route by which Heron had reached the saloon, and his object was to gain the open landing at the head of the staircase, and so leave the house at once.

But every precaution had been taken to prevent the escape of the poor victim of lawless passion.

That door was fast.

Heron had no resource but to place Amelia upon another couch, while he made an effort to force the door.

Twice he flung himself against it with all his force, but it resisted him.

He felt convinced, however, that it was only the lock which bid defiance to his efforts.

He drew one of his pistols, and was about to adopt the short, sharp, and ready mode of opening the lock, by sending a bullet crashing through it, when the door leading to the narrow passage, and at which the heavy knocking had been kept up, suddenly gave way.

Two persons appeared.

One was Quiver.

The other Lord Warringdale.

The vapour from the pistol-shot which had been fired by the Duke of Harlington still mingled with the atmosphere of the room, imparting a strange haziness to the dim twilight in which it was shrouded.

"Who called for help?" shouted Warringdale.

"There he is—shall I fire?" said Quiver.

"Fire!" echoed Warringdale.

Heron had just time to interpose himself between Amelia, as she lay upon the couch, and the discharge of a pistol by Quiver.

Heron felt at once that he was unwounded, and darting forward, he, with one sweeping blow of his sword, laid Quiver prostrate.

Warringdale made an effort to escape, but Heron detained him.

He caught him by the breast of his apparel, and held him up, as in his own natural voice, which Warringdale could never mistake, he said, "Brother, is this well done?"

Astonishment — terror — perfect fright — froz the faculties of Lord Warringdale.

He could not speak; and, thoroughly convinced as he was in his own mind of the decease of Heron some time ago, he fully believed himself to be in the grasp of some supernatural being.

That was too much for human nature.

Lord Warringdale fainted, and fell heavily to the floor, as Heron released him.

CHAPTER CCXLIV.

HERON, IN ENDEAVOURING TO FIND A WAY OF EGRESS FROM THE MYSTERIOUS HOUSE, SUDDENLY FINDS HIMSELF IN ST. JAMES'S PALACE.

HERON was a victor.

There seemed no one to oppose him now.

The thought came over him, that perchance the shortest way to leave that house would be to pass through that open doorway, and traverse the narrow passage, which surely must have some termination in an outlet to the street.

Heron picked up again his senseless burden, and with his sword still in his grasp, he made his way, in two or three seconds, to the room where the strange and villanous fraternity had held their sitting.

The lantern that had dimly lighted them was still there upon the centre of the table.

Heron thought it might be useful, and he managed to lift and carry it in the same hand that held his sword hilt.

The door through which the King had passed at the further end of that room was open.

With but a dreamy kind of idea that it might lead him quickly to the lower part of the house, Heron passed through it.

It led into a small octagonal-shaped chamber, which was in perfect darkness.

A precisely similar door, however, to that at which he had entered was opposite to him, and it yielded to a touch.

A complete change came over Felix Heron's sensations about that dim, mysterious house, and he felt that a suspicion which had arisen in his mind, to the effect that there was a direct communication between the mysterious residence and St. James's Palace, was about to be verified by an actual knowledge of the fact.

The aspect of the kind of passage or corridor in which Felix Heron now found himself, was perfectly conclusive on that point.

It was well lit by a lamp carried in the hands of a marble statue.

The floor was covered with rich carpeting, and the walls were adorned with stamped leather, so admirably fashioned that it had all the effect of a much richer material.

Heron was glad to be released from the care of the lantern, which would have interfered very much with the free use of his sword-arm.

He placed it upon the side of the pedestal which supported the statue, and then without pausing another moment he strode forward, determined that by courage and perseverance he would find a route to the open air.

He looked anxiously now in the face of Amelia, for there was light enough to enable him to do so.

A feeling of alarm took possession of him at the aspect of the deathlike face.

Felix Heron had every reason to believe that it was but a swoon, which excitement and excess of feeling had thrown her into; yet it looked so like death, that he might well be excused for looking upon it with a degree of alarm, such as any one little versed in feminine fainting might feel.

The passage was some twenty paces in length.

A gilt door was at its further extremity.

And if Heron had held any doubts that he was really within the precincts of the Palace of St. James's they must needs now have been dispelled, for over that gilt door were the royal arms in bold relief.

And perhaps any one now but Felix Heron would have hesitated about advancing further in that direction.

But he did not.

The feeling of indignation that had taken possession of him at the villany that had been attempted to be practised in the house he had just left was still dominant in his mind.

The brief, decisive conflict he had likewise had with the Duke of Harlington had produced a degree of excitement which tended in a great measure to banish calm reflection.

Bold and confident, therefore, in the justice of the cause he had espoused, Heron pushed forward, still carrying his fainting burden in his arms.

He opened the gilt door.

It led into a large and handsome room, on the hearth of which a fire, fed with some odoriferous wood, was burning.

The flickering flames that came from that fire were the only means by which that apartment was illuminated.

They were sufficient.

Probably, however, by their uncertainty and flashing waywardness, they made the room look larger than it was, and lent a mysterious brilliancy to its adornments.

A couch was drawn up near to the fireplace; and a footstool of crimson velvet, richly trimmed with bullion, close to the couch, seemed to indicate that the latter had been recently occupied.

If further evidence was wanted of this fact, it might be found in a handkerchief, trimmed with costly lace, which lay carelessly upon the couch.

One glance about him was sufficient to assure Felix Heron of where he was.

He had reached the private apartments of the King; and was actually beneath the roof of St. James's Palace.

Upon that couch the monarch who so unworthily wore the crown of England had recently sat.

Upon that footstool he had rested.

And, doubtless, the costly lace handkerchief was his.

By some natural impulse, Heron felt a distaste at the latter article.

With the point of his sword he at once jerked it into the wood fire.

He then placed Amelia gently and tenderly upon the couch, and began to ask himself, with some anxiety, whether it was not necessary to take some immediate steps towards her recovery.

For all he knew, that swoon—if swoon it were—might deepen into death, if not checked in its onward progress.

But there was nothing there by which he might aid her.

He saw no means either of summoning assistance, even should he choose to run the risk of so doing.

Heron was in dire perplexity.

But he was not long left to his own reflections.

Some circumstances soon occurred, which called upon him for the preservation of all his energies, and the exhibition of all his courage and presence of mind.

The wood fire had evidently been alight some hours; and when Heron, with his fair but senseless companion entered the apartment, the light that came from it was from its last inflammable particles.

The flame dropped.

A mass of dull-red embers only remained.

But still it was surprising to a degree how much actual light was given forth, even by them.

And this was not a flickering light; but a steady, dull, crimson glare, which, like the last rays of sunset, imparted a rare and exquisite beauty to everything it fell upon.

Such was the state of things in that chamber of royalty, when another door than that at which Heron had entered was flung open.

Two persons entered the room most hurriedly.

Heron had just time to crouch down by the side of the couch, to prevent himself from being immediately seen.

He did not hope, though, for a single moment, that he should escape observation; and he prepared himself for another conflict, the issue of which might be another death inflicted by his hands upon some of the iniquitous party assembled that night in St. James's.

But the most improbable things will happen at times; and so it occurred upon this occasion, that neither of these parties approached the fireplace, but, speaking almost together in hurried accents, they paused about the centre of the floor.

"Where is the King?"

That is the question which came simultaneously from both their lips.

"Where is the King?"

They had evidently expected to find him in that room.

Heron slightly raised his head, and looked over the edge of the couch.

Dimly, and with that red light from the fire upon them, he could see these two men.

One was Lord Clackington.

The other was Warringdale.

Each had a drawn sword, and the long, slender blades looked blood-red as the dull crimson glare from the decaying embers fell upon them.

"His Majesty is not here," said Lord Clackington.

"How terrible is this adventure!" groaned Warringdale. "It is useless to reason with me, my lord, since I shall believe to my dying day that I have seen a spectre."

Clackington laughed in his hideous, croaking fashion.

"I am not so easy of belief."

"It is possible—it is possible," said Warringdale. "You know, my lord, that there are more things in heaven and on earth than are dreamt of in our philosophy."

"Show me that there is anything but earth," sneered Clackington, "and I will believe you."

"I will not argue the point, but I have seen a spectre."

"Pooh! pooh! You have seen it in your imagination."

"No; as I am a living man, I have seen the spectre of my dead brother, Felix Heron, the true and rightful Earl of Whitcombe!"

"Absurd—absurd! The man is dead!"

"He spoke to me."

"Some one spoke to you, possibly."

"But I knew his voice, and he declared himself to me. He called me brother, and the fraternal voice sunk deep into my heart with more than mortal cadences."

"As you please—as you please; but I must seek the King wherever he is to be found, and inform him what has happened."

"It is time," said Warringdale, "for me to make my peace with heaven, if I can. Men do not receive these visitations in vain, and I feel that I am not long for this world now."

"As you please," said Lord Clackington. "I interfere with no man's superstition, and am only thankful to have none of my own. The King is doubtless in what he calls his oratory."

"I have heard of that apartment," said Warringdale.

Clackington laughed.

"Yes; all the world has heard of it as the room to which his Majesty retires to vent curses upon the head of his own son, the Prince of Wales."

"It is a disunited family; but the affairs of this world are fading from me."

"Stuff—stuff! You will be better to-morrow. Get you home, and take a bumper of burgundy with a hot toast in it, and all these superstitious fancies will fly away like a white mist before the sun."

"I have no home."

"No home?"

"None! I am a lonely man! I have slept some nights at Holland House; but that is full of strange noises and mysterious mutterings. In truth, I know not where to go, for I somewhat dread to be alone!"

"This is rare folly!" said Clackington; "but since such is your feeling, you are welcome to accompany me to my house at Westminster. But I must see the King first; and as, upon reflection, his Majesty might not exactly desire your presence, what say you to waiting for me here?"

"I will do so—I will do so!"

"Be it so, then. I will return to you as quickly as may be."

Heron made certain in his own mind that Warringdale would approach the fireplace; and such doubtless would have been the fact, but for the peculiar state of mind of Warringdale at that time.

He had a terrible dread that some one was behind him.

And as that terror increased, he feared even to cross the floor of the apartment.

He wheeled a massive arm-chair with its back against the wall, between two of the windows, and sitting down in it, he faced the fireplace, although at a considerable distance from it, and cut off from a more than very casual observation of the upper portion of the chimney-piece by various articles of furniture.

Lord Clackington went to seek the King in the oratory he had mentioned.

And now those two brothers were alone.

One so full of superstitious fear.

The other so perplexed to determine in his

FELIX HERON EFFECTS THE RESCUE OF AMELIA TRAVERS FROM THE
PALACE OF ST. JAMES'S.

Presented Gratis with No. 77, of the New Edition of EDITH HERON, the Sequel to Edith the Captive; or, the Robbers of Epping Forest.

own mind what he should do to extricate himself from his present position.

The act by which Felix Heron had made himself partially known to Lord Warringdale had been so purely impulsive, that almost from the moment he had regretted it.

By that indiscretion of a moment—for such he began to consider it—he had hazarded the discovery of his existence in a quarter where, of all others, it was likely to be most fatal to the peace and happiness of himself and to Edith.

If, however, the delusion which had taken possession of the mind of Warringdale, to the effect that it was the spectre of his brother, Felix Heron, whom he had seen, could be perpetuated, and in any way deepened, the circumstance would cease to present itself in any anxious manner to the mind of Felix.

And here fortune or providence seemed to have presented him the opportunity of exactly carrying out some such idea.

If Heron himself had had the opportunity of placing Warringdale in a particular position in that room, favourable to a continuance of his superstitious fears, he could not have devised the position better than Warringdale had done himself.

A profound silence was in and about the apartment, although, slightly and at times, Heron, for the first few minutes after Lord Clackington had left, thought he heard the murmur of voices.

These, however, died away, and all was still as the grave.

Warringdale did not speak.

But Heron heard him breathing heavily.

Situated as he was, crouching down between the couch and the fire-place, he, Heron, was perfectly free from observation; but he was, at the same time, peculiarly well s 'ed for the purpose of producing, if he so ᴄᴏᴏꜱᴇ. it, a startling effect upon Warringdale.

By the dim light of the fire, Heron stole a glance upon the fair face of Amelia.

That deep and deathlike swoon which had begun to alarm Heron so much, still continued.

But let the consequences be what they might, he resolved to free himself from the obnoxious presence of Warringdale, from whom he would receive no assistance, and with whom it seemed he could never again make up his mind to fight.

Heron felt quite confident he could easily scare him from the place.

A stealthy glance enabled him to see that Warringdale's eyes were fixed straight before him, as if he feared any wandering observation around the apartment would transfix his gaze on some sight of horror from which he could not withdraw it.

Heron now commenced operations.

He uttered a low, lengthened moan.

Amid the profound stillness of the room, the sound attracted the observation of Warringdale instantly.

He echoed the moan by a half-stifled cry of fear.

Heron's object had been exactly to attract his attention to the hearth in front of the fire-place.

With the point of his sword, then, he gently stirred the red embers of the wood fire.

The effect was to evolve from them a faint blue flickering flame, which lasted for several seconds.

Slowly, then, before it expired, Heron rose up with very much the appearance as if he had come in the accredited and approved ghostlike fashion, perpendicularly through the floor of the room.

To the terrified eyes of Warringdale, that must have been precisely the effect.

Higher and higher still rose Heron, until he attained his full height.

Then he spoke.

But he had his doubts whether speaking were not all in vain, since Warringdale remained seated in the arm-chair in perfect silence, so transfixed with terror that it was doubtful whether his senses remained to him.

CHAPTER CCXLV.

FELIX HERON HAS AN INTERVIEW WITH THE KING, AND SAVES AMELIA TRAVERS.

THE appearance of Heron reflected against the dim firelight, must have been awful and spectral in the extreme.

Even to any one who was not prepossessed with the idea that he was no more, his aspect must have partaken largely of the supernatural.

But to Warringdale there could not interpose a doubt upon the subject.

And Heron, now that he had made up his mind that his brother should recognise him, had removed the wig, which was part of his disguise as Captain Fantome, and appeared, in that dim fire-light, sufficiently like himself to render a mistake of his identity quite impossible to one who knew him so well as Lord Warringdale.

"Beware!" he said, in deep, hollow accents—"beware! and seek no more the path of evil. Repent ye, while there is yet time, and fly from further communion now with one who carries with him a surrounding air that may not be long breathed by mortality."

This was just the sort of threat to have all its effect upon Lord Warringdale.

The small amount of sense or power of action that was left him was instantly in motion to fly from that spot.

"Mercy! mercy!" he cried. "I will—I do repent! Do not kill me by another word! Already I feel the air thickening about me: it is very cold, and grasps my heart as with the fingers of the dead!"

"Fly!" said Heron. "Fly, while time is your own!"

With a cry of despair that no doubt had in it an expression of physical pain—for imagination made Warringdale believe he was choking—he rose and fled from the room.

Heron was satisfied.

He felt that he had fully substantiated in the mind of Warringdale the idea he was dead, and he hoped that the shock he had given to his superstitious fears would have the effect of altering his mode of life.

And now that this much was accomplished, Heron's anxieties and fears as regarded Amelia returned in full force.

The necessity of procuring for her some assistance, and dissipating, if possible, the swoon that still possessed her, became to his mind painfully apparent.

He crossed the room, and passed out of it at the door through which he had seen Lord Clackington make his exit.

That door led again into a small corridor, which abruptly turned to the right.

A gleam of light came through the open doorway, and Felix Heron again heard the murmur of voices.

Those voices evidently came from a room Heron was now fast appoaching.

He thought he detected and identified them both.

One was the King.

The other Lord Clackington.

Three steps more brought him to the door, which was a few inches open, and then he heard distinctly what was being said.

"All this sounds incredible," said the King; "but it must be met with the utmost caution, and, if necessary, with all the force and violence that will put a stop to any such danger."

"It shall be seen to, your Majesty," said Clackington, "but I own to being bewildered and terrified. The Duke of Harlington is killed, and some unknown power has carried off the girl, whither we know not, and by a means perfectly inexplicable."

"You talk in riddles, my lord," said the King, "or your fears have got the upper hand of your reason. Some carelessness or some folly has been perpetrated, and we are all now liable to an exposure of a most uncomfortable description."

"Will your Majesty pardon me if I tell you what is Lord Warringdale's opinion upon the subject?"

"Pardon you? What need of pardon? Tell me at once."

"I feel the need of pardon, because what I have to say will, in your Majesty's judgment, sound frivolous and absurd."

"What can it be? Speak on, my lord."

"Warringdale, then, gives a supernatural explanation of the affair."

"Supernatural?"

"Even so, your Majesty."

Felix Heron heard a chair hastily moved; and he had some idea that the fears of the King were sufficiently aroused to induce him, probably, to adopt the same plan that Lord Warringdale had done to be certain no one was behind him.

That plan was to place his chair against a wall.

He could not say that such was the fact; but the movement of the chair was suspicious.

The King now spoke in a lower tone; and, as Felix Heron had good reason to believe in the superstitious tendencies of the royal mind, he could easily account for the change.

"In what way," said the King, "does Warringdale attribute supernatural agency to this affair?"

"He states, your Majesty, in the midst of the confusion he was addressed by an apparition."

The King's chair moved again.

"An apparition, my Lord Clackington?"

"Yes, your Majesty. The apparition of his brother, the late Earl of Whitcombe."

"Ah!" cried the King. "That again? We thought that ghost was laid."

"And so did I, your Majesty; but Warringdale is so precise upon the subject that it seems difficult to contradict him. He says that not only does he know his brother's face and voice well —so well, indeed, that it is impossible he can be mistaken—but he was actually addressed by the term 'Brother.'"

"By the spectre?"

"Even so, your Majesty."

"What is the time?"

"It is nearly three o'clock."

"Then it is a good two hours yet to dawn."

"Oh, your Majesty," said Clackington; "surely, if we are to believe in ghosts, we are not obliged to adopt all the idle tales concerning them?"

"What idle tales? Who spoke of idle tales?"

"I thought your Majesty alluded to the generally received idea that it was only between sunset and sunrise that disembodied spirits could appear to the living."

"Peace, peace, my Lord Clackington! We had no such notions. Speak to us of all this in the morning. We are now fatigued, and it appears to us that we have more trouble than profit from this society of your creation."

Lord Clackington took this as a hint to depart.

How he left the royal presence Felix Heron was not aware, but no doubt there were modes of exit and entrance to that suite of apartments, which, situated as he was, he had no means of observing.

One thing, however, was quite evident.

The King was now alone.

That was the opportunity Heron sought.

He was determined to intrude himself upon the royal presence, however unbidden or unwelcome a guest he might be.

But the King was speaking to himself in low, muttered tones, and Heron paused to hear what it was that troubled the royal imagination.

He could hear, too, that the King was pacing the room to and fro, and this gave him a notion that he might be enabled to take something of a survey of the place without being himself seen.

Waiting until the royal footsteps were evidently receding from the partially-open door, Heron advanced and looked in.

He saw the King plainly.

He saw that the room was a kind of dressing closet, and he had no doubt that the royal chamber lay immediately beyond it.

Then Heron took the opportunity, after the King had passed the door again, and again turned his back upon it, to glide into the room.

He seated himself upon the first chair he came to, and quietly waited until the King should turn again and walk with his face towards him.

The King paused.

"Help! treason! What—what is this?"

The appearance of Heron was sufficiently mysterious to awaken all the fears of the King.

But Heron had put on the wig which so materially helped to disguise him as Captain Fantome.

He replied to the royal exclamation likewise in a feigned voice, for he had no desire to pass himself off to the King either as the mortal Earl of Whitcombe or his ghost.

"Your Majesty is alarmed," said Heron, "and perhaps not without reason. "It will be dangerous, however, to call too loudly for aid, since I am a well-armed, resolute man.""

The King had made a movement to a particular part of the chamber, where Heron—although he could not see it, so artfully contrived in the panelling was it—felt convinced there was a door.

"Stop, your Majesty," he said. "Your flight may be swift, but there is something here that is swifter."

"Ah!"

The King paused.

Heron had produced a pistol.

He laid its barrel carelessly over the arm of the chair in which he sat, and its muzzle pointed directly to the royal breast.

"There is not the remotest intention," added Heron, "of committing any outrage; but your Majesty's presence is desired here for a short time longer."

"This is treason!"

"Very likely!"

"And whoever you are, I would warn you that your acts are such that—that——"

The King was evidently at a loss to know what to say.

"Your Majesty may spare your breath," said Heron. "Kings are only kings, after all, by the grace of those who choose to call them so; and now, as we are here alone, we are but as two men, and I have that to say to you which you shall listen to."

The King glanced at the barrel of the pistol, and felt that he was in the power of his unknown visitor.

"Speak!" he said. "What have you to say? But tell me first who you are?"

"I am a gentleman!"

The King made a sarcastic sort of half-bow.

"Surely," he said, "I ought to have guessed as much by your unbidden and unwelcome intrusion into these apartments!"

"That sneer shall not move me!" said Heron. "I have something to say, and a complaint to make, which, perhaps, might not have been listened to so patiently under other circumstances!"

"Say on, sir!"

"Your Majesty is, or should be, a sort of father to your people; and all those who require protection, either from infancy or inability to protect themselves, or from want of friends to stand forward in their behalf, ought to look to the King, as the head and chief of the State, to be their natural guardian!"

"Well, sir, what then?"

"And more particularly," continued Heron, "should youth and innocence, when subjected to the snares of the wicked and the designing, be your Majesty's special care!"

The King winced a little.

"I can inform your Majesty that there is a kind of club, or association, of infamous men, formed for the express purpose of perpetrating, by violence, so much iniquity that your Majesty would blush to the roots of your royal hair to think you governed a kingdom that produced such specimens of depravity!"

The King made no reply.

Heron continued, in low and distinct tones; and

what he was saying, perhaps, had more effect upon the royal conscience,—and, probably, the royal fears,—than if he had directly accused the King of complicity in the abduction of Amelia Travers.

"In pursuance of the designs of this association, a young, innocent, and virtuous girl has been carried off."

"Indeed!"

"Yes, your Majesty; but I have rescued her, and she is now, not far from this spot, in a deep swoon induced by terror and exhaustion."

The King turned round, as if he fully expected to see Amelia Travers in that very room.

"Nay," said Heron, "she is not here; but I can conduct your Majesty to her; and, in her name, I have three favours to ask of you!"

"Three favours?"

"Yes. The first is, that your Majesty will supply me, from yonder well-furnished buffet, with some refreshments and stimulants which will restore the girl to sense and to existence."

"Oh, willingly!"

"The next is that you will graciously enable her, under my escort, to leave this place in safety and security."

"Be it so."

"The third is, that you will place in my hands a thousand pounds, as some slight recompense to this poor young girl for the terror she has experienced and the inconvenience she has undergone."

"A thousand pounds?"

"Yes, your Majesty, that is the sum."

The King caught at the vague idea that, after all, Heron did not mean to accuse him of any part in the abduction of Amelia.

"Why should I," he said, "pay a thousand pounds for other people's iniquities?"

"Oh, if your Majesty were yourself guilty, in any shape or way, I should name ten thousand at the very least!"

The King began to think he was getting off cheaply.

"We agree," he said; "but still I cannot help thinking that if this young person you mention is such a paragon of virtue, it is strange she puts a money value on it."

"She does not, your Majesty; for had the infamous purpose for which she was brought here been carried out, it is not a thousand pounds, but some human lives, that must have answered for it."

The King was silenced.

"Now," said Heron, "some wine from yonder buffet!"

The King brought it, and followed Heron to the room in which Amelia was lying.

A small quantity of the generous liquid with difficulty having passed her lips, restored her.

She looked about her in an agony of fear.

"Calm yourself," said Heron; "all is safe, and all is well. This gentleman will conduct us to the open air."

"Follow," said the King.

"One moment!" added Heron.

"What next?"

"The thousand pounds, if you please."

A look of chagrin came over the face of the King, and it was sufficiently marked, notwithstanding the inefficient light in that room, for Felix Heron to see it.

In fact, the one wax-candle which Felix Heron had brought with him from the King's private chamber but very dimly lighted the apartment.

The smouldering wood fire had gone completely out, although the soft and pleasant odour from the scented wood, of which it had been composed, was still manifest in the air of the room.

The King took a small pocket-book from his coat, and handed it to Heron.

"I believe," he said, "there is more than the sum mentioned in that book."

"Kings should be generous," said Heron. "The surplus will be placed to the account of royalty; and now, your Majesty having fulfilled every other condition, it only remains that this young lady and myself intrude upon your kindness to show us out of the Palace."

"This way."

The King took a key from his pocket, and opened a tall, narrow door in the wall, beyond which there appeared a flight of rather steep steps.

"Pass two persons!" he cried out, aloud.

Felix Heron, assisting Amelia, descended the steps.

They saw no one; but a door was flung open, through which came a grateful gush of cool night air.

In another moment they were in the Colour Court of St. James's Palace.

"Tell me truly," said Heron, to Amelia Travers, "is any one awaiting you at home, or will there be anxiety on your account?"

"Alas! no one. I am very lonely."

"Then you shall become acquainted with the Countess of Whitcombe, and let us hope that this night's adventure will be the dawn of a new era of happiness in your existence."

The young girl's feelings had been strongly excited, and she wept freely, as Felix Heron conducted her to Whitcombe House

---

CHAPTER CCXLVI.

TOM RIPON TAKES COUNSEL WITH DAISY.—THE COMPACT.

"WELL, Daisy," said Tom Ripon, "what do you say to a trot on the green-sward? I don't think we made so bad an affair of it, did we, beauty, the last time we went out?"

Tom was patting Daisy's neck in the stable of Whitcombe House, as he spoke.

And it would almost seem that the intelligent creature half understood him, for Daisy placed her head upon his shoulder, and fixed her large eyes gently upon his face.

"Well," added Tom, "if you say that's your opinion, as well as mine, I don't see what's to hinder us going out, and trying our luck again."

Tom had quite made up his mind that, on the first opportunity, he would saddle Daisy for the road again.

Acting upon the general leave he had from Felix Heron to take Daisy out for exercise, Tom engrafted rather a large license upon that expression.

It was ten o'clock.

The favourite hour for knights of the road to commence their excursions.

Tom's experience had told him that there was little good to be done on road or heath after midnight.

It was the quiet, orderly people, who went home early, who were best worth crying "Stand and deliver!" to.

They were the folks, likewise, who were least likely to make resistance.

The young rakes and bloods of the town, and the rather loosely-disposed characters who were out in the small hours of the night, generally had little to lose; and just in proportion as that was the case, they were inclined to fight desperately for its retention.

Tom knew all this quite well.

And having, as he imagined, secured Daisy's assent to a night of adventure, he rapidly adjusted the saddle, and made her ready for the road.

"Now," said Tom, "wait a bit, Daisy, and I shall soon be ready. Ah! here we are, all safe."

From a shelf in the stable Tom took down a parcel that contained his highwayman's apparel.

It had been his original intention on all occasions to leave that costume at his mother's house in Wardour Street. Upon second thoughts, he had brought it with him to the stable.

In that bundle, likewise, was the riding-habit, by the aid of which Tom hoped and expected to achieve some amusing adventures.

"Now, Daisy, lass," he said. "Only you wait a few minutes, and I shall be ready."

It was an intense satisfaction to Tom Ripon to be able once again to attire himself in his somewhat picturesque highwayman's costume.

Tom surveyed himself with considerable complacency in a small triangular piece of looking-glass, which he had nailed up in the stable, pretending it was for the use of Daisy.

"Well," he said, "I think that is rather the thing; so now off we go, my beauty!"

Tom folded up the lady's riding-habit into a compact parcel, which could easily be strapped to the back of the saddle.

His next care was to examine his pistols, which, in those days, was a much more important matter than at present.

Thrusting them, then, into the holsters of the saddle, Tom felt that he was fully equipped and ready for the road.

He led Daisy carefully and quietly out of the stable into the by-street at the back of Whitcombe House.

Nothing could, in a general way, be more solitary and deserted than that street.

But, upon this occasion, just as Tom emerged from the stable, a watchman, with some exalted notions of duty, came slowly down it.

"Plague take the old fool!" said Tom. "What does he want here?"

"Past ten o'clock, and a cloudy night!"

"Well, everybody knows that," said Tom, "without it being bawled out in that kind of way. I'll be off before the old stupid gets this far!"

Tom put his foot in the stirrup, and mounted Daisy; but the back street was so narrow that he could not escape being within the sphere of the watchman's lantern.

"Hilloa!" said the guardian of the night; "who are you, and what do you want here?"

"Don't you know me?" said Tom.

"How should I know you? You look like a highwayman!"

"That's just it."

"What's just it?"

"I am a highwayman, or rather, I was a highwayman. I am the ghost of the celebrated Dick Turpin, and I am bound to come on my horse, Black Bess here, once a year, to ride over the first watchman I see. You'd better stoop. Forward, Daisy! Over him!"

"Murder!" cried the watchman, as he crouched down, just in time probably to save his head from Daisy's heels, who made a flying leap over his back.

"On we go," said Tom. "I shall take the Western Road again. I had lots of luck there last

No. 78.—EDITH.

time: and who knows but some of it may come back to my share to-night?"

Daisy was full of life and spirits.

The quiet life she led in the old stables of Whitcombe House was very different to that she had been for so long accustomed to in the forest.

The feel of the night air, and the sight of the trees and herbage which then, when London had not gone so far out of town, were soon reached, appeared to inspire Daisy with the most agreeable sensations.

In fact, she seemed inclined for galloping, which would have had the effect of testing Tom Ripon's horsemanship.

"Woa! woa, Daisy!" he cried.

Daisy permitted herself to be reined in, and as Tyburn Fate was close at hand, Tom thought it better to assume an air of quietude and composure.

The keeper of that gate, however, had too much experience of knights of the road not to be perfectly well aware that Tom was one of them.

And so long as he got his toll, he cared little about it; and, in fact, at that period, the toll-bar keepers within ten miles of London were so liberally paid by gentlemen of Tom's sort, that they were generally ready to fling open the gate for them when hardly pressed, without a thought of the toll on that particular occasion.

It was always good policy for a successful highwayman to fling a guinea to a gate-keeper.

And it may be considered that it was this reckless manner in which the plunder of the road was distributed, that so greatly assisted in prolonging the career of the knights of the highway.

There never was a roadside inn at which one stopped to taste a glass of spirits, that he did not pay at least ten times the value for.

Who so popular, then, as the dashing highwayman, who took guineas from the rich, to scatter them among the poor?

Tom was highly flattered on going through Tyburn Gate on this occasion.

Being well provided with money, in consequence of his last adventure, he flung the man a crown piece with a "keep the change" kind of an air, which was not to be mistaken.

"Thank you, Captain," said the man. "Good night, and fair weather to you."

Tom was wonderfully elated.

"Good night—good night!" he cried. "Anybody in particular on the road?"

"Why, no, Captain, only the ugly one."

"Who do you mean?"

"Jonathan Wild."

"Oh, he's on the road, is he?"

"Yes, Captain. He takes a canter down it every night about this hour; and I should rather say he's looking for somebody."

The tone in which the gate-keeper pronounced the word somebody, let Tom fully understand that he was meant.

"Very good," he said. "We may meet; and if we do, it will be all the worse for one or other of us. I rather think, however, that one won't be me."

"Good luck, Captain; and good night!"

"Amen!" said Tom, "as old Mortification would say."

He gallopped onward; and was soon through the outlying district of Bayswater, and fairly on the Western Road.

There was a little public-house at the corner of a lane, not far from the long, shadowy avenue which, at that time, led to Brook Green.

Tom pulled up there, and called out aloud, "House! house!"

The landlord ran out; and then started with surprise, as he cried out, "Why, it's Daisy!"

"Hush!" said Tom. "Who are you?"

"And it's Tom Ripon!"

"Good gracious! Hold your tongue! I don't know you a bit!"

"I'm Number Ten. Don't you recollect me in the Forest? I'm a married man; and have turned quite respectable."

"The deuce you have!" said Tom. "That must be dull, isn't it?"

"Well, no, not exactly. You see, the landlord of this crib died of new rum; and left behind him a fair and elegant young creature, his widow. Quite a dove, too, in temper; and as I thought it a pity she should go cooing about by herself, why I proposed to her, and married her; and here I am, landlord of the 'Cat and Snuffers,' and getting quite jolly!"

Before Tom could make any remark upon this narrative a high, screaming voice echoed from the interior of the little hostel.

"Now, you good for nothing, idle vagabond, what are you gossiping out there for, instead of attending to your lawful business. Must I take the roasting spit again to you, you good for nothing thief?"

"Oh," said Tom, "is that the dove?"

Number Ten rubbed his head.

"Well, you know, Tom, women are precarious, and, at times, I must confess that—that——"

"You needn't say anything more about it," said Tom; "and don't give your mind to jealousy; for if you should go off the hooks, you may depend I shall not propose for the charming young widow of the 'Cat and Snuffers.' So now let us have a glass of purl."

"Directly, Tom—directly. But I assure you you have heard and seen the worst of her."

"Have I?"

"Most certainly, Tom, and, on the word of an old acquaintance, I can assure you——"

"Take that!" screamed a high voice, again; and a female, of rather extraordinary height, suddenly appeared at the door, and commenced, with the vigour of a patent threshing-machine, laying a stick over Number Ten's back.

"What a beauty!" said Tom. "I won't wait for the purl. She'd have to look at it, and it would turn it sour! Good night, Number Ten! Can't you find a bit of old rope to hang yourself with?"

Tom put Daisy to a half gallop, and rapidly left the "Cat and Snuffers" far behind him.

He reached a sequestered and lonely bit of the Western Road, not far from a narrow lane that leads to East Acton, and where a windmill was slowly moving its gigantic arms in the night air.

Tom then heard the rapid sound of horse's feet coming on at a hard trot, accompanied by the grinding of wheels upon the loose roadway.

In a few seconds the gleam of lights from an approaching vehicle shone upon the hedge-rows.

Tom drew up, and waited with some impatience a real highwayman's encounter.

He had not long to wait before a stage coach appeared.

Tom instantly darted out from his place of concealment, and, going to the door, presented a pistol, and cried "Stand and deliver!"

Scarcely were the words uttered than a pistol bullet spun through the air, grazing the side of Tom's hat.

At first, he was so taken by surprise that he almost lost his presence of mind; but, feeling assured that he was not injured, he bethought himself of a stratagem.

Slipping down from Daisy's saddle, and lying full length in the road, he managed, while in that position, to cut the traces.

By this time, Tom could attend to other matters, and soon distinguished the tones of a man, who, in piping accents, called out, "Fear nothing, ladies; I have killed the vagabond! You see, Maria Jane, it was as well that you allowed me to escort you, or goodness knows what you might not have endured from this ruffian!"

"Oh! oh!" said Tom. "They think I'm dead, do they? Come, Daisy, come!"

Tom led Daisy in the darkness to the corner of a lane where there was a finger-post, to which he tied her bridle.

"Stay there, my beauty," he said, "until I come and fetch you! I am now going to pay a visit to Maria Jane!"

CHAPTER CCXLVII.

TOM RIPON MAKES A GOOD BOOTY.—CONGRATULATIONS.

TOM quickly made his way to the coach, and again lay down upon his back, and while in that position he had no difficulty in hearing all that was said by the passengers in the coach.

"What shall we do with the fellow?" asked the gentleman with the piping voice. "I have succeeded in ridding the world of a monster, there is no doubt about that!"

"Have you, old fellow!" said Tom to himself.

"I vote," continued the man with the piping voice, "that we put the highwayman into the coach, and carry him to town. If he isn't dead, he will be long before he can offer any resistance, and then just fancy the *eclat* of capturing a knight of the road!"

There seemed to be some disagreement between the ladies on this occasion as to the desirableness of taking into the coach a known highwayman; but one of them asked, with a lisp, which she evidently intended to be youthful, "Is he young, do you think, Adolphus?"

"Young? No, of course not!" roared Adolphus. "Highwaymen are never young. He is an old, grey-headed, horrid-looking man, enough to frighten any one, even in the noonday!"

"Thank you, old pump!" said Tom to himself. "We'll see soon whether the fair Maria Jane does not think me handsome."

With this, the man who had fired the pistol-bullet at Tom Ripon alighted from the coach, and coming round to where Tom was lying, touched him with his foot, which action was not responded to by Tom.

"All's right—he is dead enough, I believe. Here, Jones, help me to stow this fellow inside the coach!"

The coachman dismounted from his box, and, with his assistance, Tom was lifted into the coach.

The coachman had orders to remount the box, and drive as fast as his horses would allow him, towards London, where it was intended to lodge Tom Ripon in the first round-house they came to.

Tom lay quite still, huddled up at the bottom of the coach, and was highly amused to hear the lady whom he supposed to be Maria Jane exclaim, "Oh, you wretch! You have killed a handsome young man! You told me he was old, and look at him!"

Adolphus, who had scrambled in as best he could, did not seem best pleased with the opinion Maria Jane had just given of the "handsome" highwayman, and contented himself with giving Tom a furtive glance and a sly kick, unobserved by his companions.

"Drive on!" roared he to the coachman.

"Please, sir, the 'osses has run away! Mr. Highwayman must have cut the traces; for, just as I was about to drive on, according to your lordship's orders, they tore away, and nearly dragged me from the box."

"Fool!" roared the voice from the inside of the coach. "I will have you——"

"Stop a bit, old boy!" said Tom, suddenly starting up from the bottom of the coach. "Stop a bit; just hand over to me all the property you happen to have about you, and then you can have a shot at your coachman, if you like—but don't keep me waiting, or it will be worse for you!"

The consternation of the passengers in the coach, on finding the supposed dead highwayman fully prepared to assert all the privileges of his profession, was immense.

The ladies screamed and huddled together, so as to leave a considerable space for Tom, who, coolly seating himself opposite to the old gentleman, threw up the pan of one of his pistols, and settling the powder around the touch-hole, said, with a preternatural kind of calmness. "Every dog has his day! It's my turn now! You've had your shot, and it's only fair I should return it."

The old gentleman uttered a cry of dismay.

He strove to drop to his knees to the bottom of the coach, but Tom propped him up with the barrel of the pistol.

"No, no," he said, "that's not fair; and, besides, it would be decidedly inconvenient!"

"Mercy, mercy!"

"Exactly so—the same mercy you had upon me."

"But I didn't mean to shoot you."

"Indeed!"

"Yes, it was only a threat."

"A threat from the barrel of a pistol!"

"But I missed you on purpose, you dear, kind youth. I assure you I did. I said to myself, 'Here is a young man, who, perchance, has been led astray in consequence of his good looks by bad company—I might shoot him, but won't—I'll pretend to do so, but miss him.'"

"Stuff!" said Tom.

"It is true, on my honour."

"Then how came you to hit me?"

"Hit you?"

"Yes—you'll pretend next that the bullet is not in my head now."

"In your head?"

"Exactly so—along with five others that I have received at different times during my adventures on the road. So now, you see, there's an end of the question."

"Mercy on us!"

"Prop yourself up in that corner, and you won't tumble on the ladies."

"Murder! murder!" shrieked the females, all in chorus. "Spare his life, and take everything we have!"

The old gentleman looked so ghastly and spectral from the state of mortal fright he was in, that

Tom thought he had carried the joke far enough.

"Very well, ladies," said Tom "To oblige you I'll let him go this time, but it is a very hard thing for me to be going about with six ounces of lead in my brains, you must allow."

"Oh, take everything!" cried all the ladies; "take everything. We are so much obliged to you, you can't think."

Tom soon found his hands full of plunder, which he rapidly transferred to his pockets.

But the old gentleman made no movement to add to Tom's store.

"I see," said Tom, "that he don't value his own life, and therefore it is just as well to put him out of the world. He gives nothing, you see."

"For shame, Mr. Bumpus!" cried one of the ladies, who evidently knew him well; "why don't you give the young man your watch and money?"

Mr. Bumpus only groaned.

"I have no time to spare," said Tom.

He seized the old gentleman by the collar, and the feminine occupants of the coach fully believed that some terrible catastrophe was about to occur.

They besought Tom to have patience for a few moments, and then they fell upon Mr. Bumpus; and, in a few seconds, rifled him of a pocket-book, purse, a watch and seals, two rings, and a breast-pin.

All these they handed to Tom, who was quite delighted at his success.

"Ladies," he said, "I have the honour to wish you good night, and it is very satisfactory to me that I have not been under the necessity of robbing you; for at any time you will be able to state that everything I take away has been freely given to me by your own fair hands."

Tom leapt from the coach, and having regained the road, he glanced up at the coachman, who sat upon the box in a bewildered kind of way, scarcely able to understand how what he called his "osses" had gone off without the vehicle.

"Good night, Samuel," said Tom.

"Bless us!" said the coachman; "he knows my name, too!"

Tom laughed, for of course it was but a guess; and then, making the best of his way to where he had left Daisy, he sprung lightly upon her back.

At the moment he did so he heard the galloping of a horse upon the road.

Bending low in the saddle, Tom listened, in order to assure himself from which direction the horse was coming, as he fully intended to take the other.

It was from the country that the horse was evidently rapidly approaching; and as Tom glanced about him, he, upon second thoughts, considered it would be better to make his way into a field which was close at hand, and which was only divided from the roadway by a gate.

The gate yielded to a touch, and Tom quietly walked Daisy into the field, closing it again behind him.

The horseman came up at a hand gallop.

"Hilloa!" he cried. "What's all this? Clear the way here! Is the King's highway to be blocked up in this fashion?"

"We can't clear the way," said the coachman "We have lost our osses!"

"Ah! How is that?"

"A highwayman."

"That scoundrel, Tom Ripon, for a thousand pounds!"

"Thank you," said Tom to himself; "I can return that compliment. I know that voice only too well; and I can say, with far greater truth, that scoundrel Wild, for double the money!"

"Yes," cried all the ladies at once, and the old gentleman likewise,—"yes, we've all been robbed by a highwayman!"

"An ugly fellow," said Mr. Bumpus.

"Oh, dear, no!" cried all the ladies in chorus, "not ugly!"

"Silence!" cried Wild. "Coachman, tell me all about it. I am an officer; and, perhaps, you may have heard my name on some odd occasion."

"What may that be?"

"Jonathan Wild. Ha, ha!"

The ladies all screamed; for Wild's evil reputation was beginning to be a matter of town's talk; and drawing near, as he was, towards the end of his terrible career, his very name carried with it an undefined terror.

Mr. Bumpus, however, was so angry at the loss of his property, that he was glad even of the alliance with such a man as Jonathan Wild.

"I can assure you, Mr. Wild," he said, "that the villain is an unheard-of villain; and that it was only by the greatest firmness I saved my life."

"That's not true!" cried all the ladies. "He might have killed you, but let you go."

"Very good," said Mr. Bumpus. "That only confirms me in my previous suspicions, that you are all of you in league with the highwayman; and I feel inclined to give every one of you into custody for helping him to rob me!"

"We in league with him! We help to rob you, you odious old wretch. Take that, and that, and that!"

"Murder!"

"We'll teach you to say we are in league with highwaymen."

"Help! help! Mr. Wild, help! I'm being scratched to death."

Jonathan Wild took not the slightest notice of the disturbance within the coach, but riding quietly up to the side of it, he spoke to the coachman.

"Tell me," he said, "what sort of fellow it was who stopped you?"

"A young chap in a scarlet coat, on a very dark bay horse."

"I guessed it," said Wild; "that's the fellow."

"You know him, Mr. Wild?"

"Perfectly. Which way did he go?"

"No way, it appeared to me, and my idea is that he is lurking about the spot here."

"Ah! Say you so? We will soon unearth that fox."

Jonathan Wild wheeled his horse round, and took as accurate an observation as he could of the trees and hedges about the shadowy spot.

Now Tom Ripon had heard the whole of this, and he had no desire to come into personal collision with Jonathan Wild.

From the abundance of his ingenuity he hit

TOM RIPON UNMASKS VILLANY OF MR. JONES.

Presented Gratis with No. 78, of the New Edition of EDITH the Sequel to Edith the Captive ; or, the Robbers of Epping Forest.

upon a plan which he thought would have the effect of throwing Wild off the scent.

It was a feasible one, although liable to failure.

Situated on the other side of the hedge as Tom was, he was on rather higher ground than the roadway.

That circumstance gave him an advantage for the execution of the little project he intended to carry out.

He took one of the pistols from Daisy's saddle, and poising it well in his hand by the barrel, he flung it right over the road into the fields on the other side.

Now Tom knew, from having frequently tried the experiment in the environs of Epping Forest, that a pistol so flung in nine cases out of ten would go off upon reaching the ground.

The present percussion pistols might be thus flung with impunity, particularly if they alighted upon soft ground; and whereas the chances were nine out of ten in favour of the explosion of the old flint and steel fire-arms, the calculation would now probably be exactly reversed.

The pistol went clearly over the hedge on the other side of the road.

There was an instant's anxious expectation on the part of Tom Ripon.

Then came the report.

Loud and startling.

The ladies in the coach screamed, and suspended their attack upon Mr. Bumpus, who, falling against the coach door, burst it open, and rolled into the road.

The coachman shrank down on his coach box, as if the bullet were specially aimed at him and there was yet time to avoid it.

"There he is!" cried Wild. "Now I know where the rascal is in hiding! That shot was meant for me, but a miss is as good as a mile!"

Wild immediately rode to the other side of the roadway, where there was a somewhat similar gate to the one which Tom Ripon had passed through.

Jonathan was well mounted, for he put his horse to the gate and leapt it.

"That'll do," said Tom; "he's on a false scent now, and I may as well be off."

Tom did not think it desirable to make his way into the road, but he trotted quietly along the meadows, now and then leaping Daisy across a little streamlet; for that part of the country lay rather low, and was intersected by numerous tributaries of the little River Brent, so well known by the picturesque aspect it imparts to many miles of country in that direction from London.

"Well," said Tom, as he emerged into the road again through a wide gap in the hedgerow, "I think I get on famously. This is the way to fortune; and if the Captain will but let me have the use of Daisy for a year, I shall be able to give a capital account of my adventures on the road."

Tom was anxious to know what the time was, and looked at Mr. Bumpus's watch as well as he could in the dim night light.

He had to light a match, however, in order to see it, for it was one of those watches with a gold face, which only show up in a good light.

"Half-past eleven," said Tom. "Time enough, and plenty to spare, for some good sport yet. What do you think of it, Daisy?"

Daisy had had but little work to do, and seemed rather anxious for a gallop.

"Let me see;" said Tom, "where am I exactly? Surely I can get down by some cross way to the Kensington Road, for I don't half like dodging Jonathan Wild about this one."

Tom's face was towards London, and therefore he knew that towards his right hand he was to look for the route he wanted.

He soon reached the mouth of one of those narrow lanes, with tall shadowy trees on each side, which are so common in that part of the country.

"This will do," said Tom; "and now good night, Jonathan Wild, I hope, for the present."

Tom trotted Daisy down the lane, and it was evident by the softness of the turf that it was a very little frequented one.

There was a feeling of intense silence and solitude about it which was not at all suitable to Tom's gay and somewhat volatile disposition.

"I don't half like this place," he said, "and I wish I was well out of it."

These words had hardly passed his lips when he was startled by a piercing scream.

He reined up Daisy so suddenly that she stood for a few seconds upon her hind feet, no doubt presenting, with Tom on her back, a very artistic-looking group, if they could have been fixed in that position.

"Good gracious!" exclaimed Tom. "What's that?"

There was but the one scream, but its echoes appeared to Tom to fill the air for the full space of a minute before they died completely away.

Then the intense stillness of the lane seemed to return with double force, and Tom felt a creeping sensation of affright, such as very seldom came over him

CHAPTER CCXLVIII.

TOM'S ADVENTURE IN THE LANE.—THE SOVEREIGN PRINCESS.

IT was some few seconds before Tom could make up his mind to proceed.

Then keeping a tight hold of the rein, he let Daisy go forward at a walk, for he seemed to consider that the quieter he was, as he made his way out of that lane, would be all the better.

But he had not proceeded above five or six paces, when he was startled again by a voice.

"Hist, hist! Stop, illustrious stranger, and listen to the woes of a Sovereign Princess."

"A what?" said Tom.

"The wearer of a diadem," repeated the voice.

"The wearer of a what?"

"Oh, pause, and render what aid you may to one who should sit upon a throne!"

"That's all very well," said Tom; "but where are you sitting now? I don't see you anywhere, high or low."

"Noble and illustrious stranger, I am in this tree."

"Oh!"

"And I need but your friendly aid to descend it, and resume my proper state and dignity as a Sovereign Princess."

The lane was very dark, but Tom's eyes were young and good, and by looking sharply about him, he saw that to his left hand there was a high, ancient-looking brick wall with a stone coping, over which projected the branches of a hugh sycamore tree, from amid which Tom thought the voice of the Sovereign Princess seemed to come.

"Are you up there?" said Tom.

"I am, noble stranger."

"But what are you doing there, and who are you, really?"

"I am the Princess Marabella!"

"You don't say so!"

"But, before we proceed further, tell me—are you noble?"

"Of course I am!" said Tom.

"That is satisfactory," said the Princess. "I can see that you are mounted on a war-steed. How many quarterings have you in your shield?"

"Well I don't know," said Tom, "There's my own four quarters here, and there's Daisy's quarters, hind and front, and that makes six; but I'm not aware of a shield just at present!"

"Perhaps your squire has it, along with your helm and vizor."

"I shouldn't wonder!" said Tom.

"Approach closer, illustrious knight, and I will descend into your arms. I have dreamt of this, many a time, and all has now brought about my most ardent wishes!"

"I rather think," thought Tom, "that I have dreamed about it, too; for if I'm really awake, this is the oddest thing that ever happened to me!"

"Speak, illustrious knight," said the lady in the tree. "Let me again hear your gallant voice."

"Here you are!" said Tom.

"Approach closer, and I will drop into your friendly grasp."

"I hope you're a light weight," said Tom. "But before we get any better acquainted, if it's all the same to you, I should like to know what it's all about."

"One question more, Sir Marmaduke!"

"Sir who?"

"Sir Marmaduke of the lion crest!"

"Oh, that's me!" said Tom. "The same to you, ma'am, and many of 'em."

"Do you come from Palestine?"

"What the deuce does she mean?" said Tom. "Perhaps that's her way of saying Pall Mall. It won't do to be stupid. Yes, yes—I come from there!"

"Did you meet a dragon on your way?"

"A dragon?"

"Yes! Tell me, illustrious knight!"

"By Jove, she means Jonathan Wild! He's the only dragon I know. Yes, I met a dragon; but I rather think he's gone on a wild goose chase now, for I was one too many for him."

"That is well. Now let me descend."

Tom was rather at a loss to know what to do, and before he placed himself and Daisy exactly beneath the sycamore tree, he thought he would like to know a little more about the Sovereign Princess.

"Perhaps you don't mind explaining," said Tom, "what's amiss, and how you came to be perched up there?"

"I am escaping from this gloomy fortress. I may find some pretender on the throne; but you shall challenge him to mortal combat, and then, when victorious, to whom am I to give my hand but to the gallant knight who has been my champion and my preserver?"

"What on earth does she mean?" said Tom. "A gallant knight and a champion!"

"Yes," added the lady in the tree; "it will need but the flash of your well-tried sword, and all will be well."

Tom was about to reply, when again the Sovereign Princess gave a half-scream.

"Why, what's the matter now?" said Tom.

"I thought—I thought," replied the Princess, "that I saw the dragon flying through the air, and that he was about to dart at thy raven locks and tear thee from my side!"

"The deuce you did!" said Tom. And he looked anxiously around him, to see if he could perceive anything of his much-dreaded foe, Jonathan Wild.

"What did you say, gallant knight?"

"Nothing."

"Oh! Approach nearer, and let me seat myself beside you, illustrious stranger, and we will speed over hill and dell until we arrive at my dominions, where you, my preserver, shall share my heart, my throne, my all!"

"Very kind," said Tom to himself, "but I do not half like it. I shall cut it short. If, now, I could manage to get hold of some of the Princess's jewellery, Hem!" said Tom.

"Did you speak, Sir Marmaduke?"

"Sir Marmaduke! Oh, I forgot! Yes, lovely Princess. Do you not think you had better hand over the wall some of your precious ornaments—your bracelets, your ear-rings, and such like, and let me secure them safely in a secret pocket I have; and then you can just give a little jump into my arms when I say the word?"

"Alas!" replied the Sovereign Princess; "when I was carried off from my home, around which waved the tall trees, in the branches of which carolled birds of every hue and colour—I say, when I was borne forcibly from my home to this fortified castle——"

"Hush!" said Tom, "What's that?"

At this moment, the murmur of voices was borne upon the night air; but the sound was at too great a distance for Tom to distinguish any words.

"It is the voice of my gaoler!" said the Princess.

"The voice of who?"

"My implacable gaoler!"

"Gaoler?"

"Even so. The voice of him who rifled me of all my possessions when he confined me within these walls; but, thank heaven, my deliverer has come at last!"

Tom could not, for the life of him, understand what to make of all this, and he was about to bid the Sovereign Princess farewell, when the sound of voices again attracted his attention.

"We have searched everywhere, if you please, sir," said a voice evidently belonging to an old woman, "and can find no traces of her!"

"Have you searched the grounds?"

At this moment, Tom was startled on feeling something strike his arm, and fearing that the

Sovereign Princess had commenced a descent which would land her on the back of Daisy, he retreated a few paces.

"Hist!" said the voice of the Princess. "Do you not hear them?" and, with the branch of the tree on which she was sitting, she struck Tom a not very light blow on the side of the head.

"I can feel, and no mistake," cried Tom. "Hold hard! What are you doing, belabouring a fellow in that kind of way?"

"Hist!" again said the Princess.

The voices by this time seemed to be beneath the very tree in which was seated the Princess; and Tom could not control the curiosity he felt at that moment to hear more of this strange adventure.

"Search every tree," said the voice again of one who seemed to be in authority,—"search every tree; but be careful not to startle the poor creature."

"Oh, oh!" said Tom. "More mysteries yet! I should think a young and lovely Princess, who has been begging of me for the last quarter of an hour to take her with me, is not in much danger of being startled."

At this moment there was a tramp as of many feet; and by the flickering light which came from a lantern carried by one of those persons, Tom could just catch a glimpse now and then of a figure seated in one of the topmost boughs of the tree.

This figure appeared to Tom to be enveloped in what appeared to be an immense counterpane, put on in the shape of a shawl; while in her hair the fair and lovely Princess wore sundry pieces of sticks, and paper ornaments, which had evidently been cut out with a pair of scissors to represent crowns, and pendants, and feathers.

"There she is! There she is!" burst simultaneously from several voices; and in a few minutes a ladder was placed against the wall, and a man's head was seen above the wall.

"Who are you?" asked the voice, addressing Tom.

"Ah! My preserver!" cried the Princess. "My gallant prince, who with his war steed has come to deliver me from this castle!"

"Perhaps, sir," said the man—who, as Tom could not make up his mind what to say at the moment, again addressed him—"perhaps, sir, you were kind enough to wish to give an alarm, when you found this poor unhappy lady trying to make her escape?"

"Not I. She asked me to help her, and I was just considering what I had best do; for the idea of a young and lovely girl being shut up a prisoner——"

"Is it possible, sir, that you do not know this to be Ashton House, a private lunatic asylum? And this is one of our patients—an old lady over sixty years of age, and who has lately got it into her head that she is a princess, or something of that sort."

"Good gracious," said Tom; "what an escape! A lunatic!"

"Indeed it is, sir! Now, Mrs. Appleby, come down quietly, and nothing will be said to you for giving us all this fright. Come in—come in, and you shall have a double quantity of snuff to-morrow if you are good."

"Snuff!" said Tom to himself. "Good gra-

cious! just fancy a Sovereign Princess taking snuff! Good night, all of you! I am in a hurry; and when I see you again, my Sovereign Princess, I will not forget your little weakness in the shape of tobacco."

Tom trotted Daisy briskly out of the narrow lane, and was once more on the high road.

The lane terminated in the Kensington Road, carrying Tom, as he imagined, so entirely clear of the scene of his recent exploits, that there was no danger of his encountering any one to challenge him concerning them.

But it was still sufficiently early in the night to look, at all events, for one other adventure before he should make his way to Wardour Street to dispose of his booty.

That adventure was not long in coming.

Just as Tom was emerging from the end of the shadowy lane, an open chaise, in which were seated a lady and gentleman, was driven towards its entrance, evidently with the intention of taking that route into the Western Road.

By the slight glance Tom caught at the occupants of the chaise, he saw that the gentleman was a very stout specimen of humanity, with fiery red whiskers, and a face that very nearly emulated them in colour.

The lady Tom could see but little of.

That little, however, led him to the conclusion that she was very young, and that she was labouring under some very extraordinary agitation.

The necessity of driving slow on entering the narrow lane made the wheels of the chaise almost pass noiselessly over the gravelly road. Tom was therefore enabled to hear that the young lady by the side of the pretentious man with the red whiskers was crying audibly.

"I should like to know what's the matter," thought Tom; "and I don't see why I shouldn't, either."

Tom was about to ride up to the side of the chaise and address its occupants, when he was saved the trouble by the man with the red whiskers speaking to him first.

"Hilloa, you sir!—hilloa!" he cried. "Does this lane lead into the Western Road?"

"What's that to you?" cried Tom, who was not at all pleased at the manner in which the question had been asked.

"Don't answer me in that way, you scoundrel, or I'll lay my whip over your shoulders. I'm a plain man, and ask you a plain question."

"I see you're a plain man," said Tom, "and something more, for I should say you were downright ugly."

"Insolence! how dare you?"

"Easily," said Tom, whose temper was a little aroused by this cavalier treatment on the part of a perfect stranger. "Easily; and if you don't like it, here's something more!"

Tom clapped the muzzle of a pistol against the rubicund cheek of the man with the red whiskers.

"Now, sir," added Tom; "who are you that call the first person you meet on the highway a fellow?"

The man opened his mouth like some fish newly stranded, and not knowing what to make of the quantity of air he was gulping down instead of water.

"Murder!"

"You may call it so, if you please, but I consider it only a little bit of justifiable manslaughter."

"Who—who are you?"

"How can you ask, when you know quite well?"

"I—I know quite well?"

"Yes; you said I was a fellow, and I am one."

The young lady was too much terrified to weep now; and stretching out a small, delicate hand, she laid it upon Tom's sleeve as she spoke to him.

"Oh, do not—do not kill my uncle!"

"Your uncle?" said Tom.

"Yes. He may not be quite so—so kind as I would wish him, but do not kill him."

By the lights of the chaise, Tom looked at the young lady, and then at the man with the red whiskers, in no small surprise.

He could not believe that there was anything approaching affinity between those two persons.

And, but that they belonged to the same species, and were unmistakably specimens of the human family, no two creatures could be more dissimilar.

"I don't believe it," said Tom. "He's no uncle of yours."

"Oh, yes—yes! he says he is; and I pray you not to delay us; for he is taking me to my father, who lies at the point of death, at Dover; and should I arrive too late to receive his blessing and last caress, the thought would be an affliction to me through life."

"Yes," growled the man with the red whiskers, "that's about it. You hear what the young lady says, so get out of the way."

"But you don't mean to say you are going to drive down to Dover in this rattle-trap?" inquired Tom.

"Yes, we are; and why not? We can easily get change of horses on the way!"

"Very well—I can't help it; and for your sake, my dear, I shall let this insolent old curmudgeon go."

"Oh, thank you!" said the young lady; "moments may be precious."

"Then be off," said Tom. "I was going to ask you for a kiss, but that would be mean, because you couldn't refuse it. Good night; and I hope you'll find the old 'un better."

It was a great relief to the man with the red whiskers to be relieved from such close contiguity to Tom's pistol.

He passed on down the lane, growling as he went.

But Tom did not feel satisfied; and, as he heard the horse in the chaise quickening its pace, so that the frail vehicle behind it proceeded at a kind of rush, that in a little time would be positively dangerous, he felt more and more dissatisfied with himself that he had allowed the man to proceed without further questioning.

The young lady had used an expression which Tom now recollected, and wondered he had not taken more notice of at the time.

She had stated that the man with the red whiskers *said* he was her uncle.

What could she mean by that?

Perhaps it was only an accidental expression.

But it sounded suspicious.

"Well," said Tom, as he looked down the lane, and heard the rapidly retreating sounds of the chaise,—"well, I suppose it's all right, and it's best not to interfere. Every mile that that young girl gets on to Dover will be some weight off her heart. Dover! Hem—Dover! Let me see! Why it's the contrary direction. They're going north, and Dover lies south."

Tom felt his heart begin to beat rapidly, and a flush came over his face, as now he felt certain something was amiss, and that interference was more than justifiable.

"Forward, Daisy," he cried; "on—on!"

Daisy crouched down for a moment as though she was about to lie flat upon the earth, and then, obeying the impulse of voice and gesture which Tom gave her, she set off down the lane in one of those terrific bounding gallops which nothing could surpass.

The chaise had got about a mile ahead, but Tom passed it like an arrow from a bow.

"Woa, Daisy, woa! Woa, lass!"

With some difficulty Tom moderated the speed of Daisy, and then suddenly wheeling round, he met the chaise and its occupants face to face.

The young lady screamed with terror, for Tom's conduct now looked so decidedly aggressive that she might well dread some catastrophe.

The man with the red whiskers stood up in the chaise, and held his whip threateningly.

"Halt!" cried Tom. "I must have something more to say to you before we part."

CHAPTER CCXLIX.

TOM NARROWLY ESCAPES A PISTOL BULLET.—HE MAKES AN AGREEABLE ACQUAINTANCE.

THE man in the chaise evidently considered now that affairs were getting serious.

From a capacious pocket of his over-coat, he produced a pair of pistols, both of which he levelled at Tom.

"Now, my fine fellow," he said, "here's one for you, and one for your horse, and you may both lie and rot by the roadside together. I give you one minute to get out of my way, and if you are wise you will take the opportunity."

"Only a minute?" said Tom.

"That's all."

"Then there's no time for nonsense."

Tom turned Daisy's head to the right hand side of the road, still advancing, and then touching her lightly both on neck and flank, he made her execute a trick which he had often taught her in the old forest.

It was to execute a sidelong leap which at once placed her somewhat further in advance still, but completely on the other side of the lane.

Bang! bang! went the two pistols of the man in the chaise.

But they were both fired to the right, and were so far from Tom, that they might as well have been discharged in the opposite direction, so far as regarded any likelihood of doing him injury.

"That'll do," cried Tom. "Now it's all plain sailing. Open your mouth, old fellow."

"Help! Murder!"

"There's no help; and as for murder, it might have been; and that it is not, is from no good will of yours."

Tom, with very little ceremony, thrust the muzzle of his pistol right between the teeth of the man with the red whiskers.

"Hark you!" said Tom; "there's only one thing you have said that I really don't like; all the rest has been fair enough; and you might shoot me if you liked,—but what did you mean by saying there was one for my horse?"

"Murder!—help!—spare my life! You are not going to kill me on account of a dumb beast?"

"A dumb beast! Call Daisy a dumb beast? Just say that again, will you?"

"I won't, if you don't like it."

"I think you'd better not. And now, my dear," added Tom, turning to the young lady, "answer me, and I am sure it will be truly. How long

No. 79.—EDITH.

have you been acquainted with this precious uncle of yours?"

"Perhaps an hour."

"An hour! And how came you to know him?"

"He came to the school at Hammersmith, and persuaded Miss Le Plomb to let me come away with him, as my father was dying at Dover, and wished to give me his last blessing!"

"His last fiddle-stick!" said Tom.

"Oh! do not be unfeeling, but let us go."

"I don't mean to be unfeeling, but I don't mean to let you go! Now, old fellow, I'm only anxious about one point. Are you sure you know your way to Dover?"

"Perfectly."

"You have been before?"

"Often—often!"

"Then that's conclusive," said Tom. "For this is exactly the contrary direction. My dear, what's your name?"

"Marian Annesley."

"And what's yours?"

"Mine? Why, mine is—is—is—is—that is to say, I am——"

"One of the reddest-whiskered, impudent scoundrels in all the world!"

"Oh, what do you mean?" said the young lady. "What am I to think?"

"Think just what you like," said Tom. "But the fact is, this man's no more your uncle than I am—perhaps not so much."

"That's false!" cried the man with the red whiskers.

"Stop a bit," said Tom, "and we'll find that out. Of course, my dear, you know your father well?"

"I have not seen him for two years, since which time he has been a foreign consul; but of course I know him well. He is——"

"Stop!" cried Tom. "Now, old carrots, do you know him well?"

"My own brother? Of course I do."

"Very well; describe him."

"He—he is—something like me; not quite so stout, but a family likeness, you see."

"Will that do, my dear?" said Tom.

"Oh, no, no! My father is particularly dark, and rather slender."

"A slight difference," said Tom. "How dare you go on in this kind of way, eh?"

Tom took the pistol-barrel out of the mouth of the pretended uncle, and knocking off his hat, dealt him two or three hard raps on the head with the stock of it.

"Murder! murder!"

"It's very likely; but are you going to confess now?"

"Confess what?"

"Who and what you are."

"My name is Jones. Don't crack in the top of my skull, and I will tell you all."

"Are you this young lady's uncle?"

"No."

"That's enough; we don't want to know any more. Get out."

"But it's my chaise."

"Get out, I say!"

The man with the red whiskers rolled out of the chaise.

"Now," said Tom, "I'll give you a start of about a hundred yards, and then I mean to blaze away. Be off, and make the best of it."

"Murder! help! fire! thieves!" shouted the man with the red whiskers, as he fled along the lane at a speed no one would have thought him capable of.

Bang! went one of Tom's pistols after him.

Then, believing himself hit, he fell, and rolled into a ditch, where he floundered about and roared for mercy like some gigantic tadpole.

"My dear," said Tom to the young lady, "you have had a narrow escape. Heaven only knows what danger this man would have taken you into."

The sudden revulsion of feeling that had taken place in the mind of Marian Annesley nearly deprived her of sensation.

She could not speak to Tom for several minutes; but with clasped hands and a face as pale as death itself, she regarded him with an expression of infinite thankfulness.

And during that short space of time which elapsed, while neither Tom nor the young lady spoke a word, he was able, by the light of the chaise lamps, to take a good look at her.

Tom Ripon fell desperately in love at once.

We are aware of the susceptibility of Tom to female beauty, and that upon more than one occasion he had believed himself enamoured past redemption; but the really singular loveliness of this young girl transcended anything he had ever seen before.

In a few short seconds all his previous predilections were forgotten, and Tom registered a mental vow that henceforth that young lady in the chaise was to be the empress of his heart.

What she thought of Tom it is hard to say.

But love may exist without reciprocity.

And, to tell the truth, Tom cut rather a grotesque appearance, for the suit of clothes he had borrowed or purchased, at his mother's fence in Wardour Street, were somewhat too large for him.

The gold-embroidered cuffs had a propensity to come down too low; and the collar, as if to make up for that little redundancy, went up too high.

But still there was an ingenuous sparkle about Tom's eyes, and the tones of his voice were pleasant.

His youth, too, no doubt, recommended him to the young girl, and she felt that sort of companionship of early life which, had Tom been ten years older, she would have shrunk from contemplating.

The silence was getting awkward, and Tom broke it by saying, "What a lucky thing it was I came up this lane! And yet no, I don't think that exactly."

The young girl looked at him with an inquiring air, as though she would have asked what was the meaning of that contradiction.

Tom answered her without troubling her to speak.

"You see," said Tom; "lucky as it looks, I think it was to be. You may depend upon it it was a kind of fate."

"Fate?" said the young girl, with a look of interest.

"Yes, Marian," said Tom; "affairs of this importance don't happen quite on the loose."

The young girl might have been a little puzzled, considering her previous education, at the phraseology of Tom; but she was quite aware that he had called her Marian, and a flush, half of pleasure and half of surprise, came across her face.

She was in the romantic period of early life, when, to a total ignorance of the real world in which she had to live, was superadded those romantic notions concerning it that were only to be acquired at that period from the shelves of the circulating library.

Of course, she felt that Tom had done her a signal service, and that was a recommendation which would go far to make him look handsome, assuming that he had been quite the reverse.

Without the least ability to decide upon who and what he was, she began in her own mind to liken him to some of the heroes of the romances with which her head was tolerably well crammed

"I am afraid," she said, "I ought not to let you call me Marian."

"Don't be afraid of anything in all the world," was the prompt reply, "as long as I'm here. You may call me Tom, if you like."

"Tom?"

"Yes, that's my name."

"It would be too familiar; I might say Mr. Thomas, and then add your surname."

"Not at all," said Tom; "call me Tom, and nothing else. But, now tell me where you want to go, and I'll take you without the slightest danger."

"Oh, yes!" exclaimed the young lady, clasping her hands, and no doubt suddenly remembering that she ought to go home to the school at Hammersmith as quickly as possible,—"oh, yes! take me back again at once. There will be a world of anxiety on my account."

"Oh, no!" said Tom; "they will think you're half-way to Dover by this time, and your coming back will be a surprise."

The young girl had forgotten, and now she smiled with an appearance of more composure; for, after all, no one was suffering on her account, and she felt a sensation of great relief from the reflection that the story about her father's imminent danger was false.

"You are quite right, Mr.—Mr. Tom," she said; "but still I would fain return at once, for I have suffered much anxiety and some regret."

"All right!" said Tom. "It's at Hammersmith, isn't it?"

"Yes. It is Mrs. Goldwinkle's establishment."

"Goldwinkle!" thought Tom: "what a name!" And then he added aloud, "I'll get into the chaise, and we will drive there together."

"But your horse?"

"Oh, Daisy will follow."

"And so your horse's name is Daisy; and the creature is so sagacious and fond of you, that you really think it will follow us?"

"I'm quite sure of it," said Tom, "and you'll soon see the fact. Now, Daisy, lass, on we go."

Tom dismounted, and got into the chaise; and as he did so, the rather preposterous size of the uniform-coat he wore could not fail to attract Marian's attention.

"I think you are in disguise," she said.

"No," said Tom; "but this is an uniform that I've been compelled to adopt on the spur of a moment, and it don't fit me so well as it might. At all events, my dear Marian, it did not have the effect of hindering me in any way, from saving you from that rascal, your pretended uncle."

The young girl now felt quite ashamed that she had taken any notice of whether the coat of her gallant deliverer fitted him or not.

CHAPTER CCL.

TOM SAFELY DEPOSITS THE YOUNG LADY AT THE ESTABLISHMENT AT HAMMERSMITH.

Daisy's sagacity by no means belied Jones's description of it, since she trotted after the chaise without the slightest hesitation, or showing the smallest disposition to diverge from the road.

The distance was not great, and the young lady pointed out a garden-wall, and an iron gate with stone supports, as the establishment of Mrs. Goldwinkle, from which she had been cajoled by the pretended uncle.

"There is my home," she said; "and I know not how to thank you for your noble conduct towards me."

Tom sighed.

"I don't know either," he said. "That is to say, I don't want any thanks at all; but I should like to be able to think that I could see you again."

Marian Annesley now sighed as she replied faintly, "That is impossible."

"How impossible?"

"None but relations are allowed to visit us."

"Can't you say I'm a sort of half and half cousin, or something of that sort?"

Marian shook her head.

"No—no; it is not possible. It must not be thought of. Farewell now, and chance only can ever let us see each other again; but be assured that I shall never forget——"

"Me?" interposed Tom.

"I was going to say that I shall never forget the service you have done me this night. And, therefore, remembering that service, it is impossible that I should wholly forget you."

"Well," said Tom, "it can't be helped; but if I don't manage, in some sort of way, to see you again, my name is not Tom Ripon."

"Ripon?"

"Yes, that's my other name; but if ever you hear of a certain old gal in Wardour Street, mind I've no connexion with that party."

Tom rang at the iron gates as he spoke, and Marian leaped from the chaise.

The progress of a light from the house, carried by some one down the garden-path, warned him that he must soon bid adieu to the fair young creature who carried away his heart in her keeping.

"Marian!" he said.

And he spoke huskily.

"Yes, Mr. Tom?"

"Did that rascal with the red whiskers, presuming upon the fact that you thought him your uncle, kiss you?"

"Kiss me—no!"

"Oh, Marian!"

"What do you mean, Mr. Tom?"

"I thought the villain had, for there's a bright spot just upon that cheek next me."

"No!"

Tom stooped over the side of the chaise, and Marian held up her cheek to let him see that the bright spot was not there; but it soon made its appearance, for Tom bestowed upon the fair cheek a couple of hearty kisses, that, in the silence of the night, and of that spot, were heard by the person with the light, who was approaching to open the gate.

"Gracious providence! What's that?"

Marian uttered a slight scream.

"It's nothing," said Tom.

"Nothing?" cried the person with the light. "I'm certain that's a he voice, and I'm sure I heard——"

"What?" cried Tom.

"Go away, you villain, whoever you are. I won't say what I heard."

"It was only a blunderbuss," said Tom. "So good night!"

He touched the horse in the chaise with the extreme end of the whip, and in five minutes Tom was half a mile from Mrs. Goldwinkle's establishment.

Daisy followed him at a smart trot, and then Tom began to wonder what he could do next; and the idea just occurred to him that among the singular pieces of booty he had acquired that night was a horse and chaise.

They might be useful.

Tom drew up, and began to consider the posture of affairs.

"What shall I do next?" he said. "It's getting towards morning. I wonder if the old gal and Mortification will take in a horse and chaise as a bit of swag. They can't put them in the melting-pot, that's for certain. I wonder what o'clock it is? I fancy the night's pretty well spent, and we shall have daylight perhaps in another hour. I will drive on to Wardour Street, at all events, for I think I have had enough of it to-night. Come, Daisy, suppose we go on another plan. I dare say you can trot first, and we can get to town in good style."

By dint of a good deal of rummaging about in the chaise, Tom found some spare reins, and with considerable ingenuity he contrived to associate Daisy with the vehicle, tandem fashion.

"On we go, now!" said Tom. "We shall get over the ground in capital style."

Daisy was quite agreeable to any arrangement Tom chose, and the only eccentricity she was guilty of was now and then turning right round, and looking the other horse right in the face, as though she very much wondered what he was doing there.

This produced occasionally a little confusion in Tom's driving; but notwithstanding, the Western Road was soon reached again, and Tom was trotting up the descent by Notting Hill, when from one of the side lanes there emerged a horseman.

"Halt!" cried a rough voice.

Tom pulled up.

The voice was strange to him, and therefore he had no particular reason to avoid its owner.

"Have you come far up the road, sir?"

"Across from Hammersmith," said Tom.

"Have you seen a fellow on a dark bay mare, with a scarlet coat?"

"No," said Tom; "looking-glasses are scarce hereabouts."

"What do you say, sir?"

"I tell you what it is!" cried Tom. "When you speak to me again, please to say Major!"

"I beg your pardon, sir—I mean Major—but I'm one of Mr. Wild's men, and we are on the look-out for a highwayman on this road."

"Oh, indeed!"

"Yes, sir. But if you've not seen him I'm sorry to have interrupted you—Major, I mean."

The man then raised his voice and shouted out.

"If you please, Mr. Wild, this gentleman, who is a Major, has not seen him."

"Let him go to the deuce, then!" growled Wild, who was in the shadow of the lane.

"Thank you," said Tom, as he trotted on, considering, as he well might, that he had had a narrow escape of an encounter with Jonathan Wild, under the very worst circumstances that could possibly have occurred.

In the chaise he would have stood but little chance; and Tom, for the moment, felt sick at heart at the idea that if Wild had come out himself from the lane, both he and Daisy might have been captured.

"This won't do," said Tom, "and shan't do any longer."

He drew up to the roadside, and jumped out of the chaise, with the intention of abandoning his prize, and trotting off alone, upon Daisy.

A new idea, however, took possession of Tom, and he thought he might as well ride Daisy, and still bring the chaise behind him.

At any moment he could disengage the extemporized traces, and gallop off.

This was a plan of operations that got Tom entirely over his difficulty; and the appearance he, Daisy, and the chaise and horse exhibited now was that of rather an eccentric conveyance, driven by a postilion.

The empty chaise rattled on for about a quarter of a mile, and then Tom suddenly checked its progress, for he felt certain he heard the clatter of horses' feet behind him.

He was on a portion of the road where there was no turning to the right or to the left, so he had no resource but to abandon the chaise at once, or to drive onwards as quickly as possible.

But yet he did not wish to act hastily, since it might be that the horseman on the road was some stranger, who would take no notice of him.

Tom, however, adopted a precaution, in order to conceal his identity.

He took off the rather large uniform coat he wore, and flung it into the chaise.

In his waistcoat and shirt-sleeves, Tom looked much more like a postilion than he had done before.

He extinguished the chaise lamps likewise, so that but a very dim view could be got of the vehicle or its horses.

"Hoy! hoy! Hilloa, there! Stop!" shouted a voice; and the same horseman who a short time before had spoken to Tom, galloped up to the side of the chaise.

"Halt!" cried the myrmidon of Jonathan Wild —"halt, or it will be worse for you."

"Very good," said Tom; "I am halting."

"Oh, I didn't see you before. You are the postilion?"

"I am."

"And where's your master?"

"Oh, he'll be here directly."

"Indeed! Give me leave to say I very much doubt that. But perhaps you've no particular objection to tell me who he is?"

"None in the least," said Tom. "He has paid me very well, and I don't expect anything more from him. He is a highwayman, if you must know, and his name is Tom Ripon."

"Thank you!" cried Wild's man. "That's the very thing we wanted to find out; and now, my fine fellow, if you want to earn a guinea, you will keep this chaise at the identical spot it at present stands in till I can bring Mr. Wild back."

TOM RIPON FINDS HIMSELF IN AN AWKWARD FIX.

Presented Gratis with No. 79, of the New Edition of EDITH; or, the Sequel to Edith the Captive; or, the Robbers of Epping Forest.

"Give us the guinea," said Tom, " and I'll stake my life on it."

"There, then; you won't find this the worst night's work you ever did."

" I don't think I shall," said Tom, as he coolly pocketed the guinea which Wild's man handed to him.

In another moment, Tom was alone with his two horses and the chaise ; but his fertile genius had already suggested what he had better do.

He contrived to stick up the chaise-whip tolerably firmly in the vehicle, and then to button loosely round it the scarlet coat he had so recently thrown off, and fixing his hat above that, he succeeded in making a very fair representation, considering the darkness, of some one sitting in the chaise.

All Tom, then, had to do was to release Daisy from the whole concern ; and giving up without a pang the horse and chaise, which, after all, he would have found it very difficult to dispose of, he started with Daisy for London.

Tom would fain have lingered to see what sort of reception Jonathan Wild gave to the supposed figure in the chaise ; but he saw the first streaks of dawn in the east, and putting Daisy to speed, he was, in twenty minutes' time, in Wardour Street.

St. Martin's clock struck four.

Tom hammered away at his mother's door ; and Mortification, after making the usual espial from the fanlight above, admitted him.

" Yea, Thomas !" he said. " Even as manna in the wilderness art thou welcome to this little receptacle for property—hem !—that has strayed from its owner."

" It's a bad job," said Tom ; " but I've got nothing. I lost my coat and hat."

" Yea, then, I can only liken thee to a howling reprobate ; and the sooner thou art hanged, Thomas, the better."

" Stuff ! Where's the old gal ?"

" She sleepeth the sweet sleep of egg-flip."

" Oh, I understand !" said Tom. " Get out of the way, do, and let me bring in Daisy."

" Yea, Thomas !"

" Forward, Daisy ; and never mind his toes."

The Reverend Mortification found it good policy to get out of the way as quickly as possible ; and Tom, leading Daisy into the open shop, closed the door quickly behind him.

Mrs. Ripon was fast asleep in the back parlour, but Tom pretended he thought she had fainted, and adroitly cutting a piece of the woollen skirt of Mortification's coat, he set it alight under his mother's nose.

The pungent essence produced awakened Mrs. Ripon, with an alarming number of sneezes.

" Mother," said Tom, " I want some more money."

" What have you brought, my jewel ?"

" Nothing."

" Then where do you expect to go to, you undutiful son ?"

Tom laughed, and was about to make some reply, when a series of violent blows on the outer door warned the whole party of the arrival of some one with whom, at all events, secrecy was not an object.

" Gracious heavens !" exclaimed Mrs. Ripon, as she slipped off her chair on to the floor, " is it fire or police ?"

" The Philistines !—yea, the Philistines !" said Mortification.

As he spoke, he dived his hands into his pocket, and produced a silver mustard-pot and several spoons, with which he ran down into the lower regions of the house, in order that they might be cast at once into the melting-pot, and all traces of their separate existence obliterated.

" Don't make a row," said Tom. " I'll go and see who it is."

Upon making his way into the shop, Tom heard the blows against the door still more distinctly ; and scrambling up to the fan-light, he took a careful observation through it.

What was his astonishment to see the very identical chaise and horse he had left in the Western Road drawn up at his mother's door, with Jonathan Wild standing up in the vehicle, and banging the upper panel of that door with the handle of the whip.

" That's clever !" said Tom. " He knows a shorter way home than I did."

With all his admiration for Jonathan Wild's alertness, Tom Ripon felt the necessity of immediate action, if he would save himself from ignominious capture.

He felt for the fastenings of the door, and, shooting another bolt into its socket, he ran back to the parlour.

" Mother," he said, " and you, Mortification, it will do neither of you any good to see me fall into the hands of Jonathan Wild. I have some swag ; there it is. Take it and welcome, and make the most of it ; but don't, for both your lives and mine too, let him know that I'm in the house, or Daisy either."

Without waiting for a reply, Tom made his way into the shop again ; and holding Daisy by a good handful of her mane, he let her through a side door into a gloomy little passage, at the further end of which was the staircase that conducted to the upper part of the house.

Tom was fully impressed with the idea that Daisy was capable of anything, going up-stairs included ; and, in fact, he had good ground for such a supposition, for her wonderful sagacity supplied in her almost the power of speech.

" Come on," said Tom, " and take it easy, Daisy."

Keeping a step or two in advance, and still holding her by the mane, Tom then slowly ascended the staircase, followed, at first very cautiously, by Daisy, who, however, after a few seconds, when she found the footing firm, went up the steps, as Tom afterwards declared, better than many Christians.

CHAPTER CCLI.

TOM RIPON AND DAISY ARE CAPTURED BY WILD.

JONATHAN WILD kept up the violent knocking at the door until Mortification opened it.

" Yea, what wanteth thou, man of wrath ?"

" Tom Ripon," said Wild ; " and I mean to have him."

He pushed abruptly past Mortification, and glaring about him like some tiger seeking his prey, he strode into the back parlour.

It was evident that Wild was much disappointed to see nothing of either Tom or Daisy.

"Transportation for life," he cried, "or else hanging, which would you like best, for keeping the most notorious fence in London; or will you save both your lives by giving up Tom Ripon?"

Mrs. Ripon thought it most convenient to fall into a swoon; and Mortification, waving his arms about like the sails of a windmill, cried out aloud, "Yea, Mr. Jonathan Wild, what would we not do to oblige you? But if Thomas is not here, what shall we do? Can we, as the psalmist says, make bricks without straw? or Tom Ripons and Daisies, when they are not here? But yea, I say unto thee, Jonathan Wild, thy 'regulars' are ready."

It was perfectly well known among the family what Jonathan Wild's "regulars" meant.

They were the sort of black mail, or percentage upon their nefarious profession, which he extracted from the receivers of stolen goods in London.

Wild made a gesture of impatience.

"I know all about that; but I will not be led this dance from post to pillar by Tom Ripon. I must and will have him. I promised to spare him, but that was on condition that he kept quiet."

As he spoke, Jonathan Wild glared about him, and, to his great disappointment, could see no indication whatever of the presence of Tom Ripon.

He evidently began to think that his information, or his surmises, had failed him.

"So, so!" he muttered; "it seems I must seek elsewhere for him who is destined to grace Tyburn Tree before long."

Mrs. Ripon spoke not a word; and the manner in which the Rev. Mortification played his part of perfect indifference was exceedingly well done.

Wild actually began to believe that he was wasting his time.

"Well," he said, "be it so. I know the business you carry on here, of course, quite well; we settled all that on my last visit; and, as for those 'regulars' you speak of, I will call for them at another time, when more convenient."

As Wild spoke, he dashed out of the shop, and jumping into the chaise, he drove off.

That is to say, he appeared to drive off; but there was no telling exactly what complicated piece of cunning he was likely to have projected.

Tom waited a good hour, and then the daylight came so strongly upon him that he felt how extremely hazardous it was to venture abroad with Daisy.

It was an irksome thing for Tom to remain at the fence for the whole of a day; and, on his own account, he certainly would not have done so.

But it was for Daisy that he was willing to make any sacrifice, and put himself to any inconvenience.

Tom procured some litter and made a bed for his four-footed friend in the first floor, so that she was comfortable enough; and from various observations he made from time to time from the front windows of the house, he felt perfectly convinced it was well watched.

Now, the fence of Mrs. Ripon was a house of very peculiar construction.

It had what may be called, for want of a better term, a back front as well as a front front.

This back looked into a narrow street—indeed, so narrow, that it made the houses look preternaturally tall.

It was towards the dusk of evening, and just as a fine, small rain began to fall, that a window in one of the houses in the back street, exactly opposite to the fence, was carefully opened.

That window, however, was only opened sufficiently far for the upper part of a head to appear at it with two ferocious-looking eyes.

If Tom had seen those eyes, he would have been able to name their owner at a glance, for they could belong to no other person than Jonathan Wild.

Now, it so happened that there was not a single house in the street that was not in a state of considerable dilapidation; and, in fact, they only preserved their perpendicularity by the various props, struts, and supports which kept them up.

Such was the state of things then as the rain began to fall and the night to darken on the evening after Tom Ripon had taken refuge at his mother's.

It was a thousand pities that neither Mortification, Mrs. Ripon, nor Tom thought of any danger from the back of the house.

It was left completely unprotected—that is, so far as vigilant observation was concerned; although, of course, its lower doors and windows were amply secured.

Gradually, then, and slowly, so as not to make the least noise, was this window to which we have alluded in the opposite house opened.

Then, Jonathan Wild, with extreme caution, stood upon the window-sill.

By so doing he could conveniently grasp one of the horizontal supports which supported that and Mrs. Ripon"s house.

It was a perilous journey he was about to undertake; but his object was evidently by that horizontal beam to pass from one house to the other.

Wild was not a dexterous man, nor by any means clever at gymnastic feats; but he made up for every other disqualification in such matters by the indomitable energy of his character, and the terrible perseverance with which he set about anything.

He slowly, but surely, made his way along the beam.

The abyss below him looked profound in the darkness, and the fall would have been fatal.

Once, too, he had a terrible fright.

The beam made an ominous sound as if cracking.

Wild paused, and the cold perspiration stood upon his brow.

His strength seemed to be deserting him, and it was almost a wonder at that moment that he did not relax his hold, and fall crashing into the narrow street below.

And what preserved him at that moment of imminent danger was perhaps the most singular thought that could occur to the mind of any man.

He recollected the prophecy that had exercised always so strong an effect upon his imagination, to the effect that he was doomed to be hanged on a particular date at Tyburn.

It was strange that such a thought as this should nerve him to overcome the terror of his situation.

He actually spoke aloud.

"If I am born to be hanged, this beam will not crack asunder, and let me be dashed to pieces upon those cold, wet stones below."

The beam visibly deflected in the centre, and Wild now, as he moved onwards, felt it shake beneath his weight.

As he neared Mrs. Ripon's house, however, the danger decreased, since he was closer to one of the points of support to the beam, and it was an immense relief to him when he rested his feet upon the sill of the window, immediately opposite to that from which he had emerged.

Twice Wild passed his hand across his brow, and twice, as he did so, he called himself some hard names for risking so much, even for the capture of Tom Ripon and of Daisy.

It was quite clear that by some means he had established the fact in his own mind that they were in the fence.

And now he cautiously opened the widow.

He bent forward to listen.

He heard a sound which was music to his ears.

The snort of a horse.

He could have shouted with satisfaction, for he felt assured now, that he was on the right track for getting possession of Daisy.

At that moment he would have compounded with Tom for the delivery of that gallant steed, and allowed him to escape; for by some strange perversity of reasoning, Jonathan Wild had always fancied he possessed a kind of reversionary interest in Daisy, after the supposed death of Felix Heron.

The nervous system of Jonathan Wild had been somewhat deranged by that terrible and perilous transit from one house to another; but that one sound which assured him he was on the right scent, and near to the accomplishment of his wishes, recovered him completely.

He spoke in low, muttered tones.

"All is well—all is well. I shall at last achieve the object of my desires; for, after Felix Heron, who shall so well bestride that noble steed to which he owed so much of his celebrity, as I?"

The capture of Tom Ripon was now quite a secondary consideration with Wild.

In fact, if Tom had appeared, and chosen to make a bargain with the much-dreaded thief-taker, he might have secured to himself at least the promise for perfect immunity from all consequences of his career on the road, provided he surrendered Daisy.

Tom was not likely to make such a bargain, but if he would have done, how gladly would Wild have ratified it.

The window was at that height from the ground floor, that to take trouble in fastening it might well appear to be useless labour.

Jonathan Wild therefore had no difficulty in making his way into the house, and he had the satisfaction of feeling certain that he was in the adjoining room to that occupied by Tom Ripon and Daisy.

If was only the lower part of the premises that was used as yet by Mortification and Mrs. Ripon for the purpose of carrying on their rather doubtful business.

That upper part, then, in which Tom Ripon now had so dangerous a companion, was otherwise deserted.

Tom was speaking to Daisy.

He was making his preparations, as soon as the darkness should deepen a little, to leave the house.

But Tom had not quite made up his mind whether to go upon the road that ensuing night, or to take Daisy directly to the stables of Whitcombe House.

Tom did not deceive himself, but knew perfectly well that the leave he got from Felix Heron to take Daisy out for exercise by no means extended to the latitude of seeking adventures with her upon the highway.

He rather, then, felt the necessity of showing himself occasionally, and, indeed, of inviting Heron's attention to the fact that Daisy was safe in her stable.

But all Tom's thoughts and dispositions upon this subject might just as well have been left alone, since Jonathan Wild was almost literally within arm's length of him and the gallant creature who had hitherto carried him in such safety through so much peril.

"Well, Daisy," said Tom, "how do you feel? Pretty well, eh? That's right!"

Tom's conversations with Daisy were of a most singular description, since he supported them all himself both in question, answer, and rejoinder.

"That's right, Daisy; and, after all, if you've no particular objection, I do think we might as well sally out to-night, and see what Fate has in store for us. Eh, Daisy—you have no objection? That's right!"

Tom carefully saddled and bridled his four-footed friend.

And all this while Wild was listening very intently.

The house on that upper floor was curiously constructed.

There were but two rooms; and at the top of the staircase was a small landing, from which merely a ladder led up to what might be called the attics, but which were in reality only a couple of lofts, situated exactly beneath the sloping roof of the house.

The two rooms had no communication one with the other, or Tom might have been taken at a worse disadvantage than he was; but the slender, old, dry, lath and plaster division that divided them was scarcely any obstruction to sound, and Wild could hear everything that Tom said with ease and distinctness.

"Well, Daisy," added Tom, after a few moments' pause; "notwithstanding, as you will, perhaps, say, I have lost my coat and my hat, we will still go upon the road! I dare say the old gal will find some other fine dress among her odds and ends; and, who knows, but we may make a better appearance still?"

If Jonathan Wild could have seen what Tom was about for the next five minutes, he would probably not have remained so easy and quiet in that back apartment.

Leaning carelessly against Daisy, who now and then gave him a push with her head, Tom was loading his pistols.

About the conclusion of that process, Wild heard the snap of one of the pans as Tom closed it.

"Ah!" thought Jonathan, "I have wasted precious time! He is armed, and we shall have a tussle yet! Well, well, what matters? If I count the bullets that have been fired at me, they would come to scores; and if, indeed, I bear a charmed life, which only can be taken from me in one particular way——"

Wild winced a little, and gave a peculiar twist to his neck, as he thought of the particular way.

"If that be true, what have I to fear from all his firearms? For what will be will be, or the word fate should not have found a place in the English language!"

There must have been a dramatic element in the character of Jonathan Wild, for we have frequently seen that he loved to do things not always, perhaps, in the safest way, but always in the most effective.

He did not desert that principle in this case; and with quite a fixed conviction on his mind that he would have to stand a shot, or, perhaps, two, from Tom Ripon, he commenced operations.

Rap, rap, rap!

Wild knocked at the partition between the two rooms.

Tom started, and uttered a loud exclamation.

"Hilloa!" cried Wild.

"Who's that?" said Tom. "Is it you, Mortification?"

"Not exactly," replied Wild. "Mortification, I take it, in the full sense of the word, is on your side of the partition! Tom Ripon, you are my prisoner! I need not tell you who I am, for you know by this time!"

"Jonathan Wild!"

"Exactly! But if you are wise enough to surrender Daisy to me without squabble or turmoil, I will give you—let me see—I will give you free range and license till the Sessions after next; and, then, Tom, I think, we must come to a reckoning!"

Tom had recovered his first shock of surprise, and now faced about to the partition.

"Johnny!" he cried.

"Bah! Don't be foolish!"

"There's an old proverb that says, 'Short reckonings make long friends!' Now, I will not give you till the Sessions after next, nor even till the next, so here goes!"

Tom calculated upon the slender character of the partition, and knowing that his pistols were accurately loaded and well rammed down, he fired both of them at once through the frail wall, in the hope of hitting Wild.

The report was prodigious in the confined space; and Tom himself was half blinded by the smoke of the gunpowder.

The first sound that met the ears of Tom, after that produced by the report of the pistols had died away, was the sardonic laugh so peculiar to Wild.

"Ha, ha! my young friend! Well done—well done!"

Tom flung his arms around the neck of Daisy, and at that moment he thought his heart would break.

"Oh, Daisy, Daisy!—what have I done, my poor Daisy? All is lost!"

In another moment Wild strode into the room. Without deigning to look at Tom, he flung open the window, shouting to some of his bulldogs who were keeping watch without.

<hr />

CHAPTER CCLII.

JOHN TARLETON AND WARRINGDALE VISIT WHIT-COMBE HOUSE.

It is necessary to our story that we should leave Tom Ripon and Daisy in their perilous situation, and return once more to Whitcombe House, and see what was there being transacted on that same evening which found poor Tom and his four-footed friend surrounded by Jonathan Wild and his men.

It is getting dark, and Edith is alone.

Alone in that same drawing-room which has been the scene of so many incidents in this history.

There is a look of anxiety upon her fair face, which sorrow has imprinted there.

Two figures, wrapped in cloaks, have been watching closely the door of Whitcombe House, and had been rewarded for their patience by seeing, at length, Felix Heron, disguised as Captain Fantome, and followed a pace or two behind by Ogle, leave the hall of the mansion, and proceed down St. James's Street.

We will listen to the conversation of these two men; and, probably, our readers will have no difficulty in recognising them.

"Hush!" said the taller of the two. "The bridegroom—ha, ha!—the bridegroom is about to leave his bride; and we shall be able to make our own terms with the fair Countess!"

"Yes, yes!" replied the other; "I am better now. I have got over the foolish idea that possessed me, that I had seen a spectre. Let us go at once, and make our own conditions with Edith."

"Come on then, Warringdale—come on at once, or the sea-Captain may return before our business is concluded."

These two men, then, Warringdale and John Tarleton, made what speed they could to gain admittance to the house of Felix Heron.

Fortune seemed to favour their design; for, at that moment, a servant in livery knocked at the hall door, which was immediately opened by Mrs. Ogle, and delivered a note to her.

Just as Mrs. Ogle was about to close the door, John Tarleton stepped forward, and, thrusting his foot inside the door, said, in a peremptory tone of voice, "Tell the Lady Edith that there are two gentlemen who wish to see her particularly on business."

Before Mrs. Ogle could recover her presence of mind, John Tarleton and Lord Warringdale were striding past her up the grand staircase of the mansion.

At the first sound of those voices in the hall, Edith had sprung to her feet, and was about to turn the handle of the door to ascertain the cause of the commotion in the hall, when she found herself suddenly face to face with John Tarleton and his infamous associate, Lord Warringdale.

For a moment Edith felt that her heart stood still, so sudden and unexpected was the appearance of the two men. But in a few minutes she recovered her presence of mind; and, but for the clutching grasp with which she held by a table, there was no visible sign of the perturbation within.

"What want you here, men of crime?" asked Edith, in as steady a voice as she could command. "What want you here, I say? Begone, or——"

Not so fast—not so fast, fair lady!" replied Warringdale, with a sneer. "We may surely

No. 80.—Edith Heron.

expect some better reception than this, when we come to offer our congratulations to the bride of Captain Fantome."

Edith's courage rose with the emergency of her situation; for well she knew there was no one in that house from whom she could hope for protection from those two bad men.

"I want not your congratulations! Leave the house instantly, or I will call for those who will quickly rid me of your hateful presence! Begone, I say!"

While Edith was speaking John Tarleton had seated himself upon one of the many luxurious couches with which that magnificent apartment was furnished, and pointed to another, saying to Warringdale, "Be seated, my lord; my sister will soon become more hospitable, I hope; and we will then tell her our business here."

Lord Warringdale seated himself with his back towards the door, evidently fearing that Edith might make her escape.

"Let us end this scene," he said, with mock gravity. "Our business here is to tell you that now you have taken the name of Captain Fantome, I intend forthwith to set up my claim to the estate of Whitcombe."

Edith made a gesture of contempt.

"Hear me out, I say. While you were the Countess of Whitcombe, you were safe; but now that you have no longer a right to that title, I claim mine; and give you fair warning that unless the thing be amicably arranged—mind, I say amicably—the law must take its course. What say you, Edith, is it to be peace or war?"

"War!" exclaimed Edith,—"war to the death, Lord Warringdale! I defy you, and scorn you; and unless——"

"Stop, stop!—not so fast!" added Warringdale. "Think again. Think of your child—Felix's child—and say if the law is to step in and arrange this little dispute between us. Give me the title deeds, and let me be Earl of Whitcombe, as I ought to be, or——"

"Or what?" asked Edith, scornfully.

"Or ten thousand pounds. Give me ten thousand pounds, and I will trouble you no more."

"And you, John Tarleton—you, too, doubtless, have some request to make?" cried Edith, turning upon him with flashing eyes.

"Yes, sister."

Edith made a gesture of impatience.

"Ah! Do you disown your brother?"

"Monster!"

"A hard word. But I, too, will tell you, Edith, Countess of Whitcombe, or Lady Fantome, whichever it may please you best, that I, too, have resolved to secure to myself some of our father's property. He must have left wealth sufficient for us both. Take your share, and give me mine; and let us see each other for the last time."

It is evident these two men, who were thus cowardly attacking a lonely woman, had quite lost sight of the fact that time was hastening on, as it does in all transactions, whether pleasant or otherwise, and that they were no further advanced in their diabolical scheme of forcing Edith to purchase their absence than they were when they first entered that room.

The fact is, Edith was trying to gain time, knowing that Felix was not far off, and that his business was not such as to detain him long from home. Still she began to feel all the peril of her situation, and it needed all her indomitable energy of character to veil from the eyes of her two heartless persecutors all the agony she felt at that instant.

"Well," said Warringdale, after a few moments' pause, "are you considering our proposal, Edith?"

"Yes," said Edith, in a low voice; and she pressed her hand tightly on her heart, for a faint footfall—the step of all others she knew the best —had fallen upon her ear,—"yes, I am considering."

"That is well!" said John Tarleton. "I would much rather part friends than otherwise."

But Edith heeded him not. She was asking herself if Felix knew in whose company she was; and when she found that he was not coming in by the door which led on to the staircase, she felt quite certain that Mrs. Ogle had encountered him, and that he would soon be by her side to protect her.

Felix Heron had seen Mrs. Ogle; and by a back staircase had made his way, with all speed, towards the drawing-room, where he could hear the murmur of voices.

To divest himself of the hat and wig, which made his disguise as Captain Fantome so complete, was the work of a moment; and then he stood with his hand on the handle of the door, ready to come to the assistance of his Edith.

John Tarleton, fancying he heard a noise, rose from the couch on which he had seated himself, and telling Warringdale he would keep guard on the outside of the door, he, Warringdale, and Edith were left alone together.

A door at the other end of the room opened quietly.

Warringdale's back was turned towards this door, and only Edith saw Felix, who made a sign to her not to recognise his presence in any way.

A glance was sufficient to show Edith what Felix Heron intended by this sudden appearance, and the effect he wished to produce upon Lord Warringdale and John Tarleton.

With that fine sense of adaptation to any circumstances presented to her where moral courage and fidelity were required, Edith at once took the hint which Felix Heron's presence gave her, and improved upon it at discretion.

But we must let the reader know exactly what that presence was, and how it was likely to have so great an effect upon the nervous system of Lord Warringdale.

Heron had had time completely to attire himself in his ancient costume of a highwayman, and it was almost with a glow of delight that Edith saw him looking handsome, picturesque, and gallant—even as she used to do, when first she surrendered her heart to the soft bondage of his affections.

A more strikingly dissimilar figure than he now presented to the Captain Fantome who was supposed to be the new husband of the Countess of Whitcombe, could not be imagined.

It was but an experiment on the part of Heron —this appearance in his old, original character— and he had some doubts of its success.

Once before had Lord Warringdale been terrified by the supposed apparition of his brother; but time had elapsed, and he had shaken off the impression which the phenomenon had first made upon him.

Its repetition was likely to be much more effective than even the first appearance.

Warringdale might have argued himself into a belief that his imagination had misled him— that some sickness of the brain, or affection of the nerves of sight, had produced the seeming apparition.

Its re-appearance now, however, would be conclusive.

And now Edith began to speak in such words as to favour the effect that was to be produced by Heron's presence.

"Be gone," she said; "nor pollute this house further by your presence. You were ever the bitter and uncompromising foe of its once master.

There were no arts or villanies that you did not practise against him!"

"Beware!" said Warringdale, savagely. "My power at Court is greatly increased."

"I care not."

"Beware, I say again; for I may be a dangerous foe!"

"Then," said Edith, "I will invoke the aid of heaven and its ministers to defend me; and if he who has gone before has but the power to look down upon earth on those he loved, he may likewise have the power to do a something to defeat their enemies!"

Warringdale laughed.

"I never really feared him on earth," he said; "and I will not fear him now that he has gone from it!"

"Then," cried Edith, "I say to you beware, lest these boastful words should beget a terrible retribution!"

"These are idle threats," said Warringdale. "Let him come!"

"Let who come?" said John Tarleton, at this moment, as he looked into the room.

Heron walked slowly forward.

"He is here!" he said.

There was no mistaking the voice.

There was no mistaking the face and figure, even if the dress could have been merely a delusion and a theatrical effect.

Warringdale fell backward into the arms of John Tarleton, who, with no real intention of supporting him, did so for a few moments in petrified amazement.

"He is here!" said Heron again.

"Gracious heavens!" exclaimed Edith.

About half a minute had elapsed, and then the agony of fear was too much for both Tarleton and Warringdale, and fighting with each other, they dashed from the room, falling down the whole depth of the grand staircase, and heedless of the wounds and bruises they received in that process, scrambled to their feet again. They made their way out of Whitcombe House, looking like men more dead than alive.

There can be no doubt but that Warringdale, in consequence of his connexion with that strange society that met at that lone house in Pall-Mall, considered that he might threaten and assail Edith with impunity.

Supernatural terrors might now, however, keep him back; for he could scarcely doubt but that he had seen the apparition of his brother.

CHAPTER CCLIII.

MRS. RIPON HAS A PITCHED BATTLE WITH JONATHAN WILD'S MEN.

WE return to Tom Ripon.

The state of affairs in connexion with Tom and Daisy seemed desperate.

Wild's shouts from the window to his myrmidons who were lurking in the neighbourhood were sure to be effective in a few moments.

And Tom had no weapons now with which to defend either himself or Daisy.

A vague idea that by one vigorous push he might send Wild out of the window, came over

him; but it was too late, for Wild turned abruptly, and, sitting on the window-sill, presented at Tom one of his short, stumpy pistols, he exclaimed, "So, so, my fine fellow. this is the end of the little game! Take things easy, and I will promise you an extra bundle of straw, to save the jolting of the cart that takes you to Tyburn Tree!"

Tom at once stepped between Wild and Daisy.

"Hold, Jonathan!" he said. "If you must fire, take care you don't hit her. I'm fair game; but I wouldn't see a hole in Daisy's sleek coat for half the world."

"I don't intend it," said Wild. "Daisy is mine, and I shall always look upon her as the legacy of Captain Heron."

A tremendous uproar was at this moment heard below, for some half-dozen of Jonathan's men had arrived, and were holding high battle with Mortification and Mrs. Ripon.

"That will do," said Wild.

He blew the call-whistle he had with him shrilly; but the reply to it was not exactly what he had expected.

The confusion below grew more intense, and so many cries and yells were mixed up with it, that even Wild began to get alarmed, and to listen with unusual attention, in the hope of discovering what the frantic tumult was all about.

The voice of Mrs. Ripon arose, like a war-cry, above all other sounds.

But Wild was surprised to hear that his men made nothing but outcries, as though they had fallen into some trap, which inflicted upon them serious bodily pain.

"Tom Ripon!" he said, shortly and sharply.

"Well, Johnny?"

"You are my prisoner."

"Something strikes me," said Tom, "you said that before."

"And," added Wild, heedless of the interruption, "as such, you ought not to attempt to escape. You have fired two shots at me, and I have not returned them. Give me your word that you will not budge from this place while I go and see what's the matter below."

"Well," said Tom, "that's about the coolest thing I've heard of for many a long day!"

"Then I must make sure," said Wild, again handling his pistol. "No one can blame me for your death; for I can easily say you resisted capture, and I was compelled to take your life in self-defence."

"Stop a bit," said Tom; "if I were alone, things might turn out differently. But——"

Tom, as he spoke, turned caressingly to Daisy.

"No," he added; "you must run no risks. A chance shot must not strike you. I yield, Jonathan Wild, for Daisy's sake."

"I don't care for whose sake it is!" cried Wild, as he dashed out of the room, and rattled down stairs.

Tom heaved a deep-drawn sigh.

"Oh, Captain Felix! Captain Felix!" he said, "where are you now? If you could but know the danger that Daisy was in, how soon you would be here! And then, not Jonathan Wild and all his men would be able to carry her off from you. But, as it is, the sooner I am hung the better; for you never can forgive me for leading Daisy into this scrape!"

The continued noise below became so outrageous, that even Tom, in the midst of all his affliction, was interested by it.

He went to the door and listened.

He heard his mother's voice declaiming at a great rate.

"Now, you wretches, you came for the swag, and you've got it! I hope you like it! And as for that mean-spirited wretch, Mortification, I've a good mind to give him a ladleful all to himself!"

These words opened Tom's understanding as to what had really occurred.

It was just this.

Wild's men, after knocking twice, and finding the outer door not opened to them so promptly as they desired, burst it in, and, like a parcel of Cossacks, or other savages, rushed into the place, scattering Mrs. Ripon's goods and chattels in all directions.

The Rev. Mortification beat a hasty retreat; and, sliding behind an old-fashioned eight-day clock that stood in a corner of the back room, he hoped entirely to escape observation.

But Mrs. Ripon's indignation took a warlike turn, and, after flinging at the heads of Jonathan Wild's janissaries every portable article within her reach, she rushed down a short flight of stairs which led to the lower regions of the house.

An excellent fire of coal, coke, and turf was always kept there, enclosed in a brick encasement, so that it looked like a chemical furnace.

On this fire was the celebrated "melting-pot," which formed so important an item in the stock in trade of a fence.

Into that were cast all articles of silver likely to be identified.

Silver spoons, snuff-boxes, plates, dishes, soup-tureens, sword-hilts, chains, watch-cases, and, in fact, every article of that metal, with crest and initial, that might be safely sworn to.

The molten silver glittered and seethed in this melting-pot from morning till night, and from night till morning. Whenever it got inconveniently full a portion was removed in a red-hot ladle, and run out to cool into a glittering slab upon the stone hearth of the kitchen.

The refiners and jewellers of the City never refused to purchase these well-known silver ingots; and their identification with any stolen property was perfectly impossible.

Gold was treated in a very different fashion.

Where the article was one of great beauty, from its workmanship, it generally found a market in some of the Continental capitals.

Otherwise the precious metal was beaten up by hammers until it had lost all its original shape and appearance, but none of its weight.

Mrs. Ripon then made her way to this laboratory of the fence.

The red-hot ladle was reposing gracefully in the silver melting-pot.

"They shall have it!" said Mrs. Ripon. "It's what the wretches come for."

In three minutes more she had reached the shop again, with a ladleful of the molten metal in her grasp.

It was scarcely necessary to say, "Take that!"

for Jonathan Wild's men got it; and the silvery shower, for once in a way, was exceedingly unwelcome.

This at once accounted for all the noise and confusion, which only ceased on the appearance of Wild.

His men, however, cut rather a grotesque appearance, with shreds and globules of the now cooled metal hanging about them.

"Handcuff the witch!" cried Wild. "The woman is a pest, and should have kicked her last at Tyburn long ago."

"Indeed!" cried Mrs. Ripon, as she placed the still hot ladle upon Jonathan's back.

Wild made a spring forward that quite delighted his men, since it is a principle of human nature that a community of misfortune is always delightful.

Having achieved this partial victory, Mrs. Ripon, like other skilful generals, effected a retreat into the back parlour.

But she carried the ladle with her in so triumphant a fashion, that Mortification, who stole a glance at her from behind the clock, thought she looked decidedly mischievous.

He glanced uneasily forth while Mrs. Ripon soliloquised.

"I only wish I could find where that wretch Mortification has hidden himself! The mean-spirited fellow, to leave a poor, lone, weak, helpless woman to fight his battles! But they shan't take Tom prisoner. I'll have at them again!"

Mrs. Ripon would have joined any *fracas* that might be supposed to take place up-stairs; but that Wild, as soon as he had seen her fairly housed in the back parlour, had had the prudence to shoot a couple of bolts in the door, and so keep her a prisoner.

Tom Ripon looked pale and calm when Wild and his men reached the upper room.

His right arm was still flung round the neck of Daisy.

There was something touching in the sight of Tom's affection for that voiceless creature, who could only with its limited instincts return the kindness and caresses he lavished upon her.

"Come," said Wild, "the time's up."

"I'm ready," said Tom. "But look you here, Jonathan; if you will take Daisy back to Whitcombe House, and ring the bell, and tie her bridle to the door-knocker, and then walk away and leave her there, you may come back and shoot me as soon as you please."

"Bah!" said Wild. "What good would it do me to shoot you?"

"Perhaps none; but it's a fair offer."

"No, Tom Ripon, I won't do it. I never, in all my life, envied Captain Heron but one thing, and that was Daisy."

Tom sighed.

"And now," added Wild, "that he is no more, I make no scruple in taking possession of her; though, if he were alive still, I don't think that even I should have the heart to separate him from her."

"You wouldn't!" cried Tom, darting forward. "Say that again, Jonathan."

"What for?"

Tom Ripon shrank back again.

"Nothing—nothing; I was only thinking."

"Thinking of what?"

WARRINGDALE ENJOYS A SHORT-LIVED TRIUMPH OVER HIS DEADLY
ENEMY, JONATHAN WILD.

Presented Gratis with No. 80, of the New Edition of EDITH; or, the Sequel to Edith the Captive; or, the Robbers of Epping Forest.

"Nothing. I have said nothing."

"And yet any one, to have looked at you at that moment, could almost have sworn you thought it possible the grave might give up its dead."

"Hold!" said Tom, with animation; "I will strike a bargain with you, Jonathan Wild."

"What is it?"

"Will you give up Daisy freely, and without a murmur, if—if——"

"If what?"

Tom sank his voice to a low, solemn tone as he added, "If Captain Heron himself should come to claim her?"

Wild retreated a step or two.

What could Tom Ripon mean by such an expression?

Could the grave give up its dead? or was that dreamy possibility which had more than once come like a shadow over the mind of Jonathan Wild, that Felix Heron was after all not dead, really a truth?

"Speak more plainly, Tom Ripon," he said. "Your own life, and the lives of others, may hang upon your answer."

But Tom Ripon was not disposed to speak more plainly, since he even began to regret that he had spoken so plainly as he had.

"They were idle words, Jonathan Wild," he said, "and idly spoken."

Wild advanced towards him, at the same moment that he snatched a lantern from the hand of one of his men, and holding the light in such a position that its full rays came upon Tom's face, he looked at him with a steady and glaring scrutiny.

Wild, indeed, held his hand up between the lantern and his own eyes, much in the manner of connoisseurs when they look at a picture in an artificial light.

Tom did his best to stand this critical examination.

"Now, say again," cried Wild, "that they were idle words, and idly spoken."

"I do so," said Tom; "and they need not disturb you."

For more than a minute Wild subjected Tom Ripon to this disagreeable scrutiny; then handing back the lantern to the man from whom he had taken it, he spoke in a low tone of voice, saying, "Be it so—but this is a matter which shall be inquired into. Now, men, look sharp, and be hanged to you all! Get the horse down stairs, and take this boy to Little Newgate."

Tom would rather be taken to Little Newgate—that is to say, to Wild's house—than to the actual prison of that name.

The fact that Wild chose personally to have possession of him was something like an intimation that he was not to be handed over to the law.

There was hope in that.

And Tom had so much faith in his own indomitable courage and ingenuity, that he had very little doubt of being able to extricate himself even from what at present seemed to be his serious difficulty.

"I'm ready," said Tom.

One of the janissaries approached him to slip a pair of handcuffs upon his wrists, but Tom protested against such an indignity.

"Look here, Mr. Wild," he said; "if I promise you that I will go to Little Newgate without trying to give your fellows the slip by the way, there can be no good in troubling me with a pair of bracelets."

"Oh, stuff!" said the janissary, "we always do."

"Let him alone," growled Wild: "upon his word that he never attempts to escape, he may leave alone the darbies."

"Stop a bit," said Tom; "never is a large word, although a little one to speak. I promise that I won't try to escape between here and Little Newgate; but never is quite another affair."

"On with them, then," said Wild, angrily, "and get the horse down stairs."

It would have been folly for Tom to resist several strong men, who, in spite of him, and most likely with the infliction of some injury besides, would have put on the handcuffs, so he quietly submitted.

By a kind of manual dexterity, however, which was well practised and known among the light-fingered gentry, Tom managed to give his wrists the appearance of being much larger than they really were, so that the pair of handcuffs put upon him were of a size he felt confident he could easily slip out of.

"Quick, quick!" cried Wild, impatiently. "Are we to wait here all night?"

It was easy to cry "Quick!" and be impatient, but a very serious obstacle presented itself to Wild's janissaries in carrying out his orders.

Daisy had no notion of being handed down stairs by somebody of whom she knew nothing, and who, her sagacious instinct seemed to tell her, was an enemy of Tom Ripon.

The moment one of Wild's men placed his hand on her bridle to lead her to the landing at the stair-head, she made a seemingly vicious bite at his arm.

The alarmed janissary dropped the bridle instantly.

"It's a vicious brute," he cried. "I can do nothing with it."

"That is too absurd," cried Wild; "the creature is docility itself, and almost has the sense of a human being."

Tom laughed.

"Try it yourself, then, Jonathan," he said. "Perhaps Daisy has heard of you, and fallen in love with you."

"Come on!" said Wild.

Snap went Daisy's teeth within an inch of his nose, and Wild retreated so rapidly, that he stumbled over two of his men.

"Confound the brute!" he muttered. "She must and shall be mine."

Tom was delighted.

"You may depend upon it, Jonathan, she won't go," he said, "and you had better give it up as a bad job. You've got me, and that's enough for one night's work."

"No," said Wild, "I don't do things by halves; Daisy goes with me, or she lies here a lump of carrion."

Wild produced one of his pistols, and shook the powder in the pan.

Tom's heart, as the popular saying goes, was in his mouth, at the idea of such imminent danger to Daisy; and for the moment he lost his keen sagacity and presence of mind, as any one is apt to do, when the feelings make war with the judgment.

Under ordinary circumstances he would have been able to decide at once that Daisy was in no real danger, and that Wild producing a pistol, with the implied threat of shooting her, was but an idle menace.

"Hold, hold!" cried Tom; "you would do a deed that the repentance of a life could not undo."

"What then?"

Tom stamped his foot impatiently.

"What must be, must be," he said. "I will lead her down stairs, and you'll obtain possession of her. Behave kindly to her, Jonathan Wild, and it may not be forgotten at some time when you may stand between life and death."

There was a certain air of dignity about Tom as he thus spoke, which had even some effect upon Jonathan Wild.

CHAPTER CCLIV.

DAISY REFUSES A NEW GUIDE.—JONATHAN WILD'S DISCOMFITURE.

TOM was released from the handcuffs, in order that he might lead Daisy down the ricketty old staircase of the fence, in Wardour Street.

The moment Tom laid his hand on the bridle, and spoke to her, Daisy followed him with the docility of a lamb.

"Come on, Daisy," said Tom, "it won't be for long. There are those who won't put up with the knowledge that you are in the hands of Jonathan Wild."

"And who may they be?" growled Wild.

"That's my business," said Tom.

"You've a long tongue," said Wild; "and I warn you not to use it so freely."

"I don't suppose," replied Tom, "that you will care much for warnings from me; but, for all that, I do warn you that the worst night's work you ever did you've done to-night. If you kill Daisy your own life is not worth twelve hours' purchase; and if you keep her, you are likely to get so hard a knock from somebody, who will come to take her from you, that you may not easily recover it."

"Thank you," said Wild, sarcastically. "Notwithstanding all these terrible threats, Tom Ripon, I will take my chance."

Daisy descended the staircase with Tom's hand on the bridle, and, in the midst of the still falling rain, the whole party sallied out into the street.

"I will ride," said Wild, "you can get a coach, and take this boy to Little Newgate."

Wild, as he spoke, put his foot in the stirrup and mounted Daisy.

Tom was rather surprised to see that she permitted him so easily to do so, but Daisy was taken by surprise, and Wild was in the saddle before she began to find out he was not her accustomed rider.

Daisy, however, quickly brought things to their proper level.

She deliberately laid herself down in the roadway, and rolled over Jonathan Wild.

"Help! help! murder! Hold her head! Help! help! The creature's gone mad!"

It was lucky for Jonathan Wild that his feet came comfortably out of the stirrups, for Daisy sprung to her feet with a snort and a bound, and dashing the mud and stones of the roadway in a blinding shower over Wild and his men with her hind feet, she went down Wardour Street at a gallop, and in less than half a minute disappeared in the Oxford Road.

"Hurrah, hurrah, hurrah!" cried Tom. "Hip, hip, hurrah! Three cheers for Daisy! How do you feel now, old Johnny?"

Jonathan Wild sat in the road with his back propped against a post, and looking about him in a bewildered fashion.

His face was plastered with mud, and if he suffered nothing but bruises from the rough tumble he had had, he was much luckier than he had any reason to hope or to expect.

There is very little doubt but that Tom, in the confusion, might have got away, but he had promised to go quietly to Little Newgate, and a romantic sense of honour of keeping his word, restrained him.

Wild's janissaries looked upon the whole scene aghast, believing that Daisy was some fiend in the shape of a horse.

Wild then burst into a series of imprecations of the most fearful character, and his own janissaries, who might be presumed to be accustomed to his particular moods and tempers, shrunk from him in terror.

Tom Ripon took things easy.

The escape of Daisy was a subject of sincere congratulation to him, since he had not the slightest doubt but that she would find her way home, and then he knew that Ogle would take good care of her.

Indeed three parts of his anxiety in regard to the *mal apropos* adventure that had taken place seemed to be removed from his mind by this gallant escape of Daisy.

And in his usual odd fashion of endowing Daisy with reason and speech, Tom shook his head, as he said to himself, "Ah! Daisy did better than I. She didn't promise not to escape, so she's off, and I'm on my road to Little Newgate. However, it's a good job one of us has got away."

Wild's breath became exhausted by the imprecations he uttered, and then two of his men approached him to help him to his feet.

The thief-taker shook himself, and one of his men picked up his hat and wig, both of which were pretty well splashed with mud.

"Where's the boy?" growled Wild.

"Here, boy," said Tom Ripon; "where are you?"

"Bah!" said Wild; "I mean you."

"How should I know that? I thought you were speaking of some boy, and not of a highwayman. However, if you think me a boy, you ought to be ashamed of yourself to come with half-a-dozen strong fellows to make me a prisoner."

"Take him along," said Wild. "Put him in number two cell. He and I will come to a reckoning to-morrow."

Wild's janissaries were glad to take leave of him, and finding an empty coach at the corner o

Leicester Fields, they hustled Tom into it, and set off for Wild's house in Newgate Street,

Jonathan, with his hands behind his back, and walking with difficulty, for he had been considerably bruised by his tumble, went up Wardour Street towards the Oxford Road.

He growled and grumbled to himself in half audible tones, as was his fashion.

"I don't know what to make of it. As for getting possession of Daisy, it's only a dream. The creature has been so petted, and pampered, and tamed, and spoken to by Heron and Tom Ripon, that she never will be worth her weight in mere horse-flesh to me or any one else. I wonder where she has gone to now."

Wild looked right and left in the Oxford Road, but saw no traces of Daisy.

"Well!" he added; "I've got that boy a prisoner, but what to do with him I don't know. He is young, active, bold as a lion, and full of a thousand tricks and ingenuities, that might in three years' time make a fortune. I wouldn't mind giving him three years fairly on the road if he would share his plunder with me; and after that—well, after that he must take his chance, and go the way of them all. A short life and a merry one, and then Tyburn Tree. Ha, ha!"

Wild laughed, but it was a laugh as unlike mirth as anything could possibly be.

He rapped at the door of a little roadside public-house; for Oxford Street, then called the Oxford Road, was quite a suburban sort of thoroughfare, having, particularly on its northern side, old-fashioned buildings of the Charles the First period, with their sharp angled roofs and gable-ends, such as have long since disappeared, except in some ancient portions of the metropolis.

"House! house!" cried Wild.

The landlord appeared, with rather a scared look upon his face.

"What's the matter?" inquired Wild: "it's early enough, isn't it, to keep open door?"

"Something has happened," said the landlord. "A mad horse."

"Ah!"

"Yes, it first went country ways, and then came thundering back as if the deuce itself was at its heels."

Wild had no doubt whatever but that this was Daisy, although the information that it had just gone country ways, and then returned, was no guide whatever to him in pursuit of it, even had he been so inclined, which he could hardly be said to be.

His last interview with Daisy had wonderfully cooled his prepossession in her favour.

Mentally he had given up the idea of ever calling her his own, or making her useful to him in his excursions in the neighbourhood of London.

"Brandy," he said, "and be quick about it."

"Yes, sir. Will you step in?"

"No."

The landlord of the little inn brought Wild out a glass of brandy on a tray. It was too dark for him to see the look of contempt with which he regarded it; but when Wild took it up, and threw it deliberately into the man's face with an oath, he became aware that he had rather mistaken the order of his brutal guest.

"When I say brandy, I mean half-a-pint. My name is Jonathan Wild."

He always gloried in the terror which his name created; and the celerity and the humility with which he was served were pretty good proofs that his evil reputation had reached to that humble little hostel.

"That will do," said Wild, as he flung the pewter measure on to the doorstep. "That will do. I'll call and pay."

The landlord was glad to compound with Wild's absence with half-a-pint of brandy; and the great thief-taker, considerably revived by the libation, which would have prostrated any one else, took his way along the Oxford Road, still pondering and speculating upon the events of the night.

"What could the boy mean by Heron himself coming to claim Daisy of me?" There was something in his tone I could not understand, and which struck me at the moment as strange and peculiar. Can it be possible that I am deceived, and that some artful plot has been constructed, to make me believe that Felix Heron is no more, while, in reality, he is in life?"

This was the first time that such an idea had really been expressed by Jonathan Wild; although the probability is that, in a vague, uncertain manner, it had found a home in his brain.

He stopped short.

The sound of his own voice, as he started the idea, sounded to him almost like a communication on the subject to him from another person.

It is strange how, when a floating supposition exists in the imagination upon any particular subject, it acquires force and likelihood by being spoken of.

And the relief was immense to Wild to think that, after all his superstitious fears, Felix Heron might be in life, and ready to vindicate his own safety and his own honour.

The sensations of Wild were quite tumultuous.

What should he do if such were the case?

What would happen in regard to the peerage of Whitcombe?

What would be his relations, then, with the man whom he had persecuted so long, but towards whose supposed widowed wife and orphan child he had certainly been a friend?

Wild leant his back against a post at the corner of a thoroughfare that led far away into the fields, and began to think over the matter.

One by one he recalled all the circumstances connected with the supposed death of Felix Heron

Wild had a retentive memory; and every little incident, bit by bit and piece by piece, rose up before his mind's eye, as though they had been enacted within the last four-and-twenty hours.

There was much in those incidents to make him doubt, now, the reality of the death of Heron.

But then his thoughts turned to Whitcombe House and to Edith.

There he was completely at fault.

What could she mean by the manner in which she had encouraged the intimacy of the Baron Von Peck?

And worse than that, what could she have

meant by actually marrying Captain Fantome, if Felix Heron were still in life?

These mental inquiries were hard to answer.

But Wild had not the highest opinion of womankind; although, certainly, if he had been asked what was his ideal of perfection in that matter, he would certainly have replied the Countess of Whitcombe.

But he was sorely puzzled.

Tightening the belt of his hanger, he strolled slowly down the narrow verdant thoroughfare, at the corner of which he had remained for so long in deep thought.

He muttered to himself, "No, no; Felix Heron must be dead. The conduct of Edith the Countess cannot be accounted for under any other supposition. I might as well believe that that wretched creature, Warringdale, after sinking like a plummet of lead deep into the bed of the Thames, should rise up again and confront me in his human shape."

Bang! went a pistol shot at this moment.

Wild's hat was sent flying from his head, as though struck off by an invisible hand.

The shot had been fired at him from amid a clump of trees growing to the right hand of the roadway.

The aim was by far too good to be pleasant, and Jonathan Wild, without losing his presence of mind, adopted at once a plan which on more than one occasion had not only saved his own life, but placed that of the person assailing him in his power.

Uttering a sudden cry, he sprang up into the air, after the manner of a person shot, and then he let himself fall prostrate on the earth, and lay apparently without sense or motion.

There were many persons who knew Jonathan Wild too well to take him at his word, even that he was killed.

Those persons would have fled from the spot, but it was not so with him who fired the shot that seemed to be so effective.

A rather tall masked figure, wrapped up in a dark brown cloak, emerged from the little wood.

"At last! at last!" cried this person—"at last I am avenged!"

Owing to the mask partially covering the mouth of the speaker, the tones of the voice, which otherwise might have been familiar to Wild, sounded strange.

He lay profoundly still, for he was determined, before he executed summary justice upon the assassin, to know who he was, and if he had any accomplices.

"This is excellent," added the man with the mask. "My life will no longer be the one of terror that it has been. I am creeping into favour at Court, and this villain Wild is the only man I had to dread."

———

CHAPTER CCLV.

JONATHAN WILD AND LORD WARRINGDALE MEET AGAIN.

As he spoke, the man with the mask leant right over what appeared to be the dead body of the great thief-taker, and by the faint night light given forth by the eastern sky regarded him attentively.

"Dead!" he said. "Ha, ha! dead!"

"Not quite!" said Wild.

Snap went the lock of one of his pistols.

There was a flash of powder in the pan, but that was all—the weapon had missed fire.

The man with the brown cloak uttered a shriek of dismay, and would have instantly fled, but his feet got entangled in that long garment, and he was near falling.

"Hold!" shouted Wild as he sat up, and presented his other pistol. "Not so fast, if you please. One may miss, but two are not likely to do so."

"Mercy! mercy!"

"Such mercy as you wished to show me."

Wild fired.

That pistol exploded in due course, but at the moment it did so the man with the cloak had completed his entanglement in its skirts, and fell to the ground.

The couple of bullets with which the pistol was loaded flew harmlessly over his head.

But the would-be assassin of Jonathan Wild had not nerve and self-possession enough to play the same part that Wild had done, and pretend to be shot.

He made frantic efforts to rise.

He struggled half-way to his feet, and with the instinct of self-preservation rather than from any impulse of real courage, he drew a sword he wore, and in a few seconds stood upon the defensive.

"Good!" cried Wild, as with a flash and a ringing sound he drew his hanger from its sheath. "Good! If that's the game, two can play at it, and I like nothing better."

With his left hand the mysterious stranger held on the mask to his face, and retreating step by step towards the wood, he feebly defended himself against the violent onslaught of Jonathan Wild.

Such a combat was not likely to last many minutes.

Wild advanced with fury, and struck down the slender sword opposed to him.

"Mercy! mercy!" cried the stranger. "By the memory of the past, Jonathan Wild, have mercy upon me now, and I can and will serve you well."

The mask dropped off.

The voice was unmuffled.

Wild started back and dropped his sword point as he exclaimed, "My Lord Warringdale! and still in life! Or does the earth breed such men?"

"No, no! shrieked Warringdale. "I am still in life. I am still your old associate—your old friend!"

"Friend?"

"Yes—yes. Whatever you may have thought, and whatever others may have told you, I was always your friend."

"Humph!"

"Oh, believe me; and what is more to the purpose now, I am in favour at Court, and can be of service to whom I please."

"Indeed!"

"It is true!—it is true! Try me—test me, Wild, and ask some favour to-morrow."

"You did not go exactly the way to work, my Lord Warringdale, to put me in a position to ask a favour of you—except one."

"One?"

"Yes—a decent funeral."

"Do not speak in that fashion," whined Lord Warringdale. "Remember one thing, Wild, and that is that you sought my life; so you see, if I sought yours, and failed, as you failed in your attempt upon me, we are only even."

"Bravo!" said Wild. "That is not so badly argued, my Lord Warringdale, considering all the circumstances."

"And so," added the trembling Warringdale, "let us be friends again. We can help each other. It is rare, Jonathan Wild, that two such men as us meet for a common purpose. Let bygones be bygones; and although neither of us can forget the fact that we have each attempted the life of the other, let us each remember that we have each failed; and if we make a compact never again to listen, even in imagination, to such a temptation, all may be well between us."

No. 81.—EDITH HERON.

"You say so."

"I mean what I say, Jonathan Wild. The time may come when you may want a friend at Court, and I tell you I have a means of befriending any one I may please, which cannot fail me."

"What means?"

"A guilty secret."

"Ah! say you so? Then I have indeed some hopes."

"A guilty and disgraceful secret?"

"Better and better still! If you had told me, my Lord Warringdale. that you relied upon the gratitude of any one at Court to do you a favour in the hour of need, I would have cracked your skull with my hanger, as you now crouch down before me; but since you tell me you have a guilty secret, you may be useful."

"I have—I have!"

"Live, then!"

Jonathan Wild sheathed his hanger, and turned his back carelessly upon Lord Warringdale, who scrambled to his feet, and spoke with more confidence than he had hitherto done.

"Is there anything you want me to do for you, Jonathan Wild?"

"Yes—tell me the guilty secret."

"I will. There is a society or association of noblemen of the highest rank, headed by the King himself, who employ inferior agents to abduct young ladies of beauty and attraction whom they have looked upon with eyes of admiration. Nothing stays their proceedings, and there is no amount of fraud, violence, or villany, which they will not have recourse to. Their funds are ample, and their impunity, in consequence, is complete."

"Funds ample?" said Jonathan Wild.

"I have said so!"

"Then you are in full feather, my Lord Warringdale?"

"I am. And if you want money——"

"I always want money—my expenses are rather large."

"Take this rouleau of gold, then," said Warringdale. "It is heartily at your service."

"Ah!" said Wild, drawing a long breath as he pocketed the gold. "This is indeed welcome, and looks like business."

"It is but an instalment of the services I would gladly do you, if you will work with me towards my ends, as I will with you towards yours; and now that I am creeping into favour in high quarters, by making myself useful, I still seem to see, suspended in the distance before me——"

'What?" asked Wild, sharply.

"The coronet of the Earls of Whitcombe."

"Indeed!"

"Yes. My hopes rise up afresh; and with your assistance, I think that I may fairly lay claim to something like an expectation of wearing the ermined robes of a peer."

"So—so!"

Wild rested his chin upon his hand and lapsed into deep thought.

It was astounding how completely he seemed to have given up all idea of personal danger from Lord Warringdale.

After a pause he spoke.

"Upon what do you found your claim?"

"The death of Felix Heron."

"But his child?"

"I mean to append one expression to that child's name, which shall stick to it through life."

"What expression?"

"Bastard!"

"Oh, oh! you are there, are you, my Lord Warringdale? I might have guessed as much, since, if report speaks truly, no man in all the world is better qualified to know sorely how that title sits upon the heart."

"My own origin will not be inquired into," said Warringdale hastily. "If I can prove, or seem to prove, that my half-brother Felix has left no legitimate heir, the King, through the instrumentality of the Marquis of Arlington, and my Lord Clackington, will issue a new patent, and that will cure all defects."

"Listen!" said Wild.

"What is it?"

"I think we are alone?"

"I am sure of it."

"Then what suppose Felix Heron were not dead?"

The start and cry of alarm that echoed this supposition on the part of Lord Warringdale mightily amused Wild, who laughed in his hideous fashion, as he added, "I only put it as a supposition. I do not say that he is alive, but I mean to say that I am not sure he is dead."

"Gracious heavens!"

"Hush! Speak of the other place as much as you like, but the less you and I, my Lord Warringdale, mention gracious heaven the better."

"But you alarm me!"

"That is likely enough. And, now, since we have made this kind of compact together, come with me to town, and we will talk the matter over."

"But tell me, as you value peace of mind and my rest, what it is that has put the fearful idea into your head of the continued existence of Felix Heron?"

"Why, look you here," said Wild, as he slid his arm familiarly beneath that of Warringdale's. "Look you here. I am one of those men who believe that the events of the world go round and round in a never-ending circle. I thought you dead, but here you turn up alive and prosperous. Why not Felix Heron the same?"

"Is that all?"

"Not quite. Come to Little Newgate to-morrow, and I will tell you more. Now, good night; I have business on hand.

*   *   *   *   *

It was just about that period, that after galloping through some of the longest streets of London, Daisy reached her own stables, at the back of Whitcombe House.

That back street was a narrow one, and the wall of the stable-yard was high.

Daisy might have tried to jump it if there had been space enough for her to take a good rush at it; but there was not, and she sagaciously forbore to make the attempt.

Ogle, who happened to be at the back part of the house, heard a strange thumping sound in the direction of the stables, and hurrying to the spot, he felt assured that some one was attempting to make himself heard by heavy blows on the gate.

There was a bell, which it seemed so much easier to ring than to make such a tumult, that Ogle paused in amazement, and felt a slight sensation of superstitious fear, as he listened to the strange sounds.

Bang! bang! bang! at regular intervals, came the blows on the stable-yard gate.

"What can it mean?" said Ogle; "and at this time of night, too."

Like most uneducated persons, Ogle was certainly inclined to think that anything he did not at once understand, must be, or at all events might be, supernatural.

That was a consideration, however, which was not sufficient, altogether, to prevent him from taking steps to ascertain who it was that on the other side of the stable-gate was creating so much confusion.

By the assistance of a short ladder, Ogle was very quickly able to look over the parapet of the wall.

A horse!

Yes, there was a horse there, who in the dim night-light looked black and shadowy.

A horse, who, standing close to the yard gate, was, at regular intervals, hammering at it with one of his hind feet.

The idea that this horse was Daisy never entered the imagination of Ogle, but as the idea of a spectre horse had likewise never found a home in his mind, he at once dismounted from the ladder, and opened the small wicket-gate in the frame-work of the larger one.

Daisy turned about immediately and trotted into the stable-yard.

Then Ogle knew her.

"Daisy," he exclaimed, "by all that's precious!"

But still the matter was one of great mystery, since the fact that Daisy had been loose at all, and outside her stables, was one that Ogle could not account for.

Tom Ripon had had such particular and special charge of Daisy, and had shown so much jealousy of any interference in that charge, that even Ogle had ceased to question him about her.

Tom, then, was the proper person now to speak to on the subject of Daisy's singular arrival home from an expedition outside the stable, apparently alone.

Tom's sleeping apartment was a small room opening from a long corridor that connected the stables with Whitcombe House.

A very brief examination of that room showed that it had not been slept in; and then the whole affair was as clear and patent to Ogle as if Tom had sat down and related it to him word for word.

"I understand it now," he said; "it's as plain as a pike-staff. Tom has been out on the road on his own account, and has got nabbed."

As Ogle thus spoke, he turned round twice, and took a survey of Tom's little sleeping apartment.

A picture hung upon the wall.

It was but the rough sketch with charcoal of Daisy, and had been drawn by one of the band in Epping Forest, whose early life was devoted to the arts.

Just peeping out cornerwise from between the frame and the wall of this picture was a slip of paper.

Ogle pulled it entirely clear of the frame, and by the stable lantern he brought with him he read upon it the following words:—

"Ogle, if there has been a row about my not coming home, nor Daisy either, I'm nabbed. Tell the Captain, so that he may look after her; but as for me, it's no matter. I suppose he'll think that I ought to be scragged for taking Daisy on to the road.

"This comes from
"Tom."

The whole affair was quite clear now, with the exception that Tom had not calculated upon the extraordinary circumstance of Daisy making her escape, and reaching her stables at Whitcombe House alone.

Ogle drew a long breath of relief.

"Things might be worse," he said. "I don't know what the Captain would have said if anything had happened to Daisy. But since she is all safe in the stable, and sound in wind and limb, he will easily forgive Tom; and as for scragging, there will be two words to that bargain."

CHAPTER CCLVI.

TOM PASSES A NIGHT IN LITTLE NEWGATE.

THE cell in Little Newgate which had been designated by Jonathan Wild as that in which Tom was to be imprisoned, was certainly one of the most wretched that the great thief-taker had constructed beneath his house, and beneath the pavement of Newgate Street.

What were his precise intentions with regard to Tom Ripon it is hard to say; but, as we have before remarked, Tom looked upon it as a good sign that he was not handed over to the law.

To all appearance, Wild had completely reinstated himself in the confidence of the authorities, and was carrying on quite his old mode of life at Little Newgate.

The establishment was about as close an imitation, on its small scale, of the great prison it adjoined as anything could well be.

There was a man upon the lock, as the technical phrase went; and a small wicket had been constructed in the street door, through which any persons demanding admittance could be questioned.

A little parlour on the ground floor had been, only within the preceding week, set apart as an office, in which sat a miserable-looking wretch, who played the part of clerk to Jonathan Wild.

He had been a pickpocket, but was lamed by being run over by a carriage at the door of the Opera one night, when he was diving under it to escape with a watch he had just dexterously picked from the pocket of a noble lord.

"What now?" cried the man on the lock at Jonathan Wild's house, as the rather strong party arrived with Tom Ripon.

"A prisoner!"

"All's right!—the more the merrier! Is he an old bird, or one of the young 'uns that's easy nabbed with a little bit of chaff?"

Tom was hustled into the passage, and a lantern was held up slightly above his head, so that its rays should fall full upon his face.

"I don't know him," said the man on the lock.

"But Mr. Wild does," said one of the janissaries.

"Yes," said Tom, "we're slightly acquainted; and it's always odds whether I take Johnny or Johnny takes me. It's his luck this time."

The men looked at each other, and laughed.

"Well, come on," said two men, who took Tom specially under their guardianship,—"come on! Jonathan Wild will get here before we have bestowed our prisoner, and then there will be the deuce to pay."

"All right! Now, young fellow."

With these words, Tom was removed from the passage, and down a flight of stone steps, which were wholly unlighted, and which looked dark and cavernous in their gloomy depths.

Tom stopped abruptly.

"Well, what now?" asked one of the men.

"Hold hard!" said Tom. "Surely you don't mean to put a fellow in a cell down in that gloomy region?"

"Those are our orders, young 'un," replied one of the men, at the same time that Tom fancied he detected a look of compassion upon his hard-featured face.

Tom was young and sanguine, and hoped that the man might perhaps befriend him in some way, so he merely said, "Well, what must be, must be, I suppose; but you give a fellow a look in occasionally, just to pass the time? When will it be supper time, by the by?"

"There will be no supper for you, I can tell you," growled the other man, "if you keep us here much longer. Get down with you, or I'll save you the trouble of walking."

Tom thought it best to make the descent without further parley, and after going down a long flight of stairs, one of the men produced a match from his pocket, and lighted a small end of candle in a lantern, which he carried in his hand.

While this man, who was addressed as Adams by his companion, was thus occupied, the other man, upon whose face Tom fancied he had detected something less ferocious, produced from his belt a massive bunch of keys.

Selecting one of these keys, he thrust it into the lock, and a heavy door grated on its hinges.

"There's your berth, youngster," said he; "it's nice and dark, so that you can sleep well until Mr. Wild wants you."

Tom stopped on the threshold.

He had endeavoured to take a survey of what was to be his prison; but so dark was it, and so faint were the rays of light emitted from the lantern, that Tom could come to no conclusion as to the size or appearance of his cell.

"Look you here," he said; "I've come here quietly, and have given you no trouble; what will prevent you giving me a light just till I get used to my new apartment?"

The man Adams shook his head surlily.

"You won't have a light if I know it; so you'd better go in, and make your life happy without one."

"Well, then," said Tom, "just take off the darbies, then. I can't do any harm in the dark, you know."

The two men exchanged glances.

"No, no!" said the man Adams; "it's Jonathan Wild's orders that the prisoner should wear the bracelets; and we can't go against orders, eh, Goff?"

This question was addressed to Tom's other gaoler.

"No, I don't see that we can take the darbies off; but I think we might as well just leave the boy this bit of candle. It will enable him to see the black beetles and toads, and such like, as are to be his companions."

"Well, for the matter of that, I don't want to be hard on a fellow; it won't last long, and Jonathan Wild will not visit the prisoner till long after it has burnt out. So good night to you, and pleasant dreams."

With these words the two men turned to leave the cell; but Tom saw Goff make a sign for him to look in a corner of the cell; and just as he was leaving it, he threw a small packet into the corner.

Then the door was banged shut, and Tom was alone with his own thoughts.

The first thing he did was to pick up the little packet thrown into the corner by the man Goff; and when he opened the paper, he found, to his great joy, that it contained six or eight of the thieves' matches.

"Thanks, friend," exclaimed Tom, as he thrust them into his pocket; " as soon as I have taken a good look at my prison, I'll put out the candle to save it, now that I have the means of lighting it again."

Tom held up the lantern above his head, and turned twice round.

"Humph!" said he; "not very unlike the little wine-cellars at Whitcombe House, barring the wine. What have we here? Ah! an old screw; perhaps we shall want you."

Tom looked about him again.

"Ah! I see a long nail in the wall! Well, that may be handy if a fellow wants to hang himself; and I don't seem to mind much whether I get out or not; for the Captain will never forgive me— he can't! Well, well, it can't be helped now!"

Tom paused and opened the slide of the lantern.

"I must not burn this any longer, that's certain. I must think what I had better do."

Puff!

Tom blew out the candle, and set the lantern down on the ground of the cell.

"Heigho! I wonder where Daisy is? If she got home to Whitcombe House all right? And whether Ogle has found my directions? He'll make the best of it to the Captain, I know that: but he'll not forgive me, I'm afraid; and then I'd much rather Jonathan Wild hung me at once."

It will be seen that our friend Tom had lost somewhat of his usual buoyancy of spirits and that his present difficulties were augmented by the reflection that he had in some measure abused the confidence of his much-loved master.

Tom was young, and fatigue began to tell upon him, so he stretched himself on some straw, and soon he was, in his dreams at least, in Daisy's stable, caressing and being caressed by her.

For two short hours Tom was happy.

* * * * * *

Tom had slept for two hours, and awoke refreshed by the sleep he had had.

He stretched out his hand, and grasped the lantern.

"Ah!" said he; "I was afraid that was a dream too, and that I really had no means of looking about me. Now for a light!"

Tom had no difficulty in obtaining a light, thanks to the man Goff, who had given him the matches, and soon he was feeling in his pocket for the long nail he had picked up from the floor of his cell.

"Here we are now," said Tom, "ready for work. We'll see if I can make any impression on the lock."

Tom set to work with his long nail, but he found it would be a work of time before he could hope to make good his escape by the door— and window there was none.

It will be recollected that Tom had still the handcuffs on when his two gaolers left him, but

JONATHAN WILD LOOKS AFTER THE SAFETY OF HIS PRISONER,
"TOM RIPON," IN LITTLE NEWGATE.

Presented Gratis with No. 81, of the New Edition of EDITH HEADER the Sequel to Edith the Captive; or, the Robbers of Epping Forest.

by the clever contrivance we have before alluded to, he was enabled to slip his hand out quite easily, as soon as he was sure that no eyes were upon his movements.

So Tom worked for more than an hour, when he was startled from his occupation by the rough, growling tones of a voice he knew too well.

They were those of Jonathan Wild.

To fly to the lantern and extinguish the light, and to replace the handcuffs, was the work of a few seconds. Scarcely had he accomplished these two feats when the key was thrust into the door, and his arch foe appeared on the threshold.

We have already mentioned during the course of this history that Jonathan Wild was not handsome, and the cast in his eye, and the knack of holding his head on one side which he had when he wished to impress any one with a sense of his power, was anything but consoling to Tom on this occasion.

"Ha, ha!" laughed Wild as soon as he entered the cell, holding above his head a hand lantern. "So the bird is quite safe. How are you, eh?"

As Wild said this, he gave Tom a kick with his heavy boot, which Tom, however, returned with interest.

"Quite well, Johnny," said Tom. "I hope you're the same, eh?"

As Tom spoke, he dealt Wild a blow with both his hands, which sent him reeling to the other side of the cell.

Wild was furious.

"Wretch!—villain! You shall pay for this, as sure as my name is Jonathan Wild! You shall hang—you shall hang!"

"Thank you, Johnny; that all depends on circumstances. I fancy I shall have the pleasure of seeing you dancing upon nothing at Tyburn! Eh, Johnny? What do you say to that, Johnny?"

Jonathan Wild winced, for he had a wholesome dread of the gallows; and the prophecy that he would one day be hanged at Tyburn was ever present to his imagination.

"Hold, Tom Ripon!" he exclaimed. "I came here to offer you terms—to offer you your freedom—upon conditions."

"What conditions?" asked Tom.

"That you will swear to me, by all that you hold most sacred, that what you said about Captain Felix Heron was merely intended to frighten me—not that there was any truth in the statement."

"In what statement?" asked Tom, coolly and calmly—for he now began to hope that he might be able to work upon Jonathan Wild's superstitious fears,—"in what statement, Jonathan Wild?"

"In the statement that Captain Felix Heron might perhaps come, and claim Daisy of me himself."

"Oh, I meant his ghost," said Tom. "I've seen it twice lately; and, what's more, I think he has some means of knowing everything that happens. So, you see, Johnny, if anything did happen to Daisy, or to anybody the Captain had taken a fancy to, there's no saying what might be the consequence."

Wild was pale as death.

He nevertheless made an effort to shake off the superstitious fears with which Tom impressed him.

He abruptly changed the subject.

"You know my mind," he said. "If you consent to my terms, you are free; and I will promise you three uninterrupted years upon the road."

"And divide all with you?" said Tom.

"Yes; you cannot do better. In fact, it is your only resource."

"I doubt that," said Tom; "and, at all events, Jonathan, I must take time to consider."

"As long as you please; only remember that that time comes out of the three years; and it is far better to pass it on horseback, in the shady roads, and on the open heaths in the neighbourhood of London, than in this cell."

Tom's agreement with Wild on that point was perfect; but still he had not the slightest idea of making the arrangement proposed by the great thief-taker.

"I leave you now," added Wild,—"I leave you now to your own meditations. You are scarcely yet a man, and yet not so much of a boy but that you are able to come to some conclusion upon what I propose to you."

Tom nodded.

Wild made an abrupt gesture of farewell, and turned to leave the cell; but he paused a moment on the threshold, and returning two steps, he spoke again.

"I will add likewise to my proposition, that I will leave your mother, Mrs. Ripon, and that bundle of hypocrisy, Mortification, free leave during the whole of that time to keep a fence; so, you see, it will be a nice little family arrangement for you."

"And I to be hanged at the end of it!" said Tom.

Wild shrugged his shoulders and left the cell.

Tom then quietly again slipped his wrists out of the handcuffs, and sat down to think upon what he had better do next.

CHAPTER CCLVII.

FELIX HERON DETERMINES TO GO IN SEARCH OF TOM RIPON.

WE return to Whitcombe House.

Felix Heron was rapidly made aware of the extraordinary circumstances attending the return of Daisy, and the safe and sound condition of his favourite four-footed friend and companion of the road.

But it was with looks of concern that Ogle made the communication.

Ogle, despite all his roughness and peculiarities at times, had many fine and noble traits in his character.

His friendships and affections were particularly sincere; and next to Felix Heron, there was no person, probably, in all the world that Ogle had a tithe of the regard for which he felt for Tom Ripon.

It was at a very early hour of the morning indeed, therefore, that Ogle sought Felix Heron with a face full of care and anxiety.

And Heron faithfully enough reflected those looks when he became fully aware of the unusual circumstances attending the return of Daisy.

"And Tom Ripon, you say, has disappeared, Ogle?"

"Yes, Captain; but if you read this, it won't be difficult to come to some understanding about the case."

Heron perused in silence the mysterious memorandum which Tom had left behind the picture in his sleeping apartment.

It was only for a moment, then, that a slight flush of indignation and anger came from the eyes of Heron, for he pictured to himself all the danger that Daisy must have ran.

He paced the long dining-room of Whitcombe House in silence for several seconds, and then, turning abruptly to Ogle, he said, "This is really too bad!"

"It's worse than that, Captain."

"Tom knows so well that the value I set upon Daisy is such, that more than once I have chanced my life for her preservation, and yet he has played with her safety in this reckless fashion."

"It is too bad, Captain: you can't say too much about it; and I have not a single word to utter in his favour."

"Who can? Who can?" cried Heron.

"Nobody in all the world, Captain; and I've not the slightest doubt but that he's either shot or nabbed."

"You think so?"

"Yes, Captain: and it serves him right, and all the better for him if he is shot, for that's better any day than a dance upon nothing at Tyburn Tree."

"Ogle!"

"Yes, Captain."

"Much as I have cause to be indignant at Tom Ripon's conduct, I am not disposed to speak of him so lightly or so severely as you do."

This was precisely the frame of mind to which Ogle wished to bring Felix Heron, and it is evident that he managed the matter with considerable judgment.

If Ogle had been so indiscreet as in any way to defend Tom Ripon, there can be little doubt but that the anger of Felix Heron would have been strongly excited against him.

But hearing Ogle speak as he did, he, Heron, was, to a certain extent, disarmed of his resentment, and began to feel a profound pity for Tom, based upon a recollection of his former services, and the great temptation it must have been for him to go upon the road accompanied by Daisy.

"It is I who have been to blame, Ogle," he said; "for I abandoned Daisy too much to Tom's care; and I ought scarcely to have expected that a boy, such as he is, would resist the temptation to endeavour to tread in my footsteps."

"That's just it, Captain."

Ogle still called Felix Heron Captain, although if any one else had dared to presume to doubt, even by implication, that he, Heron, was the Earl of Whitcombe, no one would have been so malignant as Ogle.

"There is but one thing to do," added Heron; "he must be saved. He may be killed, or lying dangerously hurt on the road; or he may have been overpowered by numbers and arrested. In either case, however, he shall not be abandoned."

"I don't think, Captain, any one runs a great risk of abandonment who has anything to do with you."

Heron reflected for a few seconds—not upon what he would do, but upon how he would do it—and then turning to Ogle, he said, "Saddle Daisy at once for me; I will but speak to Edith, to explain to her the cause of my sudden absence, and then I will be off at once to seek for Tom."

"Shall I accompany you, Captain?"

"No, Ogle. Always remember that when I am not at Whitcombe House you must be there. We should never leave it together; and you are well aware that as regards its protection, I look upon you in my absence as a second self."

In ten minutes, Felix Heron, in his full disguise as Captain Fantome, of the royal navy, issued out at the narrow street at the back of Whitcombe House, mounted upon Daisy, and prepared to seek for Tom Ripon.

And now we shall see by the first proceedings of Heron that second thoughts are not always best, despite what any proverb may say to the contrary.

Heron's first idea was unquestionably to go to the fence in Wardour Street, and inquire of Mrs. Ripon and Mortification if they had seen anything of Tom, or knew what had become of him.

And if he had carried out this determination, he would, of course, have been quickly put in possession of full particulars in regard to the arrest of Tom by Jonathan Wild.

But he did give a second consideration to that subject; and from several circumstances, he was led irresistibly to the conclusion that it was in the country Tom had met with some mishap.

One of those reasons was, that Ogle had informed him Daisy was plentifully splashed with gravel and sand.

Now those materials were scarcely to be found in Wardour Street.

Heron accordingly abandoned the idea, which, if carried out, would have saved him much trouble; and, on the contrary, determined to seek for Tom on the outskirts of the metropolis.

The only good roads out of London were, at that time, so blocked up by turnpikes, that there was little difficulty in tracing any one in any particular direction.

The pike-man was a sort of general newsmonger.

He was generally able to tell with tolerable accuracy who had passed through his gate within four-and-twenty hours.

This was, then, one of the means by which Heron thought he should be able to trace the footsteps of Tom Ripon and Daisy.

And as chance would have it, he took the Western Road as the most likely one for Tom's operations.

He well knew that the man at Tyburn Gate had a sort of speciality for the recollection of all persons passing through that barrier; and he was likewise well aware that any one who bore the appearance of a knight of the road would be looked at with more interest than usual by that man, inasmuch as it was pretty notorious among the gentlemen who got a living by crying "Stand and deliver!" that he was always open to the inducement of a stray guinea to open his gate quickly for them, and slowly for their pursuers.

Tyburn Gate has been long since swept away and even while we write, an enactment is becoming the law of the land which will clear almost all the roads leading from the metropolis of those ancient barbarisms (turnpikes), with which are associated so many of the strange tales connected with the highwaymen of the seventeenth and eighteenth centuries.

It was still early morning when, at a sharp trot, Felix reached Tyburn Gate.

The pikeman ran out with his night-cap on his head.

Heron flung him a silver piece of money; and, as the gate was slowly opened, he could not but perceive that the man looked narrowly at Daisy.

"Have you seen this horse before?" asked Heron.

"I should rather think I have, sir."

"Indeed! Upon what occasion?"

"Well, sir, I don't know if you are aware of it; but that's the famous mare Daisy, that was once the property of Captain Felix Heron, as he used to be called on the road."

"Indeed!"

"Yes, sir; and you might hunt the world through before you found a livelier piece of horse-flesh, or a better roadster."

"And when did you last see this creature, of whom you speak in such high terms?"

"Well, sir, I can hardly say; for sometimes I come out with my eyes half-shut, to open the pike."

"Perhaps this will open them," said Felix Heron, as he held out a guinea.

The man hesitated.

"I don't know you, sir; but I keep a pike, you see, and have no call to interfere with gentlemen of the law."

"Pooh, pooh! I am not a gentleman of the law; and all I want you to tell me is, if, within this last four-and-twenty hours, this famous mare of the late Captain Heron's has passed through Tyburn Gate?"

"There's no great harm in saying yes to that," replied the pike-keeper.

This seemed to Heron at the moment all the information he wanted; but after riding on a few paces, he turned again, and called out, "Tell me when you saw her pass?"

"After dark last evening, sir."

"And not since?"

"Not till now."

The fact is, that the turnpike-keeper was not in a condition to inform Captain Heron of the return of Tom and Daisy through the gate, since it was just at that time when his mate and deputy had charge of the pike.

Heron then rode into the country, with a full conviction on his mind that whatever had happened to Tom had happened on that road, and that he would have but little difficulty in discovering the particulars.

It was not at large houses or at roadside inns that Heron resolved to make his inquiries, but at the lowly cottages of the poor, whose sympa-

thies would be more likely to go with the bold dashing young highwayman than with his legal pursuers.

But Heron got no intelligence.

He rode deep into the country, some distance past Ealing, and still had heard nothing of Tom Ripon.

Even at the present day, that distance from London carries any one amid the shadowy twilight of many an umbrageous spot, where the noise and turmoil of the city is completely extinguished, and nothing but rural sights and sounds meet the senses.

Heron drew rein close to the entrance of a shadowy lane which ran across the road, presenting, both to the right and to the left, dim thoroughfares, kept in perpetual gloom by the overreaching boughs of tall trees, and the roadway of which was soft and springy with the accumulated fallen leaves of centuries.

The spot was one of great beauty, and, amenable as Felix Heron always was to the charms of nature under all aspects, it was quite a delight to him, after being pent up for so long in St. James's Street, to breathe the fresh open air of the country, and hear the birds twittering upon the boughs overhead.

He thought of his own ancient sylvan home in Epping Forest.

A sigh of regret came from his heart that he had ever deserted it.

But this romantic mood of Heron's was soon destined to be interrupted.

Up the lane that lay to his right hand there came a horseman.

Heron heard the dull beat of the horse's feet upon the soft turf and leaves before he could see either horse or rider, for the lane took a sudden turn near the point at which it crossed the high-road.

There was nothing very special or particular about the appearance of either man or horse, as the rider came into sight.

He seemed to be what the world would call a gentleman, although there was a certain style about his costume which would have induced Heron to be doubtful about giving him that title.

The stranger fixed his regards intently upon Heron, and riding close up to him, he said, in a half-confidential tone of mystery, "You're a hawk!"

Heron certainly had no idea what could be meant by this half-statement, half inquiry, and for the moment he thought it might come from some one who recognised him, even through his disguise, and who had known him during his career at Epping Forest.

He scanned the face and figure of the stranger with great attention.

Heron was convinced they had never met before.

"It may not be polite, sir, to contradict you; but why am I a hawk?"

"That's right."

"What is right, sir?"

"Oh, you needn't keep it up any longer. I have given you the word, and you have given me the answer—surely that's enough. And now I will give you the rejoinder Hawks look for doves. Will that do?"

"It will do for me, sir, if it does for you."

"Then that's all right. Let's come to the Abbey."

Heron looked with unfeigned surprise at this mysterious man, but there was nothing in his appearance to denote insanity; and as he walked his horse over the roadway and down the opposite branch of the lane, he seemed so fully convinced that Heron would follow him, and that he perfectly understood why he was to do so, that the latter almost involuntarily permitted Daisy to take the same route.

Scarcely had they got half a dozen paces, however, down the lane, when along the highway came another mounted man at speed.

"Who is that?" cried Heron's mysterious companion.

"Some chance passenger, I fancy."

"So shall I if he ride on; but if he should pull up at the corner here, he is an enemy, and dangerous to us."

The horseman did pull up at the corner of the lane, occupying very much the same spot of ground where Heron had paused with Daisy only a few minutes before.

"Look at him well," said Heron's new companion,—"look at him well! Do you know him?"

"Not in the least."

"Then I am suspicious. He may be here to thwart us. I wonder if a bullet will scare him off?"

"Would you shoot the man?"

"No, no! I only want to give him a fright. You had better wait here for me, and I will do it, and then we can go to the Abbey together. The marriage is to come off in half an hour, and by that time the chapel will be as dark as a coalpit, and the Lady Gertrude will fall into the snare."

As he spoke, this man trotted out to the roadway again, and discharging a pistol, the bullet of which whistled over the head of the horseman who had just trotted up and paused at the entrance of the lane, he called out in a threatening voice, "Take warning, sir, and ride on which way you will. You are not wanted here."

The stranger horseman did take warning.

He uttered a shout of alarm; and bending low upon the saddle to escape any other shot that might be levelled at him, he turned his horse's head towards London, and set off at a gallop.

CHAPTER CCLVIII.

FELIX HERON RECEIVES THE CONFIDENCE OF HIS MYSTERIOUS COMPANION.

THIS mysterious man, who had, so to speak, picked up Heron at the corner of the lane, had certainly, in a very few words, made to him some bewildering statements.

It was in vain that Heron strove to comprehend or arrange in his own mind what could be the meaning of the marriage coming off in half an hour, and some chapel being as dark as a coal-pit, while a Lady Gertrude was to fall into some snare.

All this was perfectly inexplicable to him; but having got so far, he thought that at least he would waste an hour, even in his search after Tom Ripon, to get at the heart of the mystery.

But Heron was not left for long to his own reflections.

The man who had fired the pistol at an apparently unoffending stranger trotted back to him.

"He's off," he said. "I don't know who he was. His stopping there might be accidental, or it might be part of a design to interfere with us; at all events, it was better to scare him away."

Heron was now determined to humour this man, in order cautiously to discover, bit by bit, what he was about.

"Yes," he said; "I think you have acted judiciously, especially as you have done him no real harm."

"Not the least; but I dare say you've heard what a dead shot I am."

"I think I have."

"But it's always better to make people take themselves off than have the trouble of disposing of a dead body; that is the greatest nuisance in life. But what is your opinion of our full success —for I suppose Sir Marmaduke has been quite confidential, and you know all about it?"

Heron was as much in the dark as ever, but he made a very judicious reply.

"Oh, yes," he said; "and my opinion always is that if you expect any good service from a man, you ought not to make half-confidences."

"Exactly so."

"I have seen the evil of that so often," added Heron, "that, feeling confident in my own mind Sir Marmaduke has not deceived me in any particular, I am rather curious to know if he has been equally confidential and sincere with you."

"Confound him!" cried the man. "If he has not, I shall not be best pleased. I have stood by him in many a scrape, and, of all men, he ought to be confidential with me."

"And yet," added Heron, "men like Sir Marmaduke are very apt to think that they may tell just as much or little as they like, and get all the service they want."

"By Jove, that's true!"

"Well, then," said Heron, "what has he told you exactly? Let me know, and then we will compare it with what he has told me."

"Yes, that's the way."

"Let me have it, then, just as if you were relating a story."

"I will; and you pull me up if there's anything in it you know to be wrong, or that you can add in any way."

"I will—I will!"

"Well, then, Sir Marmaduke Shuldham, though a man of ancient family, and indeed one of the oldest baronets of the kingdom, is not worth a rush. He has got through the whole of his patrimony, and is put to his shifts to keep up anything like an appearance."

"That's right," said Heron.

"Well, all the world knows that; but in the midst of it all he contrived to get on the weak side of Lord Dalesworth, who left him guardian to his only daughter, the Lady Gertrude."

"Exactly," said Heron.

"Her property is immense, and Sir Marmaduke has had a pretty good pull out of it; but as she attains her majority in about another week, and

as she has not the very highest opinion of her guardian, he has good reason to suppose that she will slip through his fingers, and at the same time exact from him a rather rigorous account of the past."

"Of course she will," said Heron.

"Well, then, under these circumstances, when an ordinary man would have despaired, and perhaps fled—for I rather suspect he has dipped deeply into his ward's fortune—Sir Marmaduke, on the contrary, formed the audacious design of getting the remainder of it by marrying her."

"You are right so far," said Heron.

"But there was one little difficulty."

Heron shook his head and smiled, as if he knew perfectly well what the little difficulty was.

"She hated the sight of him."

"Exactly so ; and I don't wonder at it."

"Well, I must confess he's not the most lively-looking person in the world. A worn-out, used-

No. 82—EDITH HERON.

up *debauchee* and *roue*, with a damaged charac-ter, does not present himself in the most lively colours to the imagination of a young girl."

"Good!" said Heron.

"But Sir Marmaduke is a man born to sur-mount difficulties, and this one did not appal him. He resolved to trade upon his name."

The man paused at this point of his narration, and looked in the face of Heron and laughed.

Heron laughed likewise.

"Am I right so far?" said the stranger.

"Quite," said Heron ; although what he meant by Sir Marmaduke trading upon his name, after he had declared it was so damaged an one, he had not the least idea.

It was strange to see these two persons ex-changing looks of intelligence upon a subject which, however well one of them might be in-formed of, was to the other still shrouded in the most impenetrable mystery.

"I think you had better go on," said Heron; "for he may still have deceived you in something, although up to this point we are perfectly agreed."

"Well, the young lady had a handsome young cousin, who went to India, and who, by a coincidence most fortunate for our patron, since upon that hangs his whole plot, was christened Marmaduke."

"Right!" said Heron.

He thought he began to see a little daylight through the obscurity of the narration.

"Gertrude, and her handsome young cousin, Marmaduke, were warmly attached to each other; but the old lord would not listen to any suggestion of their union, and the young man went to India, as a cadet in the Company's service, and to fight Tippoo Saib, amid the swamps and jungles!"

"I wonder what has become of him?"

"Oh, he is all right! Didn't Sir Marmaduke tell you he was on his road back?"

"If he did, I forgot it."

"Well, look here, now! In rummaging over, during her absence one day, a writing-case belonging to his fair ward, Sir Marmaduke found some letters that had passed between this young man and her. They were of no real consequence to him, except in one particular."

The man laughed as he uttered these words, and looked again intelligently in the face of Heron.

"You guess that particular?"

Heron nodded.

"It enabled Sir Marmaduke to get at the exact handwriting and style of composition of the young cousin, so that he might imitate both at his pleasure."

"Of course," said Heron.

"This, then, was the plan. He wrote a capital letter, and got it put into an Indian envelope, by some means, and addressed to Gertrude. In fact, I helped him to write it, as, perhaps, you know; and I have a copy of it about me."

"So have I," said Heron.

This was an audacious plunge, but it had its effect.

"Well," said the man, "I'll read you mine, and then you can compare it with yours."

As he spoke, he took a pocket-book from his breast, and, extracting a sheet of letter-paper from it, he halted his horse beneath the shade of a magnificent oak tree, and read to Heron, as follows, the forged letter which Sir Marmaduke had sent to Gertrude, in the name of her handsome young cousin from India :—

"DEAREST GERTRUDE,—

"I write to you half in despair, and half in hope. Intelligence has reached me that you are now your own mistress, and may bestow your hand where you will.

"Alas, it is not destined to rest in that of your devoted Marmaduke!

"I cannot—dare not aspire to the proud position of calling myself your husband.

"In a skirmish with the troops of Tippoo, I have received two sabre cuts upon the face, which have disfigured me so fearfully that, for many weeks, I made a determination to retire from the world, and in some hermitage, or gloomy retreat, permit no man to look upon my face.

"But still, at times, the idea has clung to me that real true love disregards obstacles, even of this character; and, making a confidant of a brother officer, he has urged me to make a proposition to you, which, if you accept, might restore me to happiness and to the world; but which, I think, you are quite justified in refusing.

"Will you consent to marry me without looking at me, until after the ceremony is over?

"I understand that you reside in an old manorial house, in the neighbourhood of London, called the Abbey, attached to which is a properly consecrated chapel.

"This, then, is the proposition, beloved Gertrude.

"If I arrive in England on the fourteenth of September, and reach the Abbey at twelve o'clock, will you have that consecrated chapel so darkened that it will be impossible for us to do more than see each other dimly? I will bring a proper license, and a priest, with me; and you will make yourself mine, if your love really survives this declaration of the misfortune that has occured to me.

"Should it do so, let me see hoisted, on some tower or turret of that manorial residence you occupy, a white flag.

"If otherwise, and I see no such flag, I shall retrace my weary steps to London; and, re-embarking for India, seek whatever fate may be in store for me.

"This is from your once-loved
                              "MARMADUKE."

"Is that like yours?" said the stranger, as he finished reading this epistle.

"Word for word!" said Heron.

"Then I need not trouble you to show it to me. Come on; and we shall see the Abbey in a few seconds."

"It is a good plot," said Heron. "Sir Marmaduke, in the darkness of the chapel, will assume the character of the young officer from London, and wed his beautiful ward, the Lady Gertrude?"

"Exactly!"

"But the imposture must be discovered?"

"Oh, yes! that's what Sir Marmaduke says; but the difficulty Gertrude will have dropped into will be so great, that she will be only too glad to extricate herself with the loss of half her fortune."

"Or the whole of it!"

"Well, I daresay she will give the whole of it, rather than continue the wife of such a man as Sir Marmaduke Shuldham!"

The two horses had proceeded about a hundred paces from the old oak tree, and then an opening in the mass of vegetation, which was like some fair and beautiful triumphal arch, afforded suddenly a full view of the Abbey.

Felix Heron thought he had never looked upon a more lovely spot.

An ancient manorial residence, built of that warm red brick, which maintains its beauty and freshness amid all changes of time and weather, stood at the further extremity of a lawn of vast extent and great beauty.

The grass was so exquisitely kept, and so resplendent in colour, that, with but little delusion of the senses, it might be supposed some vast expanse of bright green velvet covered the whole of this approach to the house.

It was one of those charmingly irregular mansions, which might engage the explorer weeks and months in discovering the whole interior.

Slanting roofs, turrets, ancient gable-end buttresses, and bay windows abounded in all directions.

There can be no doubt that, for many centuries, that mansion, complete in some perfect style of architecture, had been added to from age to age, and according to the fashion and spirit of each of those ages, until it became the vast, irregular, and somewhat incongruous mass it presented.

There was one turret in particular, which rose high above all the rest, having a kind of lantern or look-out of its summit, that was not unlike a modern lighthouse.

And throughout the greater part of the building there was an ancestral air.

This no doubt had given it its name of the Abbey.

And since the first portion of the mansion dated from a very early period, it is possible enough that it may have been originally erected for religious purposes.

There were deer upon the lawn.

A stately peacock sunned itself upon a balustrade, which ran the whole length of one side of the house, forming a charming terrace walk.

A rookery was established in the summits of a grove of lofty trees.

Flights of pigeons wheeled and circled round the turret tops and high-pointed roofs of the mansion.

Well might Felix Heron pause, and look with unfeigned delight upon this truly beautiful country home, so serene in its aspect, and so apparently surrounded with everything that could calm the senses and delight the imagination.

The expression of satisfaction in the eyes of Heron somewhat surprised his companion, who was a much more matter-of-fact and worldly personage than the gallant Earl of Whitcombe.

"Why, you seem quite taken with the old house!" he said.

"I am!—I am!"

"Well, these things are matters of taste."

"It is really beautiful."

"Perhaps so—but rather slow. Give me Pall Mall, and that after dark, too, when the gaming-houses are open, and there's something like life going on."

"But this beautiful lawn?"

"It's not to be compared to the green cloth on a roulette table!"

"And these antlered deer?"

"A haunch of one of them, well cooked, would be nice in the season."

"That peacock with its stately plumage?"

"Now, my dear fellow, did you ever want to sleep in the morning, and be perversely prevented by a peacock? The cry of that abominable bird is, next thing to the bray of a donkey, the most wretched sound in nature!"

"I see," said Heron, "that you have no eyes for the romantic and the beautiful. And I dare say you care nothing for the rookery, or for those flights of pigeons spreading themselves out into various forms, with such grace and beauty?"

"Pigeon pie is good; and some people say that young rooks make a good pasty. But behold all those well; and unless an earthquake takes place and swallows up the Abbey, Sir Marmaduke will be successful, and in less than half an hour he will be the husband of his young ward!"

As he spoke, this man pointed to the tall turret we have already indicated.

From one of its narrow side windows there fluttered a white flag.

That was the signal.

The signal mentioned in the forged letter with which Gertrude was to assure her cousin, the young officer, that her faith was unchanged, and that she loved him still.

Heron's companion laughed.

"That's the way with women," he said; "anything that's romantic is sure to seize upon their imaginations."

"It is something more than romance!" replied Heron.

"Hilloa! One would almost think, from your words and looks, that you were not exactly the sort of person Sir Marmaduke would have chosen to assist in a little affair of this kind!"

"I am here," said Heron, "and that ought to be a sufficient answer to your remark!"

"So it is—so it is! I was only jesting! Follow me; I know the old place well."

"But what are we required for? If this is to be a matter of fraud, what are we to do?"

"In the first place, we are to be witnesses to the marriage; and in the second, in case Lady Gertrude should decline to follow her husband, Sir Marmaduke, into the travelling carriage he has in waiting, we are to overawe the few servants in the mansion."

"I comprehend; and you may be assured I will do my work!"

"That's all right! And now come this way—for the sooner we find ourselves in the darkened chapel, the better."

There was a bridle path which wound round the lawn, and the entrance to it was only secured by a gate, which Heron's companion opened with ease, by stooping from his horse without dismounting.

CHAPTER CCLIX.

SIR MARMADUKE SHULDHAM'S MYRMIDON MEETS WITH AN UNEXPECTED DEFEAT.

THE plot thickened about the Lady Gertrude.

It seemed that she was surrounded by enemies; and but for the accidental presence of Felix Heron, the fearful plot in the meshes of which she was enveloped must surely have succeeded.

The difficulty she would have experienced in annulling her marriage with Sir Marmaduke Shuldham would have been immense.

There can be no doubt that if that marriage had taken place, it would only have been at the sacrifice of at least half her fortune that the Lady Gertrude would have escaped its terrors and entanglements.

But it was not to be.

Providence had raised up for her a protector in the person of Felix Heron.

How, and in what precise way, he was to save her, Heron as yet hardly knew; but he determined that the marriage should not take place, let the force opposed to him be what it might, unless the Lady Gertrude really knew who was the bridegroom.

He had good reason to suppose that the man who was with him and Sir Marmaduke Shuldham were the only two persons on the estate with power and inclination to oppose him.

Heron was used to fight his own way against greater odds than they could present to him; and from the language used by his chance companion, he was inclined to think that the servants of the house would gladly assist any movement in Lady Gertrude's favour.

"Who is the clergyman?" asked Heron.

"Oh, a friend of Sir Marmaduke's!"

"That, then, accounts for him consenting to perform a marriage in the dark?"

"Exactly so!"

"But if the servants should fancy anything was amiss?"

"They could do but little. There will be you and I, and Sir Marmaduke himself, and his valet, making up together, I should say, a force quite sufficient to overawe the whole household, which principally consists of women servants."

Both Heron and the man who was with him were at this moment brought to a standstill by a voice calling from the open roadway on the other side of the gate leading to the lawn.

"Sirs!—sirs!"

"Who the plague is that?"

Heron turned upon this exclamation of his companion, and saw, leaning over the gate, a dust-covered, wayworn-looking young man.

His face was bronzed, apparently by the sun of a warmer climate than England.

Those bright rays appeared to have lent a tinge to such portions of his luxuriant hair as escaped from beneath the travelling cap he wore.

He was evidently only a pedestrian, and he oked a poor one, for he carried over his shoulder a small bundle suspended from a stick.

And as this stranger leaned upon the gate he seemed faint and weary.

The voice, indeed, in which he called out 'Sirs!' as though he wished to ask a question of Heron and his companion, was indicative of great bodily fatigue and exhaustion.

"Who is that?" said Heron.

"Oh, some tramp!"

"I think not!"

"Decidedly! He is an inch thick with dust, and wants to beg a crown of us!"

The travel-worn young man's voice now seemed almost to fail him, for, although by the movement of his lips they could see that he was speaking, the words he uttered did not reach them.

It was evident, too, that he leant more heavily upon the gate.

"I will address him," said Heron. "Wait for me a moment."

"Nay—nay! Leave him alone—there is no time to lose. Sir Marmaduke will get impatient."

"Let him!"

"Now—now, this is too bad! We must not let ourselves be turned aside from what we have to do, and for which we shall be so amply paid, by any idle beggar who may look over a gate!"

"It will not take a minute," remonstrated Heron; and as he spoke he turned Daisy's head towards the roadway again.

His companion followed him, growling and imprecating.

"I'll be hanged," he said, "if I know what to make of you!"

"Perhaps you will know presently!" said Heron.

"Well, I hope I shall; but where Sir Marmaduke picked you up to assist in a little affair of this kind, I cannot imagine."

"Sirs," said the young man who was leaning on the gate, when they were sufficiently close that the low, faint voice in which he spoke could be distinctly heard,—"sirs, will you tell me who inhabits this house?"

"What is that to you?" was the rough rejoinder of Heron's companion.

"Nay," said Heron, "the question is civilly put; let us return as civil an answer. This house is now inhabited by Sir Marmaduke Shuldham, who is the guardian of a young lady named Gertrude."

The young man uttered an exclamation.

"Gertrude a ward of Sir Marmaduke Shuldham's; and in this house, the Abbey, too, once the abode of so much happiness—so much innocence—so much——"

The young man could not proceed.

Some powerful feelings evidently overcame him.

A strange idea took possession, at that moment, of the mind of Felix Heron.

He had been looking narrowly at the travel-stained, weary stranger.

He saw that he was young and handsome.

There was a certain air about him, too, that bespoke a man who had seen military service, which idea was further strengthened by a part of his dress having evidently belonged to an uniform.

Could it be possible that this was the real cousin Marmaduke, who had arrived at such a critical moment to rescue Gertrude from destruction?

And if so, how little he could imagine that the white flag he might have observed floating from the topmost turret of the Abbey merely by lifting up his eyes, unfurled itself for his sake, and for the dear love his cousin bore him.

It was but an idea of Heron's; but it grew each moment into form and strength, as though a voice from heaven had told him, "This is the man; and it is for you, Felix Heron, to rescue two young, fond hearts from destruction and despair."

The impatience of Heron's companion vented itself in coarse expressions.

"Good gracious!" he cried, "what do you want? You've had your answer, and now to off."

The young man raised himself up from his leaning posture on the gate proudly.

"Perhaps even now," he said, "I am not so weary and travel-worn but I can punish insolence like yours."

He dashed the gate open, evidently with a well-practised hand.

FELIX HERON PROMOTES THE HAPPINESS OF TWO YOUNG
AND LONG HEARTS.

Presented Gratis with No. 82, of the New Edition of EDITH HERON the Sequel to Edith the Captive; or, the Robbers of Epping Forest.

Heron's companion shrunk back.

"Confound the beggar's insolence!" he said. "Knock him on the head!"

"Not yet," said Heron. "I want to give him full information first."

"Him?—him information?"

"Certainly! You must know, young sir, that the Lady Gertrude is about this day to marry her cousin Marmaduke, a young officer in the Indian army."

The travel-worn stranger glared at Heron as though newly-awakened from a dream.

"What I tell you is true; and if you look upwards to the topmost turret, you will see a white flag there flying, which has been opened to the breeze by the Lady Gertrude herself only within the last five minutes, to welcome the arrival of her cousin."

"Five minutes? Why, it is but since that time that I have come within sight of the old, well-remembered house."

"You?" shouted Heron's companion. "And who may you be?"

"My name is Marmaduke; and I am the cousin of the Lady Gertrude."

Heron's companion opened his mouth; but his surprise and consternation were too great at the moment to supply him with any expression strong enough to give utterance to them.

He wheeled his horse round at once to make for the Abbey.

But that was a step easier to project than to execute.

Heron gave Daisy a slight touch, and she executed one of those demi-vaults which covered so large a space of ground, and which, in this instance, placed her and her rider exactly in the way of the myrmidon of Sir Marmaduke Shuldham, as he would have galloped to the mansion to give the alarm to his infamous employer.

"Not so fast, if you please," said Heron.

The bright daylight fell full upon the highly-polished barrel of one of those long, slender pocket-pistols which Heron called peculiarly his own.

Without the slightest tremor or wavering, the muzzle pointed clearly at the head of the startled horseman, who pulled up so rapidly that for a few seconds his horse looked exceedingly picturesque with his fore-feet in the air.

"Attempt to stir an inch," added Heron, "or make the least outcry, or show by action, or even by look, that you meditate mischief, and I will scatter your brains upon this green-sward as certainly as that the sun now shines above us!"

The steady look of Heron.

The tone in which he spoke.

The cool, determined aim of the pistol, and the extraordinary leap that Daisy had taken, all combined to strike terror into this man.

He was completely awed.

All the cowardice that lay at the bottom of the heart of the bully and the bravo rose up now, to the extinction of every other feeling.

How it was that the man who he thought was associated with him in the rascally service of Sir Marmaduke Shuldham, should now turn both upon him and his employer, was a mystery which he could not solve.

But there was the fact.

He was ready for any fraud or any villany, but to sacrifice his life there and then, upon that green lawn, was quite another affair.

His great effort seemed to be to shrink into as small a compass as possible.

There was something ludicrous, too, about the manner in which he took off his hat, and held it between his eyes and the point of Heron's pistol, as though that would save him, in the event of a shot.

"What have I done," he said, in a whining tone, —"what have I done to you that I should be threatened in this way?"

"Beware!" said Heron. "And let that word suffice for you! You know your danger! Your life is in your own keeping! I am not a man of many words, but prompt in action!"

The young officer, for such indeed he was, seemed, in the excitement of the moment, to overcome all his fatigue.

He rushed forward, and grasped the arm of Heron, as he exclaimed, "For the love of heaven, sir, let me know what all this means? Am I awake, or is this some vision of a weary slumber by the roadside?"

"It is true enough," said Heron. "Do you not see the flag?"

"I do!—I do!"

"It waves for you."

"Oh, in mercy, do not tantalize me! Give me but a key to all this mystery; and let me at once be the happiest or the most wretched of mortals?"

"You shall have a key to it. Your cousin Gertrude being mistakingly on the part of her father made the ward of Sir Marmaduke Shuldham, he conceived the idea of repairing his own broken fortunes by the acquisition of her property."

"Alas!—alas! Why was she not true?"

"What mean you?"

"Look at me sir. Study me well. I am weak, travel-worn, and wretched. I have deserted an honourable profession, and thrown myself a wanderer upon the world, merely that I might seek her, and hear from her own lips if a terrible letter she sent me could really convey the sentiments of her heart."

"Not yet, if you please," said Heron, abruptly.

He had kept his eye upon Sir Marmaduke's villanous associate, and saw that he was making a very slow movement to escape.

"I give in—I give in!" cried the fellow, in terror. "Don't fire."

"Now go on, Mr. Marmaduke," said Heron. "What letter is this you talk of?"

"I know you not; but I feel that I can trust you. It is here."

As he spoke, the young officer produced a torn and crumpled letter from the breast of his dust-begrimed apparel.

He handed it to Heron with glistening eyes and trembling hand.

"Hark you, young sir!" said Heron: "in me you find a friend; and it shall go hard if within the next half-hour I do not prove myself to be one such as in your wildest dreams you have scarcely hoped to look upon. But you must do something for yourself."

"Put me to the test, sir."

"I will do so. Take this pistol—or perhaps you are armed yourself?"

"Alas! no; I think if I had been, it would have been against myself."

"Take this, then, and keep a good watch over that man. You have heard me threaten what I would do if he should leave this spot; and as regards the fulfilment of those threats, you must take my place. You understand me?"

"I do, sir."

The young officer took the pistol that Heron tendered him, and effectually kept at bay the man who had fancied himself so well suited with a companion in Felix Heron.

The letter which the young officer had produced was certainly in a very dilapidated condition, and consequently difficult to read; but Heron contrived to make it out as follows:—

"The Abbey.

"MARMADUKE,

"Time was when I thought that I loved you.

"There are periods in the lives of boys and girls when they are peculiarly susceptible of the tender passion; and, thrown together as we were during that period, in the solitude and seclusion of a large country house—dependent upon each other for all the society we saw— it is no wonder that we fancied ourselves madly devoted to each other.

"That dream has passed away.

"I hope and trust it has passed away with both of us as it has with me. And now that I am no longer a child, but looking forward to a life of usefulness and domesticity, I think it but proper to write to you to say, that should you re-visit England, as my cousin Marmaduke you are quite welcome, but in no other capacity.

"Hoping that this will find you in just the frame of mind to receive such a communication, and that, therefore, you will send me no more letters similar to your last, I beg to subscribe myself

"Your affectionate cousin,
"GERTRUDE."

This letter for a few moments, but only for a few moments, staggered Felix Heron.

It was so cool, so curt, and the hand in which it was written was so delicate and so feminine, that he might well be excused for asking himself if it were really the composition and inditing of the person whose signature it bore.

But while this dubious condition of Heron's mind lasted he glanced upwards.

Upwards to the high turret of the Abbey.

There was the flag.

The white flag of lasting love and confidence, fluttering in the breeze.

Could he doubt any longer?

No. The letter which he held in his hand, and which had been addressed to the young officer in Calcutta, was as much a forgery as that a copy of which had been shown to him, Heron, by the man who now trembled beneath the barrel of the pistol held point blank at his head by the young officer.

The whole plot, in its wicked and villanous ramifications, was now as evident to Heron as the bright sunlight that sparkled upon the green lawn at Daisy's feet.

———

CHAPTER CCLX.

FELIX HERON IS THE MEANS OF UNITING TWO FOND HEARTS.

AND the plot would have succeeded.

It must have succeeded but for two accidents.

One was that Heron was mistaken for the unscrupulous assistant from London in Sir Marmaduke's service.

The other was that the young Indian officer, instead of perhaps seeking the oblivion of death, and ridding himself of life and despair together upon some battle-field; threw up his commission, and determined to hear from the lips of Gertrude herself the terrible words that she no longer loved him.

And here he was at that critical moment, with a heart heavy with despair, little suspecting that that white flag flaunting from the topmost tower of the Abbey was to him a beacon of joy and happiness.

Heron looked at him with a smile.

An expression of surprise came over the features of the young officer.

"Is it possible," he said, "that you can find in the miseries of any one a subject for laughter?"

"Not laughter," replied Heron; "but permit me to smile at your happiness."

"Happiness!"

"Yes; in the full sense of the word."

"You jest with me."

"No. Step aside."

"But this man?"

"Since our constant watchfulness of him, although necessary, becomes an annoyance, we must dispose of him in some other fashion."

"Do not kill him."

"Such carrion is not worth powder and shot. Dismount sir, or take the consequences!"

The man got off his horse with precipitation.

"You see," he said, "I obey you in all things; therefore, there is no excuse for you ill-using me."

"Still, Daisy; still!"

Heron dismounted likewise, and he knew that after what he had said Daisy would not stir an inch from the spot on which he left her.

Heron then slipped the bridle from Sir Marmaduke's man's horse, and with that and the stirrup leathers he was well provided with ample means of not only binding the fellow's hands behind him, but of fastening him securely to a young tree.

And Heron adopted the best possible mode of so fastening him.

He rather tightly buckled one of the stirrup leathers round his neck, and round the tree likewise; so that whatever efforts he might make for his extrication would go just so far towards his strangulation.

"Now," said Heron, "I sincerely advise you to keep quiet; or, otherwise, when we return, which assuredly we shall, your condition will not be changed for the better."

"The game's up!" growled the fellow.

"You are right."

"I don't know who and what you are," he added, "except that you are no friend of Sir

Marmaduke Shuldham's. I can't say, too, exactly what you are about, but if you pay me as well as he would have done, I don't see why I shouldn't lend you a helping hand."

"No," replied Heron. "Thank heaven, we have no designs which require tools of your description to carry out. Come this way, young sir, and I shall be able to tell you sufficient to drive away that look of care and depression from your brow."

Heron took the bridle of Daisy over his arm, and he and the young officer walked towards the Abbey slantways over the beautiful lawn.

Then Heron paused abruptly.

"One moment," he said. "Stay by my horse, and I will rejoin you instantly."

Heron darted back to the man whom he had left tied to the sapling.

"Give me," he said, " that copy of a letter which was forged in the name of her cousin Marmaduke, and addressed to the Lady Gertrude."

"How can I give it," growled the fellow, "with my hands tied behind me?"

Heron then recollected that he had seen him put it in the breast-pocket of his apparel; and forcing open his coat, he quickly possessed himself of it.

Making his way back, then, to the young officer, Heron placed it in his hands, saying, "This is the copy of a letter forged by Sir Marmaduke Shuldham, the guardian of Gertrude, and presented to her as coming from you. Read it, and one-half of the plot will be apparent; while, for the other half, you must likewise look in the other forged letter, which you have just shown me, and which purports to come from her to you."

"Great heaven! Can such things be?"

"Read—read, and convince yourself."

With evident signs of agitation, the young man read this infamous epistle.

Then the whole truth seemed to flash upon him.

His eyes became radiant with joy.

"She is true yet!" he cried; "and goodness, sincerity, and virtue have not yet forsaken the world!"

"Certainly not," said Heron. "But this plot is about to be carried out, and the Lady Gertrude will be, in the darkened chapel, united to her guardian, to whom she will give her hand, supposing him to be you."

The young officer uttered a cry of such despair that it alarmed Heron, and made Daisy prick up her ears, and look about her in wonder, to know what was the matter.

"Hasten!—oh, let me hasten!" he cried.

"With all my heart!" said Heron; "although, in good truth, I know not the way."

"Know not the way to the old chapel of the Abbey? It is as familiar to me as possible. This way—this way! I passed many happy years of early life in this mansion."

The young officer turned to the left, and plunged into a narrow path, overshadowed with tall trees, and which had scarcely space enough for Daisy to move forward in.

"This way—this way! We shall reach the chapel in a few seconds.

"One moment!" said Heron.

"What would you say?"

"Simply that I am some years your senior in years, and that I suspect I have seen much more of life than you have; so that I am justified in asking you to allow me to arrange this affair in my own fashion."

"I am by far too happy, and too infinitely obliged to you, to say nay."

"That is agreed, then?"

"It is; and all I stipulate for is, that I may have as early an opportunity as possible of assuring my cousin Gertrude how dear she is to me, and how constantly her image has been my companion when so far distant from her."

"You shall have that opportunity quickly, be assured; and now, as you know that Gertrude is willing to wed you in the old chapel, believing you to be fearfully disfigured by wounds, I want you to carry out that ceremony as you are."

"Ah, if I could!"

"It shall be done."

"You transport me with joy!"

"Calm yourself, and leave all to me. I will take good care that you stand by the altar in lieu of Sir Marmaduke Shuldham."

By this time, they had reached a little antique, arched door, covered with huge nails, and which was likewise so embosomed in ivy that it was difficult to detect it at all.

"This," said the young officer, " is one of the entrances to the ancient chapel; and it is one so little known, and so seldom used, that I daresay no one but ourselves, on this occasion, will enter by it."

"I have one perplexity," said Heron—"my horse."

"It will be safe here. This shadowy path that we have just traversed has, time out of mind, been believed by the whole household to be haunted; and I will take upon myself to say that, even at this nearly mid-day hour, no one will venture hither."

"Then, Daisy, wait for me," said Heron.

There was an iron ring deeply embedded in the stone wall by the side of the ancient Gothic door, and through that Heron slipped Daisy's bridle.

"Now," he said, "let us make our way into this mysterious chapel."

The door yielded to a touch, creaking slightly on its hinges; and proceeding forward three steps, Heron and the young officer stood in a little ancient Catholic oratory, which really needed but few artificial means to make it dim and obscure.

The narrow stained glass windows, each one of which represented a saint of solemn and majestic appearance, admitted but dimly the sun's rays even at their brightest and best.

But now those windows were covered with black serge, with the exception of one, which sent so dim a light of many colours through its stained compartments into the old chapel that almost absolute darkness would have been less confusing.

"Hush!" whispered Heron; "there are two persons standing by the old altar's steps."

The young officer and Heron paused; and the latter could feel, as his companion grasped his arm, in what a state of nervous agitation he was.

"Be calm—be calm!"

"You do not know what I have suffered. Who are those persons we see yonder?"

"They are speaking. Listen, and we shall soon know."

The two persons spoke, but in whispers; yet the profound stillness and repose of the little oratory was such that Heron and the young officer had no difficulty in catching every word they uttered.

"I think," said one of the speakers, "that your scruples now, at the eleventh hour, are uncalled for. It is but a whim of the lady's; and as everything else is regular, I cannot see that you run any risk in performing the ceremony."

"It is a serious thing to me if I do," replied the other person. "But, greatly beholden as I am to you, Sir Marmaduke, for many favours, I am not disposed to raise captious objections to this proceeding."

"That is well—that is well! The lady will soon be here, and the ceremony can proceed."

"Now," whispered Heron to the young officer, "you know who they are."

"The villanous Sir Marmaduke!"

"Yes; and his friend, the clergyman, who, you hear, shrinks somewhat from the part he has to play in this domestic drama."

"He will not play the part he expects."

"Only that he shall marry a Marmaduke to the Lady Gertrude, although it may not be the one he expects. And now let me make a bargain with you."

"What is it?"

"Promise me that you will not say a word to undeceive Gertrude in regard to what she thinks is the exact state of the case until after the ceremony."

"I will obey you."

"Then wait here while I clear a place for you at the altar steps."

Heron stepped lightly forward, amid the dim shadows of the chapel.

"Sir Marmaduke, Sir Marmaduke!" he said; "if you please, something so important! Sir Marmaduke, your attention for a moment."

Heron spoke in a tragic sort of whisper, which might be anybody's voice; and the rather alarmed Sir Marmaduke Shuldham darted at once towards him, uttering an exclamation of impatience anything but well suited to the sacred place he was in.

"What is it? What has happened? Are you the new fellow from London, recommended by Wrench?"

"Exactly, Sir Marmaduke; but something has happened."

"What—what?"

"Step this way, sir."

"What is it? Can't you speak—the lady will be here directly."

As Heron slowly retreated, Sir Marmaduke Shuldham followed him up involuntarily, until, in truth, they were very near the little antique door at which he, Heron, and the young officer, had entered the chapel.

"Well—well—what is it? Out with it!"

"I don't intend," said Heron, "to let you marry the Lady Gertrude!"

"Eh?"

"By no means, Sir Marmaduke; and now that you find my hand upon your throat, and feel its pressure, the propriety of submission will perhaps be evident."

A strange, gurgling sound was the only reply from Sir Marmaduke, for Heron's clutch upon his throat was far from being the most gentle in the world.

Sir Marmaduke was a heavy man, but Heron, by an exertion of that wonderful strength he possessed, fairly lifted him out of the chapel and flung him down at the feet of Daisy.

"Look to him, Daisy!" cried Heron. "Keep him, lass!"

It was a trick which Daisy had been taught in Epping Forest, to hold any one down with one of her fore-feet, without exerting sufficient pressure to do any real mischief.

Sir Marmaduke was safe.

Another moment, and Heron was beside the young officer.

"Take your place at the altar," he whispered rapidly, "and go through with the ceremony. If the clergyman speaks to you, answer as if you were Sir Marmaduke."

The young man sprung forward, and in another second he stood before the clergyman, in the precise spot so recently occupied by Sir Marmaduke Shuldham.

He was spared the necessity of playing a part repugnant to his feelings, for at that instant a distant door opened in the little chapel, and two female forms came into it.

The foremost of these advanced with rapid steps to the altar and held out both her hands.

"Oh, Marmaduke, Marmaduke!" she said, "could you think it possible your own Gertrude could be false to you, happen what might?"

"Hem!" said the clergyman—for he had a terrible fear that some explanation might take place, terminating in the confusion of all concerned; for if he did not know exactly what was doing, he at all events must have strongly suspected that some fraud was being enacted.

But the darkness of the chapel was so intense that all these people now in it could scarcely be distinguished one from the other.

For one brief moment Marmaduke clasped Gertrude to his heart, and she at least was assured that there was no mistake.

Heron stepped forward and gave away the bride.

In seven minutes and a half exactly, Gertrude was the wife of her cousin Marmaduke.

Then Heron raised his voice to a shout that rang through the little chapel.

"Unmask those windows," he cried, "and let us have all the light we can!"

Some servants, who were in a small gallery of the chapel, hastily tore down at this command the serge blinds that darkened the windows.

The change from nearly complete gloom to something like daylight was marked and instantaneous.

Gertrude uttered a cry of joy.

"You are not hurt—you are not disfigured, Marmaduke!" she cried. "Oh, what a cruel jest was this!"

"Nay, dear Gertrude, it was no jest of mine. I and this noble gentleman will explain all to you; and surely all's well that ends well, when thus I clasp you to my heart!"

"But Marmaduke, how strange you look in this dusty and travel-worn apparel—those hollow cheeks! Oh, Marmaduke! what has happened? Your face is not wounded!"

"No, Gertrude; but my heart felt a smart a thousand times more severe. Be patient, and you shall know all."

"But what is there to know, Marmaduke? I had your letter."

"Which I never wrote!"

"Never wrote?"

"No, Gertrude, no more than you wrote this one, which has caused me tears enough to dissolve it!"

Heron then spoke, and in a few short sentences he contrived to give the Lady Gertrude a tolerably good idea of the plot to which she had so nearly fallen a victim.

"And now," he said, "that all has ended so

happily here, and that you must have a thousand explanations to give each other, I bid you farewell; but be assured I shall again visit the Abbey."

"Our friend! our benefactor!" exclaimed Gertrude and Marmaduke at once, as they advanced with outstretched hands to Heron. "Give us a name that we may cherish in our memories as one we shall ever hold dear."

"You must call me Captain Fantome for the present. And now again farewell, for I have anxious business on hand."

Heron glanced round the chapel, and saw that the clergyman had disappeared.

On the other side of the little antique door, however, Daisy still held Sir Marmaduke indurance.

"Let him go, Daisy," said Heron; "and if you sir, have a particle of shame in your composition, fly from this spot; for your ward, the Lady Gertrude, is really married to her cousin Marmaduke, and it might be well for your safety that he did not meet you."

The discomfited guardian sprung to his feet, and rushed from the spot.

CHAPTER CCLXI.

FELIX HERON GOES TO NEWGATE TO INQUIRE FOR TOM RIPON.

IT was about mid-day on that morning which had been one of adventure for Captain Heron that an old woman, with grief and anxiety marked on her countenance, and ever and anon uttering a deep groan, knocked at Whitcombe House.

Ogle, restless and uneasy, was pacing the hall, expecting Captain Heron's return with some tidings of Tom.

Ogle instantly opened the hall door, and for the first time in his life felt almost tempted to embrace Mrs. Ripon, for he began to hope that, after all, Tom had been able to conceal himself at his mother's house; and, at all events, that he had sent her to give him and Captain Heron information as regarded his whereabouts.

"Mrs. Ripon!" was all that Ogle could command his voice to say.

Mrs. Ripon shook her head, and sinking into the hall porter's chair began to sob violently, rocking herself backwards and forwards like some one in great physical suffering.

"Speak, Mrs. Ripon!" cried Ogle. "Can you tell me aught of your son Tom?"

"Alas, alas!" said Mrs. Ogle, "the poor, dear boy is caught at last; and Jonathan Wild says he'll hang him, as sure as his name is Jonathan Wild!"

For a moment, Ogle's heart sank within him, but repressing his feelings, he said, "Tell me, Mrs. Ripon, has Wild, then, captured the poor boy?"

"Alas, yes! Oh, oh, oh! With all his faults, he was a good son to me; and to think that nobody can save him now!"

"Don't say that, Mrs. Ripon," said Ogle, with a deep-drawn sigh—"don't say that. Captain Heron is even now seeking him, and if he does not succeed in tracing him, he will soon be home; and when he knows that Wild really has taken him prisoner, he will most likely be able to hit upon some plan of setting him at liberty again."

When Mrs. Ripon heard that Felix Heron had gone in search of Tom, she started up, and exclaimed, "Oh, all will yet be well. He succeeds in everything he undertakes; but I thought he would be so angry with the poor boy for exposing Daisy to so much danger, that he would never forgive him, and let him take his chance with Jonathan Wild."

"No fear of that, Mrs. Ripon," replied Ogle. "It is quite certain the Captain was very angry at first with Tom, when he heard of his taking Daisy on the road; but he has too great a regard for Tom to allow him to fall a victim to Jonathan Wild, without making an effort to save him."

"He is a noble man," said Mrs. Ripon, with a sigh; "and when do you expect him to return Ogle?"

Ogle had no occasion to reply to this question of Mrs. Ripon's, for at that moment Ogle recognised the knock of Felix Heron at the hall door.

Mrs. Ripon endeavoured to conceal herself behind the leather chair which stood in the hall, when instead of the Baron Von Peck, in whose disguise she had expected to see Felix Heron, a perfect stranger stood before her, in the person of Captain Fantome, of the royal navy.

It must be understood that Mrs. Ripon had never seen Felix Heron in the disguise of Captain Fantome, and it was with evident gratification that he saw the stare of astonishment upon her face when she heard Ogle say, "Have you heard any news, Captain? Mrs. Ripon has come to tell us where he is."

While Ogle was saying these few words, Mrs. Ripon, in a perfect agony of suspense, was looking from one to the other of them.

Heron could not help smiling, although his heart was heavy, when he perceived that Mrs. Ripon, who knew him so well, had not penetrated his disguise.

"That is well," he said at last, speaking in his own voice. "Do you know me now, Mrs. Ripon?"

Mrs. Ripon burst out crying.

The events of the morning had made her nervous and excited, and she could scarcely believe her ears, when she recognised the tones of Felix Heron's voice.

"Good gracious, Captain!" she exclaimed; "who would have thought it was you? I declare nobody would know you."

"Enough, enough!" said Felix Heron. "Now tell me all you know about Tom."

Mrs. Ripon, in a short time, put Felix Heron in possession of all that the reader is acquainted with, excepting as regards the fact of where Tom was really imprisoned.

"No doubt," said Heron, "Jonathan Wild has taken Tom to Newgate. I will go at once, Ogle, and demand to see the prisoner. I think I may safely trust to this disguise?"

"I should think so, Captain," said Ogle, in a dubious voice; "but I don't half like the idea of you venturing within those walls. Let me go?"

"No, no!" said Felix Heron. "I must not lose you as well as Tom, and there's no knowing but that he might find some excuse for detaining you. I will just go and speak first to Edith, and then I will go at once and ask to see Tom Ripon."

Edith met Captain Heron at the drawing-room door. She had heard his loved footstep ascending the stairs, and had hastened to meet him.

"What news, Felix?" she asked, looking up into his face with a world of love in her glance.

"I have brought no tidings, my Edith, of that reckless boy; but Mrs. Ripon is below with Ogle, and she says he was captured at her house in Wardour Street, by Jonathan Wild, and that he is now in Newgate."

"Poor boy—poor boy!" exclaimed Edith. "What do you intend to do, Felix?"

Felix hesitated a moment, for he knew he was about to undertake something hazardous.

Edith instantly understood his silence.

"You will not go, Felix—you will not go there, Felix!" she said—and there was a perceptible tremor in her voice.

Felix folded her to his heart as he whispered, "Is my Edith going to turn coward now, my brave Edith? Must poor Tom be left without one effort to save him? Remember what he has been to both of us."

"I know—I know!" said Edith; "but may I not go, Felix? I could say something to comfort him, and no one could interfere with me."

"I am not so sure of that, Edith," said Heron, mournfully. "It will never do, I am convinced, for you—the bride of Captain Fantome—to go to Newgate to see Tom Ripon. Wild would begin to have his suspicions aroused immediately."

Edith raised her head, which she had rested upon Felix Heron's shoulder; and, looking him steadfastly in the face, she said, "Go then, Felix. I will not strive to hinder you performing what you consider a duty; but, oh! be wary; and be specially careful to disguise your voice as much as possible."

"Never fear, Edith! Why, even Mrs. Ripon did not know me! So cheer up, and believe that I shall be able to bring back good tidings of poor Tom."

"Go at once, Felix; for well I know how much he is suffering now from remorse at having given you so much anxiety and——"

Edith paused.

"And what?" asked Heron.

"Don't be very angry with him, Felix: he is but a boy, after all; and the temptation to become as celebrated as his loved Captain Heron has been too great to resist."

"Never fear, Edith," replied Heron. "All the anger I felt has passed away, and I only remember the boy's devotion and indomitable courage. Farewell, my Edith; I shall soon return to you."

Heron made his way towards Newgate, with the intention of seeing Tom Ripon—for he now entertained no doubt on the subject that he was there a prisoner—not only to say a few kind words to him, of which he felt assured he stood so much in need, but to see what terms might be offered Jonathan Wild, in order to induce him to set him at liberty.

Felix Heron knocked for admittance at Newgate.

The little wicket was opened, and a man thrust out his head, insolently demanding "What now?"

No sooner, however, did this man perceive a gentleman in an uniform belonging to the royal navy, than he instantly changed his tone, and asked civilly enough, "Who do you please to want, sir?"

"I have come to see a prisoner, a mere boy, who was brought here yesterday by Jonathan Wild's orders."

"Beg, pardon, sir; but there's some mistake. There was no such person as you speak of brought here."

"Indeed!" said Heron.

A cold feeling was at the heart of Felix Heron as he heard these words, for he now had no doubt but that Tom Ripon had been conveyed to Wild's house, or Little Newgate, as he called it.

As Felix Heron turned from the gates of Newgate, he began to ask himself what he had better do next.

He knew it would be fruitless to attempt to gain admittance in the ordinary way to any prisoner whom Jonathan Wild chose, for purposes of his own, to confine within the precincts of his own house.

At last Felix Heron came to the determination of paying his friend the young Earl of Bridgewater a visit, for the purpose of obtaining an order from a judge to search Jonathan Wild's house, if he (Wild) refused to admit him at once to Tom's cell.

A rapid walk soon brought him to the door of his friend's house, who was at the moment descending the grand staircase, and it was quite evident to Captain Heron by the look of inquiry upon the face of his friend, the Earl of Bridgewater, that he was so well disguised as Captain Fantome that even his most intimate friend failed to recognise him.

The footman who had admitted Felix Heron ushered him into the library, where he was soon joined by the Earl of Bridgewater.

"Thank you, Bridgewater," said Heron, as soon as they were alone, "for putting me perfectly at my ease with regard to my new disguise."

This was said in Felix Heron's natural voice, and instantly his hand was grasped by his friend Bridgewater.

"Is it possible?" said Bridgewater, laughing, "that I could forget your intention of assuming a new disguise. I had quite forgotten it at the moment, and did not recognise you. What is it you have come to say, for I can see that something sits very heavy on your heart?"

"In truth, I am somewhat depressed, I believe; but I want you, Bridgewater, to obtain for me, from your friend Sir Reginald, an order to search Jonathan Wild's house."

"Ah! Is there any one there in whom you are interested, Whitcombe?"

"Tom Ripon."

"Indeed!"

"Yes; the foolish boy took the mad freak into his head, of going on the road and seeking his own fortunes unknown to anybody, and this is the result of his undertaking."

The Earl of Bridgewater looked concerned, as he said, "But are you sure he is there? Has he communicated with you?"

"No," replied Felix Heron; "we found out, by the merest accident in the world, that he had been captured, by Daisy returning early yesterday morning, alone."

"What! Did he take Daisy?"

"He did; but, as I was saying, while I had gone out on the road to see if I could hear any tidings of him, his mother, Mrs. Ripon, came to my house, and told Ogle that Wild had had him taken to Newgate."

"Then what makes you think he is confined in Jonathan Wild's house?" asked the Earl of Bridgewater.

"Because I have already been to Newgate, and was told that no such person as I described had been taken in."

"I will be with you instantly. Wait here one moment."

The young Earl of Bridgewater soon made his appearance, ready equipped for a visit to his friend, Sir Reginald Selby, one of the judges.

A brisk walk soon brought Felix Heron and his friend, the young Earl of Bridgewater, to the judge's mansion.

The Earl of Bridgewater was instantly admitted, and was shown into the library, where, seated at a table, covered with papers, was Sir Reginald Selby.

"Ah, Bridgewater!" said Sir Reginald, as he rose and extended his hand; "I am glad to see you. To what am I indebted for this visit?"

The Earl of Bridgewater, in taking the hand Sir Reginald had held out to him, turned to Felix Heron, and said, "Allow me, Sir Reginald, to introduce to you my particular friend, Captain Fantome."

Sir Reginald bowed.

"Any friend of the Earl of Bridgewater I shall be happy at all times to receive as mine."

Felix Heron bowed courteously, and speaking for the first time, he said, "I am about, then, Sir Reginald, to ask a favour of you; which is, to give me an order to search the house of the notorious thief-taker, Jonathan Wild."

"Indeed!"

"Yes, Sir Reginald," interposed the Earl of Bridgewater. "This gentleman has every reason to believe that a youth of whom he knows something, has been taken to what is called 'Little Newgate,' which is no other than the house of Jonathan Wild; and where he has the means of carrying out the pains and penalties of the larger prison, for his own mere gratification."

"I have heard as much," replied Sir Reginald Selby; "but we will frustrate his plans in this case, if possible. Are you sure that the lad of whom you speak is really in Little Newgate?"

"Quite sure," replied Felix Heron; "for I went, in the first instance, to Newgate before troubling the Earl of Bridgewater, and was told by the men on the lock that no such person as I mentioned had been admitted."

"Then it is pretty clear," said Sir Reginald. "I will write you an order immediately."

Going, then, to the table on which were writing materials, Sir Reginald Selby sat down and wrote an order, by which Felix Heron and the Earl of Bridgewater were empowered to search the house of Jonathan Wild.

As soon as Felix Heron and his young friend the Earl of Bridgewater were once more in the street, the latter turned to Heron, and said, "I will go with you, Whitcombe, if you will allow me."

"Thank you—thank you!" cried Heron. "I did not like to ask you to do so; but still, if you feel inclined to assist me in this search, I shall be well pleased."

"Say no more about it, Whitcombe; say no more about it."

In a very short space of time, Felix Heron and his friend the Earl of Bridgewater ascended the steps of Wild's house.

They knocked at the door.

At the same moment that the little wicket was opened, Jonathan Wild glided into the passage,

in order to hear all that was said, unseen by the parties who demanded admittance.

The Earl of Bridgewater addressed the man who acted as porter or gaoler.

"We wish to see a boy who was brought here yesterday, of the name of Ripon."

"Ripon? Ripon?" said the man, with an inquiring look at Wild, of course unseen by either the Earl of Bridgewater or Felix Heron.

Jonathan Wild shook his head to intimate to the man that he was to say he was not there.

"Now make haste and open the door," said the Earl of Bridgewater; "we are not going to wait here all day parleying with you. We know he is here, and if you do not let us see him by fair means, we will by foul; for we are prepared with an order from Sir Reginald Selby to search every corner of this den until we do find him."

"An order!" said the man, half alarmed.

"Get out of the way!" growled Wild, as he now showed himself. "Get out of the way, and let me speak to the gentlemen!"

Jonathan Wild began to have some uncomfortable feeling with regard to the visit of two gentlemen; but when he saw that Captain Fantome, the husband of the Countess of Whitcombe, was one of his visitors, he was, so to speak, thrown off his guard.

"Open the door instantly," he cried, "and show the gentlemen into the office."

CHAPTER CCLXII.

FELIX HERON AND THE EARL OF BRIDGEWATER FIND TOM RIPON SUSPENDED FROM A NAIL IN THE WALL IN A CELL IN JONATHAN WILD'S HOUSE.

THE office was originally intended as a sitting-room, but when Wild found that his own private business increased, he thought it advisable to turn this room into a kind of office, where he kept an old man as clerk, whose duty it was to receive all visitors, whether to Mr. Wild personally or officially.

The room was barely furnished.

The floor was sanded, and a round table and a couple of chairs was all the furniture it contained, with the exception of a desk and a high stool, upon which perched the clerk.

Felix Heron and the Earl of Bridgewater entered, but it was Felix who first addressed Jonathan Wild.

"We have come to see a boy whom you have here, Jonathan Wild, by the name of Tom Ripon. It is useless for you to attempt to deny having him in custody, for we have proofs of his being here, and are determined to see him, and if need be take him away with us."

Wild, during this speech, quietly seated himself on the table, swinging his legs backward and forwards, and every now and then giving one of those leers out of the corner of his eye, which he seemed to think rather an improvement to his looks than otherwise.

"So you have come to see Tom Ripon, have you?" asked Wild.

"We have," replied the Earl of Bridgewater.

TOM RIPON EXCITES THE SUPERSTITIOUS FEARS OF JONATHAN WILD.

Presented Gratis with No. 83, of the New Edition of EDITH the Sequel to Edith the Captive; or, the Robbers of Epping Forest.

"You do not deny that he is here in this house?"

"Oh, no!" coolly replied Jonathan Wild. "He is here, and no mistake, and here he will remain; but I have no objection to you seeing him. I was actuated by motives of kindness towards the boy, and brought him here in order to keep him from further mischief, and bringing himself to the gallows before his time."

"Silence!" said Felix Heron. "Lead the way to Tom Ripon, or as sure as you are sitting there, I will find the means to make you."

Jonathan Wild did not seem inclined to put himself in the power of his visitors, so he shouted out, "Here, Jenkins—Jenkins, show these gentlemen to Tom Ripon's cell, and take care the young scoundrel does not make his escape."

Along a narrow passage and down a flight of stone steps, which Felix Heron knew but too well, the man Jenkins led the way to Tom's cell.

Arrived at a low door, studded with nails, the man stopped and produced from his belt a huge bunch of keys.

Selecting one of these, he thrust it into the lock, leaving Felix Heron and the Earl of Bridgewater to enter by themselves, while he remained on guard outside.

He was soon startled by a cry of horror which came from the hearts of Felix Heron and the Earl of Bridgewater.

"Eh? What? What's the matter?" asked the man, as Felix Heron and the Earl of Bridgewater rushed by him. "What's up?"

At a glance, the sight which was presented to the gaoler was one sufficient to account for the cry of horror which had burst simultaneously from the lips of both Felix and his friend the young Earl.

Tom Ripon was suspended from a nail in the wall, and from the stillness of every limb it was evident that he was quite dead.

Jenkins did not stop many minutes to examine the dead body, but made what haste he could to regain the room in which he and the visitors had left Jonathan Wild, and where he had no doubt of finding them.

"Bless my heart, now, who'd have thought it? A young fellow who would have made his fortune twenty times over, if he'd only just have humoured Jonathan Wild a bit. Well, it's no use a locking up of a dead body, so here goes!"

The last three words were intended as a kind of incentive to himself to hurry from that cell which contained so ghastly a spectacle, for he never ceased running until he gained the room where he heard an altercation going on between the two gentlemen and Jonathan Wild.

It is now time that we return to Tom Ripon, who, it must be confessed, for the first time in his life, found it impossible to call to his aid any of that joyousness and love of fun and mischief which seemed always at his command, no matter what were the circumstances in which he was placed.

After trying most unsuccessfully to make some impression upon the lock, Tom threw the nail down in despair, exclaiming, "It's no use! I know Captain Heron will never forgive me, so what's the use of living?"

At this moment Tom happened to cast his eyes up to the nail he had seen on first entering the cell.

"Ah!" he said, "there it is, looking quite inviting. I've a good mind to try it on. There's nobody to care for me. The old gal and that old hypocrite, Mortification, will drink their rum-punch just as well when I am gone. There's Ogle, certainly, and there's Daisy."

At the mention of Daisy the boy bowed his head upon his hands, and great tears dropped through his fingers.

"Dear, dear Daisy!" continued Tom; "if I could but know that you were safe and well, I could die cheerfully. If I could but get out of here for a few hours, and satisfy myself that she was all right, I wouldn't mind a bit coming back again."

Tom seemed lost in thought.

In a few minutes he raised his head.

"Ah, a happy thought! I have it! Yes, yes, I'll manage it! Ha! ha, Jonathan Wild! I will be as clever as Jonathan Wild!"

With these words, Tom Ripon began by taking off his tall jack-boots, his scarlet coat, cravat and wig.

He then went to the straw, upon which he had vainly attempted to sleep, and taking up in his arms a large quantity, commenced stuffing his coat with it.

Having done so, he fastened on the boots, and placed on the top of all his hat and wig.

Having made this effigy of himself, Tom tied it up to the nail which projected from the wall, and then stood some paces off to admire his handiwork.

"That's about it," exclaimed Tom. "Quite a handsome-looking fellow, I declare! I don't wonder if all the girls fall in love with me. Now, Johnny, if you would but come into the cell, perhaps you might be too frightened to give the alarm, and I shall manage to escape."

These cogitations of Tom's were brought to an abrupt conclusion by the sound of footsteps in the stone passage just outside Tom's cell.

"Ah!" said Tom; "here's somebody. I'll just hide behind the door, and watch my opportunity."

Tom Ripon had just time to get behind the cell-door, when the key was thrust into the lock to admit Felix Heron and his friend, the Earl of Bridgewater.

Our readers are aware of the result of Tom's ingenuity in imposing upon them, for they really believed that it was Tom who was thus hanging—a victim of Jonathan Wild's hatred and malice.

It was with mixed feelings of joy and sorrow that Tom Ripon heard the exclamations of Felix Heron and his friend, for it convinced Tom that whatever cause Felix Heron had for visiting him with his just anger, he still felt convinced that that cry which had come from the heart of his beloved master had in it tones of affection only, and none of anger.

It is difficult to say what Tom Ripon might not have done under the circumstances, but the inopportune appearance of the turnkey as Felix Heron uttered that cry of dismay, prevented him (Tom) from throwing himself at Felix Heron's feet, and asking his forgiveness.

As it was, Tom Ripon had just time sufficient

to hide himself behind the door of his cell, where he could hear the little colloquy of the turnkey, and was himself unobserved.

It was with a feeling of satisfaction that Tom heard the retreating footsteps of the man Jenkins, and this feeling was greatly increased when he found he had not attempted to draw the door shut behind him.

Tom Ripon allowed a reasonable time to elapse before he ventured out of his place of concealment; he then quietly returned to the hanging figure which he had suspended from the nail, and which had produced so much alarm to Felix Heron and the young Earl of Bridgewater.

Tom then proceeded to take down the figure, and again dressed himself in his coat, hat, wig, and boots, and sat down to think what he had best do next.

His best plan, Tom thought, would be to wait until dusk before he attempted to make his escape from Jonathan Wild's house; but while waiting for the hour to arrive, he did not feel inclined to sit down patiently, and do nothing.

And now that Tom had some hopes of again seeing his four-footed friend Daisy, it was remarkable how changed he was in aspect, and how soon he recovered his wonted gaiety of disposition.

Tom started to his feet; for he fancied he heard Jonathan Wild's voice close to his cell door, which Tom had partially closed.

"Hilloa there, Jenkins!" said Jonathan Wild.

"Coming, sir! coming, sir!" replied Jenkins.

"Well, make haste, then," again shouted Wild, "and don't keep one here waiting all day. Let no one go to the cell—*that* cell wherein Tom Ripon has put an end to himself—till my return. You understand, eh?"

"All right, Mr. Wild. We are none of us likely to choose that cell now to pass the time in. We don't care for live folks, but dead ones——"

"Silence!" roared Wild. "What do I care for your likes or dislikes? If you say another word, I'll make you keep watch over the body until I come back."

It was evident to Jenkins and his comrades that for some reason or another Jonathan Wild was more vexed than pleased at what that morning occurred; and knowing the hostility that had always existed between Jonathan Wild and Tom Ripon, they were at a loss to understand why his death should so affect him, Wild.

If we follow him, the reader will gather somewhat from his own words.

"Plague take the boy!" muttered Wild to himself, as he paced up and down his own particular room. "Plague take the boy, to go and hang himself just at this juncture, when I had him so completely in my power! I would have forced him to tell me what he meant by Felix Heron coming to claim Daisy himself."

Jonathan Wild paused and looked uneasily round the apartment.

"Ghosts! What folly! there are not such things. And yet—and yet——What's that?"

Jonathan Wild turned twice round on his heel, as the door of the room creaked a little on its hinges.

"Oh, only the wind!" and then Jonathan Wild sat down to think.

In the meantime Tom Ripon had taken an exploring fit into his head, hoping that he might perchance find some mode of egress from his present abode, which, to tell the truth, was not a desirable one, Tom thought.

Tom had made his way after Jonathan Wild, slowly and stealthily, intending, if possible, to watch for an opportunity of stepping out at the same time that Jonathan Wild left his house.

In fact, it was Tom who had just pushed open the door of the room in which Wild was, which had so startled him, Wild.

Tom was so situated that he could see and hear all Jonathan Wild said and did, without himself being seen.

Jonathan Wild continued.

"Yes; I suppose I shall see his ghost some day. Though I didn't kill him, that's quite certain; but still I dragged him here, and shut him up, when, after all, the boy was only doing what I would have given him free liberty to do, if he would have accepted my terms."

Tom scraped with his nail upon the panel of the door, and gave a deep sigh.

Jonathan Wild cowered down as though he had been struck by some invisible hand.

"Murder! Help! help!"

Tom Ripon opened the door, and walked into the room, looking solemn and mysterious.

He had totally altered his appearance by the addition of a large quantity of whitewash, which he had gathered from the walls of his cell, and which he had rubbed profusely all over his face, giving it an unearthly appearance.

"What want you, Jonathan Wild?" asked Tom, in a low guttural voice.

"Back! back! Spare me! spare me!" shrieked Wild. "Let me go! let me go!"

The only answer Tom gave was another deep groan, and then he closed the door and placed his back against it.

"Merciful heavens!" cried Jonathan Wild. "What want you here? I did not kill the boy! I offered to let him go free if—if——"

"If what?" asked Tom again, with a deep groan.

"If—if——Murder!"

Tom approached close to the table.

"Murder! Keep back, I say! What want you with me?"

"I am sent by Captain Felix Heron," said Tom, "to tell you that your last hour is near at hand; and that you are to go to the cell in which you caused Tom Ripon to be placed——"

Jonathan Wild stood with open mouth and eyes dilated as he cried, "But you are Tom Ripon! Say it is all a terrible joke, and I——"

"I *was* Tom Ripon," replied Tom, with solemnity, "but Tom Ripon is now no more!"

Jonathan Wild shook as with an ague.

"You are to go," said Tom, in a low, solemn voice, "to the cell in which you confined Tom Ripon, and take from the pocket of the coat which he wore when he hanged himself a paper——"

"A paper?"

"Yes."

"I will send for it, good spirit—I will send for it. But go away now—pray go away, and I promise to be a friend to poor Mrs. Ripon as long as I live."

Tom Ripon raised both his hands and pointed meaningly to the door.

Jonathan Wild understood the action, but really had not the power to move.

"Go!" said Tom, still in the same voice.

Wild got up from the chair on which he had sunk, and was about to make his way to the door, hoping that he would thus put an end to the ghostly interview, when Tom placed his hand heavily on his arm, saying as he did so, "Beware, Jonathan Wild!"

That was an unlucky step of Tom's, for Jonathan Wild's nerves were so tightly strung by this time, that he could bear no more, but uttering one loud shriek, fell to the floor insensible.

That shriek brought several of the turnkeys to his assistance, and Tom Ripon was again surrounded, even as he had been once before that day, and borne to a cell still more lonely than the one he had just quitted.

"There you are, my fine fellow!" said one of the men, as he slipped some heavy handcuffs upon Tom's wrists. "Perhaps, when you tries to frighten folks again, you'll manage matters better than you have this time!"

CHAPTER CCLXIII.

FELIX HERON MAKES KNOWN TO EDITH AND OGLE THE RESULT OF HIS VISIT TO JONATHAN WILD'S HOUSE.

FELIX HERON and the Earl of Bridgewater walked on for some time in silence after they had left Jonathan Wild's house.

It was quite evident to the young Earl of Bridgewater, who was so well acquainted with all the devotion and self-sacrifice that had marked Tom Ripon's career from boyhood, to his friend and master, that it was a recollection of his many sterling good qualities which now occupied the mind of Felix Heron, and caused a look of pain and sorrow to settle upon his countenance.

"Come, Whitcombe," said the Earl of Bridgewater, "what has happened cannot be helped. Now do not look thus."

Felix Heron shook his head. "I cannot help it," he replied. "I little thought that boy would have come to such an end. I cannot but blame myself now."

"Nonsense, Whitcombe! How could you imagine that Tom Ripon would be so foolhardy as to take to the road, without even consulting you?" replied the Earl of Bridgewater.

"Heaven knows it is the last thing I would have countenanced his doing," said Heron, mournfully, "had he consulted me about it. But it is no use talking now the deed is done, and poor Tom has fallen a victim to circumstances. And now, my kind friend," he added, "I must make what haste I can to Whitcombe House, and inform poor Edith of all that has happened; for she was no less anxious than myself when I left home this morning, determined to see and comfort poor Tom."

"Farewell, then, for the present," replied Bridgewater. "Always remember, Whitcombe, that I am ever at your service."

"Thanks—a thousand thanks, true and valued friend," replied Felix Heron, as he took the proffered hand of the young Earl of Bridgewater, and pressing it warmly, turned his face with a heavy heart towards Whitcombe House.

A very short space of time sufficed to bring Felix Heron to the door of the mansion, which was quickly opened by Ogle, without Felix Heron having had time to knock for admittance.

Ogle had stationed himself by one of the side windows in the hall, where he could command a good view of the street, and being more than usually anxious about Tom, he could not make up his mind to go about his usual vocations until he had heard some tidings about him.

A glance at the sorrow-stricken face of Felix Heron sufficed to let Ogle know that something unusual had happened.

"What news, Captain?" exclaimed Ogle, as he opened the door.

"As bad as it can well be, Ogle," said Felix Heron, sorrowfully. "The poor boy is no more."

Ogle fairly reeled against the wall as Captain Heron uttered these words, and for a moment they seemed to take from him all powers of utterance.

Then dashing his hand across his eyes, he said, "No more?—Tom Ripon no more, Captain? What do you mean?"

"I mean," said Heron, with a trembling voice, "that the poor boy has destroyed himself in Jonathan Wild's house."

Ogle looked up quickly.

"It's false, Captain—it's false, I tell you. Tom Ripon is too brave, too true a heart to do any such thing. Do you think, Captain, he would leave you, and me, and Daisy like that? I won't believe it unless I saw him with my own eyes. It is some fiendish tale got up by that villain Wild, to prevent any further inquiries being made about him. I'll go myself, Captain. Stand aside—do not look so! I will go myself, and make Jonathan Wild deliver him up."

Felix Heron placed his hand kindly but firmly upon Ogle's shoulder, as he said, "Do you think, Ogle, that anything would have convinced me of the fact, short of beholding him with my own eyes?"

"Oh, Captain, don't say so—do not say that you have really seen Tom Ripon!"

"I have, Ogle. We shall never look upon his bright young face again in life, I tell you. Now I must go to Edith."

Ogle sank into a leathern chair that usually stood in the hall—his head sank upon his breast, and the strong man's frame shook beneath the painful emotions that were struggling in his breast.

Felix Herom mounted the grand staircase, and in another minute he had clasped Edith to his heart in silence.

Edith raised her head from its resting-place, and gazing up into the face of Felix, said, in a voice which tried in vain to be cheerful, "Well, and how found you that mischief-loving boy?"

Felix Heron shook his head, and whispered, in a voice of emotion, "Alas! my Edith! you have seen him for the last time."

Edith started, and no one could have looked

upon her expressive countenance without reading there how much interest, and we may say affection, his many noble qualities and faithful services had implanted in her heart.

"Oh, Felix, Felix!" she cried, as soon as she had recovered the first shock the intelligence had given to her—"oh, Felix! are you sure?"

"Quite sure, my Edith. I saw him myself."

"How did he die?" asked Edith, clasping her hands over her eyes.

"By his own hand, my Edith," said Felix Heron, mournfully.

"Alas! alas!"

"I must leave you now, my dear Edith, for I must go and ascertain more particulars from his mother respecting his capture, and what he had been doing exactly when he was captured by Jonathan Wild; for as yet I am all in the dark, and know not really whether it may not have been some old grudge of long standing which was the cause of Jonathan Wild taking him prisoner; and I must say my suspicions point that way, inasmuch as I found him in Wild's house instead of in Newgate."

"Go, Felix, go. I need not tell you to return to me as quickly as possible. I am so anxious, and so very, very sad."

Edith's eyes filled with tears as she said these words, but she quickly restrained them, so as not to add to what she knew were the painful feelings of her idolized husband.

Felix Heron quickly made his way to the fence in Wardour Street.

His knock was answered by the Reverend Mortification.

"Yea, verily, Captain," said Mortification, as he busied himself in unbarring the door—"yea, verily, Captain, thou art welcome, for thou bringest good tidings, as the Psalmist says, to a bereaved mother."

"Where is Mrs. Ripon?" asked Felix Heron. "Tell her I wish to see her about Tom instantly."

"She is even in the back kitchen, as the Psalmist says, feeding upon sackcloth and—— Ah!—oh!"

These exclamations were caused by Mrs. Ripon rushing past Mortification, and giving him such a blow in the side that he reeled against the wall, as she made her way to Felix Heron, and, seizing his hand, she exclaimed, "Have you heard anything of my poor boy—my own Tom? Tell me—tell me, Captain, is that villain Jonathan Wild going to send him to trial?"

"No," said Felix Heron. "You must calm yourself, Mrs. Ripon, for I have very bad news to tell you."

"Oh!—oh!—oh!" groaned Mrs. Ripon.

"Yea, verily——" began Mortification.

But whatever he was about to say was quickly brought to a close, by Mrs. Ripon seizing a cup and saucer from the table and throwing it at him, while she almost screamed out, "Hold your tongue, you coward! If you had not been afraid, and hidden yourself as you did, the poor boy would never have been taken; but you left me —a poor lone, lorn woman—to do everything. Tell me, Captain, what did Tom say when you went to see him?"

"Nothing. He was beyond the power of my help. My poor woman, you have no Tom now —he is dead!"

Mrs. Ripon slid from the chair in which she had been sitting, and with one low, prolonged groan, all her mother's feelings were aroused within her, and she became senseless.

"Yea, verily," said Mortification, "I little thought that this would be the end of one of our best customers, as Thomas seemed likely to become. Yea, as the Psalmist says, blessed is he that expecteth nothing."

"Silence!" cried Felix Heron. "Assist me to remove Mrs. Ripon into the back parlour!"

While Felix Heron and Mortification were thus employed, they were startled somewhat by an impatient knock on the panel of the shop door for admittance—for Felix Heron had taken the precaution of replacing the bar of wood across the door when he entered the fence.

"Yea, verily," said Mortification, "I will even go and see whether we are visited by a friend or a foe. Eh?—oh!"

These last words were addressed evidently to the person who had so impatiently demanded admittance.

"Peace be with you, verily!" exclaimed Mortification to the new comer.

"Stuff—gammon!" rejoined the visitor. "None of your hypocrisy with me, Mortification. I want to see Mrs. Ripon."

"Verily, then, thou must wait for a short season, for she is in tribulation just at this present moment on account of that young vaga—— Hem! I mean her devoted son Thomas having bid adieu to——"

"Hold your clack, man!" interrupted the new comer; and pushing Mortification aside, he strode hastily into the parlour, holding in his hand a small piece of paper.

He paused on the threshold, however, on perceiving Captain Heron, who, being disguised as Captain Fantome, was, of course, unknown to him.

Felix Heron was the first to speak. "Your name, sir? I take it for granted you are a friend?"

"Rather!" replied the visitor, who was no other than Tom Ripon's quondam friend, Jack Sheppard.

"If your business is not urgent, you had better postpone it for a little time," said Felix Heron; "for you see Mrs. Ripon is not in a fit state just now to attend to business."

"Oh! oh! oh!" groaned Mrs. Ripon.

"Come, Mrs. Ripon!" said Jack Sheppard, giving her, at the same time, a not very gentle shake. "What's the row? Here! I've got a bit of a note from Tom!"

Mr. Ripon sat bolt upright on the floor of the apartment.

"From my boy Tom?"

"Well, I should rather say so, for he gave it to me himself this morning, and told me to bring it to you, and to say he is not dead all the time, only a make-believing like."

Felix Heron grasped Jack Sheppard by the arm.

"What say you?" he asked. "Tell me again that he is not dead?"

"Read for yourself, and then, perhaps, you'll be satisfied. You seem like a friend of the family."

Felix Heron seized the paper which Jack Sheppard had been holding towards Mrs. Ripon ever since he entered the room, and read out the following words :—

"DEAR OLD GAL,—

"Don't take on ; I'm not dead. I'm alive, and only wish I had a chance of kicking Jonathan Wild, which I hope I shall do before long. Keep up your spirits, and if you see Ogle, tell him to give my love to Daisy.

"TOM."

No sooner had Felix Heron read those few words, than he hastened out of the "fence," nor stopped until he was standing on the door-step of the Earl of Bridgewater's house, where we will leave him while we return to Mrs. Ripon's "fence," in Wardour Street, and hear from Jack

NO. 84.—EDITH HERON.

Sheppard how he became possessed of the little billet written by Tom to his mother.

When Felix Heron hastily glanced over the few hurried lines penned by Tom, he had flung the note down on the floor, as he hurried from the "fence" to seek his friend, the Earl of Bridgewater.

Mrs. Ripon stretched out her hand to reach the letter.

Jack Sheppard handed it to her, and seemed evidently relieved now that she found Tom was not really dead.

"It's always the way," she said, "with that boy ; he's always trying to frighten his poor mother in some way or another."

"Yea, verily," said Mortification, "he maketh my heart ache to think how he wasteth good opportunities of being of service to his paternal relative-in-law ; and yet——"

"Hold your tongue!" cried Mrs. Ripon, now quite herself again. "Hold your tongue, or I will find means to make you! If it hadn't been for you, the boy would never have been taken by that Jonathan Wild."

During this brief conversation between Mrs. Ripon and her affectionate spouse, Mortification, Jack Sheppard had comfortably seated himself upon a table, and was mightily enjoying the scene.

"Go it, my hearties!" he shouted. "It does a fellow's heart good to go and see a play after being shut up in Little Newgate for a couple of days."

"In Little Newgate?" shouted Mrs. Ripon. "That where my poor boy is? Tell me how you came to see and speak to him?"

"Well, that would take more time just now than I feel inclined to waste, as I do not know whether our friend Jonathan Wild may not be on the look-out for me again. There's no trusting to his word. He promised me two years' grace if I would share my profits with him during that time; so, as I promised to help Tom if ever I had it in my power, why, I promised Jonathan Wild to agree to his terms."

"What terms?" asked Mrs. Ripon.

"Why, to go partners with him for two years, then let him hang me, to be sure."

"And you mean to do that?"

"Not if I know it," replied Jack Sheppard, with a knowing wink. "But I was obliged to get out of his clutches to bring you that bit of a note. But hark! What's that?"

"Goodness gracious!" exclaimed Mrs. Ripon; "it's a knock! Go and see who it is, and don't stand there like a stuck pig!"

Mortification, to whom these words were addressed, moved warily in the direction of the shop, where, mounting upon the stool whence he usually took a survey of the person wishing to gain admittance, he beheld a man wrapped in a cloak, with his hat drawn down over his brows so as completely to hide his face.

"Who may you be?" inquired Mortification.

"Open!" replied the voice. "I have goods to dispose of, if this is Mrs. Ripon's."

CHAPTER CCLXIV.

MRS. RIPON AND MORTIFICATION MAKE A GOOD MORNING'S WORK.

MORTIFICATION quickly dismounted from his place of espial, and addressed the visitor, who proved to be a housebreaker known to both.

Mrs. Ripon hastily rose from the sitting posture on the floor which she had occupied ever since she had heard from Felix Heron that her son Tom was dead, and hastened to the shop.

Mrs. Ripon never allowed Mortification to do business without her being present, and it was she who now drew towards her a rather large parcel of brown paper, which, from its weight, she rightly imagined contained plate of no small value.

Spoons, forks, ladles, cruet-tops, sugar-tongs, and a number of miscellaneous articles, met her admiring gaze.

"How much?" asked the man, in a surly tone.

"Well," commenced Mrs. Ripon; "you would be surprised at the great fall that has taken place in silver."

"None of your cant, now!" said the man. "I don't want to hear any of your tales about the fall in silver and such like! I want to hear what you are disposed to give for the lot, and then let me go my way. I don't want to stop here all day."

"Well, if I give you two pound ten for the lot, as you are a good customer——"

"Two pound ten!" interrupted the man, bringing his hand down upon the table with such violence as fairly to make every article upon it dance again. "Two pound ten, woman! Why, it's worth at least ten pounds! and if I can't get it here, why I'll take it somewhere else; and in that case, you'll never see me here again."

Mrs. Ripon well knew that the packet before her was worth at least twice as much as the housebreaker had named.

"Yea, verily," said Mortification, coming to her assistance, "I think that we might say five pounds, as Mr. ——"

"Hold!" shouted the man; "walls have ears. Who told you to call me by my name? Give me the five pounds, and let's put an end to the affair at once."

With many a sigh, Mrs. Ripon produced the required sum; and the housebreaker, hastily sweeping the money from the table, put it in his pocket and left the house.

"That's all through you!" screamed Mrs. Ripon. "That's all through you, meddling with what don't concern you! If you'd held your tongue I should have got the whole of the plunder for half the sum; but it's the way with you. I may work and strive my eyes out, and then you step in, and away goes all the profit! Get out of my sight, or I shall scratch your eyes out —I know I shall!"

Mortification—who evidently had a wholesome dread of Mrs. Ripon—beat a hasty retreat somewhere in the direction of the lower regions, while Mrs. Ripon returned to the back parlour, where she found Jack Sheppard still seated on the table, swinging his legs backwards and forwards in a most unconcerned fashion.

"Oh, here you are!" he exclaimed, as Mrs. Ripon entered the apartment. "A good bargain, —eh?"

Mrs. Ripon shook her head and pursed up her lips, as much as to say, "Given too much."

"Well, never mind; better luck next time. Shall I tell you now how I came to get at Tom, who was snugly caged in Jonathan Wild's house?"

"Ah, yes, yes! I had almost forgotten the boy. Five pounds! Oh, dear!—oh, dear! To think of giving five pounds all for one lot!"

"Five pounds! Why, what do you mean, Mrs. Ripon? I never said anything about five pounds!"

"No; I know you didn't, Jack Sheppard. I was only thinking."

"Thinking! Thinking about what?"

"About that Mortification saying the plunder was worth five pounds, when I know he would have taken half that sum."

"Oh, bother that! I want to tell you about Tom."

"Well, go on—I'm listening," said Mrs. Ripon, putting the brown paper parcel under her arm for security.

"Well, as I was going to tell you, I was caught cracking a crib on my own account; and just as I was taking my departure, with no end of swag—which, by the bye, you were to have, Mrs. Ripon——"

Mrs. Ripon groaned.

"Who should come up," added Jack Sheppard, "but Jonathan Wild, looking more hideous than ever, and half a dozen of his bull-dogs, and I was nabbed on the spot."

"Serve you —— Hem!—I mean, what a shame!" said Mrs. Ripon.

"And taken to Little Newgate."

"And there you saw Tom?" asked Mrs. Ripon.

"No, I didn't," said Jack Sheppard; "but after being there a long time, I heard him."

"Heard him! What do you mean?" asked Mrs. Ripon.

"Heard him trying to do something at the lock of his cell."

"And did he succeed?"

"No, of course he couldn't without proper tools. At first, I had no means of knowing who was in the ceil above me; and I was too far off for him to hear my voice, so I waited patiently until I could find out who was my neighbour."

"Well?"

"So, when the fellow who had charge of me brought me my allowance of bread and water, I asked him who was overhead, as he had been making so much noise that he disturbed me."

"And what did he say?" asked Mrs. Ripon, now thoroughly interested.

"Oh," he replied, "it's only a boy that has been brought in by Jonathan Wild, and who is to be kept close until he, Jonathan, can make up his mind what to do with him."

"What did you say then?" asked Mrs. Ripon.

"Oh!" replied Jack Sheppard, "I asked the man—who seemed to be a very good sort of fellow in his way—what the boy's name was; and after a little while he told me his name was Tom Ripon."

"Ah!"

"You may be sure, Mrs. Ripon," added Jack Sheppard, "I was only too glad to hear that I had an old pal for my nearest neighbour; and I made up my mind to find some means of communicating with Tom, just to let him know he was not quite alone, you know; and I thought, too, the time would pass more pleasantly if we could establish some kind of understanding between us."

"Well, Tom, how did you begin?" asked Mrs. Ripon.

"Why, you must know that, once upon a time, when Tom and I had nothing else to think of, we agreed upon certain sounds to make from one room to another—such as knocking on the wall or the flooring, as the case might be, and so holding a kind of conversation which could not be understood by any one not in the secret."

"What a capital idea!" said Mrs. Ripon. "And you did this?"

"You shall hear."

"After the man had set down my allowance of bread and water, I commenced by giving, first of all, some raps on the floor-ceiling of my cell, which, as I thought would be the case, soon produced some answering raps on the floor of Tom's. Then I began to talk to him."

"Talk to him? Could he hear you?"

"Yes; I began to talk to him in this fashion."

Jack Sheppard began a series of knocks upon the table with the end of a stick he held in his hand.

"But how could he understand anything from that, I want to know?" asked Mrs. Ripon.

"I'll let you into the secret, Mrs. Ripon," said Jack Sheppard. "I first wanted to let him know that I was aware who he was; so I gave twenty knocks with my stick on the ceiling of my cell, which meant the letter T."

"For the life of me I can't make out what you are talking about," she said, somewhat in a vexed tone. "What has twenty knocks to do with the letter T?"

"Why, you simple creature, isn't the letter T the twentieth letter of the alphabet? And isn't that the first letter of Tom's name?"

"I begin to see," said Mrs. Ripon, as a light seemed to break upon her.

"Well," continued Jack Sheppard; "then I began again, and the next time I stopped at the fifteenth knock, which meant O."

"I see," said Mrs. Ripon.

"Then I knocked again thirteen times, and then stopped, because the thirteenth letter is M; and you see that Tom would have his name in full."

"And did he understand you?"

"Of course he did; and then we held quite a little conversation, in which Tom made me acquainted, by means of these knocks, that in the floor of his cell there was a slab of stone, which he fancied, if pushed upward, would open like a trap-door."

"And is that how you got that letter from Tom?" asked Mrs. Ripon.

"Wait a bit," said Jack Sheppard; "you women are in such a hurry to hear everything. You must give a fellow time to tell a story in his own fashion, or not hear it at all."

"Very well, Jack; go on—I will not interrupt you again."

"Well, then, as I was saying, Tom told me to look well at the ceiling of my cell; and, after climbing up and getting many a tumble in the attempt, I managed to reach the ceiling, and to my delight, there was the stone slab sure enough, but it was anything but an easy matter to push it up. I did succeed, however, in satisfying myself that it was loose, and only wanted easing all round, in order to get it into good working condition."

"And did you begin, then?" inquired Mrs. Ripon.

"There you go, again, interrupting! How could I begin without anything to work with? I had to scramble down again, and after half an hour's hard work, I succeeded in getting an immense holdfast out of the wall, which, I suppose had done duty as a gallows many a time for poor wretches who preferred that to Tyburn Tree;

and with that I intended to set to work in good earnest, and make my way into Tom's cell."

"Which you did," said Mrs. Ripon, forgetting, in the interest she took in Jack Sheppard's story, his dislike to being interrupted.

"Now, I tell you what it is, Mrs. Ripon," he cried; "if you put me out again, I'll tell you nothing, but leave you to find out everything for yourself."

Mrs. Ripon promised to be more on her guard in future, and Jack Sheppard continued.

"As I was saying, when I possessed myself of the iron holdfast, I intended to commence operations at once, but I was brought to a standstill by hearing Jonathan Wild's voice just outside my cell-door. I just had time to hide my holdfast when Wild entered, looking uglier than ever."

"The wretch!" said Mrs. Ripon.

"On that point I think we are both pretty well agreed," said Jack Sheppard; "he is a wretch, and no mistake!"

"What did he want?" asked Mrs. Ripon.

"Oh, only to make a little compact with me—namely, that if I would share with him all my profits for the next two years, that he would undertake to hold me harmless."

"And did you consent?"

"Why, how else was I to get out of his clutches? Consent! Of course I consented, but I wanted to speak to Tom first, so I said I wanted a little time to consider."

"That was well."

"I got rid of Jonathan Wild as quickly as I could, you may be sure; for I had no wish to pass another night under his roof, if I could possibly help it."

"It was very good of you, though, to wait merely for the sake of seeing my poor boy," said Mrs. Ripon.

"Not at all. Tom would have done quite as much for me any day. So, as I was going to say, when you interrupted me, Mrs. Ripon, as soon as Jonathan Wild left my cell, I set to work——"

"And did you succeed in pushing up the stone, Jack?"

"To be sure I did. With Tom's assistance we soon got it up sufficient for me to be able to creep into his cell, and then it was that Tom gave me that paper, and told me to tell you that it was only his hat and boots that he hung up in his cell, and that so startled Captain Heron."

Mrs. Ripon gave a cry of joy.

"And now, Mrs. Ripon," added Jack Sheppard, "I've told you all you want to hear, haven't I?"

"Well, I should like to know how you got away from Jonathan Wild's."

"Why, that was very easily accomplished," replied Jack Sheppard. "I only had to make my way back to the cell, where Jonathan Wild left me when he promised to favour me with his company in the evening, to learn what my decision was with regard to the little arrangement he and I had made in the morning."

"And did he see you as he promised?" asked Mrs. Ripon.

"Trust him for that! Of course he did, when there was a chance of his getting half my winnings, and none of the risks; so I told him that I had made up my mind to accept the offer, and

was content to hang at the end of the two years."

"But you didn't mean it, Jack?"

"Mean it! Now really, Mrs. Ripon, here have I been talking all this time to one I supposed to be a sensible woman, and I find, after all, that you are as green as a dairy-maid that has never left her own village. Mean it!—why of course I didn't mean it! I don't consider that there is any occasion to keep faith with such a man as Jonathan Wild; so, you see, it made no difference to me whether I said yes or not."

"I see—I see! What did Jonathan Wild say?"

"Oh, he was mightily pleased, and said a good deal about Tom being a fool for not agreeing to his terms as I had done."

"Then Tom would not consent?"

"No; Tom is a good deal too romantic, and has notions of honour which I suppose he has imbibed from Captain Heron."

Mrs. Ripon made no reply to this remark of Jack Sheppard, as she feared that it might lead to questions she would find it difficult to answer with regard to Felix Heron.

After a pause, Mrs. Ripon said, "I wish I knew what Captain Fantome intends to do with regard to Tom."

"Captain Fantome? Who's he?"

"Why, that gentleman who was here when you came in."

"Oh, I remember now. Is he a friend, then? He did seem to take a great interest in that bit of a note I brought to you from Tom."

"Yes, yes—a great friend," said Mrs. Ripon, with a little confusion. "I dare say he is going to see what can be done for him."

"Well, I wish he would come and tell us if he has been able to get Tom out of that horrid Little Newgate of his. Upon my word, I think I would rather be in the real prison, for then one might have a chance of getting acquitted; but when you get into Jonathan Wild's clutches, one never knows how long he may keep you, to revenge himself upon you for some private grievance of his own."

Mrs. Ripon stepped into the shop and looked from the window.

"I don't see any signs of him returning," she said; "but I've no doubt he will find some means of letting me know if anything has been done for Tom."

"Very likely, Mrs. Ripon; and now I will just go out a bit, and look about me, for I shall begin to-night my career on the road, the fruits of which Jonathan Wild believes are to be shared with him. Ha, ha, Jonathan! you should have kept me when you had me so snug there in Newgate Street."

And whistling a gay air, Jack Sheppard passed out at the shop door.

CHAPTER CCLXVI.

FELIX HERON SEEKS THE ADVICE OF AN ATTORNEY.

FELIX Heron was not long in making his friend the young Earl of Bridgewater aware of the state of affairs with regard to Tom Ripon, and to-

JACK SHEPPARD PAYS A VISIT TO HIS OLD FRIEND, TOM RIPON, IN NEWGATE.

Presented Gratis with No. 84, of the New Edition of EDITH IN the Sequel to Edith the Captive; or, the Robbers of Epping Forest.

gether they went and obtained an order for his release.

Another half-hour saw the two friends again standing before the door of the great thief-taker, and demanding admittance.

This time the man on the lock seemed inclined to be rather insolent.

"Now then, gents, what's your pleasure?"

"This," said Felix Heron, showing him the order of release for Tom. "We wish to see Mr. Wild immediately."

The man looked first at one and then at the other.

"Mr. Wild?"

"Yes," replied Felix Heron, impatiently.

The man opened the door, and showed them into what Jonathan Wild was pleased to call his office.

In a few minutes, Jonathan Wild made his appearance.

"I have come, sir," said Felix Heron, "to insist upon your releasing Tom Ripon, whom you have detained in your custody illegally."

"Oh, certainly," began Wild: "I am quite willing to release him upon proper authority."

"Then you have that authority," said the Earl of Bridgewater, again showing the order of release.

Wild smiled hideously, and opening a door, shouted out "Jenkins!"

"Yes, sir!" replied a voice.

There was a whispered conference outside the door of the room in which Felix Heron and the Earl of Bridgewater were, and then they heard Jonathan Wild say aloud, "Go and fetch Tom Ripon; he is released by order of a judge."

There was a look of anxiety upon the face of Felix Heron during those few minutes which elapsed while the man Jenkins was gone to execute the order which had been given him by Jonathan Wild.

In about the space of ten minutes footsteps were heard, however, outside the door.

Felix Heron moved towards it, and in another second Tom Ripon had fallen on his knees before him, clasping his hands over his face, saying, "Oh, I did not deserve this!"

"Hush Tom!—hush!" said Felix Heron. Then, turning to Wild, he said, "Mr. Wild, you understand that Tom goes with us."

"Oh, yes—he leaves the house," said Wild, dryly.

"Come, then—do not let us waste more valuable time here."

Felix Heron laid his hand upon Tom's shoulder, and led him towards the door.

There were six or eight of Wild's men stationed in the passage.

"Open!" shouted Felix Heron, "and give us free egress."

The man exchanged glances with Jonathan Wild.

"Open, I say!" again shouted Felix Heron.

The door was flung open, and the Earl of Bridgewater led the way, followed by Felix Heron and Tom Ripon, the former still keeping his hand upon the shoulder of Tom, as though he feared some treachery even then.

They had taken two steps over the threshold when Jonathan Wild ran up, and shouted in his highest accents, "Bull-dogs, do your duty! I arrest Tom Ripon for highway robbery! In with him to Newgate—in with him to Newgate! Ha, ha! He is released from Jonathan Wild's house, but only to enter Newgate, where it will go hard with him, or my name is not Jonathan Wild! Ha! ha!"

Felix Heron and the Earl of Bridgewater knew it would be in vain to resist under the circumstances, and they became the unwilling witnesses of the capture of Tom by some eight or ten of Jonathan Wild's myrmidons.

Felix Heron was pale as death, but turning to Tom he whispered something in his ear, which seemed to bring him some comfort, for the boy raised his head, and looking defiantly at Jonathan Wild, he said, "I'm ready, Johnny. I'm sorry you were so disappointed at finding that I would not turn highwayman and take you into partnership. I could not think of mixing myself up with any but honest men, you see."

"Take him away—take him away!" roared Wild, now thoroughly beside himself with rage; —"take him away, I say! He shall hang—hang —hang, as sure as my name's Jonathan Wild!"

It would have been useless attempting to do battle against such amazing odds, and Tom Ripon allowed himself to be quietly led away by the myrmidons of Jonathan Wild.

A few seconds merely sufficed to bring them within the precincts of Newgate; and, with no very gentle hands, Tom was consigned to one of, perhaps, the gloomiest cells in that gloomy building.

It was with a heavy heart that poor Tom looked about him when he found himself alone, for the sweet feeling which had pervaded his whole being in fancying himself once more at liberty, and with the assurance that he had Captain Heron's forgiveness for exposing his valued Daisy to so much peril, now rendered the loneliness of his cell particularly depressing.

Tom now took a survey of his prison cell.

It was almost a square chamber, lighted but by a grated window high up in the roof, and through the iron bars of which the bright sunlight had never been known to enter.

Tom flung himself down upon a heap of straw that was in one corner of the cell, and began to think over his situation.

"Well," cogitated Tom, "I'm in for it now, that's certain. Jonathan Wild can hang me if he is so minded, and I know I'm not a favourite of his. Well, it can't be helped, I suppose; and yet I should like to live a little longer, too."

Tom was young, and to the young death is always appalling; but when that death is to be a violent one, no wonder that they should shrink from it.

The day following, Friday, Tom Ripon knew he was to be put upon his trial; and, in his own mind, he had quite determined that his end was close at hand.

"Well," he said to himself, as he flung himself once more upon the straw, "it's no use making one's self miserable before the time. I'll try and see what a little sleep will do."

Thus saying, Tom made himself as comfortable as it was possible to do upon his rough couch, and was soon in a sound sleep.

In that dreamless sleep we will leave him, while we return to Felix Heron, who, we have seen, had been so bitterly disappointed in his efforts to rescue his faithful young follower from the dilemma in which he had placed himself.

Felix Heron, then, after taking leave of his friend, the Earl of Bridgewater, made his way to Whitcombe House.

Ogle was waiting very impatiently, in the hope of seeing his favourite, Tom, return, accompanied by Felix Heron.

It was almost ludicrous to observe the look of severity he assumed for the occasion; but when he saw Captain Heron returning alone, the expression on his countenance quickly changed to one of alarm.

"Alone, Captain?" was all Ogle could say.

"Yes, Ogle," replied Felix Heron. "The boy is now a prisoner in Newgate."

Ogle looked concerned, but Felix Heron passed him quickly as he mounted the grand staircase, anxious as he was to talk the matter over with Edith.

Edith was as much concerned as Ogle had been, and, for the moment, could think of nothing that could be done to aid Tom in his present perilous situation.

"What do you intend to do, Felix?" she asked, as she looked up into the thoughtful face of her husband.

"I scarcely know, Edith," he replied. "That man, Jonathan Wild, can so easily get the boy convicted and condemned, that nothing but a very bold step can possibly save him."

Edith turned pale, and putting her arm lovingly round the neck of Felix Heron, she said, "You will not run any more risks, Felix, now that we are on the threshold of quietness and peace?"

"Not unnecessarily, my Edith; but I am quite sure that you would not wish to see me stand idly by while that faithful, though reckless, boy perishes on the scaffold."

"I had not thought of that, Felix," said Edith. "No, that must not be; at any hazard you must make an effort to save him. But what is that effort to be?"

After a moment's pause, Felix Heron spoke again.

"I have been thinking, Edith, that you, too, would like to assist me in saving Tom."

"Yes—oh, yes! This is kind of you to let me share your danger—if danger there be."

"Nay, dearest," replied Felix, "I hope there may be no danger—but of that we will take our chance."

"Yes—oh, yes!"

"Well, then, I propose that you and I go as witnesses at Tom's trial to-morrow."

"As witnesses, Felix?"

"Yes; I will disguise myself as an old colonel; and you, Edith, must hide these luxuriant tresses," continued Felix Heron, as he fondly stroked the glossy curls that fell in such rich masses about her lovely face.

"Why, Felix?" asked Edith.

"Because, my Edith, you must personate the wife of the aforesaid Colonel Travers, you know."

"Willingly—most willingly," said Edith.

"Then let it be so arranged. Until I return, Edith, you can busy yourself in making what preparations you think necessary for the new role you have to play."

"Are you going to leave me, then?" asked Edith, in a tone of anxiety.

"Only for a short time, while I consult a lawyer as to the best way of being of service to Tom. I will return in a very short space of time. So now farewell, dearest."

Felix Heron made his way at once to a house in the vicinity of the Temple, to the chambers of a lawyer at once famed for his acuteness and eccentricity.

Felix Heron was admitted at once to the presence of Mr. Dobbs.

As he entered the apartment, the old lawyer, without raising his eyes from a sheet of parchment, which seemed to be engaging all his attention, said, in a quick, impatient tone of voice, "Now, sir; your business! My time is valuable."

Felix Heron, then, in as few words as possible, detailed candidly to the old lawyer the position of affairs with regard to Tom Ripon.

"Humph!" was the only sound that came from the lips of Mr. Dobbs when Felix Heron had finished speaking.

"I have stated the case to you," said Felix Heron, "without any reservation, and want your opinion."

"I am to understand that you wish, if possible, to defeat the ends of justice, and to aid and assist this young scamp——"

"Hold, sir!" interrupted Felix Heron. "I did not come here to have any such comments made. I came here to ask your advice as to the best means of rescuing a youth from the hands of the law, who, beyond indulging in a boyish frolic, has done nothing to make himself inimical to it."

"Boy's frolics!" ejaculated the lawyer.

"Yes," added Heron; "although, doubtless, to legal eyes they assume the magnitude of crimes of importance."

The lawyer half closed his eyes, and looked inquiringly at Heron.

"Perhaps, then," he said, "you will have no objection to define more particularly what these 'boy's errors' consisted of?"

Heron found that he was under the close scrutiny of vigilant eyes, and the natural disposition he had to be perfectly frank upon all subjects induced him now to make a confidence with this man that he otherwise would have shrunk from, inasmuch as by so doing he was certainly bearing a kind of evidence against Tom Ripon.

But after the pause of a few seconds Heron spoke.

"Emulating," he said, "the example of some of those adventurous men who have gone upon the road, with nothing but a good horse and a bold heart to sustain them, this boy, for he is little more, committed some follies on the highway."

The lawyer nodded.

"I understand," he said, gravely. "He is charged with highway robbery."

"I presume as much," replied Heron; "but I have not the particulars of the charge, and know little further concerning it, except that it will be supported by Jonathan Wild."

"An excellent support to any charge. But as a criminal lawyer it is my duty to know the particulars of every charge."

Mr. Dobbs scribbled something on a small scrap of paper, and touched some mysterious bell-handle that was in some way connected with his table.

A strange, cadaverous looking creature, who was his clerk, made an instant appearance, and almost as instantly disappeared with the scrap of paper in his hand.

A slight shade of suspicion passed across the mind of Captain Heron as he noticed these mysterious proceedings of the attorney. Was it possible that this man had penetrated his disguise, and knew who he really was?

Heron was not a likely man to be frightened at the shadow of a danger, so he sat composedly waiting for what might next occur, but keeping at the same time a watchful glance upon the attorney.

The cadaverous-looking clerk returned in about five minutes, and laid before his master a short memorandum.

"Here," said Mr. Dobbs, "are the particulars of the charge. Thomas Ripon, accused of stealing a gold snuff-box of Mr. Benjamin Mason, in the Oxford Road, in the evening of the fourth of September. Which charge is to be supported by the testimony of Mr. Mason himself, who will recognise the culprit; and by the further evidence of Jonathan Wild, who will produce the gold snuff-box, which he found upon the prisoner."

The lawyer looked up in the face of Felix Heron with a smile, as he read this memorandum.

"I would wager my life," cried Heron, "the charge is false."

"Of that there really cannot be the smallest doubt!"

"You think so?"

"I know it. It has all the charming simplicity of one of Mr. Wild's cases, and a conviction is almost certain."

"But ——"

"Hear me out, Captain Fantome. I have no doubt whatever but that there is no such person as Mr. Benjamin Mason, and I dare say the gold snuff-box that Jonathan Wild will produce is one that has done duty under similar circumstances often before."

"This is monstrous, and surely only needs to be exposed in court, not only to ensure the immediate acquittal of the poor boy, but the utter confusion and destruction of Jonathan Wild."

"Not so fast, Captain—not so fast. All these little desirable events are by no means so likely to follow as you suppose. We must meet craft with craft. Jonathan Wild has the ear of the court, and no one would be listened to for a moment who should charge him with perjury and subornation of evidence. We must meet craft by craft; and perhaps borrowing an idea from even Wild himself, we may, by fighting him with his own weapons, defeat him."

Heron rose, and paced the lawyer's room in excitement.

"To what a depth of infamy," he exclaimed, "has the criminal jurisprudence of this country sunk, when such a man as Jonathan Wild holds human lives at his disposal in this terrible fashion!"

CHAPTER CCLXVI.

TOM RIPON IS VISITED IN NEWGATE BY JACK SHEPPARD.

THE lawyer, with something of a covert smile upon his face, allowed the indignation of Felix Heron to expend itself before he spoke again.

"Look you, sir," he then said: "your object is not to vindicate the law, or even to awaken society to a knowledge of Jonathan Wild's demerits. All you wish at present is to save this boy, Tom Ripon?"

"True—true! That is the object. Let us abide by it."

"Then what say you to an *alibi!*"

"My own thought; and I would resort to such a proceeding a thousand times more cheerfully now that I feel the specific charge against which I set it up is a false one."

"Good!" added the lawyer. "That is what I call meeting craft with craft, and fighting Jonathan Wild with his own weapons. To dispute with him about the charge would be vain; it is so exceedingly simple and so well supported. Not a single word should be said about Mr. Benjamin Mason not being a respectable man, and not being robbed of his gold snuff-box; but the whole defence should confine itself to the allegation that the prisoner at the bar could not possibly have committed the robbery, in consequence of having been at least twenty miles distant on the evening in question, in company of other persons."

"Your advice," said Heron, "singularly chimes in with my own idea. I thought of personating a gentleman who has no more real existence than the Mr. Benjamin Mason who will be produced by Jonathan Wild. I thought of appearing in this boy's favour, and calling myself Colonel Travers."

"An excellent name. But we should require two witnesses for the *alibi.*"

"My wife!"

"Ah! better still. A lady witness in such a case does wonders; and I think, sir, under these circumstances, I can promise you an acquittal of the boy. But Jonathan Wild will be furious, and as soon as he can be removed from Newgate he should be conveyed at once to a place of safety and secrecy. And now, sir, if you will come to me with the lady to-morrow morning at an early hour, we will go into the minute particulars of the defence, and counsel shall be instructed accordingly."

Felix Heron's hopes ran high of now being able to rescue his faithful and attached follower from the extreme peril which beset him.

The means by which this safety was to be accomplished were certainly not those which he would have chosen had much variety of action been open to him.

Notwithstanding, however, all its perils, neither Heron nor Edith would permit themselves to shrink for a moment from the mode that presented itself of saving Tom.

And while these anxious exertions were being made for his safety, Tom's position in the miserable cell of Newgate was anything but a pleasant one.

The cell to which Tom was consigned had evidently not been tenanted by any human being for a long space of time, for the rats and other vermin had evidently long considered it as part and parcel of their own particular domain.

The stones of which the flooring was composed were damp and slippery, and the heap of straw which lay in one corner had turned almost black.

Tom sighed deeply as he looked around him, and compared in his own mind his present quarters with those he had lately been in the habit of considering his own at Whitcombe House.

The allowance of bread and water which had been brought to him by his surly and brutal gaoler were still untasted by him, but the rats, who scarcely seemed to notice him, were not so fastidious.

Tom began to dread the approach of night, for there was something truly appalling in the thought that darkness would now soon be added to his other discomforts.

He rose and paced his cell, for it was impossible for him to sit any longer; and Tom thought, too, that in all probability the rats might be scared away if he were not so still and quiet as he had been.

He had paced to and fro the narrow confines of his prison-house perhaps some twenty or thirty times, when he was roused from his unenviable reflections by hearing approaching footsteps.

At that moment, even the presence of Jonathan Wild himself would have been hailed by Tom with a feeling almost akin to pleasure.

The footsteps approached nearer.

Then they paused outside the door of the cell.

There was a rattling of keys, and then one was thrust noisily into the keyhole of Tom's cell, and two persons were visible.

One was the gaoler; the other was Jack Sheppard.

Tom almost screamed with joy as he beheld the face of his friend, and, grasping his hand, he cried, " This is kind, indeed, Jack !"

" Hold hard !" replied Jack Sheppard. " Do you think you've got hold of a pump handle ? Don't wring my arm off !"

Tom's habitual joyousness returned instantly that he found the gaoler had left them alone together.

" Have you seen the Captain ?—Captain Fantome, I mean," was the first question that burst from Tom's lips.

" Well, I can't say I haven't seen him," replied Jack Sheppard; " but that's about all I can say; for as soon as he read your bit of a letter to your mother——"

" Did he see it, then ?"

" Why, yes ; there was no help for it. He happened to be at the old crib in Wardour Street when I got there, and seemed to be the only person capable of using their wits at that moment."

" What did he say ?" asked Tom, who was much more interested than Jack Sheppard had any idea of.

" Oh, you must know your mother, or the old gal, as you call her, was in a great taking about you, and was not able to read a word of your letter; but in order to rouse her I just said, ' Don't go on so, Mrs. Ripon, about Tom being dead; he's alive and kicking, and has sent you that note to let you know all was right.' "

" Yes—yes ?" said Tom.

" Well, as I was saying, as soon as ever I mentioned your name, this Captain——what do you call him ?"

" Fantome—Captain Fantome."

" Well, this Captain Fantome picked up the letter which your mother had let fall, and before we could prevent it, and without saying ' With your leave,' he read it off, and was out of the house like a shot. I hope, Tom, it's all right—eh ?"

" Oh, yes," said Tom, " I'm glad he read it. You don't think, Jack, he seemed very angry with me ?"

" No. I should say not," replied Jack; " but what does it matter whether he is angry or not ? Now, if it had been Captain Heron——"

" Don't talk about him, Jack," said Tom; " if he knew what a simpleton I had been, I am sure he would never forgive me !"

" Nonsense, Tom ! Why, Captain Heron would only say that you had followed his example ; and you couldn't have a better, you know !"

Tom sighed.

He could not hide from himself the fact that he had given Felix Heron great cause to be very much displeased with him; and that thought, more than anything else, it was that weighed upon his spirits. He now gladly turned the conversation by asking Jack Sheppard how it was he had obtained admission to his cell.

" Ah, that's the question you should have asked before, Tom !" replied his friend. " I am sent here by Jonathan Wild !"

" By Jonathan Wild ?"

" By Jonathan Wild !" added Jack Sheppard.

Tom looked inquiringly into the face of Jack Sheppard.

" Yes, Tom," he added, " Jonathan Wild is still willing to take you into partnership, if you will accept his terms."

" What, give him half my profits on the road for two years, and then consent to be hanged at Tyburn ? Never !"

" Well," said Jack, " if I did not think it rather a foolish resolve, I should say it was brave; but why don't you accept his terms, Tom ? You needn't consider yourself bound to keep your promise to such a man as Jonathan Wild, you know !"

Tom had his own thoughts upon this subject, and his ideas of honour and truthfulness, which in all probability he had imbibed from his much-loved master, never forsook him.

" I couldn't do it, Jack; don't ask me ! I know Jonathan Wild will hang me; he may as well do so at once, instead of waiting for two years."

As Tom said this, Jack Sheppard could not but be struck with the dejection so unwonted which was depicted in Tom's face.

" Come, cheer up, old fellow !" he said, bringing his hand down heavily upon Tom's shoulder; " never say die ! There is hope yet; and if you think I care so much for Johnny Wild as to leave you here, when I may possibly get you out, you mistake Jack Sheppard !"

Tom shook his head.

" Your will, Jack, may be good to get me out, but it's easier said than done !"

" Perhaps."

There was a look of excitement and expectation about the eyes of Jack Sheppard and Tom now regarded his proceedings with not a little surprise.

Jack began deliberately to undress, singing, as he did so, a popular ditty, which was said to have been composed by himself.

"Now, Tom," he cried, "what's to hinder you from changing about a little? You've tried the road as a highwayman, and perhaps the grabs have begun to know you a little in that character. I have cracked a crib or two, and the name of Jack Sheppard is beginning to be rather often in the mouths of the nabs. I mean to make a great name yet; so, you see, I shall be rather particular who I lend it to. But you're an old friend, and that alters the case."

"Ah!" cried Tom, "I begin to understand you!"

"To be sure you do! Stand up; ain't we

both of a height? Ay, as near as a hair. Now, Tom, dress yourself in my togs, and as Jack Sheppard you may pass out of Newgate, while I take a little rest here."

Tom made a dart at Jack's clothes; and then, as quickly again dropping them to the floor of the cell, he turned and spoke to Sheppard with emotion.

"And what's to become of you if I do this thing?"

"Become of me?"

"Yes, Jack; why should I leave you here to pay, perhaps, the penalty of my acts?"

"No such thing, Tom. They can't hang a fellow for helping a pal to escape; and Jonathan Wild looks upon me as by far too valuable a property to let lie waste in Newgate."

"If I were but sure of your safety, Jack."

"Make yourself sure of it; and to convince you that I feel assured on that point, just say where I shall meet you to-night at midnight, and I will be there."

"On that condition," said Tom, "I consent; only I should like to see Wild's face when he comes here and finds you instead of me."

Neither Tom Ripon nor Jack Sheppard were persons likely to be long at their toilette, so that their transformation was soon completed.

"That'll do," said Sheppard; "it's capital! Now all you've got to do, as you pass through the hall of Newgate, is to put your hands in your pockets and whistle. I suppose you can do that?"

"Rather," said Tom with a smile.

"Then let it be the tune I was singing just now, and the chances are twenty to one not a word will be said to you."

"But if one of the warders should speak?"

"Don't answer, Tom."

"Not answer?"

"No, I've arranged all that."

"How could you arrange it?"

Jack laughed.

"Look you here, Tom! I've been in and out of Newgate half a dozen times to-day, just on purpose to see how this little job could be carried out. Some one or other of the fellows on the lock, or about the prison, has always had something to say to me, but I didn't answer them, and only went on whistling all the same. They know very well it's all right between me and Jonathan, and that some fine day he will tell them I'm to be grabbed the next time I cross the threshold of Newgate, but that won't be yet awhile; and so, you see, all you've got to do is to keep on whistling."

"That's easy."

"It is; so now be off with you at once!"

Tom held out his hand.

"Jack, when I forget all you've done for me, I shall at the same time forget that my name's Tom Ripon."

They shook hands heartily.

"Now be off with you!" added Jack. "I shall consider that in five minutes you are clear of the old Stone Jug."

"I hope so."

Jack Sheppard, as he uttered the last words, rapped at the door of the cell to be let out.

The heavy tread of the turnkey in the stone-paved passage beyond was immediately heard.

"All's right!" cried Sheppard.

The door of the cell was flung open, and Tom walked out.

He began to whistle.

The turnkey was rather loquacious, and wished evidently to talk to the supposed Jack Sheppard.

"Well, Jack," he said, "I suppose you've squared everything with Mr Wild, for I hear you're to come in and out of Newgate as often as you like?"

Tom only whistled.

"I suppose," added the turnkey, "that's an old pal of yours yonder?"

Tom still whistled.

"He's booked for a dance upon nothing, for I've heard Mr. Wild speaking of him to the Governor; and he said as he was a young cock that was done crowing, which means, I take it, that next Monday is to be the end of him."

Tom whistled louder than ever.

"Well, you're an odd fellow," said the turnkey. "There's no getting a word out of you—good, bad, or indifferent. But here's the end of my beat. Jarvis is on the lock."

Tom was an adept at whistling. It was just the sort of useless accomplishment he was sure to pick up to perfection, and the vaulted passages of Newgate echoed to the clear tones which he produced.

The vestibule of the prison was reached.

A couple of turnkeys were lolling half asleep upon the wooden benches which were placed there for their accommodation.

The "man on the lock," as he was technically called, sat upon a high stool, dangling his legs to and fro in such close proximity to the wicket, that he had nothing to do but to stretch out his hand to turn the key in the lock.

Tom, according to the instructions given him by Jack Sheppard, thrust his hands deep into the skirt pockets of his coat, and imitating exceedingly well the somewhat swaggering gait of Jack, he crossed the vestibule.

"Oh, you're off, are you?" said the man o. the lock.

Tom whistled more loudly and clearly than before.

The two turnkeys who were half asleep looked up drowsily.

"What sort of game's that," growled one, "to keep on whistling in that sort of way like a blackbird, instead of making yourself agreeable, eh?"

Tom gave a slight kick at the wicket gate, as an intimation to Jarvis that he wished to be let out.

"Oh, be off with you; you stun a fellow with all that whistling!"

The highly polished key was turned in the lock.

The little wicket opened noiselessly on its well-oiled hinges.

Tom considered himself free.

He ceased the whistling, and made a spring to clear the steps at a bound, and get outside of the atmosphere of Newgate.

An exclamation of wrath and fright came from some one at the moment, and Tom found that instead of leaping right on to the pavement of the Old Bailey, he had encountered some one who was just ascending the steps, and who, reeling with the shock of the collision, very nearly fell backwards.

"Out of the way," cried Tom, "or it will be worse for you?"

"Not so fast, my young spark!" cried the stranger. "Hilloa, there! Break gaol—break gaol! Are you all drunk or asleep in Newgate to-night?"

Tom knew the voice now.

His heart failed him for a moment, and he lost strength.

Who but Jonathan Wild could utter those tones?

The plan of escape had failed at the moment, apparently, of its success.

Before Tom could recover from the shock of the surprise that Wild's most unexpected presence had given him, the active and powerful thief-taker flung his arms round him, and fairly carried him back into the vestibule of the prison.

CHAPTER CCLXVII.

TOM RIPON ESCAPES FROM NEWGATE, BUT IS RE-
CAPTURED BY JONATHAN WILD.

"Just in time, it seems!" shouted Wild, as he
flung Tom from him, evidently with the intention
of doing him some physical injury upon the stone
floor of the hall of Newgate

But Tom was rapidly recovering his self-possession.

Slipping to Wild's feet, he seized him by the
ankle, and before Jonathan could tell what he
was about, he fell backwards, striking his head
against the projecting key in the wicket with
a force that would have fractured anybody else's
skull.

But Jonathan Wild's cranium was peculiarly
constructed; and although he looked a little confused for a few seconds, no further mischief
seemed to be done.

And Wild was so accustomed to these little
episodes in his professional existence, that they
had ceased to affect him much.

His anger was much more directed against the
turnkeys than against Tom.

The volley of abuse he levelled at their heads
transcends all description.

But if Wild's head was of such a construction
that it resisted external impressions, the feelings
of the turnkeys in the vestibule of Newgate
seemed to partake of the same character.

The abuse and imprecations of Jonathan Wild
had not the least effect upon them.

They took a hint from Jack Sheppard and
Tom Ripon, and after Wild had gone on for
some few minutes, they all took to whistling, in
which Tom joined.

"Silence!" roared Wild.

The whole party only whistled the more
intensely.

"I'll have you all hung this session or the
next!"

The whole ceased.

This was no idle threat on the part of a man
like Jonathan Wild.

"Well, Mr. Wild," said one, "we couldn't help
it."

"Not help it, three lazy scoundrels that you
are, to let a prisoner walk out of Newgate! And
you, Jarvis, too—you on the lock, you that
pretend to be a smart man!"

"Bless you, Mr. Wild, I knew him all the
while," said Jarvis. "I only meant to let him
get half down the steps, and then I could have
nabbed him again as safe as bricks."

"Bah!" cried Wild; "tell that to some fool
like yourself. Take Ripon back to his cell again.
Stop—let me look at him. Oh! I see how it is
now; it's that rascal Sheppard. I'll have them
both hung now. Let me see—let me see!"

Wild took out his pocket-book.

"Ah, yes, to be sure—yes! No. 67 Lincoln's
Inn Fields, entered on the night of the fourteenth
of August; and a basket of silver plate stolen.
Nobody knows who did the job. It will fit Jack
Sheppard, though, very well."

"No," said Tom, "that won't do, Wild. It is
true that Jack was helping me to escape, and he
is not the fellow to deny it, but all's fair in these

cases. You've nabbed me again, so now be satisfied."

"But I can't."

"Nonsense! You want to be called Jonathan
Wild the Great; don't make yourself out Jonathan
Wild the Little, nor think the worse of a fellow
like Jack Sheppard, because he tried to help a
friend at a pinch."

"Bah! Bo!"

"He won't be the worse bargain for you,
Jonathan, for the time you have him on that
account."

Wild reflected.

It was evident that the words of Tom had
some effect upon him.

"Idiots!" he cried, as he turned towards the
officers; "idiots! Take Ripon back to his cell,
where I fancy you will find Jack Sheppard, and
who you will take by the collar, and kick out of
Newgate. Look to it. You know your duty
now, and I leave you to perform it."

Wild left the vestibule of Newgate by the door
that led towards the Governor's house, and
which he opened with the master-key he had
possession of.

The turnkeys and warders had no resource,
whatever might have been their private feelings
upon the occasion, but to carry out Wild's instructions.

Tom Ripon was conveyed back to his cell, and
Jack Sheppard, without being permitted to exchange more than a few words with him, was
hustled out of Newgate.

"That's over!" said Tom, as he flung himself
on the straw that did duty for a bed in that
miserable cell; "that's over; and I don't suppose
I shall live long enough to be able to do so much
for Jack Sheppard as he has tried to do for me
to-night. I wonder how a fellow feels after he's
hung. Queer, I suppose; but I don't see that that
should hinder him going to sleep the night before
—no, it isn't exactly the night before, for this is
Thursday, and Monday's hanging morning. Oh,
if I was but on Hounslow Heath now—or on the
Western Road with Daisy; and the moon blink-
ing in and out among the clouds, and the cool,
pleasant air coming over the fields and hay-ricks!
It won't do to think of such things: it won't do
—it won't do—it won't do! Good night!"

Tom fell fast asleep.

The Friday morning came, with all its bustle
of criminal trials at the Old Bailey.

The criminal jurisprudence of the country was
carried on at that period in a strange slip-shod
fashion.

Many a highwayman or housebreaker was
brought into court without any definite idea as
to which of his numerous offences against the
laws was to be the special one taken cognisance
of on that occasion by justice.

Tom Ripon was very much in this predicament.

That Wild intended to accuse him of highway
robbery of course he knew; but as regarded the
special act laid to his charge, he was as much a
spectator and curious listener as any one in
court.

It is difficult to say if the judges and digni-
taries of the law were aware of the system pursued by Jonathan Wild.

If they were, it was a great disgrace and

scandal to justice; although, perhaps, as regarded the real right or wrong of the matter, no great harm was done; that is to say, if we assume that human life is to be taken for crimes against property—a fact which we are very far from assuming, and which is rapidly being considered as one of the barbarisms of a past age.

The system was just this.

A notorious highwayman or a notorious burglar was apprehended.

A great deal of trouble would have been involved in actually proving some particular case against him, where he had been the malefactor.

Jonathan Wild then got up a sham case, which answered all the purpose, and saved the time of the court and the jury.

The man was hanged for something he had never done at all.

But then he had really done a hundred things of the same character, and the practical injustice was considered as nothing.

Tom's trial excited no public attention, and at about half-past eleven o'clock in the day he found himself thrust forward into the dock, to answer for his life.

In a rapid, indistinct, rambling kind of way, a short indictment was read against him.

It charged him that, in contravention of the peace of our Sovereign Lord the King, he did, by force of arms on a public highway, put in bodily fear a certain Benjamin Mason, and took from him certain properties; viz., a gold snuff-box, value nine pounds ten shillings; and one ounce of snuff, value two pence one farthing.

It was only here and there that Tom caught a word or two of this indictment, and it seemed to him that he was practically charged with stealing a pinch of snuff.

The judge put on a severe look.

"Prisoner at the bar," drawled the clerk of the arraigns, "do you plead guilty or not guilty."

"Not guilty," said Tom, "though I hardly know what it's very well about."

"Silence!"

"Silence yourself!" said Tom: "you bring a fellow here about a pinch of snuff, and then won't let him speak."

"Silence!"

"Perhaps I ought to sneeze," added Tom.

There was a laugh in court.

The judge shook his wig, and looked hard and stern at Tom.

"This dreadful levity," he said, "is ill-timed, and is calculated to convey an impression to the minds of the court and the jury very detrimental to the prisoner at the bar."

"Thank you," said Tom; "let's hear all about it; but I may as well say, to begin with, that I never took a snuff-box from Mr. Benjamin anybody; and as for an ounce of snuff——"

"Silence!"

"Prisoner at the bar," said the judge, "you will have an opportunity, either by yourself or through your counsel, of addressing the court. Until then, you must preserve silence."

One of the counsel who sat just below the judge in the inner bar rose now, and said very quietly, "I appear for the prisoner, and particularly request that he should leave the case entirely in my hands, as his counsel."

"Oh, thank you!" said Tom; "I dare say it's all right."

The counsel for the prosecution rose, and, in a hasty manner, stated the case.

He was one of those small junior counsel, who get cases of no real importance, and treat them with indifference.

Human life was cheap in his estimation; and perhaps, had the question been fairly put to him, he would almost have gone the length of saying that it would be just as well, and save a deal of trouble, to bring in the prisoner at the bar guilty upon no evidence at all.

As it was, however, he was compelled to state a case, and he did so in the briefest possible fashion.

"My lord, and gentlemen of the jury,—

"The prisoner at the bar, answering to the name of Thomas Ripon, stands accused of the heinous crime of highway robbery.

"The lives and properties of his Majesty's subjects cannot be left to the mercy of depredators of this description; and consequently, my lord, and gentlemen of the jury, we are all much indebted to the vigilant officer who has arrested this young criminal in his nefarious career.

"This specific charge consists in the fact that, on the fourth of September last past, the prisoner at the bar, on the Western Road, between the hours of half-past nine and half-past ten, assailed, and put in bodily fear, a Mr. Benjamin Mason.

"Threatening him with death, and presenting fire-arms at his head in the shape of loaded pistols, he succeeded in taking from that person one gold snuff-box.

"My lord, and gentlemen of the jury, the case is so clear, that I need not trouble you with any further observations; but being convinced that you will vindicate the majesty of the law, I proceed at once to call my witnesses."

The counsel sat down.

"Benjamin Mason!" roared the crier of the court.

A rather shabbily-attired individual stepped into the witness-box.

"Swear Benjamin Mason."

The oath was duly administered, and Benjamin Mason took it with an ostentatious kind of fervour, kissing the book with a loud smack, as if he would have called the attention of everybody in court to the fact that there could be no mistake about his being duly sworn.

"Now, sir," said the counsel. "Your name is Benjamin Mason?"

"It is."

"You are a commercial traveller, I believe?"

"Yes, sir."

"Your late uncle, Mr. Aminadab Mason, presented you with a gold snuff-box?"

"He did, sir."

"Please relate to his lordship and the gentlemen of the jury what has become of it."

Mr. Mason, after a slight cough, told his story.

"I was riding down the Western Road, about a mile and a half beyond Tyburn Gate, on the evening of the fourth of September last past, when there suddenly came, out of a shady lane, a person on horseback.

"Did he speak to you?"

"Yes, sir. He cried out, 'A fine night!' and

TOM RIPON MAKES A BOLD BUT UNSUCCESSFUL ATTEMPT TO ESCAPE
FROM NEWGATE.

Presented Gratis with No. 85, of the New Edition of EDITH HERON; the Sequel to Edith the Captive; or, the Robbers of Epping Forest.

then riding up close to me, he clapped the muzzle of a pistol right into my ear, and shouted, 'Your money or your life?'"

"What did you do then?"

"I told him I had no more money than would just pay my turnpikes to Wycombe, but that I had a gold snuff-box, which I hoped he would take, and not do me any injury."

"What happened then?"

"He took the snuff-box, and, after using some very bad language, rode away."

"Was this the snuff-box?"

From the solicitor's table, the gold snuff-box that Jonathan Wild had carefully provided to do duty on the occasion was handed up to the witness.

Mr. Benjamin Mason pretended to look at it for a few minutes with great attention.

"Can you swear to that snuff-box as being the one you were robbed of on the occasion in question?"

"I can."

"By what mark?"

"A slight injury to one of the hinges."

"Very good, Mr. Mason. Now look at the prisoner at the bar, and tell his lordship and the gentlemen of the jury if that is the person who robbed you."

Mr. Benjamin Mason turned, and took a long look at Tom Ripon, as if that were the first moment he had ascertained that such a person was in court.

"Yes!" he then exclaimed, with an air of great confidence. "I can swear to him. That was the person."

"You have no doubt about it?"

"Not the least."

"Then I don't think I need trouble you any further, Mr. Mason; but perhaps my learned friend for the defence may have something to say to you."

"Nothing whatever," replied the counsel who was retained in Tom Ripon's favour.

From that moment the prosecution knew perfectly well what the defence of Tom Ripon was to be.

An *alibi*.

But they had no possible means of confuting it, or in any way providing against it.

It was the only practical means of saving Tom Ripon, inasmuch as it took the entire question out of the hands of the prosecution, and raised a new issue of defence, which had nothing whatever to do with the mock evidence of the mock robbery.

"Call Jonathan Wild."

Wild stepped into the witness-box.

It was not often that the great thief-taker condescended to become a witness himself on any of those little occasions when he thought proper to send some one to the gallows; but, in regard to Tom Ripon, he was angry and revengeful.

He would therefore trust to no subordinate the important and conclusive evidence he intended to give.

Wild was duly sworn; but he was too old a stager at that sort of thing to over-act his part as Benjamin Mason had done.

"Now, Mr. Wild," said the counsel, "attend to me, if you please."

Jonathan made no answer, but just looked the advocate in the face.

"What do you know of this affair, Mr. Wild?"

"Simply this. I heard that several highway robberies had taken place on the Western Road, and therefore considered it my duty to investigate the matter. For every night of a whole week I patroled the road, and after much trouble at last I apprehended the prisoner at the bar."

"And what did you find upon him?"

"A gold snuff-box."

"Was this the box?"

Wild pretended to look at the box almost as attentively as Mr. Mason; and then he replied, sharply and shortly, "Yes; this is the box."

"How do you know it?"

"I made a private mark on it."

"Look at the prisoner at the bar."

Wild turned, and stared at Tom Ripon.

"Is that the person from whom you took the box?"

"It is."

"Then, my lord, and gentlemen of the jury, that is the case; and I think it is one that will tax all the ingenuity of my learned friend for the defence to answer it."

Down sat the counsel.

"I suppose there is no defence?" said the judge. "The case seems to me to be remarkably clear."

"Yes, my lord," said the counsel that Felix Heron had retained in Tom's favour, "there is a defence. Clear as the case appears, we have nothing to say to this real or pretended robbery of a gold snuff-box from a Mr. Benjamin Mason; we have nothing to say to the zeal and energy, real or assumed, of Mr. Jonathan Wild.

"No, my lord, and gentlemen of the jury, all these matters do not concern us in the least, inasmuch as one grand mistake has been committed throughout the entire affair.

"The prosecution has got hold of the wrong person."

"Oh, an *alibi?*" said the judge.

"Exactly, my lord. I am in a condition to prove, upon incontestable evidence, that the prisoner at the bar could not have been on the Western Road on the evening in question, seeing that he was in the company of credible witnesses for the whole of that period, at a place called Annerley Hall, near Epping Forest.

"The prosecution has made a mistake, and Mr. Jonathan Wild will have again to patrol the Western Road in order to effect the apprehension of the real robber of Mr. Benjamin Mason's gold snuff-box."

The counsel sat down.

"Call Colonel Travers."

"Colonel Travers!" shouted the crier of the court.

Admirably got up as an elderly gentleman, with a stoop in his gait, and partially supporting himself on a large gold-headed walking-cane, Felix Heron entered the court.

He and Edith had remained in a carriage at the door of the Old Bailey until one of the clerks of the elderly lawyer they had previously employed in Tom's favour warned them that the period of action had arrived.

CHAPTER CCLXVIII.

FELIX HERON'S PLANS ARE DEFEATED, AND TOM RIPON IS CONVICTED.

THE appearance of Felix Heron was so thoroughly gentlemanly and respectable, that every one in the court felt how important a witness such a personage must be for the defence.

The counsel for the prosecution looked at the disguised Felix Heron with great interest.

But of all persons there present on that occasion, none regarded this witness for the defence with more intense interest and curiosity than Jonathan Wild.

Well he knew that the whole of the proceedings were but a solemn farce.

Whether or not they were to end in a tragedy, so far as Tom Ripon was concerned, remained to be seen.

Felix Heron was perfectly composed and calm.

He had made up his mind that that was the only course to pursue in order to defeat the machinations of Jonathan Wild; and having once so determined, he was not the man to shrink from carrying out the affair to its utmost point.

Whether the counsel for the defence actually knew, or only suspected, that this *alibi* which was about to be proved was only set up as a justifiable kind of defence against Jonathan Wild, just as a man might seize any weapon that came to hand to ward off a dastardly attack, it is hard to say.

Certainly, however, he acted as though everything was straightforward, and both the charge and the defence were to be treated in the most serious manner.

Amid a most profound silence in the court—for the trial was now becoming interesting—the examination of Felix Heron commenced.

"Your name is Travers, sir?"

"It is."

"You hold the rank of a colonel in the army?"

"I hold rank, and I am called Colonel Travers."

"Will you be so good as to look at the prisoner at the bar?"

Felix Heron turned slowly, and looked at Tom Ripon.

Was he recognised?

Yes.

Tom stretched out his arms towards him.

"Master! master!" he cried.

Tom spoke involuntarily; but if he had been tutored for twelve months, he could not possibly have said anything more to the purpose than that.

"Certainly," said Heron, as though in anticipation of the question that was about to be asked him. "I look at the prisoner at the bar, and I know him perfectly well."

"Who is he, sir?"

"His name is Jacob Gray, and he is my servant."

"Jacob Gray!" exclaimed Tom.

"Jacob Gray!" echoed Jonathan Wild.

"Yes," said Heron, calmly.

Taking a diamond-mounted snuff-box from his pocket, Heron quietly took a pinch of its contents.

The glitter of that snuff-box—worth at least a thousand pounds, as it was—had a great effect upon the minds of the jury.

How could anybody be otherwise than highly respectable in open possession of such a costly article?

"Now, Colonel Travers, if you please," added the counsel, "will you tell us where you were on the 5th of September last past?"

"From the 3rd of September," said Heron, quietly, "to the 5th, I was at Annerley Hall, near Epping Forest; and the prisoner at the bar, my servant, was with me."

This seemed conclusive.

The judge looked at the jury, and the jury looked at the judge.

The counsel for the prosecution rose, and in a voice of mortification spoke:—

"Really, my lord, and gentlemen of the jury, this man is a perfect stranger to us. It is all very well for a Colonel Travers to come forward and vouch for the prisoner at the bar; but who will vouch for Colonel Travers?"

"Hear, hear!" shouted Wild.

"Who is that?" cried the judge, angrily.

Wild saw he had committed himself.

"Bring that person before me who interrupted the court," added the judge, "and I will send him to prison."

Wild felt his danger, but got out of it with his usual audacity.

He immediately pounced upon an unoffending bystander, and dragged him forward.

"Here, my lord, is the man."

"How dared you, sir, interrupt the court by such unseemly cries?"

"Indeed, my lord, I said nothing!"

"Lock him up. It was hardly to be expected that he would admit his offence."

"Away with him!" said Wild; and he flung the man into the arms of a couple of his own myrmidons.

"If," said Felix Heron, "it be necessary to produce any further testimony on this point, my carriage is at the door, and Lady Travers will only be too happy to add her testimony to mine on this occasion."

Jonathan Wild immediately left the court.

He wanted to see who the Lady Travers was, and what sort of equipage was at the door of the court.

He was completely baffled by the disguise of Felix Heron; and although he knew perfectly well that the whole affair was some trick in order to procure the acquittal and liberation of Tom Ripon, he was quite at a loss how to meet it or combat with it.

Chance befriended Jonathan Wild in a manner he little expected.

Almost the first person he saw at the door of the court, waiting among the crowd, was the Rev. Mortification Ripon.

Mrs. Ripon was at an eating-house in the Old Bailey, in a state of mortal trepidation and rum-punch, on Tom's account.

Mortification had been craning his long neck and body over the heads of the people to hear what was going on, when Jonathan Wild suddenly gave him a blow in the stomach, which nearly doubled him in two.

"Murder—yea, murder! As the Psalmist remarks, 'We are here to-day, and doubled up like foot-rules to morrow.' Murder! murder!"

"Silence?" said Wild, "and listen to me."

"Gracious, it's Mr. Jonathan! Avaunt! Get thee behind me, Wild! Avaunt! thou Jonathan——"

"Peace, idiot, and listen to me! Step this way!"

Wild seized Mortification by the collar, and dragged him into a remote corner.

"Yea, I am even as a lamb in the hands of the spoiler."

"Silence! You come here to look after Tom Ripon?"

"I admit it; I am not aware that that is an offence in law."

"Certainly not; and as for me, I repent."

Mortification coughed.

"Yea, he repenteth, and some extra wickedness is on hand."

"Idiot, what do you mean? But it matters not. There is no time to lose. Tom is in great danger: he is believed to be somebody else, who has committed no end of crimes; and the testimony of some witness is wanted who will convince the judge and the jury that his name is really Tom Ripon."

"Yea, I can do that."

"Of course you can. Come on. You will earn his everlasting gratitude and the gushing devotion of his mother. Ha, ha!"

Jonathan Wild gave Mortification another blow in the stomach, and then one on the back, so that the unfortunate reverend father-in-law of Tom hardly knew if he were on his head or his heels as he was hustled into court by Jonathan Wild.

"Another witness in the case, my lord," cried Wild.

The counsel for the prosecution took the hint at once, and became exceedingly anxious to examine a witness introduced by Jonathan, whose animus against the prisoner was but too apparent and well known.

Felix Heron looked with a disturbed air at the Rev. Mortification, and knew not how to warn him that he might by some indiscreet words do a world of mischief.

"What has this witness to say?" asked the judge.

"A witness, my lord," said Wild, "to the identity of the prisoner at the bar."

Heron then saw all the danger of the situation.

"The prisoner at the bar," he said, "is called Jacob Gray, and he is my servant."

Heron hoped that this would be hint sufficient for Mortification, and so it might have been under ordinary circumstances, but the punches and thumps from Jonathan Wild had been so confusing and perplexing, that Mortification, with all the will in the world to be of service to Tom, became at that moment unwillingly his greatest enemy.

"Look, sir, at the prisoner at the bar," cried the prosecuting counsel, "and if you know him name him at once to his lordship and the jury."

"Yea, it is Thomas Ripon; and who should know him better than I, his paternal relative-in-law?"

Wild uttered a hideous laugh.

Heron took two steps towards the door of the court.

"Hold!" cried Wild. "If the prisoner at the bar be indeed Thomas Ripon, then this Colonel Travers is an impostor and a false witness."

"Not so false a witness, by a thousand-fold," cried Heron, "as the arch-villain, Jonathan Wild!"

Jonathan had stretched out his hand to lay hold of Heron, but the latter, with one well-directed blow, that perfectly astonished and paralyzed the bystanders, coming as it did from what appeared to be so elderly a man, laid Jonathan prostrate and insensible on the floor of the court.

Everybody made way instinctively from before a man whose arm seemed to be like a sledge hammer.

In half a minute Heron was out of the court, and jumping into the carriage at its door, he and Edith were driven away by Ogle, who was on the coach-box, before any one had sufficiently recovered from the surprise of the action to note even which way they went.

Tom was convicted.

The trial was over in another quarter of an hour, and the bewildered Mortification found himself in the Old Bailey, with some vague conviction on his mind that he had done a deal of mischief, although what it exactly consisted in he had no possible idea.

———

CHAPTER CCLXIX.

JONATHAN WILD MAKES A HASTY EXIT FROM CASTLENEAU HOUSE.

By a circuitous route, Felix Heron, with Edith, reached—not Whitcombe House—but the residence of Lady Castleneau.

Owing to the unfortunate interposition of Mortification Ripon, the attempt to save Tom from the terrible fate that seemed now to await him had failed.

Felix Heron was in a state of mind such as no danger to himself could have produced.

He paced with disordered strides the spacious breakfast room of Castleneau House, and as neither Edith nor her aunt could suggest anything that would be likely to be beneficial to Tom Ripon, they could only for a time sympathise in silence with the emotion and the regrets of Heron.

Suddenly he turned and addressed them both.

"I blame myself," he cried, "for all this."

"Yourself, Felix? How can you blame yourself?"

"In this way, Edith: because the scheme deserved to fail. It was a bad one, and I wonder at myself now for listening to it for a moment."

"Right," cried Lady Castleneau, with her usual energy.

"Yes," added Heron, "I say the scheme deserved to fail, for it was based upon deception, untruth, and perjury, and therefore it is that I blame myself most bitterly for entering into such a plan."

Edith was silent.

The truth of Heron's words struck her most

forcibly, and for the first time she shuddered at the contemplation of what the defeated plan for the safety of Tom Ripon might have entailed upon them both.

"But understand me," added Heron; "all this by no means implies that Tom is to be left to die."

"Certainly not!" exclaimed Lady Castleneau. "I will myself immediately set about making what interest I can for his pardon and release."

"It will be all in vain," said Heron. "The King is out of town; and if he were not, I am confident that any effort in that quarter would be but waste of time."

"What is to be done?" said Edith.

"I scarcely know, but I must have time to think. Be assured, however, of one thing, Edith, and you, too, dear Lady Castleneau—that whatever is done shall be done boldly and speedily."

"Then it will succeed," replied Lady Castleneau: "and it is only necessary to take care of one thing, which is that the sacrifice is not too great for the object."

Edith turned pale at these words.

She divined well what her aunt meant, and she feared that Felix Heron would adopt some course for the purpose of saving Tom Ripon that might hurry him into the greatest personal danger.

It took but a glance from Felix Heron to divine Edith's thoughts.

"No," he said, "do not think me so rash. There is ample time for reflection, and whatever I do, although it shall be done boldly and energetically, shall not be done wildly, or without ample preparation. Let us say no more about it. Here I can make the necessary change in my apparel to restore me to the outward appearance of Captain Fantome. You, too, Edith, need no longer personate Lady Travers. We will proceed homeward, and I promise that nothing shall be done without due and full consideration."

A loud ringing at the large bell which hung over the iron gates of Castleneau House at this moment attracted general attention.

"Ah!" exclaimed Heron: "you have an impatient visitor, Aunt Castleneau."

"No," she replied, "I have no impatient visitors; and when any one rings the bell of this house in such a fashion it is more likely to be an enemy."

Whoever it was that had hold of the iron handle of the bell at the gate of Castleneau House was evidently indisposed to let it go again, for the ringing continued a full minute without interruption.

There was a small room over the hall, with a pretty stained glass window, through which a view could be obtained of the whole court-yard and the iron gates.

Heron made a sign to Edith to remain where she was, and repairing to that room, he soon saw who it was that demanded admission so noisily to Castleneau House.

Six mounted men were there, headed by Jonathan Wild himself.

Wild carried his constable's staff of office in his hand, and from the expression of his countenance, it was evident that he was intent upon the execution of some deed of anger and violence.

Old Anthony stood in the hall, doubtful whether or not to answer the violent summons for admission.

Felix Heron called down to him over the balustrades of the grand staircase.

"Let them in, Anthony," he said; "but delay time for a few minutes, if you can; there will be no danger."

Heron then hurried back to the apartment where he had left Edith and Lady Castleneau.

"It is Jonathan Wild," he said, "with some of his janissaries at his heels."

"Oh, Felix, Felix," exclaimed Edith "we are lost!"

"Not so—not so. No doubt by some means he has traced us to this house; but he will seek us as Colonel and Lady Travers, not as Captain Fantome and the Countess of Whitcombe."

Even as he spoke, Heron quickly threw off the over clothing that he wore to represent the elderly officer, Colonel Travers.

In order to increase his bulk, which aided so much in an effectual disguise, Heron wore that suit of clothes completely over his ordinary dress as Captain Fantome.

The change was therefore quickly effected.

Edith went through the same process; and before old Anthony actually opened the iron gates for admission of Jonathan Wild and his janissaries, all traces of the mock Colonel Travers and Lady Travers had disappeared completely.

The discarded clothing was thrust into one of the old box window-seats, which were curious appendages in houses of that antiquity.

Lady Castleneau looked firm and resolute.

She drew a small table towards her, and commenced her work.

Heron sat on a couch, and took up a book.

Edith sat on a small footstool at the feet of her aunt, and appeared to be winding some silk.

"Mr. Jonathan Wild!" announced Anthony, opening the door of the apartment and striving at the same time to block up its entrance.

The old man was roughly pushed aside, and Wild strode into the room.

The mark of the blow that Felix Heron had given him in the court of the Old Bailey was clearly to be seen upon his face.

He glared about him like some ferocious animal, newly issued from its den in the woods, and seeking for prey.

Lady Castleneau looked up calmly.

Felix Heron put down his book.

They all fixed their regards upon Jonathan Wild, who did not utter a word until he had searched with his eyes into every corner of the apartment.

"Your servant, Lady Castleneau!" he then cried, sneeringly; "you have visitors, but I have not the pleasure of seeing all of them."

Lady Castleneau rose with dignity, and advanced two steps.

"And how dare the ruffian Jonathan Wild," she said, "intrude himself into this house, or make question about me or my visitors?"

"That's right!" cried Wild, "carry it off with a high hand. I always admired your ladyship, you have what I call pluck; but that's not to the purpose. I want to know if you honour by

your acquaintance a certain Colonel Travers and his wife, whom he calls Lady Travers?"

"I might well refuse," replied Lady Castleneau, "to answer any questions from such a man as you, but I never deny my friends. I say yes, I do know them!"

"Good! Perhaps your ladyship will likewise be candid enough to say where they are."

"I will not!"

"Good again! The answer is sufficient, since it assures me that they are in Castleneau House."

Jonathan Wild put a whistle to his lips, and blew it shrilly.

A couple of his men came roughly into the room.

"Hark you, bull-dogs!" cried Wild. "You will not leave a nook or corner in this old crib unsearched for this Colonel Travers and the female he had with him in the coach.'

"All's right, Mr. Wild!"

No 86.—EDITH HERON.

"Are your companions well posted ?

"Yes, sir. One's at each corner of the house, and they'll warrant that not a mouse shall be able to leave the old crib without their seeing it."

"Good!" said Wild; "be off, and do your duty. I stay here!"

As he spoke, Wild jerked round a chair, and sat cross-legged upon it, resting his arms upon the back.

"Mr. Wild!" said Heron.

"Sir, to you!"

"Do you know me?"

"Ha, ha! Oh, yes, I know you! You are the widow's choice—the successor of the Earl of Whitcombe. You are the new husband of her ladyship the Countess, and I wish you joy of her. I had some faith in women before she married you. Ha, ha! Perhaps you never heard of the Baron Von Peck? I know you well enough."

"And I know you. But that is no reason why you should intrude your ugly brutality into this apartment."

"My what?"

"Your ugly brutality, I said. Do you not see there are ladies here?"

"What then?"

"You must mistake them for pigs, since a sty would be your proper place."

Wild scowled upon Heron ferociously.

"Perhaps," he said, "it would be a little wiser for Captain Fantome to keep a civil tongue in his head. There's my warrant!"

Wild, as he spoke, took from his breast pocket a slip of parchment, and flung it on to the floor.

"There's my warrant to search for and arrest Colonel Travers and whoever may be in his company."

"It may be so," said Heron, quietly; "but that does not authorize your intrusion into this apartment."

"Authorized, or not, I mean to stay here till my men make their report!"

Heron took out his watch, and laid it on the table before him.

"If you don't go in three minutes," he said, "I will throw you out at that window!"

"You—you?"

"I have said it!"

"Ha, ha! There never was but one man in the world who could do that, and he is dead and gone. The Earl of Whitcombe might have managed it, and even did it once, but Captain Fantome is quite another personage."

"You will find yourself mistaken," said Heron. "Since I have had the happiness of calling the Countess of Whitcombe my wife, I feel myself quite capable in every respect of fulfilling all the conditions of my predecessor's existence."

"Oh, you do?"

"I do. Now, Mr. Wild, are you going?"

"Not if I know it!"

"Then you shall be enlightened!"

Heron had collected all his energies for a spring, as what he intended to do was just one of those actions that depended for its success upon the rapidity with which it was accomplished.

Wild either really did not expect the attack at all, or did not expect it so soon, and therefore he could not readily disentangle himself from the chair, considering the rather complicated way in which he sat upon it.

Never had Heron exhibited more completely that tremendous latent strength which he possessed than upon this occasion.

Without a pause, and apparently without an effort, he lifted Jonathan Wild, chair and all, and dashed him through the nearest window into the garden.

"Well done!" cried Lady Castleneau. "I shall never pay a glazier's bill with such pleasure as this one."

Wild was so entirely taken by surprise that he uttered not the slightest sound, and it was well for him that the vegetation of the old garden of Castleneau House was redundant and left to grow in its own wild and wayward fashion, for otherwise he might have sustained serious injury.

As it was, he fell into the midst of some bushes, from which there certainly was a difficulty in dis-

entangling himself, but which saved him from any hurt beyond a few scratches.

Heron walked quietly back to the couch upon which he had been seated, and resumed his book.

"Hilloa!" shouted Wild from the garden, "that was not badly done, and I'm half reconciled to your marriage with the Countess of Whitcombe."

A smile crossed the face of Edith, and Heron spoke in a low voice: "The rascal measures everybody merely by his strength and courage. I cannot find in my heart to kill him, because I still believe that in his rough, brutal nature he means well to you, Edith, and our little one. The very anger he exhibits at your supposed marriage with some one else is something in his favour."

"It shows," said Lady Castleneau, "that even in the most depraved natures there is something that shows humanity is not wholly lost, and which makes the whole world kin."

"Hush!" said Heron; "he speaks again."

"Captain Fantome! Captain Fantome!"

Heron went to the window.

"I give it up for the present," added Wild. "My men can't find their game, but it won't be lost for long; and if you are an acquaintance of this Colonel Travers—which doubtless you are—you'll let him know that Jonathan Wild is on his track, and that he is as certain to be run down as ever was hunted hare."

"Begone!" said Heron. "Take yourself and your men from these premises, or worse will happen to you."

"What will you do next?"

"If I have to come down to you, I will fling you and your men, one by one, over the garden wall into Bloomsbury Fields."

"Captain Fantome!"

"Well, sir?"

"Sink me, if I don't begin to like you very much, so good day to you! We're off, and if you wish to see the little hanging match next Monday at Tyburn, just come to me, and I'll get you a capital place."

Jonathan Wild called his men together, and mounting their horses, they left Castleneau House in peace and quiet.

The determination of Felix to rescue Tom Ripon at all hazards never flagged for a moment.

On the Sunday evening previous to the execution Heron held a long and mysterious conference with Ogle.

The result of this conference was that Daisy was groomed and looked to with excessive care.

Ogle might have been seen likewise carrying to the stable a valise, such as was usually carried by horsemen, fastened to the back of the saddle.

Carefully, likewise, and taking a full quarter of an hour over the operation, Ogle loaded Heron's pistols, and placed them in the holsters.

All these preparations being completed, Ogle made himself a bed on the top of an old corn-bin, and consigned himself to repose.

It was about four o'clock on the following morning that Ogle was awakened by a step in the stable.

He was a light sleeper, and was aroused on the instant.

"Who goes there? Is it you, Captain?"

"Yes, Ogle; arouse yourself—our time has come."

Ogle was on his feet before Heron had done speaking.

"All's right, Captain! I'll have Daisy out, and the other horse, in less than two minutes."

"No, Ogle, not the other horse."

"Captain!"

"Silence, and listen to me. I have considered this matter well from the only point of view at which I ought to consider it, and starting with the proposition that cannot be gainsaid, which is that Tom Ripon must be saved at all hazards. I never yet deserted a faithful follower, and, so help me heaven, at my utmost need I never will!"

"But, Captain——"

"Hear me out. I know what you would say. Our original arrangement was that you were to go with me upon what I admit will be a hazardous enterprise. In fact, so hazardous, that the only thing which gives it a chance of success is its excessive boldness."

"Do not, Captain, take away some of those chances of success by depriving yourself of my assistance."

"I fully appreciate your assistance, Ogle; and, to prove to you that I do so, I mean to go alone."

"An odd way of proving it, Captain."

"Not so. If I succeed in saving Tom Ripon, it will be by taking everybody by surprise. If once the mounted police, and the officers of the prison who will be accompanying the procession to Tyburn, recover from that surprise, they will be more than a match for half-a-dozen well-armed men."

Ogle was silent.

"Therefore, you see," added Heron, "that although I might involve you in my own destruction, I am just as likely to succeed without you as with you."

"But still, Captain, why not take me?"

"Because I want to go with a lighter heart on this enterprise; and, by you staying here to protect Edith and our little one, I shall have that lighter heart. Are you answered, Ogle?"

"I am, Captain."

"Then saddle Daisy at once, and let me be off."

Ogle obeyed Felix Heron, but it was evidently with a heavy heart that he did so.

Daisy was carefully saddled and bridled for the road, and the little travelling valise which had been brought into the stable was strapped to the back of the saddle.

"Lead her out," said Heron. "I will mount in the little narrow street beyond."

Daisy was led out from the stable, and in a few seconds Heron was mounted.

"Farewell for the present," he said. "I go forth with your good wishes, Ogle; and be assured that, as far as human judgment goes, I am doing all for the best."

"Yes, Captain—yes," said Ogle, in a choking voice. "I will try to believe that, and may heaven protect you!"

Another moment, and Daisy and Captain Heron had gone.

Ogle closed the stable door with a deep sigh.

At that early hour of the morning the streets of London were tolerably deserted, and Heron trotted down Holborn, in the direction of the City, without meeting more than half-a-dozen casual passengers.

He was dressed in his ordinary costume as Captain Fantome, of the royal navy, but over it he wore a great coat with large lappels and a couple of capes, for such was the fashion at that time.

The great coat, however, was not worn for the purposes of concealment, but merely as an article of dress and protection against the keen morning air.

The streets of London were very ill-paved at that period, and Heron had no difficulty in finding two or three deep puddles of muddy water, to splash through which enabled him to splash both himself and Daisy in a manner to give the appearance as if he had come off a very long journey.

This accomplished, he rode up to the entrance of the inn yard on Snow Hill known as the Saracen's Head.

The inn was not open, for the earliest coach had no idea of starting for a full good two hours.

A lazy-looking ostler, however, was standing at the entrance of the archway, with a straw in his mouth, in a very contemplative mood.

Heron drew up abruptly.

"Hilloa, my friend!" he said; "you seem to have it all your own way here."

"Well, sir, I'm called Early Joe, because I'm up first."

"And what wakes you up first?"

"The York fly, sir."

"York fly?"

"Yes, sir. That's the waggon as does the distance from York to London in three nights and two days. That's what I call good going, sir—ain't it?"

"I dare say it is," said Heron; "and if you will get out of the way I will ride into the inn yard."

"All's right, sir! Going to put up here?"

"I am."

"Oh, my eye, she is a beauty! Well, I never! You are a beauty! One of a thousand, you are! It's a honour to attend on yer! You are indeed a beauty!

The under ostler was walking round and round Daisy as he uttered these expressions of admiration.

"I am glad you admire my horse," said Heron, "for it will induce you to take care of her. I want to know the exact stable in which you will put her; and, as she needs no grooming, you can give me the key."

"Just as you please, sir. I'd be as particular as you if this here beauty was mine; and I tell you what, sir—the only creature in all the world that's her equal is the famous Daisy that used to belong to Captain Heron, of Epping Forest."

"Indeed! Did you ever see her?"

"No, sir; but I've heard her spoke of."

"Well, well—that will do. I want some breakfast as soon as the house is stirring."

The ostler showed Daisy into one of the best stables of the establishment; and Heron, after taking the valise from the back of the saddle, locked the stable door carefully, placing the key in one of his pockets.

The ostler rang one of the house-bells, and a half-sleepy waiter soon made his appearance, who ushered Heron into two private apartments, a bed-room and a sitting-room.

Heron at once walked to the windows.

"A good view you have here," he said.

"Yes, sir; it's beautiful. You can see the whole of Newgate; and only last week we had two men in the pillory, and it was quite pleasant to see the crowd pelting them with rotten eggs."

"It must have been. I will sit here. Let me have breakfast as soon as possible."

"Yes, sir. Hem! by the bye, sir, you will be quite amused about half-past eleven o'clock."

"At what?"

"Why, sir, it's hanging morning; and they say there's a mere boy, who is a highwayman, though, for all that, who will be taken to Tyburn, and put out of the way. You'll see it, sir, beautiful from that window."

"I have no doubt of it," said Heron.

"Yes, sir. Breakfast, sir—directly, sir."

Heron was alone.

He paced the room impatiently.

"I shall have a long vigil here," he said: "but it was quite necessary to get here early, to avoid observation and remark."

In the course of half-an-hour a substantial repast was placed before Heron, and the waiter again expatiated upon the beauty of the view from the window.

The weary hours passed away.

It was eleven o'clock.

A great crowd of people began to assemble in front of Newgate.

Field Lane and the neighbourhood of Smithfield sent forth its hordes of ruffianism on this occasion, as the escort of the death-cart to Tyburn.

Precisely at a quarter past eleven the bell of Newgate began to toll.

A pair of gates close to the entrance of the court of Old Bailey were flung open.

A large cart lumbered forth, drawn by a black dray-horse of great size and strength.

At the bottom of the cart was a quantity of straw, and placed rather conspicuously across it was a coffin.

Then there issued from the same gateway a strong party of mounted police.

There were no less than eighteen.

One of these led a horse without a rider, and the moment he was well clear of the gateway, he went at a sharp trot round to Newgate Street.

Heron had no difficulty in divining what this meant. It was Wild's horse, being taken round to his own house for him to mount.

Then the Chaplain of Newgate came down the steps of the Governor's house, and was assisted into the cart by a couple of the officers.

A yell and a shout from the crowd next announced the arrival of a personage always unpopular.

That was the hangman, who, with his head bowed down to his breast, and only glancing up now and then with a deprecating air at the angry faces about him, mounted the front part of the cart, and took the reins in his hand.

Then there was a strange cry—half shout, half groan—as Tom Ripon was brought forth with fetters on his limbs, and with very little ceremony hustled into the cart.

Heron saw all this from the window of the Saracen's Head inn, and then he darted into the back room of the two he occupied.

The valise was open, and strewed upon the bed were various articles of clothing.

Rapidly, Felix Heron exchanged his outer garments for those which the valise had contained, and in less than five minutes he stood in the complete costume which he was in the habit of wearing in Epping Forest, when at the head of that daring band of men, who for so long a period had called him Captain.

All disguise whatever was thrown aside.

As the veritable Captain Felix Heron he now appeared, with the resolution, in his own proper character, to sally forth in the open face of day and dare the observation of all the world.

Heron took one glance again from the front window.

The Sheriff had just arrived in his gilt coach.

The procession was forming.

"Forward!" cried one of the officers.

The death-cart was put into motion, and Tom Ripon commenced what every one thought would be his ride to Tyburn.

Mounted on the horse which had been taken round to his house, Jonathan Wild joined the procession at the corner of St. Sepulchre's Churchyard, and from that moment he took the command of the whole affair.

Heron could not hear what he said, but he saw him point with his heavy riding whip in the direction of Holborn Bridge.

Heron's time had come.

In half a dozen seconds he was in the inn yard, and Daisy's stable door was unlocked.

"Ho! Daisy, come forth—come forth!"

Daisy bounded out of the stable, and the ostler had only time to cry out, "Good gracious!" before Heron was on her back, and at a rattling pace sallied out on to Snow Hill.

Had he timed it in the most accurate manner in the world, Heron could not have issued forth from the yard of the "Saracen's Head" at a more exactly opportune moment.

Jonathan Wild was precisely on the spot of ground outside the archway.

Then Heron reined in Daisy, until she stood for a moment on her hind feet like some beautiful statue of a horse, and he looked straight into the eyes of Jonathan Wild.

The mouth of the great thief-taker opened as though he would have uttered a cry of terror, but the sound froze upon his lips, and for a few seconds he and Felix Heron confronted each other in petrifying and fearful silence.

Then Heron made an imperious movement with his hand.

Wild obeyed him and began backing his horse, and at the same moment his frozen up faculties found power of expression.

"Help! help!" he cried—"a ghost!—an apparition! It's the spirit of Felix Heron, and an air surrounds him that freezes me to the bones. Help! help! The dead rise up against us!"

Still Heron made that imperious gesture, and Wild, backing his horse among the mounted constables, threw them into confusion.

Tom Ripon raised a ringing cheer, and springing over the chaplain, he reached the side of the cart.

"Saved! saved!" he cried. "Hurrah! hurrah!

EDITH HASTENS TO WELCOME FELIX ON HIS SAFE RETURN FROM A
PERILOUS EXPEDITION.

Presented Gratis with No, 86, of the New Edition of EDITH HERON, the Sequel to Edith the Captive; or, the Robbers of Epping Forest.

Never say die! Who said the Captain wouldn't come, and Daisy too? How are you, Daisy? All right, eh? Hurrah! hurrah!"

Heron spoke truly when he told Ogle that Tom's rescue was to be effected by surprise, and not by force.

He gave the impulse to Daisy, and with one leap she was by the side of the cart.

Tom was on her back in an instant, and notwithstanding his fetters, he contrived to get a firm clutch of Heron's scarlet coat.

"Off and away! off and away, Daisy!" shouted Tom. "There's not a dozen horses, all rolled into one, in the whole of England, can catch you."

Heron had never spoken a word, but now, turning the head of Daisy towards Giltspur Street, where there was no crowd at all, he put Daisy to speed, and the last he saw of Jonathan Wild was his being helped off his horse, apparently in a swoon, by the officers that surrounded him.

Tom's exuberance had passed away, and now, for the first time we may almost say, the awful position in which he had been placed seemed to take possession of his mind.

It was well that he had so good a support to cling to, for he began now to feel weak and faint.

Heron spoke, but he did not relax his horse's speed.

"Come, Tom, be a man. If we succeed in distancing our pursuers, we shall have nothing to fear."

Tom gave one sob—the boy felt all the peril his beloved master had run for his sake, but he could not utter a word.

Felix Heron, with his disengaged hand, pressed one of Tom Ripon's, and said, in his own cheery accents, "It's all right, Tom; you have been imprudent, but I do not blame you so much as myself."

"Oh, don't—don't, Captain, talk in that fashion, now!" said Tom—for he could not bear to hear Felix Heron blame himself in any way. "Don't talk in that fashion, Captain! You ought to have let them hang me—I deserve it!"

"Pooh, pooh, Tom! you must be wiser next time! Ah! we must push on: there is a large mounted party of officers in pursuit. On, Daisy, on! Off and away!"

Daisy sped on like the wind; and, in the course of another half-hour, Felix Heron and Tom Ripon had ridden some miles into the country, and there was no appearance of any one in their track.

Heron drew rein.

"Now, Tom," said Felix Heron, "we must get your fetters removed at the first blacksmith's forge we come to."

"That will be a good riddance, at all events, Captain," said Tom, who now began to regain his usual cheerfulness.

Captain Heron suffered Daisy now to go at a hand-gallop; and not many paces in advance he saw a blacksmith's forge, so often to be met with on country roads.

As they approached the little hut—for it more resembled that than anything else—Felix Heron and Tom could distinctly hear the heavy blows of the smith's hammer upon the anvil, enlivened by some deep bass notes which proceeded from the lungs of the honest blacksmith himself.

Heron pulled up at the door of the blacksmith.

"Hilloa, my friend!" he said; "here's a job for you."

"Ah! it's all grist to the mill!" exclaimed the blacksmith. "I find it hard work to live in this lonely place. Has your horse cast a shoe, sir?"

"No, my man, that's not it. I want you to take these fetters off this boy here."

"Fetters, sir?"

"Yes. Don't you see it will be well worth your while to do so; and, hark you, my friend, a still tongue makes a wise head. You understand?"

"All's right, sir—here goes!"

The blacksmith, with a few blows of his hammer, soon rendered Tom quite at liberty, who threw his arms high above his head shouting, "Hurrah! hurrah! Now I'm a man again!"

The blacksmith laughed.

"A very young one, it would seem to me," he said, as he picked up some silver pieces Felix Heron had cast on the floor of his hut.

"Thanks, your honour—thanks! And if so be there be any questions asked of Tim Simpson, why, mum's the word."

"I see you are a sensible man," replied Felix Heron, as he and Tom again prepared to continue their journey.

"Where are we going now, Captain?" asked Tom, as Felix Heron still pushed forward towards the country.

"I scarcely know yet, Tom, but I will wait until nightfall at an inn, where I know we may avoid pursuit; and then, I think, we may as well return to Whitcombe House.

Tom whistled.

"We must then," continued Heron, "think of some disguise for you to adopt until this little affair is forgotten."

"All's right, Captain; anything you advise is sure to be right."

Heron could not suppress a smile.

"You did not think it necessary to ask my advice, Tom, when you got yourself into this sad dilemma," he replied.

"Don't talk about it, Captain; I feel as if I could never forgive myself. But is this the inn, Captain, you spoke of?"

"It is," said Felix Heron; and giving the reins to Tom, he entered the little hostel, and whispered a few words into the ear of the landlord, who answered,—

"Certainly, sir—certainly! Here you will be as safe as a mouse in a trap. I do say it as oughtn't; but when a gentleman asks for privacy in Ned Swallow's hostel, why Ned Swallow knows what he's about, and can keep a secret as well as anybody."

At this moment there was a pattering of horses' feet upon the road, and Felix Heron and Tom Ripon had just time to enter the little hostel, and place Daisy in a place of security, when a party of mounted officers appeared at the door.

"Hilloa! Hilloa, there!" shouted one. "Has a man on horseback passed this way, carrying a boy in fetters behind him?"

"God bless my heart, your honour!" cried the landlord. "A boy in fetters?"

"Yes, yes! Don't stand there gaping like an idiot, but answer! Have you seen two such persons?" asked the officer.

"Certainly not, sir! A boy in fetters, indeed! He would know too well that this was not the sort of crib for the like of such as he. Where might they be coming from, sir?"

"Pshaw!" exclaimed the officer who had all along been spokesman. "Don't hinder us by asking us any of your tiresome questions. Forward, my men, forward! He came this road. Let us push on, and we must overtake them in time."

The little party galloped away from the little hostel, leaving the landlord on its threshold looking very satisfied with himself, and rattling in his pocket a couple of golden guineas which had just before been given to him by Heron.

CHAPTER CCLXX.

JONATHAN WILD INTERRUPTS A VILLANOUS CONVERSATION.

IN a small but well-appointed apartment in an hotel at the West End of town sat two men.

It is late in the evening, and the remains of a substantial repast were still on the table, together with some of the choicest wine the cellar could produce.

"And now to business," said one of these choice spirits to the other; "but first fill a bumper and let us wish success to our plans—or, at least, your plans, I may say, for at present I am quite in the dark as to the business on hand."

It was John Tarleton who spoke.

His companion was none other than Lord Warringdale.

Warringdale filled his glass, and drained off its contents.

"Now to business," he said, as he looked full into the eyes of his fellow accomplice in so many dark crimes.

"Well, go on! Don't look at a fellow in that way, Warringdale! Any one would think you——"

"Hush!" said Warringdale, starting and turning pale. "What was that? Did you hear anything?"

"Nothing!" roared John Tarleton. "You are enough to make any one believe he is surrounded by spirits!"—and taking a decanter up, he again filled his glass, saying, "Take another glass, Warringdale, to give you pluck; and make haste and tell me what this precious plan of yours is, which you were so desirous of imparting to me to-night, and which you said was to give us both a fortune."

"I did—I did!"

"Well, begin, then."

"You know," said Warringdale, "that Felix Heron is dead?"

John Tarleton made a gesture of impatience as he said, "Of course I do. I did not come here to hear that as a bit of news, I hope!"

"Don't be so impatient. You know also that he left a son?"

"Of course I do, hang him! If he were not in the way, the title would go to——"

"To me," said Warringdale; and there was a baleful light in his eyes as he spoke.

John Tarleton looked at his companion for a few seconds without speaking.

"If he were disposed of," continued Warringdale, in a low voice, which now sunk almost to a whisper, "the only obstacle in my way would be removed!"

"And what should I get by the little arrangement?" asked John Tarleton, looking steadily at his companion.

"Half the property!" replied Warringdale.

"Hem! It's worth thinking about," said Tarleton. "But say how is it to be accomplished, and who is to do the deed—for it is murder of course that you propose?"

"Call it murder if you will—and you will do the deed, as you call it!"

"I?"

"Even you."

"I cannot! A little child!"

"Tush, man! since when have you become so tender-hearted? Better far send a little child to heaven, than a hoary sinner, like you or me, to the other place. Ha, ha!"

John Tarleton shuddered.

"You are a great villain, Warringdale," he said. "But, as you say, better put a little child out of the world than you or I. What are your plans?"

"These," said Warringdale, as he drew his chair closer to John Tarleton's. "These. I propose to make my way into Whitcombe House, and secrete myself in one of its many hiding places, and in the dead of night I will manage to let you in, and together we will proceed to the apartment occupied by the child and his nurse."

"And what then?" asked John Tarleton.

"Why, I will manage the nurse, while you do the business with the little one."

John Tarleton filled his glass again and drained it before he spoke; he then said, "Well, here's my hand on it. Remember, if I share the danger, I also share the plunder."

"Most assuredly you shall! But, hark! there are footsteps. Who can it be at this hour? They approach this door—we have spoken too loud. Ah!"

John Tarleton and Warringdale sprung to their feet, and encountered the eyes of Jonathan Wild fixed upon them.

"You look scared, gentlemen," he said, as he sunk into the first chair that presented itself—"you look scared, gentlemen. Your conversation must have been very interesting. You tremble, my Lord Warringdale; and you, John Tarleton, look as if you had seen——No, no! What am I saying—what am I saying?"

Jonathan Wild covered his eyes with his hand, as if to shut out some terrible sight.

Warringdale filled a glass from a decanter, and gave it to Wild.

"Drink this," he said, "and don't sit there cowering and shrinking, as though you had seen a ghost!"

Wild removed his hands from before his bloodshot eyes, and looking up, said, in a voice scarcely audible, "I have seen a ghost!"

"What? Who?" Warringdale and John Tarleton both asked in a breath.

"*His* ghost!"

"Whose? Speak, man, and don't talk fables here! Whose ghost have you seen? Speak!"

"Felix Heron's!"

Warringdale staggered back until he reached the chair from which he had risen to give Jonathan Wild the wine.

"Felix Heron's?" he gasped.

"Even so!" said Wild, in a low tone; "even so! That boy, Tom Ripon, warned me that he might appear at any time to rescue from danger those who were attached to him; and he did so to-day, when I thought nothing could save that boy from the death he so richly deserves."

Lord Warringdale and John Tarleton regarded each other in silence, while Wild continued, "Yes, at the moment when I thought all secure, Felix Heron appeared, even as he used to do of old, when he was at the head of his band in the recesses of Epping Forest."

"This is past belief," said Warringdale, now turning as pale as Wild himself had done a few minutes before. "What said he?"

"Nothing!" replied Wild. "If he had spoken, it would not have been half so terrible; but he glided through the crowd as only an apparition could do, mounted on the back of Daisy, and made his way right to the side of the death-cart."

"And what happened then?" asked Warringdale.

"Tom Ripon leaped upon Daisy's back behind the apparition, and they were soon lost to view. I believe they vanished into thin air."

"What mean you?" asked John Tarleton. "Did not the officers seize them?"

"How could they seize upon a spirit? I saw only that the crowd shrunk back, and then I fell into a swoon; for the look of that face froze every drop of blood in my veins."

As Wild spoke, a shudder passed through his frame, and he rested his head upon his clasped hands.

"Heaven knows," he murmured, apparently oblivious of the fact that he was not alone,— "Heaven knows, I would have befriended Edith and his little one. Why should he thus appear to me? I wish now I had not pursued that boy with such relentless hatred, but he drove me to it by his obstinacy."

"Since when," asked Lord Warringdale, with a sneer,—"since when, pray, have you become so devoted to the Countess of Whitcombe and her child?"

Wild started.

"Since when?" he asked. "Since when, do you ask, have I become so devoted to the Countess of Whitcombe? I will tell you, my Lord Warringdale, and you too, John Tarleton—ever since the death of that gallant, brave, and generous Felix Heron."

"Indeed!" sneered Warringdale. "You were not always inclined to be so friendly. Perhaps you will kindly favour us with the cause of this violent friendship?"

"Pshaw!" said Wild. "You would not understand me. I scarcely understand it myself. All I know is, that whatever may have been my feeling towards Felix Heron at one time, I will never relax in my vigilance in doing all I can to ward off danger or ill-fortune to either the Countess of Whitcombe or her child—his child."

"'Pon my word, Wild, it is a pity the fair Countess did not marry you, instead of bestowing her fair hand upon Captain Fantome, as she has done!" laughed John Tarleton.

"Hold!" roared Wild. "I will not have her actions questioned by you or your companion. True she has disappointed me there; but still Captain Fantome is a brave man, and perhaps he has other qualities resembling those possessed by Felix Heron, which may have won her regard."

"Doubtless!" sneered John Tarleton.

"And she may have wished," continued Jonathan Wild, "to give her little son a protector."

"I have no doubt," said Warringdale, "that was her only reason for so soon forgetting the gallant Felix Heron. Ha, ha!"

Wild rose to his feet, and looking Warringdale and John Tarleton in the face, he said, "Beware, how you speak of Felix Heron's child! The boy shall never want a protector while Jonathan Wild lives!"

In another moment the two companions in iniquity were alone.

As soon as the echo of Jonathan Wild's footsteps had ceased to vibrate in their ears, Lord Warringdale and John Tarleton drew a long breath of relief.

"What could he mean?" asked Warringdale, in a low voice, "by talking so much about that brat of Felix Heron's?"

"I can't think. But I am convinced that we were not overheard talking over our little scheme for the improvement of both of our fortunes."

"I don't know. I don't half like it," said Warringdale. "He would not let us know he had heard anything. What did he come for? I forget."

"Why," replied John Tarleton, "to tell us he had seen Felix Heron's ghost, to be sure."

"True—true! and that very naturally led him to speak of the Countess and her child."

"To be sure it did! So now let us mature our little plans. When is the business to be done?"

Warringdale started from a reverie.

"The sooner the better!—the sooner the better!" he cried, excitedly. "To-morrow night we must make our way into the stable-yard from the narrow street that runs at the back of Whitcombe House. I, at an earlier hour; you, at about two o'clock in the morning."

"All right—then, it's agreed! What death is he to die? A pistol-shot does the business quickly; but it makes such a confounded noise."

Warringdale drained off another tumbler of wine.

"Let it be the knife, keen and trustworthy."

"Be it so, then," said Tarleton. "After all, I am only her half-brother."

"Half-brother or whole-brother, what matters it when the stake we play for is so worth the having? And now, good night! I have other business on hand to-night. Adieu till to-morrow!"

* * * * *

The moon shone brightly down upon Daisy and her double burden, as she cantered through the green lanes, making towards London.

Felix Heron and Tom Ripon were each busy with his own thoughts, and it was not until the tall spires of various churches, and then long

"Are we going to Whitcombe House, Captain?"

"Yes, Tom. I think you will be safer there, for the present, than anywhere."

Tom was silent.

"What's the matter, Tom?" asked Felix Heron, in his own tones of kindness, which was like a balm to poor Tom's depressed spirits just at that moment.

"I was thinking," said Tom.

"Thinking, Tom! So I suppose; but what were you thinking about?"

"I was wondering who would have the care of Daisy in future, Captain!"—and Tom gave a deep sigh.

"Tom Ripon," replied Heron.

"I, Captain?"

"Certainly, Tom. I am not afraid of you risking her life again without my permission; and as in other respects she could not have a better groom, nor one who loved her more truly, why I think I am only carrying out Daisy's own wishes on the subject by again entrusting her to you. Eh, Daisy?"

As Felix thus addressed his four-footed friend, he patted her arched neck; and the creature, really as if she understood the little arrangement, made a snorting reply, which Tom, as was usual with him, translated into her entire approval of all that had been said.

"Thank you, Captain," said the boy; "you may rely upon me never putting her in peril again; and as for attending properly to her, why, I'd rather go without food myself than let her want for anything."

"I know that, Tom," said Felix Heron, as they reached the stable-door, at which Heron knocked impatiently.

He had not many seconds to wait, for Ogle had been told by Heron that he would dismount in the stable-yard, whether he was fortunate enough to rescue Tom or not.

The joy of Ogle at beholding Captain Heron and Tom safe and well was too great for words, and he merely said in a choking voice, "Thank heaven, Captain, you have returned in safety!"

"All right, Ogle!" said Tom: "you see Johnny has not been gratified by seeing me dancing upon nothing, as he thought he should!"

Captain Heron saw that Tom put on a look and air of playfulness to hide some deeper emotion, which was clearly perceptible in his voice.

"Here, Ogle, take Tom in, and give him a good supper, for I dare say he has not fared over well since he has been Jonathan Wild's guest; and I will go to Edith, for I daresay she is not less uneasy than you seem to have been, Ogle."

"Go, Captain, go! I never saw the Lady Edith in such a way before! She has been pacing up and down the drawing-room almost all day, except now and then, when the little one would make her play with him!"

"Dear Edith!" sighed Felix Heron, as he entered the house; and mounting two stairs at a time, was soon clasped in the arms of Edith.

"You are safe—you are safe! Oh, Felix!" was all Edith could say, as she burst into a passion of tears.

"Safe, Edith! And, thank heaven, I have

rescued Tom, who is below, with Ogle!" said Heron, as he pressed her again and again to his heart.

CHAPTER CLXXI.

TOM RIPON SAVES FELIX HERON'S CHILD FROM A HORRIBLE DEATH.

WHILE Felix Heron was endeavouring to make Edith laugh at her fears, Tom Ripon, with Ogle, had made his way to the kitchen, where Mrs. Ogle bustled about with as good a will as did her husband, in order to provide Tom with some substantial proofs of their pleasure at his safe return.

Tom's spirits had completely regained their wonted elasticity, now that he felt Felix Heron had forgiven him for exposing, not only himself, but Daisy, to so much danger.

"Ah! there she is!" shouted Tom, as he bounded into the kitchen, and clasped Mrs. Ogle in his arms. "Give me a kiss!"

"Get out!" shouted Mrs. Ogle. "I don't want to kiss any such reprobate as you are!"

"Oh, that's gammon!" cried Tom, still tormenting Mrs. Ogle. "Tell me now, Ogle, hasn't she been weeping and wailing ever since I've been gone?"

Ogle smiled;—for now that both Felix Heron and his young favourite were in safety again, he rather enjoyed Tom's good-humoured jokes.

"Me weeping and wailing?" said Mrs. Ogle, with an attempt at seriousness. "I should think not! The house has been quiet and peaceable since you left!"

Tom laughed, and sat down to a well-furnished table; and while he was doing ample justice to the good things Mrs. Ogle had provided for him, he gave them a hurried account of all that had befallen him.

Twelve o'clock struck, and Tom, rubbing his eyes, expressed a wish to retire to his own little room, saying as he did so that much as he had always liked it before, since he had been a guest of Jonathan Wild's he should value it more than ever.

In another half-hour, the inmates of Whitcombe House had retired to rest.

Tom, when he once more felt that he was free, and that he could look forward to a quiet night's rest in his own little bed, gave a long sigh of relief as he sat down, and rested his head on his hands in deep thought.

In fact, this may be said to be the first time that Tom had really reflected upon his peculiar position;—for although he scarcely could have given utterance to the belief in words, yet he had always thought, in his own mind, that Felix Heron would make an attempt to rescue him; and Tom had such unbounded confidence in whatever his Captain—for such he still called him—could accomplish, that perhaps he, Tom, was less surprised than any one else had been when, on that eventful morning, Felix Heron, in the dress he had for so long discarded, rode up to the side of the death-cart and carried him off.

Now, however, in the quiet of his little sleeping apartment, Tom knew and felt all that Felix

Heron had dared for his sake, and something very like a tear glistened in the brave boy's eye, as he murmured to himself, " Yes, I'll never forget what he has done for me to-day; and he told me, too, I might still have the care of Daisy. He trusts me again, and he shall find that——"

Tom started to his feet.

" What was that ?" he gasped, almost, rather than said. " I am sure I heard something. Daisy ! Is Daisy safe ?"

The idea of anything happening to Daisy was sufficient to drive everything else from the mind of Tom Ripon; and he carefully opened a door which conducted from his room into the stable-yard.

Tom looked out into the night air, and felt certain that he saw a figure crouching down by the outer gate.

Tom's first impression was that the figure was one of Johathan Wild's myrmidons come to seek

him; and a cold chill took possession of the boy's heart as he waited, watched, and listened in breathless suspense.

In another moment, there came three gentle taps at the gate; and the crouching figure, which, as our readers have no doubt already recognised, was none other than Lord Warringdale, opened the gate, and another figure glided in.

Tom was irresolute what to do. If they sought him, he knew resistance to the law would be in vain, so he resolved still to watch.

At length one of the figures spoke; and Tom, who had quietly retreated again into his little room, was leaning from a small window; but, from the fact of it being within the shadow of a tall stack of chimneys, he felt that he was secure from all observation, while at the same time he could be a listener to all that was said.

" Is it time ?" asked John Tarleton.

" Hush ! I think not. They have not long

retired. We must wait yet another hour, at least."

"Are you prepared?" asked Lord Warringdale. And this time Tom thought he recognised the tones of the voice, but could not at the moment recall to his remembrance where, or under what circumstances, he had heard them.

"Prepared? Of course I am! Do you suppose I should be such an idiot as to come unprepared? In which room does the brat sleep?"

Tom fairly staggered back. Was it possible that the world contained two such villains as to wish to harm the little child who was the sunshine, the idol of the house? What could it all mean?

Again Tom projected his head to listen.

"He sleeps," again replied the voice which Tom now knew to be that of Lord Warringdale, in the room they call the Yellow Chamber, quite away from this part of the premises. We must mount the staircase, and while you put an end to him, I will undertake to settle the woman, his nurse."

There was a pause, now, in the conversation, and Tom fancied that they were making some alteration in their dress.

It was no longer to be doubted that these two men, for some reason or another, were bent upon the death of Felix Heron's child.

There was a look upon the face of Tom Ripon as he clasped his hands in thankfulness, that lit it up, and made it look beautiful and heroic.

"Yes," he said, in a low voice,—"yes, I shall be permitted to stand between what Captain Heron values more than his own life—his child —and danger, perhaps death! But I, too, must not be idle. Where are the pistols—in Daisy's holsters? Ah, no! here they are. I thought I brought them in."

Tom looked to the priming, and saw that they were well and carefully loaded. Then he looked again from the little window.

The two men were silent now, evidently waiting impatiently for the time when they could carry out their villanous project.

As Tom regarded the two shadows which were crouching beneath the wall which ran along the back part of the house, dividing it from the little narrow street we have before mentioned, his mind was busily occupied in determining upon some scheme to frustrate their evil designs.

At first Tom contemplated rousing Felix Heron, and letting him take summary vengeance upon the would-be murderers of his child; but, after a few minutes' reflection, he discarded the thought, saying to himself, "No, no! I—I alone must save Felix Heron's child. Has he not this day risked his life for me, who have no one to live for? And he is so beloved; and the Lady Edith, too, will give me one of her own sweet smiles, which I value so much; and when she looks at Tom Ripon, she will remember that I saved her child! But now, how is it to be done? Shall I sally out, and put a bullet in their brains as they lie there? or shall I meet them face to face, in the presence of that innocent child they came to murder?"

Tom seemed to think the latter mode would be the most desirable; for he quickly left his place of espionage and bounded up-stairs to the door of the room which he knew was appropriated to the sleeping accommodation of the child so idolized by Felix Heron and his gentle Edith.

Having reached the door of the room, Tom paused to listen.

All was still, and he felt sure that the two assassins had not yet left their hiding-place.

Tom knocked gently at the door of the apartment, in the hope of rousing Mrs. Ogle, whom he knew had the charge of the child during the night.

There was no reply to his summons for admission.

"It's no use waiting here," said Tom to himself; "delay may be fatal. I will go in."

Tom turned the handle of the door, and entered.

Tom was convinced that not only the child, but Mrs. Ogle herself, was in a deep sleep; and the next thing to be done was to effectually rouse the latter without awakening the child.

Tom laid his hand upon her.

"Mrs. Ogle! Mrs. Ogle! Hush! don't make a row! Get up, Mrs. Ogle!"

Mrs. Ogle was fortunately too much terrified to make any outcry, which Tom felt all along she was sure to do; but she started up in the bed, and regarded Tom in astonishment.

"All right, Mrs. Ogle!" said Tom; "don't be afraid. I want you to get up directly!"

"Get up directly, you young scapegrace. What do you mean? Do you want to go and get hanged again? Get along with you!"

Mrs. Ogle was about to compose herself to sleep again, when Tom stooped down and whispered, "You'll be murdered if you lie there any longer."

Mrs. Ogle gasped for breath—and Tom, taking advantage of her position, continued hurriedly, "Look you here, Mrs. Ogle. There are two men down stairs, and from what I gathered from their whispered conversation, I believe they intend to murder that little one who is sleeping so sweetly by your side."

Mrs. Ogle raised a half scream, as she threw her arm over the sleeping child.

"Hush! do not make such a noise, and rouse the Captain and Lady Edith. I want you to get up, and let me take charge of the little one for a little while."

"You want me to leave the child, Tom? Never! While I have breath, I will protect him."

"But, after all," added Tom, "you know, Mrs. Ogle, you are only a woman, and it requires a man's arm in such an emergency as this."

"Call Ogle, then," said Mrs. Ogle, interrupting Tom.

Tom drew himself up, saying, as he pointed to the table, where lay the two pistols he had brought with him, "I am not afraid but that I shall be able to settle them both with these two friends; so just get up, Mrs. Ogle, and if you like to remain in the room, why you can, but don't make any noise, that's all."

"Gracious goodness!" said Mrs. Ogle. "I'm all in a tremble."

"Never mind that," said Tom; "I give you five minutes to put on your traps, and then I shall come back again."

"But you are not going away, Tom?" asked

Mrs. Ogle, now with terror and alarm depicted on her countenance.

"Only outside the door while you put on your things; and if you are ready sooner than I expect, just come to the door, and I will come in at once."

"All right!" said Mrs. Ogle.

Tom was turning to leave the room—

"Tom!"

"Well, what now?"

"Why, you look by this light, with the moon shining full on your face and figure,—you don't look like a boy any longer, but like a man."

"I am a man," said Tom, as he strode from the room.

While the foregoing conversation had been taking place in the child's sleeping apartment between Mrs. Ogle and Tom Ripon, the two villanous accomplices, Lord Warringdale and John Tarleton, had completed their arrangements —each drawing over their boots a pair of worsted socks, so that their stealthy footsteps might not be heard.

Then they took from their pockets a piece of black crape; much like those worn at masquerades, which they drew down over their faces.

"I'm ready," whispered John Tarleton.

"And so am I," replied Warringdale. "Follow me."

Lord Warringdale produced from his pocket a pick-lock, with which he had no difficulty in opening the door which led into the lower portion of the mansion, and the two soon made their way up a back staircase to the suite of apartments which he, Lord Warringdale, had discovered to be set apart for the use of the young heir to the Whitcombe estates.

It was just as Mrs. Ogle had secreted herself behind an old-fashioned wardrobe, and Tom Ripon had taken up his station by the side of the child's bed, that those two villains reached the door of the apartment, and listened intently.

Silence reigned in and about the house—but still they paused. Was it fear that now spoke to the hearts of those two men, that made them pause on the threshold of the room, where lay in peaceful slumber their innocent victim?

Tom had given one look at the little sleeper.

The rosy flush of childhood was upon the soft cheek, and the moonbeams played among the dark tresses.

One tiny hand was outside the coverlet, grasping a toy lamb Tom had bought only a few days previous.

Tom patted the little hand gently, and something very bright glittered in the boy's eye as he said, "No harm shall come to you, little one. I hope I shall not have to use these noisy weapons, for they will frighten you, may be, and then——"

Tom started.

A hand was laid upon the handle of the door, —but it was not turned.

Mrs. Ogle sank upon her knees, and hid her face in the bed-clothes.

Tom made a sign to her to be still, and then he reached forth his hand to grasp the other pistol, which he had laid on a chair by the bedside, while he was speaking to the sleeping child.

And now he was ready—ready to do battle for his beloved master's child, and the brave boy— for he was still but a boy in years—faced the door, with his back turned towards the bed upon which lay the child.

Both pistols pointing at the door.

There was excitement in his eyes, his head was thrown a little back, and his fingers were upon the triggers of those pistols, each one of which held the life of a man at his mercy.

Tom had not long to wait.

The door handle gently turned, and then the door opened noiselessly; and then John Tarleton, with a hunting knife—whose blade flashed and glittered in the moonbeams—entered the room, closely followed by his accomplice.

So intent were these two men upon the deed of darkness they had come to perpetrate, that it would seem they had not raised their eyes; had they done so, they must have beheld Tom as he there stood with the full light of the moon upon him.

Tom moved not; he could scarcely be said to breathe; but his heart beat wildly as he beheld these men making their way towards the bed.

Still they saw him not; but when John Tarleton was within a pace of the bed, Tom cried out, "Hold, villains! murderers that you are! Another step forward, and I'll scatter your brains as I would those of a mad dog! What want you here? Speak, or I'll fire!"

Tom advanced a step towards John Tarleton, who had shrunk back, apparently incapable of uttering a word.

"Speak, I say, villains! Why seek you the life of an innocent child? I know your plot, and have frustrated your designs. Leave this room, this house, my Lord Warringdale; and you, too, John Tarleton—you see I know you both— or worse will come of it."

The senses of both these men of crime seemed paralyzed before the majestic bearing of Tom Ripon, who followed them step by step as they descended backwards the grand staircase.

At length they reached the stable-yard, with Tom still pointing the muzzle of the pistols at their breasts, and when they were outside the little gate Tom discharged one of them.

With a yell of agony, Lord Warringdale rolled over and over.

"That's a keepsake from me. A little remembrance of this night's work," said Tom, as he slammed the little gate, and bolted it on the inside.

Tom sped up to the sleeping apartment of the child, and entering, he found Mrs. Ogle giving vent to her feelings in a violent burst of tears, while the child, clasping her round the neck, was endeavouring to make her cease weeping.

Tom caught the little one to his breast, and never had he felt so happy as at that moment.

The pistol shot had aroused Felix Heron, who, fancying he heard unusual sounds in the nursery at that time in the night, hastened thither.

The door was still open, and as Felix Heron entered, the first object which met his gaze was that of his child clinging to the neck of Tom Ripon.

————

CHAPTER CCLXXII.

FELIX HERON MAKES TOM RIPON SUPREMELY HAPPY.

IT were vain to attempt to describe in language all the various and contending emotions which found a home in the breast of Felix Heron, when he became aware of the imminent peril which had surrounded his much-loved child; nor less was he touched by the devotion of the brave youth before him, who had stood between his child and that peril.

"I can never repay you, Tom, for this!" cried Felix Heron, wringing the hand of his faithful young follower. "I can never, never repay you for such a service as this!"

Tom's excitement had passed away, and he seemed to have forgotten all that he himself had really risked in thus saving the child of Felix Heron from the hand of his would-be murderers.

"It's nothing, Captain. You wouldn't have a man stand by and see a little child murdered in cold blood, without stretching out a hand to save him. I merely did my duty."

Felix Heron looked on the flushed cheek of the boy with admiration.

"You will not make me undervalue the service you have done me, Tom, and I shall endeavour to think of something that shall at least mark my appreciation of your conduct; although, as I said before, I can never cancel the debt of gratitude both myself and Edith owe you, the preserver of our child."

As a recollection of the danger from which his little one had escaped rose up in Heron's mind, he again pressed the unconscious child to his heart, and laid his hand lovingly on his clustering hair.

Tom Ripon regarded him for a moment in silence, and then with a look of animation he said, half hesitatingly, "Captain!"

"Well, Tom, what is it? Have you thought of anything that you would like me to do or say, in order to prove to you what my feelings are on this occasion?"

Tom was silent.

"Speak, Tom—speak! I know by your looks that there is something you want to ask; and I think, whatever it is, I may promise to gratify your wish, whatever it may be."

"Daisy, Captain!"

Felix Heron smiled.

"Well, what of Daisy, Tom? Has she not all that even you can desire for her comfort and well-being?"

Tom's face flushed; and, clasping his hands, he advanced two paces nearer to Felix Heron, as he said, "Oh, Captain, if you think I have done anything to deserve all the kind things you have been saying to me—which I don't—if you would only let me have Daisy, I feel sure, with your permission and good wishes, I should, in time, become almost as good and great as you are. Let me—oh, let me, Captain—my kind master and friend—let me once more try my fortune on the road!"

As he proceeded, Tom saw a look of sorrow pass over the expressive face of Felix Heron, and once more retreating towards the door, was about to leave the room; saying as he did so, "Forgive me, Captain; it was wrong of me to ask so much. Forget that the words have passed my lips, and only believe that so long as I retain your good opinion, I am very, very happy and contented."

"Stop, Tom!" cried Felix Heron. "I meant not that you should infer from my silence that I disapproved of what you wished to do."

"Then you don't disapprove, Captain?" asked Tom, breathless with expectation.

"No, Tom, I do not disapprove of your desire to become a knight of the road; but I would fain have heard you express a desire to become something that would not be so perilous. You are young, Tom."

Tom drew himself up to his full height, as he said, "I am a good deal taller than Ogle, Captain!"

"Well, well!" said Felix Heron, smiling. "Be it as you wish, only be more careful in braving Jonathan Wild."

"Then you consent, Captain?"

"I consent."

"Hurrah! And Daisy, Captain?"

"And Daisy may go with you, provided you always contrive to let her return here to rest during the day."

"All right, Captain! and now for Ogle! Hurrah!"

"Tom!"

"Yes, Captain?"

"I think if I let you have Daisy, you will, in order to take care of her, be more careful of yourself."

"You may depend upon it, Captain, I will always contrive to send her home in safety. Oh, Captain Heron, you have made me as happy as a king! When may I start? To-night?"

"Whenever you like Tom, and good fortune attend you."

"Thanks—thanks—a thousand thanks, Captain. Hurrah! hurrah! hurrah for the road!"

Tom hastily quitted the room, and, seeking Ogle, he was giving him an animated description of all that had taken place during the last few hours, and of the change of life which was now to be his.

Ogle smiled.

"Bravo, my boy! When do you begin?"

"To-night, to be sure!"

Ogle looked thoughtful.

"What's up now?" asked Tom. "Why not to-night? What are you thinking about, Ogle?"

"Oh, nothing! What time shall you start?"

"About ten o'clock."

"All right!" said Ogle; "and now good night; or rather, good morning! I mean to turn in again for an hour or two. Your pistol-shot woke me, Tom."

"Ah! I had forgotten that! I hope I have given him something to remember for many a long day. Well, good night, Ogle! And whistling a gay tune, Tom returned to his little sleeping apartment, with a lighter heart than he had possessed for many a day.

When the morning came, Felix Heron sought Ogle.

TOM RIPON COMBINES A LITTLE PLEASURE WITH BUSINESS.

Presented Gratis with No. 87, of the New Edition of EDITH HERON, the Sequel to Edith the Captive; or, the Robbers of Epping Forest.

"I suppose, Ogle," he said, "you have heard from Tom all that he did last night?"

"Well, Captain, I can't say that Tom told me much about what his courage and bravery accomplished; for I could get him to talk about nothing else than that you had given your consent to his going on the road on his own account, and that he was to have the use of Daisy."

"Is it possible then, Ogle, that you know not how this mere lad encountered, face to face, two ruffians, who would have murdered my child?"

"Yes, Captain, I know all about it, for I was an unseen spectator of the whole thing. I knew Tom wanted to give you some proof of his gratitude for having rescued him from the horrible death which awaited him at Tyburn; and I determined not to interfere unless I found they were too many for him."

"It was kind, and like you, Ogle. But I want to speak to you about Tom's dress."

"The very thing, Captain, I was thinking about myself when you came into my room. I thought I might manage at some of the masquerading clothiers to get Tom a handsome-looking dress. He would feel more like a real highwayman, you see, Captain."

"Exactly, Ogle; and I wish you to procure him one that you think would be suitable; and let him find it all ready for him to put on tonight."

"All right, Captain! I was only debating in my own mind what sort of dress it had better be."

"Let it be something smart and dashing. scarlet coat, remember, will be indispensable."

"All right, Captain," said Ogle; "now I know what I have to do. I've no doubt I shall give both you and Tom satisfaction."

"No doubt of it—no doubt of it, Ogle," said Felix Heron; and hearing Tom's cheery voice singing in Daisy's stable, he turned his steps thither.

Tom was busily engaged in polishing up the harness belonging to his four-footed friend, and, as usual, holding a confidential conversation with her during the pauses in his song.

> "'Oh, a life on the road for me!
> With my brave and gallant steed;
> A highwayman I would be,
> And I'll gallop along with speed.'"

And so, Daisy, I'm to be a real highwayman at last! And you're quite willing to go with me, lass? I thought so. I knew it without you telling me.

> "'With my coat so fine and my spurs so bright,
> I'll ride o'er the heath on a moonlight night.'"

Eh? What, Daisy? What's up now?"

These questions were caused by Daisy suddenly springing to her feet, and giving a snort of evident recognition to some person who stood just behind Tom.

Tom turned quickly round, and beheld Felix Heron quietly contemplating him.

"So you are commencing your preparations, I see, Tom," said Felix Heron kindly, as he placed his hand on the boy's shoulder.

"Yes, Captain. Why, you see, Daisy's trappings have been a little neglected while I was a boarder and lodger of Jonathan Wild, so I just thought I'd give them an extra polish as I've nothing better to do."

"I see—I see, Tom, you have not repented of your wild project."

"Repented, Captain? Of course not. I only wish it was time to go now, I'd be off at once; wouldn't we, Daisy?"

Daisy seemed, as usual, to understand what Tom was saying, for she pawed the ground and placed her head upon Tom's shoulder.

"There, I told you so, Captain; Daisy's as pleased as I am to go and cry 'Stand and deliver!'"

Heron patted the neck of his favourite steed, and then turned and left the stable.

As the reader knows how readily Ogle had entered into Captain Heron's scheme of providing Tom with a suitable outfit for his new undertaking, he will have no difficulty in believing that he (Ogle) succeeded to his utmost satisfaction in carrying out Felix's Heron's wishes on that subject.

Ogle had purchased a smart-looking scarlet coat, a black felt hat ornamented with a drooping feather, tall horseman's boots, cravat, ruffles, and all the *et ceteras*, which went at that period of which we write to make up the dress of a veritable highwaymen.

Having made them up into a compact bundle, Ogle watched his opportunity, and entering Tom's little sleeping apartment in his absence, displayed the various articles to the best advantage on the bed and chairs and other furniture in the apartment.

The effect was almost startling—at least, Ogle thought and hoped that it would be; and it was with some degree of impatience that he busied himself as best he could while waiting for Tom's arrival from Wardour Street; for even his joy at the anticipated sport on the road that night could not induce him to forego the pleasure of paying the old gal, as he invariably called Mrs. Ripon, a visit to show that he was safe and well.

At length Ogle heard his cheery voice singing a lively air as he entered his little room.

Suddenly the song ceased, and a long whistle proceeded from Tom's lips.

Whew!

Ogle knew that Tom was regarding his highwayman's costume.

"Ogle! Ogle! Come here! Hoy! Where are you? Why don't you come? Good gracious! Just fancy! Upon my word, I am quite handsome!"

Tom was standing before a looking-glass and admiring his hat, which he had put on in the most approved highwayman's style.

Ogle was watching him, and a smile of undisguised admiration played upon his features as he did so.

Tom was still busily engaged in arranging some rebellious locks beneath the hat, when Ogle laid his hand upon his shoulder, saying, "Well, Tom, will the dress do?"

Tom turned round, and clasped both Ogle's hands in his.

"I knew it was you, Ogle! Isn't it all beautiful? What will the Captain say?—eh, Ogle?"

"Well, Tom, he knows all about it, for it was he who gave me the commission this morning to go and get everything that I thought was necessary to equip you for a veritable knight of the road."

"Captain Heron!" exclaimed Tom. "How good and kind! Hurrah! Hurrah! I say, what time is it, Ogle? It seems to me as if this day would never pass away! What time is it?"

"Just eight o'clock," replied Ogle.

"Well," said Tom, "I shall begin to dress myself at once—it will take me at least two hours to get into all this grandeur! Hip! hip! hurrah! Won't the girls be in love with me now, eh, Ogle?"

Tom soon commenced the process of dressing, and he might be excused for the look of admiration which sat upon his youthful face as he regarded himself in his little mirror.

"Rather the thing!" said Tom, as he rearranged his black hair before placing the felt hat carefully upon his head. "Yes, that'll do! Now Daisy, my lass! Off we go!"

Tom was not long leading Daisy from the stable, and in the court-yard he encountered Ogle.

"Upon my word, Tom," said Ogle, "I scarcely knew you!"

"Of course you didn't," said Tom, laughing merrily. "I say, Ogle!"

"Well, Tom?"

"Where's the Captain?"

"Here he is," said Felix Heron, who had overheard Tom's question. "I thought I should like to see how you looked, Tom."

"Thank you, Captain. I did not seem to like to go without seeing you, Captain. I fancy I shall have more luck now."

"Good-bye, my boy," said Felix Heron as he grasped Tom's hand, "and never forget that I am your debtor for life!"

There was a tremor in Felix Heron's voice, as he alluded to the service which Tom Ripon had done him in saving the life of his child, which for a moment checked Tom's hilarity.

"I'm coming, Daisy!" shouted Tom, in order to hide the emotion which he felt on hearing Captain Heron thus allude to what he had done. "I'm coming, my lass!" And raising his hat, not ungracefully, to Felix Heron, he bounded into the court-yard again, and was soon mounted on the back of Daisy.

___

CHAPTER CCLXXIII.

TOM RIPON HAS AN ADVENTURE ON THE ROAD WHICH FILLS HIS POCKETS.

TOM galloped on for some distance, until he found himself in a spot which was a very dark one, indeed; and there were tall trees upon each side; yet, from the width, it was quite clear to him that he was still upon the high road.

Tom reined in Daisy, uncertain whether or not to proceed on the course he was, when his considerations were rather abruptly interrupted by the sound of carriage wheels and a loud voice exclaiming, "Oh, there is no one here, madam, to pay any attention to you! We are alone here, so take that!"

The slash of a whip, followed by a scream from some female's lips, came plainly to Tom's ears.

"What can this mean?" said Tom to himself. "Ho, Daisy!—forward! Forward, my lass!"

Tom dashed forward in the direction of the sound.

There was a turn in the road, and the moment Tom got past it he saw a chaise with the lamps alight in the middle of the road.

Tom and Daisy were out of the line of light that the lamps cast around them: but he could see, without being himself seen, a man standing up in the chaise, while a female form was crouching down in it. The man had the chaise whip in his hand, and was preparing to strike the female again.

A flush of indignation came to Tom's face; but for a moment he restrained himself, and waited to see what more would pass before he interfered with the cowardly villain who was thus ill-using a defenceless woman.

"Oh, I saw you!" roared the man. "I saw you, madam, looking at that man on horseback, as we came through the New Road! I'll not have it—so take that!"

"Oh! you are so jealous, George!" said the female in a gentle voice. "You know I love you, and you only, and yet you treat me thus!"

"Don't tell me I am jealous!" again shouted the man. "Of course you'll say it's jealousy; but I saw it with my own eyes, I tell you; and I won't put up with it, so take that!"

"Oh! George—George!" sobbed the hapless female; "you had much better get home with that large sum of money you have about you, than stop here to ill-use me on the high road!"

"I think so, too!" said Tom, to himself, as he dashed up to the side of the chaise with one bound.

The lady gave a scream, and the man with the whip turned in alarm to see who it was who so suddenly appeared by the side of the chaise, as though he had dropped from the clouds in order to interfere with his proceedings.

"Hold!" cried Tom. "Use that whip again, and it is at the peril of your life!"

"And who may you be?" asked the man.

"That matters not," replied Tom; "but I will soon make you aware what you will be pretty quickly!"

As Tom spoke, he produced one of his pistols, and held it within three inches of the man's face.

The man turned as pale as death, and sunk on to one of the seats of the chaise, trembling in every limb.

"Oh! you are a coward, after all!" said Tom, still keeping the muzzle of his pistol in dangerous proximity to the man's eyes.

"No—no! Good sir—I only—— Oh, dear me! Let me go, if you please, my dear sir! I am not a coward—but I have not the pleasure of your acquaintance!"

"You are not a coward?" said Tom, in a voice of indignation. "Not a coward to think of striking a woman? And as for not having the pleasure of my acquaintance, I promise you that you shall not forget me the longest day you have to live!"

"Spare me!—oh, spare me! Help! Murder!"

"Another such cry as that, and I will blow

your worthless brains out," said Tom, "and thus rid this lady of your presence!"

'Mercy! Spare me!"

"As you spared her!" said Tom.

Tom pointed to the lady, who was still weeping in a corner of the chaise.

"She's not hurt!" whined the man. "She is only making this fuss in order that you may murder me!"

"Oh, no, no!" said the lady; "spare his life, and let him go."

"Now, listen to me," said Tom. "I always heard that the man who could raise his hand against a woman was a coward at heart—especially if that woman were a suffering one, and in no way capable of resisting him."

"Oh, dear, yes!" said the man. "I perfectly agree with everything you say, my dear sir—anything you please, so that you will kindly allow me to go on my way."

"You are very obliging!" said Tom; "but I have not quite done with you yet. Madam, will you kindly remove your handkerchief from your face? I do not wish to be rude, but oblige me in this one request, as I wish to be of service to you."

The lady removed her handkerchief, and gazed into Tom's face.

That one glance was sufficient to enable Tom to see that it was both young and fair, and that across one cheek there was a livid mark.

"How came that mark upon your face, madam?" asked Tom.

"Oh, do not ask me! Suffice it to say that you have saved me from further ill-usage, and that you have my gratitude. Farewell!"

"Are you this man's wife?"

"Alas, yes!" sobbed a gentle voice, and again the lady buried her face in her handkerchief.

"Ah! I thought as much!" said Tom. "Such a man would not dare to raise his hand against any other woman than the only one he was in duty bound to protect!"

Turning, then, again towards the man with a sudden fierceness which made him start, Tom cried out, "Your money, villain!—or your life and money both! Quick! I will put up with no delay!"

"Yes, certainly, my dear sir; you are quite welcome to every farthing I have about me! It isn't much, I'm sorry to say; but such as it is, you are quite welcome to it, as I said before!"

Tom rattled the pistol on the side of the chaise.

"Be quick, sir," he said; "I give you only another minute!"

"Yes, yes, if you please! There is all I have—only a few shillings, which I put into my pocket to pay the tolls! I don't know how I shall get on without them; but, nevertheless, dear sir, you are quite welcome to them!"

"I know," said Tom, "that you have a very large sum of money about you, sir; so be quick, and hand it over to me! I just give you while I can count three!"

"Oh, mercy!"

"One!"

"Yes, yes——"

"Two!" shouted Tom; and again he placed the pistol close to the man's eyes.

"Thr——"

"Here, dear sir!—here is my pocket-book, if you please! Take all that is in it; but let me have the pocket-book back, as it contains valuable memoranda, which will be of no use to you, while to me they are of the greatest importance!"

"You shall have it back," said Tom; and he commenced transferring to his pocket several bank-notes and guineas.

While he was thus employed, Tom's eyes were necessarily removed from the man who had excited so justly his indignation for his cowardly behaviour towards his unfortunate wife.

"Oh, don't—don't, George!"

As the lady uttered these words, Tom raised his eyes, and saw, but too late, the barrel of a pistol levelled at him.

He had just time, however, to jerk the man's arm, and the bullet grazed Tom's cheek, and then buried itself in the trunk of a tree which stood close by.

"Villain!" shouted Tom, "you shall pay for that dastardly act!"

"Oh, spare him—spare him!" implored the lady. "Do not kill him!"

"I will not kill him, madam," said Tom, "since you ask his worthless life; but I will give him a lesson he shall not forget in a hurry!" —then turning to the man, who had sunk down in the chaise the personification of abject fear, he said, fiercely, "Get out of the chaise, sir!"

The man sunk to his knees, and clasping his hands together, he said, "I beg your pardon, kind sir; and if you will forgive and forget——"

"Silence!" shouted Tom. "Get out of the chaise, I say, or I will drag you out!"

"Get out, George," said the lady, gently; "this gentleman says he will not attempt to take your life! Get out, or it may be worse for us, perhaps!"

Tom pretended not to have heard this admonition given by the lady to her brutal husband, but reaching down from Daisy, opened the door of the chaise, saying as he did so, "Take him out, Daisy!"

Daisy, at this order from Tom, took hold of the man by the back of the neck, and he would have been quickly removed from the chaise had not Tom again interposed.

"Quiet, Daisy—quiet, lass!"

In an instant the creature let go her hold; and the man, seeing that there was no appeal to be made, prepared with a very bad grace to get out of the chaise.

As soon as the man was fairly on the ground, Tom dismounted, fearing that he might perhaps run off.

"Guard him, Daisy—guard him!" said Tom; and the sagacious animal instantly took such a hold on his arm, that the man cried out, "Murder! murder! Help!"

Tom took no notice whatever, but quietly continued doing what he was about—viz., releasing the horses from the chaise; and then taking off the reins, he very expertly bound the man to the tree, in which was embedded the bullet which he had fired at Tom in so dastardly a fashion.

Tom then went to the chaise, and picked up

the whip which lay at the of bottom it, and returned to the man, who was trembling with fear.

"Now, sir," said Tom, "you have attempted my life; what is there to prevent me now having a shot at you, I should like to know?"

The man tried to sink to his knees, but not being able to accomplish the act on account of the position in which Tom had bound him to the tree, he clasped his hands together, and roared for mercy.

"Silence!" said Tom. "If you make such an uproar as that, nothing shall induce me to spare your life! I now intend to make you take a solemn vow!"

"Yes, good, kind sir—anything you please! You have my money, and in my pocket you will find a gold repeater,—only don't—pray don't look so angry!"

Tom quickly transferred the watch to his own pocket.

"Now, sir," he said, "promise me that you will never raise your hand against your wife again!"

"But she is so provoking, my dear sir! Oh! Help! Murder!"

Tom began to use the chaise-whip pretty freely without any regard as to where the blows fell.

"Then do you like that? Now, will you promise?"

The man was silent.

"Oh, very well! You shall have a little more, then, if you wish! Take that—and that—and that!"

"Mercy! mercy, noble sir!" roared the man. "I will promise you anything you wish!"

"Say, then, that you will never again raise your hand to strike your wife!"

"Well, sir—yes, sir—I daresay she will not give me cause again; and then you see, sir——"

Slash! slash! went the whip again over the face and shoulders of the cowardly wretch who had not scrupled to use that same instrument of torture to a helpless woman.

"Stop! In mercy, stop! I shall be killed! I shall never get over this—I know I shall not!"

"Do you promise, then?" said Tom.

"Yes, yes—anything—everything!"

"That won't do," said Tom. "Repeat after me."

"Yes, sir."

"I promise that I will never again raise my cowardly hand——"

"I promise that I will never again raise my hand——"

"No," said Tom; "that won't do! I said cowardly hand; and there's something to brighten up your memory a bit.

Slash! slash!

"Mercy! mercy! Yes—oh, I forgot—I promise that I will never again raise my cowardly hand——"

"Against my wife——" continued Tom.

"Against my wife——" repeated the man.

"Who is a thousand times too good for such a scoundrel——" Tom went on.

The man hesitated.

Slash! slash! slash! again went the whip.

"Who is a thousand times too good for such a scoundrel——" repeated the man.

"As I am," said Tom.

"As I am," repeated the man.

Tom now returned to the chaise, where the lady was still weeping bitterly.

"Don't be alarmed, madam," said Tom; "you will have reason to be thankful of having met me. I have given your brutal husband a lesson that I think he will not easily forget; and now I will bid you farewell!"

Tom raised his hat as he spoke, and mounting Daisy, he rode away, well knowing that his prisoner would soon be released from his unpleasant position by his late victim.

Tom now put Daisy to a gallop, and did not draw rein until he came in sight of a little inn, which rejoiced in the title of "The Hungry Man."

"Woa, Daisy, woa!" said Tom. "I'll just look in here, and find out if Johnny is on the road to-night. I've not made a bad night's work of it. That cowardly vagabond's pocket-book was pretty well filled; and it's quite certain that I am much more deserving of the guineas than he could have been."

By the time Tom had come to this conclusion he reached the door of the little hostel, and knocked loudly for admission.

"Hoy!—hoy! House!—house! Open!"

"Goodness gracious me!" exclaimed a female voice; "I declare if it ain't a highwayman as beautiful as anything!"

Tom smiled as he heard the exclamation, and said to himself, "I knew how it would be, but Ogle wouldn't believe me. All the women will be ready to fall in love with me; but I must speak to this susceptible young damsel, and find out if Wild is on the road to-night."

Then raising his hat, and speaking in a lower tone, he said, "Mary, my dear, come and open the door; I want to speak to you."

"La! good gracious! I daren't, for the life of me, come down—master has gone to bed."

"Well, never mind that," said Tom. "My life is in danger, perhaps, and you can save me!"

"Poor young gentleman!" said the girl. "I'll come down in a minute if you wait."

Tom had not long to wait before the door was opened by a blooming damsel, who certainly looked anything but averse to receive the compliments Tom lavished upon her.

"I want to know, my dear," said Tom, "if you have had any company here to-night?"

"No," said the girl, "nobody to speak of, only that vile-looking wretch who squints with one eye."

"Who's that?" asked Tom, feeling uncomfortably assured that his friend Mary was speaking of his implacable foe, Jonathan Wild.

"Well, I don't know now what his name was. Stop a bit—yes, I do—Savage, I think. No, that wasn't it either! Dear me! what could the wretch's name be?"

"Wild?" suggested Tom.

"Ah! yes! Wild!—that was it. I knew it was some dreadful name. Yes, Wild was his name. Do you know him? He isn't a friend of yours, is he?"

"I should rather think not," said Tom, "when, if he could lay hands on me, he would hang me at Tyburn with less remorse than I would hang a cat."

"Merciful Providence!" almost shrieked the girl. "Go away—go away!"

"Why, what on earth ails the girl?" asked Tom, in surprise. "Are you mad?"

"Oh, no—no! but go—go at once; for that man Savage—no, not Savage, I mean Wild—said he would look in again in about an hour's time, and there's the clatter of his horse's feet, I declare!"

Now most unmistakably came upon the ears of Tom the sound of horse's feet, and he had just time to drag Daisy towards the back portion of the house, when he heard the voice of Wild shouting, "Open! open! You have a highwayman concealed here—I saw him come in!"

The tumult which Jonathan Wild made effectually aroused the landlord from his slumbers, who, as soon as he heard Jonathan's voice, quickly descended.

No. 88.—EDITH HERON.

"Eh? What? What is all this?" he asked "Oh, Mr. Wild! I did not know, sir!"

"I want that highwayman you have concealed in this house!" shouted Wild.

Now the reader is well aware that the worthy landlord really had no idea of Tom's appearance beneath the roof, for the servant girl had adroitly slammed shut the door as soon as the first sound of the horse's feet met her ear, and had herself retired unobserved.

Hearing now, however, what Wild said about the highwayman, and hoping to save the handsome young man from his enemies, she now rushed into the room, saying, "Yes, I saw him! I saw him!—he rode past here, just as I was looking out of the window; and I believe he intends to murder sombody—he looked awful!"

Jonathan stopped to hear no more, but rode away in the direction indicated by the girl.

CHAPTER CCLXXIV.

LADY CASTLENEAU MAKES A COURAGEOUS DE-
TERMINATION.

NEVER in the history of his chequered existence
had Felix Heron, Earl of Whitcombe, passed so
complete a period of repose as that which had
characterized his recent life.

Many and anxious were the consultations he
held with the Earl of Bridgewater, regarding the
succession to his titles and estates of his son.

And these consultations assumed a character of
redoubled anxiety from a piece of intelligence
which was brought to him by Colonel Trelawney.

That intelligence was just this.

The question of the succession to the title of
Earl of Whitcombe was about to be complicated
by the erection of a new Earldom of that
name.

My Lord Clackington, practising upon the
weakness and vices of the monarch, had claimed,
as a reward for all his past services, a step in
the peerage.

That step was to have the effect of creating
him Earl of Whitcombe.

How this was to be combated became the
subject of a conference which took place at
Whitcombe House, in the dusk of the evening;
and at which were present the Earl of Bridgewater, Colonel Trelawney, the young Marquis of
Ormond, and Lady Castleneau.

Of course, Heron and Edith, as the principal
personages concerned, listened and took part in
all that occurred, with intense interest.

Colonel Trelawney made his statement again;
and although he endeavoured to word it in such
a manner that it should be in the least degree
offensive to the feelings of Edith or of Heron,
yet there was much in it which could not fail to
give them many a pang.

"It is scarcely necessary," said the Colonel,
"that I should acquaint you with the name of
my informant; but upon the authenticity of my
information you may rely; and I can assure you,
Whitcombe, that it is intended to bestow your
honourable and ancient name, and title, upon one
of the basest of men!"

"Rather," cried Heron, "ten times rather
would I that the coronet of my earldom rested
even upon the brow of Jonathan Wild, than that
it should fall into the possession of such a man
as Clackington!"

"Yes," added Colonel Trelawney; "Clackington is the man; and I call upon our mutual friend,
Bridgewater, here, to confirm my statement."

"I can confirm it," said the young Earl of
Bridgewater.

"But upon what pretence," exclaimed Edith,
"can this new earldom, upon an ancient title, be
engrafted? Does the King and his Council forget that, although to all appearance, and in the
world's estimation, my husband is no more,
that I have a son who inherits his name and
titles?"

The Earl of Bridgewater and Colonel Trelawney exchanged uneasy glances.

The young Marquis of Ormond seemed afraid
to meet the gaze of any one present.

It was evident that some secret sat uneasily
upon the minds of all the gentlemen.

And old Lady Castleneau, who had hitherto
not spoken, saw with her habitual acuteness that
such was the fact.

"Let us know all," she said. "I can well presume that there is something upon your minds,
which you hesitate to give utterance to."

"We do hesitate," said Colonel Trelawney
"and yet it is necessary that we should make a
statement clearly and distinctly."

"Make it, then!" cried Lady Castleneau. "We
are not children, to be frightened at a shadow."

"Then I call upon our friend Bridgewater to
make it, since from him I just heard it."

"I do not shrink," said the Earl of Bridgewater;
"and in answer to the observations which have
been made by Lady Whitcombe, I may say that
the reason put forth by Lord Clackington for
asking the King to confer on him the earldom of
Whitcombe, consists of an allegation on his part
that the—the——"

"Gracious heavens!" exclaimed Lady Castleneau. "What is the matter with my Lord
Bridgewater? Has he lost his senses or his
powers of speech?"

"Neither, my dear Lady Castleneau; but I
naturally shrink from saying a very disagreeable
thing to a dear friend."

"Whatever it is, Bridgewater," said Heron, "it
will lose its sting by coming from your lips."

"Then," added the Earl, "I will state that the
legitimacy of your son is questioned."

"Indeed!"

"Yes. That is the ground upon which Lord
Clackington goes. You are believed to be no
more, and it is alleged that the marriage; if
marriage there were, was of too informal a character to entitle your son to claim either the name
or honours of his father."

"Is that all?" cried Lady Castleneau, at the
highest pitch of her voice. "I only wish I had
my Lord Clackington here; I fancy I could alter
his opinion."

"No, aunt," said Edith sadly, "you would
not alter his opinion; for he cannot doubt the
truth of my position or the legitimacy of my
child, however it may suit his purposes to affect
to do so!"

"Let me speak, now," said Trelawney. "I
am quite convinced that such an allegation would
not be put forward unless some means had been
taken to carry it out; and you may depend, Whitcombe, that unless you are in actual possession
of clear and substantial proofs of your marriage,
there will be the greatest difficulty in substantiat-
ing it."

Both Heron's and Edith's thoughts flew back
to that time of difficulty, trouble, and danger,
when they became united in defiance of a thousand
obstacles.

The possibility likewise of all the substantial
proofs of that union being obliterated, came but
too clearly before their imaginations.

"This will never do," cried Heron; "it seems
to me, my good friends, that I shall have to come
to life again, for the purpose of confounding this
new iniquity."

"But will that answer the purpose?" asked
Bridgewater.

"Rather the reverse," said the young Marquis
of Ormond. "For it seems to me it would only
complicate the transaction."

Lady Castleneau rose and advanced two steps towards the table in the centre of the room.

"And all this trouble," she said, "is to be taken and endured in order that my Lord Clackington should receive the reward of an infamous life spent in crime and iniquity, at the hands of a Sovereign to whom he has been the basest of menials?"

"Aunt," said Heron, with a smile, "you call things by their right names, and I cannot help thinking, with all due deference to my friend Ormond, that I must re-appear again upon the busy scenes of life in my true character, and let Captain Fantome, of the royal navy, be for ever obliterated and forgotten."

"No," said Lady Castleneau; "something better that, Felix, can be done."

The eyes of all present were turned towards the courageous old lady, who thus continued: "Instead of Felix re-appearing, and exposing himself to the enmity and villany of those who we know seek his life, let the subject of this difficulty disappear."

"Disappear?" exclaimed Heron.

"Disappear?" cried the Earl of Bridgewater and Colonel Trelawney with one voice.

"Yes. Let my Lord Clackington disappear, and with him will likewise pass away his troublesome and pertinacious attempt upon the peerage of Whitcombe."

"That is a bold measure, aunt," said Heron, with a smile.

"Not very; but I think you misunderstand me. I do not mean to take the wretch's life, but to keep him somewhere in seclusion and in secrecy, until some change takes place that will render him harmless for further mischief."

"Good!" cried the Earl of Bridgewater.

"In truth," said Colonel Trelawney, "it might be done; and as we all know the King's physicians do not give him six months of life now, the plan approves itself to my mind each moment."

"Moreover," said Bridgewater, "the heir to the throne, as we well know, detests the very name of Clackington."

They looked at each other then for a few seconds in silence, and then Colonel Trelawney held up his hand as he cried, "Agreed! I vote for the temporary suppression of my Lord Clackington, and trust that we shall be unanimous on that point."

"Agreed!" cried everybody.

"Then I will set about it at once," said Lady Castleneau.

"You, aunt?"

"And why not? Do you think that I am so helpless and harmless that I cannot seize upon such a poor wretch as my Lord Clackington? The only question is where to put him, even for the six months that the King's physicians think the present reign will last?"

This was a question which no one seemed able to answer at the moment, and Lady Castleneau, after looking from one to the other for a few seconds in silence, exclaimed, "I see how it is. I must not only make this man a prisoner, but keep him too."

"No, aunt, no!" said Heron; "that will never do. You would be involved in future trouble on his account."

"The trouble would be nothing," replied Lady Castleneau; "and I particularly desire that this plan be left to me to carry out. Let me see, Felix. What is the name of that boy you have in your household, who wanted to be a highwayman?"

"Tom Ripon: he not only wanted to be a highwayman, but is one."

"Then send him to me, and with his assistance only I promise effectually to remove my Lord Clackington out of the way of being further troublesome."

"Then," said the Earl of Bridgewater, "our conference comes to an end. Of course you are aware, Whitcombe, that your half-brother, Warringdale, is intent upon the same project, but his chances of success are too slender to permit them to give you the slightest uneasiness."

The party rose, and as the shadows of evening began to render objects in the room indistinct, they took leave of Heron and of Edith, leaving Lady Castleneau to make her own arrangements for the temporary seclusion of my Lord Clackington.

"Let me see this Tom Ripon," said the old lady, "and I will explain to him what I wish him to do."

"But, dear aunt," said Edith, "are you not going to let us know exactly your course of proceedings?"

"No, dear niece, I am not. I have read and heard quite enough regarding all such matters as these to feel convinced that the more one keeps one's own counsel the better. The best general is the one who has the fewest confidants; so let me alone, my dear, and you may depend I shall dispose of my Lord Clackington."

Tom Ripon was sent for, and made his appearance in that drawing-room, with a very dubious expression of countenance.

Tom was afraid that some abrupt end was about to be brought to his experiences on the road, but he was speedily reassured by the first words of Lady Castleneau.

"Tom," she said, "if you have no fear, and are in want of an adventure that may produce both profit and satisfaction, you must get into my coach, and come to my house at once."

"I'm your man, Lady Castleneau!" said Tom. "I suppose the Captain knows all about it?"

"Yes, Tom," said Heron; "and I wish particularly that you should place yourself completely under the orders of Lady Castleneau."

"All's right! Shall I take Daisy, Captain?"

"No," interposed Lady Castleneau, "there will be no occasion."

The old lady consulted her watch, which was one of those huge old time-pieces weighing at least a pound, that were then thought quite wonders of the mechanical arts.

"Half-past eight," she said. "I hope between this and midnight to have that wretched man, Clackington, in safe keeping. Come along, Tom, and don' tread on my skirts."

Tom made a comical face to Edith and Heron as he followed Lady Castleneau from Whitcombe House.

He would have got upon the coach-box along with old Anthony, or hung on behind that wonderful vehicle which Lady Castleneau, in defiance of time and fashion, still used; but as she had her plan to explain to him, she insisted upon him riding inside.

What that plan was we need not here detail, since, in its progress, it will sufficiently explain itself.

By nine o'clock the state of affairs at Castleneau House was just this.

Lady Castleneau, still attired for the open air, and with her hands reposing in a wonderful muff of enormous proportions, sat in that breakfast-room with which the reader is so familiar.

In the court-yard of the house was the carriage, with its two sleek, well-fed horses; while old Anthony, wondering what his mistress could be about to wish to go out at such a time of night, stood by their heads as if in deep consultation with them.

There is a foot upon the staircase of Castleneau House.

There is a rustle of garments in its old hall.

A faint scream, evidently in female tones, makes Lady Castleneau impatient and a little angry.

She taps the floor impatiently with her foot.

The door of the breakfast-room is then opened, and Martha, with the corner of her apron stuffed into her mouth to suppress her laughter, enters, exclaiming, " Here he is, my lady! No, I mean here she is! That is, I mean Tom Ripon, my lady! Here she is, if you please!"

What appeared to be a female form, attired in a very elegant dress of pale blue satin, sailed into the apartment, and executed such an elaborate curtsey, that it seemed impossible to conceive she would ever rise to the perpendicular again.

"Nonsense! said Lady Castleneau; "you must be perfectly serious."

"All's right!" said Tom Ripon—for it was, indeed, none other than that personage, who was attired in the elegant satin dress, and whose hair had been frizzed and powdered by Martha until he really resembled, as old Anthony afterwards remarked, a very fine young woman.

"Tom Ripon," said Lady Castleneau, with some severity of tone and manner.

"Yes, my lady."

"Recollect that upon the expedition we are going, the less you say the better; and we must have no levity whatever."

"All's right!" said Tom. " I have my pistols with me, and I'm going to carry them in this little bit of a bag that Martha calls a *ridicule!*"

"Which I suppose is a reticule," said Lady Castleneau. " I, too, will go armed, for it may be quite necessary to frighten that wretched old sinner within an inch of his life."

CHAPTER CCLXXV.

LADY CASTLENEAU AND TOM RIPON PROCEED TO
ST. JAMES'S PALACE.

ALL the passive resistance in the world, and all the remonstrances against the perpetration of such a piece of iniquity contemplated by my Lord Clackington, could not have produced a hundredth part of the effect which these energetic proceedings of Lady Castleneau certainly promised.

Probably there was not another nobleman about the Court of St. James's who would have striven to place himself in possession of the dormant peerage of Whitcombe, even if it had been proved to be so.

And although vice had its votaries in those quarters as well as elsewhere, still the kind of natural odium which would attach to any man who would seek to make war against the rights of the widow and the fatherless, might well cause even the most grasping and avaricious of the hangers on of royalty to hesitate before they would seek to arrogate to themselves the Earldom of Whitcombe.

But my Lord Clackington had no such scruples.

And if, under ordinary circumstances, the slightest shadow of any such sensations had crossed his mind, his continued anger and rage, both at Edith and her husband, the deceased Earl, as he was supposed to be, would have overcome them.

It was a kind of triumph over the dead that Lord Clackington looked to.

And, inasmuch as he could not fairly contend with, or overcome, the Earl of Whitcombe in life, he gloated over the idea of despoiling his widow of her fair fame, and his infant son of his name and his inheritance.

We shall see how he fared.

Probably my Lord Clackington was well armed against any ordinary resistance.

He expected remonstrances from the friends of Edith.

Perhaps he expected a petition from the Countess of Whitcombe to the King.

And, probably, in addition to that, he looked forward to no inconsiderable amount of public obliquy.

But for all that he was prepared.

The prize he wished to grasp seemed to him to be well worth all these considerations.

But in his most discursive dreams upon the subject, he never contemplated such an action as that which had been advised by Lady Castleneau, and which we now see she was prepared, with her usual energy, to carry out.

"Now, Tom!" said the old lady; "follow me and be discreet.

"I mean to," said Tom. "Some young women are a disgrace to their sex; but I shall set a public example."

"The first effort in that direction," said Lady Castleneau, rather curtly, "should be to keep silent."

"All's right, my lady!" said Tom.

Tom Ripon gallantly offered his arm to old Lady Castleneau; but she declined it, informing him that that was not the way to keep up his supposed character.

"You look the young gentlewoman well enough," she said; " but the slightest indiscretion would betray you; and recollect, that upon the proceedings of this night probably depend the peace and happiness of those who, I believe, are very dear to you."

These words had a great effect upon Tom Ripon.

The kind of levity of air and demeanour that had come over him since he had been attired by Martha in female apparel, subsided at once.

TOM RIPON COMES ON A NEW CHARACTER.

Presented Gratis with No. 88, of the New Edition of EDITH the Sequel to Edith the Captive; or, the Robbers of Epping Forest.

"Lady Castleneau." he said; "you may depend upon me. I may be a wild sort of fellow at times, but when there really is anything serious to be done, I can look as grave, and be as silent, as any of those old owls in Epping Forest, that used to stare at us all when we were going out on an expedition with the Captain, and then sit on the stump of a tree all the night long, asking no questions, but, no doubt, wondering who we were, and what we were about."

"Come on, then!" said Lady Castleneau; "I feel assured that I can trust you."

The court-yard was reached, and old Anthony, as usual, assisted his mistress into the antiquated coach.

Tom followed, looking as demure as possible, and only replying to Anthony's blank stare of astonishment by the slightest possible wink, and a kick, which made the old man jump again.

"Good gracious!" muttered Anthony; "what's going to happen now?"

"To St. James's Palace!" said Lady Castleneau.

"Yes, my lady."

The old sleek horses were set in motion, and through the now tolerably crowded streets—for it was that time in the evening when a number of persons were returning to their homes—the ancient vehicle made its way to the Court end of the town.

Upon reaching the gateway of the Palace, the carriage was stopped, since none but known visitors and members of the household were permitted to drive into the Colour Court.

Lady Castleneau spoke from the window of the vehicle.

"I wish to see my Lord Clackington," she said; "and I have an appointment with him of importance."

The name of Clackington was too well known as that of the King's prime favourite, for it to be otherwise than a good passport of admission to St. James's.

After a little hesitation, the carriage was allowed to proceed, and it rattled over those old stones, on which so many illustrious feet have trod, into the Colour Court.

A couple of dim oil lamps lighted this court, or, rather, made darkness visible within it.

A soldier off duty, however, had been sent from the guard-room with a lantern, and marshalled the way for Anthony. He directed him to pull up his horses at a particular doorway; and then, informing him gruffly that there he would hear of my Lord Clackington, he made a surly kind of salutation to Lady Castleneau, and was about to leave.

"Stop!" said Lady Castleneau; "we never allow any one to do us a service without being paid for it."

The soldier looked perfectly astonished at the guinea which Lady Castleneau placed in his hand.

He paused, as if expecting some extra service would be required of him for so large a payment.

"If you wish," said Lady Castleneau, "to do us more service, you will probably be at the gate as we leave the Palace?"

"That will I, marm, if you should be half the night before you do so!"

Lady Castleneau felt that at all events she had secured one ally who would be quite ready to do her any service; and however obscure he might be, there was no telling how useful the good opinion of such a man as that even might be in an emergency.

Anthony alighted and knocked at the door indicated by the soldier.

The demand for admission was answered by one of the Yeomen of the Guard, who evidently looked with intense surprise at the extraordinary equipage that was drawn up in the court-yard.

"My mistress would speak to you," said Anthony.

"Who is she? A lady?"

"What else should she be?"

"But I mean title—title?"

"Certainly, a lady."

"All's right."

The Yeoman stepped to the door of the carriage, and, glancing into it, he exclaimed, in a mysterious tone of voice, "Clytemnestra!"

"What?" exclaimed Lady Castleneau.

"Media!"

"Eh?" exclaimed Lady Castleneau again.

The Yeoman of the Guard and the occupants of the carriage now gazed at each in silence for a few seconds, which was interrupted by Tom's natural loquacity, which could be kept quiet no longer.

"What do you mean?" said Tom, speaking in an affected falsetto voice,—"what do you mean by calling us such names? I believe you're a gay deceiver; and as a respectable young woman, I beg you will keep your distance, you misleader."

"That's it," said the Yeoman. "That'll do."

"What'll do?" said Tom.

"Why, marm, you might as well have said it at once!"

"Said what at once?" asked Lady Castleneau, with some impatience.

"Why, marm," said the Yeoman, "if the young lady had said she was Miss Leda at once, I should have known all about it, for that's one of 'em. And if the young lady will be so good as to alight and follow me, I shall be very happy to lead the way."

"What does it all mean?" whispered Tom to Lady Castleneau. "I never said I was Miss anybody."

"Hush! it's the man's mistake."

"Rather!"

"Don't alight."

"I don't mean."

"Now, miss, if you please," added the Yeoman. "His lordship is in the Yellow Cabinet, and a certain person is at supper."

"Get out!" said Tom. "What do I care about your certain person and yellow cabinets? I want to see my Lord Clackington. And all you've got to do, my good man, is to go and tell him that a young, tender, and delicate female, subject to kicking hysterics if she don't have her own way, is waiting in the court-yard to see him."

The Yeoman shook his head.

"His lordship never comes out; and as you are one of them, Miss Leda, you ought to have known that."

"Tom!" whispered Lady Castleneau.

"Yes, my lady."

"You will have to go. I trust all to your discretion. You must see my Lord Clackington, and, upon one pretext or another, get him to come down here and step into the coach."

"Very good," said Tom, "I'll try it; and if he won't come in a proper way, I'll carry him."

"Now, miss, if you please," said the Yeoman; "are you coming?"

"I am," said Tom; "but it's a very hard thing that a delicate young female should ask for a gentleman to come out to her coach, and be told he won't."

"That's not my business, miss," said the Yeoman; "only I know he never does come out. Allow me to assist you."

"Thank you," said Tom, as he alighted from the carriage, taking care to come with all the weight he could upon the Yeoman's toes; and then, pretending to trip a little, Tom thrust his elbow into the stomach of the Yeoman with such force, that the man was nearly doubled up with the concussion.

"Dear me!" said Tom; "mind what you're about! Is this the way to treat a female in her teens?"

"I don't know!" growled the Yeoman; "but my toes are smashed, and I haven't a bit of breath left in me!"

"Then you should be more careful and considerate, you horrid earthen jar!" said Tom.

"Earthen jar!" exclaimed the Yeoman.

"Yes. A fair young being like me is a real chany tea-cup—delicate as a piece of tissue paper, and as pretty as puff-paste; but wretches like you are nothing but common earthenware!"

"Well, it may be so," said the Yeoman; "but the chany tea-cup has got a deuce of a point to its elbow!"

"Lead the way, fellow," added Tom. "I wouldn't have you come behind me on any account. You'd have you're hoofs on my skirt every moment. There, now, go on!"

The Yeoman preceded Tom into the Palace, muttering to himself some not very complimentary expressions in regard to Miss Leda.

Tom thought he was playing his part to perfection; but it will be seen that his notions of the habits and behaviour of young ladies in general were rather crude.

The Yeoman led the way across a small corridor, and up a staircase very thickly carpeted.

The stairs, however, were rather steep; and Tom was not in the habit of ascending any steps whatever, steep or shallow, in female costume.

The consequence was, that he slipped twice or thrice, and each time made such a grasp at the Yeoman, that he nearly brought him down the whole flight.

"Good gracious!" ejaculated the Yeoman; "whenever shall I get rid of this dreadful young person?"

"There you go again!" said Tom, as he slipped again for the fourth time, just at the head of the stairs.

This time, the tug that Tom gave to the Yeoman's coat fairly overthrew him; and Miss Leda, as he supposed, scrambled over him without the least ceremony, and leaped on to the landing.

"I have a good mind to scream," said Tom; "and I'll tell my mother, as sure as you're born!"

"Go to the deuce!" cried the Yeoman. "I believe you're mad; and I'm only sorry I let you in at all!"

"Men," said Tom, "were deceivers ever; but I didn't come here to be made game of by a low fellow like you!"

"I won't go any further," said the Yeoman; "You may find your own way, and be hanged!"

"Be off, then!" said Tom. "And the next time you have a delicate young lady to show up a staircase, don't be tumbling about and pretending to be drunk. Take that, and be off! Nervous and delicate as I am, too!"

The kick with which Tom accelerated the movements of the Yeoman was so heartily bestowed, that he made but one flying leap down the whole flight of stairs into the corridor below.

"Well," said Tom, as he re-arranged his somewhat disordered apparel,—"I think, if Lady Castleneau had seen all this, she would have been quite delighted at my supporting the character so well. Any other fellow, now, might have walked in looking as demure as a cat, but that wouldn't have answered a bit, and I dare say that fellow thinks I'm a girl of spirit. I wonder where I am now?"

Tom pushed open a door very handsomely covered with crimson velvet, and studded with a profusion of gilt nails.

It led him into a picture gallery, where hung portraits of many of the monarchs of England, and various members of their families.

The gallery was lit by lamps held in the hands of marble statues, and it was quite evident from the rich carpeting that was laid upon the floor that it formed one of the royal thoroughfares within the ancient building.

But as Tom saw no one, and did not know very well which way to go in order to find Lord Clackington, he began to regret having knocked the Yeoman down stairs, and to debate in his own mind the propriety of seeking that individual again.

A few seconds, however, put an end to this perplexity, for Tom saw approaching him from the further end of the gallery a rather richly dressed personage, with a bow of ribbon on each shoulder, and who walked in a manner which seemed to indicate that if St. James's Palace and all its dependencies did not actually belong to him, they ought in his estimation to do so.

"I wonder who this is?" thought Tom; "and what I ought to say and do now? However, I think I can hold my own; and if the worst comes to the worst, I can fight him and defend my virtue."

CHAPTER CCLXXVI.

TOM RIPON APPEARS IN A NEW CHARACTER AT
ST. JAMES'S PALACE.

THE personage with the shoulder knot made a low bow to Tom Ripon, which he returned with a courtesy so profound that Tom had the greatest difficulty in recovering his balance again, and rising to his feet.

This elegant solution of Tom's seemed to make a great impression upon the gentleman with the bows upon his shoulders, for he advanced six steps something after the fashion of a dancing master, and placing his hand upon his heart, he executed another bow considerably lower than the former.

Tom Ripon had advanced about the same distance, so that they were now tolerably close to each other.

"May I," said the gentleman with the shoulder knots, "take the liberty of inquiring to whom I have the honour of addressing myself?"

"Certainly not!" said Tom. "I don't permit any liberties."

"Eh?"

"And, if it comes to making inquiries, who may you be, old pump?"

"What?"

"I ask you who you are? Can't you answer a plain question?"

"I have the honour to be Sir Adolphus Jingle."

"You look it!" said Tom.

"Madam!"

"Don't madam me, old Jingle! Can't you say what you want at once, or I'll scream and raise the house."

"Scream?"

"Certainly. Why not? What else can we delicate females do to protect ourselves from wolves in sheep's clothing, and with bows on their shoulders?"

"But, madam, I have done nothing."

"I know that as well as you, old Jingle, but you wanted to kiss me, and I won't have it.'

"I, madam?"

"Yes—you, to be sure. I saw you screwing up your old mouth, and your wicked old eyes all of a twitter."

"Madam, I am his Majesty's groom in waiting, and I presume that you are either Clytemnestra, Media, or Miss Leda?"

"Your presumption is not at all astonishing," said Tom; "so you'll be so good as to get out of the way?"

"Certainly, madam.'"

The King's groom in waiting made another low bow, and as Tom sidled past him he suddenly lowered his head, and, to the bewilderment of Sir Adolphus Jingle, butted him up against one of the walls of the gallery with such a crash that his head went through one of the royal portraits.

"Now, clumsy!" said Tom. "Where are you going?"

"Confusion take you!" cried the groom in waiting. "Was there ever such a female in all the world? And this is royal taste, too!"

"Be off with you!" cried Tom; "and don't be getting your stupid old head into trouble. I'll tell of you, I will. You first of all want to kiss me, and then you abuse his most gracious Majesty. Be off with you, do!"

The groom in waiting was only too glad to be off, and rushed down the staircase, muttering some expressions that were anything in the world but complimentary to the supposed Miss Leda.

"Well," said Tom, "I've got his watch, and if all's gold that glitters, it's a good one. What a fine long chain too, and a bunch of seals at the end of it! Well, it wouldn't do to come here for nothing; but I wonder what I'm to do next? I suppose some of these doors lead somewhere. I'll try this one."

About half-way down the gallery a very elegantly ornamented door presented itself, and Tom was on the point of opening it, when he recollected that wound round the pretty fanciful hat he wore was a gauzy kind of veil of the palest possible pink.

This veil Tom drew over his face, and tied in a coquettish manner under his chin.

He then opened the door, and he did so with his usual abruptness, and perhaps a little more than usual, for there seemed a kind of opposition to his doing so, which he had to exert some force to overcome.

It did not strike Tom Ripon that this opposition arose from the fact of some one opening the door at the same time from the inner side.

But such was exactly the state of affairs.

The personage, whoever he was, ran full against Tom, and Tom ran full against the personage.

It probably was but an accident, but Tom thought the personage kicked rather unmercifully, and he retaliated with such interest that the personage uttered a yell of pain.

Tom, then, in the confusion of the moment, saw nothing but a very elaborately curled and powdered wig bobbing about in confusion before his face.

To seize it, and fling it to the other end of the apartment into which that door opened, was the work of a moment to Tom; and then a voice yelled lustily, "Murder! murder! help!"

"Guard! treason!" shouted another voice; and a door at the further end of that first room was opened, at which a gentleman appeared with a drawn sword in his hand, and shaking from top to toe with the direst apprehensions.

This gentlemen was attired in a plain brown suit of half-worn-out velvet.

His countenance was long and cadaverous, and the only thing noticeable about him was a star upon his breast of the purest and most sparkling brilliants.

There was plenty of light in the gallery.

There was more light still in the room in which Tom had intruded.

And through the open doorway of the apartment from which the gentleman with the star had just emerged, there came still more light.

The richness of the furnishings of these apartments, and the general style of costly decoration that met Tom's eyes as he gazed about him, convinced him that he had reached some of the rooms specially in the occupation of royalty.

"Good heavens, my Lord Clackington!" cried the gentleman with the star; "what is the meaning of this unseemly uproar?"

"Craving your Majesty's pardon," said the bewildered Lord Clackington, as he looked gloomily about him for his wig,—"craving your Majesty's pardon, I have not the slightest idea."

"You never had," said Tom.

"Audacious!" said the King, for it was none

other. " Who and what are you, and how came you hither ?"

" Ah !" cried Clackington ; " I guess."

He darted forward to the King, and whispered something.

" Indeed !" was the reply.

" Yes, your Majesty ; so entirely unsophisticated, as I remarked."

" Ah, ah ! Something fresh ! Well, my Lord Clackington, we have had sophisticated ladies of this school enough."

" What do you mean," said Tom, " going on about fisty-cuffs in that way ? If you want to fight, come on !"

" This is indeed original," said the King. " She seems a fine young woman."

" A remarkably fine young woman, your Majesty," added Lord Clackington ; " although I must confess her conduct now perfectly puzzles me, for Mrs. Marables reported her only fault to ber excessive bashfulness."

" Indeed !"

" Yes, your Majesty, and if such a thing were possible with one so young, I could almost imagine she was under the influence of some vinous excitement. Oh, there's my wig ! Your Majesty has your royal foot upon it."

" You'd better say I'm drunk at once," said Tom. " It's hard, it's hard indeed to be abused and called all manner of names by a wretched old reprobate like that. Let me get at him ! I'm long-suffering, but when I'm once roused, I can take my own part, and I've much need to do so. My mother brought me up with much tenderness and care, and she used to say, 'Juliana, my tender and delicate dove, if any one insults you, give him one in the eye !'"

" Hold, hold !" cried the King. " This has gone far enough !"

" Do you think so ?" said Tom.

" We have said it. My Lord Clackington may have erred in his over-zeal in my service. Forgive him—let it pass."

" I don't bear malice," said Tom. " Put on your wig, old 'un."

" And you remove your veil," added the King ; " for report calls you charming."

" Wait a bit," said Tom. " I feel all of a fluster with the conduct of that man—or rather that baboon, I should say, in the shape of a man ; and the only thing that will reconcile me to him would be his coming down to the court-yard at once, and apologizing to my second aunt's mother's sister, who is waiting for me below."

" Well, well," said the King, " he shall apologize—he shall apologize ; but at present, my dear girl, let me invite you to a little repast which is laid in the adjoining chamber. Pray take my hand."

" La ! your Majesty," said Tom ; " how precipitate you are!"

" This way—this way. Come, my Lord Clackington, let bygones be bygones. We have no attendants but yourself on this auspicious evening, for we have dismissed Sir Adolphus Jingle from further waiting until to-morrow."

" And look sharp !" said Tom, as he seized Lord Clackington by the back of the neck, and gave him a shake that nearly lifted him off his legs.

" Bashful, indeed !" muttered the King ; " she's the most violent piece of goods I ever saw in my life."

Lord Clackington was thoroughly bewildered ; and when Tom released him he made a rush into the supper room, with a total disregard of all etiquette, and uttering some expressions which the King found it politic and prudent to seem not to hear.

But his Majesty had evidently great expectations of the beauty of Miss Leda ; and holding Tom by the hand, he led him with a smirking sort of gallantry into the adjoining room, where an elegant repast for two persons only was laid on a small oval table.

The dishes and covers were of gold, and the spoons and forks of the same costly metal, while the richness of all the appurtenances of the table was such as to dazzle and confound any imagination not accustomed to such costly details.

" Pray be seated, " said the King, " and let me again entreat you to remove that envious screen, which, I am quite certain, hides so much beauty ?"

" Not yet," said Tom. " I'm afraid I'm being deceived. I shall be taken in and done for, if I don't look sharp—what's that ?"

Tom directed his eyes, with a frightened look, up to the ceiling.

Both Lord Clackington and the King followed his example, and during the temporary and mystified examination of a painting, which adorned the ceiling, Tom managed to pocket three table-spoons and two forks.

" I see nothing unusual," said the King.

" Nor I, either," said Clackington.

" No more do I," said Tom. " But lor' ! its getting late."

" By no means !" cried the King. " And, besides, time is of no account within these walls."

" You don't say so ? Bless us ! what a pretty watch !"

Tom adroitly whipped the King's watch out of his pocket, and put it to his ear.

" It's going," he said.

" I hope so," said the King.

" You're right, then," said Tom ; " for it's gone !"

A he spoke, he put the watch into the bosom of his dress.

The King looked a little chagrined, which Lord Clackington observing, induced him to say, " Miss Leda, I am sure, is only jesting, and——"

" Take that !" said Tom ; " and speak when you're spoken to !"

A gold soup-ladle came with such force upon the head of Lord Clackington, that the sound was quite alarming.

" Really ! really !" cried the King, " this is too much ! You are reckless, my dear Miss Leda. There will be some mischief done."

" Only a little bump," said Tom, as he looked at the bowl of the ladle, which was slightly indented.

The Palace clock at that moment struck the hour of eleven.

Tom Ripon uttered two vigorous screams.

" Gracious heavens !" cried the King ; " what's the matter ?"

" My aunt's sister's second cousin's wife !"

"Who?"

"Down in the court below. I forgot her."

"Oh, heed her not—heed her not."

"But I must tell her. Oh, you wicked men! if I'm to stay here and have some supper, I must tell her. Don't you think, you old seducing creature,—don't you think she ought to be told to go away and come again at breakfast-time?"

"Certainly, if you please. But why are you holding one of the dish-covers over your face?"

"To hide my blushes," said Tom; "but I'm better now."

Tom put the dish-cover upon Lord Clackington's head, apparently in a moment of abstraction.

"Well, well," said the King; "we will see to all that—we will see to all that, Juliana, I think you said your name was?"

No. 89.—EDITH HERON.

"Juliana Matilda Mary Ann Emily Jane, if you please."

"What a chorus of names!" muttered Lord Clackington. "Is it your Majesty's wish that I should go down to the court, and send the female relation away?"

"Certainly; go, Clackington."

"Not if I know it!" said Tom, as he put out his foot and sent Lord Clackington sprawling,—"not if I know it! She won't go till she sees me, and then not for nothing. Stop! I have it! I have it! The old woman is mercenary. We must give her something to go away. Let's see—these plates and dishes——"

"Stop—stop!" cried the King.

"This cruet-stand."

"Hold! hold!"

"This star."

Tom made a grasp at the brilliant decoration on the breast of the King.

"Are you mad? Do you think that wholesale robbery is to take place in this fashion? I am quite willing that the person you named should be rewarded, but it must be done with some sort of discretion. My Lord Clackington, I leave this business to you. Go to the court-yard and despatch it, and then return to us, for we shall require these covers removed, and your attendance at supper."

"I obey your Majesty's orders."

"Stop," said Tom. "Your Majesty don't know her, or you would never suppose she would go away for anything my Lord Clackington could say to her. I must go myself, or she will create a riot and a scandal in the court-yard of the Palace."

"But how can I be sure of your return?" remarked the King.

"My Lord Clackington will go with me, and, if needs be, bring me back by force, although that will not be needed."

Tom Ripon, as he spoke, gave the King a sudden dig about the region of the ribs which nearly deprived him of breath.

"Gracious heavens! don't do that! And this," added the King to himself, "is the modest young creature whose bashfulness was considered her only drawback! Go, my Lord Clackington,—pray accompany this young lady to that terribly complicated female relative who is below! Give her this purse, and tell her she may call for her niece, or forty-fourth cousin, whatever their relationship may be, in the morning!"

"I'll carry the purse," said Tom, as he intercepted it before Lord Clackington could reach out his hand to receive it. "Now, come along, and mind you behave yourself! I'm afraid this is a bad place for a tender, young, delicate creature, still in her teens, to come to; but if you say half a word to me, I'll knock all your teeth down your throat, and scalp you!"

"She's a perfect virago," whispered Lord Clackington to the King.

"But you reported her as the mirror of modesty and bashfulness!"

"I was deceived, your Majesty!"

"You are a fool, my Lord Clackington—an idiot!"

"I have the honour to be anything your Majesty pleases!"

"Go—go! Dismiss the female relative, and bring the girl back again! I long to see her face, since you have praised her beauty to the very echo!"

"Come on, old 'un!" said Tom.

As he spoke, he seized Lord Clackington's arm, and pulling it under his own, he dragged him out into the gallery, whither they were both followed by the wondering eyes of the King, who began to doubt, after all, whether it would be prudent to wait for the return of so violent and precarious a personage as Miss Leda.

Tom took care not to release my Lord Clackington for a moment; and even when the staircase was reached, he managed to drag the half-scared old nobleman down the steps by his side.

That confidential Yeoman of the Guard was still there on duty.

Seeing Lord Clackington, he officiously opened the door which led into the Colour Court.

There stood the carriage of Lady Castleneau.

"Come," said Tom, "you must just say a word or two to assure my female relative that all is well, and I can give her the money."

Tom opened the coach door, and still holding Lord Clackington by the arm, he adroitly leaped into the vehicle.

"Now, my lord," he said, as he reached out his other hand, and caught the elderly nobleman by the collar, "you will be so good as to step in here, and if you utter half a word above your breath, I will blow your brains out with as little compunction as I would those of a mad dog!"

"Mur——"

"Hush! Your life is in your own hands!"

By a vigorous effort, Tom dragged Lord Clackington into the coach; and then placing over his head and face the reticule he had brought from Castleneau House, he tied the strings rather tightly round his neck, and to Lord Clackington all was darkness, danger, and terror.

CHAPTER CCLXXVII.

TOM RIPON PAYS ANOTHER VISIT TO WARDOUR STREET.

THE capture of Lord Clackington had occupied so short a space of time, that, in the dim light of the Colour Court, he had not observed the appearance of the vehicle into which he had been hustled and dragged.

Lady Castleneau had not uttered a word, therefore he had no means of identifying her with the transaction.

Tom Ripon, however, spoke in his own voice now, as he gave Lord Clackington a slight tap on the head with the barrel of a pistol.

"Do you know what that is?" said Tom.

"Mercy, no!"

"It's a pistol, well loaded and carefully primed. Silence is necessary, and if you break it, any further noise is of little importance. Therefore, I shall fire, and make an end of my Lord Clackington."

"I am silent. Spare my life—that is all I ask."

"And a great deal, too," said Tom. "Hush! Sit there!"

Tom thrust Lord Clackington into a corner of the carriage, on the opposite seat to that occupied by himself and Lady Castleneau.

Old Anthony had previously had his instructions, and now he put his horses in motion to leave the court-yard of the Palace.

A feeling of desperation must have come over Lord Clackington at this moment, and even the dread of death did not overcome it.

The idea of being carried away by persons he knew not, and he could not guess whither, produced such a feeling of despair, that even at a risk of a realization of those threats that had been held out to him, he could not refrain from calling for help as the carriage was about to roll under the archway at the Palace gate.

"Halt!" cried the sentinel on duty. "What is that?"

Tom Ripon thought for a moment all was lost.

Lady Castleneau laid her hand upon his arm.

"Don't speak!" she whispered; "leave me to manage this."

"It is I," she said, as she looked from the carriage window. "Where is the man who kindly showed me to the Colour Court?"

"Another guinea, by Jove!" cried a voice. "It's all right, sentry; this is a most respectable lady, and a friend of his Majesty's."

"But it is too late," added the sentinel, pertinaciously,—"it is too late without the night pass-word."

"Why, she told it you, didn't she? Brunswick—didn't she tell it you?"

"Certainly," said Lady Castleneau,—"Brunswick."

The sentinel was rather confused, and scarcely liked to take upon himself to say that the pass-word had not been properly given.

Another guinea was dropped into the willing palm of the corporal who had made so good a night's work by unconsciously assisting Lady Castleneau in an adventure which had much more important results than he anticipated, and for which assistance, had he but known its value, he might have received a much larger sum.

The Palace was left.

Lord Clackington had made his last effort at freedom, and now he sank back in the corner of the coach in a state of absolute despair.

It was half-past eleven o'clock, and no doubt the old, pampered horses in Lady Castleneau's coach were anxious enough to get home, and as the distance from St. James's to Bloomsbury was but short, Tom Ripon fully expected to arrive there in the course of the next twenty minutes.

But Lady Castleneau was conducting the whole affair with an amount of finesse that Tom had no conception of.

In pursuance of his instructions, old Anthony certainly drove to Bloomsbury, but instead of proceeding direct to Castleneau House, he astonished the horses and Tom Ripon by going up and down all the new bye-roads in the neighbourhood.

He drove right through the narrow lane that led to the fields at Camden Town, and then back again past the mansion and grounds of Lord Mornington.

For a short distance, likewise, on to the stony way of Tottenham Court Road was the carriage driven; and in this way, although the distance from Castleneau House never exceeded half a mile, a whole hour was consumed in driving round about the neighbourhood.

"You understand," whispered Lady Castleneau to Tom Ripon,—"you understand now that the impression on the mind of Lord Clackington will be that he is taken some miles into the country, and made a prisoner in some old house, from which there will be no chance of escape, or of succour coming to him."

"Good!" said Tom. "That's the right way to do it, but I must own I didn't think of such a dodge."

Lady Castleneau now touched the check-string that was round the wrist of old Anthony, and that was the agreed upon signal at which he was to drive into the court-yard of Castleneau House.

"You will bring the prisoner along," said Lady Castleneau, in the same low tones in which she had been speaking, "and follow me."

Tom took a firm grasp of Lord Clackington by the collar, and helped him out of the vehicle.

"May I speak—may I speak? Let me speak!" moaned Clackington.

"If you cut it short," said Tom, "you may. What is it?"

"I will give a hundred guineas for my liberty."

"What do you say?" cried Tom, addressing an imaginary personage,—"what do you say, Captain? He offers a hundred thousand guineas for his liberty."

Tom then answered himself by speaking through his doubled hand, in the form of a trumpet, in growling accents, "Not for a million."

Lord Clackington gave himself up for lost, and with a shambling gait, allowed Tom to lead him across the court-yard, and up the steps of Castleneau House.

Lady Castleneau herself led the way, and on the topmost storey of the mansion a small room was opened, which was sufficiently well lighted, although only by a skylight, so that my Lord Clackington could make no observation of his whereabouts, unless such information could be derived from the flying clouds or the blue sky to be seen through the skylight.

Tom Ripon then spoke: "My Lord Clackington, it has been determined to be necessary that you should be out of the way for a time. Some people thought that the best way would be to put you under ground; but others, more merciful, suggested that you be made a prisoner. If, however, you would rather go out of the world altogether than out of it in this kind of way, you've only to say so, and you can be indulged."

"No, no—life!" cried Lord Clackington; "at least let me have life, for while there is life there is hope."

"Agreed," said Tom; "but I warn you that any attempt to escape will be visited upon you with certain death."

"Tell me, then," said Clackington, in a dreary tone of voice,—"tell me what is the motive of my imprisonment. What have I done to you, whoever you are, or to anybody else, that I should be captured in this fashion? Who and what are you? You cannot be the Miss Leda expected at the Palace, for it is not your interest to behave in this way."

"It's best to ask no questions," said Tom.

As he spoke, Tom closed the door of Lord Clackington's prison, and turned the key in the lock.

"There he is, all right, my lady; and now I'll go and tell the Captain and Lady Edith what has happened. But, after all, I think it'll be best to hang him, for he will be no end of trouble."

"Leave that to me, Tom Ripon," said Lady Castleneau. "We have secured him, and put an end to that one complexity which, perhaps, might have caused Felix to discover his continued existence to his enemies. This wicked old man shall not escape from his imprisonment while the present King sits upon the throne of England."

Tom departed from Castleneau House exceedingly well pleased with the night's adventure.

But before he proceeded to St. James's Street, to give an account of what had taken place to Felix Heron and to Edith, Tom thought it prudent to get rid of the little plunder he had brought with him from the Palace.

He accordingly bent his steps towards Wardour Street, and a little after midnight was rapping at the shutters of his mother's house, in that peculiar manner which was sufficient to indicate to her and to Mortification that a customer was at hand.

The opening at the top of the shop door was again resorted to as usual by Mortification as a point from which he could reconnoitre the visitor.

"Open—open, old boy!" cried Tom.

"Yea, it is Thomas! Yea, the prodigal returneth! Is it spoons, Thomas, or what?"

"Don't be stupid," said Tom; "but let me in at once. I've been having supper with the King, and he's made me a present of some gold spoons and forks."

Mortification was so astonished at this statement from Tom Ripon, that he made a false step on the three-legged stool he stood upon behind the door, and came down to the passage with a rattle and a dash that made Tom wonder what had happened.

Then Mrs. Ripon's voice could be heard inquiring the cause of the uproar; and, as Tom began to amuse himself by flinging some of the royal spoons through the fanlight, Mrs. Ripon began to think the house was besieged.

But Tom's voice quickly reassured her.

"Open! open!" he cried. "Am I to stand here all night, with no end of swag?"

"Gracious providence, no!" said Mrs. Ripon. "Get out of the way, you handless wretch!"

"I can't," said Mortification. "Yea, light of my soul, you are standing on my back!"

In a few minutes, however, the door was opened, and Tom Ripon entered his mother's house.

The shop was very dark, and as it was the policy of Mrs. Ripon and Mortification to keep it so, in order that the prying eyes of intruders from without should not learn too much of the little transactions taking place within, Tom Ripon and Mortification had to grope their way to the back parlour.

Now, Mortification was a step or two in advance of Tom, so that the latter could hardly understand how it was that some one trod upon one of his heels.

"Hilloa!" cried Tom; "what's that?"

"Yea, what is what?"

"Are you behind or before me, Mortification?"

"Yea, I am here, Thomas; and, as the Psalmist remarks, one cannot be in two places at once. Come on, Thomas—worthy youth, come on. Yea, thou shall have the fat of the land, and the lean of the land likewise, judiciously mixed; for, as the Psalmist remarks, he who brings silver spoons to the melting pot shall be welcome, but for him who bringeth gold ones, yea, there shall be a clashing of cymbals."

"Hold your row!" cried Tom.

"And, yea, a braying of horns."

"Hold your braying!" cried Tom again. "I want to listen."

"And yea, a dance."

"I tell you what it is, Mortification; there shall be, yea, a broken head if you don't be quiet."

"Yea, a fatted calf with onions."

The next utterance of Mortification consisted of a shout of dismay, for Tom Ripon, turning on the threshold of the back room, fired both his pistols right into the shop.

The flashes lit up the dingy place for a second, and exhibited unmistakably a man seated on the counter, and swinging his legs to and fro with all the unconcern imaginable.

"I knew it," cried Tom. "Mr. Wild, what do you want here? But it's come to this, you or I must be a dead man to-night."

"Take things easy," said Wild, as he undid the slide of the dark lantern, and held it out at arm's length,—"take things easy, Tom Ripon. I admire you very much, and knowing that you would be sure to come here to-night, I was determined to tell you so. Let bygones be bygones. I promise you three years from this date, and I'm sure I shall not lose by leaving it to your generosity to pay me well for my forbearance. Mortification, what's for supper?"

Tom was perfectly staggered and surprised at this cool behaviour on the part of Jonathan Wild.

It was quite evident, however, from the manner and looks of Mortification, as well as from his previous conduct, that the appearance of Jonathan was not all unexpected by him.

In fact, it was a little speculation of Mortification's own to let Jonathan Wild, for a consideration, sit in the dark on the shop counter of an evening, in order to take notice of the customers that came to the fence.

It was not for the purpose of apprehending them, or bringing them to justice, that Jonathan Wild required such information.

On the contrary, his sole object was to be able to confound them by saying, "On such a night you sold so much plate to Mrs. Ripon, or you parted with a gold watch and seals, without giving me my share."

In this manner he acquired the extraordinary ascendancy he possessed for so long over the criminals of the metropolis, who began to believe him to have a preternatural means of acquiring a knowledge of their proceedings.

Tom Ripon looked from one to the other with doubt.

But whatever might be his opinion of Mortification, he could scarcely believe that he would actually betray him into the hands of Jonathan.

"Come, come," said Wild, "I see you doubt me; and perhaps it will take some time to convince you that I bear no malice."

Tom started.

A heavy knocking came at the shop door.

"Good!" said Wild. "I have an opportunity of convincing you now that I mean you no harm!"

"What opportunity?"

"Listen!"

The knocking came with redoubled force.

"Those pistol-shots," said Wild, "with which you favoured me a short time ago have reached the ears of some of my bull-dogs, and alarmed them. There is a party outside strong enough to take possession of the whole of this place, and secure every one of you as prisoners; but you will no longer doubt me when I send them away!"

Wild advanced to the door, and struck it heavily with the handle of his hanger.

"Hilloa! hilloa, bull-dogs!" he shouted. "Away with you! No scent here! Away with you! All is well!"

The knocking at the door ceased.

"You hear?" said Wild; "and I think, after the manner I have trusted you, you might show an equal confidence in me."

"Trusted us!" said Tom. "In what way?"

"Why, you might have taken my life ten times over, while I had my back to you just now, when I was speaking to my men."

CHAPTER CCLXXVIII.

FELIX HERON RESUMES HIS OLD LIFE ON THE ROAD.

TOM RIPON had no occasion to be particularly well pleased with this sudden and unexpected appearance of Wild at the fence in Wardour Street.

But, under the circumstances, what was he to do?

True, he might, at some odd moment, take Wild's life, but that would be so like assassination, that Tom Ripon was not the sort of person to bring himself to the commission of the act.

There seemed no resource, then, but to allow Wild to pursue his own course.

Jonathan, with the most careless air in the world, walked into the back parlour of the fence.

"Come," he said, "now that we are all agreed, and understand each other, let us to supper."

Mrs. Ripon was anything but pleased at such a guest, and the look she darted at the Rev. Mortification was quite sufficient to let that personage know what kind of remonstrances were likely to be made to him when Jonathan Wild should have left.

And Tom Ripon was uneasy.

He could not entirely divest his mind of the idea that, after all, this was but some cunningly laid trap for his recapture.

And Tom Ripon adopted a very ingenious expedient for leaving the house.

Mrs. Ripon kept scales and weights in that back parlour, by the use of which, after purchasing silver plate, she arrived at something like an approximation to its value.

The parlour was not brilliantly illuminated by the single candle that burnt in it; and Tom Ripon, affecting to walk about in it in a careless manner, was able to possess himself of one of the smaller weights.

Watching his opportunity, then, of when the door of communication between the shop and the parlour was open, Tom Ripon flung the weight right across the shop at the upper panel of its door.

The effect was very similar to some one knocking loudly from without.

"Ah!" said Tom; "a customer!"

Wild looked a little suspicious.

"Yes, I will go," said Mortification; "it may be that some person actually mistaketh this respectable establishment for a fence."

"I will go," said Tom. "Shall I ask him in, whoever it is?"

"Certainly," said Wild, speaking for Mrs. Ripon, to whom the question was addressed,—"certainly; but, as the sight of me might not be agreeable, I will hide myself behind this door."

"That'll do," said Tom, as he passed out of the back parlour.

Crossing the shop, he opened the door, and making his way at once into the street, he closed it with a loud bang; and then, at a pace which it would have been difficult to follow, or keep up with, he made his way towards Whitcombe House.

Felix Heron had been by far too anxious regarding the success of Lady Castleneau's undertaking to retire to rest that night, and he received from Tom a relation of what had taken place with mingled feelings of admiration and gratitude.

If the necessity for declaring his own continued existence had still maintained, he would have been embarked in a sea of troubles.

An attempt would no doubt have been made by his enemies at the Court of St. James's to procure his attainder, on the charge of having offered personal violence to the monarch, which, of course, would have involved the disinheritance of that son whose future interests formed the basis of all these transactions.

Heron drew a long breath of relief, with the conviction that his worst foe, Lord Clackington, was no longer able to do him a mischief that might be irreparable.

"Tom Ripon," he said, "I owe you many thanks, and I suppose I cannot better repay you for the service you have done than by reiterating my promise to you, that Daisy shall be at your service whenever you require her; but always bear in mind one thing, which is, that her safety is very dear to me, and should you be hard pressed at any time, rather give in and surrender than let her run the chance of danger to life or limb."

Tom replied with some emotion to this speech of Captain Heron's.

"I mean to be careful of myself, Captain, but ten times more so of Daisy; and even now that you are so willing to lend her to me, I seem as if I shrunk from taking her."

"I do not wish you to have that feeling, Tom, and yet——"

Heron paused, and paced the room for several seconds in silence.

"Yet what, Captain?"

"I will make a confidence with you, Tom. The kind of life I lead stagnates me. I have neither the health nor the spirit I had in the free air of Epping Forest."

"Hurrah!" cried Tom; "we shall be on the road and on the heath again before we are four-and-twenty hours older!"

"Hear me out," said Heron. "I no longer

speak to you as a boy, for you have now come to an age when you can understand these things."

Tom listened with the most absorbed attention.

"You must know, Tom, that the revenues of the earldom of Whitcombe are so large that their possessor might, even in a country like this, where every article, either of necessity or luxury, is at its highest value, live like a prince."

"I've heard as much," said Tom.

"And yet, owing to the strange position which I now occupy, those revenues are not available."

Tom nodded.

"I've heard Ogle say, Captain, that the tenants of the Whitcombe estates won't pay."

"You have heard right, Tom. Taking advantage of the real or apparent fact that the peerage is in abeyance, not one of them will pay rent for their farms or their houses; and the consequence is, that at this present moment, although sixty thousand a year at least ought to come into our hands, we have pecuniary distress staring us in the face."

"That's soon put right, Captain," said Tom; "we have but to sally out and cry, 'Stand and deliver!' and live upon the plunder."

"It is a necessity from which there is no escaping; and so, Tom, I think that you, and I, and Ogle, to-morrow night, will take a trot down to the old forest, and see what may be in store for us on the road there and back."

"Ah," cried Tom; "old times are coming back again! This is just as it should be. Never mind the estates and rents of the earldom of Whitcombe, Captain. We shall make quite enough on the road, you may depend, and be all the healthier and all the happier to make it in that way."

It might be that Felix Heron really mourned over the necessity of again embarking in that precarious profession of a knight of the road, which had characterized his early career.

But still it had for him its secret charms.

The only person that looked with a kind of mournful distaste upon a recommencement of those scenes of difficulty and danger, which she had seen so much of, was Edith.

She shuddered at the necessity that Heron should again go upon the road, even for the purpose of procuring a subsistence for herself and child.

Well she knew that Lady Castleneau would only too gladly appropriate the larger part of her income for the purpose of meeting any necessities of that description.

But that was a resource that Heron could not reconcile himself to, for well he knew that, what with her numerous charities, and the high-minded liberality with which she conducted her whole affairs, that that income was sufficiently absorbed.

And so it was that Captain Heron once more determined to go upon the road, accompanied by his faithful followers, Ogle and Tom Ripon.

It seemed to him easier to embrace that line of life once more than to make himself dependent upon those friends who would otherwise gladly have stepped forward to save him and Edith every possible pecuniary inconvenience.

Had it for a single moment crossed the imagination of the Earl of Bridgewater, or of Colonel Trelawney, or of the young Marquis of Ormond, that the inhabitants of Whitcombe House required subsidizing, they would freely have done so.

But Felix Heron never, by word or action, engendered such an idea.

It was on the following evening, then, after this conversation with Tom Ripon, that the stable door of Whitcombe House was opened cautiously, about the hour of nine.

From it emerged Ogle.

A remarkable change had taken place in his appearance.

In Whitcombe House Ogle had contrived to make himself look like a confidential servant, and, by powdering his hair, and wearing a decorous suit of black, he passed very well for a great man's butler, or confidential valet.

Now, however, Ogle had all the appearance of a rough-rider.

He wore top-boots.

A faded plum-coloured coat, that had once been a gay article of attire, although it was buttoned across the chest, partially exhibited a flowered waistcoat.

His hat was placed rakishly on one side of his head, and a lace cravat of considerable value encircled his neck.

Ogle carried a riding-whip in his hand.

His object was to make an observation of the little street into which the stables opened, in order to be certain that no spies of Jonathan Wild were lingering about the spot.

It was the hour at which the night-watch came on duty, and it might be supposed that the particular watchman who had charge of that neighbourhood might be sufficiently awake to be troublesome.

During the whole of the day the night-watch were not supposed to do anything but sleep; and, so far as the privilege of idleness went, they fully availed themselves of it.

But, inasmuch as they took upon themselves to repose the whole night long in their watch-boxes, there was certainly no extra vigilance at the commencement of their duty.

"Past nine o'clock, and a showery night!"

"Hang you!" muttered Ogle; "why can't you get along?"

The watchman came drawling past.

"Stop!" cried Ogle.

"Hilloa! What now; do you want to be taken up?"

"Certainly not; but I want to know what wages you get?"

"Wages? Don't obstruct me in my duty!"

"Is this the way you answer a nobleman?"

"A nobleman, your honour's worship? I get seven shillings a week, and my coat."

"And you look sharp after this street?"

"I believe you, your worship! You see, it's a by-street, and, as Mr. Wild once said to me, 'the stables of Whitcombe House look into it; and, if anything extraordinary about them happens, it's a good half-crown to you to come and tell me.'"

"Half-a-crown?"

"Yes, your honour; half a crown extra, to keep wide awake and look about me."

"I comprehend. For five shillings, then, you

see nothing, hear nothing, and are as stupid as an owl?"

"Certainly, your honour."

"There's the money. Be off! You will get the same sum every week."

"Bless your honour! that makes seven-and-sixpence; for I'll go to Mr. Wild, and get his half-crown, by telling him I've seen something very strange at Number Eight!"

"Do as you please, so that you are discreet."

The watchman made the best of his way from the street.

Ogle then tapped at the wicket-door of the stables, and Tom Ripon soon came forth, leading two horses.

One was for Ogle, and one was for himself.

No doubt Tom thought himself gorgeously attired; for he was in his new, full costume as a highwayman, with every appointment about it in exact imitation of Captain Heron.

Strapped, however, to the back of the saddle of the horse which he was to ride, Tom had a small bundle, which consisted of a complete disguise, which he could slip on over his highwayman's clothes.

In a few seconds Heron himself emerged from the stable, followed closely by Daisy.

Then Ogle spoke, in a low tone.

"I think, Captain, every possible arrangement has been made."

"I am sure of it, Ogle. Have you the keys to the wicket-gate?"

"I have."

"Keep one yourself, give Tom one, and hand me the third. There is just a possibility that we may be, by some circumstances, separated; and if so, it will be of the utmost importance that we should individually be able to get into the stable here, without a moment's delay."

"All right, Captain. I've tried the keys, and they fit like an old glove."

Heron patted the neck of Daisy.

"So," he said, "once again on to the road, in search of adventures, you will carry your old master, Daisy, to whom you have been so good a friend on many an emergency."

Daisy pushed her head caressingly against the breast of Heron; and then Tom Ripon looked at her with a sigh, and shook his head, for now that Captain Heron had determined to go upon the road again himself, Tom was forced to put up with one of the other horses from the stables of Whitcombe House.

"Follow me, both of you!" cried Heron, as he mounted. "We will take, as I have said, the road to Epping Forest; and our two places of refuge will be the stables of Whitcombe House and the deep recesses of those leafy glades which we know so well."

"All's right, Captain!" said Ogle. "We have met many an adventure upon the road between here and there, and may meet with many still."

"Yes," replied Heron; "the world may be older somewhat, but the times are still unchanged."

As he spoke, he touched the neck of Daisy lightly with his gloved hand, and at a smart trot the little party started from the neighbourhood of St. James's, to gain as soon as possible the open country.

Heron was in his full costume as a knight of the road, but it was less noticeable than it might have been, because over it he wore a roquelaire cloak, which permitted little more than one arm and his boots to be visible.

It was a strange and new sensation now, for Felix Heron to find himself mounted upon Daisy, and going in search of adventures.

His thoughts flew back to the past. When in Epping Forest, leading the rough, rude life he there did, he was a great deal happier than he had ever been in the gilded saloons of Whitcombe House.

The evening was cloudy, and now and then a scatter of rain, accompanied by a slight squall of wind, which seemed to threaten an inclement night.

Such a state of weather, however, was favourable enough to such proceedings as were contemplated by Felix Heron and his party.

Half an hour's sharp trotting took them quite clear even of the suburbs of London; and the fresh, cool, grateful air of the country came pleasantly upon their senses.

The slight rain that had fallen at intervals seemed to have brought forth the fragrance of the fields and flowers; and but for those near and dear ties that bound him to London, Felix Heron would gladly have bidden farewell for ever to the wilderness of bricks and mortar, and taken up his abode once again in the picturesque recesses of the forest.

Heron was riding on considerably in advance, when he became conscious that he was rapidly gaining upon some horseman who was somewhat before him on the road.

Without in the least accelerating the speed of Daisy, Heron soon came up with a dusky-looking figure mounted on a very tall horse.

The horse had what is called plenty of action; but, as is very common in regard to such steeds, the progress made was by no means commensurate with the bustle of making it.

The dark-looking horseman drew quite away to the shadow of the hedges on his own side of the road as Heron came up.

It was evident that the stranger wished to avoid any encounter or colloquy with Heron; but it was a rule with the latter, which he rarely infringed, to speak to any one he saw on the road, in order that he might know them again.

CHAPTER CCLXXIX.

FELIX HERON MEETS WITH A MYSTERIOUS STRANGER ON THE ROAD TO EPPING.

"A PLEASANT night, sir!" cried Heron, as he slackened the speed of Daisy.

The horseman muttered something in reply which Heron could not catch, and evidently made an effort to ride on more quickly.

As he did so, even in the dim light of that country road, Heron could see that he wore spurs, which glittered as though they were of some costly material.

He fancied, too, that he saw, slightly projecting beneath the cloak which the stranger horseman wore, the scabbard of a sword.

That scabbard, too, had a glittering, rich aspect about it which awakened Felix Heron's curiosity.

A touch to Daisy was quite sufficient to let her know that she was to keep up with the other horse.

That was done without the slightest effort whatever.

Heron spoke again.

" I remarked, sir, that it was a pleasant night."

" And I told you, sir," replied the horseman, " that you were quite welcome to your opinion."

" You are very obliging."

" Take it as you will. Good night, sir."

" Nay," said Heron ; "companionship, upon such a road as this, is never a bad thing, and may be a good one."

" You are welcome likewise to that opinion ; but as I do not require any companionship whatever, permit me, without offence, to dispense with yours."

" But, sir, have you not heard that this road, in particular, is the haunt of highwaymen ?"

" No, sir."

"Then I am most happy to be able to inform you of so interesting a fact."

" Sir, good night."

" Nay, sir ; allow me likewise to add that one of these highwaymen has had the audacity to claim the road as his own property, and to allow no one to pass over it without paying such a toll that, heavy as the exaction is, few persons care to resist it at the price of a life.'

" Ah !"

" I fancy you comprehend me."

" A highwayman ?"

" At your service."

"Scoundrel ! Do I look like the sort of man to be robbed by a single highwayman upon a road like this ?"

"Of that you are the best judge," said Heron ; "but as far as my experiences go, I do not see anything the least extraordinary in the transaction. Now, sir, your money or your life, or perhaps both !"

" Well," said the stranger, " if it must be so."

As he spoke, he flung aside the cloak, showing that he was in a military costume beneath it ; and from the character of that costume, it seemed to Heron that he must be an officer of some distinction.

Almost simultaneously with the throwing back of the cloak, the stranger seized on one of his holster pistols from the saddle, and making his horse suddenly rear, he said, calmly, " Now, Mr. Highwayman, fire away ! It will be my turn next !"

Heron had heard quite sufficient of military service to be well aware that the officer was pursuing exactly the tactics prescribed for such an emergency as he now found himself in.

" No," said Heron, " I will not fire, because I do not see that your horse or mine should be involved in this little transaction ; but still, having commenced it, I carry it out—thus !"

As Heron spoke, he sharply turned Daisy, and making her give one of her vaults which she was so expert at, he was on the other side of the mounted officer in an instant.

Stretching forth his right arm, then, Heron grasped the wrist of the officer, and pointed his pistol in the air.

" Fire now, sir !" he said, "it is your most prudent plan."

" Fire yourself !" was the reply.

"Certainly not," replied Heron. " Give me your word that you will take no further advantage, and at the same time pay me some reasonable toll, and you may go free."

The officer hesitated for a few seconds, and then, in much more conciliatory tones than he had hitherto spoken, he said, " I don't believe you are a highwayman at all, and I charge you, upon your honour and faith, to tell me if you have any knowledge of Sir Hugh Durban ?"

"Not the least. I never heard the name before."

" Do you happen to know, then, General Gaston ?"

"Certainly not. But will you permit me to ask, sir, the reason of these strange interrogatories ?"

" The full reasons were too tedious to mention ; but if you are a gentleman, or even a highwayman with so much of the gentleman about you as your conduct seems to have shown this night, I would fain ask a favour of you."

" Hush !"

" What is it ?"

" Ride aside, sir. I hear a clatter of horses' feet, and suspect that some strong party is on the road."

Felix Heron was right ; for, although the party was not a very strong one, four mounted men passed them at a sharp trot, the clatter of their horses' feet quickly dying away in the distance.

General Gaston—for such was the name of the officer who spoke so mysteriously to Felix Heron —uttered a deep groan.

" You suffer, sir ?" said Heron.

" Alas ! alas ! It is as I suspected ! The villain Durban is upon the expedition I was warned of, and carries with him associates sufficiently powerful to have made my interference worse than useless. Alas ! alas !"

The distress of General Gaston was evidently so unaffected and real, that Heron replied to it promptly.

" Why, sir, if you allude to those men who have even now passed us, there were but four of them."

" But I am only one."

Heron hesitated for a few seconds ; and then, although to engage in an adventure of the kind that seemed to present itself, was something of a departure from the ideas with which he had started that night upon the road, he quickly descended to offer his services to the distressed officer.

By the time Heron spoke again to General Gaston, his mind was quite made up that whatever mysterious adventure that personage was bound upon, he, Heron, would assist him.

There was a tone of grief, a sighing utterance of despair, about General Gaston's manner, which much affected Felix Heron.

Close and accurate observer as he was, he could not but observe the catching of the breath, and the half-smothered sighs, that burst from the heart of the General.

"Treat me frankly, sir," he said. "Can I be of any assistance to you?"

General Gaston hesitated for a few seconds, and then he said, rather as if communing with himself, than replying to Felix Heron, "You are bold and resolute?"

"Men account me so."

"We live in a world of mysteries; and who shall say that heaven, having its own way of doing which no human judgment shall fathom or question, may not have sent you across my path to-night?"

"Think and believe so."

"I will—I will trust you."

"You may do so freely; and all that one human being can do to aid another, that will I do."

"Listen to me, then. I will not ask you for a name by which to address you, but I will speak to you freely."

"I listen."

"A dear friend, and brother companion-in-arms, who met his death upon the battle-field in India, made me the guardian of his only child—a girl eighteen years of age, of delicate constitution, and fragile structure. Her father left her a competent fortune, which, for convenience of transit from India to England, was converted into jewels of the richest and rarest description.

"I have heard," said Heron, "of such being a favourite mode with Anglo-Indians of transmitting their wealth to Europe."

"Yes, it is common enough."

"And did the young lady arrive in safety, or are you mourning her loss?"

"I can answer 'yes,' to both those questions."

"Then she is no more?"

"To appearance, certainly no more; and yet I cannot divest myself of the belief that we shall meet again; and it is not that kind of belief which is based upon a reunion of spirits in another world, but I have never been able to realize to myself the fact that she has departed from this."

"It is a common feeling," said Heron.

"Yes, I know to what you would allude—the well-known difficulty of believing that any one we knew well in life has passed away from it for ever."

"And is not that your feeling?"

"Scarcely. But let me hurry on with my narration, for we have, indeed, much to do to-night."

The General spoke in a tone of deep emotion, and Felix Heron became irresistibly attracted by the words he uttered.

"This young, fragile girl, in all her beauty and all her innocence, reached my home in London. I am single, and have always led the life of a solitary man, but from the first moment I beheld my young and lovely ward, I felt that she was dearer to me than life itself."

The General, as he spoke, turned upon the saddle, and looked full in the face of Felix Heron.

The night was a dark one.

And yet there was that mysterious kind of reflected light in the night sky which, although it was not sufficient to enable Felix Heron to detect the features of the General, he yet could see sufficient to enable him to come to the conclusion that his new acquaintance was a singularly handsome man.

He was, at the same time, by no means sufficiently advanced in years to put him out of the pale of female society, even when represented by so young and lovely a personage as he stated his ward to be.

"Proceed, General," he said. "I am deeply interested in your statements."

"And I feel irresistibly compelled to trust you. I loved my ward dearly—fondly—devotedly."

"And she?"

"I know what you would ask. Did she return the passion?"

"Yes."

"I cannot answer you, It is a question I cannot answer to my own heart, for looking at the disparity of our years, I dreaded to intrude the feelings of a veteran on the attention of one as yet only on the threshold of existence."

"But what happened, sir?"

"A distant relation of my own, and a sort of forty-fourth cousin, or something of that degree, to my young and lovely ward, suddenly begun to visit at my house. His age did not exceed eight-and-twenty, and he was singularly handsome."

"Ah, I begin to see!"

"You think he was my rival?"

"Was it not so?"

"No. Along with that singular beauty of person, which he inherited from a father who was one of the noblest gentlemen who ever lived, he bore about him an expression of libertine recklessness which no polish of manner or hypocrisy of words could suppress."

"Your ward, then, General, did not love him?"

"At first, she was indifferent to him."

"And then?"

"Then, sir, she loathed him."

"Some act of his probably, then, had outraged her feelings."

"It may be so, but I never heard exactly what it was. A great calamity was hovering above my house, and this day week I was aroused early in the morning by the cries of my ward's maid, and in ten minutes more it was established beyond a doubt that the fair young girl who had been committed to my charge, and who might have formed the sunshine of my future existence, was no more."

"Dead?"

"Alas, yes! Some mysterious ailment of heart and brain had hurried her from a world she had seen so little of, and I was left lamenting."

The General was silent for several minutes.

The curiosity of Felix Heron was strongly excited, not so much by what he had heard, as from the conviction on his own mind that he had yet something to hear more curious still.

"I will tell you all that followed," added the General, "as briefly as I can. A letter was found in Ida's dressing-case directed to me."

"Her name was Ida?"

"It was. Oh, when shall I forget it? The letter was brought to me in the extremity of my grief. It is here, and has rested since that moment next my heart."

The General produced the letter, but it was by far too dark to enable Felix Heron to see more than its outlines.

Up to this moment, however, they had trotted on side by side, and had reached a portion of the road where stood a lonely cottage.

That road was as familiar to Felix Heron as the doorstep at Whitcombe House.

The old woman, who was an inhabitant of the cottage, had been many a time recipient of his bounty during the period when he held possession of Epping Forest, with the gallant band who had obeyed his orders.

The night was still young, and a thin stream of light showed itself from one of the cottage windows.

"Let us pause here for a moment," said the General; "and you shall see this letter upon which I have acted, but which, notwithstanding is a great mystery to me, and has filled me with many strange doubts and fears."

Heron trotted up to the cottage door and tapped at it with his riding whip.

"Hilloa! hilloa!" he cried. "Dame Fearon, if you are up yet, let us have a light!"

"Gracious providence!" cried the old woman as she flung open the window. "It's the Captain himself!"

"Captain!" said the General. "Have you likewise served?"

"Oh," said Heron, with a light laugh, "we knights of the road are called Captain."

"But you are no highwayman in reality, although you affected to be one?"

"Indeed, and in truth, I am, General; and if you are trusting me upon any other supposition, I beg that you——"

"Hold, hold!" interrupted the General. "I will trust you upon any supposition, for I feel confident you will aid me, and that I am right in obeying the impulse which prompts me to open my heart to you."

CHAPTER CCLXXX.

GENERAL GASTON MAKES A CONFIDANT AND FRIEND OF FELIX HERON.

THE old dame, with officious haste, opened the cottage door and trimmed the little light which burned within the humble dwelling.

"Let us enter here," said Heron, "and if you still wish to do so, you can permit me to read the letter you allude to."

"Your horse," said General Gaston, "which appears so sagacious and under your control that it will obey a word of command, might probably wait for you, but I am afraid mine can scarcely be so far depended upon."

"We will get assistance, then."

Heron produced two sounds upon the silver whistle he carried with him, and, to the surprise of the General, Ogle and Tom Ripon rode up to the spot.

"Ah, I perceive you have followers!"

"I certainly was not alone," replied Heron; "and it may be that I shall be able to render you more efficient assistance than you at first supposed."

"Doubtless—doubtless!"

"Tom, mind the horses!"

"Yes, Captain; though Daisy don't want minding."

"Daisy!" ejaculated the General. "Surely I have heard that name before?"

"It is a name of some repute," remarked Heron; "but dismiss from your mind all that you may have heard either of Daisy or her master, only believing that they are both ready on this night to do you a service."

"I do believe so, and at the same time I shall ever consider that it is not mere accident that has brought us together on the present occasion."

Tom took charge of the horses, and General Gaston, accompanied by Felix Heron, entered the cottage.

The General threw aside his cloak, and Heron could scarcely forbear a smile to himself at the excessive modesty of his companion in supposing he was past the period of life even for evoking the tenderest sentiments in the breast of one so young as his ward.

The General was singularly good-looking, and set off as he was by a brilliant uniform, it would have been difficult to find a more gentlemanly and attractive man than he presented.

"I perceive, sir," said the General, "that you are somewhat surprised that I am in full military costume, but the Duke of Cumberland held a levee at the Horse Guards to-day, where I officially attended, and I have not had time to change my dress. Here is the letter to which I alluded. Pray read it; I submit it to your attention unreservedly."

The letter was written in a very delicate female hand.

Felix Heron took it, and sitting down close to the little light in the cottage he read it with great surprise.

"TO MY DEAR GUARDIAN, GENERAL JOSEPH GASTON.

"A presentiment, which I cannot shake off, is ever present to me, and warns me of some sudden and mysterious decease.

"Perhaps in the midst of some gay scene, when so stern a monitor as death is completely forgotten.

"Perhaps with joyous music ringing in my ears, when human existence would seem immortal and full of delight.

"Perchance in the solitude of my own chamber communing with my own heart, and dreaming of a long and happy future, death will come to me, and I shall pass away like a vapour, to be forgotten by all save those who have loved me and will with tears regret me.

"I cannot resist the belief that such will be the case.

"It is in that belief, then, that I address these few words to you as my last wishes.

"You are well aware that the whole of my considerable fortune was brought by me to England in the shape of jewels, and acting on your advice, after your kind inquiries of competent persons, those jewels still remain in my possession, since it is understood that the price of precious gems of their quality is rapidly rising.

"There is one thing, however, dear guardian, that you do not know, and that is that these jewels, or the money which purchased them, were acquired in India in a manner that neither you nor I could approve.

"It is not for me to cast a stain on the memory of a beloved father, but he was too anxious that his adored Ida should be lifted far above the possibility of want of any of the luxuries of existence.

"I look upon these jewels, then, as unsanctified, and I do not believe that they will ever bring peace or happiness to their possessor.

"I implore you, then, to listen with favour, and to carry out implicitly what you will no doubt consider a strange wish I have regarding them.

"If the presentiments I have regarding my decease should prove true, and if you should find some day that I have passed away from you into the silence of death, I charge you before I am consigned to the tomb to take an opportunity to place the whole of these jewels about me.

"They will not perish as the poor clay which they belong to will, but in the silence of the grave they will no longer exist as a temptation and a snare to human hearts and human virtue.

"And one more request I have to make.

"I am almost sufficient of a Hindoo to have a horror of burial after the European fashion.

"Let me repose in some vault, upon an open bier, so that my mortal frame may exhale into its elements untrammelled by stone or earth.

"And do not think me, dear guardian, wild and fanciful in these matters, but, as you love me, and I think you have always loved me, I charge you to carry out these, the last wishes of

"Your IDA."

Felix Heron finished the letter, and looked at the General with no small surprise.

"Well, sir," said General Gaston; "what think you of that strange epistle?"

"It is the production of some over-heated fancy."

"It may be so."

"Of course, however, you paid but little attention to these feverish dreams of what must have been a sick person?"

"I perceive that you will think me weak," replied the General, "when I tell you that I obeyed the injunctions contained in this letter literally."

"Is that possible?"

"Yes; as I have already informed you, this day week Ida was found dead in her own apartment. Yesterday only she was consigned to her last resting place, in a vault which I purchased in the old church at Woodford."

"And the jewels?"

"I myself obeyed her request by placing them upon her silent breast."

"And the open bier, how was that managed?"

"I expected opposition from every one, and on the pretence of taking a last adieu and a last look of the coffin that contained Ida, I remained in the vault after all had quitted it, and with an instrument I had ready with me for the purpose, I wrenched off the lid of the coffin and so left her, with the jewels sparkling upon her dead form, on the open bier she desired."

"This is indeed a strange story," said Heron.

"You think me foolish, perhaps superstitious, and you will think me more so before I have done."

Heron might have replied that that was hardly possible; but the General, as he rested his head upon his hand and sat by the table of the little cottage, added, in a low voice, "Last night I had a strange dream."

Heron could not forbear the smile that sat for a moment on his lips.

"Bear with me," added the General; "there may be more in these things than is dreamt of in our philosophy."

"I should fancy your imagination was powerfully excited by the events you have detailed as taking place yesterday, and which would no doubt people your slumbers with strange visions."

"It may be so; but, after a short, uneasy slumber, I awakened about the midnight hour, fancying I was called upon by name, and that the voice was Ida's.

"So strongly impressed was I with this vision, that I started from my bed and hastily replied.

"All was still then; and, concluding that it was merely a passing dream, I fell into repose again, but was again startled into wakefulness by a similar call.

"A third time was this singular episode repeated before the night passed away; and from that time to this, the intense desire to re-visit the tomb of Ida has grown into a longing I cannot resist."

"It is very strange."

"It is so, and yet may be nothing more than a disordered fancy. But now, having heard the whole of these particulars, I ask you still to accompany me on this expedition; for my mind is troubled, and a cooler judgment than my own may be required to grapple with possible events."

"I will accompany you with pleasure. We are but two miles from Woodford. You have perceived that I have a couple of trusty followers with me; and let what will happen, I think that we four will be able to direct things as we wish."

A look of satisfaction came over the face of the General as he hastily rose.

"At once, then!" he cried,—"at once let us proceed; and if all is well in the tomb of Ida, I will not nourish such fancies again, but believe them only to arise from a distempered imagination, and a grief-laden heart."

Felix Heron and the General left the cottage.

"Keep close, Ogle," said Heron; "and you, Tom, likewise."

"Yes, Captain."

A sharp trot for a quarter of an hour brought the party to the little village of Woodford, which since that period has grown to be a place of more importance.

The church was rather an ancient structure, and looked picturesque and solemn in the faint moonlight, which now had made its way through the clouds, and was rendering objects much more distinct than they had been an hour previously.

There was an ancient grove of trees close to the church, which afforded a perfectly secure covert for the four horses, as well as for Ogle and Tom Ripon.

"Remain here, both of you," said Heron. "This gentleman and I are going into the church."

"Goodness gracious, Captain!" said Tom; "you don't expect anything is going on there at this time of night except ghosts."

"That's just it," said Heron.

"What, Captain! you don't mean to say you're actually going to look for one of them on his own grounds?"

"Perhaps I am," said Heron; "but, at all events, attend well to the instructions I now give you. If you hear my whistle three times, make your way to yonder iron gates, at which one of you can keep guard, preventing any person from passing, while the other will come into the church to look for me."

"Mind you don't forget, Ogle," said Tom; "you're to go into the church to look for the Captain and the ghosts, while I hold on to the iron gate."

Ogle did not seem very well pleased with this arrangement; but he made no audible objection to it.

"We'll see about it, Tom," he said; "but in the meantime just help me to tether the horses to one of these young saplings."

"Be vigilant," added Heron.

He then rejoined the General; and, passing through the iron gates that have already been mentioned, they took their way towards the church, treading very lightly, and not exchanging a word until they stood beneath its ancient porch.

The place was profoundly still.

The light rain that had been falling in the early part of the night had ceased.

The wind, which in gusty squalls had made its own rough music among the tree-tops, had

FELIX HERON MEETS WITH AN ADVENTURE IN THE OLD CHURCH
AT WOODFORD.

Presented Gratis with No. 90, of the New Edition of EDITH HERON; or, the Sequel to Edith the Captive; or, the Robbers of Epping Forest.

now quieted down to the lightest possible air that could blow.

The General spoke in a whisper.

"I have the key of the vault," he said; "but we must find some means of entering the church, if its doors, as I suppose will naturally be the case, are locked."

"We will try," said Heron.

The heavy, nailed, Gothic, studded door, that opened from the porch, was tried, and found to be perfectly secure.

Heron then went a little distance into the churchyard and looked about him.

A range of small windows ran along one side of the church; and as the lower portion of them was not about five feet from the ground, they were easily accessible.

After trying several of them, Heron found that one of them could be easily opened, although it was at the expense of one of the small, diamond-shaped panes of glass, which he had to break in order to get at the fastening within.

"I will enter the church," said Heron, "and then help you in, General."

Felix Heron had more practice, probably, in dexterous climbing than General Gaston, and certainly he insinuated himself through the small window into the church in a manner that would have done credit to any harlequin.

Heron was somewhat puzzled at first in regard to the object upon which his feet rested, after he had entered by the little Gothic window.

On looking more closely, however, he found it was a tomb, on which lay in effigy the full length figure of an armed knight.

When once Heron ascertained the reason of the uneven surface on which he trod, he was easily able to accommodate himself to it.

Resting one foot upon the mail clad-breast of the warrior, and the other upon the window-sill, he assisted General Gaston to enter the church.

How still and solemn the place was!

"Alas!" said the General, in low tones, "little did I suspect that six-and-thirty hours would not pass over my head before I stood again beneath this roof."

"Courage!" said Heron. "It is always best to remove imaginative fancies from the mind as quickly as may be."

"True—most true."

"You would never have been happy until you had re-visited the tomb of your fair ward, and it is far better to have the opportunity of doing so in my society than by yourself. Lean on me— I can support you. That will do; now leap; and here we are, General, in safety, on the marble floor of the church."

These words had scarcely escaped the lips of Felix Heron, when a strange noise resounded through the ancient building.

It was not a loud noise by any means, but sounded like the dull, heavy echo of some disturbing influence in the immediate vicinity.

The General grasped the arm of Felix Heron, and in a voice of some alarm, he whispered, "Tell me—oh, tell me, you who are younger and have sharper senses than my own, what sounds are those?"

"Hush! let us listen!"

Heron could hardly convince himself that the sounds—strange though they were—had any-thing to do with the church; but he soon found that that idea was fallacious.

The strange sounds not only were connected with the church, but soon localized themselves as coming from one of the old oaken doors that led from the churchyard into the sacred edifice.

"You hear—you hear?" again whispered the General.

"I do."

"Tell me, then, if in your experience you can give a name to those sounds?"

"Easily! Some one from without is trying to effect an entrance into the church."

"For what object?"

"That, at present, we can scarcely guess; but we can easily seclude ourselves in one of these ancient pews, and there, free from all observation, be mute spectators of whatever may happen."

"It was to be—it was to be!" whispered the General. "All these events I feel convinced are following each other in regular pre-ordained succession."

"We shall see," added Heron. "Follow me and trust that all may yet be well. Providence ordains no mischief, although we are not always good judges of the paths that lead to good."

There was an ancient pew in the church, nearly as large as a room.

It was deeply enclosed by curtains, likewise, which cast a funereal gloom about it, and singularly adapted it for a place of espial or secrecy.

CHAPTER CCLXXXI.

FELIX HERON PROVES TO GENERAL GASTON THAT HE IS A FRIEND INDEED.

A VERY strange light now shone through the sacred edifice.

As the moon rose higher on that night of partial rain and squally winds, it seemed to bring a softening and gentle influence with it.

The dark clouds were scattered.

Through a long rift, extending many thousand miles in boundless space, the bright pale face of the silvery satellite of this earth shone down in all its beauty.

But the moonbeams had to pass through the old coloured glass of the Gothic windows of the church.

That circumstance it was which gave them their strange appearance.

The ancient edifice seemed full of faintly coloured light; and, if anything could tend more than another to produce a feeling of reverential and almost superstitious awe, it was certainly that singular preternatural-looking atmosphere which pervaded the whole building.

The mysterious noise at the door continued.

Rattling, scraping.

Heron understood the signification of those sounds instantly.

Some one, by no means an adept at that kind of work, was engaged in trying to pick the lock of the church door.

Heron whispered as much to the General.

"I knew it!" was the reply. "I was sure of it!"

"But who can it be?"

"The villain Durban!"

"And his errand?"

"The spoliation and robbery of the dead!"

This idea of the General's was too congruous and likely to be the truth for Heron to doubt it.

"Be at ease, General Gaston," he whispered; "and let us thank heaven that we are here to defeat so unholy a project."

"Yes; thank heaven!" sighed the General.

The little, low, Gothic door of the church yielded.

The bungling picklock had, at last, effected its purpose; and, slowly creaking on its hinges, the door opening wide, admitted a stream of moonlight, perfectly white and silvery, to fall upon the floor of the church.

General Gaston was about to utter an exclamation, but Heron caught him by the arm, and whispered "Hush!"

From the open air there stepped into that broad gleam of moonlight on the marble floor of the old church, the figure of a man.

He turned and beckoned to his comrades without, and then three other persons entered the church.

The person who had first made his appearance, spoke in low, angry tones.

"Confound the moon, and all moonlight, say I; give me a lantern for this sort of work. Close the door, one of you!"

The door was closed, and then within the church the only light that remained was that mysterious-coloured atmosphere which had already greatly charmed and interested Felix Heron.

He whispered in the lowest possible tones to the General.

"You saw those persons, and, in particular, the man who first entered?"

"I did."

"And you heard his voice?"

"Too well."

"You know him?"

"It is Durban. I pray you, sir, take your hand from off my arm. Thank heaven, I am armed! And now that I feel confident I know the purpose of these wretches, I will no longer tolerate their presence even so near as they are to the tomb of Ida!"

"Hush—hush! Let me implore you to be silent!"

"What manner of light is this?" said the man who was named Durban, still speaking in low, guttural tones to his companions. "I feel half-dazed by it! What does it mean?"

"It's the moonlight," replied another, "through the coloured glass windows."

"Hang the moonlight! I thought we had shut it out when that door was made fast again."

"I don't half like this job," growled another of the men.

"Indeed!" cried Durban, raising his voice; "there spoke Tom Croaker, as a matter of course. I wonder what job you would like except that of playing at dice from night till morning?"

"Don't be bullying me! I never was partial to churches, and churchyards, and family vaults, and those sort of things."

"Then, if you don't like the job, leave us and let us manage it among ourselves.

"No, I won't do that as I've come thus far."

"Ha, ha!" laughed another. "I thought, Tom Croaker, you were quite proud of your ancestors; for, sometimes, you talk about family tombs and statues, and all that sort of thing, belonging to what you would make us believe were your great progenitors."

"Oh, that's all very well! I like to have great ancestors as well as anybody; but I've an earnest desire to keep out of their company as long as possible."

"Peace, all of you!" cried Durban; "Have you your lantern here, Jack Loder?"

"To be sure I have."

"Open the slide and let us look about us. This odd kind of light puzzles and confounds me."

A broad gleam of light from the lens of a lantern radiated on the wall of the church, and, in an instant, the beautifully-coloured atmosphere, compounded of the moonbeams and the stained glass windows, seemed to vanish.

"Hold a moment," said the man who was called Tom Croaker. "Let us all understand, Durban, what is to be done."

"I will tell you; gather round me here."

The three associates of Durban stood close to him, and the iniquitous little group of men were thrown into strong relief by the rays of the lantern, the slide of which was still kept open.

"I could not venture," said Durban, speaking in low tones, which, however, in the silent repose of that place were distinctly audible to Felix Heron and General Gaston,—"I could not venture to tell you what I am now going to tell you anywhere but here."

"Out with it, Durban! We are snug enough and quiet enough."

"To be sure," said another; "and I would venture to say that there's not another living soul but ourselves within earshot."

"Of that I am well convinced," added Durban; "and now listen to me. A person, whom I may as well call a young lady, has been buried in a vault in this church with a diamond ring upon her finger worth a thousand pounds."

"Indeed!" exclaimed the other three.

"Yes; and I thought as we were all somewhat out at elbows and bare of pocket, that two hundred and fifty guineas or so to each would not be amiss."

"Then you mean to share and share alike, Durban?"

"I certainly do."

"Well, that's liberal!"

"The villain!" whispered General Gaston. "Poor Ida's jewels are worth at least thirty thousand pounds!"

"Hush!" said Heron, in his lowest possible tones. "Do you not understand that he wishes to purchase the assistance of his comrades in crime as cheaply as he can, by deceiving them as to the amount of the booty?"

"Yes--yes! I comprehend now."

"Let us listen further."

"Yes," added Tom Croaker, "it's what I call liberal; and I'm only surprised, Durban, that you did not keep the whole affair to yourself."

"It is not a pleasant thing to come to a place like this alone at night."

"Ah, that's it!"

"Partly so; but I wish to do you all a good turn."

The three men coughed, to intimate their doubtful reception of this idea.

"You may believe me or not, as you like," said Durban; "but such was partly my motive; and now I will proceed to point out to you the door of the vault."

"Ay—ay! we lose time!"

The General made a movement to sally forth from the pew, and laid his hand upon his sword-hilt, but Felix Heron restrained him.

"Not yet—not yet! Let us hear more!"

The state of agitation of General Gaston was extreme, and it was evident he scarcely had the power to speak.

"If I could only persuade you," whispered Heron, "to leave the whole of this adventure now to me——"

"No—no!"

"Believe me, it would be better. Your feelings will only be harrowed by a sight of those mournful remains which have to be defended against these despoilers of the dead."

"I will steel my heart against such feelings, and do my duty!"

"Hush! they speak again!"

"This low iron door in the wall," said Durban, "opens upon a flight of steep steps, which lead down to the vault we have to visit."

"It's locked."

"We hardly expected to find it open. Come, Jack Loder, you pretended to be an adept with the picklock, although it seemed to me you bungled at the church door."

"The old lock was so heavy," muttered the man; "but this one seems more modern, and I shall make a better job of it."

"You will understand," added Durban, "that I will descend myself and procure the diamond ring, while you all keep watch above. Not that I fear any interruption, but it's better to do a job like this in good company. The vault is a new one, and, with the exception of the remains of the young girl I speak of, contains nothing that any man might shrink from."

The scraping and rattling of the picklock in the keyhole of the vault door now came plainly upon the ears of General Gaston and Felix Heron.

The state of agitation into which these sounds threw General Gaston rendered him almost incapable of following the advice of Felix Heron, to keep still until the proceedings of Durban and his villanous associates had assumed more importance.

A very few minutes must suffice to make a great change in the state of affairs.

And those few minutes were rapidly passing away.

"That will do, I think," suddenly exclaimed the man who was working with the picklock.

"Yes," said Durban, "the door yields."

"It is open."

"Then our object is all but accomplished. One of you keep watch at the church door—one, too, had better go outside, to be sure that there are no interlopers in the churchyard. You, Loder, stay here with your picklock, for when all is done we must fasten up this door again so as to give it the appearance of it never having been tampered with."

It will be seen in all these arrangements that Durban reserved to himself the task of proceeding into the vault.

But yet the circumstances were sufficiently mysterious, that neither Felix Heron nor General Gaston were able to come to a direct conclusion in regard to them.

That is to say, they could not imagine how Durban had come to his knowledge of the fact that Ida was placed in the tomb so richly adorned with the Indian jewels.

It was a circumstance that had never passed the lips of General Gaston to any human being until he communicated it to Felix Heron.

Durban's criminal associates now, however, began to distribute themselves in the manner suggested by him.

Felix Heron felt that the time for action had come.

"Follow me, General," he said; "and although your rank might entitle you to command, permit me, as more used to adventures of this kind, to direct you."

"I will obey."

"Prevent, then, that man at the door of the church from interfering?"

"Certainly."

The General, by a few hasty steps, crossed the pavement of the church, and to the astonishment of that one of the associates of Durban who was there on guard, he faced him, and hastily drawing his sword, placed its point within an inch of his throat, as he cried, "Stir hand or foot, and you are a dead man."

Terror took possession of the gambler and roue, for such indeed he was; and, but for the door behind him, against which he leant heavily, he would have fallen to the floor of the church.

While the General was thus playing his part, Felix Heron was not idle.

Half a dozen rapid strides brought him to the little iron door in the wall, which led down to the vault.

And Heron's progress so far was completely unnoticed by the man named Loder, who was there waiting for his iniquitous principal Durban, who had descended the narrow staircase to the home of the dead.

The curiosity of Loder had been strongly excited, and he was projecting his head and body as far as he could down the staircase, while he held with one hand to the side of the door.

Felix Heron had had no such precise intention when he reached that spot, but seeing the favourable position of Mr. Loder for such an act, he, with one hearty kick, loosened his hold upon the door-post, and sent him with a flying rush down the vault staircase, before he had time even to utter a cry of alarm.

Heron's next act was to close the iron door of the vault.

The pick-lock was still in it.

A slight turn, and the door was secured.

Some loud yells and shrieks came from the vault, which sounded all the more fearful from the half-smothered, strange, echoing way in which they reached the upper air.

Another moment, and Felix Heron was by the side of the General.

"What has happened? What have you done, good friend?"

"I have disposed of two of them, General."

"Spare my life, and I'll confess all," cried the man, at whose throat General Gaston still held his sword.

By slipping down quite close to the door the fellow got upon his knees, for he fully believed, from the expression that Felix Heron had used, in the death of two of his companions.

"If you would save your worthless life," said Heron, "call in your comrade from without."

"I will—I will; and if you will have the kindness to settle him instead of me, I shall take it as a great favour. He is a much greater rogue than I am, I assure you, gentlemen."

"Silence!"

"But let me explain that I am rather a poor innocent sort of fellow than otherwise. I'm only twenty-eight years of age, and the villain that's outside is thirty-seven, so I've not had time, gentlemen, to be quite so bad as he is."

"Silence, I say, or it will be worse for you."

"I will go to the vault," said the General.

"Not alone."

"There are only two of them there."

"True; but let me accompany you. We will first of all secure these rascals, and then pay our attention to the others."

"But they are alone with Ida."

"With the dead, General—you forget."

"And yet it seems a kind of desecration."

"And it is what it seems; but we will soon put an end to that. Now, you fellow, call in your comrade, or prepare for instant death."

"I will—I will! Heath! Heath!" cried the man. "Heath! Heath!"

"Is that you, Croaker?"

"Yes, come hither; you are wanted!"

"What's up now? Is it all done?"

Mr. Heath rather started at the church porch, for Felix Heron blew shrilly the whistle which was a signal to Tom Ripon and Ogle that they were wanted.

"Now be off," said Heron to the trembling wretch who was in the church, and he believing that he was released and permitted to escape, made a dash out to the porch, overthrowing his companion by the suddenness of the shock with which he came against him, so that they both fell together by the side of the old tomb close to the spot.

Tom Ripon and Ogle were at hand instantly.

Heron, as he looked out from the church saw them in the moonlight.

"Take care of these felows!" he cried.

"All right, Captain," said Tom.

"They're as safe as diamonds in cotton," said Ogle.

As he spoke, he pounced upon the two men, and holding each by his collar by his main strength, forced them to their feet.

Heron then turned his attention to affairs in the inside of the church.

General Gaston was standing with his drawn sword a few paces from the porch.

The state of agitation in which he had been for some time past had mainly arisen from inaction.

But now that he had something to do he was calm, cool, and self-possessed.

"You manage these things, sir," he said

"with a practised hand. Let us now to the vault, and clear it of the presence of those men, who I little suspected would ever have the chance of looking in this world upon the face of Ida."

"I am with you," said Heron; "we will descend instantly."

To cross the pavement of the church, and reach the little iron door of the vault, was the work of a moment.

———

CHAPTER CCLXXXII.

FELIX HERON AND GENERAL GASTON MEET WITH A SURPRISE IN THE VAULT OF WOODFORD CHURCH.

A SHRIEK so fearful, so concentrated, so terrible in its agonizing cadences came from some one in the vaults, that even the tolerably well-strung nerves of Felix Heron were shocked and staggered by it, and he involuntarily fell back several paces.

"Gracious heaven!" cried the General, "what is that?"

Heron recovered himself instantly.

"We will see," he said. Follow me, General, and that cry shall no longer be a mystery."

The skeleton key was difficult to move in the locked door.

A terrible fear came over Felix Heron that he had broken it.

He dreaded lest too late he had recollected that such things must be managed by skill and by tenderness rather than by force.

The General became fearfully impatient.

"Open, open!" he cried; "for the love of heaven, open the door!"

"Hush!" said Heron; "it must done quietly, or not at all."

The key turned.

The lock was shot back.

"Oh, where are my senses?" cried the General. "I have the real key of that door in my pocket."

"It matters not."

Heron forced the door open.

Immediately he did so, with a rush, Durban and the men who had been kicked down the stairs flew into the church.

But it happened that Durban encountered Felix Heron, and the shock was sufficiently great to give the ruffian so severe a fall upon the stone pavement that he lay insensible.

General Gaston had closed with the other man, and exerting a strength and energy Heron would hardly have given him credit for, he raised him in his arms, and flung him bodily into one of the pews with such a force, that he was not likely to move for many minutes.

Without a moment's hesitation, then, the General plunged down into the vault.

Heron quickly followed him.

Lying on the floor, half embedded in the thick sawdust, was the lantern Durban had taken with him.

It shed but a sickly ray about it; and Heron, by that light, saw that he was in a small stone chamber, the roof of which was vaulted.

But soon his eyes became riveted to the living and the dead occupants of that last sad home of mortality.

On a raised bier, about the centre of the vault was a coffin, the lid of which lay by its side.

Kneeling by that sad memorial was General Gaston.

His head rested on his hands, and he seemed either to have dropped into a swoon, or to be so overcome by his feelings on the occasion, as to be incapable of speech or motion.

Heron raised the lantern.

He looked upon the face of the dead.

As he did so, a surprised expression came over him, for he had seen death before, and this was altogether unlike his remembrances of such a sight.

There was a faint flush upon the face.

Nothing whatever indicated the presence of the Destroyer, and what imparted a life-like slumbering appearance to the young girl, was the fact that one arm hung over the side of the coffin, while the other was raised above her

No. 91.—EDITH HERON.

head, partially resting upon the fair brow, that lay there apparently in the calmness and stillness of its last repose."

By the light of the lantern, Heron could see the sparkle of the magnificent jewels which adorned the wrists and neck of Ida.

"Rise, sir—rise!" he cried to the General. "There is nothing here to look upon which can give you a pang, for whatever remembrances you may have of this fair young creature in life, they will not be outraged by beholding her now apparently in deep repose."

The General looked up.

"Death, death!" he cried,—"the repose of death!"

"Hush! Be calm!"

"Ida! Ida!"

"It is but sleep."

"The sleep that knows no awaking! Ida, Ida! I did love you, and I have let you pass away for ever!"

"General, this is no time for giving way to such feelings. Take the opinion and the judgment of one calmer, although, perhaps, not wiser, than yourself!"

"What judgment?—what opinion? What can I do, but suffer and weep?"

"Listen to me. So long as you could keep secret to yourself the fact of leaving these jewels with the dead, all was well; but now that it is known to others, these sad remains will never rest in peace!"

"What would you wish?"

"I counsel you to remove these glittering gems, and leave the dead to the calm rest which otherwise would be broken by the cupidity of those who have no sense or feeling but their own greed of gain."

"It is true—it is true! And what can she know either of compliance, or otherwise, with her last wishes?"

The General slowly stretched one hand towards the bier.

"I should not shrink from you," he said, "for even death here is beautiful."

Tremblingly he raised the hand of Ida, which hung over the side of the coffin.

With fingers that shook at the task, he essayed to unclasp the brilliant bracelet that encircled the wrist.

Then he uttered a cry.

"What is this?—what is this? The hand is warm—there is life-blood in it yet! Ida, Ida! what is this?"

Was Heron deceived?

Could it be real?

Did fancy play him the trick?

Was it but the quivering of the lantern light upon the dead eye-lids?

Heron could have sworn at that moment that he saw a slight movement of the eyes of the dead girl.

And the General had seen it.

Another moment, and he had wound his arms about the supposed corpse.

"She lives! She lives! This is a cheat—a delusion — a horrible mockery of death only! Ida, Ida! Speak to me, if it be but one word, to assure me that you live!"

General Gaston might have been deceived by these appearances of life, deeply interested as his feelings were.

The over-wrought imagination might impose upon the judgment, and even the senses.

But such could not be the case with Felix Heron.

With surprise, and a feeling of heartfelt felicitation at the extraordinary event, he saw indeed that life still lingered in the frame of Ida, and that this world was still for her and for those who loved her.

The breath of the girl heaved with emotion.

She seemed to be struggling with the vitality which was coming back to her in full force.

Short, sharp screams burst from her lips, and then a flood of tears relieved her over-charged heart, and she sank sobbing on the breast of General Gaston.

"Tell me, my friend — tell me," cried the General, addressing Heron, "is this a dream, or have I indeed lived for so much happiness?"

"It is no dream," said Heron. "The lady lives."

"In the tomb?"

"Yes, General, this adds but another to those remarkable cases where some deep swoon, or a suspension of all the ordinary faculties of nature, has looked like death."

Ida now looked up, and gazed around her with a shuddering consciousness of where she was.

The vault.

The thick-lying sawdust on its floor.

The raised bier.

The coffin.

All these objects struck her gaze; and then, as the truth seemed slowly to dawn upon her that she had been placed in that fearful home of death while life still lingered at her heart, a shudder pervaded her frame, and Heron was fearful she might again lapse into that state of forgetfulness of life from which she had been just rescued.

"Fight against this depression," he cried; "you are saved, and all will yet be well."

Heron ran to the foot of the stairs leading from the vault to the church.

"Ogle, Ogle!" he cried.

"Yes, Captain."

"You usually carry a dram-bottle with you."

"A bad habit, Captain. I have it not."

This being the only occasion on which it was ever required.

"All right, Captain!" cried Tom, who heard the question and answer. "If one fellow hasn't a thing of that sort, another one may. Here you are! Shall I come down, Captain?"

"Yes, at once."

Tom descended into the vault, and the moment he saw the state of affairs there, he would have turned and fled into the church again, had not Heron caught him by the coat, and stopped his flight.

"Give me the case-bottle, if you have it."

"Here, Captain, here! But let me go. This is rather out of my line. After corpses are properly put into vaults, they ought to stay there."

"The young lady lives," said Heron, as he took the case bottle containing some strong *eau-de-vie* from Tom Ripon, and prevailed upon Ida to taste a small portion of it.

While this process was rapidly going on, Tom Ripon stood at the foot of the stone steps leading to the church, with his eyes fixed upon the beautiful girl that had been rescued from a fate worse than death.

Tom heaved a deep sigh.

"This is the one," he said. "I thought I could never change—but I do. All the others ain't fit to hold a candle to her. Yes, this is the one! and now I'm fixed as fate. But I wonder if she's really alive, or only pretending to be so, as she seems to have pretended to be dead for ever so long."

"Ida! dear Ida!" said the General. "You are stronger—better?"

The girl shuddered.

"What has happened? How has it all come about?"

"You shall know all in good time. Let us now hasten from this place. Oh, what a happy night is this, and how changed does all the world appear to me!"

in a swoon, seems to have been mistaken for death."

The General was about to make some reply to these words, when another tap came at the drawing-room door.

It was some one wishing to see the physician—the nurse, in fact, whom he had hastily sent for to attend upon Ida, and who brought word that the fair patient would not be quieted until she had seen the General.

General Gaston glanced at the physician.

"Of course I consent," said the latter. "The shortest way is to humour a patient in these fancies, for the perils of contradiction are much worse than those of indulgence."

The General hastily left the room, and Felix Heron was alone with the physician.

"Sir," said Heron, "we have a prisoner below in the person of the young lady's-maid, who, the moment she saw her mistress brought home, made a desperate attempt to leave the house."

"Then my suspicions are more than confirmed," said the physician.

"What do you suspect, Doctor?"

"That some one has administered to the young lady a narcotic drug of such potency that although it failed to destroy life, it threw her into that state of seeming death which has lasted so long."

"She had a bitter enemy!"

"Which is further confirmation! This affair must be well sifted, Captain Heath. Pray excuse me for a few moments, and I will send for some one who will materially assist us."

The physician left the room, and during his absence General Gaston returned, looking radiant with happiness.

"Congratulate me, dear friend!" he said. "Ida is not only well, but——"

A flush came over the General's face, and then he smiled with sincere happiness.

"Let me conclude the sentence for you," said Heron, "and congratulate you upon your approaching union with your fair ward, who I am sure will be enviably happy."

"It is so—it is to be! Oh, what a change is this! I can scarcely believe in my own felicity!"

"Such is life," said Heron. "Hope and happiness succeed despair; and, alas! too often, when we think ourselves securely armed against the shafts of malice or misfortune, we stand in the most imminent danger."

"It is so—it is so! But Ida has informed me of strange things!"

"Indeed!"

"Yes, Captain Heath: she never wrote that letter about the jewels being carried to the tomb with her! It was a rank forgery!"

"I guessed as much."

"The villain Durban!"

"Yes, General, you name the man; and there can be little doubt but his accomplice in this house has been the own maid of your ward, Ida!"

"By heavens, yes! I will question her, and force a confession of her guilt! Ah! here is our friend the Doctor returned, and he shall assist us in unravelling all this guilty mystery."

The Doctor walked into the room with a well-contented smile upon his face.

"Sit down, both of you," he said.

"With pleasure, Doctor, but——"

"I like to see the end of everything, and after what this gentleman, Captain Heath, has told me, I felt myself justified in taking a step which I am certain you will both approve."

"What step, Doctor?"

"Answer me first. You are sure your prisoner down stairs is secure?"

"Quite," said Heron. "There is the key of the room."

"Good! Then what do you think I have done?"

"Doctor, you are quite mysterious!" said the General.

"And something of an old woman, beside," thought Heron, to himself.

"Well," added the Doctor, "not to keep you longer in suspense—ha, ha!"

"In the name of heaven, Doctor," cried the General, "what have you done?"

"I have sent for Jonathan Wild."

"Who?" cried Heron, starting to his feet.

"Jonathan Wild, the famous thief-taker!"

"The villain!"

"Well, well, my good sir, I do not say for a single moment that Mr. Wild is an estimable personage."

"A mighty scoundrel, I believe," said the General.

"Well, gentlemen, well, that may be; but these kind of men, you see, have a sort of tact in managing intricate criminal affairs, and I have always heard that Jonathan Wild is on the side that pays him best."

The General looked vexed.

Heron caught up his hat.

"Good night, General!"

"Nay—nay——"

"Do not stay me!"

"My dear Captain Heath," cried the Doctor, laying his hands upon him, "you must stay. Did you ever see Jonathan Wild?"

"I think I have, once."

"I assure you he is a most remarkable man. I am visiting physician to Giltspur Street Compter. I quite long to introduce him to you."

"By no means!" cried Heron. "General, good night, again!"

"Ah!" cried General Gaston. "Yes, yes! Hang it, Doctor, what on earth has induced you to contaminate my house with the presence of such a scoundrel as Jonathan Wild?"

"But, my dear sir, I thought——"

"Mr. Wild!" announced a servant.

The drawing-room door was flung open.

With one bound, Heron passed through the folding-doors that led to the back drawing-room, and slammed them shut behind him.

The Doctor was so astonished at this sudden movement, that he slipped off his chair to the floor.

General Gaston advanced a step or two, and Jonathan Wild stood in the doorway, glancing about him.

"I think Doctor Fletcher sent for me," said Wild, producing a card from one of his capacious pockets.

"Certainly, Mr. Wild, I did," said the Doctor. "Something has taken place in this house which I am sure ought to come under your cognisance."

"Excuse me, sir!" said General Gaston, with dignity. "Doctor Fletcher, you seem entirely to forget that this is my house. I have not the slightest doubt but you are a well-meaning man, but give me leave to say that all this is troublesomely meddlesome in the extreme."

"Sir!"

"I repeat my words!"

"General!"

"That is my opinion, Doctor; and as regards Mr. Wild, all I can say is that I do not require his services."

"Well, General, if this is the way my kind offices are received," said the Doctor, "I will take my leave of you, and of Captain Heath, likewise; only I don't see him, for at the mention of Mr. Wild's name, he shot off like a rocket, either up the chimney, or out of the window, or into the back drawing-room, or somewhere!"

"Ha, ha!" cried Wild.

CHAPTER CCLXXXIV.

JONATHAN WILD IS MADE A PRISONER, AND CONVEYED TO THE COMPTER BY HIS MEN.

WILD stepped further into the room.

The ordinary suspicious look upon his countenance deepened into one of gloomy ferocity.

"What is the meaning of this?" he said. "Who is it that has mysteriously disappeared?"

"Captain Heath," said the Doctor.

"Captain who?"

"Captain Heath."

"Bah!" said Wild; "there is no Captain Heath, except he be of the road; but of all your suppositions, Doctor, in regard to where this mysterious gentleman has gone, I prefer that that points to the back apartment here."

Jonathan Wild made two strides towards the back drawing-room, but General Gaston was too quick for him, and gliding between him and the door, he drew himself up proudly, as he glanced at the vulgar, ruffian-like figure before him.

"Hold, sir!" he cried. "I am the master of this house, and I neither sent for you nor will I tolerate your presence here any longer!"

"Then why was I sent for?" asked Wild.

"That you may settle with your friend, the Doctor, whose services I no longer require."

For a few seconds Wild seemed as though about to spring upon the General, and force a passage into the back drawing-room.

The significant manner, however, in which General Gaston handled his sword-hilt was something of a caution to Wild, and he adopted another line of tactics.

Suddenly stepping towards one of the windows, he blew a long clear note upon the whistle he always carried.

The sound was so prolonged and shrill that it was heard by every one interested in the proceedings of the great thief-taker.

Felix Heron well knew that it was a signal to Wild's janissaries and bull-dogs to gather about the house.

If he were to escape at all from his present predicament it must be done at once.

And easy, indeed, would have been Heron's evasion of the danger that beset him in General Gaston's house, but for one accidental circumstance.

The door opening from the back drawing-room on to the landing from the head of the stairs would have been quite a natural mode of exit for him.

Unfortunately, however, it was closed, and some one had turned the key in the lock on the outside.

What was Heron to do?

Nothing but boldness would now save him.

But if that were an element in the transaction, his safety was pretty well assured; for when did Felix Heron ever shrink from any act of which courage was the principal ingredient?

He made up his mind what to do at once.

While the echo of Jonathan Wild's whistle still filled the entire house, Heron quietly opened the door leading from the back to the front drawing-room, and walked forward without the smallest hesitation.

For the instant, Wild's attention was to the window towards which he had turned when summoning his myrmidons by the whistle.

Heron had just time to sink into a chair some half-dozen paces from Wild, and there he sat profoundly still until Jonathan, turning his eyes upon him, seemed transfixed with mingled terror and astonishment.

Wild opened his mouth several times as if about to speak, and retreated backwards as he did so.

"This is Captain Heath!" cried the Doctor.

"Captain—Captain Heath?" gasped Wild. "Captain Death, you mean!"

Wild had reached the door, which was partially open; but as he did so, a couple of arms were flung about him, and he felt himself in the iron grip of Ogle.

A blow upon the crown of his hat sent it at once so far down over his eyes, that, as far as Wild could be cognisant of what was going on in that apartment, he might as well have been in the next street.

Ogle did not utter a word, for he had no wish to be identified by Wild, but he made some gesticulations over the head of Jonathan Wild to Felix Heron.

"Goodness gracious!" cried the Doctor; "what's the meaning of all this?"

"It's only a little drama," said Heron; "and it is called 'The Biter Bit; or, Caught in His Own Snare.'"

General Gaston started at the sound of Heron's voice, which was so entirely different to any he had hitherto spoken in, that it could scarcely be supposed to come from the same person's lips.

But Ogle was still busily engaged with Jonathan Wild, about whose face and head he tied a silk handkerchief so quickly and scientifically that he was completely hoodwinked, and at the mercy of circumstances.

"That roquelaire, Captain," said Ogle, now speaking for the first time.

And Ogle had taken the hint from Heron, altering his voice so much that, particularly muffled up as he was, Wild had no chance of recognising it.

Another moment, and Wild was wrapped up

The General would fain have carried Ida from the vault, but the state of agitation he was in precluded the possibility of his doing so.

He could only fold her to his breast, and strive to look at her through his tears.

"You cannot walk, Ida," he said—"you cannot walk. I will convey you hence. We will find a carriage, and in one short hour you will be in your own home again."

"If you please, sir," said Tom, "I don't mind carrying the young lady up-stairs, now that I see she's alive and kicking. I shan't think it's any trouble. Ah, me! she is the one!"

"Out of the way," said Heron. "General, permit me. The sooner this young lady is at home, the better."

Even as he spoke, Heron raised Ida gently in his arms, and sprang up the stone steps.

The General followed him.

"That's always e way," said Tom. "I get cut out by somebody, just at the moment when I can make myself agreeable; and now she'll go to fall in love with the Captain; but I'll put a spoke in his wheel before it goes any further. Captain, Captain!"

"What is it, Tom?"

"How pleased your wife and family will be when they hear how kind you've been to this young lady!"

"What do you mean, Tom? Are you mad?"

"Ha, ha! I'm not mad — but I shall be soon. I could have had her up on my back in a moment."

Heron might or might not suspect what Tom's notions were for making this speech, but he turned and spoke to him with great gravity.

"You can still do the young lady a great service, Tom."

"Only mention it, and it's as good as done."

"Stay in the vault, then, and take care of the coffin."

"I think I see it!" cried Tom, as he darted up the steps. "I'm sure you feel cold, miss. Shall I lend you my boots."

"Be off, Tom, and don't make yourself absurd."

"Yes," muttered Tom, "there he goes again. I'm absurd when I fall in love, and everybody else is quite right and romantic."

"Ogle," said Heron, "where are the prisoners?"

"All here, Captain; we've taken the liberty of tying them all together in a string."

"General," added Heron, "I think the most righteous retribution that can happen these fellows is to leave them in the vault from which Ida has so miraculously escaped."

"Be it so, sir."

"Ogle, bring them forward."

Durban and his three rascally associates with terror in their looks, were led to the top of the steps conducting to the vault.

"You will please to descend," said Heron—"unless you prefer death here above. Make your election quickly, for we have no time to spare. If you choose death, my men here will shoot you. Ogle, are your pistols handy?"

"Yes, Captain."

"No, no!" shouted Durban and his comrades: "let us live, and we will go anywhere."

"Descend, then, at once."

While Ogle was shaking the powder in the pans of his pistols, Durban and his associates, trembling in every limb, and looking like so many ghosts, descended the steep stone steps into the vault.

Ogle slammed the iron door shut, and turned the skeleton key in the lock.

Both Heron and the General had been provided with ample cloaks, and these were now wrapped around Ida, till she looked more like a mummy than a living being of modern times.

"Ha, ha!" cried Tom. "I've an idea, Captain, and I'm sure you'll give me credit for it."

"What is it, Tom?"

"Why, you see, Captain, we've only one horse a-piece, so I think the lightest weight among us ought to take the young lady. If she sits behind me, and puts both her arms round my neck——"

"Silence, Tom! I shall take her on Daisy."

"Oh, yes!" muttered Tom; "of course you will. Well, miss, you'll be very comfortable on Daisy. The Captain's family and little wife often rides on Daisy."

"What on earth do you mean, Tom, by these constant allusions to my wife and family?"

"Oh, nothing, Captain, nothing! Only I wish I had a wife and family. I'm a single man—single—single—single—and I never fell in love, even with anybody, till to-night."

"Be quiet, Tom, be quiet. General, I ask you to let me carry out this adventure. My horse is swift and sure, and I am rather more cool and collected than you can possibly be; but if you have the remotest shadow of an objection to Ida riding with me, say so, and I will lend you my horse, and you shall take charge of her yourself."

"No," said the General—"no. To whom could I entrust this treasure of my soul, more truly than to him who has so gallantly helped me this night to life and happiness again?"

"That's the way! — that's the way," said Tom,—"they settle it among 'em, and think no more of a man's agonized feelings than if he was nobody in the world. Ah, yes! this is the one. I am in for it this time, and no mistake!"

CHAPTER CCLXXXIII.

FELIX HERON HAS A NARROW ESCAPE AT THE HOUSE OF GENERAL GASTON.

OGLE rode by the side of Heron.

The General followed closely.

Tom Ripon brought up the rear.

It required such a horseman as Heron to ride with safety encumbered as he was by Ida, who, wrapped up in those roquelaire cloaks, was, perforce, compelled to be perfectly inert, and to rely entirely upon what support she might receive from the disengaged arm of Heron.

The little party rode at good speed.

"Farewell, Captain," cried Ogle, "to our projected expedition to the Forest."

"There is a destiny in such things," replied Heron; "and this adventure is surely worth a thousand expeditions, even into those fair and beautiful glades, which are endeared to us by so many recollections."

After a time General Gaston led the way.

He was in a state of feverish impatience to reach his home, for although Ida had thus certainly been snatched from the very grave, there was so much of mystery in the whole transaction, that he longed to see her perfectly recovered, in order to hear from her own lips what account she could give of the strange occurrences of the last week.

And Felix Heron was not without his apprehensions.

He feared that upon reaching the General's house, it would be found that death had completed his victory.

The arrangement by which, however, General Gaston went first, materially increased the speed of the whole party, for Heron was not so apprehensive of distancing everybody else by the swiftness of Daisy.

At length the mansion of the General was reached.

It was a handsome house, at the West End of the town.

The General knocked rapidly and furiously at the outer door, which the alarmed hall-porter flung open wide.

"Permit me, dear friend," said the General, addressing Heron, as he took from his arms the apparently lifeless body of Ida.

Then, before he could cross the threshold of his house, a woman, in the dress of a servant, appeared coming down the grand staircase.

The moment she cast her eyes upon the burden the General carried, she uttered a shriek of dismay, and would have fled from the house.

Heron, however, had just dismounted, and barred the way.

"No!" he cried. "Hear me, General Gaston. I think it will be prudent, until we know further of these affairs, that no person should be permitted to leave your house."

"You are right!" cried the General. "I agree with your suggestion. By all means keep the door."

The servant actually fought with him for a few seconds in her anxiety to escape, and it was only by main strength that Heron forced her into a room leading from the hall, and turned the key upon her.

"Follow me!" shouted the General. "The person you have just captured is the personal servant of Ida. Follow me, sir, and we will come at the heart of this mystery. Yet what am I doing? I have not your cool judgment. We need a nurse and a physician instantly."

The General tore up the staircase as he spoke, and Heron ordered Tom to look right and left, and see if a physician's door-plate was visible, and if so, to request his immediate attendance.

There was much hurrying and scurrying in the General's house for the next ten minutes, with the minute details of which we need not trouble our readers.

But supposing those ten minutes to have passed away, we will look into a large and handsome drawing-room, where General Gaston is seated in company with Felix Heron.

"Hope for the best!" said Heron. "The phy-

sician's first report was not unfavourable, and the second one may calm all your fears."

"I pray heaven it may!"

There came a low tap at the drawing-room door.

General Gaston sprung to his feet.

The door was opened, and a quiet, gentlemanly-looking man entered the apartment.

One glance at his face was quite enough.

"She lives?" cried the General.

"She not only lives," replied the physician, "but will live. Youth has conquered all."

General Gaston was overcome by his feelings, and sunk into a chair.

"Come, come, General," said the physician: "you will be in a worse way than my patient up-stairs; and I am sure this gentleman, whose name I have not the honour of knowing, will join with me in begging you to be calm and tranquil."

"Joy does not kill," said Heron. "He is better already."

The General sighed deeply.

"I ought to be better. I ought to be thankful. I ought to be full of peace and contentment."

"Well—well! All is well that ends well! And as we physicians are a sort of privileged gossips of the community, I would fain know how the strange events of this night have come about."

"I am indebted," said the General, "to this gentleman for the life of your fair patient, and, I do honestly think, for my own likewise."

"I shall be happy to know the gentleman."

There was an awkward pause.

Twice had the physician thus intimated his desire to be introduced to Felix Heron.

But General Gaston knew no name to call him.

And Heron was in doubt, under the circumstances, what name to give him, since, it will be remembered, his first introduction to the General was in the capacity of a highwayman

"I am Captain Heath," he said, after a few moments' pause.

The physician coughed slightly, as if to intimate that he by no means believed that to be Heron's name.

In fact, the pause that had taken place, and the hesitation with which Heron had pronounced it, would have been quite sufficient to engender suspicion in any one.

But the General took up the name instantly.

"Allow me, then, Doctor," he said, "to state that Captain Heath is the dearest friend I have in the world, and I am under infinite obligations to him."

The Doctor bowed.

"Allow me, now," said Heron, "to take my departure. It is a great delight to me that I leave a happy atmosphere behind me, and at some future time I shall be glad to hear from you, General, the solution of all the mysteries of this night."

"And I, too," said the Doctor. "I was aware of the domestic calamity that had overtaken you, General, being so near a neighbour to you, although I had not the honour of attending your fair ward in the illness the termination of which, n one of the roquelaire cloaks, and perfectly helpless.

The Doctor turned quite red in the face, as he energetically protested against the proceedings.

"Gentlemen—gentlemen, this must not be. It is quite an outrage—this is Mr. Jonathan Wild, the well-known officer. This must not be, gentlemen! General Gaston, I call upon you to interfere."

The General shook his head.

"There has been a great deal too much interference already," he said, "and that of the most unauthorized description."

A confused bustle was at this moment heard upon the staircase.

There seemed to be some contention going on between General Gaston's servants and some persons who were forcing their way into the house.

That these persons were Jonathan Wild's myrmidons Ogle felt perfectly assured; and holding Wild by the collar, he dragged him to the landing, while he called over the staircase balustrades, "Mr. Wild orders a sedan chair."

Several of the janissaries—for such, indeed, they were—ran back into the street to procure one.

"Here's the sedan, sir."

"Mr. Wild," added Ogle, "desires that this prisoner may be conveyed at once to the Compter."

With a dexterity that only practice could have given him, Ogle, with a short piece of rope that he had in his possession, had effectually gagged Wild; so that, with all the disposition in the world to yell and roar out his disapprobation of the whole proceedings, the great thief-taker could only utter a low gurgling sound, which was very expressive of the last stage of strangulation.

Ogle flung Wild, thus wrapped up and disguised even from the observation of his men, right into the arms of his janissaries.

He was hustled into the sedan chair, and carried off at once in triumph.

"Any orders, Captain?" said Ogle.

"Where is Tom?"

"Minding the horses."

"That is well. General Gaston, good night; and as for you, Doctor, I warn you that the least said in matters of this sort is the soonest mended; and if you value your own safety, you will be prudent enough to keep a still tongue in regard to the proceedings of this night."

General Gaston stepped forward to Heron and took him by the hand.

"Let us not part thus," he said; "or I shall fear we part for ever."

"No, General; we shall meet again, and that shortly. I have need of friends, and have already a few, among whom I am certain you will be glad to be enrolled; but, for the present, farewell!"

In the midst of a storm of indignant remonstrances from the Doctor, Heron left the house, accompanied by Ogle.

In two minutes more, he was mounted on Daisy, and making the best of his way towards Whitcombe House.

It was on the evening of the next day that Felix Heron, in his carefully got up disguise as Captain Fantome of the royal navy, made his way once more to the house of General Gaston.

In reply to his question as to whether the General could be seen, the servant ushered him into a room on the ground-floor, that same apartment which Heron had converted into the temporary prison of the maid of Ida.

In a few seconds, General Gaston entered the room; but upon beholding one whom he believed to be a perfect stranger, he merely bowed courteously, and begged his guest to be seated.

"Do you not know me, then?" asked Felix Heron, with a smile, as he held out his hand to General Gaston.

"Is it possible?" exclaimed the General, grasping Heron's proffered hand in both of his,— "is it possible that any disguise could hide from my eyes the dear friend to whom I am so much indebted?"

"I am not surprised," laughed Heron. "This same disguise, General, has stood the test of eyes who have known me much more intimately. But how is your fair ward?"

"Well—well—quite well; and, I hope, as happy as myself, Captain Heath; for by that name alone I know you."

"Nay—nay; to you I am no longer Captain Heath; and it was as much for the purpose of telling you who I really am, as to inquire after your ward, that I hastened here to-night."

"That is well," said the General. "I would fain feel that I am accounted by you as worthy of being one of your dearest friends. Nevertheless, had you seen fit to withhold from me your confidence, I should still have been your debtor as long as I live."

"I know—I feel that my confidence will not be misplaced. Have you ever heard of Captain Felix Heron?"

"Often, often; and not unfrequently has his name been mentioned to me with feelings of love and admiration by many a poor creature who has been a receiver of your bounty."

"Then you guess that I am he?" asked Heron.

"Certainly."

"You are right, General. And now I tell you who Captain Felix Heron is."

"How? Have you yet another name?" asked the General, laughing.

"Even so," replied Heron, mournfully. "The proscribed Earl of Whitcombe."

General Gaston fairly staggered back, as he repeated, "The Earl of Whitcombe!"

"Yes, my friend," replied Heron.

"But—but I thought it is believed that the Earl of Whitcombe is no more?"

"I know it. But, General, you will understand my motives for lending myself to such a deception when I tell you that I have a child—a son; and had I not allowed myself to be considered dead to the world, the title and estates would have passed away from that child by an act of attainder."

"Ah! I see—I see," said General Gaston. "But have you no friends at Court, Whitcombe?"

"Yes," replied Heron, "I have a few tried, sincere friends; all of whom, probably, you know. The Earl of Bridgewater——"

"Ah!" interrupted the General; "I know him

well, and esteem him as one of my dearest friends."

"Colonel Trelawney and the young Marquis of Ormond complete the little circle of my friends," added Heron, with a faint smile.

"I know them all, I am rejoiced to say," said General Gaston.

"And may I now add the name of General Gaston to the list?" asked Heron.

"You may, indeed," replied the General, extending his hand to Felix Heron; "and believe me that you will not find me backward in doing all in my power to restore you to your rights."

"I know I may count on your friendship," said Felix Heron. "But now, General, may I not see the fair Ida; or am I to wait until she is the wife of General Gaston?"

"You shall see her at once, my dear friend. Come with me. I left her but now in the drawing-room when Captain Fantome's card was brought to me."

The General led the way up the grand staircase, and opening the door on the landing, a flood of light streamed out, lighting up every object with beauty.

Seated at a table in the centre of the room was the Lady Ida, with her back towards the door, who said, without turning round, "So you have returned at last, truant. I have a great mind——"

"Not to let me introduce to you my dear friend the Earl of Whitcombe, eh?" said the General, playfully, as he led Felix Heron towards the blushing girl.

"Forgive my seeming rudeness," she said, rising and holding out her hand to Felix Heron; for by General Gaston's manner his ward perceived that the gentleman whom her guardian was so anxious to introduce to her was a very old and dear friend.

Felix Heron raised the fair hand of Ida to his lips as he said, "I ought to apologize for intruding at so late an hour; but I was very anxious to hear how you were after the exciting events of last evening, and so ventured to call as early as possible."

Ida looked first at her guardian, and then at Felix Heron, with a puzzled look.

"I will explain," said the General, taking Ida's hand in his. "This gentleman, the Earl of Whitcombe, is none other than the kind friend who so gallantly assisted me in rescuing my Ida from her perilous situation in the tomb of Woodford Church."

With one bound, Ida was by Heron's side, in an instant clasped both his hands in hers, but was too much overpowered by her emotions to articulate a word.

The General, thinking that perhaps this scene might be productive of evil consequences to his fair ward, now said, playfully, "Come, cheer up, my Ida. Let that be all forgotten. We have gained another friend; let us make him welcome, Ida."

Ida raised her beautiful eyes to Heron's, and said, in a sweet voice, as she took General Gaston's hand in hers, "I can never make the Earl of Whitcombe aware of all that he has done for me. May heaven bless him!"

"There is one thing which I may as well make known to you now, Whitcombe, and then let this subject never more be mentioned between us. The woman whom you locked in the apartment below was, as we both supposed, the accomplice of the villain Durban. It was her duty to take my ward a cup of milk every night before retiring to rest. On the night of Ida's supposed death, there is no doubt but that a powerful narcotic was therein administered by this wretched girl, for Ida tells me that no sooner had she drank it, than she felt giddy and fell to the floor in that deathlike swoon, doubtless, from which we recovered her."

"No doubt—no doubt," said Heron. "Now, General, having satisfied myself as to the state of health of your fair ward, I will now take my leave, hoping that I shall soon have the pleasure of introducing you both to the Countess of Whitcombe, who is most impatient to become acquainted with your ward."

When Heron left the mansion of General Gaston, he made the best of his way to Whitcombe House, intending, as soon as he arrived again, to give his permission to Tom Ripon to have a night on the road.

———

CHAPTER CCLXXXV.

TOM RIPON HAS A NARROW ESCAPE, AND SLAYS HIS ANTAGONIST.

TOM RIPON was busily engaged with Daisy, when he was startled by hearing Felix address him.

"Well, Tom," he said, "are you preparing to have a night on the road?"

"Well, Captain, I was in hopes that Daisy would be wanted for that purpose, although I must say I've been a little bit afraid that, so sure as you have made up your mind to have a regular highwayman's night of it, there would be sure to come some horrid adventure or another to put a stop to it."

"You do not mean to say, Tom, that you regret having saved that young girl from the horrible death which awaited her?"

"No, Captain, certainly not: and isn't she a beauty?"

"Who?"

"Why, the young lady that you wouldn't let anybody carry but yourself."

"Ah, Tom," laughed Heron, "I see that you are jealous of my attentions to the young lady."

"Well, Captain, if married men do all the business that might be the means of recommending the single men to the hearts of beautiful, angelic——"

"Stop, stop, Tom! Why, I declare you are getting quite poetical!"

"It's enough to make a man get poetical, Captain, when he finds he hasn't a bit of his heart left in his bosom. I used to think that Martha was a lovely creature, but——"

"Well, Tom," said Heron, good humouredly, "don't think any more about General Gaston's ward, for she is going to be married."

"Going to be married?"

"Yes, Tom. Why not?"

"Oh, nothing, Captain; I ought to have known it, that's all. It's always the way; as sure as

ever I make up my mind to make a young lady an offer, somebody else is sure to step in and cut me out. Who is she going to marry, Captain?"

"General Gaston."

"General Gaston!" exclaimed Tom in a tone of incredulity. "Oh, then I'll go in and try my luck with her. Why just look at me, Captain! Young and not bad-looking—certainly not bad-looking; and then think of that old pump of a General, old enough to be her father, or grandfather I might say! It's perfectly absurd Captain."

"But it's quite true, nevertheless, Tom; so I would advise you to look out for some one who does not happen to be engaged, and then I have no doubt you will succeed in gaining her affections."

Tom shook his head wofully.

"It's no use, Captain. I suspect no one will

No. 92.—EDITH HERON.

care for me half so much as Daisy here does, so I'll have nothing to say to the fickle sex."

"Until the next opportunity, Tom." added Heron. "But now, Tom, if you feel inclined to go on the road to-night by yourself, you can take Daisy with you; only mind you don't get into any mischief."

"All's right, Captain. It's the only consolation after being treated as I have been by Miss Ida."

"Hold, Tom!—no more of this," said Felix Heron. "I must not have the young lady's name mentioned by you any more."

Tom saw that Felix Heron was in earnest, as he quietly busied himself grooming Daisy.

Between nine and ten o'clock, Tom Ripon led Daisy from the stable, and equipped in his costume of a highwayman, mounted and rode away in the direction of Hampstead Heath.

"I'll pay the old heath a visit to-night, as I was disappointed last night, and see if I can have any sport. Ho, Daisy, lass! away!"

Daisy who always seemed to understand what Tom wanted, went off at a brisk trot, and soon houses and trees were left far behind.

Tom now drew rein and listened.

Was he mistaken, or did he hear the crushing of wheels upon the hard roadway?

Nearer and nearer came the sound.

"All right," said Tom; "now for a breeze. I hope I shall be able to fill my pockets."

Tom could see by the light of the carriage lamps, as the vehicle approached, that it was an old-fashioned coach with a hood almost as large as that of a waggon, which was making its way towards him.

The coachman was in a faded livery suit, and the horse came along lazily enough.

With one bound, Tom was by the side of the vehicle, and resting his hand on the door, cried "Halt!" so suddenly, that the drowsy old coachman was so startled, that he pulled in his horse with such force, that for a moment the creature rested on its haunches.

Tom now looked in at the coach window, and was saluted by a series of little screams, which could only come from the lips of very young girls.

"Bother to it," said Tom to himself, "they're only a lot of female kind; there's no credit in robbing them;" and added aloud, "Good evening, ladies!"

"Get along with you, you masculine man," said a female voice from within the vehicle, which certainly did not belong to a very young personage, "Get along with you, or I will call the watch."

Again the young girls screamed, but this time it was in a lower key.

"Don't be alarmed, my dear girls," said Tom, "I'm not going to harm you. Tell me where you are going with this old virago?"

The old woman uttered a scream of rage, and one of the young girls said to Tom, "We are going back to school after the holidays, and this is one——"

"Hold your tongue," interrupted the elderly female. "Miss Clare, you are a bold, forward girl, and as soon as I get home to Lawn House, I——"

"Go on, my dear," said Tom, who at this moment glanced uneasily about him, for clear upon the night air came the unmistakable tramp of horses feet.

A party of horsemen now rapidly approached the carriage.

Tom presented a pistol right in the face of the coachman.

"Mercy, Mr. Highwayman—spare my life, and I'll give you my watch, which goes like St. Paul's, if you'll only spare my life."

"Be silent—utter not a word in reply to any question which may be asked, and you will save your own life."

"All right, sir."

"James! James!" screamed the lady from the coach, "call to those gentlemen I see, and tell them we are being murdered and robbed by a——"

"Oh, no, no, ma'am!" exclaimed the young ladies in chorus, "the gentleman has done no harm to us."

"And he's much handsomer than Adolphus," cried one of the young ladies.

Whatever the elderly lady might have said to this speech was abruptly put a stop to by the foremost of the horsemen riding up to the coach and saying, "Did I not hear some one calling for assistance?"

"You did, sir," replied Tom, who had drawn closely around him a roquelaire cloak, with which he was provided; "and hearing that cry for assistance, I took the liberty of offering my services to these ladies."

"Yes, yes! that's it," shouted all the young ladies.

"He's a——"

"You were somewhat nervous, it would appear," added Tom, "from hearing that a highwayman has just passed on this road."

"A highwayman! Which road did he take?" asked the first speaker.

"Straight up here," said the young lady, who was nearest the door, pointing in the opposite direction to the one they were pursuing.

"Let us away at once," said the one who seemed to take the lead; and Tom Ripon had no difficulty in recognising them as officers of police.

At a smart gallop they urged their horses on, and left Tom alone again with the coach and its occupants.

"Now, madam," said Tom, "you tried to do me a bad turn, so I shall not let you off scot free as I intended; so just hand over to me that gold watch and chain which graces your fair neck, or I may be compelled to help myself to it."

The elderly lady evidently thought that it would be best to accede to the demand, and quickly handed him the watch and chain, saying as she did so, "Take it, you monster, and I hope I shall hear of you being hanged!"

"Thank you for your kind wishes, which, nevertheless, will, I hope, disappoint your expectations. Ladies, I have the honour of bidding you good night!"

As Tom raised his hat he galloped away, leaving the discomforted elderly female in anything but a serene state of mind.

The night had become cloudy, and Tom was wondering what he should do next, when his attention was attracted by the sound of voices speaking in high tones.

"I tell you what it is," said a voice; "I have promised to ride over to the Grange to-morrow with these papers, and deliver them into the hands of Lord Willoughby; and once in possession of them, he will be able to force the Lady Hilda to bestow her hand upon me."

"True, true!" replied another voice; "but is her fortune settled on herself?"

"Yes; but after we are married I shall find means to induce her to make the whole over to me, her lord and master.

"That's it," said Tom to himself; "that's it, is it? I'll try and spoil your sport, my beauties!"

In a moment Tom had divested himself of his roquelaire cloak, and giving the impulse to Daisy, came so suddenly upon the two speakers, that they shrunk back in dismay.

"Stand and deliver!" shouted Tom. "Your money, gentlemen—or your life first, and your money afterwards!"

"A highwayman, by Jove!" said one of the gentlemen. "Here goes!"

As he spoke, he drew a small dress sword, and made a dash at Tom, but missing his foothold, slipped upon the soft turf.

Bang went one of Tom's pistols.

"Take that, coward!" cried Tom; "and now give me your purse!"

The bullet from Tom's pistol had disabled the sword arm of his antagonist, and Tom hoped that he should have but little further trouble.

"Your money!" again shouted Tom; "and be quick, or I will scatter your brains to the four winds of heaven!"

There was a deep groan from the gentleman whose arm was disabled, and he sunk to the ground.

Tom was not sorry to see that he now only had one enemy to contend against.

At this moment Daisy made a plunge, and by that means, in all probability, saved her own life, for the other gentleman made a slash at her with his sword, and had the dastardly action been successful, Felix Heron would have had to mourn the death of his valued and much-loved Daisy.

Tom's young blood was heated by passion. Indignation flashed from his eyes, and seizing the other holster pistol, he fired it at the head of the coward who had assailed the inoffensive animal.

"Take that, villain!" shouted Tom.

There was a yell, half of pain, half of rage, and the cowardly dastard fell lifeless at the feet of Daisy.

"Your blood be upon your own head!" said Tom, as he dismounted, and knelt beside the companion of the dead man.

Tom was not, as we have seen during the progress of this veritable history, devoid of feeling, and he was more shocked than he chose to confess, even to himself, at the result of his night's adventure.

Kneeling down, then, by the side of the wounded man, Tom said, "Are you much hurt, sir? You forced me to do it."

"I know it! I know it! I deserve all I have met with. It might have been worse. Is that wretched man dead?"

"As dead as a door nail!" said Tom, after examining the man whom he had shot. "The bullet must have passed through his head."

"And with such a load of guilt upon his head!" groaned his companion.

Tom began to wish himself well out of the affair, but had some compunctions with regard to leaving the wounded man in his present situation.

"Try to rise, sir," said Tom, "and I will see you to a place of safety."

"No, no! leave me here," replied the wounded man. "I shall do well in a few minutes, but leave me in peace and quietness."

"As you will," replied Tom; and then he added to himself, "I would rather it were you than myself in such company."

Tom gladly mounted Daisy, and taking a hasty leave of his strange companion, he trotted off as fast as he could, taking the direction towards Kensington.

"Well," said Tom, "my night's adventures have not brought me much gain, but there is yet time for some sport—eh, Daisy?"

Tom had gone some distance without taking much heed as to whither Daisy was taking him, and looking up, Tom, to his surprise, found that he was riding just beneath a garden wall, the trees of which were branching out and extending far over the roadway.

Tom reined in Daisy and held his breath, for he heard a sound which made his hair stand on end—a deep, prolonged groan, and then followed a piercing shriek from one of the rooms in the upper portion of the mansion, which he could just see through the trees.

"Goodness gracious!" cried Tom. "What in the name of all that's horrible can that be?"

CHAPTER CCLXXXVI.

TOM MEETS WITH A STRANGE ADVENTURE, AND AN OLD FRIEND.

TOM was debating in his own mind whether to ride on or not, when again the cry came upon his ears.

"What shall I do?" asked Tom of himself. "If the Captain were here, I know he'd go in and see what it was all about: but then, he's not afraid—I mean he doesn't mind ghosts; and perhaps I may find another girl like the General's ward, all laid out ready to be buried, covered with jewels from top to toe. And who knows but that I may yet find a lovely young creature, who will be only too glad to let me carry her back to her father's house, just in the same fashion as the Captain carried Miss Ida?"

Tom seemed to gather courage from this reflection, and he hastily tied Daisy to a lamp-post while he scrambled over the wall just above a door, which he hoped he might be able to open without any difficulty on the inside.

It was fortunate that the little gate was only secured by two heavy bolts on the inside; and, from their rusty condition, it was evident that gate was but little used.

Tom was not many minutes opening this gate, and, darting out into the lane, he led Daisy into the garden, and made her fast to the trunk of an elm tree.

Just as he had completed these arrangements, Tom heard another shriek, and then a voice cried out in piercing accents, "Approach not nearer if you value your life, or you, too, will meet with the same horrible fate as he who now addresses you. Begone—begone, I say!"

Tom stood irresolute for a moment. He then remembered that he had discharged both his pistols in the lane; so grasping one of them nervously, he commenced reloading it.

This done, he performed the same office for the other, and placing them both in his belt, he made his way towards the house whence proceeded the cries, and knocking at a door which presented itself, he called out in an authoritative voice, "Open—open, I say!"

All was still.

"I believe it's only a trick, after all," said Tom. "I don't feel a bit nervous. I shall try to get in at one of the windows."

There was a balcony to the windows on the ground-floor, and Tom had no difficulty in pulling himself up by the iron railings, and finding one of the windows yielded to a touch, Tom was just in the act of jumping into the room, when the voice again addressed him: "Beware! If you approach another step, you are a dead man!"

"Ah!" exclaimed Tom; "Do my ears deceive me? I should know that voice. Speak again, and tell me, whoever you are, if you recognise me?"

There was no reply, but Tom was now fully persuaded in his own mind that the voice which had just addressed him was none other than that of his old companion, Jack Sheppard, but why he should be enacting such a part, and in that house, Tom was at a loss to explain.

As soon, therefore, as he had decided in his own mind that there really was no danger, Tom boldly proceeded in the direction of the sounds he had heard.

A few steps brought him to the door of a room, at which Tom listened intently; and he was rather relieved than otherwise by hearing a low moaning sound proceeding from some one within the chamber.

Tom placed his hand on the handle of the door, and entered instantly.

The room was in profound darkness, but a stream of moonlight fell full upon the figure of a man lying prostrate on the floor of the apartment.

"Speak," said Tom, "whoever you are, and tell me why I find you here at such an hour, and why you give utterance to those unearthly shrieks. Are you ill? Speak to me."

The dark figure raised itself on its elbow, and gazed upon Tom, and in a voice faint and weak, said, "Tell me your name, and let me know if I have at last found one whom I knew in happier times."

"Before I answer your question," said Tom, who was very much interested, "let me ask you another. Is your name Sheppard?"

"Ah! you know me?"

"I should think I do," replied Tom, rushing forward and throwing himself down by the prostrate figure of his friend; "and do you not know me, Tom Ripon?"

Jack Sheppard uttered a cry of joy, and then fell backward in a swoon.

Tom was alarmed. What could it all mean? What was he to do?

"Ah!" he cried—"my bottle. Ogle says it's a bad habit to carry a dram-bottle, but I don't think so. Didn't it save the life of that beautiful —no, not beautiful, because she's going to marry that old fellow, old enough to be her grandfather —but didn't a drop out of my bottle save her life? And now I'll try what effect it will have upon Jack's."

From one of the capacious pockets of his coat, Tom produced the dram-bottle, which had already had such happy results in Ida's case; and gently raising Jack's head, he poured a few drops of the *eau-de vie* into the lips of the insensible Jack.

A few minutes, and Tom had the satisfaction of hearing his friend heave a deep sigh, and then he opened his eyes, and glared about him like one in a dream.

"Where am I?—oh, where am I?"

"All's right!" replied Tom's cheery voice. "All right, old pal! There—there, you look better now! Take another drop, Jack, and tell me why I find you here in such a condition."

Jack Sheppard raised himself, with Tom's assistance, into a sitting posture, but refused to take another drop from the bottle, which Tom was so anxious he should empty, apparently.

"No, no, Tom!" he said. "What I've had has put new life into me; but I am not strong enough to take any more until I have eaten something."

"What!" cried Tom, in amazement,—"what, in the name of all that's stupid! do you stay here for, in such a ghostly-looking place as this, when you might have as much to eat and drink as you like at any of the old inns where you are so well known?"

Jack shook his head as he said, "I forgot, Tom; you do not know I am badly wounded."

"Good gracious!" exclaimed Tom; "I did not think of that. Where are you hurt, old fellow?"

Jack moved aside his vest, and then Tom saw what looked like a very ugly sword-thrust just above the region of Jack's heart.

Tom was not inexperienced, however, in these kind of things, so he spoke cheerfully to Jack, while he busied himself in bathing with water the wound in his friend's side.

"That'll do—gently! There! Soon be all right again! Looks like one of Jonathan Wild's digs. There! Eh—what? Ho, Jack, don't be stupid now—don't go to faint like a girl! Where's my bottle?"

Tom seized his bottle again, and succeeded, with some difficulty, in pouring some of its contents through the clenched teeth of his friend Jack.

Tom had to wait some minutes before the few drops he did succeed in getting into Jack's mouth produced their desired effect. At the end of that time, however, Tom had the unspeakable satisfaction of again seeing his friend open his eyes.

"Come, Jack," said Tom, hardly knowing what to say,—"come, Jack, be a man! You're better now, and when you can sit up, we'll both get upon Daisy's back, and I'll take you to some place of safety, where you will have better nursing than I can give you."

Jack Sheppard made an effort, and succeeded in scrambling to a sitting posture, saying, in a voice more like his natural one than Tom had yet heard him speak in, "I shall soon be all right now, Tom; but how to get away from this place I don't know."

"We'll see about that," replied Tom, overjoyed at seeing his friend look and speak so differently to what he had hitherto done,—"we'll see about, old fellow; but I can't make out why you came to such a dismal-looking place as this. And now I come to think of it, I heard the most horrid, unearthly sounds in the world as I came through the garden, that I wonder at myself for having the courage to enter."

"I made those sounds," said Jack, faintly.

TOM RIPON DISCOVERS HIS OLD FRIEND JACK SHEPPARD IN A STATE
OF GREAT DISTRESS.

Presented Gratis with No. 92, of the New Edition of ED. PERRON, the Sequel to Edith the Captive; or, the Robbers of Epping Forest.

"You, Jack? What on earth for? I thought the place was haunted by ten thousand ghosts."

"Ah!" said Jack, "I'm glad to hear it."

"Glad to hear it? Why, what do you mean?"

"Glad to think I managed so well; for, if I had not managed it so well, I should have been nabbed to a certainty."

"How?"

"Why, Tom, I was caught cracking a crib not far from here, but contrived to make my escape. I gave chase to the officers, and being a practised hand at such things I climbed over the garden wall of this house, which I knew to be empty, and succeeded in eluding pursuit."

"But how did you get that wound?" asked Tom.

"In the scuffle that took place I had the misfortune to lose my foothold, and then one of the nabs thought he'd settle me then and there by giving me a dig in the heart."

"But you got off?" interrupted Tom.

"Yes—yes, I got off; and it was not till I got snug in here that I was aware that blood was pouring from the wound. I just managed to place my handkerchief inside my vest, so as to staunch the blood, I suppose, and then I must have fainted."

"Poor Jack!" said Tom.

"When I came to myself I was conscious of some sort of uproar—it might have been only in imagination, I now think—but when I attempted to rise, my limbs, I found, refused their office."

"What did you do then?" asked Tom.

"Why, I thought I would make those unearthly noises you heard, Tom, in order to scare away any one who might be desirous of paying me a visit."

"Yes," said Tom, "and you almost succeeded in scaring me away, I can tell you. for I never was, and never shall be, partial to ghosts."

Jack laughed, and Tom was glad to perceive that his friend had nearly recovered his wonted spirits.

"Jack!"

"Well, Tom—what now?"

"I should like to explore——"

"Explore? Explore what? What do you mean?"

"Explore this house. Who knows, perhaps, we shall find something worth having—eh, Jack?"

Jack shook his head incredulously.

"I think not," he said. "However, I don't mind trying to accompany you, if you will lend a fellow your arm, Tom."

"Ay, that will I!" said Tom; "and my legs, too, if necessary. Gently, now—here we go!"

Tom led Jack from the apartment in which they were, and proceeded along a wide corridor, which extended the whole of the length of the mansion.

There were doors opening from this corridor both right and left, and the two friends were in doubt as to which door should be first opened.

They tried one—it was fast.

"Ha, ha!" laughed Jack; "I can manage that little business, Tom. I happen to have my pic lock with me. But that reminds me, Tom, I've not told you——"

"Not told me what, Jack?"

"I am going to give up my line of business—it's got to be too hazardous."

"And what do you mean to do, then, Jack?"

"Become a knight of the road, and cry 'Stand and deliver!' like you, Tom."

"Hurrah!" cried Tom, slapping his friend on the back with such goodwill that Jack almost lost his footing.

Tom flung his arms round his friend in a moment, saying as he did so, "What a confounded harum-scarum I am, Jack! I quite forgot, in the delight of the moment, that you were unable to stand such rough treatment just now. Here, take my arm again. All right! I'm as steady as a judge now."

Tom twined his arm within that of Jack Sheppard, and they both proceeded towards the door of the apartment which they had found was locked, and which they had left some paces behind them during their brief conversation regarding Jack Sheppard's contemplated change of life.

Jack applied the picklock, and soon they had the satisfaction of beholding the door turn gently with a creaking sound upon its hinges.

The apartment which met their view was vast in extent, and was still partially furnished.

"Humph!" said Tom, "you've quite comfortable quarters here, Jack. I'd no idea you were in possession of a furnished house."

"Nor I either," replied Jack. "How cold it strikes!"

Tom glanced uneasily about him.

"Come, Jack, suppose we leave it. There is nothing very inviting, that I can see, in all this musty, frowsy-looking furniture. Let us go, Jack."

"Nay! but I thought we were to explore," said Jack, with a smile.

"But I have altered my mind now, Jack," said Tom, "I see—I see there's nothing worth looking at. Let us come away."

"I should just like to see where that door leads to, Tom. Come along."

"What door, Jack?"

"Why, that one at the end of the room. There, don't you see it is not quite closed?"

Tom did look; but as he did so, an unpleasant sensation of fear took possession of him.

"Stuff, Jack! what is it to us where it may lead? Confound it! Only to another room, I've no doubt, in the same state of dilapidation as this. Come along, and let us mount Daisy, and be off."

"I must look into that room, Tom. Wait for me here, if you will," said Jack, disengaging his arm from that of his friend as he spoke.

"Wait here, alone, while you go there to be murdered, perhaps! Not if I know it. If you must go, why, I'll come with you."

Jack and Tom Ripon made their way along the whole length of that apartment, and reached the half-opened door.

Jack pushed it gently, and entering cautiously, closely followed by Tom, they were somewhat surprised to see the remains of a recent repast still upon the table, which occupied the centre of the room.

"Tom," said Jack, turning round, "we must be off, for I suspect we are not the only occupants of this house."

"It looks like it," replied Tom; "but look, Jack! Do you see anything more attractive than the remains of somebody's supper on the table?"

"By Jove, yes! I did not see them at first. I wonder if they are loaded?"

Jack and Tom approached nearer to the table, upon which lay a pair of beautifully mounted pistols.

"Why, Jack, they are the very thing!" exclaimed Tom. "Some good fairy must have placed them there."

"Hem! They don't seem exactly the sort of things to be clasped by fairy fingers," said Jack; "nor do I think a fairy could have loaded them."

"Don't you understand what I mean, Jack?" said Tom, impatiently. "I mean they are the very things for you, as you intend to go into another line of business."

"Ah, I understand! I will accept these pistols as a good omen of my successful career as a knight of the road. Now let us be going, Tom. There does'nt seem to be anything else worth taking, so we'll make the best of our way to the garden, where, I think I remember, you said you secured Daisy."

"All right! Yes, let us be going; there's no telling but that the owner of the pistols may return, and dispute our right to their possession; so the sooner we're off the better."

In less than five minutes, Jack Sheppard, accompanied by Tom Ripon, stood beneath the wall of the garden, close to which Daisy was secured.

Another moment, and they were mounted, and soon left the apparently deserted house far behind them.

CHAPTER CCLXXXVII.

TOM RIPON AND JACK SHEPPARD PAY A VISIT TO MRS. RIPON.

WHEN the two companions found themselves clear of the green lanes, Tom reined in Daisy, and asked the very pertinent question, "What are we going to do, Jack?"

Jack was silent for a few seconds, and then he said, "I wonder, Tom, if your mother has anything in the way of a highwayman's costume that would suit me—eh?"

"Of course she has," replied Tom. "I wonder I never thought of that before. There is a good suit of clothes that once belonged to a captain in the navy, or something of that sort, that would just do, except that they would be a trifle too large in some places, and too small in others."

"Oh! I won't stand out, providing I can get into them. I am able to use my arms and legs. What say, you, Tom, to coming with me at once to Wardour Street; and then, if there's time, we'll go together and seek an adventure?"

"All right, Jack! I'm your man. Let's push on, for the dawn cannot be far off. But what was that? Did you hear nothing?"

"I hear the tramp of a horse's feet, if you mean that, Tom; and here is the rider. Halt!"

As Jack uttered the word "Halt!" Tom reined in Daisy.

"Halt yourself!" growled a voice; and at the same time the horseman made a slash at Daisy with his heavy riding-whip, which so exasperated Tom that he stretched forward his arm, and grasped his antagonist by the throat, giving him at the same time so vigorous a shake that he nearly unhorsed him.

"Don't let us waste valuable time, Tom, upon such a ruffianly coward! I'll give him a bullet first, and rifle his pockets afterwards," said Jack, at the same time producing one of the silver-mounted pistols he had so strangely become possessed of.

The horseman made frantic efforts to free himself from Tom's grasp, but this was a very difficult thing, for his arms had become entangled in the folds of an ample roquelaire cloak he wore, and consequently he was almost helpless.

"Are you going to murder me?" he asked, in tones of terror. "Spare my life, and I will give you all I have about me!"

"I don't know yet," replied Jack, "whether it will be murder or not—that depends upon yourself. Who are you, and where are you going at this time of night?"

"That's my business," sulkily replied the horseman.

"Oh, that's your answer, is it, to a civil question?" said Jack. "I'll find a way to make you speak very differently."

As Jack said this, he touched the cheek of the horseman with the cold muzzle of the pistol.

"Help! Murder!"

"Silence!" shouted Tom. "Deliver to me everything you have about you, without another word; or, as sure as you are alive now, you shall become food for the ravens before another hour passes over your head."

"There's my watch and seals," said the horseman, as he placed them in Tom's hands.

"And that ring—it looks like a diamond."

"Take it; and now let me go!"

"Not yet," said Jack. "I have taken a fancy to that nag of yours. Dismount instantly!"

"Never! This horse cost me a hundred guineas."

"All the better," said Jack; "it had better cost you a hundred guineas than your life, which it assuredly will, if you make much more ado. I'll give you time while I count five. One!"

"Hold!" shouted the horseman. "You know not what you are doing, or who I am!"

"Two!" said Jack.

"I am an officer of His Majesty's——"

"Three!"

The officer still seemed irresolute; but Tom, who had never taken his eyes off him since he had grasped him by the collar, saw by the moonlight that he had managed to get possession of the handle of his sword, which hung by his side.

"Did you think we were as green as all that, now?" said Tom, as he wrenched the sword from its scabbard. "You'd better give in, for we are two to one; and, moreover, we are well armed, while you have nothing to defend yourself with."

"Four!" cried Jack; and again the officer felt the close proximity of the muzzle of the pistol against his face.

With something like a yell of rage, the officer dismounted.

"That is well!" said Jack, who, with Tom's

assistance, made short work of securing their prisoner by tying him to a tree.

"Remain there until we are out of sight, my friend," said Jack; "and the first person who passes, ask him to be kind enough to release you. And now, good-bye!"

Jack was soon mounted on the officer's horse; and Tom was again in Daisy's saddle, and they both trotted off at a brisk pace, nor turned their heads once to look at their victim, who was in anything but a charitable frame of mind, and was kicking and shouting till the whole air seemed filled with his outcries.

"Well, that was a good stroke of business, Jack," said Tom, as soon as they thought it safe to draw rein. "Here you are, with a horse almost equal to Daisy, and a pair of as handsome pistols as you can desire, and all for nothing!"

Jack laughed.

"Shall we make our way to Wardour Street now?"

"No, Tom; I've altered my mind. With my horse and my pistols, I think I may manage to have some sport, even to-night, without troubling myself about my highwayman's dress. What think you, Tom?"

"I should think you might; but I've had enough for one night, so I'll just say good-bye, old fellow, and wish you good luck!"

"Good-bye, Tom! When we meet again, I will tell you what adventures I've had!"

Tom still pursued his way towards town; while Jack Sheppard turned his horse's head again, and seemed as though he intended to retrace his steps.

There was a look of dissatisfaction upon the usually bright face of Tom Ripon when he found himself trotting quietly along the road; and from the few words which he uttered aloud, it will be seen that Tom was disappointed.

"That's what I call selfish! As soon as he gets everything he wants, off he goes, without even thanking me for, perhaps, saving his life! Ah, well! I suppose it's the way of the world!"

Tom still continued his onward course; but he had not proceeded far before a cry of distress fell upon his ear.

"Why, what sort of adventure are we going to have now, Daisy, eh?"

A very few minutes sufficed to bring Tom up to a scene which at once called forth all that was chivalric in Tom's disposition.

A lightly-built chaise, drawn by a fine bay horse, had been overthrown by something in the road, which in the darkness the coachman had not seen, and a young girl was kneeling by the side of an elderly lady, vainly endeavouring, by tears and caresses, to restore her to sensibility.

"Can I be of any assistance, miss?" asked Tom, as he quickly dismounted from Daisy,— "can I be of any assistance?"

"Oh, sir, if you would—if I might beg of you to fetch a surgeon! I fear my dear aunt is killed!"

Tom, at the moment, was at a loss what to do. He was not very anxious to show himself in his costume of a knight of the road; but he could not disregard the accents of entreaty and alarm in which he had been addressed by the young being who still knelt by the insensible form of her aged relative.

"I think, miss," said Tom, "matters are not so bad as you think, perhaps; but it would be some time before I could reach the house of any medical man. Let me try, with your coachman's assistance, to right the chaise, and then he had better drive to the nearest house."

"Oh! aunt, aunt! Look up! Speak to me! Do not leave me yet!"

A bright thought came into Tom's mind.

"My little flask bottle—my little flask bottle!"

The young girl removed her hands from before her eyes.

"What—oh, what did you say?"

"All right! Here you are! Now she will be all herself in a twinkling! Here, ma'am, please to take a pull—I beg your pardon, take some of this, and you'll be yourself again, and no mistake!"

"Oh, what is it?" asked the young girl.

"Brandy, miss—the very best that can be had! Don't be afraid—you are quite welcome to it all! It's not the first time it has saved people's lives!"

"Oh, thanks, thanks!—a thousand thanks!" cried the young girl, as she eagerly seized the bottle, and with great skill dropped a small quantity of the liquor into the mouth of her aunt.

Almost instantaneously the old lady moaned feebly.

"She lives!—she lives yet!" cried the young girl. "Oh, what do I not owe you, sir?"

"Don't mention it, miss!" cried Tom. "You are quite welcome to it all, if you please. Suppose I begin to get the chaise right, and then we'll place the old 'un—I mean, your dear, respectable aunt—carefully inside, and you can order your coachman to drive you slowly into town."

"Do so—do so; and in the meantime, I will give my dear aunt a few drops more of this life-giving liquid."

Tom and the coachman now set to work, and in a few minutes the chaise was righted.

Tom drew near to the young girl, who was still bending anxiously over the elderly lady, who, at the moment Tom approached, had opened her eyes, and was speaking in a low voice.

"My poor darling, I shall leave you alone and friendless! I feel that the hand of death is upon me! Oh, that I could have lived to place you in safety!"

"Oh, say not that you are dying, my dear, my only friend!" sobbed the young girl, in accents that went straight to Tom's heart;—"say not that you are dying, dear aunt! All may yet be well!"

Tom coughed, in order to draw the attention of his strange companions.

The young girl started. Then holding out her hand to Tom, she said, "Dear aunt, be comforted! This gentleman has been the means of restoring you to consciousness; and he has kindly offered to place you in the chaise, with Robert's assistance. You shall then be driven to the nearest house, where, with the assistance of a skilful medical man, and the blessing of providence, you will be able to continue your journey."

The elderly lady shook her head.

"Too late—too late, my darling child! But

let me see this gentleman who has so timely arrived to our assistance; and let me speak to him, and confide you to his honour and protection, should I die before we reach our destination."

"Oh, lor'! oh, lor'!" said Tom to himself; "the old lady is going to bestow the hand of her beautiful niece upon me, without even inquiring what or who I am! I'm glad the Captain isn't here to step in and spoil all!"

The elderly lady raised her head from the bosom of her niece, where it had been resting, and looked at Tom long and steadily.

"Do I see a highwayman?" she asked.

Tom winced a little.

"Confound her!" said Tom, to himself. "What occasion was there for her to say that? She's too knowing by half."

The young girl shrunk closer to her aunt, and looked somewhat alarmed.

"Are you a highwayman, sir?" again asked the elderly lady.

"I am here as a friend, madam," replied Tom, as he raised his hat in imitation of Captain Heron. "I am here as a friend, and await your commands."

The light from the carriage lamps fell full upon the face of Tom.

"It is an honest face, young man, that I look upon, and I would fain believe that the heart does not belie the face. Are you willing to undertake to escort us some few miles further, so that——"

The elderly lady paused, and her head sunk again upon the breast of her niece.

"Have patience, dearest aunt; you will soon be better, and then all will be well."

Tom Ripon was now beginning to get interested, and was by no means willing to forego the task of protecting the fair young being whose aunt seemed to be so prepossessed in his favour.

"You had better let your coachman assist me in placing you within the chaise," he said, addressing the old lady; "and I will then mount the box with him; and I shall be most happy to escort you wherever you may wish to go."

"Thank you! thank you!" sobbed the young girl. "Shall we return to Elm House, dear aunt? Are you not too unwell to continue your intended journey?"

"By no means," faintly replied the elderly lady. "Go on to Lady Travers, in Berkeley Square, by all means, and then I shall die in peace, for you will be in safety, my child."

"Speak not of dying, dearest aunt," said the young girl. Then turning to Tom, she continued, "If you will kindly go with us, sir, we shall feel greatly indebted to you."

"Don't mention it, my dear—at least, I mean, miss. I never was so happy in all my life before."

"Sir!"

"Oh, nothing, miss! I was only saying that we had better be moving, as the old 'un—I mean your dear, respected aunt—might get cold."

"Agnes!" moaned the old lady, as Tom, assisted by the coachman, placed her in the chaise.

"That's it!" said Tom. "I was longing to know what the angel's name was. Agnes—oh, beautiful!"

It did not take long to accomplish the distance to Berkeley Square; but Tom, who had secured Daisy to the back of the chaise before mounting the box, could not be said to pay any attention as to the course taken by the coachman, for he was engaged during the whole of the drive in looking into the chaise at the beautiful girl whom he now verily believed would reign supreme in his too susceptible heart as long as life remained.

At length the chaise stopped before a pretentious-looking mansion; and, after some delay, a sleepy-looking hall-porter opened the door, demanding civilly enough who asked for admission at that late hour.

"Say Lady Clareville," said Agnes to Tom.

"Lady Clareville!" announced Tom sententiously.

"Good gracious! At this late hour!" exclaimed the hall-porter, as he sprung down the steps to assist the visitors to alight.

Tom now assisted the hall-porter in conveying the invalid to a room on the ground-floor, and then he turned to Agnes.

"Anything else, miss, in a small way?"

There was a smile upon the lips of the young girl, who seemed to be somewhat amused by Tom's evident admiration.

"Only my best thanks," she replied, holding out her hand to Tom.

Tom took the proffered hand in his, and looked into the eyes of Agnes as he said, "Good-bye, miss! Shall I see you again?"

"If you wish to do so, certainly. We shall remain here some time, and we shall, of course, be happy to see one who has so materially assisted us this night. Now, good-bye!"

Tom bent down and kissed the hand of the fair girl; and then he said, "I suppose I must be satisfied with that, eh, miss?"

Agnes nodded.

In another moment, Tom was making his way towards Whitcombe House.

CHAPTER CCLXXXVIII.

FELIX HERON AND TOM RIPON TOGETHER SEEK AN ADVENTURE ON THE ROAD.

THE morning after the events detailed in our last chapter, and which had made a rather serious impression upon the somewhat too susceptible heart of Tom Ripon, Felix Heron delighted him—Tom—by the announcement that he should himself require Daisy on an expedition on the road; and that Tom was to have her and his own horse in readiness to accompany him.

"Hurrah!" shouted Tom; "I'm glad you're going, Captain, for it seems as though I should never meet with a right-down good adventure when I am alone."

"Then you are not satisfied with your last night's expedition, Tom?" interrogated Captain Heron.

"Satisfied, Captain? Is it likely that robbing a parcel of women could give satisfaction to any one calling himself a man?"

"Well, Tom," said Felix Heron, "we will see what we can do together."

"What time shall we start, Captain?" asked Tom.

"Ten o'clock, Tom."

"All right, Captain; we will be ready."

The evening set in with a small, steady rain; the clouds were dark and lowering.

At the appointed hour, Heron found Tom at the little gate leading into the narrow street which ran along the back of Whitcombe House.

"Not a very inviting night for a ride," said Heron, as he sprung into Daisy's saddle; "but we will not be disappointed Tom."

"I think, Captain, there looks to be a break in the clouds already, and we shall yet have a fine night."

Felix Heron shook his head incredulously, and gave the rein to Daisy; and, at a sharp trot, took his way towards the Oxford Road.

They had proceeded some distance, when the wind changed, and it was with difficulty that

No. 93.—EDITH HERON.

Felix and Tom could keep folded around them the roquelaire cloaks with which they were provided.

A distant peal of thunder came upon their ears, and already the lightning began to flash from one end of heaven to the other, while the rain now descended in torrents.

"This is pleasant, Tom!" laughed Felix;" I can think of no expedient in our present dilemma than taking refuge in the haunted house, a little to our right."

"Good gracious, Captain!" exclaimed Tom; "for goodness sake don't think of it! The people about here are scared out of their wits by the unearthly sounds that proceed from different parts of that old tumble down place! Come on, Captain; we shall find shelter somewhere, without disturbing all kinds of evil spirits. Come on, Captain—don't go there!"

"I am sorry, Tom, to disoblige you," answered

Heron; "but I have often had a fancy for exploring this very house; and it seems to me that chance has directed me here this evening. Nevertheless, Tom, if you prefer taking shelter under these trees——"

"Oh, as for that, Captain, I'm not afraid. If you have made up your mind to go in, why, of course, I'll go too; but I think it much better to leave such folks to themselves.

"Folks, Tom? Why, it has been uninhabited for years past; you may be quite sure we shall encounter no folks."

"Well, Captain, I mean ghosts; for, of course, only ghosts live in haunted houses."

Felix Heron smiled as he drew up before a little gate, nearly concealed by the thick growth of ivy which had formed an almost impassable barrier to any one who wished to effect an entrance by that same little gate.

Felix Heron soon, however, tore down sufficient of this natural screen to enable both himself and Tom, with their horses, to enter the garden of the deserted mansion.

It was intensely dark, but Felix Heron continued his way, cautiously followed by Tom Ripon, with the horses; and in a few moments he had the satisfaction of knowing, by the gritty tread under his feet, that they were upon a gravel path.

The rain was still coming down, but it was not so heavy as it had been, and by the shifting character of the wind that kept coming in squally puffs, it was pretty clear that a change in the weather was at hand.

Felix Heron went on fearlessly enough through the garden, and he felt quite satisfied that he should come to a house soon. More than once he diverged from the path, and got upon what had once been the turf edging of the flower-beds, but the soft tread always warned him of that, and he, followed always by Tom leading the horses, regained the path again.

Suddenly, upon making an abrupt turn, he saw, standing in bold relief against the night sky, a large and dusky-looking house.

From a window in the upper storey there gleamed a faint ray of light.

Tom darted forward, and touched Felix Heron on the arm.

"Look there, Captain!"

"Where? Can you see any of the ghosts?"

"I think it very likely that that light proceeds from a room in the occupation of one of them."

"Ah!" exclaimed Heron, "I had not observed it, Tom. We will go and see who is keeping watch so late."

"Not for the world, Captain!" cried Tom. "I'll wait here with the horses, and be in readiness, if you should want me."

"As you will," said Felix Heron. "I must find my way into the house somehow. I fancy there must be all sorts of windows and doors to such a house as this, and it will be hard indeed if I don't get in at some of them."

There was a kind of lawn in front of the house, and Felix Heron, in a stooping posture, walked quickly across the lawn, and reached the house.

There was a terrace running along half the front of it, and a range of windows opened upon that terrace. Felix Heron broke one of those windows, and noiselessly entered the house.

"Here I am!" was Felix Heron's first exclamation.

The first thing he did then was to run against a chair in the room, which gave an ominous creak upon the collision.

Not a sound came upon his ears, and the room was so profoundly dark that, as for seeing anything, he might as well have been in a dungeon.

"Ah! What is that?"

Felix Heron knocked his head against something that gave him rather a sharp rap, and then feeling out carefully in front of him, he found that it was a key in the lock of a door.

The fact is, Felix Heron had been so afraid of tumbling over anything, that in his progress through the room he had, as people are apt to do when they are uncertain what obstacles may be in their route, stooped considerably, until his head came on a level with the key. But that little accident did not disconcert him much.

"Where there is a key there is a lock," said Heron; "and it strikes me forcibly that by its size, it is in a door."

Felix Heron was not mistaken, he felt round about where the key projected, and found the handle of a lock. He turned it, and at once opened the door.

A footstep, close at hand, fell upon his ear, and Felix began to ask himself if he had been seen; but, hearing the footsteps taking an opposite direction to the room in which he found himself, he felt somewhat reassured.

Felix Heron, as soon as the footsteps had died away, came cautiously out of the room and looked about him, and seeing a staircase just opposite, he lightly sprang up it, and was soon upon the landing of the upper storey of the mansion.

He then crossed the landing, and entered a room, the door of which was partially open.

The room in which Felix Heron now found himself, was one that was dimly lighted by a lamp hanging from the ceiling immediately over the table, upon which was laid a rich but small repast of cold meats, wines, and pastry.

Felix Heron glanced about him to see if there were any possible means of hiding himself in that apartment, if such a precaution became necessary, for he knew not how soon the personage whose footsteps he had heard on first entering the mansion might think proper to begin his supper, for Felix had no doubt but that that repast was prepared for that individual.

In that apartment there were no means of concealment, but he saw, however, that there was a door in one of its sides, partially open. To make towards that on tip-toe was the work of a moment.

He went into the adjoining room. It was fitted up as a bed-chamber, and upon a table was a small hand-lamp.

A large bed was against one of the walls, the hangings of which were drawn; but, still on tip-toe, Felix Heron advanced towards it, impelled by a curiosity he could not resist.

He gently drew aside the curtains. Upon the bed lay two beautiful girls—children in years, evidently—locked in each other's arms.

"What can be the meaning of this?" said Felix, half aloud. "What can such children as these do in this deserted mansion? I wish they would wake."

At these words, one of the children opened her eyes, and then she looked at Felix Heron, and placed both her hands together in an attitude of prayer. No doubt at the moment catching but an imperfect view of Heron, whose back was towards the lamp, she took him for some other person.

"Oh, have mercy upon us! Take us back to the school, where, at least, we were contented! Oh, spare us—spare us! and heaven will bless you yet, and forgive you the past!"

Felix stepped forward, and clasped both the girls' hands in his, as he said, in his own gentle tones, "They shall kill me before they shall injure either you or your sister, as I presume her to be. Don't be afraid, I will protect you both."

With a faint scream of joy, the child clung to him.

"You are not, then, in my step-father's service. You will befriend us, then?" she asked.

"That will I," answered Felix Heron.

At this moment, the other sister moved uneasily, probably disturbed by the little conversation between Felix Heron and the elder one.

"Wake up—wake up, Amy dear! Here is a friend who will take us back to Ullesthorpe."

Amy sat upright in the bed, and gazed doubtingly upon Felix Heron.

"Will you not make friends with me, little one?" asked Felix. "I am going to see in what way I can serve you both; but in order to do so better, I must know who has placed you here, and for what reason."

"That is soon told, sir," replied the elder of the two children. "Our dear, kind father died about a month ago, leaving the whole of his property to our mother, little imagining that almost as soon as he was dead she would marry Mr. Sharples. As soon as he married our mother, she made over all the property to him, and we could see that we were regarded as standing in his way; so one night, after pretending to be kinder to us than usual, we were brought here under pretence of being taken for a drive; and here he has kept us ever since, only giving us just sufficient food to keep us alive. Oh, how much we——"

"Hush!" said Amy.

"What is it?" asked Felix Heron.

"He comes!" she cried. "Oh, we are all lost!"

"Not yet. Do not say a word; I will get behind this great easy chair."

Felix Heron remained some time in his place of concealment, and then he whispered softly, "Whoever it was, he's gone down stairs again. Can you not manage to dress yourselves, for I have made up my mind to take you both home with me?"

The two children gave a scream of joy.

Felix Heron again retired behind the great easy chair; and he could hear that the toilette of these two innocent beings was satisfactorily progressing.

Perhaps Felix Heron never felt more unalloyed happiness than at the moment when he raised both the orphans in his arms, and commenced the descent of the stairs.

The door of the room, with the windows opening on to the terrace, was only slightly closed: a touch with Heron's foot soon opened it sufficiently for him to pass through with his light burden, and in another moment he took them across its threshold.

They none of them spoke for some few moments; but, having placed the eldest of the two children on the floor, Felix Heron felt with his right hand before him, moving it about, so that they should not—as he had done when he was in that room before—encounter sharply any of the furniture.

He knew that if he made his way right across the floor, he must come to the windows; and he was rather surprised that through them he did not see the night sky.

"Some one must have closed the shutters," he said, in a low voice. "You, Amy, stand down, dear, close to your sister, and I will soon open one of them."

"Yes, yes; I will."

He quitted his hold of the children, and groped his way to one of the windows. It was, as he supposed—the shutters of them had been closed; and it took Heron some few moments to find the fastenings of them in the intense darkness that reigned within the apartment.

He did so at length, however, and with great care removed an iron bar.

The shutters, then, were easily opened, and through the windows he saw the drifting clouds; and amid the moving branches of the trees he could perceive the dim outline of Tom Ripon and the horses.

CHAPTER CCLXXXIX.

FELIX HERON AND TOM RIPON MEET WITH AN ADVENTURE ON THE ROAD.

THE light that now fell faintly into the room showed Felix the two children, looking more like spectres then aught human; but he could not go to them then, as he had the window to open, and that was a delicate and nervous thing to do, as it would make a slight creaking noise, in spite of all his care.

Felix Heron was fearful—not for himself, but for those fair, innocent beings whom he hoped to rescue from the cruelty and tyranny of their cruel step-father—lest that a slight creaking noise should be heard amid the silence of the night by that person to whom the footstep he had heard belonged, and whom he doubted not was the step-father of his two *protegees*

It did not seem, however, as if such were the case, for he got the window open far enough for himself and the children to easily creep out, and no one came.

"Now, my dears—now!" he whispered.

"Yes—oh, yes, dear sir!" exclaimed both the children in a breath.

They tottered to the window, and Felix Heron helped them out on to the terrace.

Amy's dress threw something down that was leaning against one of the trellis-work supports of the canopy over their heads.

Felix stooped to feel what it was, and found

that it was a fowling piece, with two barrels to it. There could be no doubt but that the man who had been prowling about the house had placed it there before entering.

"There's no saying what use this may be to me," thought Heron to himself. "At all events, I will not leave it here to be used by its owner." Then turning to the two children, he asked them if they could walk quietly across the garden to where they could see two horses and a boy.

"Yes—oh, yes! The fresh air is so reviving after being so long confined in that close room," said Florence, the elder of the two.

"Come, then," said Heron, leading the youngest by the hand, while the other held the fowling piece. "Keep close to me, Florence, and you will soon be free and in safety."

The children were, as Florence had said, considerably strengthened and encouraged by finding themselves in the open air, and they now almost ran from that gloomy house, which they believed, and believed truly, was to be their grave as well as their prison.

At the rate they went, the distance between the mansion and the back wall under which Tom Ripon was taking charge of the horses was soon traversed, and they dashed into the flower beds, close to the old ivy that grew right up from that spot in such luxuriance.

"Tom!"

"Captain!"

"Help me to get these little girls mounted as quickly as possible, for we must off and away ere it is too late."

Whatever reply Tom Ripon might have made to this order was lost to Felix Heron, for at that moment a blaze of light came through the trees, and a man with a large stable lantern appeared, rapidly approaching the spot where they stood.

Perhaps they might have succeeded in mounting the horses and distancing their pursuer, if the children had not in their agony of apprehension uttered a scream, that of course immediately attracted the man's attention, and he cried out in a loud, harsh voice, "Ah! just in time! If you, either of you, stir another step, it shall be your last!"

"Tom!" said Felix.

"Yes, Captain?"

"Take charge of these children, while I settle accounts with that villain."

"Oh, he will kill you! He will kill you!" shrieked both the childrn eat once.

Felix Heron did not stop to hear more, but hastily snatching his pistols from the holsters in Daisy's saddle, he walked to meet the man, who was rushing onwards like some wild animal in search of its prey.

The light of the lantern carried by Mr. Sharples, the step-father of the two children, fell full upon the figure of Heron, and displayed at the same time the two barrels of his pistols pointed at his head.

The effect was instantaneous.

The man came to an abrupt standstill.

"Have a care!" shouted Felix Heron. "Both these pistols are loaded, and their contents shall find a place in your brains if you come another step forward!"

"I don't want to come another step forward, but I demand the right of claiming my dear children at your hands, whoever you may be."

"Never more will you have the chance of imprisoning them in yonder deserted house. By a decree of Providence my steps were this night directed hither for the purpose of exposing your villany, and forcing you to make restitution, as far as may be, for the past.

"Never!" roared the man, as he rushed past Heron, and was clasped tightly in the arms of Tom.

"Now, then, old 'un!" said Tom; "you might as well say, another time, when you're coming this way, and I should be prepared."

So unexpected was his capture, that the villain remained perfectly passive in Tom's arms until Felix Heron came up, but seeing that the man was unarmed, he (Felix) placed his pistols in the holsters again, and then came to release Tom.

"Now, sir, are you anxious to try who is the better man of the two, now it has come to a trial of strength?"

The children had lost all thought for themselves now that they saw their brave deliverer closing with their cruel step-father.

"We will return—we will return with you, Mr. Sharples!" shrieked Florence, "if you will not injure that gentleman! Let me go, sir!"

Tom had enough to do to keep his hold upon the generous girl, without hurting her, but Felix Heron's voice re-assured her.

"Do not be afraid, my dear. I cannot come to any harm from such a man as this. Now, sir!"

Mr. Sharples had been gathering strength during the brief conversation between Florence and Felix Heron, and as the latter finished speaking, he twined his bony fingers in Heron's cravat, who, but for his agility, must have fallen a victim to this treacherous attack.

In another moment it was Felix Heron who had his adversary at his mercy, drawing him backwards, intending to fasten him to a staple in the door of an outhouse, which was only a few yards from the spot.

"Hold! stop! mercy! You know not what you do!" shrieked the helpless villain.

Felix Heron was at a loss to conceive what such outcries could mean, for up to this moment the man had shown no want of courage.

Too soon, however, the truth flashed upon him, and he had just time to save himself from a horrible fate.

The cruel step-father had disappeared; and as Felix Heron, with difficulty, disengaged himself from the falling man, he could now understand the meaning of those dreadful shrieks for mercy.

Mr. Sharples was dashed to pieces at the bottom of a stone quarry in his own grounds.

*   *   *   *

"It was no use, Captain," said Tom, when Felix Heron reappeared upon the spot where he had left his young follower in charge of the two little girls,—"it was no use. I could not persuade either of them to mount until they were assured of your safety."

"Have you sent him away, sir? Will he let us go with you?" asked Amy.

"Most assuredly he will never interfere with you again," replied Felix Heron. "But now let us mount instantly, and I will take you to my house, unless you would rather go anywhere else."

"To your house—oh, to your house! We have no friend but you. Our mother no longer loves us, or she would not have allowed that man to treat us in such a manner as he did."

"Be it so, then," said Heron; and taking Amy on the saddle before him, he told Tom to do the same with her sister, who, to judge from the readiness with which Felix Heron's orders were carried out, was not averse to the arrangement.

Proudly and gently the gallant Daisy cantered into the high road that led to London.

Felix Heron drew rein suddenly. "What's that?" he said. "Listen!"

"What is it, Captain?"

"Do you hear nothing?"

"Hush! The sound's approaching!" said Felix.

Felix now backed Daisy close to the hedge on one side of the road, and then he waited, with a pistol in his right hand, for the approach of the carriage, the grating of the wheels of which upon the road came more distinctly to his ears every passing moment.

There was the crack of a postilion's whip —the tramp of horses' feet—and then, at a turn in the road, there came into view a chariot drawn by a pair of handsome grey horses, one of which was ridden by a postilion.

The postilion was a mere youth.

The moment for action had come; and, stooping down, he whispered to Amy, "Fear nothing, my child; no harm shall happen to you!"

"Not with you—not with you!" was the artless reply.

The carriage came on at a rapid rate.

Tom Ripon hid himself completely behind a tree, and was doing his best to reassure Florence.

"Oh, they will kill him—they will kill him!" she almost shrieked.

"Nonsense! It's only some friends of master's coming along in that carriage, and he's going to speak to them."

"Oh!"

Felix gave one touch to the bridle of Daisy, and, with a leap, the creature was in the very middle of the road.

The horses of the carriage were not above thirty paces from that spot.

"Stand!" cried Heron, in a strong, high, clear voice—"Stand!"

The postilion drew the rein of the horse he rode, rather instinctively than from any desire he had to do so, and the carriage swerved, owing to the other horse not obeying with the same quickness the impulse to stop, and was partially swung round towards the hedge.

"Stand!" shouted Heron again. "Another step, and your life is lost!"

"Murder!" cried the postilion, as he saw that Heron levelled a pistol at his head. "Oh, good Mr. Highwayman, don't shoot me! Lor' bless you, I'm only a poor fellow!"

"Still! Keep still! On your life!" added Heron.

Another touch to the rein of Daisy, who was quite at home in what was going on, and under-

stood apparently all about it, brought the beautiful creature to the side of the carriage.

"Your money and valuables, if you please," said Felix.

There were two gentlemen in the carriage, and as Felix uttered these words, he was answered in a voice the tones of which he knew too well.

They were those of his half-brother, Lord Warringdale.

"Take that!"

Bang! went a pistol, as he at once fired it with the full intent of lodging the bullet it had contained in the brain of Heron.

Fortunately, the bullet flew some six inches aside of his face and that of his helpless young charge.

Another moment, and the barrel of Felix Heron's pistol rested on the edge of the coach panel, as he said, "Now, sirs, your lives, as well as all that you have of value about you!"

"No, no! Oh, do not murder us!" shrieked Warringdale.

"Quick, my Lord Warringdale, or it may be a bad night's work for you!"

"Ah, you know me, villain!"

For one moment the recollection of all that he had endured, and was still likely to endure from Lord Warringdale, came over Felix Heron, and a strong desire to avenge himself by taking his life at once came over him, but it was only for a moment.

Even that pause, short as it was, would, to his mind, full of high and noble feelings as it was, have converted the act into murder.

He could not do it.

"Villain," he said, "I know you, and your life is at my mercy! That I do not take it is because I am not, as you are, unscrupulous, murderous, and with the heart of an assassin!"

"Ah!"

"It is contamination to parley with you. Had you the revenues of that earldom you would fain usurp, with you, I would wrest from you every coin. Quick, my lord, quick! I will not brook delay. False brother — false man — ignoble wretch, who, with wickedness beyond all human villany, are not what you seem to be to the world—I demand of you your money, and all that may be money's worth about you!"

Lord Warringdale's eyes flamed with rage; and he turned white and cadaverous-looking with concentrated wrath.

"Oh! give him all!—give him all!"—cried his companion in tones of affright.

"That is wise counsel, John Tarleton: I trust you will follow it yourself, when your turn comes."

There was evident fear about the bad heart of that man of iniquities; and he was, in vain, endeavouring to subdue the shaking of his hands.

"Take what you want, then," he said, "and let me be free of your presence."

He held out a pocket-book, which from its bulky appearance seemed to be well filled.

It was in his right hand that he so held it. And Heron did not see that his left was busy in a pocket of the carriage, where he had another pistol, and which he thought he should be able to use with deadly effect the moment the highwayman, as he thought him, should turn away from the vehicle.

But my Lord Warringdale was foiled in the perpetration of this little piece of treachery.

There was a sudden shadow cast into the coach, and from the other side an arm was projected through the window, and the voice of Tom was heard.

"Oh, dear, no, my lord! that won't do at all."

Tom, with Florence still grasping his horse's mane, had made his way up to that other side of the coach, in order to reassure his trembling companion that Felix Heron was in no danger, and had, therefore, heard and seen all that had passed; and now he pulled Lord Warringdale's hand out of the pocket where the other pistol was; and so suddenly was this done, that he (Warringdale) had no time to let go of the stock of the weapon, and he brought it out of the pocket, but only dexterously to be snatched from his hand by Tom, who, as he got hold of the barrel, dealt Warringdale such a crack with the butt of it, on the top of the head, that he half fell back, confused and stunned by the blow.

"He's a treacherous vagabond, Captain! Take the plunder, and let's away."

Tom dexterously relieved Warringdale of his watch, seals, rings, and then Heron turning to John Tarleton, said, "Now, sir, it is your turn!"

With a pistol, the barrel of which felt cold and deadly against his cheek, there was not much difficulty with the cowardly John Tarleton, from whom Heron took a full purse and a roll of papers.

"Stop! They are useless to any one but the owner. Give me those papers, and take everything else I have."

"I will take these as well as everything else," coolly replied Heron, as he placed the papers in one of the pockets of his coat.

Little did Felix Heron think that those papers so nearly concerned his interest. But we will not anticipate.

"Help!—help!" cried the postboy, at this moment.

He had heard the sound of horses' feet on the road.

Another moment, and Felix Heron and Tom Ripon had both ridden onwards at a smart gallop, and were soon lost to sight in a curve of the road, as it wound down the hill.

In another half-hour, the children, pale and jaded, were seated beside Edith on one of the sofas in the drawing-room of Whitcombe House.

———

CHAPTER CCXC.

TOM RIPON MEETS WITH A SINGULAR ADVENTURE AT THE "WHITE HORSE."

THE night succeeding the events detailed in our last chapter set in wet and dreary, but that did not prevent Tom Ripon availing himself of Captain Heron's permission to make use of Daisy, and seek his fortune on the road.

The wind blew in wild gusts, but still Tom trotted on; but when he found himself in a lonely lane, and a heavy storm evidently at hand, he hailed with delight the sight of a little roadside hostel, hoping there to find shelter until the storm had blown over.

The porch of the old inn was huge and deep; and as Tom Ripon crossed the threshold, a kind of shudder came over him, he knew not why. But he shook it off; for although his vigorous and rather untutored fancy strove hard to make him superstitious, his endeavour to emulate Felix Heron in all things would not allow him to give way to the feeling.

Tom, as we know, was rather inclined to be superstitious, and, for the moment, he called this shudder that came over him at crossing the threshold of the inn, a presentiment of something wrong about the place.

At all events, he did his best to forget the uncomfortable impression that had come over him; and having assured himself of the safety of Daisy by locking her stable door, and placing the key in his own pocket, he felt somewhat reassured—especially when one of the most motherly-looking women in the world came forward, saying, "Are you wet, young gentleman? Pray, sit down by the fire, and make yourself at home."

"The fact is," replied Tom, now perfectly at his ease, "I rather missed my way, owing to its being so dark a night; so, if you will allow me to stay here until the storm has passed away, I shall be greatly obliged to you, and will pay you well for the accommodation."

The landlady of the "White Horse," as the little inn was called, was most profuse in her offers and attentions, and Tom began to feel quite delighted to think he had fallen into such capital hands.

To Tom, one word of kindness was a complete passport to his heart, and he never knew when he had said or done enough in recompense for it.

The landlady now turned, and left the room, after wishing her guest "Good night."

The room in which Tom found himself was the kitchen, or common room of the inn, where the people who kept it sat; but, by some mysterious means, the only person left in the house now appeared to be the landlady herself, and thus Tom was able to account for being quite alone.

The landlady had taken the only candle, but yet the wood fire that burnt upon the hearth shed a sufficient light about it to emit a slight glow over the quiet old room, and every article in it.

Tom felt very tired, and his eyes were half shut as he gazed upon the fire, when suddenly he heard a deep sigh in the room.

The sound was so clear, and so startlingly earnest, that Tom, in a moment, sprang to his feet, saying, "Who's that?"

All was as silent as the very grave; but a strange fear now suddenly crept over him, for in the distance of the apartment, which was but partially lit up by the rays from the wood fire, he saw—or fancied he saw—the dim outline of a figure, and it was actually moving along the wall.

Tom, as we have said before, was naturally superstitious; and such an appearance as this, being, as it was, so very evident to the senses, was enough to appal any one.

He kept his eyes steadily fixed upon it; and, indeed, if he had wished ever so much to do so, he would have found it impossible to withdraw the gaze, which was fastened upon the object by a kind of fascination that overcame every other feeling.

How long a time the figure took to move along the wall Tom had no means of knowing, but when it got to the foot of the stairs, which opened from the room, it paused, and he heard a low, soft voice say, " Beware!—oh, beware! Danger! Death! Death!"

The figure then seemed to ascend the stairs, still keeping the face towards him, and rather to float up than to walk, and, finally, it disappeared, leaving Tom so bewildered and terrified, that he was quite incapable of speaking or moving for some minutes.

The first thing he did, when he recovered himself sufficiently to do so at all, was to rush to the staircase, and cry out aloud, " Hilloa!—hilloa! Help!—help! Who is there?"

A flash of light came upon his face, and he saw the landlady coming slowly down the stairs looking as if nothing were the matter.

" What do you want?" she said. " Did you call?"

" Yes, I—that is, I think I did. It is nothing!"

Tom staggered back to the seat he had been occupying before, and sank down upon it, looking as white as a sheet.

" Good heavens!" cried the landlady,—" what is the matter? What has happened to you? Are you ill?"

" Oh, no, no! I——Nothing!" was all Tom could gasp.

The woman shaded the candle with her hand, and, as she shook in every limb, she said, in a strange whisper, " Did you see anything?"

" Ah, that's it!" said Tom. " You know something of it?"

" Oh, no, no! There is no apparition here!" said the woman, turning as pale as Tom himself.

" But I tell you there is, and you know there is! I saw it! A figure, in a strange, grey looking dress, that went right along the wall yonder," said Tom, " and then mounted those very stairs you just descended! You must have met it! Is your house haunted?"

The woman shook so much, that she was compelled to place the candle upon the table, or it would have fallen from her hand, and then she tottered to a seat, and stared at Tom for some few minutes in silence, as if he, too, had been something not of this world.

" What's the meaning of it all?" said Tom, excitedly. " Are you out of your mind, woman, or am I mad? How is it that your house, of all others, has got a ghost in it, and that it takes the first opportunity of appearing to your guests, to terrify them out into the night air at once, as many people would go?"

" I know nothing," was the reply.

" But you have seen it, woman?" said Tom.

She shuddered from head to foot, as she said, " Once—once only! I think if I were to see it again it would be the death of me!"

She covered her face with her hands, rocking herself backwards and forwards for a few moments; and then, before she took them away, the door of the room was opened, and a head was thrust in, while a rough voice said, in suppressed tones, " Is it all right?"

" Oh, fool, fool!" cried the landlady.

" Confusion!" said the voice; and then the rough-looking head was as suddenly withdrawn again.

" Upon my word," said Tom, his courage rising with the emergency, " this is a very nice sort of house! I wish you would explain to me what is the meaning of it all?"

" Oh, dear! oh, dear!" groaned the woman.

" Yes, it's all very well to cry, ' Oh, dear!' said Tom; but I want to know what is the meaning of it all?"

" I will tell you," replied the woman, making an effort,—" I will tell you, sir! The fact is, sir, my son is a little wild, and it's only when he thinks there is nobody here that he comes to get a trifle from me to keep him, for he has been poaching in the neighbourhood, and he is afraid to show himself in the daytime, the dear fellow."

" Oh, indeed!" said Tom.

" Yes, poor fellow! That's the real truth."

" Then, that was the poor fellow with the great head of hair, and who didn't seem to have taken the trouble to shave himself for the last six weeks, who just now popped his head into the room?"

" Yes. Alas, yes!" moaned the woman.

" Well, I wish you joy of him!" said Tom. " I suppose the poor fellow is his mamma's darling?"

" One can't help loving one's own flesh and blood, you know, and he is as like his poor dead father, sir—who is now a saint in heaven—as one parched pea is like unto another."

" Then his father must have been a remarkably handsome man, ma'am, I should think," said Tom. " But what explanation have you got to give about the ghost—that is what I want to know?"

" That I know nothing about, indeed, sir," replied the woman; " except that it once appeared to me when I was darning the stockings of that poor fellow, sir, you saw just now, and whom you were good enough to call handsome."

" And pray what did you say to the ghost when it paid you a visit?" asked Tom.

" Of course, sir, I screamed and fainted dead away, and since that time I know nothing of it whatever."

" Well, it's an odd thing," said Tom; " but of course you cannot be answerable for a ghost taking it into its head to come to your place."

" Did it—did it say anything to you, sir?" faltered out the landlady.

Tom thought it best not to tell the woman the words that had come to his ears from the lips of the supposed apparition; and as the strange being had certainly said more than one word, Tom excused himself very well for the little deception he intended to practise upon the landlady.

" Not one word," he said, in reply to her question.

The woman seemed greatly relieved at the news that it had not spoken to him, and evidently got much more composed in consequence.

" I hope, sir," she said, " you will not let anything that has happened here to-night disturb you. You will soon go to sleep and forget all about the ghost; and I feel quite sure there will be no complaints from you in the morning."

Tom thought the last words of the landlady had a very strange significance in them, and accordingly he began to get anything but easy.

"Very good," he said, assuming what he was very far from feeling, a careless air; "very good. Where is my room?"

"Up-stairs, if you please, sir; and if you are so inclined, I will show it you at once."

The landlady rose with such alacrity, that it seemed as though she were delighted at the thought of getting rid of Tom for the night; but he pretended not to take any notice of the fact, and he rose too, and followed her to the staircase, up which she rather hastily ascended.

"You will be as comfortable as possible, sir; and I am quite sure will have never slept so soundly as you will here."

"That's quite a comfort," said Tom, "for I am dreadfully tired, and I dare say I shall sleep like a top."

"This way, sir—this way, if you please," said the woman, still hurrying on.

They had by this time reached the landing of the stairs, and a long, gloomy-looking passage that seemed to run along the whole length of the house.

It was to the right of this passage that the landlady conducted Tom, who stopping suddenly, said, "Where does that passage lead to?" indicating the one to the left.

"Oh, sir, only to a few rooms which are seldom used, unless, sir, the town is very full."

"Well, I think I should prefer sleeping there," replied Tom, "because it must overlook the stables."

"Oh, certainly, sir," she replied, "if you prefer it; but you will not be near so quiet there as you would be here."

"Never mind," said Tom; "I have a fancy for them; so show me the way."

She opened a door that led into an old-fashioned, gloomy-looking room; but there was no vestige of a bed to be seen.

The landlady drowned Tom's thoughts, for she said, instantly, "The bed is in the inner room, sir, if you please."

"Oh, this'll do," said Tom. "I see that there is an old sofa in this apartment, and upon that I will lie down and take what rest I require, without undressing, as I want to be off by daybreak."

"What! upon the sofa, sir?"

"Certainly, ma'am. I have slept many a time upon a sofa, and I don't see anything extraordinary in it at all."

"Oh, but, sir, for the honour of my house I cannot allow a gentleman to pass the night on a sofa. You must, indeed, sir, conform to the rules of the house, which is a most respectable one, and go to bed in a Christian-like manner!"

"Oh, indeed!" said Tom. "Then I tell you that here I shall remain, whether it be against your rules and regulations or not. But as you are so particular, who is to know that I pass the night here instead of going to bed, unless you inform them? I will have a light, too, if you please, ma'am; so no more nonsense."

The landlady seemed upon the point of saying something very angry; but, as if some new thought had entered her mind to change the current of her ideas, she said, suddenly, "Oh, very well! Of course, sir, it is just as you please, sir. I will leave you this light. Good night, sir!"

CHAPTER CCXCI.

MORE MYSTERY.—A STRANGE VISITOR.—THE PISTOL-SHOT.

WITH these words the landlady immediately turned and left the room, and Tom Ripon was left alone to his reflections, which, it must be admitted, were none of the most cheerful description.

"Well," he said, when he could no longer hear the footsteps of the landlady,—"well, this is about the most mysterious inn I ever stopped at in all my life. I wonder, now, if that was a ghost or not that I saw in the room below, gliding along so very mysteriously. The worst of it is, ghosts are never clear and explicit about what they come to tell you; but they rely so much upon your powers of guessing, which, in nine cases out of ten, is decidedly wrong. Ah! what's that?"

Tom flew towards the door, and was about to open it and look out to satisfy himself that all was right, when he made the rather disagreeable discovery that he was a prisoner, the door being locked on the outer side.

At the moment that, without a doubt, this conviction came over him, Tom felt a pang of dread upon Daisy's account, but certainly none for himself; and he mechanically put his hand to his pockets to feel for his pistols.

It was a consolation to find that they were safe; for while he was well armed, he, at all events, held the lives of some of his enemies in his power.

After thus finding that the door was really locked on the outside, Tom made a vigorous effort to open it, and effectually convinced himself, at length, that there was no chance of breaking it open, as it was most frightfully strong.

"Very good," he said to himself; "I will do the best I can, if I can't do just what I would."

Tom thought it best to await the course of events, and not give any indication that he was aware of the fact that he was a prisoner, so he retired from the door, and began to consider what he had better do next.

He was anxious now to discover if there were any other mode of leaving the room, except by the door by which he had entered; but, although he glanced carefully round the apartment, he felt confident that there were no means of egress.

The fireplace was enclosed by a chimney-board, but Tom did not disturb it, as it would have required much more urgent circumstances than those in which he now found himself, to think of getting up the chimney.

Tom had just finished this investigation, when he heard a singular tapping sound in the inner room, and snatching up the light, he rushed into the bed-room.

The rapping sound continued, as Tom made his way into the inner-room; and, holding

the candle high above his head, in his left hand, he grasped one of his pistols with his right, as he said, "What is it? Who is there?"

All was still in the apartment, and he could see no one—athough he strained his gaze into every corner of the place. Tom began to fancy that he should see the ghost again, perhaps; and that this was the mode by which it was pleased to make it presence known.

This thought, it must be confessed, produced a kind of terror as he looked about him; for what human breast can preserve its usual calmness when it believes itself to be in the presence of some being of another world, the capabilities and powers of which are all unknown.

It was a relief to Tom to see nothing.

"That knocking must have been a matter of imagination," said Tom; "it can't be real, or I should —— Ah!"

Tap! tap! tap! came the sound again, and

No. 94.—EDITH HERON.

Tom had no difficulty whatever in tracing it to some window in the room.

Settting down the light upon the table, he went at once to the window, and shading his eyes with his hand, he at once saw something like a human face behind one of the panes of glass.

This was rather a startling fact, for, after all, Tom thought it might be some sepulchral-looking being he had seen in the apartment below, but he was rather desperate this time.

The fact of the locking of the door of the apartment upon him by the landlady had too much impressed Tom with the idea that there was more of human than supernatural agency at work in the matter, to permit superstitious fear entirely to get the better of him, and he at once made an effort to open the window.

It did not require a second to let him see, and feel, both, that whoever was outside was holding the window down against his efforts to open it, and then a voice from without said, "Gently—gently!"

Tom nodded, although, probably, his visitor from the outside could not see the action very well, and then, with great care, so as not to make any noise, he opened the window, and the person who was outside made no sort of opposition to his doing so, which proved to Tom that he was right in the translation he had put upon the word "Gently!" and that it did indeed apply to the opening of the window with as little noise as possible.

If Tom Ripon had paused, only for a moment, to think about the matter, the whole affair would have seemed so very mysterious to him that, probably, he would have hesitated very much before he went so far as to open the window, but the rapidity with which he acted prevented him from having any fear.

Intense interest and curiosity in what was going on was the only dominant feeling in his mind on the occasion.

The moment he succeeded in opening the window, Tom found that the person outside it was a female.

"Good gracious!" exclaimed Tom; "who are you?—and what do you want here?"

"Hush! Oh, do not speak above your breath, for the love of heaven!" said the female; and, by the voice, Tom felt quite convinced it was a young girl who addressed him. "Help me into the room at once. I am standing upon a ladder, and am afraid of falling off!"

"Oh, to be sure—certainly!" said Tom. "I have not the slightest objection!"

And he at once assisted the girl into the apartment, and then she hastily closed the window and sank into a chair, and began to sob as if her heart would break.

While she was thus singularly conducting herself, Tom was able to take a good look at her, and see what she was as regarded appearance, and he came to the conclusion that her age did not exceed fifteen—possibly she was younger, but she was very pale, and appeared to be in a great state of excitement, and dread of something or somebody.

"For goodness sake," said Tom, "what is the matter?—and tell me if you are the ghost?"

"Oh, do not ask me!" she sobbed; "I only hope he will be here soon;" disregarding altogether Tom's last question.

"Who?"

"Jonathan Wild."

"The deuce!"

"Oh, no! I mean Mr. Wild, who they say catches all the thieves, and is so very active. I read about him in a newspaper, so I thought that the best thing I could do was to send for him, and I wrote the letter early to-day, so he will be sure to be here soon."

"Well," said Tom, "if he only comes while I am here, I shall hardly be able to express my obligations to you. He is, of all others, the most delightful gentleman to meet that I know! But tell me, did you climb up a ladder and get in at this window on purpose to tell me that?"

"Oh, no, no!"

"Well, that is some consolation," said Tom, half-amused, and greatly perplexed as to how all this would finish. "And now, perhaps, miss, you will have no objection to say who and what you are, and what you want?"

"I am the orphan niece of the landlady of this house, and I want to save your life. That is my errand now."

"Save—my—life?" asked Tom.

"Yes—you are in a house where you will be murdered if you are not put on your guard. There has been one murder here already since I have been in this place, and I was so terrified and shocked at it that they shut me up, and have made me a prisoner ever since; but I was determined to see you if I could, so I watched my opportunity, and have escaped to come to you. But Jonathan Wild—that good Jonathan Wild will be here soon, and then all will be well."

"Humph!" said Tom. "There may be two opinions about his goodness. But tell me more. I can scarcely understand why they wish to murder me."

"I fear I am confused," replied the girl, "but I cannot tell you any better than I have done. I was brought here to assist my aunt and her son, and they thought I could be frightened into holding my tongue with regard to their villanous proceedings. But I will tell the truth. They murder every one who stops here."

"Murder them?"

"Yes, they do indeed, but it drives me nearly mad to think of it. They shut me up in one of the old rooms, and only give me enough to eat just to keep me alive—and that little is of the very coarsest and worst description of food—because they began to fear that in my horror I should tell of their proceedings."

"But how came you to be able to convey a letter to Jonathan Wild, if you were locked up?" asked Tom.

"I succeeded in flinging a letter addressed to him into the road, from the window of the room in which I was confined, when some one was passing, and in addition to his name on the letter I wrote these words:—'Please to post this.' And by the person who picked it up nodding his hand I knew that it would be done, and then I felt some degree of satisfaction."

"Hem!" was all that Tom could reply to this very unsatisfactory communication.

"I am sure he will attend to it," added the girl, "for I have read in the newspapers what a wonderful man Jonathan Wild is."

"Well," said Tom, "it may be very consoling to you to have written to Jonathan Wild; but it is not so to me, for I happen to know him, and when we meet we never agree."

"Oh, how sorry I am for that!" said the girl; "for I am sure he must be a very nice person. He is always hanging highwaymen, and such bad people."

"Goodness gracious me!" said Tom. "I always expected to hear a great many funny things as I got on in life, but among them I never expected to hear any one say that Jonathan Wild was a very nice person."

"Is he not so, then?"

"Rather the reverse," said Tom; "but this is not the time to settle the character of Jonathan Wild. Let us leave this house at once, which which you tell me is such a bad one. But can you give me any proof that I may trust you?"

"Alas, yes!"

"Why do you say 'Alas, yes!'" asked Tom.

"Because the proof that I can give you of the truth of what I have told you is such a horrible one that I dread to show it to you."

"What is it? Tell me at once—be quick!"

"Oh, yes, sir, I will tell you! There is a large cupboard in the other room, and if you open the door you will see a sack, and in it a dead body!"

"A dead body!" gasped Tom.

"Yes, it is a frightful and a melancholy truth. You have only to look to convince yourself in a moment."

"Just wait here for me," said Tom, "while I take a peep. I won't keep you long."

Tom snatched up the light and hurried into the next room.

Tom gently opened the door of the cupboard, and at the moment a huge sack fell into the room, and bursting open, disclosed to his horrified gaze, the head and hands of a dead body.

Tom now made his way back to the room where he had left the girl, who was still weeping and wringing her hands; for as yet she had great fears that both Tom and herself would be murdered in that house.

At the sight of Tom she appeared to gain a little more courage. She said, "Oh, sir, it is you who must save me now! I have no hope but in you!"

"Don't say another word," said Tom. "It is you who have saved me, brave, courageous girl. If you could manage to get up to this window by the aid of a ladder, as you did a little while ago; the ladder is still there, and we can surely descend by it; so let us come away at once, for this is anything in the world but a desirable place for us to remain in."

With a faint scream of joy, the young girl clung to Tom.

"You will befriend me, then?" she asked.

"To be sure I will!" said Tom. "Didn't you risk everything to save my life, and do you think I will be less generous? It will be a joy, indeed, to think that I have saved you from these dreadful people; for, do you know, I love you dearly already. What is your name, dear?"

The young girl blushed as she spoke, and said her name was Ellen; but Tom placed his arm round her waist, and drawing her close to him, kissed her, saying as he did so, "Perhaps this is the last kiss, after all, that I may be able to give you, Ellen. Bless you, dear! I shall always love you! You must call me Tom!"

"Oh, do not fancy, Tom, that I am ungrateful!"

Her lips just touched his cheek, and moved slightly. It was like the flutter of a little bird upon his face.

"Ah, Ellen!" said Tom: "if I were to live for a thousand years I should never love any one but you. It was my fate to meet with you, and to think there is no one in all the world like you. I am quite sure there is not, either, you beautiful, dear Ellen."

"Hush! oh, hush! they may hear us!"

"Ah! I had forgotten, dearest; we must be quick, for Jonathan Wild may be here, and then I should be lost."

They now approached the window; but, just as Tom had opened it again, they distinctly heard footsteps in the passage outside the door, and the rattle of the key in the lock.

"Lost! lost!" said the young girl.

"Not quite," replied Tom, as he stood calmly facing the door with a loaded pistol in his right hand.

In another moment there came a flash of light from the corridor, and the door was opened.

CHAPTER CCXCII.

TOM RIPON AND ELLEN ARE PURSUED BY JONATHAN WILD.

A ROUGH-LOOKING head was projected into the apartment.

Bang! went Tom's pistol, and the head was immediately withdrawn again, and the light that had flashed into the room disappeared.

A lumbering noise down the stairs proclaimed that the head, and the body that belonged to it, was descending those stairs with much greater expedition than they came up.

"Now for it, dear one!" said Tom. "Open the window as wide as you can, and let us be off, for we don't know how many there may be in readiness to come to this fellow's assistance."

Ellen was deathly pale, and she stood by the window trembling so much that it was quite clear she would not be able to descend the ladder without the greatest assistance.

Tom, however, preserved the most perfect self-possession that it was possible to assume, and approaching the window, he said to the young girl, "Come, dear, pluck up courage, and descend from the window. It is but a few steps, and then we are safe."

"I will try, Tom; but you will come at once?"

"Assuredly I will."

Ellen began the descent of the ladder, while Tom followed so closely that she did not let go her grasp of his hand during the whole descent, and, in a minute or two, they were on the ground in safety.

"Come! come!" said the young girl. "This way—this way!"

"Stop a bit," said Tom. "Where's the stables?"

"Oh, never mind the stables!"

"But I do, though," said Tom. "I am not going to leave Daisy here. She goes with us, or I do not go at all. Don't you fancy there is any great risk in that determination. Only show me the way, for I don't know it in the dark. For the love of heaven, be quick!"

"Come, then, if you must."

The young girl laid hold of Tom by the arm, and led him hastily across a portion of the garden in which they were now, and in a minute or two, by turning an angle of the house, they came upon the stables, and Tom then knew exactly where he was.

The fact was, the window from which they had escaped had opened upon a part of the little kitchen-garden, and he had not before been to that side of the house at all.

"Wait for me half a minute," said Tom. "I did not unsaddle the horse, so I shall be with you again directly. Don't stir."

"Oh, Tom, I hear footsteps! They are coming!" said Ellen. "Let us both hide in the stable!"

As she spoke, she ran into the stable, whither Tom had just gone, and it was not a minute too soon that she did so, for the landlady came along the garden like a madwoman, crying out, "Where are you, boys?—where are you? Oh, my poor son is murdered! He has killed him—that he has! Come and finish the job, or he may get away, and then it is all up with us! They have killed my dear son!"

There was a rushing sound, as of people breaking through the hedge, and then a voice said, "What! has he got his deserts at last? I thought he would some day. He was always so mighty fond of cutting a throat by himself, and it was only to get more of the share of the plunder, nothing else, for he always pocketed something before we came in for any of the affair."

"Come, come!" again screamed the woman. "He is a young body, and we can sell it well. The doctors will give a good price for him. Come and finish the job, lads, for my poor son is breathing his last in the kitchen."

The men who were called lads by the landlady went hurriedly past the stable door after her, thus narrowly escaping Tom and his helpless and terrified partner in the adventure.

But even while the great danger was apparent, Tom had not lost a moment in feeling that Daisy's harness was all right; and as soon as the voices had died away in the distance, he led Daisy into the garden.

"Oh, let us go—let us go!" said the young girl. "The very air of this place seems as though it would kill me. Let us go at once, Tom."

"Yes, dear. Can you ride on horseback?"

"Alas, no! But I will try. I will do anything in the world to escape from this place."

Tom mounted, and then assisted Ellen to do so, and then off they went out of the garden into the high road.

The clatter of the horse's feet was evidently the first intimation that those who were in the inn had of the escape of the fugitives, and then one of the "lads" ran to the door and called out, "The gun, Ned! The gun! Bring me the gun! There they are, and they will be off if you don't be quick!"

"They?" screamed the woman. "Who do you mean by they?"

"Why the young chap and our Ellen."

The landlady threw up her arms, and with one shriek fell senseless to the floor.

"The gun!" again shouted the man, who had seen the fugitives.

"Perhaps the pistol will do as well," cried Tom, as he fired at the man, who he saw clearly and distinctly in the doorway of the inn, and then, without waiting to see if he had hit him or not, on he went, keeping a hold of the bridle of Daisy with one hand, while with the other he pressed that of Ellen.

At this moment it was that the clatter of horses' feet coming at a brisk pace along the road fell upon the ears of Tom and Ellen, and Tom drew aside to let the party of horsemen go by them quietly, for he did not wish to come into collision with friend or foe just then.

"Halt!" cried a voice, and they all stopped, in a straggling kind of mob, for there was about a dozen of them.

"Who are you?" added the voice.

"Travellers on the road," said Tom. "I hope you are honest people."

"We are the police, and we want to know whereabouts the 'White Horse Inn' is upon this road. Perhaps, young sir, you can inform us?"

"You will see it a few paces down the first turning you come to on your right," said Tom.

"A lantern here!" growled a fierce voice. "I must see who these good folks are, before I let them go by me so easy. A lantern here, quick!"

It was Jonathan Wild who uttered these words.

"Oh, we won't trouble you about the lantern," said Tom. "Our names are Smith, and we belong to the great family of the Smiths, of Smith Hall.

Tom now gave the rein to Daisy, and away they went at such a gallop that Wild was thunderstruck at the moment, and let them get considerably ahead before he could recover from his surprise.

"After them!" he shouted, in a voice hoarse with rage. "After them! Shoot them!—shoot them! Anything but let them go; for I do believe it is that young villain, Tom Ripon. I'm sure that's Daisy."

The pursuit now began in right earnest, and Tom and Ellen soon heard the clatter of the armed men coming after them

Jonathan Wild and his company had gained considerably upon Tom in that short space of time. Still Tom had confidence in Daisy, and he had confidence too in his pistols, which he had found means to load again, so that he by no means despaired of the result of the affair.

"Come, Johnny," said Tom, "since you seem bent upon it, we will have a race. I don't pretend to have any clue as to where this road leads to, but at all events it is a good one, and there don't seem to be any obstruction in the way, so now for it."

With these words, Tom put Daisy very nearly to her utmost speed, and off he went.

Nothing could be more self-evident now to Tom than the fact that he was distancing Jonathan Wild, and he felt quite elated at the idea that in a very few moments he should be able to tell himself that he had escaped.

But, alas for Tom! for some reason or another Daisy came to an abrupt standstill, and refused to go a step forward.

Spur and bit were of no avail, and in another moment poor Tom found himself surrounded by Jonathan Wild's men.

"Seize him!" roared Wild.

A couple of the officers laid violent hands upon Tom, for they saw that he was feeling most probably for his pistols.

With their practical skill in such matters, they speedily enough disarmed him, and bound his arms behind him with a cord. It was quite useless to struggle against these proceedings. Twelve men were something more than a match for Tom Ripon.

"Now," said Jonathan Wild, who stood by, with his hand on Daisy's bridle—" now, my dear fellow, how do you feel?"

"I feel rather better than you did, Johnny, when the ghost of Captain Heron took me out of the death-cart on Holborn-Hill."

It would be quite impossible to describe the change that came over the countenance of Jonathan Wild as Tom uttered these words.

Rage and terror appeared to be struggling for mastery in his mind, and both these expressions found a place in his hideous physiognomy.

"Wretch!" he cried; "is it from you that I am to put up with such taunts?"

"Yes, to be sure, Johnny," said Tom.

"Then die the death you have provoked!"

With these words, Wild drew a pistol from his pocket, and fired it, as he thought, full in Tom's face; but he, Tom, instantly stooped so low, that the couple of bullets with which the pistol was loaded flew over it.

"Don't do that again," said Tom; "it's dangerous."

"What!" roared Jonathan Wild, "has he a charmed life? Will nothing kill him?"

One of Jonathan Wild's men now stepped forward. Probably this man's heart was not quite dead to every kindly feeling; and Tom's youth and courage, too, might have inspired him with something like compassion.

"No, no! don't kill him, Mr. Wild—don't you take his life. The law will do that soon enough. It will not sound well to say that twelve of us, with yourself at our head, could not take this mere lad without first shooting him."

"Ah! well, be it so. Hanging is worse than shooting. Bring him along!" shouted Wild. "Mount him on one of the horses, and bring him along at once! And mind you look to him!"

"Shall I strap him behind me, Mr. Wild?" asked the man who had interceded for Tom's life.

"Yes; that will do, Jenkins. You will then know that he is quite safe. That is the best way you can get on with him."

"How kind you all are!" said Tom, assuming a cheerfulness he was far from feeling in reality, for he was in alarm for the fate of Ellen and Daisy, for he knew not what had become of them during the first part of the fray.

"Now, young fellow," said Jenkins, "mount, if you please."

"Dear Jenkins," said Tom, "are you afraid I shall fall off if I am left by myself?"

"Rather!" said Jenkins, sulkily.

The night continued to be intensely dark—so much so, that Tom could scarcely see the dusky forms of Jonathan Wild and a couple of the officers, who rode on in advance of those who might be said to form his special escort.

The party, with their prisoner, now proceeded in silence, and the darkness seemed rather to increase each moment than to diminish.

"Well," said Tom to himself, "I can't say, for certain, where we are; however, we are in a lane, or by-road, now, that's quite clear from the size of it; and when we get a little further, I may see some familiar object, for all I know to the contrary, that may tell me whereabouts we are. In the meantime, I have work before me."

The work that Tom alluded to was to get his hands out of the piece of cord that tied them together behind his back.

It was no easy matter for him to squeeze one of his hands out of the bondage in which they were both held.

The skin was much torn by the rough state of the cord, and Tom felt his hand was dripping with blood before he got it free; but extricate it he did, and he kept his teeth so firmly shut, that not the least sigh or sound of pain escaped him in the process.

What a relief it was to him, though, when he did, at last, get his hands fairly free!

Of course Tom took care that no notice should be taken of his partial state of freedom by any exhibition of his arms or hands, which, even in the intense darkness, might possibly have been seen by the officers who were following him, but the next thing he wanted to do was to release himself from the belt that was round him, and which bound him to the man Jenkins, who rode upon the same horse.

Tom had a knife in a narrow pocket, made by himself to hold it, in the lappel of his coat.

"Now," thought Tom, "if I can manage to get hold of my knife, I can, at any moment, cut the belt, and give Mr. Jenkins a little dig with the point of it at the same time, and then I can slip off the horse, and as there is a capital state of darkness in the road, I shall have a pretty fine chance of life and liberty, and of regaining Daisy and Ellen."

Such was the calculation upon which Tom went; and now, with the knife in his hand—for he managed to get hold of it, as the trotting of the horse effectually prevented Jenkins from noticing any little movement—he waited for a good opportunity of putting his daring project into execution.

"Halt!" said Wild.

The officers stopped their horses.

"Is the prisoner all right?" he asked.

"Quite right, Mr. Wild! He is fastened to me, you know, sir, by the belt, and he can't get away."

"He seems pretty quiet now," said Wild.

"Yes, Jonathan Wild," said Tom, in a dejected tone; "it's a dead beat this time. Jenkins," said Tom, in a whisper.

"Well, what is it?"

"Do you pity me?"

Jenkins was silent for a minute or two, and then he said, "Well, Tom, upon my word, I do; for you are as good-looking and likely a young lad as I ever saw; but, for my sake, don't speak to me, as you know what Wild is when he is thoroughly enraged."

"That will do!" said Tom.

Now Tom had fully intended to have accommodated Mr. Jenkins with about three or four inches of the knife in the small of the back, but when the man said that he pitied him, Tom could not find it in his heart to do any such thing; but if he had had a rough and brutal answer from Jenkins, why, he certainly would, with some degree of satisfaction, have perpetrated the act he had contemplated.

"No," thought Tom, "I must try my luck without that! I can't hurt him Bother fellow! why didn't he answer me like a b

Jonathan Wild now turned and spoke to his men.

"Be careful, now, and look to your prisoner. You had better come singly, for this infernal old bridge even shakes under me and my horse as I go over it."

"All's right, sir!" replied Jenkins.

"Come on, then, and follow me!"

"Now or never!" said Tom to himself. "If I can do any good, it will be on this same shaky little bridge."

No one could be more fully alive to all the hazards of what he was about to undertake than Tom himself; but he had made up his mind that Jonathan Wild should not take him a prisoner into London if he could by any possibility avoid it; and the risk of present and sudden death even was to him preferable to being again an inmate of the dreadful cells that Wild had beneath his house, and of which Tom had already had a taste that was quite enough to last his life.

Exactly in the centre of the little bridge, Tom, with one sharp and sudden stroke of his knife, cut the belt that held him to Jenkins, and slid off the horse close to the parapet of the bridge.

The first sensation Tom had was, that he had struck his head a sharp rap against a large stone that lay against the parapet, and then he heard Jenkins cry out, "Help, help! Catch him! He's off!"

Wild uttered a perfect yell of rage and incredulity.

"I'd rather drown than hang!" cried Tom, and then he threw over the parapet the huge stone against which he had struck his head.

Splash! it went into the water, and then Wild cried out, "He's over—he's over! Fire at him! Kill him if you can, any of you! This way—this way! Dismount, and follow me! Never mind the horses!"

Leaving his horse to take its chance, Wild rushed to the brink of the stream with both his pistols in his hand. The officers followed him, and Tom was left alone on the bridge.

───

CHAPTER CCXCIII.

TOM ELUDES JONATHAN WILD, AND BECOMES POSSESSED OF ANOTHER HORSE.

"THERE he goes!" cried one.

Bang went one of Wild's pistols at a bundle of weeds that was floating under the bridge.

"Have you hit him, sir?" asked Jenkins.

"Yes; to be sure I have."

"Don't make too sure of that, Johnny," thought Tom, as he made a dart at the first horse he saw, and was in the saddle in a moment.

Bang! bang! bang! went three more pistol-shots.

And now there was nothing to hinder Tom from riding off at once, and leaving them all to their own mistakes and errors, but he thought he would say a word to Jonathan before he went.

He had, indeed, opened his mouth to do so, when another idea occurred to him, and he shut it again without uttering a sound.

"No," he said,—"no; it is better not!"

Still, without letting Wild know where he was, Tom made a strange, yelling scream, that came very horrible upon the night air to the ears of the officers, and then he walked his horse some distance, and only very gradually increased its pace as he got far enough off for the clatter of the horse's feet upon the road not to be heard. Then he put it to a trot; and, finally, at a full gallop, Tom tore across the road, and retraced his steps, in hopes of encountering Ellen on Daisy.

Successful pursuit, as long as Tom kept on horseback and the horse kept his feet, was out of the question upon the part of Jonathan Wild and his myrmidons, even supposing that they had any idea that he had galloped off upon one of their horses.

Tom had now reached, as well as he could guess in the dark, the turn in the lane close to the "White Horse," where he had been separated from Ellen.

Looking, then, cautiously to the right and left, Tom said, in a low voice, "Ellen! Ellen! Daisy!"

Tom fancied he heard a slight movement in the hedge.

"Who is there?" said a voice, in female accents.

Tom looked about him, but could not, at the moment, guess where the voice came from; but at last he fancied he saw a face looking over the hedge.

"Who speaks?" asked Tom.

"Oh, heaven be thanked, it is he!" cried Ellen; for it was indeed she, still seated on the back of Daisy, but the intense darkness prevented her from seeing who it was that had called her by name.

In another moment Tom had the satisfaction of holding to his breast that young and innocent girl whom he had been the means of rescuing from her villanous associates at the "White Horse."

That virtuous young girl did not refuse an embrace and a kiss to him who had done so much for her, and who had more than once risked his life in her service.

"Tom, Tom!" she sobbed, "is it a miracle by which you escaped from Jonathan Wild? How was it possible that he did not capture you? And to think that I was the cause of all this! Oh, you do not know, Tom, what I have suffered while waiting here for you!"

"He did capture me, dear Ellen."

"He did?"

"Yes; but I managed to give him the slip again, I am happy to say. But all that is past now, and I feel much happier than I have been for a long time."

"I am glad of that," said Ellen.

"And now, dear, we will make our way towards London as fast as we can; but I think you can manage to ride Daisy, and in that case I will take possession of Jonathan Wild's horse."

"Oh, yes!" said Ellen; "I can ride him. But where am I to go? Alas! I have no home now!"

"No home now?" said Tom. "Why, surely, Ellen, you never called that horrid place, the 'White Horse,' a home?"

"It was all I had."

"Well, don't regret losing it! I will take you with me, Ellen."

"But——"

"But what, dear?"

"It is not quite——I mean, I will not be a burden to you, Tom. I will get a situation."

"We'll talk about that afterwards, Ellen; in the meantime, I am going to take you to my home."

"Is your home in London?"

"Yes."

"Have you a father and mother?" asked the young girl.

"I have a mother."

"Oh, I am so glad! because I think I shall love her."

"Hem!" said Tom. "I don't think, Ellen, the old gal—that is, my mother—is exactly the sort of person you would care to know, and I have no father."

There was a long silence, broken only by the patter of the horses' feet.

Tom was busy with his own reflections. He wondered if Captain Heron would approve of all he had done, and his conscience whispered "Yes."

Ellen, too, was lost in thought. She knew nothing of her companion but that he was brave, handsome, and evidently loved her.

Ellen was tolerably well educated. Her father had been a respectable tradesman, and had taken care to give what he considered better than a dower to his only child—namely, a good education.

When he died, he bequeathed his greatest treasure, Ellen, to an only sister, leaving her in possession of whatever money or other valuables he had saved, in trust for his precious child.

How the faithless sister fulfilled her duty we have already seen.

The clouds had cleared away, and the sun was just rising, as Tom took from his pocket a key which opened the little wicket gate leading to the stables at the back of Whitcombe House.

"Where are we?" asked Ellen.

"This is where I live," said Tom, with a smile. "Let me assist you to dismount, and then, when I have got both the horses in, I will take you into the house."

Mechanically, Ellen obeyed, for she felt faint and weary with the night's excitements and exertions; and having been kept so long without food, it was with difficulty that Tom could support her with one arm, while with the other he led in first Jonathan Wild's horse, and then Daisy, into the stables.

"That'll do for the present," said Tom, closing the gate with a breath of relief,—"that'll do for the present! I'll come back in a minute, Daisy, and attend to you. Now, dear, cheer up! You will be safe here, and in the morning I will speak to the Lady Edith about you."

"Lady Edith?"

"Yes, dear one. She is the wife of Captain—Captain Fantome, the gentleman who lives here—as noble and brave as you can imagine, Ellen."

"And you, Tom—who are you?"

"Oh, I am Tom Ripon, and Captain Fantome's confidential valet. Ah, here's Ogle!"

At this moment, Ogle, who had heard voices below, came into the servants' hall, where Tom and Ellen were talking.

"Here, Ogle, I wanted to see you. Just go and fetch Mrs. Ogle. I want her to take care of this young lady until I can speak to Lady Edith about her."

Ogle looked from one to the other in amazement; but there was a look of innocence and helplessness about Ellen that went at once to his kind heart.

"All right, Tom! Wait for me here, and I'll fetch Mrs Ogle."

Ellen had sunk down on a chair, and sobbed.

Tom was in vain trying to comfort her.

"Nay, why do you weep so, dear Ellen? I tell you you have nothing to fear now; and do I not love you dearly, Ellen?"

"Oh, yes! I know—I feel that you love me, Tom; but yet I cannot but fear that this lady of whom you speak—the Lady Edith—will condemn my conduct, and yet, heaven knows, I have done all for the best!"

"No doubt of it, Ellen. And as for the Lady Edith, why, I tell you you do not know her. She is the sweetest, gentlest creature in all the world, and will only be too glad to hold out a helping hand to us; and besides, Ellen, in a very little while I shall ask you to give me the right to protect you and watch over you. Shall you say 'Yes,' Ellen?"

As Tom uttered these words, he took Ellen's hand in both of his, and looked into her eyes.

No words came from her lips, but Tom felt from that moment that he was all in all to that young and virtuous being.

At this moment Mrs. Ogle entered the room, and, going up to the young girl, she took her kindly by the hand, saying, "You look pale as a ghost. Come with me, and I will give you something to put a little life into those poor chilled limbs. Deary me! why her hands are like ice!"

"Don't stand talking here, Mrs. Ogle," said Tom, "but take Ellen to your room, and do the best you can for her, and in the morning I will speak to Lady Edith."

"Good night, dear Ellen!" whispered Tom, as he pressed her hand; but this time he did not kiss her—there were too many spectators, for Ogle, too, had returned—and young, pure love is bashful; and if Tom had before fancied himself in love with every pretty face that had met his eyes, he was quite convinced, now, that Ellen had inspired him with a very different feeling to any which he had experienced before.

"Well," said Tom, when he was once more left alone,—"well, this has not been altogether a bad night's work! I have got Jonathan Wild's horse, and—yes, I feel sure of it this time—a wife into the bargain; for I mean to tell the Captain all about it in the morning, and I'm sure he'll not say no when he knows that my love is returned by Ellen."

It was with a smile that Edith greeted Tom Ripon the next morning, as the latter entered the green drawing-room, with which the reader is already so well acquainted.

"And so, Tom," she said, kindly, "I hear that you have made me a present of a well-educated and virtuous young girl as a nurse to your little favourite here,"—pointing to the child who was playing at his mother's feet.

Tom looked somewhat confused. He tried to speak, but the words he would have uttered seemed somehow to refuse to pass his lips.

"Speak, Tom," said Edith. "I already know something of the occurrences of last night, and of your gallant conduct with regard to that young girl, but I wish to hear from your own lips something more than Mrs. Ogle can tell me."

Tom took courage, as he glanced at the face of Edith; and then he said, "Oh, Lady Edith, I really do love Ellen; and if I can only get your consent, and that of Captain Heron, I shall be the happiest man in the kingdom."

"But what does Ellen say herself, Tom?" asked Edith.

"Well, Lady Edith, I should say there would be no difficulty in that quarter; for, look you, Lady Edith, she has no father—no, mother—no friend but me!"

"And myself and Felix," said Edith.

"Oh, thank you—thank you!" cried Tom, in an excited voice. "If you befriend us, then we shall do quite well, and I can go out every night on the road, or on the heath, and make a fortune; and when we have got enough, why, then we will settle down, and open a quiet little inn somewhere."

At this moment, Felix Heron entered the apartment, and placing his hand kindly upon Tom's shoulder, he said, "And so, Tom, at last you think you have really have found the person who is some day to be Mrs. Tom Ripon—eh?"

"Don't joke about it Captain, don't," cried Tom. "I was a fool ever to have thought I cared for anybody, before I saw Ellen Shackle; but now I know beyond a doubt that I am quite in earnest."

"Well, Tom," said Heron, "I believe you are, and you may be quite assured I shall not stand in the way of your happiness, if at the end of three months you still continue in the same mind."

"I see how it is, Captain," said Tom: "you won't believe I'm in earnest until I've really been and gone to church, and got married out and out. Then, I suppose, you'll have no doubt on the subject?"

"Not the least, Tom. Now, tell me if you feel inclined to go on the road again after what occurred last night?"

"Most certainly, Captain, if you'll trust me with Daisy. I fancy I should not take half so much interest in my adventures if it were not for her."

"Take her, Tom, and welcome. Remember what we both owe to you."

As Felix Heron spoke with some emotion, he drew to his bosom his little child, who, all unconscious of what Tom had done for him, threw his arms round his father's neck, and asked coaxingly for a game at romps.

"Not now, not now, my boy," said Felix, as he sat the child upon the floor, at his mother's feet. "I must read those papers this morning, dear Edith, that Tom and I were fortunate enough to despoil Warringdale of."

"Then I may take Daisy to night, Captain?" asked Tom.

"Yes, and I need not warn you to be very, very careful of her, Tom."

"All right, Captain. I want to make some money now you, know. I feel as though I had somebody else to work for."

As Tom left the apartment, Edith turned to Felix and said, "I really think this time, Felix, that Tom is in earnest."

"So do I, Edith, and I am very glad of it. Nothing makes a man so estimable as a good and kind wife, and I think from the little I saw of Ellen this morning, she is well calculated to make Tom a happy man."

At this moment, there was a gentle tap at the drawing-room door, and in answer to Edith's "Come in," Ellen entered, looking very modest and pretty in her little smart cap and a snow-white apron.

"Oh, here is Ellen, mamma!" shouted the child, springing to his feet. "She tells me such beautiful stories about birds and flowers. Me want to go to Ellen, mamma."

"Go, dearest," said Edith, as she imprinted a fervent kiss upon the lips of her much-loved child.

CHAPTER CCXCIV.

TOM RIPON IS AGAIN PURSUED BY JONATHAN WILD.

TOWARDS nine o'clock, Tom Ripon was standing with his arm round Ellen's waist, trying to make her believe that he was going out merely for a ride.

Ellen sighed.

"Now, my dear Ellen," said Tom, "you know that I love you as dearly as one human being can love another; and do you not think, therefore, that for your sake I shall take all the care of myself in the world. Since I have known you, I value life so much more than I did before, so you may be quite sure I shall take the greatest care of myself."

"Then you will come back soon, Tom?"

"Yes, as soon as possible, Ellen; but I have to meet some friends, and they may detain me, you know, perhaps beyond the hour of your retiring to rest."

As Tom gave utterance to this speech, it must be confessed he had some qualms of conscience.

He then kissed her as lovingly as possible before he left Whitcombe House.

In another moment, Tom was mounted on Daisy, and leading Jonathan Wild's horse by the bridle, he intended as soon as he saw a good opportunity to let the riderless horse go.

He soon came to a long, narrow lane, where Tom started off, and had the satisfaction of seeing it go at a smart gallop right down the lane.

Tom now put Daisy to a gallop.

"Hilloa!—hilloa, there!" shouted a voice.

Tom did not slacken his speed. He turned round in his saddle, and saw three or four mounted men galloping after him.

"Now for a race, Daisy, my lass!" said Tom.

"Hilloa!" shouted the voice again. "Pull up, or we will fire at you!"

"Fire away!" said Tom; and as he spoke he urged Daisy on at increased speed, and with his light weight the creature was able to get on tremendously.

Bang! went a pistol-shot, but it did no harm

"Hold hard! Halt, I say again!" shouted the voice.

"Forward, forward, Daisy!" was all Tom said; and on he sped at a rattling speed. But now an obstruction presented itself in the shape of a toll-bar.

The toll-bar keeper evidently guessed that there was something wrong on the road, for he rushed out of his little house, and shut the gate.

"I'll not forget you for that," thought Tom.

In another moment more Tom reached the gate, and over went Daisy.

"Murder! Stop him! stop him!" cried the man.

Off he went again; but the gate was an obstacle to his pursuers, who were not so well mounted, and were not so reckless as to what

leaps they took as Tom had been, for they all stopped till the man had opened the gate again; and his fright made him bungle so that he delayed them nearly a minute.

"You idiot!" roared Jonathan Wild. "If it had not been for you shutting the gate we should have had him! What is the use of me losing my time watching for that scoundrel here all this evening, only to lose him through your confounded stupidity?"

"Very sorry, sir," said the man; "but I thought I was doing the best thing to assist you, Mr. Wild, I am sure I did!"

"Confound you!" muttered Wild. "There were papers in the saddle of that horse he stole from me last night that I would not have lost for all I possess!"

"What did you say, Mr. Wild?" asked one of his men.

"Nothing, idiot! Speak when you're spoken

to, and don't listen when what is being said is not intended for your ears!"

The man slunk back.

Tom had got considerably the start of his pursuers now, and really began to think there was a chance of his escaping.

"Well," said Tom to himself, "I think Jonathan Wild might have waited till I had had some sport on the road before he hunted me down again. Never mind, Daisy, lass; we'll have another try before we go home, won't we, lass?"

Daisy moved her head up and down as she was wont to do when Tom was holding any of his mysterious conversations with her; and then Tom made up his mind to get out of the high road as soon as he possibly could, and seeing a lane to his right, he made a dash round the corner of it.

Tom now began to walk Daisy; but presently he heard the unmistakable clatter of horses' feet, and then he knew that his pursuers were again on his track.

He happened at this moment to be just beneath the hedge of what seemed to be a very pretty garden.

There was no time to lose, so he contrived to drag Daisy by the bridle through a gap in the hedge into the garden beyond.

This little garden adjoined a cottage he could just see through the boughs of the fruit trees, and over the tops of the beans and peas, with which it was well stocked.

Tom made Daisy crouch down as she had been taught to do, and then threw himself flat down beside her, between two rows of peas, and then he heard his pursuers pass by.

"Saved!" he said, as he scrambled up again.

As he did so, Tom was quite taken aback at the moment, for coming down one of the garden paths was a beautiful young girl about sixteen years of age.

"Don't be alarmed, miss," said Tom. "I would not harm you for the world."

"Oh, who are you?" said the girl, suppressing her inclination to scream for assistance.

"A hunted man!" said Tom. "Don't you hear the bloodhounds?"

It must have been the cheerful and kind tone in which Tom Ripon spoke that reassured the alarmed girl, but she looked puzzled, and Tom thought he had never seen such eyes before, that had in them such a world of tenderness.

"Oh, tell me who and what you are?" she said.

"I am——"

Tom stopped short, for, to tell the truth, he did not know what to call himself to that young girl. The word highwayman was upon his lips, but he did not like to say that to her.

"Why do you not tell me who you are?" she said, still regarding him earnestly.

"Because I hardly know myself," replied Tom; "and that's the real truth," in his pleasant and ingenuous way, that always had a sort of charm about it.

"But how can that be?" persisted the girl. "You must know who you are!"

"Never mind now who I am. Is it not sufficient for you to know that I am in great danger—perhaps in danger of my life. I am

pursued by eight men on eight horses; and, as sure as they see me, as surely they will shoot me."

"Oh, this is dreadful!" exclaimed the young girl. "What have you done to be so hunted?"

"I don't know. I don't think I deserve it," said Tom.

"No, I am sure you don't," said the young girl.

"Thank you for that kind speech! I think you will save me if you can."

"Oh, yes, I will!"

"Ah, I knew you would!"

"I hope you are not very wicked. You don't look as if you were."

"Well, I don't think I am," said Tom; "but I might, perhaps, be better, and I will some day."

"That's right!" said the young girl, with a sweet, bright smile. "Come this way, and mind your horse does not trample down any more beans. I don't know what aunt will say when she sees this bed."

"Oh, say a pig got in by accident."

What further might have passed between Tom and the young girl was put to an abrupt termination, for the horsemen seemed to be returning.

The beautiful girl trembled very much as she ran along a little pathway, the sides of which were adorned with flowers of many hues, and then opening a rough looking door at the end of it, she said, "Go in there. It is where we keep our fruit."

"I understand," said Tom; "good night! But first tell me how I can thank you?"

"Not at all. I am afraid——"

"Of what?"

"That I am doing wrong."

"No; a kind action can never be wrong, dear. Tell me what your name is; but if you don't I shall never forget you; and I can't think why people are made with such pretty faces as yours, except it is to ruin the wits of the rest of the world. Oh——"

The young girl shut the door abruptly in Tom's face, to put an end to his compliments, so that he was left to himself in complete darkness.

"What a smell of apples there is here!" said Tom, as he stretched out his hand and secured a very fine one, which he began eating.

Tom had not got past the age when he could relish an apple with all the gusto of youth.

"Capital!" said Tom. "I feel myself very much refreshed; and, if it were not that the image of Ellen is at my heart, I should take it into my head that this young girl was the prettiest and gentlest creature in the world; but, at all events, she is the next best. Heigho! what a thing it is a man can only have one wife!"

Tom thought then it would be just as well to examine as well as he could in the dark the mode of exit which the young girl told him he would find at the back of the apple-house, and he found that it was a small door on the latch, which opened close to the margin of a little pond, evidently a duck-pond.

"That'll do," said Tom.

All Tom's reflections were now put an end to, for it appeared that Jonathan Wild and his men had become so impressed with the belief that he must be hiding somewhere in the lane, that they dismounted, and leaving their horses in charge of one of their number, they began hunting about the bushes at a great rate.

During their search they soon came upon the garden, and the idea struck them at once, from the rather dilapidated state of the hedge, that he and Daisy might have made their way through it.

"Here's a gap!" cried one.

"It's too small," cried another.

"Oh, I don't know! Besides, the hedge can be easily pushed together on the inside, and he is cunning enough for that, I take it."

"No doubt of his cunning."

"Very well, then. You all of you keep a watch on the hedge," said Jonathan Wild, "while I and Jukes go into the garden by the house gate."

"Very good, Mr. Wild."

Then Jonathan Wild and his bull-dog made their way to the front entrance to the cottage, and demanded admittance in the King's name.

The young girl's aunt was dreadfully alarmed; but she let the officers into the cottage, and thence, at their request, into the garden.

"Oh, gentlemen," she said, "who do you want? I am a lone widow, and live here by myself, with my niece Mary!"

"Who do we want?" asked Jonathan Wild. "Why, a highwayman, to be sure, whom you have concealed in this house!"

"Gracious providence!" exclaimed the elderly woman, raising her hands. "Me hide a highwayman? Oh, oh, oh! There's no highwayman here, gentlemen, that I'll take my solemn Bible oath of! I'm not a highwayman, neither is Mary!"

"I don't say you are, ma'am," said Wild, with a brutal laugh; "but we mean to look for ourselves, for all that! Your garden has not a very good hedge, and we suspect the person we are after has concealed himself and his horse in t"

"A man and a horse in my garden?" almost shrieked the woman. "Merciful providence, what will become of the fruit and vegetables?"

Mary and her aunt had followed the officers out into the garden, and were standing upon the little grass plot in front of the cottage.

Poor Mary was the picture of fright. Her face had turned quite white, and she trembled very much.

"You needn't be afraid, my dear," said Wild's bull-dog, as the gleam of the lantern he carried fell upon her pale features. "We don't mean to harm you."

"No, no—I'm not afraid!" gasped Mary.

"That's right; but you look as if you had seen a ghost! You'd better go indoors!"

"Why!"

"Because, you see, if we do find the young fellow we're after, there'll be a bit of a disturbance, for he's sure to show fight!"

"Oh, how cruel!"

"What is cruel?"

"Of you—two big men as you are—to be pursuing such a mere lad—almost a boy!"

"Ah, you have seen him! Did you hear that, Mr. Wild? This here gal says he's only a mere lad!"

"Does she? That is capital!" shouted Wild, who had been busily engaged searching the garden. "Now, my dear, all you have to do is just to say quietly where he is!"

Poor Mary was ready to sink to the ground with remorse and terror at what she had said, for she saw in a moment, after the words had passed her lips, what she had done, and that nothing now could save him.

"Oh, no, no!" she cried, as she clasped her hands imploringly. "I know nothing—indeed, I know nothing! I did not say I knew anything, did I?"

"You did, though," said Wild.

"Do not say that! Oh, aunt, what did I say?"

"Come, come!" said Wild, as he drew a pistol from his pocket. "Come on! We shall get him at last! This way! Shoot him, so as to disable him, if he should resist at all!"

"All's right, Mr. Wild!"

Poor Mary uttered a shriek of despair, and had sunk upon her knees on the grass plot. She had really wished to save Tom. There was something in his looks which seemed so pitiable, and withal so frank and good-tempered, that she could not believe that he had done anything so very bad; but now she found by her own want of tact she had probably destroyed him.

And yet what could she do now? Nothing but pray for him, and that she did most fervently.

Tom knew nothing of all this, as he was in a distant part of the garden; but if he had, he would have felt no indignation at the innocent girl, whose very innocence and anxiety to save him had caused her to utter words that were so much against him.

Poor, poor Mary, and poor Tom, also—for, with all his faults, we must pity him.

Jonathan Wild and his men soon came to the apple-house, in which Mary had shut Tom.

Tom heard them.

"Now for it!" he said. "I suppose my fate hangs upon the next five minutes!"

"Here's a door!" said Wild. "I'll fire through it, if I can't open it! Oh, it's all right—it's only on the latch!"

It must be confessed that Jonathan Wild, notwithstanding his brutal kind of courage, was well aware of the danger that might be in store for him, for he felt certain that if Tom happened to be on the other side of that door, a couple of bullets would be the salute he should meet with. That idea was none of the most agreeable, and we can scarcely wonder at Jonathan Wild hesitating.

It was with a feeling of relief that he called out when he had opened the door, "All's right!"

"Not there, Mr. Wild?" asked his man.

"No," shouted Wild, "he is not there."

"What door is that at the back, sir?"

"I don't know," said Wild; "let's open it."

"Confound your curiosity," thought Tom, and he tried to get cautiously round the corner of the storehouse, leading Daisy by the bridle; but his foot slipped and he half fell.

"Hilloa!" cried Wild; "I hear a noise!"

"Take that, then?" said Tom, as he fired a pistol at Wild's head.

His hat and wig flew off, but he was himself uninjured.

CHAPTER CCXCV.

TOM RIPON SUCCEEDS IN FRIGHTENING JONATHAN WILD, AND IS ALLOWED TO GO IN PEACE.

FROM the moment that Tom found his presence in the garden was discovered, he felt that there was no possible chance of escape, and the shot he had fired was rather from impulse than from reflection.

"Has he hit you, Mr. Wild?" asked his man.

"I don't know, confound him," was the reply.

"Tom Ripon!" Wild then shouted, "you are my prisoner! We are two to one here, and there are four more in the lane: so give in, or it will be worse for you."

At that moment Mary appeared, and clasping her hands she cried, "Oh, he is taken! They will kill him—they will kill him! He is taken!"

"Never mind," said Tom, kindly; "it is all right."

"But you are hurt! I heard fire-arms! They have shot you!"

"No, thank the Fates, I'm not hurt! As for me, don't think ever again that you saw me. Forget me. Our acquaintance began this hour, and this hour let it end."

"I am very—very sorry for you."

"That I know," said Tom; "and it is some consolation to know that there is one kind, gentle heart that is sorry for me."

"I did all I could to save you," said Mary.

"Hush!—oh, hush!"

"Oh, you did, did you?" said Wild, savagely; "in that case, I believe it is my duty to take you prisoner, likewise; for it is a high crime to aid a criminal."

"Are you a man," said Tom, "and utter such words to an innocent young girl, who is still almost a child?"

Wild pretended not to hear what Tom said, and his man took an opportunity to whisper to her.

"Don't cry, my dear; no harm will come to you. Don't mind what Mr. Wild says to you; he's always blustering out stupid things."

"I am not thinking of myself," said Mary; and then she looked at Tom with such a mute eloquence, that there was no need, upon her part, to tell any one that it was of him she was thinking.

"Don't think of me, either," said Tom; "all are not lost who are in danger, you know."

The young girl shook her head, and sighed deeply.

At this moment, Jonathan Wild, who had been hailing the men whom he had left in the lane, returned, and producing a pair of handcuffs from a capacious pocket in his coat, he advanced to Tom.

"Now, then, we'll make sure of you this time, young fellow," he said, with a brutal laugh.

A flush of colour mounted to Tom's cheek at this proceeding; he would have given something not to have been subjected to such an indignity in the presence of that fair young girl.

"Hold, Jonathan Wild!" he said; "you know I keep my word if I make a promise. I will not try to escape if you leave my hands at liberty."

"Not if I know it," replied Wild, who appeared to enjoy Tom's discomfiture greatly. "Not if I know it. A bird in the hand is worth two in the bush, you know, any day. So, here goes!"

Tom felt that resistance would only make matters worse, so he quietly surrendered his hands, and Jonathan Wild roughly placed the handcuffs on them.

"As nice a fit as if they had been made for you," he said, looking triumphantly at Tom.

Tom made no reply to Jonathan Wild; but, turning to the young girl, he said, as cheerfully as he could, "Good-bye, dear Mary!"

"Oh, can you ever forgive me?" she asked, as she placed her warm, soft hand upon his manacled wrists.

"Forgive you? why I have nothing to forgive; but I have a great deal to thank you for. You are a good, brave girl, and I should be a great deal more contented if I thought the day would ever come when I might be able to do you a good turn."

Jonathan Wild chuckled malignantly, as he said, "I wouldn't make any promises if I were you, as you'll only have time to make your will; and if you have anything to leave to this girl, why, that would be the greatest service you will ever have an opportunity of rendering her."

"Oh! cruel—cruel!" said Mary.

"Cruel or not cruel, I can tell you this is the last time you'll see him, unless you like to attend his execution. In that case, I will, for a consideration, undertake to procure you a good view."

Poor Mary clasped her hands over her eyes and wept bitterly.

"I'm ready, you villain!" shouted Tom, roused now past all forbearance. "Lead on. Good-bye, Mary; you'll see me again before long."

In another minute the party left the garden, and Jonathan Wild had Tom placed behind one of his men for the greater safety.

"Forward!" shouted Wild.

Now it must not be supposed for one moment that Tom, notwithstanding all his anxiety for his own personal safety, had forgotten his dear companion, Daisy.

He had never taken his eyes off that noble creature during the whole of the proceedings which we have been detailing; and it was with a feeling almost of agony that he beheld Jonathan Wild seize her by the bridle, and seem to appropriate her to his own use.

Still Tom had a scheme in his head, and he waited for an opportunity to carry it out.

Wild, in his anxiety to keep Tom continually in his sight, lest, by some means or another, he might again make his escape, gave Tom every facility for keeping close to Daisy also.

They were just about to mount, when Jonathan Wild turned and glared at Tom, as he said fiercely, "Tom Ripon, you have not many days to live, and you may just as well be on good terms with me as not, for I have the power of making the remainder of your life very miserable if you continue to defy me."

"Oh, indeed!" said Tom, with a careless air. "And pray what do you want me to do in order that my life in Newgate may be so jolly as you seem to intimate it may be?"

"Return me those papers you found in the pocket of my horse's saddle, and all personal enmity will be at an end."

"No, no, Johnny!" said Tom; "I must have something more than you promise for those papers, because I am in hopes I shall be able to get you hanged by giving them up to the proper authorities."

Wild uttered a yell of rage, and his men could scarcely suppress a laugh at what they considered the courage of Tom in thus speaking to their redoubtable leader.

"Wretch, I will search you myself, but I will recover them!" roared Wild.

"That won't be quite so easy, Mr. Wild," replied Tom; "for I have given them into the hands of a friend of mine, who, if I am hanged, will at once deliver them into the hands of the Lord Chief Justice."

Tom began to have some hopes of working upon the fears of Jonathan Wild, now that he found he attached so much importance to those papers, which, it will be remembered, he (Tom) had found in the pocket of the saddle of the horse he had seized when he left Jonathan Wild and his men looking for him on the little bridge.

Jonathan Wild now made Tom mount behind one of the men, which little operation he was so intent upon watching, that he somewhat slackened his hold upon Daisy.

"Ho, Daisy! Oh! oh! Fly, Daisy!" cried Tom.

The intelligent creature, with one bound, tore herself loose from the slight hold Wild had on her bridle, and flew, rather than aught else, down the road as swiftly as an arrow from the bow.

"Confound you!" shouted Wild, as he dealt Tom a blow with his hanger.

It will be remembered that Tom was almost helpless, for his hands were fastened behind his back; but as good fortune would have it, he happened to be behind the same man who had before been constituted his keeper under similar circumstances, and who, it will be remembered, had told Tom that he pitied him.

This man now parried the blow, which must otherwise have fell upon Tom's defenceless head, saying as he did so, "Hold hard, Mr. Wild; if you knock the boy's brains out now, you will deprive us all, and yourself at the same time, of the pleasure we are looking forward to of seeing him hanged at Tyburn."

Tom understood what the man was doing, and he immediately made a mental vow to himself that if ever he could be of any service to the rough man he would not forget that act of kindness.

"Ride on!" said Wild, "and you, Davis, lend me your horse, and I will ride behind to see that this scoundrel does not escape us a second time."

Tom began to think his case looked rather hopeless, but he had removed a great load off his mind by setting Daisy free, for he had no doubt in his own mind that she would find her way back to the stables of Whitcombe House.

The little party now moved on in silence; but ever and anon, Jonathan Wild could be heard muttering to himself, "Fool! fool that I was to trust those papers to the safe keeping of a horse. Why did I carry them about with me? I would give any price for them—any price in reason, if I but had them in my own possession again."

"Would you, Johnny?" asked Tom. "Then why don't you strike a bargain with me at once, for their redemption?"

"What would you ask for them?"

"My freedom, Johnny; nothing less would suit me, I'm sorry to say."

"Silence, wretch!"

"Oh, very well, just as you like. I thought I was obliging you," said Tom. "Look there! Who's that?"

"Who's what?" asked Wild.

"Why, there, between the trees," said Tom. "I could almost declare it was Captain Heron himself, mounted upon Daisy! That's jolly! Hurrah! hurrah!"

Wild clutched by the mane of the horse upon which he was riding, and would have fallen but for that support. The sudden movement, however, startled the creature, and it reared violently.

"Confusion take you!" growled Wild. "What do you mean? I see no figure."

"Why, there, to be sure!" cried Tom, glad to perceive the advantage he had obtained over Wild, and hoping to profit by it. "Why, there to be sure! I have no fears now, Johnny: he has come to rescue me, no doubt."

"Tom—Tom Ripon, hear me!" said Wild, in choking accents.

"Well, go ahead; I'm all attention."

"If I let you go this time, will you promise me that you will destroy those papers?"

"You'll be obliged to let me go, whether you like it or not. See, he comes!"

Jonathan Wild was ghastly pale, and glanced about him on every side.

"Do you see anything or anybody, Davis?" he asked of the man behind whom Tom was riding, highly amused at the turn affairs had taken.

"Can't say as I do, Mr. Wild," replied the man.

"Why, of course not," said Tom; "ghosts only make themselves visible to those whom they wish to be seen by. I've no doubt but that you will see him as plainly in a few minutes as you did on Holborn Hill that day, you know, when he took me out of the death-cart."

Jonathan Wild breathed heavily.

"Look you, Tom; I never intended," he said, "to hang you this term."

"Indeed!" interrupted Tom. "Why, I thought you said I had only a few hours in which to make my will."

"Mere jest—mere jest; nothing more," said Wild.

"And these handcuffs?" asked Tom. "Are they mere jest also?"

"A matter of form."

"Oh, indeed! Then perhaps, Johnny, you will, just for form's sake, produce the little key that belongs to them, and set me at liberty."

"I will—I will."

"That is something like! Now, Johnny, I feel as if I could almost forgive you for spoiling my night's sport by detaining me all this time. Come, make haste! I see Captain Heron has been standing still all the time we have been talking, as if to give you a chance of doing the right sort of thing without any interference on his part."

"But he is too far off to hear what we are saying," said Jonathan, his teeth chattering as he spoke.

"Oh, distance is nothing; ghosts hear miles off. Why, the day you were going to hang me——"

Wild made an imploring gesture with his hand, but Tom pretended not to see it, and continued.

"The day you were going to hang me he was at the furthest end of Hampstead Heath just as the cart was leaving Newgate. He knew all about it, and knew a few minutes would be amply sufficient for him to rescue me from what seemed certain death."

Wild took the key of the handcuffs from his pocket, and unfastened them, but his hands shook so violently that it was some minutes before he succeeded in freeing Tom's wrists from the manacles.

"That is well," said Tom, as he felt himself comparatively at liberty. "Now you must let me go free."

"But Captain Heron——" began Wild.

"Oh, as soon as I am free I shall ride on, and tell him that you have done the right thing without being made to do it; but now I must be untied from behind this man, as I feel quite capable of riding alone."

"Undo the belt," said Wild to the man upon whose horse Tom was riding.

The order was instantly obeyed, and Tom quickly dismounted.

"Forward!" shouted Wild.

"Not so fast!" cried Tom. "Do you suppose I am going to be turned loose in this fashion, Jonathan? I must have a horse, as I intend to have some sport to-night before many hours have passed."

"And the papers?" asked Wild.

"Give me a horse first, and then I'll give you the papers," said Tom.

"What?" cried Wild. "Have you the papers about you?"

"To be sure I have. Here they are."

Jonathan Wild made a clutch at them.

"Not so fast, Jonathan, if you please," said Tom. "I said that as soon as you gave me a horse I would give you the papers. Is it to be a bargain?"

"Agreed!" said Wild. "Davis, dismount, and let him have your horse."

In another moment Tom was in the saddle. He then handed the papers to Wild.

"There are the papers, although I feel almost as bad as you are in thus giving them up; but a promise is a promise, and so good-night!"

Tom dashed along in the direction of a clump of trees, where he had pretended he saw Captain Heron, knowing that he would be safe from all pursuit from Jonathan Wild if he took that course.

"Well," said Tom to himself as soon as he had placed some distance between him and Jonathan Wild—"well, at all events I ought never to speak against ghosts; they have stood me in good stead this night."

———

CHAPTER CCXCVI.

TOM RIPON HAS AN ADVENTURE, AND ACQUIRES SOME BOOTY.

"ELLEN—my dear Ellen!" were the first words that Tom uttered as he stood beside that gentle girl on the morning succeeding the events detailed in our last chapter.

It is not too much to say that Ellen was too completely overcome by the emotions of that happy moment, when she found herself clasped in the arms of Tom Ripon, to speak.

The silence, however, was far more eloquent than language could have possibly been, and she could only sob out her thankfulness to heaven that had permitted her again so much happiness; for it will be remembered that it was with the greatest reluctance she had parted from Tom on the previous night.

"Ellen, I cannot yet hear you say one word," said Tom, "to assure me that you are glad to see me returned safe and well."

Upon this, Ellen did manage to make an effort to say something, but somehow the words seemed to choke her; but she did contrive at last to say, "Tom—Tom—my Tom!"

This was quite sufficient for Tom Ripon. Once more he heard that sweet voice, which was to him more welcome than anything in all the world.

Once more he listened to those soft, tender, accents that he had at one time began to think he should never hear again—viz., when he found himself once more in the power of Jonathan Wild and his officers.

For a few moments now they neither of them spoke, and Ellen wept on the bosom of him whom she loved, and who loved her with a truthfulness, and we may say with a purity and innocence, seldom to be met with in this world.

When Tom managed to speak again, his voice was broken and unsteady; but it was with the truthfulness of pure joy that it was broken—the tears came from the heart's overflowing.

"My own darling—my pretty Ellen—do not cry. All is well now."

"Oh, Tom—Tom! I thought——"

"What did you think, dear?"

"That you would be captured by that dreadful man whom I used to think so differently of."

"What made you think so, dear Ellen, when I told you I was merely going for a ride?"

"I do not know, Tom, but I had a presentiment. Did you encounter Jonathan Wild?"

"I did, dear."

Ellen shuddered as she said, "What should I do now if I were to be deprived of you, Tom?"

"Oh, never fear, Ellen," said Tom cheerfully. "I am cased in armour now, you know."

"In armour, Tom?"

"Yes, Ellen. I do think that when any one loves sincerely, and without offence to heaven's virtue, as I love you, Ellen, that that one is specially under the protection of angels; and so, in a manner of speaking, is encased in the proof armour of that affection which shall save him from peril in this world, and, perhaps, be his passport to the world to come."

It was a gentle and happy thought that of Tom's. After a few moments Ellen strove to smile, as she replied, "Tom, then I, too, have that armour."

"You, dear?"

"Yes, Tom; for do I not love you?"

"Oh, Ellen, Ellen! this is too much joy! I do not deserve it!"

"Nay, Tom, it is not often that I have allowed those words, 'I love you,' to pass my lips; but they have ever been at my heart. From the first moment that you entered that house of those wicked people who kept the 'White Horse,' I loved you. From that time my love has increased, and I know that it will never diminish; and now I think that I love you as well as it is possible for any one to love."

Tom was too much delighted by these words of Ellen to recollect anything but that he held her in his arms, and that she avowed that feeling for him which he had for her in such intensity.

For a time, surely, their young hearts were very, very happy indeed.

"But now, Ellen," said Tom,—"now that you see, dear girl, that I come back to you safely, you will not object to my going out again to-night, will you?"

Ellen shook her head, as she said, "What do you do, Tom, on these expeditions, taken at such a late hour?"

"Do not ask me, Ellen, there's a good girl. I am engaged in an undertaking by which I hope to hasten the time when I shall be able to call you really my wife."

Ellen did not reply; but it was with an aching heart that she saw Tom depart on the following evening, mounted, as before, upon Daisy, who, it is needless to inform our reader, who is already acquainted with that noble creature's sagacity, had found her way back to the stables at Whitcombe House, when Tom so successfully bid her.

Tom now took a different route, in hopes of having an adventure without encountering any of Jonathan Wild's myrmidons.

He had proceeded some paces down a narrow lane, when he heard a vehicle rapidly approaching.

"Shall I stop that chaise — for chaise I believe it to be by the sound—or not?" said Tom to himself.

Before Tom could satisfactorily answer this question, which he had put to himself, he became very much interested in the appearance of the person in the chaise, and in the very odd manner in which he contrived to manage the horse that was in it.

From the light from the lamps on either side of the chaise, Tom could see that its occupant was a very old man, with white hair. He had on a faded suit of livery, and on his arm he carried a bundle, about which he seemed to be dreadfully anxious, for he held it close to his heart, and drove with the aid of his left hand only.

The look of terror that was upon the face of the old man was such that Tom found it difficult to withdraw his gaze from him.

The horse was going at a good pace, and must have been a very docile creature to keep his route as well as he did, notwithstanding the very odd and wayward manner in which he was driven by the old man, who seemed to pay no attention whatever to where the creature was going, so very intent was he upon the bundle that he had on his knees.

The bundle was wrapped up in an old shawl.

Tom saw all this, of course, in much less time than it has taken us to describe it.

Tom walked Daisy right out into the middle of the road, and called out, "Stop!"

The old man, with a cry of despair, clutched the bundle that was rolled up in the old shawl closer to his heart, and, dropping the reins, took from the seat upon which he had been sitting a double-barrelled pistol, and, pointing it at Tom, he cried, in tremulous accents, "Off, off! or I must take a life! Oh, do not stay me! I see that you are a young man, and it will be better for you to live, and say that you let me go free, than that I should have your blood upon my head."

"Hold!" cried Tom.

"No, no! Off—off, I say—off! Are you alone?"

"Yes, but don't shoot me on that account," said Tom. "What have you there?"

"Nothing—nothing but a few trifles that I am to convey to a place of safety."

"Oh, indeed!" said Tom. "Perhaps you will allow me to see these same trifles?"

"Stand back, I say! stand back! I am dangerous!"

"And so am I!" said Tom, as he coolly produced a pistol from the holster of Daisy's saddle, and presented it full in the face of the old man.

"Now see," he said; "perhaps you will allow me to see what you have so carefully tied up in that bundle?"

The old man seemed terror-stricken, and Tom began to think that the double-barrelled pistol which he had produced was not really loaded.

Slowly the old man began to untie one end of the shawl, and as he did so, Tom was surprised and delighted to find that it contained gold and jewels to a considerable amount.

"Why, what on earth, you old sinner, are you going to do with all this wealth, and how did it come into your possession?"

"Oh, kind sir," whined the old man, "do not ask me—do not ask me; it is not mine—it belongs to a lady."

"A lady?"

"Yes, kind sir; she owes me a deal of money, and as she could not pay me, I have consented, as a favour, to take these little nick-nacks as a kind of security."

"Oh! and who may the lady be, pray?" asked Tom.

"Well, sir, I—that is, I never was good at names. Dear me! what is her name?"

The old man rubbed his furrowed brow, and put on an air of deep reflection.

"No nonsense!" said Tom, clicking his pistol

so as to frighten the old man out of his senses almost,—" no nonsense ! It cannot be possible that you should forget the name of any one who owes you so much money as to entrust all those jewels to your keeping, as security for the payment of it. Speak, and tell me the lady's name, I say, or I'll fire and scatter your old brains to the night wind."

" Help !—oh, help !"

" Speak, I say !" shouted Tom.

" Well, then, if you must know, it's the Countess of Whitcombe,"

" Oh, you old scoundrel !" said Tom, as he grasped the old man by the neck, and shook him backwards and forwards.

" Murder ! murder ! Spare my life, kind sir, and I will tell you all about it."

" I want to hear no more. Hand the bundle over to me instantly, just as it is."

" Never !" roared the old man.

" Never ? We'll soon see about that,", said Tom. Here goes ! When I count five I shall fire this pistol, and off will go your head."

" Mercy !"

" One !"

" Help !"

" Two !—three !"

" Mercy—mercy ! Spare an old man's life ?"

" Four !"

Before Tom could count five, the old man shrunk down to the bottom of the chaise, apparently unconscious.

" Well," said Tom, " that makes it all the easier. I will relieve you of this bundle, old chap, and when you come to yourself you will find you have been eased of an inconvenient load. Forward, Daisy—forward, lass !"

With a bound, Daisy sprung forward, and Tom, quite satisfied with his little adventure, began to ask himself what he should do next.

Just as Tom had put this very pertinent question to himself, he became aware of the sound of carriage wheels.

" Oh !" said Tom to himself, " the night's sport is not yet over."

It did not take many minutes to let Tom see that the usual canter of Daisy would suffice to bring him up with the coach ; so he felt at that moment a conviction that he could, at any time, get up to the side of, and astonish, the occupants, whoever they might be.

In this way, then, on he went, keeping the vehicle just in view, and waiting until the most unfrequented part of the road should afford him the best possible opportunity of putting his plans into execution.

The carriage now seemed to go at a rapid rate —perhaps the horses thought they were going homewards, and did their work more energetically.

Tom had slightly to increase his speed.

A gloomy part of the road was just nigh at hand.

Tall trees on each side nearly met overhead, forming a natural leafy arch, and a trickling, rivulet ran by the roadside.

There was no house near, and interminable fields seemed to stretch away to the right and left as far as the eye could reach.

Another moment, and Tom dashed up to the side of the carriage, and called out in a loud voice

to the coachman, " Stop, coachman, or you will get an ounce of lead in your brains !"

" Oh, lor', who's that ?" said the coachman, as he pulled up at once in a fright.

A man's head was suddenly projected from one of the windows of the carriage, and a voice called out to the coachman, " Go on—go on, coachman ! On your life, go on !"

" I can't sir," said the man. " Here is a highwayman, with a pistol as long as my arm."

" Go on, I say !" still roared the occupant of the carriage.

" No, he won't !" said Tom, as he let down the window of the coach,—" he will not go on !"

" Who are you ?" asked the voice which had just issued such peremptory orders to the coachman.

" A highwayman !" said Tom. " Come, come, sir—no nonsense ; you must have guessed who I was long before this."

Tom stooped down and looked into the carriage, and was surprised to see that it contained also a lady.

While Tom was taking this cursory glance in at the carriage window, he saw the gentleman draw a pistol stealthily from a pocket in the breast of his coat.

" Take that !" he said, as he levelled it at Tom, and fired at the moment.

Tom, young as he was, had had too many pistol shots discharged at his head to be much alarmed at this one, and with a cool dexterity that few men could have effected, he moved aside just in time to avoid it.

The horses in the coach were a little alarmed at the noise of the discharge, and began to plunge, so Tom called out to the coachman in a threatening tone, " Get down, coachman, and hold your horses' heads, or it will be the worse for you."

" Oh, lor', yes, sir !" cried the coachman ; " anything you like sir, so that you won't put that ounce of lead your worship's honour spoke of in my brains, sir—that's all, sir !"

The coachman rolled off his box, and held the horses by the head ; and then Tom, looking into the vehicle, said, " If you would like another shot at me, pray have it at once, my good sir, and satisfy your mind. My turn is sure to come, but I am in no sort of hurry about it, I beg leave to assure you."

The lady uttered a scream.

" Now, sir," said Tom " be quick, if you please. You know what I want."

" You are a highwayman, you say, and want to rob us. Do so, and go your way. Give him what you can, my lady. I have no money myself, but you can give him all you have. I didn't mean to shoot you."

Tom opened the door of the carriage, and he said fiercely, " Come out—come out, I say !"

" No, no ! I tell you I didn't mean to shoot you ; it was all a mistake."

Tom hesitated a moment, but springing from Daisy's back, he made a dash at the legs of the gentleman, and fairly dragged him out on to the roadway.

Desperation now lent the gentleman courage, which he was far from possessing in its better and more ennobling condition, and he, with a yell of rage and despair, clung to Tom, and tried his utmost to throw him to the ground.

CHAPTER CCXCVII.

TOM RIPON CHASTISES A COWARD, AND OBTAINS SOME VALUABLE BOOTY.

THERE is little doubt but that if the coachman had come to the assistance of his master, Tom might have been overcome in the encounter; but although he had quitted his horses, he was by far too much alarmed to interfere in the brief contest that was raging between Tom Ripon and his master.

Tom Ripon had profited by the many lessons given him by his friend Ogle, who had once been an expert thief-taker. He, therefore, knew how to lay hold of a struggling man better than most folks.

By a kind of sleight of hand he got hold of the gentleman by the back of the neck with his

No. 96.—EDITH HERON.

left hand, and then, by severely kicking him, he drove him close to the little rivulet by the road-side, which we have already mentioned.

It was then that the gentleman, finding he was in the hands of a man who was his master in strength—for Tom looked much older than he really was—called out in a voice of wild, shriek-ing agony, " Murder! murder!"

It was but twice that Tom permitted that cry to ring through the night air.

Taking a holster pistol from the ample skirt-pocket of his coat, Tom placed the muzzle about an inch from the head of the gentleman as he said, "Now, sir, I want your ill-gotten gains, and shall not allow you many minutes. You see I know you."

Now Tom was speaking at random, for he had no idea of ever having met the man in his life before; but he fancied he looked like a disre-putable kind of man, and, as fortune would have it, Tom was right, for the man was an inveterate, unprincipled gambler and sharper.

"Now, sir, be quick!" said Tom, still keeping the muzzle of the pistol close to his eyes.

"Yes," gasped the man. "You—you know me?"

"I do. I know you are a rascal, and so I have no sort of hesitation of at once ridding society of your presence."

"Mercy!"

"Ha, ha! Mercy? Why that is a good joke! Why, my dear sir, you can have no idea of who you are speaking to when you ask mercy of me."

"Who are you, then?"

"That doesn't signify," replied Tom. "Hand over your plunder."

The man saw that he was at a disadvantage, so he handed to Tom a pocket-book and a watch.

"Is this all?" said Tom.

The man was silent; and then he said, after reflecting for a few moments, "Yes, all—all."

"I don't believe you. I shall go and search the carriage, and if I find anything secreted there I will return and blow your brains out."

"Stop!—oh, stop!"

"Well, what now?"

"There is some money in one of the pockets of the carriage. I had forgotten that until this minute."

"Oh, indeed! Well, then, come along with me and find it."

As Tom said this, he laid hold of the man by the collar of his coat, and dragged him towards the carriage.

A very few minutes sufficed to put Tom in possession of the whole of the gains of the gambler.

"That'll do," said Tom, as he counted a roll of bank notes into his pocket with one hand, while he still held the pistol in the other. "That'll do; and now good night."

Tom had no difficulty in recovering Daisy. A word from him brought the intelligent creature to his side with a bound.

"Woa, Daisy!"

In another moment Tom and Daisy were flying down the lane at a tremendous rate, and were lost to the wondering gaze of the coachman, who had lain quietly beneath the carriage ever since Tom had told him to get off his box, but who now scrambled to his feet, crying, "Stop him! stop him!"

"Hold your noise, idiot!" shouted the man in the coach. "If you had not been such a coward, we might easily have got the better of the villain."

"Lor', sir, what was a poor fellow to do? Didn't he fire two pistols right through my head, and tell me if I dared to get up he'd kill me on the spot?"

"Fool! idiot!" roared the man. "I wish he had killed you. Drive home, instantly."

"All right, sir. I wish you hadn't stopped me just now, that's all; I should have had him, and no mistake."

"Drive home!" again roared his master.

The man mounted the box, and after some little delay managed to make both the horses understand that they were to move on, and not consider that they had come to the end of their journey, as they seemed inclined to do.

The night, as we have stated, was a dark one, and it was indeed just such a night as suited highwaymen.

If it had been positively bad weather, which it was very far from being, Tom would have felt that such a state of things was against him, inasmuch as it would have kept people at home.

But such was not the case, and the night was not one to deter any one from going out in it, whether on business or on pleasure.

So Tom now put Daisy to speed, and trotted as far as Ealing Common before he thought it at all wise to look about him for anything in the shape of an adventure.

"Now," he said, "I have the road pretty well to myself, I reckon, and we will see what we can do, eh, Daisy?"

Hardly had Tom uttered these words when he became aware of a strange light flashing across his path, and on glancing about him he found that it came from a lantern that some one was holding up at a gate in a garden wall, a good distance from where he then was.

Tom did not by any means wish to be seen, so he took a round course to get out of the way of the direct rays of the lantern, and then he slowly walked Daisy in the direction of the house to which the garden wall belonged.

By the aid of a clump of trees that grew close at hand, Tom was able to get so close to the door of the garden wall that he could see a man in the sort of undress of a gardener standing at it.

In a few minutes a female figure, with a shawl thrown over her head to protect her from the night air, came to the door.

Tom could hear their voices in the silence of that spot quite plainly, for at that time Ealing Common was very considerably more in the country than it is at the present day.

"Do you see the chaise, John?" asked the female.

"No, ma'am."

"But it is past ten."

"Yes, ma'am, it is."

"Then they really ought to be here. Dear me! dear me! I objected to her going."

"Yes, ma'am."

"Hold up the lantern higher, John."

"Yes, ma'am."

"It is a very dark night."

"Yes, ma'am."

"I wish you would go out on the common, John, and look for them. There is that ditch, you know, that people are so very apt to dive into."

"Yes ma'am; I should say they were."

"Then do you go out with the lantern, and if you hear the sound of wheels you can call out."

"Yes, ma'am."

John did not appear to be the very brightest specimen of domestic servants in the world; but he sallied out with the lantern in his hand, and kept looking about him as far as the halo of light which the lantern shed about the spot upon which he was as a kind of centre, would permit him.

In this way John approached pretty close to Tom Ripon, without knowing it.

"Hoy!" cried Tom.

"Hilloa! Who's there?"

"A gentleman," said Tom. "I am afraid, though, that I have lost my way on the common."

"Oh, have you, sir?"

"Yes. What house is that opposite? Is it called the Cedars?"

"Lor', no, sir! I don't know of such a place as that about here, sir. That there house opposite, sir, is Mrs. Grimstead's school for young ladies, sir."

"Oh, indeed!"

"Yes, sir."

"Are you looking for some one? I presume you are," added Tom, "as you have your lantern with you, my man?"

"Yes, sir; I are."

"Some of the young ladies, I suppose?"

"Yes, sir, I are."

"Ah! I know her very well. It is Miss ——Good gracious, I shall forget my own name soon! Miss—Miss——"

"Miss Johnson, sir."

"Oh, yes; Johnson—Johnson!" said Tom.

"Miss Amy Johnson, sir, as has been up to town to see her uncle, you know, sir, who is very ill, sir; and our boy Ted, as works in the garden with I, sir, and is a kind of a sort of a page, do you see, sir, to the young ladies, is with her in the pony chaise, sir, and brings I and her back, sir!"

Now, Tom had no intention of having anything to do with Miss Johnson and the chaise; and it was more for the love of mischief, and to pass the time, that he had entered into conversation with the servant; so now, wishing the man good night, he walked slowly off, making up his mind to wait patiently for some adventure.

With this view, then, he kept across the common, every road and path of which he knew so well, towards London; and just as he got in the rather narrow part of the road that leads towards Acton, he heard the grating sound of wheels approaching him from London.

"Perhaps this is the chaise," said Tom to himself, "with the boy Ned driving the young lady."

Tom placed himself close to the hedge, in a very dark part of the road.

The chaise—for it was the chaise—came on at a very creeping pace, and, to the surprise of Tom, it stopped just at the spot where he had chosen to halt at.

A young and sweet voice then said, "Why, Ted, won't Lightfoot go on?"

"Yes—oh, yes," almost groaned another voice; "I stopped him, miss."

"Then don't stop him again, my good Ted, I beg of you; but go on at once. You know I promised Mrs. Grimstead to be home by nine o'clock at the latest, and it has struck ten, as you yourself heard."

"Oh! oh! oh!" groaned Ted.

"Why, what is the matter, Ted?" asked the pretty voice again.

"Oh, Miss Johnson—oh, Miss Johnson! I've stopped Lightfoot, the pony, on purpose in this here quiet spot, miss. Yes, I've stopped him on purpose, because, Miss Johnson, I've got something to tell you, miss!"

"To tell me?"

"Yes; you, miss!"

"Nonsense, Ted! Go on."

"It's very likely, miss; but it's true, for all that!"

"Then, Ted, I will listen to anything you may have to say to-morrow; but not now."

"Oh, but it won't do to-morrow."

"Oh, yes, it will, Ted. Come, do drive on, there's a good Ted! I am so cold! If you don't, I shall certainly complain of you to Mrs. Grimstead!"

"You may, Miss Johnson—you may, and your Ted will be gone, miss, I can tell you that. But oh! oh! oh!"

"Are you ill, Ted?"

"Yes, miss."

"Then give me the reins, and I will drive the pony home. If you had told me at first that you were ill, I should have known what to do."

"But it isn't a regular sort of illness, Miss Johnson. Only look at everything about you. The waving trees, miss, that you can't see; the blue sky, as is now as black as pitch, miss: only look at the face of nature, miss."

"I think, Ted, your brains are turned, for I don't understand you."

"Then I—I—oh, I——"

"You what?"

"I'm blessed, miss, if I can say it!"

"Do give me the reins, Ted! If you do not, I will get out of the chaise and find my way home by myself!"

"Well, then, miss, I love you!"

"What?"

"I love you! Oh, Miss Johnson, from the first day—the first hour—the first moment that I clapped eyes upon you, I adored you; and I said to myself, 'Oh! ye heavens! but she's beautiful, and she shall some day be Mrs. Ted Smallboy!' Yes, I've said it now—I love you!"

Miss Johnson laughed, and so she could not reply.

"Oh, don't laugh now, Miss Johnson—Mrs. Ted Smallboy that is to be. This is just the opportunity."

"So I should think, Ted."

"Now, do you, though?"

"Yes; I'm sure of it, and so I can't help laughing!"

"Oh, but I didn't think you'd laugh!"

"Then what did you think, Ted?"

"That we might run off to Gretna Green, Miss Johnson, at once. Only look here, now! I have got fifteen shillings and sixpence in my pocket, and here is this here chaise and pony; and here is you, and here is me. Now what, miss, is to hinder us driving off all at once to Gretna Green and getting married, and being happy for ever after, as they say in the books?"

"Oh, nothing is to hinder us, Ted."

"Then let's be off."

"But there is one objection."

"Objection! What's that?"

"Yes, Ted; I won't go!"

"You—won't—go?"

"No!"

"Then you don't love your Ted?"

"Certainly not."

"Then I'll go and 'list for a soldier!"

"There is one objection to that, too, Ted."

"Oh, lor'! is there?"

"You are not big enough!"

And again came the little silvery laugh upon the night air.

With a deep sigh, Ted jerked the bridle of the pony, and had made two or three steps forward, when a man darted from the shadow of the trees, and cried out in high tones, "Halt!"

Ted pulled up.

"Another step, and you die!" said the horseman.

"Oh, murder! It's a highwayman, with a pistol as long as a rake!" cried Ted.

"Silence!"

"Yes, sir—yes, your worship!"

"Oh, then," cried Miss Johnson, "we are close at home. Drive on, Ted, or you risk your life and mine!"

"If he attempts to move an inch," said the horseman, "I will shoot him dead on the spot. Now, young lady, I want whatever valuables you may happen to have about you!"

"Help! help! help!" shouted the young girl.

"Hilloa!" cried Tom, darting from his hiding-place. "What cry was that?"

"Protect me!" cried the young girl. "Protect me, sir, if you be a gentleman! I am going to Mrs. Grimstead's, and this man will not let me proceed. Oh, protect me, sir!"

"I will soon do that," said Tom. "Who are you, sir, I should like to know?"

"Find out," said the horseman.

"Very well, we can soon do that. I suspect you are a highwayman!" said Tom.

The man at first seemed inclined to hold his ground, but perceiving that Tom had drawn a couple of holster pistols from Daisy's saddle, and had levelled them both at him, he seemed to think all of a sudden that discretion was the better part of valour, and giving his horse, which was undoubtedly a good one, an impulse with the spurs, he dashed off across the common.

Bang! went one of Tom's pistols.

CHAPTER CCXCVIII.

TOM RIPON OVERHEARS AND FRUSTRATES A PLOT.

"I DON'T think you will be annoyed any more now, my dear," said Tom, to the young lady in the chaise. "And as for you," he said, turning to the boy who was driving, "if you don't drive on as quickly as possible with this young lady, I shall discharge my other pistol at you, and teach you how to behave in future to young ladies who honour you so much as to allow you to drive them."

"Yes, sir! I'm off at once, sir—but she is very beautiful——"

"Silence!" shouted Tom. "Another such word, and I keep my word!"

Ned evidently thought it advisable to proceed as quickly as Lightfoot would allow of his doing, and in a few minutes Miss Johnson's adventures for that night were brought to a conclusion.

Tom now turned Daisy's head towards the Edgeware Road, and from there took a field-road to the right, and got amid the green lanes between Edgeware and Finchley.

Now, Tom knew the bearing of the roads thereabouts tolerably well, but so dark was the night that he could not be said to know very well each particular lane, so that the real fact was that, about three o'clock in the morning, he found himself what might with truth be called benighted.

Tom drew rein, and tried to look about him, but the most positive darkness reigned about the spot, and the only sound that met his ears was the sighing of the wind among the branches of the tall trees.

A feeling of great loneliness crept over Tom, and he began to wish most devoutly he had taken some other route.

He walked Daisy so close to the hedge on one side that the creature stepped into a little ditch, but the depth was so very trifling that Tom thought it best to let her stay there.

The sound of footsteps came each moment more and more clearly upon his ears.

In the course, then, of a few minutes he heard voices. One of those voices was that of a female, and the other that of a man.

It so happened that the persons who were talking had some little difference of opinion about something which they paused to discuss close to where Tom had drawn up, in order to hear what sort of people they might be who, at such an hour, were abroad in the green lanes.

"It's no use, I tell you, mother," said the man's voice. "I can't manage it that way."

"But it's the only way," said the female voice, "I tell you, it's the only way!"

"But there's such a lot of 'em, I tell you!"

"What of that?"

"What of that, mother? Why, everything of that! There's enough of 'em, I tell you, to swallow me, if they all set about it."

"Stuff! Nonsense! Coward!"

"Oh, it's all very well to say 'Stuff, nonsense, and coward,' but it's a fact, for all that—and I don't seem as if now I half liked the job."

"You fool!"

"Come, now, don't begin to abuse me, for that's of no sort of use. I like the girl's money well enough, and I like her well enough—but I don't like the danger. Come, now, think of some other sort of way of managing it, do."

"I can't," replied the female voice.

"Then I don't think it will be managed at all, for I don't seem as if I were at all equal to it."

"Ah, Sam, you don't understand me, I see."

"What on earth," thought Tom, "can all this be about, I wonder? I will listen a little longer.

Sam raised rather a little laugh when the old woman said he did not understand her, and he replied, "Oh, yes, I think I do, mother. You want me to run off with Miss Woods, from the school over yonder, under the pretence that her father is dying. I understand you well enough, and I'm afraid they will find me out."

"Good gracious! was ever anybody half so trying as you are? How could they find you out?"

"How?"

"Yes, how can they find you out?"

"Oh, a thousand ways. Girls are so knowing!"

"But, Sam, now just let me tell you how safe you are. Haven't I bought you a beautiful suit of groom's livery, which you have on now, by the by?"

"Yes—yes!"

"And how nice you look in them!"

"Stuff!"

"Not at all. I don't say it because you are my boy, but you know you are good-looking."

"Oh, well, I never doubted that fact, mother; and another little one into the bargain—and that is, that you are a woman of taste."

"And haven't I bought you that hat, with the silver lace round it and the cockade at the side of it—and don't you look as nice as nice can be?"

"Well?"

"Then don't talk to me about being found out, don't! Miss Woods is only fifteen years of age, and she is an orphan, and she has got ten thousand pounds, all of her own; and if you can once get off with her out of the school, and get to town with her, and to a very nice house in the City Road—where, thank goodness, there's no lodgers, just now—I'll take good care that she shall marry you!"

"Well, mother, you are clever, I grant you; but what, suppose——"

"Suppose what?"

"Why, suppose everything goes right, and you get her to our house, and then she turns out as obstinate as a pig, and won't be persuaded to marry me?"

"Indeed!"

"Well, she may, you know, mother."

"Well, then, my dear Sam, I'll put something into her tea—that is all!"

"Something into her tea?"

"Yes, my dear Sam!"

"Why, you don't mean to say, mother, that you would go to poison her, do you?"

"Oh, dear, no; but something that'll make her so sleepy and so stupid that there'll be no sort of difficulty after that."

"Oh!"

"Yes, you may say oh! but I know how to manage all that."

"Well, you are clever, mother, and no mistake, so I think I will consent."

"That's right, Sam; and mind you have all right what you are going to say."

"Oh, yes—yes!"

"But if you make any blunders they will find you out, and then all our trouble and expense will go for nothing at all."

"Oh, trust me! I am to say that I have come from Captain Jordan for Miss Woods, as he is at the point of death, and cannot die happy unless he sees her."

"Now you know the way to the gate bell, and all you have got to do is to say what you have just repeated to me."

"Oh! I shan't forget."

"Then go at once, and I shall not be far off, and the coach will wait for us near; so be off at once."

The woman and her hopeful son went along the lane, leaving Tom a little amused by what he had overheard.

"You're a couple of beauties!" said Tom, when they were at a sufficient distance to enable him to speak without what he said being overheard by them. "You are a nice couple; but I'll try to put a stopper upon this little transaction."

A pitchy darkness now reigned around, and Tom was at a loss to think how he should find the house which had been spoken of by the old woman and her hopeful son.

Just as Tom, however, was beginning to think that he must give up the idea of finding the house, the sky began to get of a hazy, streaky outline in one quarter of it, and presently there peeped out just one corner of a bright moon, and then, on his right hand, Tom saw the chimney pots of what appeared to be rather a large mansion among a thick grove of trees in the meadows, and although it was certainly about twenty yards off, yet he could not doubt but it was the school.

"I will rouse them," said Tom.

With this view Tom walked Daisy slowly along, and presently came to a little gate, which, upon dismounting, he found he could easily lift off its hinges.

"That'll do," said Tom.

In another moment he had lifted the gate, and thrown it down in the meadow, and then he, with ease, walked Daisy past the obstruction.

To mount again, and to trot towards the house, was the work of another moment.

All was darkness in the mansion; and it was in vain that Tom sought for some window at which the presence of even a faint light might lead him to suppose that some one was up.

There was no time to lose; and Tom tied Daisy to a branch of a tree close at hand, and then he dashed up a flight of steps to a door on which there was a handsome balcony.

After a little searching, Tom found a bell-handle, and gave it a couple of as vigorous pulls as he possibly could; and, in fact, he heard, each time that he did so, a bell ring very loudly and violently somewhere or another inside the house.

"That'll rouse them!" said Tom.

For a time all was still; and then a window just above the balcony opened, and a female voice demanded, "What do you want?"

"Open the door, my dear madam," replied Tom, "and you shall know all."

"Go away, young man, go away; or I will set the house dog upon you."

"You will not open the door?" asked Tom.

"Certainly not."

"Then all is lost."

"Yes, your trouble is lost, that is all, young man. So you can go back as wise as you came."

"Well, madam," said Tom, "if you will not allow me to protect you against possible violence, I will put you upon your guard against possible fraud. You have a young lady in this house of the name of Woods?"

"Well, what of that?"

"Then you will soon have an application," said Tom, "at the front door of your house, from a pretended servant in livery, who will come and say that her father is at the point of death, and that he desires to see her at once. If you yield to that application, and let her go, you at once place her in the hands of fiends in human shape, and you will never see her more."

"Is this possible, young man?"

"It is true."

"But—but——"

"Nay, madam," said Tom, "you can take the warning or not, just as you please; I have done my duty."

"Stay a moment. Let me look at you."

"Very well," said Tom, "I am quite willing."

The schoolmistress came out on to the balcony; and as well as the very faint light of the moon enabled her, she took a look at Tom, who stepped out on to the lawn, in order to enable her to do so.

"Well, you don't look like a young man that ought not to be trusted, I must confess. Who are you?"

"A gentleman," said Tom. "If you feel that you can protect yourself and your house, after what I have told you, I will no longer trouble you, madam, for I've my own affairs to look to; but if you cannot, I will adopt any course you think proper."

"Oh, sir, you terrify me!"

"Well, well! Have you the means of defence?"

"No, no; indeed I have not!"

"Is there no man in this house?" asked Tom.

"Man in this house? Certainly not."

"Then what do you propose to do?"

Before any reply could be made to this question, there came a ring at the gate bell in front of the house, and the consternation of the schoolmistress at this sudden confirmation of Tom's story was very great.

"Oh, if I could truly believe you, I would open the door, and get you to come in and afford us all the assistance and protection you could."

"Well, my good lady," said Tom, "I have no means of convincing you of my good faith. If you won't believe me, I can't help it, although I shall be sorry to leave you in such an unprotected state."

"I will trust you—you shall come in; I will not, I cannot doubt you any longer. Heaven forgive you, if you are deceiving me! I will open the door directly."

Another ring at the bell in front of the house gave another shock to the nerves of the schoolmistress, and she hastened to let in her ally from the back of the house.

The schoolmistress was evidently in a state of great agitation; and she was very anxious to catch a glimpse of Tom's face, in order that she might come to some judgment about the propriety of the course she was pursuing.

By the light of the wax candle she had with her, she soon got that glance, and then she said at once, "Oh, I feel that I may indeed trust you. You cannot deceive me."

"Indeed, I will not," said Tom.

"Come in—come in at once; but you are very young to defend us."

Tom drew himself up, as he said, "I am young, but I am well armed; and I have that without which all the mature strength in the world is valueless."

"What is that?"

"Courage, ma'am."

Tom had fairly now got into the house, when a very loud knock as well as a ring came at the door of the mansion; and from somewhere on the floor above, there arose quite a commotion.

"Madam," said Tom, "you will have the goodness, I am sure, to permit me to reply to the person who is now at your door, so very importunately demanding admission to this house?"

"Oh, yes—yes."

"Very good, then. There will be no danger, then, allow me to assure you."

The confusion above was now rather on the increase than otherwise; and as Tom glanced up the staircase, he could see quite a collection of heads and eyes looking down upon him.

He could hear, too, occasional expressions from the young girls concerning himself which very much amused him.

"Oh, isn't he a love?" said one.

"Yes, he is," said another. "Only look at him, Lucy! He must be some officer."

These and such like expressions of admiration of Tom from the school girls came so thick and fast down the stairs, that at last the mistress called out, "Young ladies, I am surprised at you. Repair to your dormitory instantly, and close the door!"

"Yes, ma'am."

"Go, then."

"But, if you please, ma'am, we are all in such a fright about the thieves."

"Thieves! There are no thieves; go directly."

"No," said Tom, looking up, "there is no danger to any of you now; for I am here to protect you all."

"There! you hear that," said the mistress. "Now you can all go to bed again."

The girls still lingered.

"Oh, dear! oh, dear," said the mistress. "They don't mind me in the least to-night."

"I'll soon make them all go, ma'am," said Tom. "Young ladies, since you are too much alarmed to go to bed, I'm coming to help you all to do so. Here I am!"

Tom, as he spoke, made a dart at the staircase, and got up some half-dozen steps, when all the girls, with loud screams, disappeared in a moment.

Another ring at the bell, and another knock at the door, now announced that the pretended groom was not disposed to give up the plan of carrying off Miss Woods, just because there was some delay in opening the door.

"Oh! there it is again," said the schoolmistress. "I am afraid we shall all yet be murdered."

"Oh, dear, no, you won't," said Tom.

"But what will you do, sir?"

"Have you any window above that commands a view of the front door?"

"Oh, yes! yes!"

"Then it is from that that I would rather let the rascal see you are not so unprotected as he seems to suppose."

"But oh! how can I take you to the window above, when that is the very room in which the young ladies sleep?"

"Well, ma'am; I don't want to eat the young ladies."

"But it would be dreadful—so unusual——"

"Nonsense, ma'am—nonsense!" said Tom, losing patience. "I will follow you, and you can explain to the young ladies that I am neither an ogre nor a mad bull; but that it is absolutely necessary that I should intrude into their room for a few moments."

The schoolmistress led the way up the staircase, followed closely by Tom, who, as the reader knows, was the very spirit of fun and frolic, and who enjoyed the whole transaction amazingly.

"Will you wait here one moment, sir, if you please?" said the schoolmistress, when they reached the dormitory door.

"Certainly."

The schoolmistress opened the door, and Tom heard her say, "Ladies, it cannot be helped. There is some one at the door who has evil designs upon us; and the young gentleman who has come to protect you cannot see who it is, or tell him to be off, except from one of these windows."

A general scream followed this speech.

"So, young ladies, don't be shocked; for it cannot be helped, I assure you."

"Let's put our heads under the clothes," said one."

"Yes, and blow out the light," said another.

"Silence!" said the schoolmistress.

"Here I am, young ladies," said Tom, stepping into the room. "I hope you are quite well."

There was no direct reply to this for a moment or two, but there were very many suppressed giggles. Then a voice said, "Pretty well, sir, thank you! How are you?"

There was now a general laugh, and Tom thought it was high time to go to the window to question the intruder.

CHAPTER CCXCIX.

TOM RIPON PUNISHES AN INTRUDER.

THERE can be no doubt but that such a circumstance happening at the school was really, even with all its alarm and all its terrors, one of the pleasantest diversions of the monotony of such a course of existence that could possibly be imagined.

Every eye was fixed on Tom, and his really handsome appearance fascinated more than one of the young ladies in the dormitory.

He opened the window—which was a French casement one—and stepped out upon a balcony outside it, and cried out, in a loud voice, "Who's there?"

"Me, sir!" said the mock groom.

"What do you want, fellow?" Tom demanded, fiercely.

"Please, sir, I come from Miss Woods' father, sir, the Captain. He is at the point of death; and he says, sir, that he can't leave this world, sir, without giving his daughter his last blessing, you see, sir!"

Now this was spoken quite loud enough for all the young ladies to hear it, and consequently Miss Woods heard it among the rest. Such a message was sure to seize upon her imagination; and forgetful of everything but the terrors and the sympathy with which it inspired her, she sprang from her bed, and was by the side of Tom Ripon in a moment, crying out, "Yes, yes—I am here! Oh, my dear papa! I will come at once—I will come at once!"

"Thank you, miss!" said the pretended groom. "I've got a coach waiting, if you please, miss!"

"Hush!" said Tom—and he flung his arm round the young girl, and half carried her back into the room. "Go to bed again, I beg of you, my dear girl! It is all false!"

"False?"

"Yes, I assure you it is!"

"But my poor papa——

"Allow me to assure you that it is all a fabrication. Your father has sent no such message; it is nothing but a trick to get you away from the school."

"Oh, are you sure of that?"

"Quite—quite sure!" said Tom.

"I am so frightened!" said Miss Woods, clinging to Tom.

"Come, come!" said Tom, gently. "Don't tremble so! Let me help you back to bed."

Tom now led Miss Woods to the side of the bed, for the poor girl was too much agitated to think of who was attending her; and then he fairly lifted her into it, saying, as he did so, "Come, come; make yourself quite easy. Be assured your father never sent for you!"

"Oh, yes, yes! Thank you!"

Tom now returned to the balcony, and called out, "Hilloa!"

"Yes, sir," said the groom.

"You can go back, and take all our compliments to the Captain, and tell him Miss Woods declines to obey his orders."

"Declines to obey his orders?"

"Yes."

"Oh, but, sir——"

"It's of no earthly use your talking there," said Tom. "If you were to stay for a month, she would not come."

"Sir, sir!" said somebody, pulling Tom by the sleeve,—"sir, if you please!"

Tom looked round, and saw, standing on the balcony by his side, an unusually stout female, with a couple of pails of water.

"Bless me! and who may you be?" asked Tom.

"Please, sir, I'm the cook; and hearing as there was murderers and thieves, I got up; and, if you please, sir, and many thanks to you, sir, for coming to protect poor, defenceless females, I'll just throw these here pails o' water on 'em!"

"Hush!" said Tom. "You shall! All right! I'll just speak to the rascal again, and hear what he has to say!"

"Do, sir, if you please, sir!"

"Now, are you off, fellow?" shouted Tom.

"Dear me, no, sir! But you don't mean, sir, as to say that the young lady is so hard-hearted that she won't come to see her poor father, who is going to breathe his last, sir?"

"She is, though," said Tom.

"Then, sir, it will be a terrible reproach to her, in time to come, sir! I'm only a servant, sir; but it seems to me as you ought to make her come! She will be back here again before the morning, if you like, sir; and if so be as you'll call up the school-mistress, I'm certain sure she won't refuse to let her come."

"Yes, she will; so you have your answer at once. I am here at all times to defend this house; so if you thought it was defenceless, you have made a very great mistake."

"Oh, lor', sir, you don't suspect me of anything wrong—do you, sir?"

"Not at all," said Tom.

"Then let the young lady speak for herself; and if she don't want to come, why, of course, I'll go away."

"No, I shall not," said Tom.

"No?"

"I won't!" said Tom.

"You'd better mind what you're about! It's no business of yours; and if you don't let her come, I'll——"

"Hold!" cried Tom. "Do you threaten me?"

"I do!"

"And what then?"

"Why, then, I ain't going to be put off in this way; and I tell you, Mr. Jackanapes, whoever you may be, that I will come into the house, and I will see Miss Woods herself!"

"You shall not," said Tom, coolly.

"Oh, we'll soon see that! There is one of the windows on the ground-floor that I can get in at, for I see that it is a little way open."

"Now look!" said Tom.

Dash! went one of the pails of water right over the groom, and with such a fair aim did it come, and there was such a deluge of it, that it took away his breath for a moment, and he stood stock still.

Dash! went the other.

"There!" said the cook, as she flung the empty pail out at him; "I hope as you feel a little damp now, you horrid wretch!"

"Murder!—oh, oh!—murder!"

The pail had fallen right over the fellow's head, and he roared and plunged about with it on him, without really knowing what he was fighting with. At length he fell down, and the pail rolled off his head, and he sat on the garden path, opposite to the door of the house, half dead with fright, and drenched to the skin.

"Well," said Tom,—"well, my friend, how do you feel now; or do you want another bath?"

"Oh, no, no!"

"Very good. If you don't be off now out of these premises as quickly as possible, I will put an end at once to the state of misery you are now in, by shooting you. I can see you nicely, and am now taking aim at you with a pistol I can depend upon."

"Oh, mercy! Oh, don't! I'm going! Oh, murder!"

The cowardly rascal rolled over several times; then, scrambling to his feet, he made a rush to get away, and Tom, by way of completely frightening him, fired one of his pistols in the air.

The moment he heard the report of the pistol, the rascal uttered such a yell, that if Tom had not felt quite sure that he had fired some twenty feet over his head, he must have thought him a dead man.

In another minute the school premises were perfectly clear of the intruder, and Tom closed the window, and turned with a smile into the dormitory of the young girls again, who were not a little alarmed at the pistol shot.

"I think you are all quite safe now," said Tom; "and, therefore, as my presence here may be an intrusion, I will leave you, if you please."

The girls did not speak.

"Young ladies, good night," added Tom; "or rather I ought to say good morning, for I perceive the daylight is very close at hand."

Tom made towards the door, and then, making a very low bow, he left the room, closely followed by the schoolmistress, who was not a little pleased at the general good conduct of the handsome young gentleman, as well as at the service that had been rendered to her establishment by him.

"I don't know how to thank you, my dear sir," she said, "for you have indeed done me a great service."

"Don't mention it," said Tom. "I'm only too glad to think I have been the means of saving one of the young ladies of your establishment from disgrace and ruin. And now farewell, madam; perhaps we may meet again."

Tom now mounted Daisy, and, putting her to a smart trot, soon reached the neighbourhood of Whitcombe House, where he found Ellen anxiously watching for him.

CHAPTER CCC.

JONATHAN WILD AND WARRINGDALE MAKE A COMPACT.

WE must now return to Jonathan Wild.

It is evening, and from the appearance of wine-bottles, glasses, and pipes scattered on the table, it would seem that Jonathan expected visitors.

He is seated in an old-fashioned easy chair, covered with chintz, which looks rather the worse for wear; his feet are placed upon another chair, and altogether the great thief-taker looks tolerably comfortable.

"Ha! ha! ha!" comes in low, guttural sounds from his lips.

Evidently Jonathan Wild's reflections are, in his own estimation at least, rather clever than otherwise.

"Ha! ha! ha! He thinks he has succeeded in blinding me to the fact of Felix Heron's existence. The young scoundrel! Ha! ha! ha! Tom Ripon, a mere boy, to suppose that his wit was a match of Jonathan Wild! Ha! ha! ha!"

Jonathan Wild's laugh, however, was anything but mirthful, and to judge from the manner in which he set down a glass which he had just drained of its contents, one would have thought he was anything but in an amiable mood.

"He is late," he muttered to himself. "I want company; this room is gloomy. I wish he would come."

At this moment a bell rung.

"Ah! That's Warringdale."

"The very same," said that personage, entering the room. "Ah! I see you were expecting me."

As Warringdale spoke, he seized one of the

bottles which contained brandy, and pouring out nearly half a tumblerful, he drained it.

"That's done me good, Wild; and now I want to speak to you about Felix Heron."

"Oh!"

"Why, what do you mean by that? You don't seem to care to hear what I have to communicate," said Warringdale. "We thought he was dead, you know."

"No, we didn't—at least, I didn't."

"Well, then, why on earth, man, have you been allowing him to live in comfort and security all this time, when, by giving him up to justice, we might have obtained such a reward as his capture would have afforded us?" asked Warringdale.

"I had my own reasons for letting things take their own course," replied Jonathan Wild.

Warringdale looked at him suspiciously; then he said, "Tell me, Jonathan Wild, are we to part

company here, after having worked so far together, or are we still to work in concert?"

"Just as you will," said Wild; "but if we are to work together, it is necessary that we should have no secrets from each other. Tell me what reason you have for supposing that Felix Heron still lives."

"Because I have seen him," replied Warringdale, "too frequently of late to believe that it was a mere trick of the imagination, or to think that it was his ghost."

"Ghost! Bah, man! There are no such things," said Wild.

"Well, then, if there are no such things, as you say, why, then, Felix Heron is still in life, and is laughing at you and me, to think he is cajoling us both, while in reality he is going about at large enjoying himself."

"I doubt whether he is enjoying himself," said Wild, "because he is in constant dread of yet being made a prisoner, and taken to Newgate, where he knows but too well he will only remain just long enough to enable me to give the directions for his committal and condemnation."

"But where do you suppose he is?" asked Warringdale.

"Where you know him to be," said Wild, with a look about his eyes that made Warringdale drop his immediately.

"Well, you need not be so hard upon me, Wild. I came here on purpose to tell you all I knew or thought I knew about our enemy, and you seem to regard me as though I were anything but what I am—a friend."

"A friend!" sneered Wild.

"Why, what on earth are you taking up my words in that way for, Wild? I am as anxious as you can be to rid the world of him, and yet you seem as though you distrusted me. What ails you to-night? Here, take another glass of brandy, and be like yourself again."

Wild mechanically raised the glass to his lips, and drank off the brandy.

"Now," said Warringdale, "let us make our arrangements. How are we to proceed?—for we must bear in mind that we have not a fool to deal with in Felix Heron."

"Or Captain Fantome," said Wild.

"Right—right! I see we are both agreed as to his whereabouts. Now how are we to get at him?—watch for him, and so take him into custody?"

"No."

"No?"

"I have laid my plains," said Wild, smiling hideously,—"I have laid my plans. I will make him repent having played me so many tricks, and for having at one time made me almost believe that there were such things as supernatural appearances in this world."

A pallor spread itself over the features of Jonathan Wild as he uttered these last words.

"What are your plans, then, for unearthing this fox?" asked Warringdale.

"Ah! you have said it—unearthing the fox. I mean to smoke him out."

"Smoke him out? Do you mean to burn him out?"

"Even so. He shall have a little trouble and anxiety, too, for all the trouble and anxiety he has given me in his time."

"But he will escape?"

"Yes, he will escape from the burning flames, but he will then find that Jonathan Wild has made his own arrangements, and that there are such things as bull-dogs, who will be stationed round the burning pile in such a manner that escape will be impossible."

"Capital! capital! When will you do this!"

"Do what?"

"Set fire to this house—Whitcombe House."

"Never!"

"Never? What mean you."

"I shall not do it myself, but I shall depute some one else to do it."

"He must be some one whom you can trust fully, then," said Warringdale.

"I intend it should be. Some one whose interest it will be to place his death beyond all doubt. Somebody, in fact, who hates this man as much as I do."

"Ha! ha! ha!" laughed Warringdale. "We shall yet have the laugh on our side. Who do you intend to give the job to, eh?"

"To Lord Warringdale," said Wild, carelessly.

"To me? I—I——"

"To you, my Lord Warringdale, I said. What are you afraid of?"

"Oh, I am not afraid, only I—that is, I fancied——"

"That you are a coward!" shouted Wild. "You will willingly share the plunder, but you are too mean and cowardly to take a step that would put that plunder in our grasp. Bah!"

Wild rose and seized his hat.

"Stop, Wild, you are so strange to-night. There is no doing or saying anything to please you. What do you want me to do. Tell me, and I will do it."

"Indeed!"

"There you go again! I don't know what to make of you to-night."

"Let it pass—let it pass," said Wild, giving Warringdale his hand. "Let us be friends, or we shall never effect anything."

"That's something like. Now let us to business. What plan have you decided on, Wild?"

"I intend you to make your way into Whitcombe House by the stables, as you did once before."

"Ah! that time I failed in what I attempted."

A malignant look came over the features of Wild as Warringdale gave utterance to these words.

"Yes, did I not say you were a coward? Who but a coward would attempt to take the life of an innocent child?"

"Ah! you know that?"

"I do know it, Warringdale, and you may thank me for not at once knocking you on the head, and dashing your cowardly brains out."

Warringdale turned pale, and placed the table between himself and Wild.

"Tush, man!—you need not fear me now. Enough for me that you failed in your dastardly attempt. I care not to quarrel with you, for, as I told you just now, I intend to make you useful."

Warringdale looked somewhat more reassured.

"Tell me, Wild," he said, "what it is you want me to do, and I will do it."

"Well said! I shall begin to think you brave, Warringdale!" replied Wild, with a sneer.

Warringdale winced, but made no answer.

"You must effect an entrance into Whitcombe House, and when all is quiet you must contrive to set light to some of the draperies on the ground floor—or, at all events, you must produce a fire. I care not how, so that it be done effectually."

"And burn down Whitcombe House, do you mean?"

"And burn down Whitcombe House!" said Wild.

"But what will be the result?" asked Warringdale.

"Oh, I understand you. You would ask what you will get by it?"

"Exactly."

"Only this. In all probability the only obstacle which remains to you becoming the Earl of Whitcombe!"

"Then you want to kill Felix Heron?"

"I want to see him hanged!" replied Wild.

"Well, I don't half like the job, somehow. However, I don't mind trying; and, at all events, I know Felix Heron too well to have any fears as to my personal safety. I will try it—I will try it; but, as I have much to arrange before I enter upon this little affair, I will wish you good night, Wild."

The two villanous accomplices parted.

Lord Warringdale immediately directed his steps towards a low public-house in an obscure street, where he felt pretty certain of meeting with John Tarleton, with whom, indeed, he had an appointment.

Warringdale pulled his hat low down over his eyes as he entered the public-house, and inquired if a gentleman of the name of Smithson had made his appearance there.

"Yes, sir," replied the landlord. "He is now awaiting you in the parlour. There is a gentleman of that name, and he gave directions that if any one inquired for him he was to be shown in immediately. This way, if you please, sir."

"The gentleman you were expecting, Mr. Smithson," said the landlord, as he threw open the door of a dingy-looking apartment.

John Tarleton had his back towards the door, but, on being addressed by the landlord, he faced about and encountered the gaze of Warringdale, full of meaning.

"Thank you, friend," said John Tarleton. "Ah! I am glad to see you," he added, turning to Warringdale. "Here, landlord, bring us a bottle of your best old port, and see if you can find anything in the larder for supper while we are discussing the wine."

The landlord withdrew, well pleased with his guests.

"Gentlemen, evidently," he said, to himself; "though they don't look of much account, to be sure. But, then, what are looks?—it's the money that makes the man! Here, wife! wife! A bottle of that old crusted port we never touch except when we have such guests as these."

"A nice pair they seem, in good truth. I said they were a couple of ——"

"Hist, wife! What is that to us, so long as they've got money to pay for what they order? Their money is as good as the best man's going, isn't it?"

No sooner did Lord Warringdale and John Tarleton find themselves alone than the former said hurriedly, "I have seen Wild, and he is as assured as we are that Heron still lives."

"What do I care whether Wild believes it or not? What are we to do, is the question, in order to rid ourselves of his detestable presence?"

"I was just going to tell you, but you interrupted me. There is a way, and a way in which your aid would be most valuable."

"How?"

"We were talking it over, Wild and I, and he thought that the best method would be to smoke him out of Whitcombe House."

"Smoke him out? What mean you?"

"Set fire to the house, that's all; and when he is making his escape—which he will most assuredly try to do, with Edith and the child—Jonathan Wild means to pounce upon him with a strong party of his bull-dogs, take him prisoner, and carry him off to Newgate."

"And how am I to assist you, pray?"

"Why, we thought that we would keep watch outside while you contrived to enter the house by the back offices, and lie in concealment until all was quiet, and then it would be easy to set fire to a few handfuls of shavings saturated with oil, which I have no doubt you will find plenty of in the stables, and leave them to burn, say, in some little cupboard. Having accomplished this, you could then, of course, make your escape before there were any indications of fire; for it will probably take some time before the flames make any show."

"But supposing I should encounter Felix Heron himself in the meantime? What do you think is likely to happen then?"

"Oh, there's not the slightest fear of that, for he never visits the stables after dark, unless he happens to be going out."

"Then I'll do it to-night," said Tarleton; "for I owe Edith a grudge I am not likely soon to forget, and if her ladyship perish in the flames I shall not take it much to heart."

"Nor I either; but I should like to see Felix Heron die on the scaffold, so I hope he will get safe out of the house."

"Well, so long as we get rid of him, it does not much signify whether he perish in the flames or on the scaffold. It will be all one to us."

"True, true."

At this moment the landlord entered the room, bearing a bottle covered with dust and cobwebs, which sufficiently testified to the good condition of its contents.

"That's right, landlord. We will amuse ourselves with this while you prepare us a nice little supper; but mind, we must leave in less than an hour's time from now."

"All right, gentlemen. My wife is now busy preparing something which will, no doubt credit to the 'Old King's Head.'"

The two companions in wickedness now drew their chairs towards the table, and drank glass after glass of the really excellent wine which had been set before them.

* * * * * *

It is past midnight, and a stealthy figure might be seen hovering around the precincts of Whitcombe House.

It stoops, and places an eye to the key-hole of a gate which led into the stable yard.

It glances to the right and to the left, and then apparently satisfied that it was not observed, it commences to climb the rather steep wall that shuts in the outer offices of Whitcombe House from the narrow street that runs at the back of the premises.

Higher and higher glides that figure until it reaches the top, and then again it seems to take a glance about and around before making its final descent on the other side.

An attentive listener would, in a few minutes, have heard a heavy thud on the other side of that gate as the figure now leapt from the slight hold his foot had retained in the wall.

All was then still.

John Tarleton—for, as the reader has already surmised, it was he—crept along almost on all-fours until he reached the shelter of a kind of outhouse, used as a sort of storehouse by Tom Ripon for stowing away superfluous articles which were for use in the stable and harness-rooms, such as oil, bits of rag, pieces of stick, and any kind of rubbish that was not exactly to be classed in the category of useless articles.

John Tarleton drew a match from a box he carried in his pocket, and having ignited it, gazed around him, in order to see what kind of abode was to be his probably for the next few hours.

Suddenly he crouches down close to the wall, for he hears a footstep, and fear takes possession of his craven heart.

And truly he had reason to tremble in every limb, for now he hears a voice the tones of which he recognises but too well.

"Yes, Tom, as you seem to make such a point of doing so, I have no objection to your accompanying me."

The tones were those of Heron.

What if they should have occasion to enter his temporary abode?

The voices are further off, and John Tarleton hears them unlock the stable-door, and Daisy and another horse are led into the stable-yard.

There is a pause in the whispered conversation, and John Tarleton devoutly wishes he had not undertaken the affair.

"Are you ready, Captain?" he hears Tom ask.

"Yes, Tom," replies the voice of Felix Heron; "but there is a weight upon my heart to-night, and I seem as though I should linger here, instead of doing what I feel to be a duty."

"Oh, come on, Captain," said Tom. "You've often felt like that before, and nothing has come of it. It's because you've had no exercise for so long."

"May be that it is so, Tom. I am ready."

John Tarleton had the unspeakable satisfaction of hearing the horses led out of the stable, and the gate closed behind them.

He breathed more freely.

"That's just as I would have had it," he murmured to himself. "I shall, at least, have no one stronger than myself to oppose me. I will make my way into the house now, and seek an interview with my sister. Sister, indeed! A pretty sister she has ever shown herself to be! Yes, yes, Edith Tarleton, I will seek you, and wring from your fears a sufficiency to make me amends for whatever risks I may run this night."

He walked towards the servants' entrance, and found the outer door yielded to his touch.

"So, so!" he said to himself. "Fortune favours me to-night!"

He entered, and found himself in a stone passage that ran the whole length of the basement, and then he came to the stone steps which led to the upper regions of the mansion.

A little oil lamp lighted this passage, and John Tarleton, therefore, had no difficulty in finding his way to the hall, and thence up the grand staircase of Whitcombe House.

On the first landing he paused, undecided which room to enter. At last he determined to try the door of the nearest that presented itself.

As he did so, the door slightly creaked on its hinges.

John Tarleton paused to listen.

All was silent as the grave.

In which room should he seek his intended victim?

Where was Edith?

Where was that fond mother who, to save her little one, would willingly have coined her heart's blood?

"Ha, ha! Countess of Whitcombe!" muttered John Tarleton to himself. "If I drive not a hard bargain with you this night, it shall not be my fault."

He entered the room, but it was tenantless.

CHAPTER CCCI.

EDITH AND HER CHILD ARE SAVED BY JONATHAN WILD.

THE apartment in which John Tarleton found himself was a kind of study. Between the windows was an old-fashioned bureau.

A desire to look into that bureau took possession of him, hoping to find therein, if not money, at least something that might be valuable.

He approached, and was glad to find that he could easily open it; but he was disappointed to find that it contained nothing but a few old books, a few manuscripts, pieces of twine, and such like useless articles.

"Bah!" he said, with a look of disgust; "there is nothing there. But stay! Let me see what is in this drawer; it seems as though it were full of something."

He drew out a long drawer at the bottom of the bureau, and found that the contents were carefully covered over with some sheets of brown paper.

He raised one corner, and to his surprise found that it was a complete highwayman's suit.

There was the scarlet coat, the lace ruffles, large boots, three-cornered hat, with a long white feather, the embroidered waistcoat and rich cravat, all complete.

"Ha! ha!" laughed John Tarleton; "I will dress myself in these, and perhaps, as my lady has a taste for highwaymen, I may be more welcome in this costume than in any other."

In an incredibly short space of time John Tarleton equipped himself as a knight of the road; and as he glanced at himself in a mirror that hung in the apartment, a smile of satisfaction was visible upon his features.

"I fancy I look rather the thing," he said to himself. "Surely my lady sister will consent this night to whatever I may propose. Ten thousand pounds, either in gold or jewels, I care not which, is all that I propose asking her for, and if she gives it me, then, perhaps, I may show her some means of escaping from this burning house, for it will most assuredly be a mass of ruins in less than six hours from this time."

There was a swaggering gait about John Tarleton as he walked from that apartment in order to seek Edith, where he hoped to find her, viz., in the drawing-room.

His hand was upon the handle of the door, but he paused to listen. Was he mistaken? No, that was surely Edith's voice, as she sung,

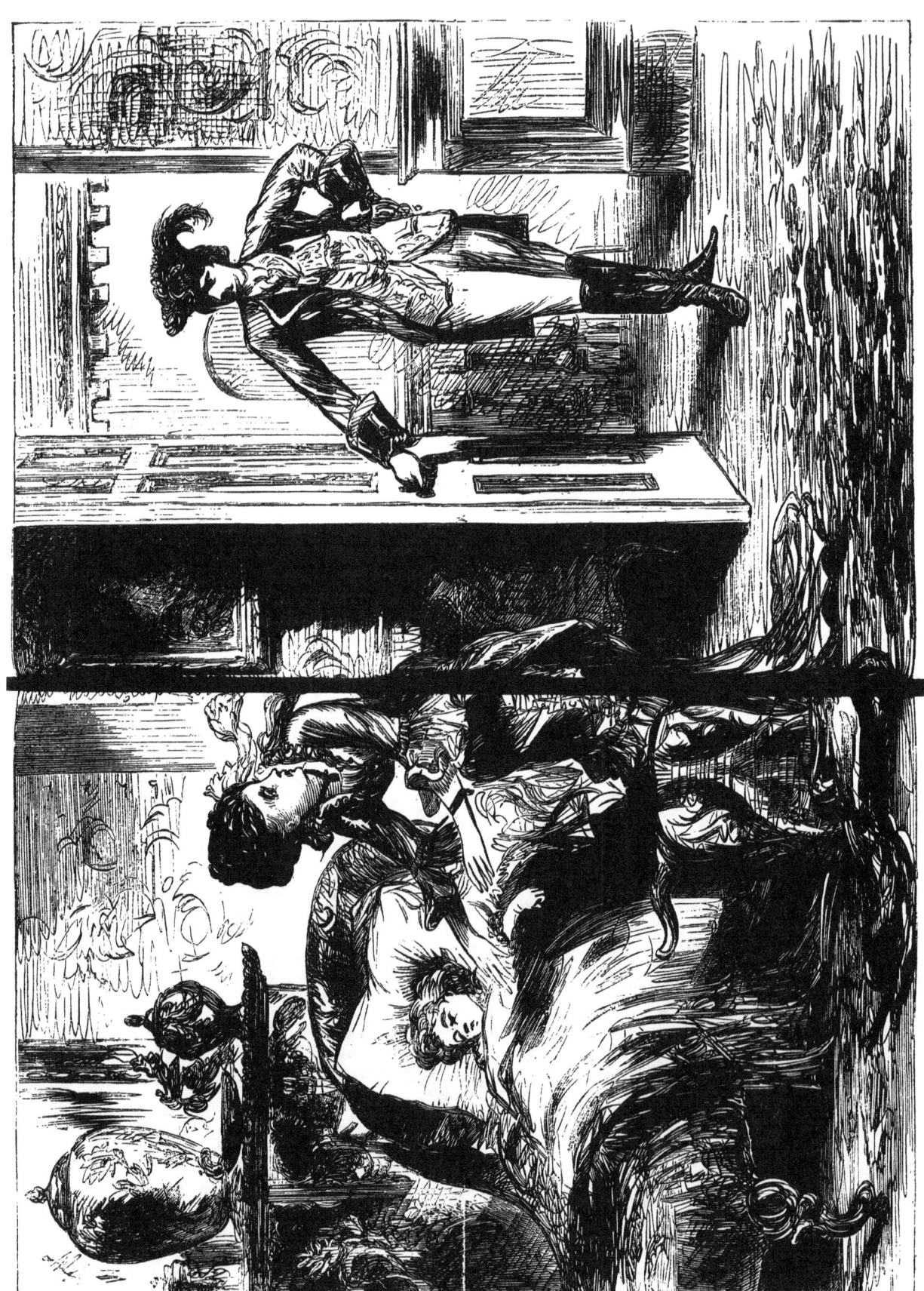

JOHN TARLETON MAKES A FINAL ~~ET~~ TO SUBDUE EDITH TO HIS WILL.

Presented Gratis with No. 97, of the New Edition of EDITH ~~he~~ Sequel to Edith the Captive; or, the Robbers of Epping Forest.

low and sweetly, a few lines of an old nursery ballad.

A sneering smile curled the lip of her unnatural half-brother as he said, "Oh, solacing herself with her child, to while away the time, I suppose."

He opened the door quickly, and stood before the terrified mother.

A half scream burst from Edith's lips as she sprung to her feet, clutching, as she did so, at the covering beneath which lay her precious child.

"Ah!" said John Tarleton, "have I startled you, Edith? Pardon me, but I was so anxious to see you, that I forgot everything else."

"Wretch! Leave me!"

"Why, come now, that is scarcely hospitable, when I have come to show you that in all things I consult your fancies. See here, Edith, I have actually, knowing your predilection for knights of the road, become one of them. Look at me; do you not think the costume becomes me?"

Edith was silent.

That brave heart shrunk from what might be in store for it to suffer; for well she knew that no help was at hand in that house. Oh, how she wished that Felix had not left her and his helpless child!

"Come, speak to me, Edith," added John Tarleton. "You surely do not bear malice?"

"Can I ever forget, John Tarleton, to whom I am speaking when addressing you?" asked Edith, with a shudder.

"Why, your brother, to be sure; and——"

"And the murderer of the father of my Felix!"

'Oh, stuff! I didn't come here to talk upon such gloomy topics."

"What then is your object, John Tarleton, in thus thrusting your unwelcome presence upon me?"

"Merely this, Edith; to tell you that I am just now desperately in want of money, and that I am resolved to have it from you before we part."

"And if I refuse?" asked Edith, gazing steadily at her unnatural brother.

"Simply this, that you will be left to perish—you and your child—in the ruins of this old mansion. Accede to my demands, and I will save you both."

"We are, neither of us, in any danger," quietly replied Edith, although her heart sunk within her at she knew not what.

"Ha! ha! ha!" laughed John Tarleton. "We shall see—we shall see. Even now I can detect the subtle smoke of the smouldering fire careering through the house."

As he said this he approached the door and threw it open, and immediately there came into the room a dense body of smoke.

"Oh, heaven!" shrieked Edith, "what means this? John Tarleton—brother—speak to me! Help me! Save my little one!"

"Give me the money first."

Bang! bang! bang! came at the outer door of the mansion.

"Felix!" cried Edith—"my Felix, save us, oh, save us!"

A sudden panic took possession of John Tarleton, who had a wholesome dread of encountering Felix Heron under any circumstances, more especially under the present; and he turned and fled through a door opposite to that which he had entered, and which led on to a back staircase.

In the meantime, Edith heard voices in the hall, and a hasty footstep ascended the grand staircase—a footstep which Edith did not recognise.

In another moment, Jonathan Wild stood before her, with a look of sorrow and compassion upon his features that she could not mistake, which at first made her almost doubt the evidence of her senses.

"Edith," he said, "thank heaven I am in time to save you and the child! I meant not to have done this. I was maddened by drink and rage, or I should never have planned such a means as this of getting Felix Heron, if he be in life, into my power!"

"What mean you, Jonathan Wild? Was it you, then, who plotted our destruction in so fearful a manner?"

"It was! it was! But I was not myself, I tell you, Edith! No sooner had Warringdale left me, than I repented, and hastened hither in order to put a stop to the fiendish project. For that, I am too late; but not too late to save you and his little one!"

As Jonathan Wild spoke, he stooped over the child, who was sleeping peacefully, as though nothing uncommon were taking place around it.

Wild raised the child in his arms as gently and tenderly as a woman; and taking Edith by the hand, he led her out upon the staircase.

A puff of smoke met them, and the effect was so overpowering, that Edith staggered backward a pace or two.

"Not this way! not this way!" cried Wild; "follow me;" and he turned and again entered the room they had just left, in order to reach the back staircase, through the door which John Tarleton had passed.

Jonathan Wild seemed to know the house as well, or better, than even Edith did, for he immediately made his way towards the back stairs.

Just as he did so, a heavy beam fell across their path, and cut off all retreat in that direction.

But what was it that made Jonathan Wild gasp for breath, and almost let the child fall from his encircling arms?

What was it that made him turn to Edith, to see if she, too, had witnessed the fearful sight that had met his gaze as the falling beam descended?

"No, no!" he muttered to himself; "she is in ignorance of it. She saw not that form she loves so well crushed and bleeding beneath that burning beam!"

In truth, Edith had seen—had heard nothing. Her eyes were riveted on her beloved child; for although Jonathan Wild appeared to wish to do all in his power to save her child, still she could not bring herself to trust that man who had so long persecuted both Felix and herself. But had she really seen the sight which had filled Wild with so much horror and regret, it would not so have affected her, for she knew that Felix was far away, whereas Wild, seeing only the scarlet coat, believed it to be none other than Felix Heron.

"This way! this way!" he shouted, dragging

Edith after him. "Hold on to me Edith, and speak not. The grand staircase is of stone, and we may yet descend it in safety. Why, oh, why did I come this way?" he almost shrieked.

They retraced their steps, and when they reached the hall they encountered Mrs. Ogle and Ellen, who were too much alarmed to be able to speak.

"You are safe, Edith," said Wild, as they reached the door of the mansion. "Ah! who is this? Ogle?"

"Lady Edith! Lady Edith!" was all Ogle could say.

"Take this child among you, and see that the Countess of Whitcombe is placed in safety somewhere."

"To Lady Castleneau's," said Edith, faintly; for now the reaction had begun to take place, and she felt as weak and helpless as a child.

"Shall I go with you, Lady Edith?" asked Ogle.

"No—oh, no! Call a hackney coach, and you, Ogle, watch for Felix to return, and break to him, as gently as may be, the sad calamity that has overtaken us."

"I will—I will, Lady Edith!" And after seeing Edith and her child, with Mrs. Ogle and Ellen, placed in a hackney coach, and giving the driver directions where they were to be taken, Ogle turned in the direction where he expected to see Heron and Tom Ripon return.

"I must walk briskly," said Ogle to himself. "I would not have him come within sight of that burning pile for more than the world contains. The dread that some dire accident had happened to those he holds so dear would be too much for even his brave heart."

And what became of Jonathan Wild when he had seen Edith and her child safely bestowed in the hackney coach that was to convey them in safety to Castleneau House?

Again he rushed into that burning house, and fearlessly made his way to the back staircase, in order again to look upon that still silent form, which he believed to be Felix Heron.

Might he not even yet be able to drag him from his perilous position, and perhaps save his life?

He would try.

He soon found himself kneeling by that figure, but after many ineffectual attempts to remove the beam he gave it up, for it would require much greater strength than he (Wild) unaided could bring to bear upon it.

"Help! help!" he shouted.

The roar of the flames alone responded to his cries.

"Alas, alas, it is too late—too late, Felix Heron! I never dreamt of thus causing your death!" he murmured, as he sank almost exhausted beside the dead. "I intended only to force you out—to penetrate the disguise you have so long worn as Captain Fantome, and then to have arrested you; for I wanted above all other things to let you see that I was a match even for you, Felix Heron. Then, when you felt and confessed that I had you entirely in my power, I would have stirred heaven and earth to have saved you. Nay, if necessary, I would have ransomed your life with my own; but it is too late—too late—too late!"

Wild clasped his hands over his eyes.

"Mr. Wild—Mr. Wild!" shouted several voices. "Where are you. Another minute, and you cannot be saved. Mr. Wild—Mr. Wild!"

"Ah, they call—the men I brought with me to take him prisoner."

"Mr. Wild—Mr. Wild!" again shouted some of his men, and two appeared at the head of the staircase.

"Here he is—here he is!" they shouted, as they leaped down the stairs, and between them raised Wild, and carried him out of what would most assuredly have been his grave.

Jonathan Wild was perfectly passive in their hands. He had swooned.

* * * * * *

The moon had not risen. The sky, which had been calm and serene when Felix Heron and Tom Ripon had left Whitcombe House, was now covered over with long lines of dark grey cloud, heavy and near the earth, when the two horsemen entered a shady lane which led by a new cut across the country to London.

It was a dim and sombre scene that met the eye of Felix Heron—unsatisfactory to the eye, but exciting to the imagination. Everything was vague and undefined in the shadows of that hour, and the long streaks of deeper and fainter brown which varied the surface of the landscape.

A tall, solitary, mournful tree might be seen here and there, adding to the feeling of vastness and solitude.

It was an hour and a place fit for sad thoughts and dark forebodings, and Felix Heron sat upon Daisy in an attitude of one full of mournful reflections.

He had sat there about a quarter of an hour, and so intently was he gazing around him that Tom did not venture to break the silence.

There was not a breath of air stirring; no change took place in the aspect of the earth or sky; it was as if Nature were dead, and the feeling seemed to become oppressive—contagious—for Tom Ripon heaved a deep sigh.

"Ah, Tom!" said Heron, in his kindly tones; "I had forgotten. I never pass this spot without a feeling of depression, for which I can scarcely account. Let us, however, push forward."

"That's just what I was thinking, Captain: it would be better to get home, for the Lady Edith did not seem to like our coming out much tonight, and I think we may as well get home as quickly as we can."

"We will—we will, Tom, for my heart is heavy, and I cannot account for the feeling. If I were superstitious, I should say I had a presentiment of evil," added Heron with a smile, which, however, had very little mirth in it.

Felix Heron and Tom Ripon now put their horses to a gallop, nor drew rein until they were within sight of the busy city.

"There has been, or is, a great fire somewhere," said Heron, as he looked up at the lurid sky; "and methinks I can hear the shouts of a multitude, as they gaze upon the wreck made by the devouring element."

Tom was of the same opinion, and was most anxious to reach the scene of confusion, that he too might bear his part in the general commotion.

Suddenly a solitary figure was seen running with the speed of lightning in the contrary direction from whence could be heard the roar of voices.

"Halt!" cried Felix Heron. "Tell me, my friend, where——Ah! Ogle?"

"Yes, Captain!" said Ogle, almost breathless with the speed at which he had run; "I've come to meet you, Captain."

"Speak! What have you to tell me? Edith—my child—my boy——"

"Are well and safe."

"Safe! What mean you Ogle? That fire? Ah! I see. It is Whitcombe House."

Ogle drooped his head, and something like a sob burst from his lips.

"The worst is over, Ogle. Where is Edith?"

"At Castleneau House, Captain."

"And she was alone in Whitcombe House, Ogle?"

"Yes, Captain, but Jonathan Wild, by some means or other, arrived just in time to save her and the child."

"Jonathan Wild! Impossible! You amaze me, Ogle!"

"It was even so, Captain, and he himself was in such a state of grief, I may say, that I could scarcely believe my own eyes."

"It is strange," said Heron. "Let us proceed."

At this moment Ogle felt a rather rough twitch at his hat, and looking up, perceived Tom close to him.

"Where is Ellen?" he asked, his voice trembling with emotion.

"At Castleneau House, with Lady Edith," replied Ogle.

"That is well!" replied the boy. "I feared almost to ask."

Felix Heron now rode on, leaving Ogle to follow more at his ease, and arrived just in time to see the roof of the noble mansion fall in, burying within its ruins many objects of value that had been collected through many generations within its walls.

"Let it go—let it go!" sighed Heron; "there is more of unhappiness than happiness connected with that old mansion. I will not regret its loss, since I know my priceless treasures are in safety."

He turned Daisy's head, and putting her to a hard gallop, was soon ringing the great bell at Castleneau House, where old Anthony, from the speed with which he responded to the summons, seemed to have been watching for him.

"You know all, sir?" asked the old man, with affectionate sympathy.

"All that has happened to Whitcombe House.—yes, Anthony; but where is Edith?"

"In the little breakfast parlour," replied the old servitor, "with Lady Castleneau."

Even as he spoke, Edith came out, and throwing herself into his arms, sobbed forth her thankfulness and joy at again beholding him.

"And our little one, Edith?" asked Heron, as soon as he could command his voice sufficiently to speak.

"Is well, and sleeping soundly," was the reply.

CHAPTER CCCII.

JONATHAN WILD APPEARS IN A NEW LIGHT.

It is early morning, and the bright sun is shining through the tall, old-fashioned windows of Castleneau House.

A happy and contented party is assembled in that ancient breakfast-room, where so many scenes have occurred in connexion with this story of actual life.

It is true that Whitcombe House, so long the head-quarters, so to speak, of the earls of that name, is no more.

The flames have done their work, and that magnificent, although somewhat gloomy mansion, with all its associations, sad and happy, has passed away.

Is it regretted?

No! A thousand times, no!

On the contrary, about the eyes of Edith there is a lightness of expression, for although she had passed some happy hours in the old house at St. James's, it was at the same time associated with gloomy recollections.

And did Felix Heron regret it?

Certainly not. The world of his affections did not embrace bricks and mortar and the old stone portico of that family mansion.

And when he looked about him in the breakfast-room of Castleneau House, and saw there all the human hearts he held dear, he felt that there was nothing of which he could accuse Fate or Fortune in the shape of unhappiness.

"Now," cried Lady Castleneau—"now, my dear children, let us hope that that bold, bad man, Jonathan Wild, will be content, since he believes that you, Felix, are no more."

"No, aunt," cried Heron; "believe me, he will be far from content; and I do not think any of you really understand the kind of hostility Jonathan Wild had against me."

"He sought your life."

"Perhaps so, in the regular way. It is probable that, if we had fought, he would have tried to kill me."

"He could not!" exclaimed Edith.

"Ah!" added Heron, "you believe me invincible. Still, I believe he would have tried to kill me, although he would much have preferred taking me into custody, and letting me be condemned to death in the regular manner."

Edith shuddered.

"And then," added Heron——

"I will hear no more," said Edith. "I cannot contemplate such things."

"Nay, I was only going to say, 'And then I feel assured Jonathan Wild would have striven might and main to save me.'"

"Indeed!"

"Yes, Edith, and you, aunt, likewise, I think you both judge wrongfully of that strange, eccentric man. He wants to conquer me, to overpower me, to hold me at his mercy; and then I believe he would risk his own life rather than mine should be destroyed."

"But he thinks it destroyed now," said Lady Castleneau.

"Perhaps."

Before Felix Heron could add another word, a

tap came at the door of the room, and old Anthony put in his head, with a scared look.

"Mr. Wild! Mr. Wild!" he cried: "he is even now alighting at the gate!"

Edith turned pale, and sprung to her feet, clasping the child in her arms as though she imagined Wild could have no other errand than to tear it from her.

Lady Castleneau put on a look of firm resolution.

Heron smiled.

"Fly, Felix, fly!" cried Edith. "There is danger!"

"I think not," said Heron. "Whatever may be Wild's object in calling here, I do not think it involves danger to me. He either thinks me no more, or that I have escaped. Do you not remember, aunt, that long ago I listened to an interview between you and Jonathan Wild in this room, and was only separated from you by one of the folds of yonder screen?"

"Yes—oh, yes!"

"It shall again hide me from him; for although I might easily take his life, I will not do so, except under the pressure of some dire extremity."

"He is coming!" cried old Anthony—"he is coming! I have looked out into the courtyard from the window on the staircase, and he is coming! He did not stop to ring the bell, but clambered over the gate. Hush! that's his footstep in the hall!"

Heron glanced about him.

He was anxious to leave no evidences of his presence that might meet the scrutinizing glance of Jonathan Wild.

Darting, then, behind one of the folds of the screen, he was completely hidden.

A heavy blow came upon the outer panel of the door.

Old Anthony hastily opened it, and in a high, cracked, trembling voice announced "Mr. Wild."

Jonathan stood upon the threshold.

At sight of Lady Castleneau and Edith, he pulled off his hat with such a jerk, that it brought with it the eccentric and loosely fitting wig he usually wore.

Wild's wig was not ornamental, but without it he presented rather a hideous spectacle, from the numerous scars that were upon his bald head of sword-cuts he had received in his many encounters with knights of the road.

But the expression upon Jonathan Wild's face was something wonderful to see.

It was positively human.

His voice even faltered.

He advanced in a stooping posture into the room.

"Lady Whitcombe," he said, "and you, Lady Castleneau, you see me before you both, but not as an enemy."

Lady Castleneau had risen and confronted Wild with that calm dignity of manner which had always had such an effect upon him.

"Jonathan Wild," she said, "what want you here?"

"I will tell you. I want to banish a fear, and to awaken a hope."

He looked wistfully at Edith as he spoke.

"The fire no longer blazes," he added, "and Whitcombe House is a mass of ruins."

"Your work," said Edith.

"Partly."

He made a gesture of impatience.

"But I did not intend it," he added, hurriedly. "What's done, however, is done. It is past for ever, and may not be recalled. I have now come to ask a question."

"What question? Ask it," cried Lady Castleneau, "and then——"

"I know," said Wild. "And then be off as quick as I can, you mean."

Lady Castleneau inclined her head.

Wild took from his pocket an immense, dingy-looking handkerchief, and passed it twice across his brow before he spoke again.

Then, in strange accents for him, because there was some emotion in them, he said, "Where is the Earl of Whitcombe?"

"I ask that of you," replied Edith. "Where is the Earl of Whitcombe?"

"Ah!" said Wild, as he passed the handkerchief across his brow again; "you ask that of me, do you?"

"I do, Jonathan Wild."

"Then I am sorry to hear it, and I have something more disagreeable to say still."

He paused a few moments, and turned towards Lady Castleneau.

"I think," he said, "I would rather say it to you, for you have the courage of a man, and can hear something that would blanch ordinary checks, and strike ordinary people dead with grief."

By the slight movement of one hand that Jonathan Wild made, it was evident that he alluded to Edith.

But she was strong in the consciousness of the safety of Felix Heron, and she spoke boldly and fearlessly.

"Say on, Jonathan Wild; I am prepared to hear all that you can state, and I will try to be as courageous as my Aunt Castleneau in regard to whatever you may utter."

"The object," said Wild, "of setting fire to Whitcombe House, was to ascertain if the Captain Fantome there residing with you was not in reality my old friend the Earl of Whitcombe himself in disguise."

A faint flush came over the cheek of Edith.

"And if it were so?" she said.

"That's an answer!" said Wild—"that's an answer!"

"An answer to what?"

"To all my doubts and suspicions. Edith, Countess of Whitcombe, if you had taken twenty oaths that Captain Fantome and Felix Heron were one and the same person, you could not more perfectly have convinced me of the fact, than by that look, and those few words."

"Nay, Jonathan Wild."

"Hush! You were there!"

He pointed down to the floor as he spoke.

"And now you are there!"

He pointed up to the ceiling.

"Perhaps you don't understand me. I'm not very good at saying things out of my own plain, blunt way; but what I mean is, that you had sunk very low in my esteem as the wife of Captain Fantome, but he and Felix Heron being one and the same person, you rise again to your former height. You comprehend that?"

"I do; but I have not yet said——"

"Bah! you have. Now I want to break something gently to you. A dead body has been dug out of the ruins of Whitcombe House, with the remnant of a scarlet coat upon it, but the face was so charred and destroyed by the flames that no one could recognise it. I want to know if it be Felix Heron or not."

"And you call that," said Lady Castleneau, "breaking things gently."

"Never mind!" shouted Wild. "I'm a fool— an ass! I know it. I lent myself in a moment of weakness and frenzy to the plan of setting fire to Whitcombe House; and now look at me! The mere thought that I have destroyed that man in it shakes me to the soul, and there would be tears in these eyes, only that you wouldn't believe in them, because they would be half brandy, half blood. But, in a word, Edith, Countess of Whitcombe, I want you to come with me and look at the—the——"

No. 98.—EDITH HERON.

Wild had to wipe his brow again with the handkerchief before he could utter another word, and then he added, "Well, it must come out. I want you to come and look at the body."

Edith and Lady Castleneau exchanged glances.

"Be at peace, Jonathan Wild!" said Edith.

"At peace?"

"Yes; the poor, charred remains you speak of are not those of Felix Heron."

"You say that; and in such a tone, and with such a look? Then it's true; and I'm a double ass for not seeing how the game lay, when first I came into this room. He has escaped."

"He has."

Jonathan Wild picked up his wig.

He put it carefully on, and then turning to Lady Castleneau, he made one of his most hideous faces, as he said, "A small drop of brandy, my lady, if it's only half a pint, would be very acceptable."

"Anthony," said Lady Castleneau, "you will give Jonathan Wild whatever refreshment he requires."

"Thank you," said Wild; "and look here. I promise one thing, that henceforward I will try to forget the existence of such a person as Felix Heron. I have fought him hard now for six long years, and, therefore, naturally enough, I begin to like him. Tell him, Lady Edith, Countess of Whitcombe, that he has nothing to fear—no, that's not exactly the word, for he never did fear me; but tell him that he will never have any more trouble of any kind or description from Jonathan Wild."

"I will."

"And in that case," said Heron, stepping out from behind the screen, "there is no longer any further necessity for my remaining concealed."

"Ah!" cried Wild.

Heron smiled.

"Yes, by Jove! it is the man! Felix Heron, Earl of Whitcombe!"

"And the Baron Von Peck!" said Heron.

Wild uttered a shout.

"And Captain Fantome of the royal navy!"

"Blind! blind as a bat!" yelled Wild. "Blind as a mole! I not to know you! I am getting old—old and past work. My eyes grow dim—my limbs totter. I'm not the man I was; and it seems to me now that the career of Jonathan Wild is near its close. Strange thoughts come over me at times, that those who have made most use of me, as the tool for their own purposes, will turn against me, and, perhaps, seek my life; but if they do I will die game—game to the last, and——"

Wild turned abruptly.

There was a sharp rap at the door of the room.

Old Anthony looked in.

"Mr. Challener!" he said.

There was a dead silence for a few seconds, during which the persons assembled in that breakfast-room looked at each other as if they would ask, who is Mr. Challener?

Heron rose from the chair he had taken beside Edith, and took one step towards the screen again.

"Challener! Challener!" said Wild. "Who is Challener?"

Old Anthony shook his head.

A heavy footstep was heard in the hall.

Wild drew himself up to his full height, and glanced at the half-open door.

A quiet, gentlemanly-looking man appeared at it, and glancing round the room, his eyes settled upon Wild.

An evident access of fear came over the heart of the great thief-taker.

The stranger advanced towards him, and laid his hand upon his shoulder.

"Jonathan Wild," he said, "you are my prisoner."

"Prisoner?"

"I have said it!"

"Prisoner?" echoed Wild again, as though he could hardly believe in the verity of the word.

"Yes. I arrest you on the virtue of a warrant issued by the Home Secretary. Resistance is of course quite out of the question, as I have a suffi-cient force in the court-yard of this house to render it as vain as it is foolish."

"Arrest me?"

"Even so!"

"Upon what charge, Mr. Challener?"

"For receiving stolen goods, which, under the recent statute, is a capital felony. Surrender, Mr. Wild, and give me up whatever arms you may have in your possession."

"I receive stolen goods!" exclaimed Wild. "Ha! ha! Certainly, once I did it; but that was to restore a gold snuff-box, stolen from the Home Secretary himself."

CHAPTER CCCIII.

A HAPPY RE-UNION.—THE FAMILY COUNCIL.

JONATHAN WILD, for the first time in his life, now occupied a cell in Newgate as a prisoner.

A strange feeling came over Felix Heron and Edith.

It seemed to them both that in some mysterious way their fortunes had been mixed up with those of Jonathan Wild.

And now that justice seemed about to overtake him, there was a sensation of relief in both their minds, such as they had not experienced for many a long day.

During the course of the morning at Castleneau House, the Earl of Bridgewater arrived with Colonel Trelawney.

The destruction of the old mansion of the Whitcombes, in St. James's Street, had created quite a sensation at the West End of the town.

"Thank heaven!" exclaimed the Earl of Bridgewater, as his eye wandered from Felix Heron to Edith, and from her again to the little child, whom he knew so well—"thank heaven, you are all safe!"

"We are, Bridgewater," replied Heron; "and, believe me, we have no regrets for the bricks and mortar of old Whitcombe House."

"Who, then," said Colonel Trelawney, "is the mysterious stranger in the scarlet coat who now lies so grim and stark in death at the 'Thatched House Tavern' in St. James's Street?"

Edith glanced at Heron.

Her face was very pale.

He saw that she caught her breath convulsively.

"You are avenged, Felix," she said; "and, thank heaven, not by your own hand!"

"What mean you, Edith?"

"It is the act of heaven, and I will not repine at it. That person you speak of, Colonel Trelawney, was once John Tarleton."

"John Tarleton?" exclaimed every one.

"Yes; the unworthy brother of her whom you have been pleased to be so kind to, and to make so happy with your friendship and esteem."

As Edith spoke she left the room, carrying her child with her.

There were tears in her eyes.

"Nature," said Felix Heron, as he closed the door after her,—"Nature speaks out with a stronger voice than Reason for a short time: but Edith will soon remember who and what John

Tarleton was, and the shock of his terrible death will pass away."

"I have further news for you," said the Earl of Bridgewater.

"It is good! I can see it in your eyes!"

"The Government has determined upon the arrest of Jonathan Wild."

"That I am aware of, Bridgewater, for it has taken place here in this very room!"

"You surprise me!"

"It was so. Wild was here a short time since, where he was met by Mr. Challener, a King's pursuivant, and marched off, I presume, to Newgate."

"Better times, then, are in store for you, Whitcombe, for the King is very sick; and although he rallies wonderfully at times, and denies being in the slightest degree indisposed, the royal physician declares that his death will be sudden and soon."

"Yes," added Colonel Trelawney; "we have received this news in confidence, and we come with a piece of advice accordingly."

"I shall listen to it," said Heron, "as to the voice of an oracle. What would you have me to do?"

"The advice, then, that we have to offer," added Bridgewater, speaking in a low tone, as if he feared his words might reach some hostile ears, even through the walls of that apartment,— "the advice that we have to offer is that you seek an interview with the heir to the throne."

"Indeed!"

"Yes. You are aware, Whitcombe, that by the mysterious death of the Prince of Wales, his son George, now only eighteen years of age, and residing in strict seclusion at Kew, will, upon the death of the present King, ascend the throne."

"Exactly! But is it not probable he will be already prejudiced against me?"

"Not so. He looks upon Trelawney and myself as his prime friends."

"That alters the case."

"It does materially; and we shall have no difficulty in procuring an audience, either at the Palace in Kew Gardens, or somewhere else that Prince George may appoint."

"I will be guided by you entirely," said Heron. "I ask nothing for myself; but I wish that the titles and estates of Whitcombe should be assured to my son."

"No, no!" said the Earl of Bridgewater; "that will not do. We must have free immunity for all the past. You are yet a young man, Whitcombe, and the future of your life must not be under a cloud, which would dispel much of its happiness."

Some further discourse now ensued with respect to the best plan of operations to arrange this meeting between Felix Heron and Prince George.

Lady Castleneau was taken into the council; and it was finally arranged that Colonel Trelawney, who was on duty at Kew, and who had acquired great influence over the young Prince, should sound him upon the subject of the proposed interview, and take his orders accordingly.

This being arranged, Felix Heron took Bridgewater aside, and speaking to him with some emotion, said, "You are aware, Bridgewater, by what I have told you of my history, that my poor father, the late Earl, in his repentant state, and after reviewing the errors of his life in such a light that they could never be repeated, met a cruel and terrible death at the hands of John Tarleton!"

"I know it, Whitcombe."

"You know, too, that I spared the murderer for Edith's sake?"

"I do know it, and I am likewise well assured that you have not repented of so doing."

"I have not; but it will be a weight off my mind if I can thoroughly assure myself that that most unexampled villain is indeed no longer of this world."

"I understand you. You want to see the dead body now lying at the 'Thatched House,' in the scarlet coat."

"I do—I do. I wish to be assured that that is the body of John Tarleton, and that the world is rid of such a fiend in human shape. In truth, Bridgewater, I hold that man to have been—you see, I speak of him in the past tense, believing him dead—much worse than even Jonathan Wild in his most savage excesses of fury."

"Come, then, at once. As Captain Fantome, you can have no difficulty in accompanying me to the 'Thatched House.' Trelawney, you will walk with us?"

"With pleasure."

Felix Heron only delayed to run up-stairs, and say a few words to Edith; and then, with many instructions from Lady Castleneau to take heed of his personal safety, he departed on his gloomy errand.

Three gentlemen stopped opposite old Whitcombe House, and contemplated for a time its still smouldering ruins.

"Let it perish!" said Heron. "I could not like the house. I never knew the love of kindred within its walls. The words that passed between me and my father beneath its roof were those of dissension, and never shall I forget one episode of my life in connexion with that house, which nearly crushed me utterly."

Felix Heron alluded to that terrible time when, by the arts and practices of Le Jenne and John Tarleton, he was reduced to doubt even the truth and constancy of Edith.

"Oh, how blind I was!" he exclaimed. "I should have doubted my eyes, my ears, all my senses, and believed that they had risen up as traitors against my peace and happiness, before I should have doubted her."

"Come along," said Bridgewater. "These are but gloomy fancies. Do not summon back even the shadow of the clouds that have passed away."

"And here we are at the 'Thatched House,'" said Colonel Trelawney. "Ah, Mr. Staples, a fair morning to you! We want to see that fellow who was dug out of the ruins at Whitcombe House."

"Hem!" said the landlord of the "Thatched House." "Really, gentlemen, knowing all your worships quite well, I am sure I'd gladly do anything to pleasure you; but the coroner, or rather I should say the coroner's clerk——"

"Oh, never mind the coroner or his clerk either," said Colonel Trelawney. "We want to identify the body; so, you see, we are on a legitimate errand."

"I believe," said the landlord, looking at Heron, " I have the distinguished honour of seeing, for the first time in the ' Thatched House,' Captain Fantome, who married the Countess of Whitcombe ?"

Heron slightly inclined his head. .

He was scarcely aware that he was so well known to his neighbours as was really the case.

"Come, come !" said Bridgewater; " let us see the fellow !"

The landlord of the ' Thatched House' put on an air of preternatural cunning as he spoke: " Well, you must know, gentlemen, the coroner's clerk came here and put his seal on the door of the room where the dead body lies; but, gentlemen, he was not exactly aware that there was another door. Ha, ha !"

"Precisely !" said Trelawney. "That is the great advantage of these old houses. You have all sorts of doors, and exits, and entrances, in every direction."

"This way then, gentlemen—this way. Of course, you will say nothing about it ?"

"Not a word—not a word."

The landlord of the " Thatched House" led his guests up one of the back staircases, and from thence threading a number of intricate passages, they arrived in a small apartment that had evidently been long used as a lumber-room to store away odds and ends of broken furniture.

"It's the next room to this," said the landlord ; " and here's a door that hasn't been opened, I should almost think, since the house was built."

The landlord produced a bunch of old keys, and with some difficulty fitted one to the lock, which turned with extreme difficulty.

The door creaked upon its hinges, and let fall a cloud of dust, and with difficulty it was opened inward.

The room, in which lay the mutilated, charred body from the ruins of Whitcombe House was a long, low-roofed apartment, probably thirty or five-and-thirty feet in length, and eighteen or twenty in width.

It had evidently been used for dinner parties, and the tables were ranged along the walls, so as to leave the open space in the centre perfectly clear.

On one of those tables, covered with a large coarse piece of baize, lay an object, which, from the outlines it presented, had evidently once been human.

There is something even in the presence of death, when associated with those who in life are least entitled to respect, that awes the bolder part.

Felix Heron had good reason to suppose that the still form before him presented all that remained of his father's murderer.

And yet he approached what might be called the bier of John Tarleton with a look of solemnity.

The green baize was turned aside.

Heron shook his head.

"No, no !" he said ; " I cannot recognise those features—the flames have done their work too effectively."

"It is a sickening spectacle," said Bridgewater.

"It is indeed," added Trelawney : " let us leave it."

" Yes," said the landlord ; "and it's a very hard case that they should have brought him to the ' Thatched House;' for what's drunk down stairs at the bar is nothing at all compared to the bother of an inquest, and all that sort of thing."

"Hush !" said Bridgewater ; "be quiet, all of you."

He held up his hand, demanding silence.

They were all perfectly still, and a rather scared look sat upon the countenance of the landlord.

"What is it ?" he whispered.

"Hush—hush !"

A confusion of voices was heard without.

It appeared as if some one was demanding admission to that room, so carefully sealed up by the clerk of the coroner, and that the officials of the hotel were protesting against the intrusion.

A deep-toned voice spoke, and although it could be heard but indistinctly through the thick panelling of the ancient door, its tones struck upon the ears of Felix Heron with a strange familiarity.

But yet he did not recognise the voice sufficiently to give a name to its possessor.

"Resist me at your peril !" said the voice. " I hold an order from the Secretary of State to examine the dead body that lies here, and, therefore, my authority over-rides all others."

The Earl of Bridgewater now suddenly grasped the arm of Felix Heron, and whispered in his ear.

"You hear, Whitcombe—you hear ?"

" I do."

" That voice—do you not recognise it ?"

"Scarcely ; I feel that I have heard it, but cannot name its owner."

" It is a voice that I can never forget ; and for the same reason that you could never forget, Whitcombe, the voice of him who lies still in death now before us."

Felix Heron now understood what the Earl of Bridgewater meant.

The name of the person who was speaking without, came like a flash of lightning to his mind.

" Warringdale !" he said.

" Yes," exclaimed the Earl of Bridgewater "The murderer of your father lies here before us, and is beyond human vengeance; but the murderer of mine still lives, and it is his voice we have just heard demanding admittance to this chamber."

The landlord of the " Thatched House" looked alarmed.

The tone and manner of the Earl of Bridgewater were full of excitement—so much so, indeed, that Colonel Trelawney laid his hand upon his arm, as he said, "Be calm, Bridgewater—be calm—be calm, or you will know not what you do !"

There was a rustling at the door, and a voice, now undoubtedly recognised as that of Lord Warringdale, was heard, in louder accents.

" I will hold you harmless. I tell you again,

WARRINGDALE RIFLES THE DEAD BODY OF JOHN TARLETON.

my authority is quite sufficient. Open the door, for I can no longer delay!"

"What is to be done?" whispered Heron.

"Let us ascertain," said Colonel Trelawney, "what the villain wants here; and to do that we must be in secret. Come this way; we can easily all of us hide on the other side of this small door."

A few seconds before the ordinary door of the apartment was opened to admit Lord Warringdale, our little party, as we may call it, retreated from the room in the occupation of the dead John Tarleton on to the narrow staircase up which the landlord of the "Thatched House" had brought them.

They closed the narrow door all but a crevice, and waited anxiously the appearance and proceedings of Lord Warringdale.

CHAPTER CCCIV.

LORD WARRINGDALE RIFLES THE CORPSE OF JOHN TARLETON.

"REMAIN where you are!" cried Warringdale to the officials of the tavern who had accompanied him to the room. "Remain where you are; I require no services."

He closed the door upon them.

Then he thought himself alone with the dead.

Alone with the man who had been his unscrupulous associate while living, and who, now that he was no more, was looked upon without regret.

"One by one," said Warringdale, in a low voice to himself,—"one by one they go, and I am left alone, master of the field. Le Jeune is no more, and now John Tarleton is but a senseless clod."

He stepped up to the table on which the body lay.

He contemplated it then for some few moments in silence.

Then he spoke in a careless, jesting tone.

"Under ordinary circumstances, John Tarleton, to see you thus I should not have known you; for, in good truth, the fire at Whitcombe House has not improved your beauty; and yet, even through all its ravages, I fancy I can still detect the downward villanous look that always belonged to you. It is strange that so great a difference should be between the brother and sister; for, antagonistic as I have ever been to her, I am free to confess that Edith is beautiful."

Through the crevice of the door, Felix Heron and the Earl of Bridgewater could easily command a good view of the proceedings of Lord Warringdale.

"Yes, in truth," added Warringdale, "this is a strange meeting; and, however satisfactory it may be in some respects, it is one I do not wish to prolong."

He busied himself about the corpse, and tearing open the vest, he found a secret pocket, from which he extracted some papers.

"Good!" he said. "I would not have these fall into the hands of that half-brother of mine, Felix Heron—assuming him to be still in life which I verily believe—for the value of half the estates of Whitcombe."

As these words were spoken by Lord Warringdale, the Earl of Bridgewater whispered eagerly in the ear of Heron.

"You must have those papers, Whitcombe."

"Assuredly."

"I will get them for you."

"Thanks."

"No!" whispered Colonel Trelawney.

"No?"

"I mean, let me get them. It is better for neither of you to interfere with that man. I shall be a much more disinterested witness than either of you."

"As you please, Trelawney," said the Earl; "but I shall have something yet to say to my Lord Warringdale before he leaves that room."

"Be careful, Bridgewater—be careful. I can see by your eyes, and the flush of colour on your cheek, that your heart is full of excitement."

"Trust me," replied the young Earl. "But go, Trelawney, since you wish it, and take the papers from him."

"Certainly."

Colonel Trelawney was a man of action.

When he made up his mind to do a thing, it was done with that calm exhibition of power and resolution, which won half the battle before it was commenced.

He opened the little door at once, just sufficiently wide to allow him to pass into the room.

Warringdale heard the footstep.

He uttered an exclamation of alarm.

He made a rush at the door by which he had entered to escape, but his own haste impeded him, and he forgot which way the door opened, inward or outward.

The two seconds he lost were quite sufficient for Colonel Trelawney.

With a bound, the active officer reached Warringdale, and, seizing him by the shoulder, he swung him round from the door, and stood between it and him.

"Not so fast, my Lord Warringdale," he said. "I have a word to say to you before you go."

"To me, sir?"

"Even so."

"And who are you that dare——"

"I am Colonel Trelawney, of his Majesty's Guard. I need not ask you who you are, because I know you."

"Know me, sir?"

"Yes, you call yourself Lord Warringdale, although you know well, and I know likewise, you have no right to the tile."

"No right?"

"Not the least. It belongs to the infant son of Felix, Earl of Whitcombe!"

"And is that," said Warringdale, with a sneer, "the precious piece of intelligence that Colonel Trelawney, of his Majesty's Guard, has taken the trouble to come here and tell me?"

"No; that has arisen incidentally. I am here to receive from you those papers you have just taken from the dead body of your rascally associate, John Tarleton, lying there."

"Ah!"

"Be quick, sir!"

"What papers? I have no papers!"

"This is an occasion on which lying will not

answer your purpose. I saw you take the papers!"

"These are harsh words, Colonel, from one gentleman to another."

"They might be. I would never use them to a gentleman."

"Colonel, you shall answer to me for this language. I will be at my lodgings for the remainder of the day, and will send a friend to demand satisfaction of you. If you conquer me you may take the papers from me—even, as you say, I have taken them from him who lies so still and cold before us."

"That subterfuge will not answer your purpose," said Colonel Trelawney. "I must and will have them now; and as for fighting you, that, you know, I will do with the greatest pleasure in the world, at any time and place you may appoint."

"This is an outrage!"

"You are welcome to call it what you will, but I must have the papers, and if you will not surrender them by fair means, I warn you that I mean to take them by foul."

"There, then!"

Warringdale took from his breast pocket some letters and newspapers, and flung them on one of the tables.

"No," said Trelawney.

"What do you mean, sir? You are inconsistent."

"Not at all. The papers I require I saw you place in your left hand skirt pocket."

Warringdale changed colour.

"And since," added the Colonel, "you have so great a disinclination to part with them, I will end the matter thus."

As he spoke, he drew his sword and rushed upon Warringdale, who expected nothing less than instant death.

He raised yells of fear, and called loudly for help.

But Colonel Trelawney had no such intention. Seizing the skirt of Warringdale's coat in his left hand, where he knew the papers he required had been deposited, he with one stroke of his sword, fairly severed it from the rest of the coat.

"That is sufficient," he said: "you may now go."

But Warringdale had called aloud for help, and when he did so, the Earl of Bridgewater had whispered to Felix Heron, "It is our turn now. Let us appear."

From the look that was upon the countenance of the young Earl, Heron would fain have kept him back, but it was not possible to do so.

Bridgewater strode into the room, and Heron had no resource but to follow him.

"You cried out for help, my Lord Warringdale," said the Earl; "pray what is the matter?"

If Lord Warringdale had seen a spectre appear in answer to his call, he could not have been more astonished than he was at the sight of the young Earl of Bridgewater.

And the landlord of the "Thatched House" tavern was so alarmed at the whole proceeding, that he thought his most prudent course would be to leave the whole party to settle their affairs in their own way.

"Gentlemen," he said, "you are all men of rank, and I am quite sure my best plan is not to interfere."

"A wise decision," said Trelawney; "you had better go."

"Thank you, Colonel. I know nothing, see nothing, and don't want."

The landlord speedily made his exit, and then the young Earl of Bridgewater stepped forward, and spoke in a voice of great emotion and animation.

"It seems to me, Colonel Trelawney," he said, "and——"

He paused a moment, and fixed his eyes on Felix Heron.

It was quite a chance that he had not pronounced that name, but he saw Heron's finger on his lips, and then he added—

"It seems to me, Captain Fantome, that we are all in the hands of a superior destiny, that shapes our actions according to its own will. We have frequently to do something which must be done; but however impelled we may be to do it, we cannot, and dare not, until the proper time arrives."

"Be calm, Bridgewater," said Trelawney.

"I am calm, Colonel, but I know and feel that it has been my duty, and that the time would come when I must avenge my murdered father."

Lord Warringdale staggered back, and leant upon one of the tables for support.

"Am I to be assassinated?" he gasped—"assassinated by you all?"

"What matters it to you,' said Colonel Trelawny, calmly, "unless you happen to be the murderer of his father?"

This logical speech of the young Earl's seemed to be anything but a reassuring character to Lord Warringdale.

He still trembled and turned pale, and yet he was far from guessing at that moment the real extent of the danger that menaced him.

He strove to put on an air of confidence, and to assume a courage that he did not feel.

"It appears, gentlemen," he said, "that I am well known to you; and if so, there can be no difficulty in finding me, if you wish to question my proceedings. The outrage to which I have already been subjected I shall of course report in the proper official quarter."

Warringdale made again a movement to reach the door of the room, but the Earl of Bridgewater interposed between him and it.

"No!" in a voice, he cried, that was strange even to Felix Heron, well as he knew his young friend the Earl—"no! I say again, the time has come!"

"What time?" gasped Warringdale.

"The time when I should be something worse than a stick or a stone—a human clod, if I did not cast off from my soul the weight that has for so long oppressed it!"

"Be calm—be calm," again interposed Colonel Trelawney.

"Nay, Trelawney; this is an opportunity that will not occur again. It is fate, I tell you, and I must embrace it."

Again Warringdale moved towards the door.

The young Earl, however, with flashing eyes, placed his back against it.

"Listen to me, all of you!" he said. "I have good reason to believe this man, who calls himself Lord Warringdale, to be the murderer of my father!"

"False!" cried Warringdale.

The Earl made a gesture, as though to command his silence, and continued: "The act was done long ago, and the reputation of it fell upon the innocent head of Felix Heron!"

"Hear me—hear me!" said Warringdale.

"Hear him!" interposed Colonel Trelawney. "Let him be the blackest criminal the world ever saw, he is entitled to a hearing."

"I ask but one question," said Warringdale. "Is the witness alive that I would call to exonerate me from this charge?"

"Witness alive? What mean you?"

"I speak of that Felix Heron you have just mentioned. Does he live?—for if he does, I would cite him to appear, to say no to this monstrous charge!"

Heron at this moment stepped forward, and so confident was he in his disguise as Captain Fantome, that he had no hesitation in submitting himself freely to the observation of Lord Warringdale.

They looked at each other earnestly.

It is well known to the reader that Warringdale had been of opinion, along with Jonathan Wild, that Felix Heron was still in life, and if he were so, he could only be identical with Captain Fantome.

And never had Warringdale obtained so good a look at his half-brother in that admirably got-up disguise.

And never had Heron so fully succeeded in putting on a look and expression entirely different from his own, as upon that occasion.

He managed to settle himself down, likewise, in a manner that took several inches off his height.

Warringdale was baffled.

All the vague suspicions of the identity of Captain Fantome with Felix Heron seemed to scatter to the winds before this ocular demonstration that such could not be the case.

He breathed more freely.

A great weight seemed to be lifted off his mind, and his voice was more free from embarrassment, as he spoke.

"My Lord Bridgewater," he said, "you have nourished now for some years this terrible and injurious suspicion regarding me."

"I have; and I nourish it still."

"It has been fostered, I know well, by the cunning and duplicity of Felix Heron."

The Earl of Bridgewater was about to make some violent reply to these words, but Colonel Trelawney stopped him.

"Hold!" he said. "It is but right and just that we should hear what this man has to say. In what way, my Lord Warringdale, can you exonerate yourself from suspicion of this fearful crime?"

"In this way," said Warringdale. "Felix Heron himself confessed his guilt!"

Again the Earl was about to speak furiously, but again he was hushed to silence by Colonel Trelawney.

"Upon what occasion," he said, "did Felix Heron confess himself the perpetrator of the murder?"

"I overheard him by chance confess it to his man, Ogle; although, I am bound to say in common justice and candour, that he confessed it with regret, saying, it partook much more of an accident than a premeditated crime; and if he were now in life——"

"What then?"

"I am quite certain he would not see me exposed even to danger, or forced into conflict with any man on such a subject."

"You believe that?" added Trelawney.

"I do. On my soul, I do."

"Keep the door, Bridgewater."

"I mean to do so."

"Then, gentlemen," added Colonel Trelawney, "I will take you into my confidence upon so singular a subject, that it may well excite your admiration and even your incredulity."

CHAPTER CCCV.

THE FALSE ACCUSER MEETS WITH HIS DESERTS.

COLONEL TRELAWNEY pronounced these words in so mysterious a tone of voice, that neither Felix Heron nor the Earl of Bridgewater knowing what his plans were, looked at him with surprise and expectation.

As regarded Lord Warringdale, he knew not whether to extract hope or fear from the manner of the Colonel, but he listened with the most absorbed attention to what might follow.

"It's well known to you all," added Trelawney, still speaking in the same mysterious voice,—"it is well known to you all that I have travelled in the East; and, while in Egypt, I got accidentally into communication—in consequence of saving his life—with one of those extraordinary men who seem, in some manner, to have gathered together the lost links of that mighty chain of occult knowledge only known to the seers of antiquity."

Warringdale was gathering courage.

When people began to talk in that way, he thought there could not be much danger to him.

The Earl of Bridgewater was more composed, for, from an occasional glance that Colonel Trelawney gave him, he was quite convinced that what was being said and done was exactly in the direction he wished.

"But the most extraordinary piece of knowledge," added the Colonel, "that I acquired at that time, and from that person, was a secret formula, or set of words in the old Sanscrit dialect, which would suffice to bring before me the spirit of any one who had departed this life."

Warringdale started.

"I propose to try the experiment," added Colonel Trelawney.

"In what way?"

"I think if I should be successful in summoning before us in his image, as he lived, this Felix Heron, we might get the truth as regards this unabsolved, unavenged crime."

"Oh, this is midsummer madness!" cried Warringdale. "The thing is too absurd—and here in broad daylight, too!"

"But if it were possible?" said the Earl of Bridgewater.

"Then I feel confident," added Warringdale.

" that I should be immediately absolved a. ex-
onerated from all part in the murder—if murder
it were. But the thing is, I say, too absurd.
You were deceived by your Egyptian seer,
Colonel Trelawney, and it cannot be."

Trelawney shook his head.

" Answer me one question," said the Earl of
Bridgewater, who began now thoroughly to see
the drift of his friend. " Did you ever try the
experiment of a repetition of those strange and
terrible words ?"

" I did."

" And the result ?"

" It came."

" It ? What it ?"

" The spirit that I summoned."

Lord Warringdale turned pale, and again
grasped the edge of the table for support.

There was a consciousness in his mind that all
this boded no good to him, but in what precise
way it was to affect him he scarcely, as yet,
knew.

Felix Heron, however, and the Earl of Bridgewater were, by this time, perfectly well aware of
Colonel Trelawney's mode of action, and they
were prepared to second him to the utmost of
their power,

" My opinion is," said the Colonel, " that a
man possessed of such means as I have of summoning so awful a witness, should exercise it
sparingly, and never wantonly."

" This is all absurd," cried Warringdale.

" You think so ?"

" Most assuredly I do ; and any rational man
would think so likewise."

" But since this spirit of Felix Heron, which
I propose to summon, seems, by your own account, to be a witness in your favour, you can
have no objection to the experiment ?"

Warringdale hesitated a moment, and then
uttered but one word—

" None !"

He strove, by putting on an appearance of
bravado, to give himself the only hope there could
be of escaping from the present predicament.

Then Colonel Trelawney spoke again with
mysterious and low tones.

" Captain Fantome," he said, " you will oblige
me by going out at that door."

He indicated the little door that led out on to
the staircase.

Heron left the room at once.

" My Lord Bridgewater !" then added Colonel
Trelawney, " you will leave by that other
door."

The young Earl obeyed him.

Warringdale was alone with Trelawney, who
spoke to him earnestly.

" Will you abide this trial ?" he said. " Will
you now, before the spirit of another world appears, call upon heaven to witness to your innocence of the charge brought against you ? But
I want you, before you speak, that if you do so
with a consciousness of guilt at your heart, the
consequences may be far more fearful than you
can imagine."

Warringdale hesitated.

" Speak !"

" I will not be catechised in this way."

" That is enough."

" When a man is accused of a great crime, it
is sufficient if he answer the tribunals of his
country, and not private individuals."

" It is enough ! I will summon the spirit."

Lord Warringdale turned as pale as death,
and caught his breath now convulsively as Colonel Trelawney spoke, using a strange jargon
of unmeaning words, which might pass for Sanscrit, or any other obsolete tongue.

And during all this time Felix Heron had been
an attentive listener from the other side of the
small door that led to the staircase.

It needed no further explanation to enable him
thoroughly to understand the part he was to
play.

During the few minutes he had been there he
had divested himself of the wig, and carefully
rubbed off some of the lines upon his face which
had so effectually disguised him as Captain
Fantome.

By throwing likewise open the lappels of his
coat, he imparted to himself quite a different
appearance ; and any one who had once seen
Felix Heron undisguised and in his own proper
person, could not have failed to recognise him
instantly.

And who knew him so well as Warringdale ?

Heron heard Colonel Trelawney use the outlandish words.

He felt that they were the signal for his appearance.

Opening the small door instantly, he took two
steps into the room.

Warringdale's eyes were fixed in that direction.

It needed but one glance to convince him that
there stood before him the veritable Felix Heron.

That half-brother to whom he had been so
bitter an enemy.

The generous man, who, with such abundant
incentive to kill him, had on so many occasions
spared his life.

He could not speak.

Terror froze his faculties, and he could only
glare at the seeming apparition in mute despair.

" Speak !" said Colonel Trelawney—" speak,
Felix Heron ! Did you ever confess to this
man that you were the accidental murderer, or
the designing one, of the late Earl of Bridgewater ?"

" Never !" said Heron.

" Let me go !" shrieked Warringdale. " Let
me go ! I will stay here no longer ! A plot !
a plot ! It is my life that is sought ! I appeal
to the law ! If I am accused of a crime, let the
law decide my guilt or innocence ! I appeal to
the law of the land ! I will not stay here to be
baited by beings either of this world or another !"

He rushed past Colonel Trelawney, and reached
the ordinary door of the apartment through
which the Earl of Bridgewater had so recently
gone ; and so sudden was his movement, that he
evaded the grasp of the Colonel, and perhaps
even then might have escaped, but that he fell
exactly into the arms of the Earl of Bridgewater, who was on the landing.

And sooner would Warringdale have encountered one of the wildest creatures that ever made
its home in a forest, than that accuser.

He recoiled into the room again.

The young Earl followed him, and closed the door.

He drew his sword at once; and speaking in a voice that sounded calmly, because his feelings at that time were too highly wrought to admit of noisy demonstrations, he addressed Warringdale.

"It is true that I might give you up to the law—it is true that I might bring this charge against you, and support it by evidence that would bring you to a shameful death on the scaffold; but you shall have another chance for your life. You shall fight me."

"Fight you?"

"Even so. Moments are precious. To your guard, villain, and murderer!"

"It is so," said Warringdale—"an assassination! Here are three men ready to murder one."

"Not so," said Colonel Trelawney. "There lives not the man who is hardy enough to doubt my honour. I am merely here to second my friend the Earl of Bridgewater"

"And who is to second me?" shouted Warringdale.

"I!" said Felix Heron.

"You? you?"

"Yes—let the supernatural farce with which this business commenced here end. I am the Earl of Whitcombe, and as much a being of flesh and blood as yourself; and let your conduct have been what it may, I cannot obliterate the fact from my mind that we are of near kindred, therefore, Warringdale, I will second you."

"No, no; I will not fight!"

"You shall fight!"

They all three spoke as with one voice.

Warringdale looked about him like a wolf at bay.

"You shall fight," added Colonel Trelawney; "or we will leave you to the consequences of the

No. 99.—EDITH HERON,

long-cherished vengeance of the son of a murdered father!"

Then Warringdale glared about him, and the conviction came over his mind that there was no escape.

His last hour had either come, or by some fortunate chance he must succeed in taking the life of the young Earl of Bridgewater.

Or, perhaps, he might escape with some wound of too serious a nature to enable the contest to be continued.

But be that as it may, he saw in the implacable eyes of those men around him the fact that fight he must.

The Earl of Bridgewater quietly took up his position at one end of the room. Colonel Trelawney leant his back against the door, which was the ordinary mode of entrance.

Felix Heron imitated him so far as to take possession in the same way of the little narrow door leading to the obscure staircase.

"Now!" said the Earl of Bridgewater.

He advanced upon Warringdale, who reluctantly drew his sword.

"Heaven defend the right!" cried Heron.

"Amen!" said Colonel Trelawney.

The swords clashed together.

Warringdale had, but one hope, and that lay in the state of extreme excitement which was visible in every movement and in every look of the Earl of Bridgewater.

Moreover, a slant of sunlight came into the room at that inopportune moment, pouring full upon the face of the young Earl.

Warringdale took advantage of the accidental circumstance, and made so furious an assault that he wounded the Earl of Bridgewater in his left arm, ripping up with his sword's point the sleeve of his coat at the same time.

The wound was slight as regarded the Earl.

But it was fatal to Warringdale.

There was a slight entanglement of his sword's point in Bridgewater's sleeve; and that pause, although it was but for a couple of seconds, ended the conflict.

The Earl of Bridgewater shortened his right arm; and, pressing forward, heedless of the wound he had received, ran Warringdale through the body as cleanly as though he had stood up to have the operation performed upon him without attempting to defend himself.

A shudder pervaded the frame of Warringdale.

"Enough!" cried Trelawney.

Warringdale stood, then, for the space of another moment or two, and then fell heavily back, leaving the blood-stained sword in the hands of the Earl of Bridgewater.

"It is over!" said Felix Heron, as he knelt down and looked in the face of Warringdale. "He lives still; but his life is ebbing fast. Confess, Warringdale! I call upon you at this awful moment not to leave the world with defiance and untruth on your lips. Confess the murder with which you are charged; and seek that Eternal Judge, in whose presence you will soon stand, with the word repentance on your lips."

Warringdale made a dying effort.

"A fable!" he gasped—"you did it! Ha, ha! You did it!"

Those were his last words.

The expression of his countenance was something fearful to see in the concentrated hatred that sat upon it.

Heron rose, with a sigh.

"He has died as he lived," said Colonel Trelawney; "false as any fiend that ever disgraced the likeness of man."

"It is justice," said the Earl of Bridgewater, as he sheathed his sword. "This is justice, Heron. There lies the murderer of your father, and there the murderer of mine."

"Let them rest together," said Heron. "I cannot blame you, Bridgewater, although the man was of such close kindred to myself. I have often prayed that he might not fall by my hand; and, now that he is no more, I feel a weight lifted off my heart which has sat upon it for many a year."

"Come away, both of you," said Trelawney: "this is no place for us; and I should advise that when we see Prince George, at Kew, we make him a confidant of all these circumstances."

CHAPTER CCCVI.

FELIX AND EDITH AGAIN BECOME TOM'S DEBTORS.

IT was on that eventful evening on which Felix Heron had, by the advice of his best friends, gone to Kew, there to seek an interview with the heir to the throne of England, that strange occurrences were taking place in the usually quiet mansion of Castleneau House.

It is about seven o'clock in the evening, and Lady Castleneau and Edith are seated in that drawing-room which is already so well known to the reader as being so intimately associated with some of the most interesting episodes of this history.

Perhaps the sweetest hour of a sweet season is that which precedes the setting of the sun. All the world is taking holiday. The aspect of the sky and earth too, clear, calm, and tranquil, are full of repose. The mistiness of the mid-day sunshine is away, and the very absence of a portion of the full daylight, and the thin, colourless transparency of the evening air, afford that contemplative, but no way drowsy, charm which well precedes, by thought tending to adoration, the hour when, in darkness and forgetfulness, we trust ourselves unconscious to the hands of God.

The heart of man is but as an instrument from which the great musician, Nature, produces grand harmonies; and the most soothing anthem that arises within the breast is surely elicited by the soft touch of that evening hour.

There was in the heart of Lady Castleneau a deep memory, a powerful feeling, which had their harmonious connexion with that particular hour, and with that particular room; and as she gazed, and saw the sun sinking slowly in the west, one image, one sensation took possession of her bosom.

She thought of him—the lover of her girlhood —who, in that very room, at that very hour took leave of her he hoped, in one short year to make his happy wife.

She spoke not; she tried to suppress the feeling—or, rather, to indulge the feeling, while she suppressed its expression.

Lady Castleneau's eye was tearless, but her brow was sad; and as she withdrew her gaze from the setting sun, and turned her looks upon Edith, it was with a sigh.

Edith, too, had been recalling some of the events of her past life; and as she regarded the high-souled gentlewoman beside her, and remembered how true a friend she had ever been to her and to Felix, she cast her arms about her, and kissing her cheek, said, " Dear aunt, you are sad and silent to night! May I not share your thoughts?"

" It is past, dear child," replied Lady Castleneau, returning her caress. " I was but thinking of what might have been, had not heaven ordained it otherwise."

" Ah, I see!" said Edith; " you are thinking of your girlhood's days; and will you not now, dear aunt, tell me something concerning that portrait which hangs in yonder room?"

" No, no—not to-night, dear Edith—not to-night! I know not why my thoughts recur to the past, as they do of late. Perhaps—perhaps, Edith, it is because I am soon to join those who have gone before."

" Oh, speak not so, dear—dear aunt!" cried Edith. " What—oh, what would your Edith do without your kind guidance and fond affection?"

" My Edith?" said Lady Castleneau. " When a woman marries a man of such high intellect and such deep affections as are blended in Felix, that woman no longer requires any other arm to lean upon, or any other adviser. Do you understand me, my child?"

" I do—I do! But, oh, aunt! I hope you may yet be spared to us both for many years. And now, too, that brighter days are beginning to dawn upon us!"

" Yes," said Lady Castleneau; " yes, I would fain stay long enough to see those I love so fondly as happy as they deserve to be; and then I hope I may be able to close my aged eyes upon this world in calmness and peace."

At that moment, however—for it is still at the time when the deep, shy feelings of the warmest hearts peep forth to enjoy some cool, secluded hour, that the world is sure to burst upon them, like the cry of the hunters upon the timid hare,— at that very moment, one of the servants opened the door of the apartment in a hurried manner, saying as she did so, " My lady! my lady! Anthony is——"

Lady Castleneau and Edith both sprung to their feet. A dread of they knew not what took possession of their hearts.

" What of Anthony?" asked Lady Castleneau, endeavouring to speak calmly.

" Is shut up in the room where Lord Clackington was, and we cannot open the door!"

" He has escaped!" said Edith.

Lady Castleneau turned calmly to the servant who had just entered, and telling her to precede her with a candle, made her way, accompanied by Edith, to that disused suite of apartments which had formed, for the time, a temporary prison for my Lord Clackington.

When they arrived at the door, Lady Castleneau tapped gently with a huge key she held in her hand, saying, as she did so, " Anthony, are you there, and alone?"

" Yes, my lady. He overpowered me, and locked me in here."

Lady Castleneau opened the door.

" Tell me, Anthony, how long ago is it since this happened?"

" About half an hour, my lady."

" So long!" said Lady Castleneau, thoughtfully. " Come with me, Edith; we must talk over this matter seriously, and see what is to be done."

At this moment a scene of terror and alarm was taking place in another part of the mansion, and when Lady Castleneau and Edith once more reached the drawing-room, the sounds were unmistakably those of grief—wild, unchecked, heart-wrung grief—that Edith and her aunt looked at each other in mute astonishment, each fearing to ask the other, " What can this mean?"

It was Edith who first spoke.

" Let me go, dear aunt, and ascertain what all this commotion can be about?"

Lady Castlenean had sunk into a chair, and merely assented to Edith's proposition by a look.

Another moment, and Edith had left the room, —and then there was one piercing shriek—a murmur of voices—some hurried footsteps, and then all was still.

Lady Castleneau rose to her feet.

" Heaven help me now!" she murmured, as she left the room.

In the hall, a spectacle met her gaze which was well calculated to make her heart stand still.

On the floor of the hall, half-supported by Martha and Ellen, lay Edith in a death-like swoon; while old Anthony, with clasped hands, approached his mistress, but was unable to articulate a word.

" What is the cause of this?" asked Lady Castleneau, pressing her hand upon her heart. " What has caused this death-like swoon? Tell me, Anthony! Keep me no longer in suspense!"

" The child, my lady!—Lady Edith's child is nowhere to be found!"

" Merciful heaven!" exclaimed Lady Castleneau. " What new grief is in store for us?"

Edith was raised from the floor, and conveyed back again to the drawing-room, which she had so lately left. For the time being, all other thoughts were absorbed in the all-engrossing one of her recovery.

Old Anthony had been despatched for a physician, who, on his arrival, pronounced Edith to be in a dangerous state.

Lady Castleneau took her place beside Edith's bedside.

It is an awful thing at any time to sit by the side of one who is struck down in the midst of this life's hopes and joys; but when the being whom we see so situated is dear to our heart by the ties of kindred or of love, it is still more awful to see that strange and inexplicable thing, human life, oppressed and beaten down like a crushed butterfly, waving its faint wings with the energy of suffering, but not the freedom of health.

Edith fell into swoon after swoon, and upon awakening from one of them she gazed about her wildly, and Lady Castleneau almost dreaded to approach too near to the sick couch, lest she should find that she was unrecognised still.

It was towards midnight when Edith spoke in a low voice.

"Aunt, dear aunt, tell me, have they yet discovered any tidings of my child?"

"Hush!" said Lady Castleneau, bending over her, affectionately; "be still. We all hope for the best."

"And Felix—has he returned?"

"Not yet, dear Edith."

The effort had been too much for Edith, and she could say no more, but lay passive as an infant.

Suddenly she started up.

"He comes! I hear him, aunt!"

There was, indeed, a footstep on the staircase, which the wife's ear had not failed to catch, but which had escaped that of Lady Castleneau.

There was a pause at the chamber door; and then a well-known voice was heard to say, "Joy never kills! Look up, my Edith! Our little one is safe, and here, closely clasped in my arms. Here, Edith, love; kiss him, and believe that all is well."

With a cry of joy, the little one was folded in his mother's fond embrace.

"Tell me—oh, tell me how you came to know——"

"Hush, dear one—not now. Suffice it that your darling is restored to your arms. Ask no questions now, as you love me," said Felix, bending over her fondly.

With the habitual gentleness which ever characterized Edith when Felix Heron expressed a wish, she laid herself gently back on the pillow, still clasping her darling in her arms, and seeming to have no other wish on earth but to gaze into those innocent eyes.

Felix now made a sign to Lady Castleneau, and, turning to Edith, he said, "I will return in a short time, Edith; and then you must consent to part with that little fellow, as you are keeping him awake much beyond his usual bedtime."

There was a light-heartedness about Felix Heron which imparted itself to Edith, and she cheerfully assented to his leaving her in charge of Ellen.

As soon as Felix and Lady Castleneau were left alone, the former, taking her hand, said, "I know how anxious you are to know how it was that I should be the happy means of restoring my Edith to herself."

"Yes, yes, Felix; tell me how and where you found the child."

"I will. Again, dear aunt, have we to thank that brave boy, Tom Ripon. It was he who saw and recognised Clackington as he was hastening from the house with the child beneath his cloak, evidently in search of a vehicle which would convey him and my child to some place of concealment."

Lady Castleneau seemed almost overwhelmed with this intelligence.

"I cannot understand——" she began.

"And I can scarcely enter into particulars now, dear aunt; for I heard only a few hurried particulars from Tom, who was as anxious as I was to relieve Edith's mind, but was afraid to do so until he had talked the matter over with me.

But it appears that Tom had been paying his mother and Mortification a visit in Wardour Street, and was just turning down the Oxford Road, when he observed a man walking at speed with a child beneath his cloak. There was something about the furtive glances which the man cast about him, which drew Tom's attention to him; for he stood aside and watched him; and just as he approached the spot where Tom was in hiding, the child struggled to free itself from the folds of the cloak, and called out ' Mamma! Ellen!' in the, to Tom, unmistakable accents of little Arthur."

Lady Castleneau drew a long breath.

"This was sufficient, you may be sure, for Tom. He strode out of his hiding place, and confronted Clackington, holding a pistol to his head as he cried out, ' Hold hard, there! What are you doing, my Lord Clackington, with that child?' As soon as Arthur heard Tom's voice he made a desperate struggle, and succeeded in freeing himself from Clackington's grasp. This was all Tom wanted, for he was alone; and he thought with the charge of Arthur he would be no match for his lordship, so he wisely determined to let him off, and to be satisfied with getting possession of the child, who clung to him as to a well-remembered friend."

Clackington, it seems, saw his advantage, and took to flight, leaving Tom master of the field.

"Thank heaven!" said Lady Castleneau. "I will now go to Edith."

"And I will go with you, dear aunt; for I, too, am most anxious to see them both again."

As Felix and Lady Castleneau entered Edith's chamber, their hearts throbbed with delight to hear again the gentle tones of Edith's voice, talking to her newly-found treasure.

Little Arthur, too, was doing his share of conversation; and on seeing Felix Heron he held out his little arms, exclaiming, "Here comes papa! Look, mamma! He is not going out any more to-night."

"I know all," said Edith, looking at Felix, and then smiling at Ellen, who was standing by the bed-side. "How shall we ever be able to repay Tom the debt of gratitude we owe him."

"Oh, that will not be so very difficult, I fancy," said Heron, glancing mysteriously at Ellen, who immediately withdrew behind the shadow of the curtain. "I think the best way will be to make him a present of Ellen, there, and let her tell him all we think about him."

"What say you, Ellen?" asked Edith, in the same strain. "Are you willing to become the exponent of our feelings towards Tom?"

What answer the blushing Ellen might have made must still remain unknown; for when Edith drew aside the curtain, Ellen was gone. She had made her escape from that room, her heart thrilling with every joyful emotion.

"Is that the way you pass me, Ellen?" were the first words which greeted her ears, as Tom laid his hand upon her arm, and gently detained her.

"Oh, don't—don't keep me now, Tom! dear Tom—I—I——"

"Why, what's the matter, Ellen; don't you love me to-night?"

This was too much for the gentle girl, who had gone through so much during the last few hours,

EDITH IS OVERCOME WITH GREAT AT THE LOSS OF HER CHILD.

Presented Gratis with No. 99, of the New Edition of EDITH HERON; Sequel to Edith the Captive; or, the Robbers of Epping Forest.

and she burst into a flood of tears which were finished, however, upon Tom's shoulder, and the brief half-hour which succeeded those tears was perhaps one of the happiest of her life, for she felt that she loved and was beloved, and what more does the heart require in this world than that blessed assurance?

CHAPTER CCCVII.

HERON AND HIS FRIENDS PAY A VISIT TO PRINCE GEORGE AT KEW.

It is now necessary that we should more specially record to the reader the particulars of the visit of Felix Heron and his attached friends to the young Prince George, at Kew, immediately after the death of Lord Warringdale.

Some remarkable changes had taken place in the position of Felix Heron and those who were dearest to him on earth.

The sudden and awful death of John Tarleton, although it certainly was an event which made no material change in the prospects of Heron and Edith, yet removed a weight and sense of oppression from the mind of the former, which had sat there long.

The struggle which had taken place in his feelings between the urgent desire to take summary vengeance for the murder of his father, and his shrinking horror of taking the life of Edith's brother, had been painful and intense.

But now all that had passed away.

John Tarleton was no more.

He had met his death as he deserved to meet it, in the pursuit of one of those nefarious and villanous plans which helped to make up the sum of his existence.

But if the death of John Tarleton was a relief, as regards Heron's domestic life, how much more so was that of his half-brother, the so-called Lord Warringdale?

By a strange coincidence, one of his most notable offences had been a murder, partaking very much in its character of that which Tarleton had committed.

But the young Earl of Bridgewater had none of the considerations which had swayed Heron in sparing the murderer of his father.

And now that half-brother was no more; and Heron, strange to say, felt a sensation which, but for those dear ones he had at home, would have partaken of loneliness.

He felt that he stood, so to speak, the last of his race; and in all the wide world there was not another Whitcombe, so far as he knew, in existence who could claim kindred with him.

But regrets were in vain.

He did not fashion the mind and heart of Lord Warringdale.

The mysterious secrets of Nature, and the hidden aims of Providence, by which such men are created, and play their part in the drama of existence, were not to be questioned by Heron.

Warringdale was no more, and gladly would Felix Heron have forgotten his existence, burying alike in oblivion his crimes and their terrible retribution

The sadness that spread itself over the face of Felix Heron could not but be observed by those trustworthy and affectionate friends who were with him.

"Cheer up, Whitcombe!" said Colonel Trelawney. "You have nothing to regret."

"Nothing," said Heron.

"Then throw aside all consideration of the past. Turn your attention to the present, and the bright and radiant future, for something seems to tell me that all will be well with you."

The Earl of Bridgewater was still in a state of excitement, and he spoke rather gloomily.

"I think I shall go to Vienna," he said, "until all this affair is blown over."

"Nay," interposed Trelawney; "it is a fair fight, with two credible witnesses."

"It was so!" exclaimed Heron; "and, as heaven will judge us all upon this account, we cannot be accused of the slightest unfair conduct in regard to that man."

"But yet," said Bridgewater, "there may be some disturbance about it. I, too, have my enemies!"

"Come, come!" added Trelawney, "you must not take too serious a view of this affair. I propose that we at once go to the young Marquis of Ormond. You know, Whitcombe, he occupies an official position there now."

"Do not let us involve him in any of our troubles," said Bridgewater.

"Certainly not! But I am sure he will think himself very much neglected—always bearing in mind his great friendship and romantic affection for Whitcombe—if we do not take him into consultation as to what is to be done."

"But you still adhere to your advice," said Heron, "that we should proceed to Kew as quickly as possible on our visit to Prince George?"

"I do."

"And you think we should take Ormond with us?"

"Of that I am quite convinced. He is a great favourite with the young Prince, and may look forward to some of the highest offices of the State."

"Then let us proceed at once. I am only too anxious, for the sake of those who feel deeply interested in my welfare, to carry out any suggestion that may put an end to the sea of troubles which has so long surrounded me."

The distance to the lodgings at Warwick House of the young Marquis of Ormond was but short.

The little party soon occupied a handsome apartment in that semi-regal establishment.

Then with that perfect sense of security among gentlemen of honour, that anything and everything can be communicated freely and without reserve, the young Marquis was made acquainted with all that had taken place at the "Thatched House Tavern."

He took precisely the same view of the circumstances that Colonel Trelawney had done.

"There was everything," he said, "to constitute a fair fight. The weapons were equal, and two gentlemen of unblemished honour and reputation acted as seconds. What on earth more would Lord Warringdale desire?"

"Yes," added Colonel Trelawney, with a slight smile, "you are quite right, Ormond, and I think Lord Warringdale must be hard to please, indeed, if he be not abundantly satisfied."

"Let us to Kew at once; the day is wearing on," remarked Heron.

"But yet listen to me, Ormond, a moment," said the Earl of Bridgewater.

"What is it you would say?"

"Just this—that I fear by appearing before the young Prince at present I may prejudice the cause of my friend Whitcombe."

"Not in the least."

"That is really your opinion, then, Ormond?"

"It is, and I will tell you all why."

The Marquis of Ormond glanced around him suspiciously before he again spoke.

He then lowered his voice to a whisper.

"If the old saying be true, that walls have ears, those walls must certainly belong to palaces; but I am quite certain, speaking in the tone I do now, that no word I utter will reach any other persons than those to whom they are addressed."

Neither Heron, Trelawney, nor the Earl of Bridgewater could form any notion of what the young Marquis of Ormond meant to say.

But he continued speaking in, if possible, a lower tone than before.

"It is one of the most singular thoughts connected with your destiny, Bridgewater, that Prince George will have the keenest possible sympathy with you."

"Indeed!"

"Yes, he will almost wish that he had been in your place at the 'Thatched House;' and, instead of Lord Warringdale, the murderer, who there met with his deserts, had been a personage much more illustrious by courtesy."

Colonel Trelawney nodded.

"I comprehend you, Ormond," he said: "you would imply that the Prince himself is not altogether heedless of the reports which have gone abroad regarding his father's death."

"Exactly so; and you will understand that the Prince, of all others, is least likely to know how richly that father deserved any fate that came over him."

"True, true; he has been brought up in strict seclusion."

"Exactly so, and although neglected by Prince Frederick of Wales, his father, it is said that when they did meet he was always treated with lavish generosity, and, at all events, an external show of affection."

"I begin to understand," said the Earl of Bridgewater, "why it is that I shall secure, then, the sympathies of Prince George."

"But can it be true," said Heron, "that this antagonism between the King and his son Frederick, Prince of Wales, assumed so deadly a shape?"

"It is strictly true; but it is a subject upon which we should not further converse. I am happily at leisure, and advise that we immediately proceed to the Palace at Kew."

"Would you tell all?" asked Bridgewater.

"Certainly, I would conceal nothing; for there is a moral and physical certainty that the young Prince will sit upon the throne of England before many weeks have passed away."

Heron would gladly have ridden to Kew on Daisy, but there was no time to send to Castleneau House.

The young Marquis had no difficulty likewise in mounting his friends well from the stables of Warwick House, and the party of four gentlemen went at a sharp trot to the beautiful old palace amid the shadowy groves of the far-famed gardens of Kew.

The evening was rapidly approaching as they neared the ancient red-brick building now so utterly deserted by royalty.

The name of the Marquis of Ormond was a passport immediately to the Prince's presence.

In a rather large apartment looking out upon one of the pleasant lawns of what was called the private garden of the palace, they found a youth, who, as George the Third, reigned for so many years over England.

The young Marquis made himself spokesman, and very briefly, but with sufficient clearness, detailed the whole story connected with Felix Heron.

The episode at the "Thatched House" was not forgotten.

At the conclusion of the narration the Prince seemed to reflect a little.

Then, proceeding to the window, he said, very quietly, "What sort of a summer do you think we shall have, my Lord Whitcombe?—eh? eh?"

Prince George's manner partook very much of those peculiarities of style which became so marked and observable as he advanced in life.

"A warm summer, your Highness," replied Heron.

"And are you of the same opinion, Bridgewater."

"I am not very weatherwise, your Highness, but I am inclined to that opinion."

"Then, gentlemen, if it should ever happen that I am King, we will talk over these matters again, and I shall be very happy to receive the Earl of Whitcombe at any time."

This was quite a sufficient royal acknowledgment of the validity of Heron's claims to the titles and estates of his ancestors.

Then the Earl of Bridgewater spoke.

"Does your Royal Highness think I had better travel?"

"I should not travel," said the Prince, "if I were so lucky as to slay in fair fight the murderer of my father; but if you would like a journey, the Princess Ernestine, my cousin, is at the Court of Hanover. Go and ask her how she is, with my compliments; but don't go unless you feel inclined."

"I will not."

"Or unless necessity prompts you; and if it does, I do not think any one will be bold enough to stop, on any pretence whatever, a special messenger from the heir to the throne of England."

The four gentlemen bowed; for they felt that their mission to Kew was perfectly accomplished, and, that let what would happen, they had the voice of Prince George with them, with the certainty that sooner or later he must sit on the throne.

Then that voice would be effective enough for all possible purposes.

The Prince then lifted a letter from the table, and said, in a tone of cheerful curiosity, "I have here a note from Lord Mandeville, who tells me that justice is at length likely to overtake that notorious rascal, Jonathan Wild."

"He is certainly arrested," said Heron, "since I was an eye-witness of the fact."

"Mandeville says he must certainly be hanged."

"I am sorry for it, your Royal Highness."

"Sorry? sorry? Eh? Sorry for such a man as that?"

"Yes, your Royal Highness; sorry because I do not like any man to be hanged under false pretences."

"Indeed! False pretences?"

"Yes, your Royal Highness; Jonathan Wild is as bad as he can possibly be, and has, in all probability, committed a hundred crimes for which he may deserve the gallows; but I should like to see him hanged for some one of them, and not because——"

Heron paused.

"Not because what? Not because what, my Lord Whitcombe?"

"Perhaps I am going too far, and ought not to utter the words which were upon my lips."

"Yes, yes, say them—say them. You may say what you like here."

"Then I was going to say, your Highness, that, although Jonathan Wild deserved hanging, he ought not to be hanged merely because my Lord Mandeville, the Secretary of State, had no further occasion for his services."

"Oh," said the Prince, "that's it, is it? Good day! good day! See you all again—all again, some fine day. Good day! good day!"

The Prince bustled out of the room.

The four gentlemen looked at each other with smiles.

"So far so good," said Colonel Trelawney. "Bridgewater, you need be under no trouble whatever as regards the death of my Lord Warringdale."

"And I," said Felix Heron, "amid all the clouds that have obscured my fortunes for so long, begin to see a steady light breaking, which may lead me on to happiness and peace."

The party left Kew, and mounting their horses, again made the best of their way to London.

They alighted once more at Warwick House, where Heron was compelled to stay for a short time, that he might not cast a slur upon the hospitality of the young Marquis of Ormond.

He then made his way on foot to Castleneau House, for he was exceedingly anxious to impart to Lady Castlenau, and to Edith, the stirring and remarkable events of that day.

We are already aware of how fortunate was the arrival of Felix Heron at the peculiar conjunction of affairs at Castleneau House, which made his presence so intensely to be desired.

———

CHAPTER CCCVIII.

JONATHAN WILD IS AN INMATE OF NEWGATE.

"They can't hang me! They shan't hang me! They dare not do it! You may all look at me as you please, and no doubt you think the last days of Jonathan Wild have come; but they have not; it's the spring time of the year, and come what come may, I can't hang till autumn."

Jonathan Wild stood in the vestibule of Newgate.

He glared about him ferociously.

Every face that looked upon him he knew so well.

The warders—the turnkeys—even the hangman himself was there to take a look at the great thief-taker in the hour of his misfortune.

There was little pity in any of those faces.

There was no hope whatever.

The general impression was strong and prevalent that Jonathan Wild's days were numbered.

It was not that they thought him one whit more criminal than he had always been.

Nor was it that they viewed that criminality with any peculiarly distasteful eyes or strong sense of its iniquity.

But they believed that such a man as Jonathan Wild was tolerably sure to be hanged at last, and they had good reasons to suppose that the time had come.

"Do you hear, all of you?" shouted Wild. "I tell you it won't be, and it can't be! They may pretend to prosecute me; but I am too useful. And besides, there's another reason."

"What may that be, Mr. Wild?" said the head turnkey, stepping forward.

"You'd like to know, wouldn't you?"

"If it's all the same to you, Mr. Wild, I should."

"Then I will tell you. I know too much, and I might open my mouth too wide, and let some of it out. Ha! ha! ha!"

This was a strange idea of Jonathan Wild's.

Strange, because he was generally so acute, and had a rough and ready mode of coming at the motives of actions, particularly when those motives were lying near the surface.

He thought, because he knew so much, that the Government would not venture upon his execution.

There could not have been a more fatal mistake.

It was just on account of that very knowledge that he stood in such imminent danger; and Jonathan Wild, like every one else similarly situated, had to learn the fact that the baser tools of men in power are always sacrificed so soon as they know so much as to be dangerous on account of that very knowledge.

"What are you all staring at?" cried Wild again. "Did you never see a man in trouble before?"

"Often, Mr. Wild—often!"

"Then don't be making a show of me, as if you didn't know me."

"Well, Mr. Wild, don't be in a passion; and if your time has come——"

Wild uttered a yell of rage.

"My time come!" he shouted. "No; all your times will come first; and I hope to see every one of you dangling at the end of the rope before a noose is knotted that will fit my neck. It's all a sham, I tell you."

"Very good, Mr. Wild," said the clerk of the prison.

"Oh, you're there, are you, idiot!" shouted Jonathan; "and you think it very good, do you? I will tell you all now what will be very good; and that is for every man Jack of you to be civil and obliging, for the time will come when I shall have more power than ever, and then look out for squalls."

The turnkeys and warders of Newgate were quite abashed at this effrontery of Jonathan Wild's.

With the great majority of minds, it is only necessary to assert something in a bold, confident, impudent manner to have it implicitly believed; and whether this self-confidence of Jonathan's was real or assumed, it certainly had all its effect upon the men who surrounded him.

"I suppose, Mr. Wild," said the head turnkey, "you have a great deal of respect for the old customs of Newgate?"

"What do you mean?"

The turnkey held out his open hand.

"Garnish," he said.

Wild laughed.

"Oh, yes, I understand that perfectly well, and I intend to distribute a hundred pounds among you."

"A hundred, Mr. Wild?"

"Yes, a hundred. It is fit that I, of all men, should be liberal in the old Stone Jug."

"You are very good, Mr. Wild."

"Of course I am. A hundred pounds, recollect, among you. It will be a nice little sum a-piece."

Wild had been released from his handcuffs, and now he plunged his hand deep into one of his pockets, as though to get out the hundred pounds which were for distribution among the ten or twelve warders and turnkeys that surrounded him.

Even the prison clerk put on an amiable look, and uttered something about Mr. Wild always being a gentleman when he liked.

"Yes," added Jonathan, "a hundred pounds among you; and let me see, it shall be payable—yes, payable on the day I walk out of Newgate a free man."

A sort of groan came from the warders and turnkeys.

"He always was the greatest blackguard in life," said the prison clerk.

"And so," added Wild, "you will all of you be interested in that charming result—I mean, my liberation. How delighted you all look!"

"But, Mr. Wild," said the head turnkey, "if things should go wrong, what are we to do then?"

"Ah, to be sure, that's true!"

"You know we can't help it if you are hanged."

"True again—true again! Well, then, if it should happen that things go wrong——"

"Yes, Mr. Wild."

"If my enemies should get the better of me, and I should really take a ride to Tyburn——"

"Yes, Mr. Wild?"

"I will leave you all——"

"What?"

"My blessing."

The turnkeys fell back.

They muttered maledictions loud and deep upon the head of the great thief-taker.

The prison clerk walked away thoroughly disgusted.

Wild laughed loudly, with a fiendish kind of roar, that echoed through the vestibule of the prison.

Then one of the turnkeys called out in a loud voice, "Make way for his honour the Governor—make way! make way!"

The Governor made his appearance, and looked with some curiosity on Jonathan Wild, who had exercised a sway in the prison of Newgate almost equal to his own.

"Well, Mr. Wild," he said, "things have come to a bad pass with you."

"Not at all," said Jonathan. "I intend, after this little brush is over, to take a steady, respectable situation."

"And what may that be, Mr. Wild?"

"Governor of Newgate."

"Confound your insolence!"

There was a trampling of horses' feet and a rattling of wheels in the Old Bailey.

"The Sheriff!" cried the man on the lock.

The little wicket at the top of that narrow flight of stone steps, up and down which so many unfortunates had proceeded with lagging feet, was flung wide open.

The Sheriff made his appearance with his chain of office round his neck, and looking unusually grave and solemn.

He had a long, official-looking letter in his hand, with a broad seal upon it.

For a single moment there came a sallow flush over the face of Jonathan Wild, for he thought it might possibly be his release from the Secretary of State's office.

The letter had evidently been opened, and the Sheriff was glancing at it now and then as he came into the vestibule of Newgate, as if it were the special cause of his visit.

The most important personage, as we have before had occasion to hint, that can cross the threshold of Newgate is the Sheriff for the time being.

The Governor always treats him with marked respect.

The words that fall from his lips are listened to as though they were the words of an oracle.

"Mr. Governor, you have one Jonathan Wild in custody," said the Sheriff.

"Yes, sir; here is the man."

"Oh! very good! Then I may as well read you a paragraph in this letter, which I have received this morning from the Right Hon. the Secretary of State."

"Ah!" cried Wild.

"Silence!" said the Governor

The Sheriff gave a slight cough, and then he read.

"'And more especially I call upon you, in your official capacity as Sheriff, and, consequently, responsible keeper of His Majesty's gaol of Newgate, to be heedful of the safe custody of its prisoners, several of whom, to the great scandal of the administration of the law, have recently escaped.'"

The Sheriff looked at the Governor at this juncture, as though he would have him mark these words well.

Then he raised his voice a little, and read on.

"'I would, therefore, suggest to you, that when a criminal of no ordinary magnitude is in your hands, that you would take the most stringent means for his safe custody; and you will understand me when I give you, as an example, the name of Jonathan Wild.'"

The Sheriff ceased reading.

He slowly folded up the letter, and looked at the Governor.

Wild glanced from one to the other of them, like some caged animal, who felt that his chances of escape from his captors were becoming each moment more slender.

"I comprehend," said the Governor. "Griffiths—Mr. Griffiths!"

"Yes, sir."

"Send for Martin."

"Yes, sir."

"And get your heaviest set of irons ready."

A roar burst from Wild.

"Since when," he cried, "is a man like me, taken up for petty larceny, to be loaded with the heaviest fetters Newgate can afford?"

"It is not petty larceny," said the Governor; "but capital felony."

"There hasn't been a man executed for re-

No. 100.—EDITH HERON.

ceiving stolen goods," added Wild, "all this session."

"Are you coming, Martin?"

There was a tremendous noise, as if some great mass of iron had fallen down immediately adjoining the vestibule of Newgate.

Then a man of herculean form and strength made his appearance, carrying over his shoulder a huge forge-hammer, while, under his other arm, he brought a small portable anvil, consisting of an upright block of oak, iron-bound, and heavily capped with the same metal.

With a grating, discordant noise across the stone flooring of the vestibule of Newgate, a turnkey dragged in a complete heavy set of fetters.

Those iron manacles of an age past, specimens of which may still be seen by the curious in such affairs if they would only now proceed to the Old Bailey, and glance upwards at the stone doorways of Newgate.

Those grim old rusted set of irons that are now to be seen over the narrow entrance porch, may, for all we know, be the very set that on this occasion were dragged lumbering into the vestibule of Newgate for the special use of Jonathan Wild.

The smith set down his anvil.

The operation of fettering some notorious malefactors was what Jonathan Wild had often himself seen performed upon others.

The shrieking terrors of the poor wretch thus encased in iron had never brought a thrill of pity to the heart of the great thief-taker.

But then he had never contemplated wearing those manacles himself.

"Now, Mr. Wild, if you please," said the smith. "One foot up here; whichever you please first; we give everybody their choice."

Wild hesitated a moment.

He seemed half inclined to resist.

But then the hopelessness of doing so with anything like effect must have come instantly across his mind.

He put up his foot.

The manacle was clasped round his ankle.

A loose rivet was placed into it.

Then a piece of iron of rather soft texture, and shaped like a large flat nail, was thrust in by the side of the rivet or bolt.

This nail—if we may so call it—could only be pushed about half-way into the narrow space left for it.

The hammer was to do the rest.

"Steady, Mr. Wild!" said the smith.

Wild shut his eyes.

He felt the whiff of air pass his face, as the huge forge hammer was raised and swung round the head of the smith of Newgate.

Bang! it came on the head of the nail.

The soft iron was crushed down and flattened.

The manacle was tight.

Then Jonathan Wild opened his eyes again.

There was an awful look of hate and vengeance lurking in them.

But in five minutes more he was completely fettered.

One compassionate turnkey lent him a couple of pocket-handkerchiefs, with which the loose portion of the fetters could be tied up in a manner so as to be the least inconvenient to wear.

Then Wild drew himself up, and, in spite of the inconvenience of the action, folded his arms across his chest.

The iron bars and links about him rattled as he did so.

"Listen to me, all of you," he said. "I don't believe I shall be hunted to death this time; but if I am, and it is then possible for any ghost to make Newgate a horror that none of you can abide in from sunset to cock-crow, mine shall be that ghost. You shall meet me in the long, gloomy passages at night; you shall encounter me in the cells; I will dart out upon you from the corridors, and as you ascend the staircases, you will hear me rushing after you, and feel my skeleton fingers clutching at your skirts. Ha! ha!"

CHAPTER CCCIX.

JONATHAN WILD'S INDICTMENT

THE indictment against Jonathan Wild was of two sorts.

He was first of all accused generally for setting up, as general profession, the business of receiving stolen goods, and that indictment ran in the following form :—

"That for many years past he had been a confederate with great numbers of highwaymen, pickpockets, housebreakers, shop-lifters, and other thieves.

"That he had formed a kind of corporation of thieves, of which he was the head or director, and that notwithstanding his pretended services in detecting and prosecuting offenders, he procured such only to be hanged as concealed their booty, or refused to share it with him.

"That he had divided the town and country into so many districts, and appointed distinct gangs for each, who regularly accounted with him for their robberies. That he also had a particular set to steal at churches at time of divine service, and also other moving detachments to attend at Court, on birthdays, balls, &c., and at both Houses of Parliament, circuits, and country fairs.

"That the persons employed by him were for the most part felon convicts, who had returned from transportation before the time for which they were transported had expired, and that he made choice of them to be his agents because they could not be legal evidences against him, and because he had it in his power to take from them what part of the stolen goods he thought fit, and otherwise use them ill, or hang them as he pleased.

"That he had from time to time supplied each convicted felon with money and clothes, and lodged them in his own house the better to conceal them; particularly some against whom there are now informations for counterfeiting and diminishing broad-pieces and guineas.

"That he had not only been a receiver of stolen goods, as well as of writings of all kinds for near fifteen years past, but had frequently been a confederate, and robbed along with the above-named convicted felons.

"That in order to carry on these vile practices, and to gain some credit from the ignorant multitude, he usually carried a short silver staff as a badge of authority from the Government, which he used to produce when he himself was concerned in robbing.

"That he had under his care and direction several warehouses for receiving and concealing stolen goods; and also a ship for carrying off jewels, watches, and other valuable goods to Holland, where he had a superannuated thief for his factor.

"That he kept in pay several artists, to make alterations and transform watches, seals, snuff-boxes, rings, and other valuable things, that they might not be known, several of which he used to present to such persons as he thought might be of service to him.

"That he seldom or never helped the owners to the notes and papers they had lost, unless he found them able exactly to specify and describe them, and then often insisted on having more than half their value.

"And lastly, it appeared that he had often sold human blood, by procuring false evidence to swear persons into facts of which they were not guilty. Sometimes to prevent them from being evidences against himself; and at other times, for the sake of the great rewards given by the Government."

It was quite clear that an indictment of this description, however much it might prejudice a man in Jonathan Wild's position, was of by far too general a character to be convicted upon.

We must not weary the reader with the full details of Jonathan Wild's various appearances at the court of the Old Bailey; but we proceed at once to that important day when he was fairly put upon his trial, with an intention on the part of the prosecution to strive every nerve to bring him in guilty.

It was the middle of the month of May

A bright and beautiful season, for at that time winter and summer seemed more decided in their aspects, and to come and go with more decided hues of demarcation, than they do at present.

The protracted prosecution of Jonathan Wild had made it not only the town's talk, but had awakened a strong interest throughout the whole of the United Kingdom.

And if the vanity of the great thief-taker at that moment could have overcome his sense of great and paramount danger, he might well have looked about him with pride and satisfaction to see the dense crowd of faces about him in the court of the Old Bailey.

Many persons of rank and note had seats upon the bench.

It was surmised that every barrister in London made at least an attempt to get into the court on that occasion.

The heavy irons had been struck off from the limbs of Jonathan Wild previous to his being placed in the dock.

He was rather pale, but he had dressed himself with great care.

No costume, however, or colour, could do more than transiently hide the brutal ferocity of his appearance.

Previous to the judge taking his seat upon the Bench, and the trial fairly commencing, Wild industriously distributed hand-bills from the dock.

These bills contained a long—real or pretended—list of malefactors whom he had brought to justice.

The list might have been essentially true, but Jonathan Wild forgot to add, that almost in every case these malefactors had only been brought to justice because they either refused, or were no longer capable of being useful to him, in the nefarious business he carried on.

It was a quarter-past ten o'clock when this important trial commenced.

One of the most eminent counsel of the day was engaged to prosecute; and Wild listened with a darkening visage to the trenchant terms in which his guilt was depicted.

"My lord, and gentlemen of the jury,

"It becomes necessary, even when a criminal of so deep a dye as the man who now stands before you is brought to justice, that he should

have the full benefit of the laws under which he lives.

"It is not that we think him a bad man, or that we believe him to have been guilty of this or that offence against justice and morality that we must judge him.

"No, gentlemen of the jury, we must allege some specific charge, and that must be supported by the clearest and most substantial evidence.

"Upon that evidence the prosecution must stand or fall; and in relation to that evidence the prisoner at the bar stands before you, in no greater peril being what he is, than as though he were the best and purest of human beings."

The counsel suddenly sat down.

He had said all he wished.

It was left to a junior counsel to state the facts of the case as against Wild, and to call the witnesses.

"My lord, and gentlemen of the jury," said the junior counsel, raising almost immediately his superior had sat down; "the case against the prisoner is just this.

"There resides in Holborn a Mrs. Catherine Stretham, a lace mercer, who finds it necessary, in the course of her business, to keep a stock of exceedingly expensive Foreign and English laces.

"On the evening of the twenty-second of January last past, Mrs. Stretham was in her shop alone—having sent her assistant out on some business of importance.

"Two persons came into the shop—a man and a woman, and engaged her attention for a considerable time in looking at laces, which, however, appeared not to please them; and they left without making any purchase.

"At the door of Mrs. Stretham's shop they met her assistant, who was returning from her errand; and who, consequently, forms an additional witness to their identity.

"Within five minutes of the departure of these persons, Mrs. Stretham missed a tin box, containing eleven pieces of valuable lace, coming, collectively, to the sum of fifty pounds.

"No trace could be found of the thieves for a considerable time, until they were accidentally seen in the street by Mrs. Stretham's assistant, who immediately raised an outcry, and gave them into custody.

The male prisoner's name was Henry Kelly, and the woman's Margaret Murphy.

Finding that they were distinctly sworn to before the magistrate, both by Mrs. Stretham and her assistant, they confessed their crime, at the same time stating that they were incited to its commission by the prisoner at the bar.

Under these circumstances his Majesty's Government considered it would be desirable for the ends of justice to permit these two persons, Henry Kelly and Margaret Murphy, to become King's evidence.

"My lord, and gentlemen of the jury, they will appear before you this day to depose to these facts as against the prisoner at the bar, who you will perceive is indicted as an accomplice in the stealing."

The counsel who had been employed, and most enormously feed by Jonathan Wild to defend him, was an elderly man.

No one was better versed than he in what was called "Old Bailey law."

He rose now and addressed the judge.

"I hope, my lord, we clearly understand what is alleged against the prisoner!"

"I hope so, too," said the Judge.

"Perhaps, your lordship will have no objection to state it."

"The prisoner," said the Judge, "is indicted for stealing, in complicity with Henry Kelly and Margaret Murphy, eleven pieces of lace, the property of Catherine Stretham, and of the value of fifty pounds."

"Will your lordship kindly state where the alleged felony is said to have taken place?"

The slightest shadow of a smile crossed the Judge's face as he replied, "In the dwelling-house of the said Catherine Stretham."

"Very good, my lord."

Wild's counsel sat down as if there was nothing at all the matter.

"Call Henry Kelly!" cried the usher of the court.

A low-browed looking ruffian, who was perfectly well known to Jonathan Wild, since he had been one of his own men for a considerable period, was brought into court in custody and ushered into the witness-box.

The oath was immediately administered to him, and then the senior counsel for the prosecution rose to examine him.

"Your name?"

"Henry Kelly."

"Anything else?"

"Well, the family calls me the Artful Grabber."

"Look at the prisoner at the bar."

"I sees him."

"And you know him?"

"Rather. Why everybody knows Johnny Wild."

"You will please, then, to relate to the court what took place in relation to the robbery at Mrs. Stretham's, the lace merchant, on Holborn-Hill, on the twenty-second of January last past."

"I was at Jonathan Wild's house, and as he came by me he gave my skirt pocket a bit of a shake, and he says, 'Why, Kelly,' says he, 'there's nothing to jingle here. What do you say to a bit of business that'll bring in a few odd guineas?' So I says 'I'm your man, Mr. Wild.'"

"Stop a bit!" said the Judge; "not so fast, if you please!"

The Judge finished his notes, and then, looking up, he added, "Now, go on!"

The villainous witness proceeded.

"'All's right,' says Mr. Wild; 'but it'll want two of you, and the other ought to be a woman.' 'I knows of one,' says I. 'Very good,' says he. 'Then do you know Mrs. Stretham's warehouse on Holborn Hill?' 'I does,' says I."

"Stop!" said the Judge again.

In a few seconds more, the witness was allowed to proceed.

"'Then,' says Mr. Wild, 'you and the woman you knows of go in there at the dusk of the evening and grab some lace. I'll wait here at home for you and give you the best price going for the swag!'"

"Go on."

"Well, we went and did the job, and Johnny Wild he gave us ten spangles, and after that a young woman 'dentified us on Snow Hill, and we were both grabbed, and here I is!"

"That will do."

Kelly evidently thought that his examination was over, and was about to descend from the witness-box, but the counsel for Jonathan Wild rose, and said, in a calm, cool voice, "Not so fast, Henry Kelly, if you please! I have a few words to say to you!"

"Wery good, sir."

"Were you ever convicted?"

"Sir?"

"Were you ever convicted of any offence against the law?"

"I've been took up on suspicion!"

"And found guilty!"

"Well, they was all dead set agin me, so they did say as I was guilty; and what was a poor chap to do all alone, with no end of people swearing agin him?"

"How often has that happened?"

"I always was bad at recollecting!"

"Have you been convicted twenty times?"

"I should say not."

"Recollect you are on your oath, and that records are kept in this court. Now, will you swear that you have not been convicted fifteen times?"

"Can't recollect."

"But you won't swear to the contrary?"

"Well, I won't."

"How many times have you been convicted of perjury?"

"Why, only twice. You knows that well enough!"

"A capital witness!" said Wild's counsel. "I quite congratulate the prosecutor upon this just specimen of King's evidence they have had the temerity to bring before you, my lord, and you, gentlemen of the jury."

"Anything else, sir?" said Kelly.

"No, you may go down, and a greater ruffian, I may say, I never saw!"

"The same to you, sir, and many of 'em!"

"Take that man out of court!" said the Judge.

The officers hustled the witness away, and in the countenance of Jonathan Wild there sat a covert smile.

He began to breathe more freely.

The certainty of his escape, at all events from the consequences of this indictment, began to put him into better spirits.

The atrocious character of the witness almost made Jonathan Wild look not so bad as he really was.

Wild was a clever tactitian.

He thought, now, that if he could raise a laugh, it would be in his favour.

He had observed that when juries laughed they seldom convicted.

Suddenly, lifting off his wig, he clapped it on the head of one of the warders of Newgate, who was close to him, and then, with an immense silk handkerchief, gave his bald head, with its numerous cuts and contusions, a general scrub.

The effect was ludicrous.

There was a general laugh in Court.

Wild had effected his object.

JONATHAN WILD MEETS WITH SYMPATHISER IN HIS ADVERSITY.

Presented Gratis with No. 100, of the New Edition of EDITH FALCON, the Sequel to Edith the Captive; or, the Robbers of Epping Forest.

He had amused the jury, and was accordingly hopeful.

CHAPTER CCCX.

JONATHAN WILD FINDS THAT HE HAS A FRIEND IN NEED.

WHILE these preliminary proceedings were going on at the Court, there was another scene enacting, which it was hoped by Jonathan Wild would go far towards liberating him from his present dilemma.

It is necessary that the reader should be made aware that two hours before the commencement of the trial of Jonathan Wild, a man had presented himself at the door of Newgate, with a request to see the prisoner.

The visitor was dressed in a sober suit of black, with a white cravat, and when the man who was "on the lock" beheld a respectable looking, even gentlemanly man, demanding admittance, he asked more civilly than was his wont, "Who did you please to want, sir?"

"One Jonathan Wild," replied the visitor, in calm, solemn accents; "it is necessary that I should see him, for in good truth I apprehend he has not long to live. His many crimes——"

"Oh, you are not a friend of his, then," said the turnkey with a jerk of his thumb, which the visitor took for granted indicated that portion of the building in which Jonathan Wild was confined.

"Not in the sense that you mean, my man; but I am a friend to the friendless and unfortunate, and I would fain make this one see the error of his ways."

"Well, he is a bad 'un, and no mistake," rejoined the turnkey; "and if so be as you can make an impression upon his heart, why, I for one, will call you a clever fellow."

"Peace, my good man. I have no time to lose, my flock require almost my hourly attention, therefore, admit me at once to this lost sinner's cell."

"Yes, sir."

The turnkey turned the key in the lock, and admitted the visitor.

He led him to a door, where he called to a warder, saying, "Admit this gentleman to Jonathan Wild's cell, Peters; it's all right."

The visitor followed his guide, until they stopped before a low arched door, the present abode of the great thief-taker.

"Here's a visitor, Mr. Wild," said the man, as he flung open the cell door; "and much good may he do you."

Jonathan Wild spoke not until the door was closed, and then he raised his eyes to the visitor's face.

"You, Bradshaw?" he exclaimed.

"Yes, Mr. Wild. I always said, that if ever you did get into a scrape of this kind, Jem Bradshaw would not desert you, and here I am. What's to be done; tell me, and I'll do it."

A look of gratification passed over the face of Jonathan Wild, as he listened to these words. He had good reason to know that it was only because he possessed so large a share of interest in high quarters, that his janissaries were faithful to him, but now that he was, as it were, displaced from his high position, the great thief-taker could not but be aware that there was scarcely one of them who would have held forth a helping hand to save him even from death.

We say, then, that Jonathan Wild looked gratified as the man gave him this proof of his fidelity, and, stretching forth his hand, he said, "Thanks, Bradshaw, I see you are at least faithful. I have really no fears for myself, but still it will be as well to provide against all contingencies."

"I should say so, too, Mr. Wild, for from what I can gather outside the stone jug, matters will go hard with you."

"I tell you, no such thing," roared Wild. "What have I done now, more than I have done for the last fifteen years of my life?"

"It is just that, Mr. Wild," replied Bradshaw, "it is just that—it is an offence of long-standing."

"Bah! you are a fool, Bradshaw; and if you only came here to try and make matters look worse than they do already, why you had better take yourself off again."

"As you please, Mr. Wild," returned the man; "only I thought it would be just as well not to feel quite so confident, and then, most likely, you would take better steps to extricate yourself from your present trouble."

"That's just what I am going to do, idiot that you are! only you interrupt me at every turn by some drivelling argument or other. I tell you you can help me materially, if you will."

"That I am willing to do so is sufficiently proved, I should think, by my being here, Mr. Wild."

"Well, well, I was to blame, perhaps; but it enrages me to hear you talk as though everything were arranged, and I was actually cast for death. No, no! That can't be! I won't believe it!"

The warder at this moment rapped at the cell-door.

"Time's almost up, sir."

"Five minutes more," said Bradshaw, in the voice he had assumed in conversing with the warders and turnkeys of the prison. Then, turning quickly to Wild, he said, "Quick, Mr. Wild—tell me how I may serve you."

"You must know, then," said Wild, "that one clause in the indictment against me is that I have never returned stolen property to its rightful owners without exacting more than half its value."

"Yes, yes," said the man, glancing uneasily at the door.

"Then you must go to Mrs. Ripon, who keeps a fence."

"Yes; I know them well. She married a hypocritical vagabond, who goes by the name of Mortification Ripon now."

"The same. Go there, and tell them that, to save my life, and make me their friend, they must both be prepared to swear that they know of several instances where I have returned stolen property without demanding a single farthing."

"Enough; I understand. Is there any one else more influential than these people, who are known to be no good themselves, to whom I can go."

Jonathan Wild looked down upon the floor of the cell, and seemed lost in thought.

"Yes," he muttered to himself; "surely she will aid me. I have done more than this for her."

"What did you say, Mr. Wild?" asked Bradshaw.

"Nothing; a habit I have contracted of thinking aloud."

"Time is up," suggested Bradshaw. "Is there any one else I can go to?"

"Yes. Go to Castleneau House; ask to see Lady Castleneau, and see if you can induce her to intercede for me. If she will, she can save me at my utmost peril."

"Now, sir," shouted the turnkey, "time's up."

"I thank you, my friend," said Bradshaw, assuming his solemn voice again; "I will leave my charge now, and will return again to-morrow to see if what I have said has been the means of melting his obdurate heart."

"Heart!" said the turnkey, laughing hoarsely; "heart? I think it is a long time since he was troubled with such an incumbrance. The idea of Jonathan Wild's heart—it's positively amusing."

"My friend, be more charitable; try to think well of your fellow-creatures, and seek not to add to the sorrows of one who is already so crushed down by misfortune."

"Then I suppose he's not swearing and tearing about his cell now like a wild beast in his den, as he was a little while ago."

"He is penitent, I trust."

"Humph! It may be so, for all I know," said the turnkey "Only he didn't seem so very penitent awhile ago, when he said he should like to see me and everybody else hanged, and that as soon as he got free he would use his influence to procure himself that little gratification."

"You should not take any notice of what a fellow-creature says when he is cast down, as Mr. Wild is just now, but you should pray."

"Oh, bother! I leave that to better people than Joseph Jebb; so, good day to you, Mr. parson—for, I take it, you are of that kidney—and joy be with you."

Bradshaw was passed on from what may be called beat to beat of the warders, and soon had the satisfaction of hearing the wicket-gate of Newgate closed upon him.

He walked at a rapid pace through by-streets, looking neither to the right nor to the left until he reached Wardour Street, where dwelt Mortification and Mrs. Ripon.

The latter was just indulging in a cup of extra strong tea with Mortification; and this couple, who were usually anything but agreeable company for each other, on this day appeared to be on the best possible terms.

"I wonder what on earth has become of Jonathan Wild, that we have not seen him, as he promised to receive his share of the plunder of——"

"Hush! Don't mention names."

"Hold your tongue! Do you think I don't know what I am about?" retorted Mrs. Ripon. "I say, I wonder he has never been to receive his share of the plunder of——"

Bang! came at the shop-door.

"Lor' bless me!" shrieked Mrs. Ripon. "Talk of the——Well, never mind! We were not saying anything against Mr. Wild."

Bang! bang! came again at the outer door.

"Go and let him in," said Mrs. Ripon. "It is Mr. Wild, I've no doubt; and he can have a cup of tea."

Mortification went to reconnoitre in the shop, as was his custom when any visitors demanded admission to that respectable-looking little dwelling.

He came back in a minute to the parlour, and whispered, "I don't know him; he's not one of our customers. Perhaps, it is one of the nabs in disguise."

Mrs. Ripon uttered a half-shriek, as she grasped a paper parcel which lay on the table by her side.

Bang! bang! bang! came again the blows on the outer door.

"Open the door, now, Mortification," whispered Mrs. Ripon, after having hidden the brown paper parcel behind a cushion on an old easy chair which stood by the fireside.

Mortification went to the outer door and threw it open.

"Sorry to keep you waiting so long, sir, but I was in the back part of the premises with my wife, and we did not hear you knock the first time."

"How did you know, then, that I had knocked more than once?" asked Bradshaw; "but, pshaw! don't keep me parleying here. Let me come in; I have something particular to say to you and to Mrs. Ripon."

"Certainly, sir, certainly!" said Mortification, as he ushered the visitor into the parlour at the back of the shop.

Mrs. Ripon glanced at him, and it was evident that she did not recognise her self-bidden guest.

"Jonathan Wild is going to be hung!" he said, without losing another moment.

"Lor's a mercy!" screamed Mrs. Ripon, "what a good thing!"

"Oh, you think so, do you?" asked Bradshaw, sternly.

"No—no. That is—I—a—oh, lor'! oh, lor'! Poor Mr. Wild!"

Here Mrs. Ripon raised the corner of her apron to her eyes.

"No nonsense, Mrs. Ripon," continued Bradshaw; "Jonathan Wild has been a good friend to you."

"Yes, that he has, sobbed Mrs. Ripon."

"And it is your turn now to do him a good service."

"Yes, Mr. What's your name—yes, I'm sure I'll do all I can for him to the last, and so will you, Mortification, won't you?"

Mrs. Ripon was spending her breath in vain, for her loving spouse had returned to the shop to make fast the door, so that he did not hear the assurance of his better half that he would be willing to assist Jonathan Wild to the best of his ability.

"Mortification! Mortification! Come here I say, and ask this kind gentleman what we can both do to help dear Mr. Wild, who it seems has been unfortunate enough to get into trouble."

It did not take long to make Mrs. Ripon and Mortification understand what was required of them, and after partaking of a cup of tea, Bradshaw bent his steps towards Castleneau House.

Old Anthony replied to his summons for admission, and in answer to his question as to whether Lady Castleneau were visible, said he would go and see, in the meantime conducting the visitor to a small room on the ground floor.

" Your name, sir," asked Anthony.

"Mr. Makepeace!" replied Bradshaw.

Old Anthony withdrew.

"Makepeace? Makepeace? I do not know the name, but nevertheless I will see him."

"Very good, my lady," as he preceded his beloved mistress down the grand staircase of the mansion. "This way, your ladyship," he added, as he threw the door open, and stationed himself outside, to be in readiness should his services be required.

Lady Castleneau advanced into the room with that dignified step which characterized the aged gentlewoman, and said, " I have not the honour of knowing Mr. Makepeace, but if I can be of service in any way——"

"You can, my lady," interrupted Bradshaw. " You can, perhaps, be the means of saving a human life."

" Me? How? What mean you?"

" Of saving the life of one," continued Bradshaw, who has befriended those dear to you more than once."

"Of whom speak you?" asked Lady Castleneau.

" Of Jonathan Wild."

Lady Castleneau held up her hand.

"No," she cried; " I cannot do it. Ask me not. True, he has saved the life of one very dear me ; but I cannot forget, also, that he has likewise been the bane of that dear one's life ; that he persecuted the husband of that dear one, and would have taken his life more than once."

" But listen——"

Lady Castleneau waved her hand for silence.

" I can only promise to do nothing that may in any way make his present prospects worse than they are ! but I cannot—dare not interfere with the course of justice."

Lady Castleneau bowed gently, and turned to leave the room.

" Stay yet one moment," said Bradshaw, when I tell you that he is penitent, full of remorse."

"No more, no more," said Lady Castleneau. " If he be penitent, he may yet be happy ; if not in this world, at least *there*."

Lady Castleneau pointed upwards, and with a sorrowful look upon her face, left the apartment.

CHAPTER CCCXL.

THE TRIAL OF JONATHAN WILD CONTINUED.

WE resume the trial of Jonathan Wild.

Up to the point at which we left off our account of that remarkable judicial investigation, the proceedings seemed rather in favour, than otherwise, of Jonathan Wild.

The characters of the witnesses for the crown were of that nature materially to damage their evidence.

Certainly Mr. Kelly had not come scatheless out of the cross-examination to which he had been subjected.

But still the prosecution had something to say to Jonathan Wild.

The jocular look he had put on faded as the junior counsel again rose.

" Call Margaret Murphy."

The name echoed through the corridors and avenues of the court.

Wild looked a little anxious.

He of all men knew well the effect of corroborated evidence on the minds of a jury.

Margaret Murphy might not be able to depose to one fact more than had been sworn to by Henry Kelly; but she would no doubt substantiate what he had said.

An ordinary-looking young woman stepped into the witness box.

Wild knew her well.

But she would not look at him, although it was quite evident he strove to catch her eye

She was duly sworn

Very few questions were asked, because, after all, the case lay in a nut shell, and all she could do was to corroborate Henry Kelly.

Wild's counsel paid no attention to her whatever, feeling no doubt in his discretion and practice, that the sooner she was gone and her examination over, the better.

Then a more important witness stepped forward, viz., Mrs. Catherine Stretham, the owner of the lace.

She was a quiet, rather lady-like person, and appeared in a state of great trepidation, at being dragged up as evidence in a court of justice at all.

The senior counsel examined her.

" Now, Mrs. Stretham, you will be so good as to relate to the court how and under what circumstances you lost a box of lace on the twenty-second of January last past."

" I was alone in my shop when a man and woman came in."

"Should you know that man and woman again ?"

" Most certainly."

"Then." said the counsel, I have to apply to your lordship to order that the two witnesses Henry Kelly and Margaret Murphy be brought forward."

" Let it be so," said the judge.

The two King's evidences were placed side by side, and although they knew that they were perfectly safe, long habit made them exceedingly chary of being recognised.

And Henry Kelly in particular made the most hideous grimaces, such as he was accustomed to do on the former occasions when he was brought up at the bar of justice, and wished to puzzle witnesses as to his identity.

Margaret Murphy looked perfectly stolid, and put on that air of vacant stupidity which persons of her class frequently assume, when they are in an objective mood, and will not understand anything that is said or done.

"Now, Mrs. Stretham," said the Counsel, " look at these two persons."

" I do, sir."

"Do you recognise them ?"

"Oh, yes."

"On what occasion have you seen them?"

"They are the man and woman who came into my shop and stole the lace."

"That you swear to?"

"Oh, yes; most certainly."

"Now tell us what happened after that?"

"Having heard that Mr. Jonathan Wild was the most likely person in London to hear of my stolen lace, I——"

Wild's counsel was on his feet in a moment.

"Stop!" he cried, in a voice that rang through the Court.

Mrs. Stretham looked terrified.

"We have nothing to do with what you did after that. I call upon his lordship, in the name of Justice, to confine the evidence within the limits of the indictment."

The Counsel for the prosecution interposed, then, with an air of vexation.

"What does my learned friend mean? Of course there is an indictment, and of course we are all here, including his lordship as well as my learned friend, in the interests of truth and justice."

"I beg your pardon," said Wild's Counsel. "I am here in the interests of my client, and you may depend upon it I mean to take care of them."

"But——"

"There need be no buts, I object to the evidence you are endeavouring to procure from the witness, Catherine Stretham, and I call upon his lordship to decide the point."

The judge paused a moment, and then glancing at the counsel for the prosecution, he said, "May I ask if there are any more witnesses to call for the prosecution?"

"No, my lord."

"Then I feel bound to say, that the evidence, as at present rendered, does not support the indictment."

Wild's counsel at once sat down, and calmly took up the newspaper.

The case was over.

Or if he did not think it over, it was his policy to pretend as much.

The prosecution looked vexed.

Or they pretended to look vexed.

Which was it?

There was an enormous deal of finesse among those lawyers.

The judge then addressed the jury.

"Gentleman," he said. "I shall direct an acquittal of the prisoner at the bar upon all matters of fact, inference or reason, and as regards the case brought before you, it is your particular province to decide, but this is a matter of law, and it is quite clear from the evidence adduced by the prosecution, that the prisoner at the bar did not steal the lace which is the subject of the indictment, that is to say, as far as we are concerned, he did not steal it because we have no evidence that he did."

The jury upon this consulted together for a few moments—or seemed to consult, and then pronounced a verdict of not guilty.

Did Wild rejoice?

Did he believe himself safe?

Certainly not, no one knew better than he that there was a second count to the indictment, upon which he might be convicted, and the penalty of which was likewise death.

It was upon that second count that the great battle was likely to take place, for there Wild had his answer, and the whole matter was sure to be a conflict of evidence.

That second indictment charged him with an offence actually committed while he was in Newgate.

There was a clause in an act of Parliament, passed in the reign of George the First, which made it a capital felony for any person to act as agent or go-between for fee or reward, between thieves and persons who had been robbed for the purpose of restoring the stolen property.

Surely if any man breathing was inimical to such an indictment, that man was Jonathan Wild.

Such acts had been the business of his life.

He had reduced them to a system.

He had thriven upon them.

He had grown rich upon them, and the very golden fee that lay snugly in the pocket of his counsel, was a result of the very business that that act of Parliament was levelled at.

Affairs looked serious.

The semi-jocular appearance which Wild had put on departed from his face.

It was remarked that he put his hand up to his ear, which had become a rather frequent action of his of late, and it now arose from his intense anxiety, that not a word should escape him of what was about to take place.

The senior counsel rose again to speak to this second alarming count in the indictment?

"My lord and gentlemen of the jury. I entirely agree with the learned judge, that the evidence we had to offer fell short of proving the first count in the indictment against the prisoner at the bar, and therefore I rejoice and heartily connive in his acquittal."

Wild made a hideous grimace.

"But!" added the counsel, "the second count presents features of quite a different character.

"It is a fact patent to you all, gentlemen, and especially to you, my lord, that if there were no receivers there would be no thieves.

"It is the facilities which are daily and hourly presented for the disposal of stolen property, that makes robbery so easy to accomplish, and so difficult to detect.

"It is a notorious fact to the administrators of justice, that there is a regular organised system in this great city, by which, the moment a robbery is effected, a series of negociations are set on foot between the receiver of the stolen goods, the thief, and the person who has been despoiled of his property

"I am quite sure that, when I state that the prisoner at the bar is the man who, of all others, has brought that system to perfection—if I may use that expression—I am saying nothing but what is warranted by the truth.

"I now proceed to state the facts to you, gentlemen of the jury, which bear upon this second indictment, and which I shall be able to prove to you on incontestable evidence.

"Mrs. Stretham, of course, upon the loss of her lace, had a two-fold anxiety.

"She wanted to recover her property.

"And she wanted to bring the criminals to justice.

"Making inquiries with regard to this two-fold

G.B.

object, she was informed that the best person she could possibly apply to, was Mr. Jonathan Wild, the prisoner at the bar.

• "She accordingly repaired to his house, Little Newgate, as it is familiarly called, and there she saw him, when he at once entered into the transaction, promising her the return of her lace upon an adequate reward.

"She offered five guineas, which Jonathan Wild declared to be utterly inadequate to the return of property valued at fifty pounds.

"He then put on an air of unconcern, and told her she had better advertise, and say what she would give if the property were left at her shop, stating at the same time in the advertisement, that no questions would be asked.

"She did so advertise, but in vain.

"Then Jonathan Wild paid her a visit, at which he told her he had received a mysterious communication, to the effect, that if she deposited the

sum of twenty pounds upon the doorstep of his house, between the hours of eleven and twelve at night, her lace would be brought to her by eight o'clock on the following morning. •

This Mrs. Stretham declined.

"Well, my lord and gentlemen of the jury, negociations went on in this manner between the prosecutrix and prisoner until his Majesty's Government thought proper to apprehend him and place him at the bar of this Court.

"And now I come to a remarkable circumstance, which shows that, to a man like Jonathan Wild, no circumstances would be sufficient to deter him from carrying on his nefarious practices.

"My lord and gentlemen of the jury, he actually carried out this negociation between the prosecutrix, the thieves, and himself, for the return of the stolen lace, while a prisoner in Newgate

"It is for the authorities of that prison to explain how it is that a prisoner, confined there on a charge of felony, could be permitted so much liberty of action.

"On the tenth of March last, Mrs. Stretham received a letter, signed by the prisoner at the bar, stating that if she came to him at Newgate, and brought ten guineas with her, she should have her lace restored.

"The object of this course was to quash the prosecution.

"We are all thankful that in the interests of justice that object has not been accomplished.

"Well, my lord and gentlemen, the prosecutrix did go to Newgate, and took the ten guineas with her. She saw the prisoner in one of the rooms appropriated to the interviews between prisoners and their attorneys.

"Now what happened at that interview is exceedingly important as bearing upon the guilt of the prisoner in respect to the present indictment.

"He held the ten guineas in his hand, and then laid them on a table, after which he wrote a letter, which he told her was addressed to the person who would return her her lace.

"Placing the ten guineas then on the letter, he handed them both back to Mrs. Stretham, saying as he did so: "Go, now, where that letter is addressed, and pay the money, when your goods will be restored to you.

"This she declined to do, but, eventually a porter was sent with the letter and the money, and upon the return home of Mrs. Stretham, she found a box that had been left at her shop, containing the whole of the lace, with the exception of one piece.

"Now, my lord, and gentlemen of the jury, that is our case.

"The Act of Parliament clearly specifies the case to be 'holding a secret correspondence with felons,' in the shape of negotiations for the return of stolen property.

"That is what the prisoner at the bar stands charged with; and I apprehend, gentlemen of the jury, that you can have no difficulty in coming to a conclusion as regards his guilt."

The counsel sat down.

Then the junior rose.

"Call Catherine Stretham."

If possible, in a greater state of perturbation than before, Mrs. Stretham now again made her appearance in the witness-box.

As she had already been sworn, and had not left the Court, her examination was at once proceeded with.

"Now, madam," said the junior counsel; "did you receive a letter dated from Newgate, and signed by Jonathan Wild?"

"I did."

"Where is that letter?"

"It is here."

The letter was handed up, and read by the Clerk of the Court, as follows:—

"MADAM,

"Owing to the machinations of my enemies, who, in all probability, will suffer for it, both here and hereafter, I am, at present, confined in Newgate; and, as under such circumstances, I am desirous of the prayers of all good people. I wish, in order to entitle myself to yours, to do my best to restore to you your stolen lace.

"Please call here for further particulars, and ask for

"Yours faithfully,
"JONATHAN WILD."

"An exceedingly proper letter," said Wild's counsel, as if speaking to himself.

There was a laugh in court.

The rank hypocrisy of such an epistle from a man like Jonathan Wild was so great, that it was almost too much for the gravity of the Judge.

"What did you do then, Mrs. Stretham?"

"Nothing, sir."

"Then, I presume, you had some further communication?"

"Yes, sir, Brandy Bill."

"What?"

"He isn't a what, sir, he is a who. A gentleman called Brandy Bill, with a dreadful odour of spirits about him, called and said he had come from Mr. Wild for an answer to the letter; and that if I would take ten guineas with me to Newgate, I might have back my lace."

"And what did you do then?"

"I took the ten guineas, and went and saw Mr. Wild."

"Please relate to the court what passed at that interview."

"He said there was a good deal of wickedness in the world."

"You had no doubt of that?"

"None in the least, sir."

"It is quite evident," said Wild's counsel, "that my client was in a most proper and improving state of mind. The chaplain of Newgate himself could not have made a juster remark.

"And what did he say next, Mrs. Stretham?"

"Must I tell, sir?"

"Certainly—certainly!"

"I hope," said the Judge, sternly, "the witness does not intend to prevaricate?"

"Oh, dear no, my lord! He asked if I was a widow, and how long I had been so, and whether I thought it was a happy state——"

There was a general laugh in Court.

"And what next took place, Mrs. Stretham?"

"I told him I was and it wasn't."

"What do you mean?" cried the Judge— "what do you mean, woman, by 'I was and it wasn't?' Are you simply ungrammatical or idiotic?"

"Anything your lordship pleases, I'm sure; but, as I've got back my lace, I'd rather not persecute Mr. Wild any longer."

"Certainly not!" cried Wild's Counsel. "A most proper remark to make."

"My learned friend," said the Counsel, who was examining Mrs. Stretham—"my learned friend will have an ample opportunity by and by of making any remarks he thinks proper; but, at present, silence would be judicious. Now, Mrs. Stretham, what further passed at this interview?"

"He told me that it was very curious that he, too, was a widower, as five of his wives were dead, and he didn't know what had become of the other four."

There was a roar of laughter at this.

The Judge checked it to the utmost of his

power, but Jonathan Wild thought he would again improve the occasion, and put himself on good, mirthful terms with the Jury.

He placed his hand upon the region of his heart, and made a gallant sort of bow to Mrs. Stretham, who returned it with a profound courtesy.

This was too much even for the gravity of the Judge, and well schooled as he was in keeping his countenance, he had to hold up his notes before his face to hide his laughter.

"Well, Mrs. Stretham," continued the counsel, "after you had become on such excellent terms with Mr. Wild, I suppose you began to talk about your lost lace?"

"Yes, sir."

CHAPTER CCCXII.

JONATHAN WILD'S TRIAL CONTINUED.

ALL that had taken place hitherto in regard to the examination of Mrs. Stretham had been merely badinage.

The real evidence that was of importance to Wild was coming.

And now there was a more profound silence in the Court as the witness continued:

"I offered him the ten guineas for the return of my lace, and then he wrote a letter, which he said if I took to the person to whom it was addressed, I should get back my property."

"Now, Mrs. Stretham, be so good as to attend to the next question."

"I will, sir."

"Who was that letter addressed to?"

Mrs. Stretham shook her head.

"I don't know, sir. I refused to take the letter, and therefore did not look."

"Are you quite sure of that, witness?" asked the judge.

"Quite, my lord."

"What happened next?" asked the counsel.

"He proposed that a porter should take the money and the letter, and get the lace for me, and take it to my house."

"You consented to that arrangement?"

"I did."

"What then?"

"Then I went home, and I found the lace had just been left in a box, and that it was all right with the exception of one piece."

"Then, my lord and gentlemen of the jury," said the counsel, sitting down, "that is the case."

Mrs. Stretham thought she was released from further examination, and was about to leave the witness box, when she was stopped by Wild's counsel, who said, with an air of great severity, "A few words more, madam, if you please."

"Yes, sir."

"Did Mr. Wild put the ten guineas in his pocket?"

"Oh, dear no."

"What became of them?"

"He gave them to the porter."

"And what did he get for his trouble in the transaction?"

"Nothing."

"Nothing? Did you offer him nothing?"

"I asked him what satisfaction he was to have for his trouble."

"And what did he say?"

"He said he required only the satisfaction of doing his duty. That he acted from principle in assisting people under misfortune, and that all he required of me was my prayers for his welfare, since he had many enemies, who were exceedingly unscrupulous persons, and who, notwithstanding a man might be as virtuous as he could, would think nothing of swearing away his life on the first opportunity."

"That will do, madam," said Wild's counsel. "We need trouble you no further."

Mrs. Stretham was released, and then Wild's counsel, with an air of great candour, appealed to the Judge, saying, "I apprehend, your lordship will be of the same opinion in regard to this indictment as with the first."

"I don't know that," said the Judge.

"Will your lordship allow me to make a few remarks?" interposed the counsel for the prosecution.

"You have a right to be heard, although, of course, you will, by your speaking, as you well know, give a right of reply to the counsel for the defence."

"Certainly, my lord; and what I have to say will be comprised in a very few sentences.

"This second count in the indictment against the prisoner is framed in exact accordance with the Act of Parliament.

"If the correspondence, which the prisoner at the bar is proved to have held with the thieves who stole Mrs. Stretham's lace, had been for the purpose of their apprehension, of course the case would have been different, but it was merely a kind of traffic, having reference to the restoration of the property for a reward.

"It is not necessary that I should trouble your lordship with any further remarks, since the Act of Parliament is quite clear, and the indictment is framed under the Act, while no one will be hardy enough to dispute that the evidence is fully sufficient to support the indictment."

The counsel sat down, and then he who acted for Jonathan Wild rose to address the jury.

"If there be anything, gentlemen, in this country which we esteem above all others, it is that thing which we call even-handed justice, and I would appeal to your hearts and your consciences, asking if the prisoner at the bar is having that even-handed justice?

"What is it that is alleged against him?

"An every-day occurrence.

"Some goods are lost or stolen—a reward is offered for their recovery, and they are brought back and no questions asked.

"Why, gentlemen of the jury, these are the very terms in which advertisements are drawn up and inserted by the score in the daily papers.

"But I have used the words lost or stolen, and some of you, upon a mere casual consideration of those words, may think that there is an essential difference between them.

"In the eye of the law, however, gentlemen of the jury, there is none; for whether I pick up eleven pieces of lace in the middle of the roadway, or take them from Mrs Stretham's shop counter, and retain them one moment after I know who is their rightful owner, I am feloniously in possession of them. Therefore, gentlemen of the jury, all that the prisoner at the bar has done, is the common every-day act of helping some one, by the offer of a reward, to recover lost property.

"And how did the prisoner act throughout the whole transaction?

"Did he take any of the reward himself?

"Certainly not.

"Did he ask for any material advantage?

"Certainly not.

"I call upon you, gentlemen of the jury, to look at this matter conscientiously, and not to allow yourselves to be swayed by prejudices or irrelevant stories which may be afloat regarding the prisoner at the bar.

"If he is to be convicted and sentenced to death, let it be for something that your consciences will approve as a cause of offence, and do not lend yourselves to the designs of those persons who want to put the prisoner at the bar out of the world, for reasons of their own, and would fain get your assistance in doing so upon the flimsiest pretences."

The counsel sat down.

The jury looked rather solemnly at each other.

It was quite evident that he had produced some effect upon them, and that they were rather in doubt as to the course they should pursue.

But the Judge had to sum up.

There was the danger to Jonathan Wild.

He arranged his notes, and immediately commenced.

"Gentlemen of the jury, the prisoner at the bar stands arraigned before you on an indictment framed under a very special Act of Parliament, the penalty of which is death.

"It, therefore, behoves you very carefully to consider the evidence.

"That evidence resolves itself to this.

"The prisoner at the bar, knowing that a felony had been committed, places himself in communication with the person who has been robbed, and, in tolerably plain words, informs her that he knows who is in possession of her property.

"Now, gentlemen of the jury, the person who was so in possession of that property—namely, Mrs. Stretham's lace—was the thief, because, as has been very properly stated to you by the counsel for the prosecution, that person is in felonious possession, whether he found it or stole it.

"It is quite clear, then, that the prisoner at the bar had established communications with a felon or felons, for other purposes than his or their apprehension.

"What were those other purposes?

"Clearly, the return of the property on the payment of some money.

"Gentlemen of the jury, if that evidence does not support the indictment, I do not know what would?

"My learned brother who appears for the prisoner, has urged that this kind of transaction is so common, that we ought to think nothing of it; but you must dismiss that consideration from your minds, since we are here to dispense the law as we find it, and not to consider how many times it has been evaded.

"Gentlemen of the jury, I leave the case in your hands."

This summing up was so thoroughly against the prisoner, that there could be no doubt at all as to the result.

Indeed, they never left their box, but after staring at each other for a few moments, the foreman, who, of course, was the biggest, bulkiest, and most stupid of the lot, shook his great fat head, and whispered to the one nearest to him.

The ominous whisper went round.

Then the jury settled themselves in their box, and stared at the judge.

The foreman got up, and gave two coughs.

He struck his thumbs into the arm-holes of his waistcoat, which is thought an elegant attitude by some folks, and waited to be asked what was the verdict.

The clerk of the arraigns rose.

"Gentlemen of the jury, what say you? Do you find the prisoner at the bar guilty or not guilty?"

"Guilty."

All eyes were turned to Jonathan Wild.

He had so fully expected the verdict, however, that no one could see the slightest change in his countenance.

The Judge then turned towards him.

"Jonathan Wild, after a patient and impartial trial, you have been declared guilty by a jury of your countrymen. Have you anything to say why the sentence of the law should not be passed against you?"

"I have," said Wild.

"Then the Court is bound to listen to you."

"Many thanks," said Wild, rather sarcastically. "What I have to say is just this. I have been twenty-two years in the public service, and any time within those twenty-two years an indictment like this might have been framed against me. I know there's the Act of Parliament quite well—we all know it—but it's a dead letter.

"And not only, my lord and gentlemen of the jury, might such an indictment as this have been got up against me at any time, but it may be got up, to-day or to-morrow, against any police-officer in the kingdom, or against the City Marshall, or the Governors of Newgate, Bridewell, or the Compter."

"That," said the Judge, "will not avail you. The criminality of others, if they comprised half the population, can have no reference to yours."

"Thank you, my lord. I was only drawing your attention to the fact that it was just possible to make fish of some people and fowl of others; and now I come to something else.

"It was perfectly well known to the authorities, including the Secretary of State, that I did busy myself in restoring people their property, after they had been robbed of it by malefactors.

"It was one of the modes by which I brought the malefactors themselves to justice.

"It was the trap which I laid for them, and if I had been continued at liberty, the two persons who stole Mrs. Stretham's lace, instead of being paraded here as King's evidence against me, to tell all sorts of lies, would have been hanged this session.

"But that's not it, my lord and gentlemen of

FELIX HERON HAS A FINAL INTERVIEW WITH JONATHAN WILD BEFORE
HIS EXECUTION.

Presented Gratis with No. 102, of the New Edition of EDITH HERON, the Sequel to Edith the Captive; or, the Robbers of Epping Forest.